GILDED PATH TO NOWHERE

Elaine L. Orr

GILDED PATH TO NOWHERE

ELAINE L. ORR

BOOK 4 OF THE
FAMILY HISTORY MYSTERY SERIES

Gilded Path to Nowhere is a work of fiction. All characters and story lines are products of the author's imagination.

Lifelong Dreams Publishing

www.elaineorr.com
www.elaineorr.blogspot.com
ISBN 13: 978-1-948070-84-3
Library of Congress Control Number:

DEDICTION

As we age, we begin to lose people close to us.
If you have a small family, this could leave you
alone.
This book is dedicated to the people who need
to learn to have friends become family.
May it be a smooth transition.

ACKNOWLEDGMENTS

All of my books have heroes off the pages – friends,
critique group members, and family who read many
drafts. Because of a severe back injury that put me
behind, this book had exceptional helpers in all three
categories. My Decatur critique group
stepped up, of course.
Special thanks to J.D. Webb and Angela Myers,
critique group friends who volunteered to go
through the entire book one more time. And to my sister,
Diane Orr-Fisher and fellow author Karen Musser
Nortman, who did the same.
I wish I could give those extra hours back to you!

.

CHAPTER ONE

"TREASURE HUNTER FINDS Stash of Gold Coins from Late 1800s."

Digger Browning almost dribbled her cereal. Marty Hofstedder had told her to look for an interesting article in Friday's *Maple Grove News,* but she hadn't expected gold coins.

She scanned the piece. The unnamed finder had hunted for the coins many times. He had heard stories about some that were stolen from a retired banker in the early 1900s. Supposedly the thief, an itinerate blacksmith making his way West, arrived in Maple Grove on a warm June day and left town a few days later.

The date of departure was uncertain, but the blacksmith, Gerard Morton, was found dead on June 9th on Meadow Mountain, a mile above Maple Grove – minus any coins.

Uncle Benjamin floated into the remodeled kitchen and listened as Digger gave him the gist of the article. "*I never believed that story. That banker, Robert Heller, had a gambling problem. I think he lost 'em at the poker tables."*

"You weren't quite born then," Digger said.

He snorted. *"Not 'til 1935. But my parents said every now and then, especially during the Depression, somebody'd organize a search in the woods for those coins."*

"What do you know about the man who supposedly stole them?"

"Marty's article said his name was Morton, and that's what I always heard. Blacksmith. Cars were getting popular in Baltimore, and he thought he'd go to Nevada or someplace where they still used a lot of horses."

"And what?" Digger asked. "He ran out of money in the Western Maryland mountains and thought he'd burglarize a house?"

Uncle Benjamin shrugged. *"Like I said, I think old man Heller made up the stolen coins. Maybe the guy did break into his place. No way to know now."*

Digger looked at the clock on the stove. "I have to get to the office. You coming today?" She picked up her cereal bowl and put it in the sink.

"I 'spose. Do I look okay?" He smirked.

"Do you really think I have an opinion?" As a ghost, Uncle Benjamin could simply imagine himself in a different outfit and he would be wearing it.

At the moment, he wore what had been his favorite home outfit before he died – a yellow, long-sleeve shirt with frayed cuffs and a red cardigan. He didn't sport his green tie, but he usually reserved that for the Christmas season. He had added a daffodil to one of the sweater's buttonholes and carried a goldminer's pick.

Digger envied him sometimes. She was most comfortable in jeans and a cotton sweater, but to the office she wore a blazer with either slacks or a skirt. She glanced down to be sure she hadn't dribbled any cereal on her hunter green blouse.

"I'll bring the paper so we can finish the article."

"Meet you in the car." He floated out the closed back door. Uncle Benjamin could remain at the Ancestral Sanctuary without Digger, but he couldn't go other places unless he was with her. He often came to her office and roamed through the building.

Digger put food in Bitsy's bowl and rubbed her dog's head. The German Shepherd made a small whine. He'd been out twice already, but he hated it when Digger left for the day.

"Don't let Ragdoll boss you around." Bitsy's ears perked up and he looked around. With no cat in sight, he wandered off, apparently to secure a friendly hiss.

Uncle Benjamin's cat was the only other mammal in the house who seemed able to see and hear him, not that Digger could be positive about that. The long-haired feline followed him around and perched on tables in whatever room he occupied, just has she had before he died.

MARTY'S ARTICLE DOMINATED conversation in the Coffee Engine that morning. By the time Digger had ordered a cup for her and one for Holly, she had overheard four theories from other patrons.

1. A collector had dropped them while hiking on the mountain.

2. Someone died in the woods long ago and the coins weren't found until the wallet they were in disintegrated.
3. There were rumors someone wanted to buy land on the mountain for a camping resort. Maybe they were rich and had dropped the coins.
4. The Bank of Maple Grove was robbed in 1910. The thieves were never caught. Maybe they buried the coins in the woods and an animal finally dug them up.

Digger was tempted to ask the most voluble man why he thought a bank robber didn't retrieve them, but stopped herself. It would lead to more speculation and a long conversation. Was 1910 also the year Heller's coins disappeared?

She parked in the small lot behind the office of You Think, We Design, and carefully balanced the coffees as she walked around the building to the front door. The crisp, late Spring air gave her an incentive to think of a reason she could be outdoors today.

Digger sat one of the coffee cups on the sidewalk so she could pull open the door to the two-story, frame commercial building where she and Holly rented much of the second floor. A few flecks of green paint had chipped from the trim near the door itself. That was new.

"Too bad you can ride the banister up." Uncle Benjamin demonstrated.

When she arrived at the second floor office she and her partner shared, Digger heard a fifth theory from Holly. Her grandmother, Audrey, speculated that the coins were related to building the railroad through

Western Maryland. She had heard that John W. Garrett, after whom their county was named, had paid workers in gold coins if they laid so many miles of track in a day.

Digger frowned as she placed Holly's coffee on her desk. "She does know that the Meadow Mountain tracks were only a spur off the main B & O System, right?"

Holly waved a hand as she reached for her cup. "That doesn't bother her. She figures a paymaster absconded with some of the gold and hid it away from where they were laying track."

Digger grinned. "And then he couldn't find it?"

"I managed to get away before I heard the rest of the theory."

Along with Digger, Audrey was active in the Maple Grove Historical Society, but she had what Uncle Benjamin referred to as an active imagination. This was when he wasn't calling her a busybody.

"Why were you with your grandmother early on a March morning?"

Holly sat the coffee cup on her large desk, which occupied the center of their graphic arts and marketing firm. "I stayed at her place last night to help her do more research on our slave ancestors. We went over to the historical society yesterday after work and I photocopied pages from the 1860 and 1870 census for Allegany County, you know, before we were Garrett County."

"She can't look at the paper copies when she volunteers at the society?" Digger asked.

"Her eyes really are getting worse. I mean, she's eighty-something. She has a really thick magnifying glass at her house, and she pores over stuff. She's too vain to take the magnifier to the society. She can use her key after hours to copy pages and read them at home."

Uncle Benjamin added a decorative pair of glasses to his outfit. "*She's so vain.*"

"I believe she doesn't want to own up to her bad eyesight. I'm amazed she was willing to pay for the copies."

Holly raised an eyebrow. "I didn't say *she* paid."

Digger smiled. "How old is she? I thought you found her christening records."

"I did. She's eighty-six. But she doesn't own up to it, so I don't let on I know."

Digger shook her head as she sat at her desk and opened a folder. "I'm revising the new tourism brochure to focus less on the Visitor Center itself."

"Why?"

"The Chamber of Commerce board wants to mention things people can do in and around Maple Grove, especially hiking. They also want more about the B&Bs."

"What made them want something different?"

"Abigail told me yesterday that they want to attract more young people. They mostly go down to Deep Creek Lake."

Holly frowned. "Did you tell them to pay for a couple hours more work, since you were almost finished with a mock-up? "

"I did. What are you up to today?"

"Menus." She laughed at Digger's raised eyebrows. "I'm going to come up with a standard design for all the restaurant menus in town. Then we can plug in the specifics and some graphics that go with whatever they serve."

Uncle Benjamin, who now sported a chef's hat and apron, sat on top of a bookcase. *"Maybe you can include smudges that look like spilled chocolate milk."*

Distracted, Digger stumbled over her words. "What made you think of that?"

"Audrey and I had Sunday breakfast at the diner. Their menus are so old they've crossed out prices when they raised them. And I swear mine had some egg yolk on it."

"Told you," Uncle Benjamin said.

"Menus are usually pretty labor-intensive, but if they use our standard design, we could do them quickly."

"Yep," Holly said, "and they could update them more easily. Because we'd use a standard format, we wouldn't have to charge a lot and our company name would be somewhere on the menus."

"Free advertising. Great idea." Digger faced her computer and turned it on. "Let me know if you need any help.

"I'm just getting started. I'll ask if I need it."

"Hey. Aren't you going to talk some more about Marty's article?"

Holly couldn't see or hear Uncle Benjamin. More than once she'd come into a room when Digger was talking to him and she had to say she was talking to herself.

Digger had arranged her computer so Holly couldn't see the screen from where she sat. She typed, "I have to work. Go away."

"You need to be more polite to your elders. At least spread out the paper so I can read the rest of it."

Digger typed, "In a minute."

She turned to Holly. "In the Coffee Engine this morning, someone mentioned there might be people who want to buy land on the mountain to create a campground. Have you heard about that?"

"Last time I stopped in the Chamber, Abigail asked me the same question. Audrey heard it at the grocery store. Though she thought she might have heard blood hound instead of campground."

"Gee, if Abigail heard it, there must be something to it." Digger paused. "Or it's a rumor that really gained steam."

Holly shrugged. "Not much up there."

"Can't think of any easy access to water. Guess I'll wait for something more concrete than a rumor." Digger eyeballed the hand-written mock-up of the revised tourist brochure to decide how much text would fill up one of the tri-fold pages.

Uncle Benjamin floated over and sat cross-legged on her desk. *"Maybe you and Marty could take sleeping bags up there and see how rocky the ground is."*

She glared at him.

The phone rang and she reached around Uncle Benjamin to grab it.

He laughed and floated toward the ceiling.

"You Think, We Design. This is Digger Browning."

Marty sounded cheerful. "What did you think of the article?"

"I'm glad you called. It's a reminder to finish it." She opened the paper and spread it on her desk.

"It was so dull you didn't read all of it?"

She laughed. "I was rushing to get to work. I brought it with me. Who's the guy who says he found the coins?"

"I'm not supposed to tell anyone who he is."

"Even your girlfriend?" Digger asked.

Holly raised her voice enough for Marty to hear her. "Or her best friend?"

Digger put Marty on speaker. "Don't gang up on me," he said. "Professional ethics."

"He's not exactly a source who needs to be protected, is he?" Digger scanned the rest of the article. "It says the person is an 'Average Joe,' whatever that means."

"He didn't even want me to let on a guy found them, but I told him I wasn't going to say 'he or she' throughout the article."

Uncle Benjamin waved a hand in front of Digger's face. "*Ask him if he's seen the coins.*"

"Exactly what kinds of coins are they?" she asked.

Marty didn't say anything for a couple seconds. "The one I saw was an 1888 five-dollar coin."

"*Those coins aren't all that rare.*" Uncle Benjamin said.

"How do you know he has more than one?" Digger asked.

"He had a draw-string bag."

It didn't seem that Marty had insisted on definitive proof that the man had more than one five-dollar gold coin. "If he found it outside, wouldn't a cloth bag have deteriorated?"

"I asked him about that. He said he put them in the pouch after he found them. Soft leather, which he made himself from deer hides he'd tanned. Full of coins. He let me hold it."

Uncle Benjamin floated onto Holly's desk. *"That sounds like Bruno Sampson. He lives above Maple Grove on the west side of the mountain. Not exactly a hermit, but close."*

"Hmmm," Digger said. She decided not to ask if Sampson had found the coins.

Marty seemed to sense Digger's doubt. "The bag was a lot heavier than it would have been if it'd had quarters."

"Heavier than if he'd had more recent dollar coins in there?"

Softly, Holly said, "Uh-oh."

Marty's tone had an edge to it. "I wouldn't have written about it if I didn't believe the guy."

"Of course. You'll be pleased to know that the article had everybody talking at the Coffee Engine when I stopped there."

"Oh, yeah? You think they'd read a follow-up piece?"

Digger rolled her eyes at Holly and took the phone off speaker. "I think you'd have to give them a more complete account of what the guy found and where they could have come from."

"I'm not supposed to say where on the mountain they were. He plans to look for more."

"More power to him. I have to get to work."

"Lunch?"

Digger glanced at Holly, hard at work on the menu design. "A short one at the diner. Twelve-thirty, okay?"

"Bringing your uncle?"

"God, I hope not. Bye."

Holly looked up. "What are you so fervently not hoping?"

Digger could have slapped her forehead. "I don't want a bunch of people offering their theories on the coins."

"I can just hear your former neighbor going on for half-an-hour. What's his name?"

"O'Bannon. And he's at the diner every morning with a couple other old-timers. Should be gone by the time Marty and I get there."

DIGGER WAS UNLUCKY on both counts.

Uncle Benjamin wanted to go to the diner and promised to stay away from her and Marty. "*I'll go into the kitchen and practice smelling, and then I'll wander around away from you two and eavesdrop.*"

Uncle Benjamin grinned when he saw Doug O'Bannon in a booth, joined by a man from the VFW and one from the Knights of Columbus. He headed that way and Digger made a beeline for a spot just around the corner from them. She returned Doug's wave, but pretended she didn't hear the eighty-something man call to her.

The diner wasn't the traditional cigar-shaped, stand-alone building. The customers sat in a U-shaped space, and the interior of the U was filled in with the kitchen. For some reason, few people sat at the old-fashioned counter. Maybe because they went to the diner looking for companionship.

As she made her way to a booth, she passed one with Lucas, a Chamber board member who had given her ideas for the tourism brochure. "Digger, how's the new pamphlet coming along?"

"I should have the revisions you wanted in the next couple of days."

"Great. We really need to boost income for all the businesses, but especially the B&Bs. Have to have places for people to stay."

"We sure do. Enjoy your lunch."

She slid into a booth. Menus stood behind napkin holders at each table or booth, and Digger studied one before Marty arrived. A sticky substance attached to the side of her pinky finger and hand.

She saw Marty and waved. At six-two, he was usually easy to find. Since he'd moved to Maple Grove from Baltimore only a few years ago, he also dressed like a city guy- more likely khakis than jeans, no baseball caps or hoodies, and either a blazer or dressy sweater. Today was no exception.

Marty slid in across from her and squeezed her hand. He picked up his own and looked at the back of his fingers. "What is that?"

"Syrup, I think. Have to hope it's from today."

"Sheesh." He grinned and then grew somber and lowered his voice. "Are we alone?"

Digger was tempted to gesture around the room, but she knew what he meant. "He's in the kitchen and promises to stay away."

They ordered – BLT on wheat for Digger and corned beef for Marty – and waited until the server was en route to the kitchen to talk about the article.

"You really can't tell me who found the coins?"

Marty shook his head. "He specifically said not to tell anyone from the Maple Grove Historical Society."

Digger didn't mention Uncle Benjamin's idea. "That makes me wonder if it's a made-up tale and he wants to avoid people who might know more about the thefts."

He shrugged. "Or the coins. He's somebody who keeps to himself a lot. I think he doesn't want to be bothered."

"Does he have any theories about where the coins came from? You mentioned the burglary at the Heller house, but the Maple Grove Bank was supposedly robbed in 1910. According to one of the experts in the Coffee Engine this morning."

"The guy doesn't know or care. I mentioned the Heller burglary because someone brought it up in a talk about local banking at a Rotary Club meeting." Marty paused. "Or maybe it came from that history book on Garrett County. I have it in the notes I did for the article."

Digger lowered her voice. "You saw a five-dollar coin. Did he mention the different denominations he found?"

"No, but when I looked up information on a collectors' website, it mentioned the coins can be different diameters and weights. The bag clearly had different..." He stopped as he seemed to take in the strange expression on Digger's face.

She was trying to ascertain whether the forty-something man approaching them wore a perennial frown or if he was really angry about something. I should know him, she thought. At least that camo jacket and canvas hat.

He stopped at their booth and Marty looked up. His expression grew guarded. "Hey, Bruno. Haven't seen you for a while."

"The hell you haven't! It's all over town that I found those coins. You said you'd keep your mouth shut!"

CHAPTER TWO

A FLECK OF SPITTLE flew toward Digger. Fortunately, their food hadn't arrived yet.

Marty sat up straighter and turned toward the man. "Bruno, I told no one. Absolutely no one."

Uncle Benjamin rounded the corner and headed for Digger.

Bruno leaned closer to Marty. "Then how's come a bunch a people come up to me and asked can they see the coins?"

"Because people who hunt for food are in the woods a lot. Especially him." Uncle Benjamin had whispered into Digger's ear, not that anyone else could hear him.

"Think about it," Marty said. "I talked to you about a second article. You wouldn't let me do that if I told your secret."

"You're damn…"

Forcefully, Digger said, "Bruno."

He turned toward her, mouth still open.

"Marty didn't even tell me. And I've asked him at least three times." She remembered Bruno Sampson now. He made his living helping hunters display their glory on their walls or, for a small animal, a fireplace mantle. He was not popular with the no-kill animal shelter in town.

Bruno leaned toward Digger and Uncle Benjamin came between them, not that Bruno could tell. "And who are you, Miss?"

Calmly, Digger said, "I own a business in town, and I collect information on local history." She turned her head slightly so she didn't rub noses with Uncle Benjamin — not that she could feel him.

The diner's owner, Ashley Grund, wiped her hands on a white chef's apron as she came toward them. "Sir, please. May I seat you for lunch?"

Digger almost laughed. No one seated anyone at the diner.

Uncle Benjamin sat on the back of Digger and Marty's booth. *"Maybe she'll make the SOB shut up."* He now wore the short pants and thick gloves of a boxer and moved around doing punches in the air.

Bruno glanced at Ashley. "No."

Ashley's eyes met Digger's and she shrugged slightly before moving to the counter, where she stayed instead of returning to the kitchen.

Marty spoke quietly, but with an edge to his voice. "Bruno, if you don't want people to know what you found, yelling in the diner won't keep it a secret."

Bruno's eyes darkened as he returned his gaze to Marty. "You're a liar."

Marty reddened, but as he stood, his voice was even. "You're entitled to hold that opinion, but saying it publicly is slander. Maybe you should go somewhere to cool off."

Bruno straightened his spine, but said nothing.

Uncle Benjamin continued to dance around him, throwing punches. Digger tried to ignore him.

Ashley had stepped closer again. In a voice much higher than usual, she said, "You like my apple pie. How about a complimentary piece to go?"

Bruno turned his head to Ashley. "Sure." He turned fully and followed her to the counter.

Uncle Benjamin sped after him. Thankfully, his spindly legs were now ensconced in long pants.

Digger wondered what her uncle thought he could accomplish. As Marty again lowered himself into the booth across from her, she realized the diner had grown completely silent. Not even the sound of cutlery striking the thick ceramic plates.

Marty cleared his throat. Before he could say anything, their server appeared with two plates. The clunk of placing them on the booth's table was the apparent signal for conversations to resume.

Digger smiled at her. "Thanks, Jen."

The server widened her eyes at Digger as if to say "whew." Aloud, she added, "The corned beef is especially good today."

"No doubt," Marty said.

From the booth next to them, a man asked for more water and Jen turned toward him.

Digger took a potato chip from her plate and grinned at Marty. "Guess I don't need to try to pry the source out of you again."

"If he knew anything about reporters, he'd know we don't disclose sources unless they want us to."

Digger lowered her voice. "Do you really think Bruno is that sophisticated?"

Marty took a huge bite of his sandwich and moved it to one cheek. "Maybe not, but he's no dummy."

"I know who he is, but haven't ever talked to him in the hardware store, which is the only store I've seen him in. He's the perfect example of someone who lives in a cabin in the woods and keeps to himself."

Marty swallowed. "Says he's a taxidermist."

Uncle Benjamin spoke from a few feet away. "*He's more a poacher who stuffs the heads of what he kills.*"

Digger had looked at him as he spoke, and she returned her eyes to Marty as Uncle Benjamin turned back toward the main room of the diner.

"He came over when Bruno was yelling, but he's left." She picked up her BLT. "He says the guy is more of a poacher who stuffs what he kills."

"I thought taxidermists mostly worked with what hunters brought to them."

Digger nodded. "Best way to get paid. Maybe he sells the ones he kills to people who are lousy hunters."

"He let me visit his cabin. Bruno does his work in an outbuilding behind it. He wouldn't let me in there. "

"So, what's his place like?"

"Very basic lifestyle. He uses a wood stove for heat. His cabin is about halfway up on the west side of the mountain. You get off the state road onto Jessup Lane, which doesn't go to any homes now, just gets narrower and finally ends. His place is back from Jessup, and he has a bunch of No Trespassing signs by the road and around his cabin."

"What's his E-9-1-1- address?" Digger asked.

"I asked so I could use GPS, and he said there wasn't one. He gave me directions."

"Every residence has to have one. I'll look at the county plat book to see if he owns land up there."

Marty grinned. "Your family history research skills come in handy." He nodded toward Digger's left shoulder. "Button today?"

She lifted the lapel of her blazer. Under it was a button that said Family Tree Hugger. "Did he take you to where he found the coins?"

Marty swallowed. "Nope. Wouldn't even say whether it was east or west of Maple Grove."

"If he found them above the west side of Maple Grove, you know there's a lot of parkland up there."

"And a lot less traffic," Marty said, "especially in the evenings. But I doubt he found them in the dark."

Digger looked behind Marty to see her former neighbor, Doug O'Bannon, coming toward her.

He met her eyes and grinned. "Hey you two. I want to know if a rumor is true."

Marty kept his expression impassive, but he winked at Digger before he turned to face O'Bannon. "I don't know, Doug. You usually come to me with ideas."

The elderly man steadied himself on the back of their booth. "I heard the city has a big tourism campaign lined up. There's a couple new B&Bs so there'd be more places to stay in town. And there's been talk of a campground, though I don't know much about that."

"I know about the B&Bs," Marty said. "Makes a total of four. But even if they were all filled to capacity, that's only seventy-two beds."

"Well, here in town. But people could do stuff up here and stay in a motel down by the interstate."

"That'd be great," Marty said, "but what would they do all day?"

Uncle Benjamin had floated behind O'Bannon. "*I heard a guy from the Chamber just now say there's going to be a parade on Memorial Day. I can wear an Uncle Sam costume.*"

"Was there something about a parade on Memorial Day? Or was it the 4th of July?" Digger asked.

O'Bannon seemed pleased. "I thought that was just a rumor, but if Digger Downing heard it, it must be true." He did a small wave and limped back to his booth.

"How come you didn't tell me that?" Marty asked.

She smiled. "Someone recently put a bug in my ear about it."

THE OFFICE PHONE WAS ringing as Digger entered You Think, We Design.

Holly waved at her as she picked it up, but before she had time for the greeting, someone apparently started talking. She listened and said, "Uh-huh."

Holly rolled her eyes in Digger's direction. "Just a minute, Grandmother."

Digger laughed quietly as she sat at her desk.

Holly placed the receiver on her shoulder and held it there so Audrey couldn't hear her. "She said you and

Marty got accosted at the diner and Bruno Sampson is the one who found the coins."

Digger nodded. "You can tell her yes because he yelled at Marty quite publicly. Apparently, people guessed it was Bruno and talked to him about it. He's ticked because he thinks Marty let on."

Holly repeated that and kept listening. To Digger, she mouthed, "Know anything else?"

"Nope. Marty's closed-mouthed."

Uncle Benjamin floated out of the kitchenette cabinet where they kept the coffee. *"Tell her I was ready to beat up the guy."*

Digger ignored him and opened the folder where she had the tourism brochure.

"Humph." He floated through the ceiling to the attic.

"If I find out more, I'll let you know." Holly put the receiver firmly on the handset. "I know her. She'll tell everyone she has the inside scoop."

"Marty said Bruno wouldn't say where he found them, just that he'd been looking for them for a long time. I never heard about them before I read his article." She almost said Uncle Benjamin didn't think a burglar had taken coins from Robert Heller's home.

"If she calls again soon, would you tell her I've gone out for a few minutes? She'll lose interest in an hour."

Digger grinned. "Sure. How's the menu design coming?"

Holly brought two rough draft pages to Digger's desk. She had no food items on them yet, but X's and dollar signs gave an idea of the format. "I think we'll probably need two basic sizes. A place like the Coffee Engine could be front and back of a standard piece of copy paper. The diner would probably need legal size. They can be laminated so stains get wiped off."

"Sure. Places that have specials usually put them on a chalkboard by the entrance or above where you order, like at the Ice Cream Shoppe."

They spoke for another couple minutes and then Holly went back to her desk. Digger worked on the brochure for another half-hour, all the while thinking about the coins and their provenance.

She went to Ancestry.com on her computer. She and Holly did small projects for the historical society and sometimes they designed ads for the paper or cable TV that featured historic scenes of Maple Grove and other parts of Garrett County.

Beyond that, Digger tried to separate her family history hobby from work. Otherwise, she'd explore one topic and go to another for hours at a time.

Now, however, she went to her Garrett County tree on Ancestry. She had a tree for her families, but in this one she entered any early resident and linked them to others. The linkages always fascinated her.

She'd listed Robert Heller and his family – wife, three sons, and one daughter – by name and approximate dates of birth, but she'd never had reason to explore them in detail. With hints from the website, she filled in dates of birth and death and eventually came across an obituary for Robert Heller.

His wife Caroline's maiden name was Shaw, and the children were Robert Jr., Helen, Herbert, and Herndon. "Helen Heller," she murmured to herself. That could have brought on some teasing in middle school.

Robert Heller, Sr. died in 1917, lauded as a "banking visionary" who helped Maple Grove grow from a sleepy town with one sawmill, a general store, and a tavern to an "expanding metropolis" that connected to the mighty Baltimore and Ohio Railroad. Even in the flowery language of the early twentieth century, Digger had never seen Maple Grove referred to as a metropolis.

The obituary did mention the theft of "a large number of nineteenth century gold coins of varied denominations." It continued to say that Mr. Heller had planned for them to bring ease to him and his wife in their advancing years, and that they sorely missed the added comforts.

Mental calculations told Digger that Heller did not live to tremendously advanced years. He had been born in 1857 in Frederick County, Maryland, meaning he died at age sixty. The obituary mentioned the "scourge of bowel cancer."

The phone rang again, which gave Digger a guilty start. She'd been looking for information on the Heller family for almost fifteen minutes. She picked up the phone. "Digger Browning speaking for You Think, We Design."

A rough voice said, "I don't want you asking no more question about me or my bizness."

"Uh, Bruno? Mr. Sampson?"

Uncle Benjamin appeared on her desk, wearing a gold miner's outfit more appropriate for the California gold rush.

"You know full well who this is, Miss. You said you'd been askin' that reporter about me. You stay out of my bizness!"

"I apolo…" At the sound of a loud click, Digger took the phone away from her ear. She glanced at Holly. "Meet Bruno Sampson, he of the gold coins. Oh, wait, you can't. He hung up on me."

Holly grinned. "I heard him. How did you get into his business?"

"When he accused Marty of telling folks he found the coins, I told him Marty wouldn't even tell me who found them, and I'd asked three times." Digger picked up the receiver. "I guess I should let Marty know he's probably not going to get follow-up interviews."

CHAPTER THREE

DIGGER AND UNCLE BENJAMIN left the office just before four o'clock on Friday, which was the longest she could be away from home without worrying that Bitsy would soil the floor.

Uncle Benjamin sat in the passenger seat. *"You concerned about that Bruno fellow bothering you?"*

"Not really. He might call again, but he doesn't like to be around people, so I doubt he'd show up on my front porch."

"You're probably right. We should go to the historical society tomorrow to look up articles about Robert Heller and that supposed burglary."

"I'll see what I can pull up on the Internet tonight." She didn't add she didn't want to spend time there tomorrow.

"You could do some more research about the railroad spur that came through here. For the Visitor's Center history material."

"I know you like to prowl through the society's collection, but I have stuff to do around the house, and Franklin might come up tomorrow."

"*Good. I love to follow my son around.*" He floated to the back seat.

Digger turned from Crooked Leg Road onto the one that went up the east side of Meadow Mountain, toward the Ancestral Sanctuary. Mention of her cousin Franklin tightened her stomach muscles. She had to tell him about his father's post-funeral return to life – or whatever it was. But how?

Maybe she could send him an email. No, she had to tell him at least on the phone. Could she make herself do it tonight? No, she had to plan the conversation.

Tonight, Digger planned to take Bitsy for a walk on the property, eat dinner, look at county land records online, and see what she could learn about Robert Heller. She hoped the Internet would have info on the supposed home burglary that might – or might not – have contributed to Bruno Sampson's discovery.

If he had been someone who craved attention, she might think he made up his story and showed Marty a coin he'd picked up at a hobby shop or flea market. But Bruno seemed to be a genuine loner; hardly a hermit, but a man who didn't want notice.

Uncle Benjamin floated onto the dashboard and peered out the front window. "*You see those spots of yellow by the road?*"

Digger smiled. "Crocuses, not gold. Please stay on your side of the car."

"*Humph. Have to see if they've come up around your Great Aunt Clara's grave.*"

Digger pictured the small Browning family plot behind her house. It reminded her that she needed to repaint the metal arch that bore the family name.

Uncle Benjamin had said that when they put the last shovel of dirt on his coffin, he found himself sitting on the joint headstone he and his late wife shared. Had he imagined his spirit would still be hanging around a year later? She now felt much older than her twenty-six years.

Digger turned from the road into the long driveway that led to the Ancestral Sanctuary. The maintenance needs of the large home, the third residence on the property, were unpredictable. She dreaded the day when the small stipend Uncle Benjamin left for the large, 1878 brick home ran out.

But she loved it. The lawn and garden had begun the transition to spring. Buds on the trees promised a lot of leaves to rake for fall, but for now all she thought of was the smell of damp earth and fresh air.

"You want to come with me while I walk Bitsy?"

"That dog does not need a minder when he does his business."

"No, but I don't enjoy giving him a bath after his every romp in the woods. Plus, getting the porcupine needles out of his nose wasn't fun."

DIGGER TOUCHED BASE WITH Marty after dinner. "Anyone else call you about gold coins they found?"

"Nope. It was an interesting story to write, but not much feedback."

"And you still believe him?"

"I believe Bruno found them. He said they glinted up from the dirt, so I guess they were lying in that spot for a while. Eventually rain and snow washed away whatever covered them."

"When I was cooking dinner, I looked for information about the coins stolen from Heller's house. Didn't find any so far, but I found an article about the 1910 bank robbery. Some kid wrote it for a school project about ten years ago, and a parent posted it on their Facebook page tonight."

"Huh. Who's the parent?"

"Sylvia Taylor. She works in the convenience store at the gas station. She didn't say which kid wrote it. Hang on, I'll grab my laptop."

Digger sat the kitchen wall phone on the counter and almost tripped over the cat, who was sitting by her food bowl. "Sorry, Ragdoll, I forgot." Digger reached into a canister on the counter, took out half a handful of dry cat food and placed it in the cat's bowl.

Ragdoll meowed to express displeasure at the cavalier treatment.

Digger grabbed her laptop from the dining room table and went back to the phone.

"You know," Marty said, "if you break down and buy a cordless phone, you could carry it to the laptop. And other places."

"Still paying for the new granite kitchen countertops. Listen to what the kid wrote about the 1910 robbery."

"The good citizens of Maple Grove were shocked to learn that the town's only bank was robbed on

Thursday. Miss Phyllis Tuley required smelling salts afterwards, but she was able to provide a description of the ill-attired man."

"Would you have required smelling salts?"
"Pipe down," Digger said.

"The man wore a red kerchief well over his nose and a flat cap pulled down to nearly cover his eyes, and Miss Tuley said he did not give off an air of familiarity. She thought he was older, perhaps in his mid-thirties, with brown hair and a thin frame. His knee-length coat was cut too big for him, and was a coarser cloth than a gentleman's attire.

Police Captain Jeremy Willard said the man showed cunning to arrive at the bank at approximately two PM, when there were generally fewer customers than at the lunch hour or just before the bank's three PM closing.

"Does it say how much was taken?" Marty asked.
"The kid's piece goes on to say that police couldn't immediately say how much was robbed, but a couple days later they said it was about $710 in paper money and gold coins."

Digger thought about that amount. "That was a lot of money back then. I didn't find any information about people whose money was stolen. If I knew some names, I'd talk to any family I could find still in the area.

"Your article said this blacksmith's body was found June 9th, and that he was suspected in the theft from

Heller's home, but doesn't say anything about the bank robbery."

"Bruno said he'd heard about the home burglary and searched off and on for years," Marty said. "My editor had heard about it, but didn't mention the bank robbery. I should have done more research, though. I thought the story was more about finding the coins than how they got there."

"No way to really know," Digger said.

"Yeah. I didn't put the blacksmith guy's name in my draft of the article. Who knows what was true? My editor knew the name, said it had to go in."

"Uncle Benjamin said people would look for those coins, especially during the Depression."

"Which is exactly what my editor's parents did."

Digger didn't see that they could learn a lot more. "Uncle Benjamin said the blacksmith was from Baltimore, heading west. Doubt he has any descendants here."

"Did your uncle have any other comments?"

"He hasn't seen the Facebook piece yet. He's up in Franklin's apartment on the third floor."

When Uncle Benjamin surprised Digger and her cousin by leaving the Ancestral Sanctuary to her and the bulk of his money to Franklin, she'd been worried he would resent her.

Franklin was initially surprised. But he figured, and Digger agreed, that Uncle Benjamin knew his son liked his life as a lawyer in Washington, DC. Franklin might be fond of Maple Grove, but if he'd wanted to live in the Western Maryland mountains, he would have opened a law practice in Allegany or Garrett County.

After Uncle Benjamin's death, Franklin built a small apartment on the unfinished third floor, which used to serve more as an attic. He came up a couple times each month, more often than when Uncle Benjamin was alive.

The twelve-year age difference meant the cousins hadn't been close as kids, but they liked each other. Digger thought Franklin saw it as his responsibility to be sure she was okay rattling around in the huge house.

"What does your uncle do up there?"

"Franklin has old family photo albums on his shelves, and I asked him to put some of his dad's stuff that he wanted to keep in those storage cupboards he built under the eaves. I figured it would give Uncle Benjamin a lot of his things in one place."

"You're going to have to tell Franklin eventually," Marty said.

"I know. At first I didn't know how. Now, I'm afraid he'll be furious with me for not telling him right after Uncle Benjamin came back. Or whatever you call what he did."

"Franklin still has a room on the second floor, doesn't he? Maybe you could tell him your uncle popped up in Franklin's childhood room a day or so ago?"

Digger laughed. "I'd get in trouble later if I referred to Uncle Benjamin being with me at the old depot when I found that body."

"We," Marty said.

"You were there, but I had the gross privilege of uncovering it. Anyway, Franklin is slowly moving the stuff he wants to keep up to his apartment. Then we'll give away his old bed and dresser and…"

"Hey. Franklin collected coins."

"True," Digger said. "But I don't know that he had gold ones."

"I doubt I'll do more on Bruno's find, but next time Franklin's up, I'll tell him he can be my consultant."

From the doorway that led from the back hall into the kitchen, Uncle Benjamin said, *"Tell him Franklin'll charge a stiff fee."*

Digger turned her head toward her uncle and frowned, not that Marty could see through the phone. "I've been joined by an obstreperous ghost."

"So weird. Tell him I said hello."

Digger did, then repeated Uncle Benjamin's thoughts about a fee from Franklin.

Marty laughed. "I'll ask for a discount. Have fun looking for more gold coin stuff."

Digger hung up and picked up her laptop to return to the dining room.

Uncle Benjamin frowned. *"Did he get off because of me?"*

"Nope. I had already told him about something I saw on Facebook." She shook a finger at him. "You aren't supposed to listen to my phone conversations."

"I try not to. But Marty's voice is loud and my spiritual hearing is perfect."

"Nothing spiritual about it," she muttered. Digger put her laptop on the table and went back to the handwritten class project Sylvia Taylor had scanned and posted. "Check this out. A kid wrote it for a class project years ago."

Uncle Benjamin peered at the screen. "*You know how I can go into a book and look around? You suppose I could do that with a computer?*"

"Interesting question. Is there a magic button I can push if you don't reappear?"

"*Oh. Guess I don't want to know that bad.*" He glanced back at the screen. "*Interesting, but I really want to find out about the burglary at the Heller house.*"

"I'll do more of a Google search now, but that would probably be on the newspaper's microfilm at the historical society. If an article was even written."

"*Your buddy Marty has access to that microfilm at work. He can look.*"

"Okay, but it's at his office. I'll send him an email tonight."

"*Guess it doesn't do any good to grumble.*"

Digger smiled to herself. She was glad Marty would probably be willing to check the microfilm, but it brought up the whole Marty/Uncle Benjamin conundrum.

Since Uncle Benjamin could stay at the Ancestral Sanctuary alone without fading away, she and Marty could be together at his place. They trusted Uncle Benjamin not to poke his head through a wall to spy on them in her bedroom. Still, it was awkward to know he could. Especially for Marty.

Digger was planning to move her bedroom from one of the two guest rooms on the second floor to the nearby master bedroom, which could help. Or not. It had been Uncle Benjamin's and Aunt Clara's room. After his beloved wife died decades ago, he had left it much as she had it arranged.

Digger might not have made the move even now, but Franklin had emphasized that she needed to make the house feel like hers. Moving into the largest bedroom would help with that. She appreciated his logical thinking, but still wasn't sure about it.

After selling the small bungalow she had in town, Digger had gotten rid of some of her things. She'd also put others in storage. The master bedroom would be large enough that she could create a sitting area using some of her former living room furniture. It would be cozy.

Cozy for two people and an ornery ghost.

CHAPTER FOUR

MARTY SATURDAY BROUGHT SUNSHINE and warmer air. Once it got close to sixty degrees, Digger figured winter might really have ended. Nights still tended to drop to freezing or below, but as long as it didn't get too low, the crocuses would soon be followed by tulips and blossoming dogwood trees.

After breakfast, Digger texted Franklin to see when he might arrive. Anytime was fine, she just liked to know.

He texted back before she had put her cereal bowl in the dishwasher, her favorite item in the remodeled kitchen.

"Be there about two," the text said.

Uncle Benjamin floated through the kitchen window. "*Maybe we could pick up some sticks and dead leaves from around your Aunt Clara's headstone.*"

"Please don't come in through the window when I'm standing in front of it. And I love your pronoun."

He sat on the old, red Formica-topped table. As promised, Digger had left the ugly thing in the new kitchen, but she'd removed a leaf so the table took up less space.

"*Believe me, if I could hold a leaf bag open for you, I'd do it.*" He'd added a gardener's apron and floppy straw hat to his outfit of brown jeans and a t-shirt with the name of the store he used to own, Maple Grove Hardware.

"I'm going to do twenty minutes of spit and polish on this floor, then we can see if Marty found any articles about Robert Heller being burgled."

DIGGER FINISHED HER VERSION of weekend housework and jogged to the second floor to take a quick shower. She dressed for the day in blue jeans and a deep red cotton pullover and headed downstairs. She figured eight o'clock was an okay time to call Marty.

"You're underway early for a Saturday," he said.

"I'll have you know I've wiped down the kitchen, dusted the living room, and taken Bitsy for a walk to the end of the driveway and back."

"*Ask him,*" Uncle Benjamin said.

"Hush," Digger said.

Marty grunted. "What's he up to?"

"Actually, we both want to know if you had a chance to look in the newspaper morgue for an article about a burglary at Robert Heller's place."

"A bunch of microfilm pages around that time are blurred. Want to come down to the office and look in the archives with me?"

"Sure." Digger figured he meant only her.

"I have to help my grandparents later today. Why don't you bring your uncle this morning, and this evening we can do something by ourselves?"

Digger could have kissed him through the phone. She knew Uncle Benjamin would love to spend time in the huge *Maple Grove News* storage room. Lots to explore. "He'll be delighted. Thanks. What time?"

"Let's say nine."

"See you then." Digger saw the hopeful expression on Uncle Benjamin's face. "He said you're welcome to join us."

"*That guy's a keeper.*"

NOW THAT HE'D been in spirit form for a year, Uncle Benjamin had become adventurous. He had not figured a way to be away from Digger or the Ancestral Sanctuary for long without what he called fading.

But he had learned that he could ride on the roof of Digger's Jeep without falling off. As she turned out of the Ancestral Sanctuary driveway toward town, Digger heard a loud, "*Yippee!*" from above.

She didn't care about him riding on the roof, but she'd asked him not to yell as she rounded a corner or passed another car. What would she say to Sheriff Montgomery if she jumped the curb and hit a fire hydrant? Perhaps, "You know how you helped fold the flag for Uncle Benjamin's coffin? The joke's on you."

Digger's thoughts turned to the gold coins and Bruno's obsession with secrecy. She couldn't blame him, but his outburst in the coffee shop pretty much ensured his identity would be all over Maple Grove by now.

Did any of Robert Heller's descendants still live in Garrett County? Or anyone who had money stolen from the Maple Grove Bank in 1910? There was no bank insurance back then. Maybe Bruno thought somebody would want payback.

After she and Marty searched the newspaper's morgue for articles on the burglary of the Heller home, she'd go back into Ancestry.com to trace Heller's family tree to current time. Ancestry didn't permit any living people to appear on a public family tree. She could add them to her own tree, but only she and people she had allowed to view her entire tree could see them.

The policy also meant Digger couldn't find living people on trees other people maintained. However, she could usually find obituaries with names and locations of living descendants.

Uncle Benjamin's upside-down head appeared at the passenger side window. "*Slow down so you can see all the crocuses.*"

The steering wheel jerked as Digger reacted to his appearance.

"*Uh oh.*" The head vanished.

If he weren't dead, she'd kill him. She turned off Crooked Leg Road and drove to a parking space in front of the *Maple Grove News*. Uncle Benjamin wisely chose to move ahead of her and floated through the locked door into the paper's reception area. Digger knocked and Marty came toward her from the hallway that led to his office.

He waved through the door's glass and unlocked it. "Welcome to the search of a dusty newspaper morgue."

He sneezed and his glasses slid down his nose. He pushed them up.

"Can't wait. Had any luck yet?"

Marty shut the door and flicked the bolt. "Some, but I just started. Those really old editions are heavy, and the pages are pretty fragile."

Digger knew what he meant. She'd worked with Uncle Benjamin and his friend Thelma Zorn to do an index of Garrett County marriages in the first half of the 20th century. County records were the primary source, but when a name, especially a bride's name, seemed improbable, she'd checked the huge, bound newspaper folios.

Sometimes the person who wrote an article about a wedding knew the families and was more precise than the county clerk or judge who signed the marriage certificate. She almost always checked the name on the certificate with what the paper used. If she went with the paper's name, she'd list a judge's scribble as an alternate spelling.

Marty led the way to the large storage room at the back of the newspaper office. "You know why we have such a huge room for records?"

Digger took in the tall shelves on three sides and the leather-bound folios of past editions. "Printing presses used to be in there."

"*The place really stunk with ink when they printed the papers here,*" Uncle Benjamin said.

Digger didn't glance in his direction.

"Can't surprise you," Marty said. "I pulled the paper's articles about the 1910 bank robbery. Lots more detail than the piece the kid wrote and his mom posted on Facebook."

He had placed a large folio on the lone wood table, which was more like a basement workbench. "That Miss Tuley later added a lot to her description of the robber, but it sounds phony." He pointed to a page of the oversized old newspaper, dated June 7, 1910.

On further reflection, Miss Phyllis Tuley allowed that while the robber wore a cap, his hair seemed to be a brownish red, and he was approximately five feet ten inches tall."

Digger glanced at the date on the article. "Her memory got better three days after the robbery. Seems as if she would have initially remembered at least the height and hair color. Especially the height. Five-ten was taller than a lot of men at that time."

Uncle Benjamin floated out of the pages. "*My guess is somebody wanted her to identify a guy who matched that description. They probably suggested those features to her.*"

Digger repeated Uncle Benjamin's assumption, and added, "In crime shows, the police like to interview witnesses separately, so they aren't influenced by what any other people say they saw."

"Hello, Benjamin. Could be. The paper was a daily back then, so there's an article a day for two weeks. And your uncle will like this, the pages I couldn't see well on microfilm have a couple articles on the burglary at the Heller house."

"*Hot dog.*" Uncle Benjamin dove back into the folio.

Digger shook her head slightly. "He's gone into the paper to look around."

"Creeps me out," Marty said

"You don't know the half of it. How many days separated the two thefts?"

"Just four." Marty carefully turned a group of the fragile pages to get to a spot where he had placed a blue sticky note. "It's good we can look at the originals. In the old days, they referred to events as happening 'last Friday' or whatever. Easier to see dates this way."

Digger looked to where Marty pointed on the yellowed page.

Robert Heller, head of the Maple Grove Bank, reported that a large number of gold coins and several other items were stolen from the family home on approximately June 2nd. The date is not certain because the family was visiting Mrs. Heller's sister and her family in Hagerstown for several days.

Digger stared at the page as she thought. "Bank was robbed June 4, Heller home burglarized about June 6, and Mr. Morton's body found in the woods June 9th. Lots of action for such a short time."

"Yep. No follow-up on the Heller home burglary after a few days. I read every paper for a week, then just searched the index," Marty said.

Uncle Benjamin floated out of the folio and Digger jumped. "You've got to stop surprising me like that."

Marty smiled. "Keep it up, Benjamin."

"*I can't see where I'm coming out. Told you not everyone thought Heller's money was stolen from him.*"

"Marty said there wasn't much in the way of follow-up to the supposed home burglary."

Marty looked up from notes he was taking. "What did he find?"

Uncle Benjamin sat cross-legged on the worktable. *"Wasn't an article specifically about stolen coins. Heller was at the town 'gentlemen's club' playing cards. And his more highly skilled compatriots were kidding him about, and I quote, 'losing money from his home.'"*

Digger repeated what he said. "Sounds as if they were implying he lost it in some other way."

"Guess it's not a big deal now," Marty said. "The Morton man wasn't from here, so any accusation probably didn't damage his reputation. His posthumous reputation."

"Wish we had Baltimore papers here," Uncle Benjamin said. *"We could see if there was an obituary for him there."*

"Good idea." Digger turned to Marty. "Later I'll use Newspapers.com to see if I can find an obit for Gerard Morton in a paper in or near Baltimore."

He looked amused. "Why bother now?"

"The original *Maple Grove News* article called him an 'itinerate blacksmith.' Was he some sort of traveling vagrant, or was he simply a man traveling west who happened to be a blacksmith?"

He frowned. "Guess I picked up on language from the 1910 article about finding him."

"Never good to make assumptions," Uncle Benjamin said.

Digger decided repeating that would not contribute to a fun date that evening.

HALF AN HOUR LATER, Digger and Marty stood in front of the *Maple Grove News* trying to decide where to go for dinner that evening.

"If I didn't have to take my grandparents to Frostburg to buy jellybeans my grandfather likes, I'd say go over there. But I probably won't feel like going back."

Digger raised an eyebrow. "They go to Frostburg for jellybeans?"

"Supposedly we go for meat from a butcher they like, since we don't have one here. But it's an excuse to go to a specialty candy store by the university."

Uncle Benjamin floated onto the roof of Digger's Jeep. "*Good for them.*"

"Guilty pleasures when you're almost ninety, I guess," Digger said.

As she finished, a rust-colored, almost metallic-shiny, BMW pulled up to the curb and a man of about thirty jumped out. He pointed a finger at Marty. "I recognize you from your photo on the editorial page. You need to issue a retraction."

Marty's expression stayed impassive. "What story are you talking about?"

"You accused my great uncle of stealing gold coins before he died in the woods near here. That's wrong. Gerard Morton sold his blacksmith shop in Baltimore and had the proceeds with him. They vanished when he did."

"Was it a lot of money?" Marty asked.

"Nine-hundred and eighty dollars, assuming he hadn't spent any of it. Neither my great aunt or anyone else could get the sheriff in this backward county to believe them."

CHAPTER FIVE

DIGGER'S FIRST THOUGHT WAS to wonder what the guy thought he would get out of being rude.

Marty didn't appear annoyed. "So, your great uncle was the blacksmith. I only knew what was in the paper back then."

The nephew's six-feet-two height and dark expression gave off a menacing vibe. He walked a few feet closer, and Marty held up a hand, palm toward him. "That's close enough for an accusatory conversation. Unless you're just here to vent rather than talk to me."

He stepped back. "I...I just...He was my great aunt's brother. She talked about him a lot. He's not here to defend himself."

Digger said, "If you want Marty to write something different, what can you tell us about the sale of his blacksmith business? That would be a good place to start."

The man's attention shifted. "Who are you?"

"I'm Beth Browning. People call me Digger because I like to search in graveyards for family history information."

He gave her a blank stare.

She smiled. "Dig up information on relatives. Or anybody in Garrett County, really."

The man, who still hadn't introduced himself, looked from Marty to Digger and back. He seemed to deflate, as if he'd planned on a fight and they were too calm.

"Is your last name Morton?" Marty asked.

"It's Henry. I'm Josh Henry." He reached into the right pocket of his slacks and pulled out a folded piece of paper. "I have a copy of the contract he signed when he sold his shop. My great aunt kept it." He unfolded it and held it out to Marty, and Digger leaned closer to him as Marty unfolded it.

By 1910, some documents were typed, but this transaction was in flowery lettering with the first word of each paragraph indented and almost a half-inch high.

"In the city of Baltimore, Maryland, I, Gerard Morton, do hereby sell my business known as Morton Blacksmith and Ironworks to Mr. Houghton Clifford on this day of 27 May 1910 for the sum of nine-hundred and eighty U.S. dollars. This includes the building on South Eden Street as well as all tools, metals, and conveyances."

The yellowed paper described the building as brick with a flat, tarred roof. The forge -- with "modern bellows" – sat against the east wall. The contract continued with the list of the tools, metalworks underway (which included three fireplace sets), a two-seat buggy, a wagon used to transport finished products, as well as an assortment of horseshoes and nails.

The May 27, 1910, document was notarized, but the notary's signature was barely legible. It looked like Notting or something similar.

Uncle Benjamin had hovered over Digger's shoulder as she read. "*Sounds like a decent business. Morton could have done a lot with that $980.*"

Digger raised her eyes from the paper and smiled at Josh. "I can almost see his shop and what was in it."

Marty added, "The newspaper morgue has a photo of the last blacksmith shop in Maple Grove. It closed in the early 1930s."

"There's still one in Grantsville, but it's more artistic metalwork," Digger said.

Uncle Benjamin sounded hopeful. "*We should visit that place. Maybe a blacksmith ghost hangs around there.*" He now wore a rubberized, long apron and held a hand bellows.

"Yeah," Josh said. "Manufacturing was the death knell for blacksmithing, for the most part. And as the city expanded, there was less demand for rural-type needs."

Marty and Digger exchanged a quick look. She smiled and turned to Josh. "You want to head over to the Coffee Engine for a few minutes?"

Marty glanced at his watch. "I can join you for about fifteen minutes, but I have an errand to run in Frostburg. I'd like to do a piece on your…what is he? Your great uncle?"

"He's the brother of my great aunt so, yeah, my great uncle. I really appreciate you guys. I came on pretty strong."

"Always good to stick up for family," Digger said. She gave him directions for the short distance to the Coffee Engine and she and Marty headed to their cars.

Uncle Benjamin climbed into the front seat of Digger's Jeep. *"Thought at first that guy was going to throw a punch at Marty."*

"Me, too." Her phone buzzed and she took it from her purse and pressed the speaker button.

"You okay with being with him by yourself, if I leave to take my grandparents?"

"What does he think I am, a potted plant?" Uncle Benjamin asked.

"Yep. I think he worked himself up on his drive here, but he's calmed down. Hey, did he say where he's from?"

"Don't think so. And I'm sure Benjamin reminded me he's with you."

"I like this guy more every day."

Digger laughed. "He did. See you in a couple minutes." She pushed the end call button and briefly turned her head toward Uncle Benjamin. "If there was an article about the sale in a paper in Baltimore, somebody might have figured Morton'd be carrying the money and followed him out here."

"And gone for a walk up the mountain with him?" Uncle Benjamin sounded sarcastic.

Digger pulled into a parking space two shops down from the Coffee Engine. "Guess anything could have happened. The guy wasn't an itinerant blacksmith, that's for sure."

She didn't see Marty's car, so Digger followed Uncle Benjamin into the shop, though he floated through the door and she entered more traditionally. He had already made it to the display of bagged coffees to practice smelling when she reached the counter.

"Morning, Leslie. I'm going to pay for three coffees, one check. I'll let Marty and another guy give you their specifics."

"Sure. We have a new strawberry latte that I'm calling an Easter blend. Want to try it?"

"Sounds good." Digger gestured to the basket of plastic Easter eggs next to the cash register. "Goes with your decorations."

The door opened again, and Digger waved to Josh. "My treat. Just tell Leslie what kind of coffee you want."

He looked around. "Thanks. Marty's coming?"

"Think so. He probably had to take a call."

Digger carried her latte to the condiment counter and added a pinch of sugar. She grabbed a few napkins and headed for a booth at the far end of the shop. Just before lunch, there weren't many people at the fifteen tables or booths.

She sat and felt her phone vibrate. A message from Marty.

"Did a quick Internet search on our new friend. All looks okay. Be right in."

Digger put the phone in her purse and smiled at Josh as he slid in across from her. "Marty'll be here in a second."

He held up the coffee cup. "Thanks. Again, I'm sorry I came on so strong."

"I used to have a great uncle." No need to tell him she still did, in a way. "I would have defended him, too."

Uncle Benjamin made a heart sign with his hands.

Marty came in and waved. When he got to the counter, Leslie handed him a cup, and he laughed. Then she shook her head, and nodded toward Digger.

He sat next to Digger. "Leslie knows what I like. Thanks much."

Digger took another sip of her latte and nodded to Josh. "How did you come across Marty's article from yesterday?"

"I didn't. I have a cousin who's into anything tech, and he has alerts set up on Google."

From above her, Uncle Benjamin asked, "*What's that mean?*"

Digger inwardly cursed him. "It means he gets notified when certain family names appear on the Internet?"

"Yep. But he's also Gerard Morton, so he has an alert notification for himself. It picked up my great uncle."

Marty put his hot coffee on the table. "It took me a year to get the editor to put portions of the *Maple Grove News* online. Can't wait to tell him it led you to us."

"What do you know about what your uncle took with him from Baltimore? At least some of the money, obviously," Digger said.

Josh nodded. "He had two large suitcases – my great aunt called them valises – and that was it. She said he was trying to decide what to do next and didn't take much."

"Traveled by train?" Marty asked.

"Yeah. At first I couldn't figure how he got up here, but I found a couple articles online that said there used to be a rail spur into Maple Grove."

Uncle Benjamin's tone was excited. "*I bet I wrote that! Ask him if there was a picture of the old depot with the article.*"

"Was it an article from this historical society's newsletter?" Digger asked.

"Yep. Had a drawing of the oldest station and a photo of the last one in use."

"*Told you,*" Uncle Benjamin said.

"So, he took his money with him as far as you know. Was some of it in gold coins, do you think?"

Josh raised his eyebrows. "I don't know. I just knew he wouldn't steal someone else's money."

Marty looked up from his phone. "I did a quick Google search. If he put $980 in a bank in 1910, it would be worth almost $29,500 today."

"What!" Josh almost yelled.

From where he perched on the back of the booth, Uncle Benjamin said, "*That's assuming his bank didn't fail in the Depression.*"

"So, if somebody took it from him, I could say they owe me $29,500 today?" Josh asked.

Gently, Digger said, "Since the person would be dead, that'd be tough. And you'd have to prove he would have put it in a bank and not spent any of it. Kind of a hard case to make."

"I suppose," Josh said.

"However, if he did have some in gold coins, they would be worth many times the face value today."

"Like how much?"

"Let's see." Marty tapped his phone's keypad and studied what the search engine told him. "For example, some twenty-dollar gold coins from just before 1880 could bring $5,000 today."

"Whoa!" Josh said.

"We should talk more to Franklin about that," Digger said, quickly. She nodded to Josh. "My cousin collected coins. I don't know that he has any gold ones, but he would know about them."

Digger had hoped this might delay discussion of coin value, because others in the Coffee Engine had taken notice of the discussion. But Josh was not to be waylaid.

He leaned forward, "What do you think the chances are that he had money in coins?"

"Well, Marty said, if he was heading west, he knew he'd be crossing rivers and sitting by campfires. Paper money wouldn't survive any flames, and if it got wet enough it could be hard to separate bills.

Josh shrugged. "That's no different than today."

"Just look around this town," Digger said. "Many older buildings have been preserved and they're all wood. Almost any hotel he stayed in would have been, too. And there weren't fire hydrants like today. Sometimes entire city blocks – or more – burned because a bucket brigade wasn't enough to put out the fire."

Marty's expression indicated he wished he hadn't mentioned the current value of Gerard Morton's money.

"I couldn't see anything that said how old he was when he died."

"He was born in 1874, so late thirties. Thirty-six, I guess."

"No kids?" Digger asked.

He grinned. "My great aunt said he was a ladies' man, but she didn't know of any."

Digger took a small notebook from the miniature backpack she used as a purse. "So, there was your great aunt, your Great Uncle Gerard, and I take it you descend from one of their other siblings?"

"Always the genealogist," Marty said.

"My grandmother was Great Aunt Beatrice's younger sister. Her name was Angela. Beatrice and Gerard were closer in age, which is why she talked to my grandmother about Gerard a lot. Grandmother was quite a bit younger. She barely remembered Gerard."

Digger wrote Gerard, Beatrice, and Angela across the top of a page, and put an X under Gerard's name since he had no descendants. "So, one of your parents is Angela's son or daughter? What was her married name?"

"My grandfather was Leon Henry, so my grandmother became Angela Henry. My dad's name is the same as mine, Joshua." He frowned lightly. "Does it matter?"

Marty grinned. "She likes to put puzzles together."

Digger smiled at Josh. "I didn't mean to be nosy, Josh. I think in terms of family trees. Now I know how you fit in relation to Gerard Morton."

Marty slid his hand over and took Digger's notebook. "Mine's in the car. Tell me some more about

Gerard Morton. I'll write a piece about him. Make him more than a name on paper."

"My Great Aunt Beatrice, who was alive until I was nineteen, talked a lot about his shop. He was really proud of the business he built. So was she."

He described the blacksmith business Gerard Morton bought in 1896 as a fledgling concern that had lost customers when nails began being mass-produced in the 1880s. "Before that, the prior owner made a lot of his money by making nails for Baltimore's homes and small businesses. He shod horses and made stuff farmers used, like plows. But farms were being sold all around him as the city sprawled."

"Why did the prior owner sell to your great uncle in 1896?" Digger asked.

"Grandmother said the guy, I don't know his name, was going to close up shop and sell land with the building, but Gerard saw an opportunity."

"What did he do differently?" Marty asked.

"I was told he made metal railings for homes, metal fences. I guess when people had the money, they didn't want to go with wood fences and railing, not outside anyway." He nodded to Marty. "I had a laugh when your article said he left because he didn't shoe as many horses."

"He didn't shoe horses?" Digger asked.

"Some, but that wasn't where the money was, according to my great aunt and grandmother. He was sort of a free spirit, too. Made fancy belt buckles, hinges…all kinds of stuff."

"So why leave Baltimore?" Marty asked.

"My grandmother said he was tired of smithing. Hot work. And he simply wanted to go west. I have no idea what he planned to do, and I'm not sure he did either."

Marty asked a few more questions, then tore out the pages he'd written on and handed the notebook back to Digger. "Sorry I have to head out, but I need to run an errand in Frostburg." He turned to her. "You're going to hang out here for a while?"

"For a while. Call me when you get home."

Marty shook hands with Josh and left. Uncle Benjamin slid into the booth next to Digger. *"Ask him where he lives."*

"I take it you aren't from Garrett County. But you must be close."

"I live in Bethesda, not too far from DC. I've driven by here on Interstate 68, but never stopped in any of the small towns. It really is quaint."

Digger never thought of Maple Grove as quaint. Small, yes, but there were many thriving shops and some beautiful homes. Not a very diverse community, but more than some in Garrett County.

"Are you staying over? If you are, you might try the small bed and breakfast at the end of Main Street. It's nicer than going to one of the motels closer to the highway."

"I had planned to go back home this afternoon, but I think I'll stay. I'd like to walk around a little. It's an odd feeling to think that my Uncle Gerard walked these streets 110 years ago. Do you know where the coins Marty wrote about were found?"

"You probably noticed he didn't name the person who found them. I've heard who it was, and if he found them near where he lives, that would mean on the west side of Meadow Mountain, about three-quarters of the way up."

"Aunt Beatrice kept the letter a local doctor wrote about my uncle's death. That sounds kind of like the same area he referred to. I know it was above Maple Grove."

Digger frowned slightly. "I don't recall a mention of exactly where your uncle's body was found."

"I'm not sure. I guess there's no way to know if he died where he was found or if his body was moved there."

Uncle Benjamin interjected. *"Maybe we should go up there and look around. I can snoop in places that you can't."*

Digger didn't acknowledge him. She nodded to Josh. "I don't think there was much up there at the time that your uncle died. A couple of small houses, perhaps. Likely long gone."

Uncle Benjamin said, *"There must be coroner records down in Oakland."*

Digger hadn't thought about that, but she didn't see that knowing the cause of death would matter much. Unless it was clear that he was murdered. She nodded to Josh. "The newspaper at the time said that gold coins could have been stolen from a local banker, though I've heard people say they didn't think that was true. Maybe the banker lost the money gambling and a burglary was the story he came up with."

"The more I think about someone robbing him, probably leaving him for dead, the angrier I get. What do you think happened?" he asked.

"News stories say there was a bank robbery a few days before Gerard Morton died, and some of what was taken included gold coins." She shrugged. "I say there isn't any way to know whether the found coins were taken from your uncle before he died or were from a bank robbery or burglary."

"Huh." Josh stared at his coffee for a moment and then looked at Digger. "Would you be willing to drive me up there?"

Digger thought about work she had to do at home, her evening date with Marty, and the many No Trespassing signs he said littered Bruno's property. "I'll tell you what, we can take my Jeep and drive by the area, but I really don't want to walk around."

He frowned. "Why not?"

"Couple reasons. There aren't any paths, hardly even a lane off the state road. Also, the guy who found the coins is really ticked off that people guessed he found them. He blamed Marty and yelled at both of us in the diner."

"Are you afraid of him?"

"*You maybe should be. At least a little bit,*" Uncle Benjamin said.

"No...but it would be fair to say he likes to intimidate people. He's the classic loner in the woods and he has No Trespassing signs everywhere."

"I can follow. Then you can leave and I'll look for the guy."

Digger felt irritated. She wasn't responsible for Josh, but she didn't want to lead him into a fight. "Sorry." She smiled to soften her words somewhat. "It's a take it or leave it offer."

CHAPTER SIX

MARTY STOOD AT THE entrance to Fabulous Frostburg Candies Saturday afternoon and watched his grandfather tell the counter clerk he wanted a full pound of black jellybeans. Malcolm Wilson maintained he was entitled to eat all the candy he wanted after working hard for fifty years. Maria Wilson maintained he was a very hard worker, but there was no need to eat himself into an early grave.

True, his grandfather had gained a few pounds in the fifteen years since he retired from driving long-haul trucks, but he was hardly obese. Marty thought if his grandmother was so worried about her husband's weight, she could switch to egg whites and turkey bacon. She wouldn't, of course.

He'd been taking them to the old-fashioned shop in Frostburg at least twice each month, ever since they stopped driving the year both turned eighty-two. Maria passed her vision test at Motor Vehicles, but Malcolm had not. She decided if they kept a car he would try to sneak the keys and head to the lake to fish. She was probably right.

Marty asked the local senior center if they could schedule fishing outings in the summer. Malcolm was pleased, and Maria was glad to have the time to herself while he fished for walleye and smallmouth bass in Deep Creek Lake.

The elderly pair finished their purchases, with Maria buying her usual six chocolate-covered cherries. "Okay, chauffer, bring the car to the door, please," Malcolm said.

They both laughed.

Marty opened the door to the street, "At your service."

He pulled away from the curb to his grandfather's complaint about car doors with automatic locks. "What would happen if you crashed and we couldn't get out?"

Marty looked at his grandfather in the rearview mirror, noting he was surreptitiously starting on his jellybeans. "If I drive over the side of the mountain, you'll have bigger problems than getting out of the car."

Maria smoothed the skirt of her shirtwaist dress so it lay evenly under the seatbelt. "No one's crashing the car."

"Everyone should stop buying these so-called modern cars until Detroit does away with these automatic locks," Malcolm said.

"They'll just buy Toyotas," Maria said.

Before his grandfather could respond, Marty asked, "Did you two read my article about the coins found on the mountain?"

"We read all your articles," Maria said.

"Of courshe." Malcolm spoke through a jellybean.

"This morning a guy in his late twenties or so caught up with Digger and me at the paper. He said he was the great-grandnephew of the blacksmith whose body was found in 1910."

"No kidding," Malcolm said.

Marty relayed what he'd learned about the not-so-itinerate blacksmith and the options for how gold coins might have ended up on the west side of Meadow Mountain. "So, what did you two hear about that 1910 bank robbery? It's the only one I know of in Maple Grove."

"That was a good deal before our time," Maria said.

"I heard different versions of the bank story and that Heller fellow who ran it." Malcolm's paper bag crackled. "Couple guys at the VFW said their parents had money in the bank. No insurance back then."

Marty heard his grandfather fish yet another jellybean from his sack. At the rate he was popping them, he'd be done before they got back to Maple Grove.

"I don't think anybody believed the blacksmith angle. Seems to have been made up after the poor man's body was found," Malcolm said.

"If this man who came to town was the blacksmith's great nephew, what did he think happened?" Maria asked.

Marty thought about the conversation with Josh. "I don't think he had a clue about what was going on in Maple Grove at the time. His great aunt tried to convince whoever was sheriff back then that her brother had to have been murdered."

"Did you find a death certificate?" Malcolm asked.

Marty headed up the ramp onto Interstate 68. "I need to delve into that more. Seems it would have been obvious if he didn't die of natural causes."

"You don't read much Agatha Christie," Maria said.

"True," Marty said.

"We had supper at the diner last night," Malcolm said. "Heard about that Bruno Sampson fellow hollering at you. You should watch out for him."

"Seems harmless," Marty said.

"So did his father until his wife left him after one too many beatings."

"One beating is too many," Maria said.

"Obviously," Malcolm agreed.

"How old was Bruno when they split?" Marty asked.

"Not sure, junior high school maybe," Maria said.

Marty figured witnessing those beatings would have been horrible for a kid. "So, Bruno left with her and came back?"

"She left without him," Malcolm said.

"She left him with an abusive father?"

"Yes," Maria said, "but the school paid attention to him. I never heard that Silas Sampson hit his son."

"Some abusers make a point not to hit people where it would show," Marty murmured.

Malcolm leaned forward and tapped Marty on the shoulder. "All the more reason to keep away from that Bruno. He could have a lot of hostility built up in him."

MARTY DROPPED HIS GRANDPARENTS at their house just outside of Maple Grove and refused an offer to stay for supper. "Digger and I are doing something, not sure what yet."

Malcom gave him an exaggerated wink as he climbed out of the car. "Have fun."

"Planning on it." He forced a wide smile. Both his grandparents were anxious for him to develop what they called a serious relationship. He figured they thought it would ensure he would stay in Maple Grove.

He had no particular plans to leave, but if he and Digger fizzled it would probably be time to think more about his future. There weren't too many single women in their late twenties in town. Not that many in all of Garrett County.

Marty parked in front of the newspaper office. He'd decided to check a couple online databases to see if he could find death information for Gerard Morton. Years as a reporter in Baltimore had led him to the Maryland Archives to look up death records. There were some indexes, but people pretty much had to go to the Archives to use state computers. Or mail a request to Vital Records for a certified copy of a death certificate and wait for weeks. He didn't feel like waiting.

He had a friend at the *Baltimore Sun* who could probably be talked into sending an intern to the state Archives. But from his desk he could check newspaper collections for hundreds of papers throughout the United States.

He lucked out. *The Baltimore World* ended publication in 1910, when it was sold to become the Baltimore *Evening Sun*. The *Baltimore World* had been a smaller paper. Maybe since Gerard Morton had just sold a business and left town, his death – especially if it was a murder – would have been noted.

Marty searched by Morton's full name, then remembered many men used initials back then. However, they used first and middle initials and he didn't know Morton's middle name.

He signed onto one of Digger's favorite genealogy sites and searched for Baltimore birth records. That sent him back to the Maryland Archives, so he switched tacks and went to the 1900 Federal Census for Baltimore.

When he entered Gerard Morton he found several, but only one in a household with Beatrice and Angela. "Bingo!"

Gerard David Morton was twenty-five, born in December 1874. Beatrice's birth showed as January 1882 and Angela as April 1892, eighteen years younger than Gerard. Though it looked as if the children were evenly spaced, Marty knew there had probably been other children who died young.

Armed with Gerard's birth month and year as well as his initials, Marty searched for news articles about G.D. Morton. He immediately found a short one in 1896 that described the man's purchase of the blacksmith works on Eden from Horace T. Hill. Following that were several quarter-page ads for fireplace andirons and metal fences "for the discerning Baltimore home."

All well and good, but didn't help Marty learn more about Morton's death. He tried different keywords, and when he put "death" and "woods" in the same string, he finally had a useful hit.

"Local Man Found Dead in Garrett County." Marty skimmed the three paragraphs before he printed them. Misses Beatrice and Angela Morton had been notified the previous day that their beloved brother Gerard, recently of the family home in Baltimore, had been found dead in the woods near the small mountain town of Maple Grove.

Marty glanced at the date of the paper. June 11, 1910.

Most of the piece described the blacksmith business Morton had sold and his desire to "seek his fortune" in the Western Expanse. The next-to-the last sentence noted he had been found with a head wound, which the local sheriff assumed had been from a fall while walking in what were termed city shoes. The final point was that Mr. Morton's only local acquaintances were at the hotel in Maple Grove, and no one knew why he had ventured out alone on the mountain.

No mention was made of any money or other valuables Morton might have had with him.

An even shorter article three days later announced that Misses Beatrice and Angela Morton had held a viewing in the family home the prior day and had buried their dearest brother in Green Mount Cemetery.

Marty had viewed the grave of John Wilkes Booth, the most infamous resident of the very large Baltimore burial ground. He shut down his computer. He'd verified what Josh Henry had told him and Digger, but hadn't added anything substantial to the story. If Gerard Morton had had a large sum of cash or coins with him, he'd carried the information to his grave.

JOSH HENRY DID NOT take Digger up on her offer to drive him up the mountain. He said he'd walk through town and then drive back to Bethesda. That was fine with Digger. She found it hard to maintain a conversation with someone she barely knew.

Uncle Benjamin wanted to head up the mountain to look for more coins. "*I can go places you can't in those woods. Hey, I wonder if there are Geiger counters for ghosts?*"

Digger grinned as she pulled into the Ancestral Sanctuary driveway. "I think you mean metal detector. How would you use it?"

"*I'd...Look, Franklin's here!*"

Digger hadn't finished putting the car in park before Uncle Benjamin floated out the window to stand next to his son. She waved through the windshield and laughed as her uncle tentatively put his hand on Franklin's shoulder. It simply went through Franklin's arm.

Other than the guilt she felt about keeping Uncle Benjamin's so-called existence a secret, she was always glad to see her cousin. He came up from DC at least twice a month now, in large part to be sure she was okay rattling around in the large house.

Digger climbed out of her Jeep. "Have a good drive?"

"Very peaceful. Once I got about ten miles north of DC." He walked down the porch steps and kissed Digger on the cheek as Bitsy barked from inside the house.

"*I'm damn jealous,*" Uncle Benjamin said.

"Marty coming up tonight?" Franklin asked.

"We'll probably eat dinner here with you and then head into town again. Saturdays are always an exciting time at the Ice Cream Shoppe."

"And then come back here, right?"

Digger knew her cousin worried that if Marty didn't stay over, it was because of Franklin's presence. "Once a month he goes to church with Malcolm and Maria Wilson, his grandparents. They go out for pancakes before the service. So, maybe not."

Franklin opened the screen door and Bitsy bounded out. "You aren't invited?"

Digger stooped to pet the excited German Shepherd. "I'm sure his grandparents would love to include me. But that might seem like a sort of…"

"Commitment?" Franklin asked, with a smirk.

Uncle Benjamin said, "*She's kind of guy-shy.*"

Digger wished she could tell him to butt out. "We get along great, but I don't want to rush anything, like I did with the last guy."

Franklin followed her into the large entry hall. "I hear you, but Marty's nothing like what's-his-name."

"Damion. I try to forget the name. Have you unpacked?"

"I just brought a duffel bag. I'm resigned to having two sets of toiletries and some other basics. No sense hauling them around all the time."

"Good. Come out to the kitchen while I throw together a box cake. Cupcakes, anyway."

"*I used to love the smell of the chocolate ones,*" Uncle Benjamin said.

"What kind?" Franklin asked.

"Strawberry with chocolate icing."

"I've seen strawberry cake in the baking aisles but haven't tried it. Let me check the shepherd's hooks I put by Mom and Dad's stone. I'll be right back." He headed out the back door, toward the gentle rise that led to the small family plot.

Uncle Benjamin floated through a porch window to follow his son.

Digger gave Bitsy a treat and washed her hands at the kitchen sink. It gave her a chance to switch into 'secret-keeping mode.' She took two eggs from the fridge and retrieved some cooking oil from the pantry near the steps that led to the cellar.

Before she began to mix the ingredients, she texted Marty that Franklin had arrived and asked him when she should put the frozen lasagna in the oven.

He wrote back, "Just leaving the paper. See you in a few minutes."

DINNER WITH MARTY AND FRANKLIN always involved a certain amount of teasing in Digger's direction. It sometimes flustered her, which guaranteed more.

They'd finished the cake when Marty asked, "Do you play bridge, Franklin?"

He shook his head. "I always think of it as an old person's game, I guess."

"Takes just enough brain power to keep me interested," Marty said. "I've been trying to talk Digger into learning."

"Takes four people, right? Who do you have in mind?" she asked.

"So, we'd have Franklin. You could ask your lovely business partner," Marty said.

"Holly knows a little, but she's afraid if she plays her grandmother will get wind of it and she'll have to play a lot with her."

"*I heard Audrey cheats,*" Uncle Benjamin said.

Digger turned a smirk into a light sneeze. "Excuse me."

"You can keep a secret," Marty said. "What do you say, Franklin?"

He shrugged. "I'll give it a shot, but I don't want to become one of those people who eats and sleeps bridge."

"Okay," Digger said, "but before we switch gears, I want to talk more about gold coins."

"I may have told you most of what I know during dinner," Franklin said.

"In 1910, would the blacksmith have been carrying coins from that year or the year before, or coins that went way back?" Marty asked.

"He might've had mostly recent ones," Franklin said. "In 1910, the Indian Head five-dollar gold piece was issued. It'd be worth more than $1,000 today. There were smaller denominations, like the $2.50 Indian Head. I don't see how you'd figure out if he had older coins."

Marty leaned his chair back until it almost touched the mahogany buffet. "If a lot of his money came from the person who bought Morton's blacksmith business, he could've been saving his money and had some much older coins."

"That's true," Franklin said. "People put their gold coins in a home safe. Maybe a bank safe deposit box, but even some middle-class folks had safes."

"And I suppose all it was worth to them was the face value of the coin," Digger said.

The kitchen phone rang and Digger got up from the dining room table. "Be right back."

"I'll clear the rest of the dishes," Marty said, and Franklin stood to help him.

She took the receiver from the kitchen wall phone. "Digger Browning here."

"Digger, this is Sheriff Montgomery. You know a fellow named Josh Henry?"

"Josh Henry?" She met Marty's glance. "Marty and I met him today."

"Somebody took a pot shot at him. He's lucky to be alive."

CHAPTER SEVEN

DIGGER AND MARTY MET Sheriff Montgomery in the waiting room of the urgent care clinic, the closest thing Maple Grove had to a hospital.

"Your friend's back there getting his ankle wrapped and a couple decent scratches bandaged. Who the heck is he?"

"He came to the paper today." Digger nodded to Marty to indicate he could pick up the story.

"Josh has a cousin who was named after Gerard Morton, the blacksmith who died while traveling through this area in 1910. The cousin has one of those Google alerts on his name and he had a note yesterday because the name Gerard Morton was in my story about the gold coins on Friday. Not the living man, but Google doesn't necessarily differentiate."

Montgomery shook his head in frustration. "What does that have to do with this Josh being up the west side of Meadow Mountain?"

"He didn't tell you?" Digger asked.

"If he did, do you think I'd be asking?"

"Right." Digger said. "He wanted to see the area where the coins were found. I told him I'd drive him up there…"

"To Bruno Sampson's place?" Marty asked.

"As I was saying, I would drive him up there, in my Jeep, but we wouldn't get out." She looked at Marty. "You mentioned the No Trespassing signs and Bruno had already told me to stay out of his 'bizness.'" Digger put the last word in air quotes.

"So, you drove him?" Montgomery asked.

"No. He wanted to get out and roam around. When I said I didn't think that was a good idea, he said he'd walk around town and head back to where he lives, Bethesda, I think he said."

Marty nodded toward a door that said Treatment Area. Staff Only. "I take it he didn't go home."

Montgomery nodded. "According to the good Mr. Sampson, who was checking some traps, he heard rustling on his land and hollered at whoever it was to get the hell off the property. When he saw the back of a man not long after, he fired a shot – he says in the air."

"So, Josh didn't actually get shot?" Digger asked.

"No. And though I question whether he needed to fire that shot, this Mr. Henry was on Sampson's property and had been warned off. Never yelled who he was or anything."

"How'd his foot get hurt?" Marty asked.

"Ran off in a panic and tripped over a bush or root or something. Doc here says it's a really bad sprain. Swollen and purple. Scratched up his face. Lucky he didn't poke out an eye."

Digger shook her head. "I told him Bruno was grouchy, or something to that effect."

"He admitted that." Montgomery sighed. "He doesn't have any records of arrests. I mostly wanted you to verify who he is, what he told you about being here."

"While I believed him," Marty said, "all we can say is what he told us. Though…" he hesitated, "I did look up more about the Gerard Morton who was killed in 1910."

"You did?" Digger asked.

"And?" Montgomery said.

"Pretty much what he told us earlier. His great uncle sold his blacksmith shop in Baltimore and was heading west. No information on why he was up here, but a Baltimore paper had short articles about his death here and burial in Baltimore. Article mentioned the Garrett County sheriff of the time said Mr. Morton died from a wound on his skull from walking in the woods in city shoes."

Montgomery frowned. "What the heck was he doing up that far? Even back then weren't but a couple houses there."

Digger shrugged and Marty said, "Maybe there's something in some old sheriff records."

"I don't have time to go through stuff from 120 years ago. Will you two see he gets to one of the motels? He can't drive." The sheriff's phone rang, and he answered it as he walked away. "You at that accident on 68?" And he was out the door.

Digger and Marty looked at each other and then sat on hard plastic chairs in the minuscule waiting room.

Digger glanced at a reception desk behind a now-closed glass. "Guess the rest of the staff went home."

"Yeah, they close at eight. You want to flip a coin for him?"

Digger sighed. "I'll take him. My dog can't turn around in your place."

"Your bedrooms are all upstairs."

"Franklin can help me get him settled on the couch. I wonder where his car is?"

"I'll find out," Marty said. "But I have some better information."

"So, you did some digging?" she asked.

Marty grinned. "Yes, *Digger*. You'll be pleased to know I went to the 1900 census to find Morton. He still lived with his sisters. I guess that wouldn't have been too long after he bought the blacksmith business."

"I'm glad you learned a lot of techniques from me."

He wiggled his eyebrows and Digger blushed. He continued, "And that got me his middle name, which was David. The later articles referred to him as G.D. Morton."

"So, what does that tell us?"

"Nothing, just lets me write a better update piece; I don't want him remembered as an itinerate blacksmith."

"Any mention of him having money with him?"

Marty shook his head. "If he didn't leave some of it with his sisters or a bank in Baltimore, I don't see what else we can learn about that."

"Kind of makes sense that someone figured out he had money and enticed him to a place to try to rob him."

"Mmm. He's buried in Green Mount Cemetery in Baltimore."

"Where John Wilkes Booth is?" Digger asked.

"You do know your history."

The door to the treatment area opened and Dr. Webb preceded a visibly shaken Josh Henry, who was very unsteady on the crutches he used. Large scratches on his right cheek seemed to have some sort of salve on them.

Dr. Webb's expression changed from a frown to a smile. "Oh, good. You two can help Mr. Henry, can't you?"

Josh, concentrating on his foot and crutches, hadn't noticed them. He paused and tilted to one side.

Marty took two long strides and put a hand on Josh's right bicep. "Steady there."

Josh stopped and looked at Dr. Webb "Thanks a lot. Especially for staying late." He nodded to Marty. "Thanks."

The doctor smiled. "You got here just in time." He looked at Marty. "You're taking him to a motel?"

Digger spoke as she looked at Josh. "We were thinking of the couch on my first floor. There's a half-bath nearby, and we'll keep the cat off your foot."

He winced and mumbled. "Thanks a lot."

"I'll let you be off then." Dr. Webb hurried into the treatment area.

Marty looked at Digger. "I think your Jeep would be better than my Toyota. I could follow you up there."

She shook her head. "Franklin's there. No need to waste the gas." To Josh, she asked, "Where's your car? Is there stuff in it you need?"

He shook his head. "A couple sheriff deputies came up with the ambulance. One of them drove it to a lot he said was behind their Maple Grove office. I have my phone."

"Let me get the door," Marty said, and opened it, letting Digger go out ahead of Josh.

She walked quickly to the Jeep, a couple car lengths from them, and opened the door to the back seat. Marty stayed with Josh, who rested after every couple of crutch steps.

With much assistance and a few groans, Josh managed to slide into the Jeep, leg extended across the back seat.

Digger took a blanket from the back and rolled it up so his foot was slightly elevated. "I have some gel ice packs in the freezer; that'll help."

Josh met her eyes for the first time. "If I'd listened to you, I wouldn't be in this mess."

From the open Jeep door, Marty said, "Digger is familiar with ignoring sound advice at times."

Digger slid into the driver's seat. "Pot calling the kettle black. See you tomorrow afternoon, maybe?"

"Yeah, I'll bring up enough ice cream for four."

"Say hello to your grandparents," Digger said, and Marty waved and shut the car door.

She fastened her seatbelt and turned her head to look into the back seat. "I'll try to avoid bumps, but our roads in spring are known for potholes."

"I really appreciate this," Josh said.

As they drove, Digger explained that the Ancestral Sanctuary was on the east side of the mountain and that her great uncle had left it to her. She mentioned Franklin, Bitsy, and Ragdoll, and said she'd try to get Ragdoll to sleep on the third floor with her cousin.

"She's the only one in the house who would try to investigate your ankle."

"It sounds so idyllic – an inherited family home, pets, a cousin, good friends."

Digger thought he sounded wistful. "I guess it seems ordinary to me. Franklin's life as a lawyer in DC sounds a lot more interesting to most people."

He asked where Franklin lived – Dupont Circle – which Josh said was just a few Metro stops from Bethesda.

They pulled into the long drive and Josh whistled at the sight of the large brick house with its large porch and many gardens. "I bet this is stunning in the daytime."

"And a lot to mow," Digger said.

Franklin came onto the front porch as she parked in the circular drive in front of the house. "Hang on a minute, and I'll let my cousin know why you're here."

Franklin met her at the bottom of the porch steps, with Uncle Benjamin standing silently behind him. Both listened to why she had brought a relative stranger to the house. The Jeep windows were up, but Franklin still lowered his voice. "You feel safe with him here?"

Digger spoke equally softly. "Before we went to the Coffee Engine today, Marty did a quick Internet search. He said he doesn't seem to have any kind of record or anything."

Franklin's light frown cleared. "Let's get him into the house. Living room?"

Digger opened the door to the back seat. "Yep. Josh, you ever climbed stairs on crutches?"

He had not, and it took a full ten minutes to get him into the house and seated on the couch, leg aligned in front of him. Franklin grabbed a batch of pillows from the guest room and Uncle Benjamin's old room as Uncle Benjamin hovered around all the activities.

"You have to be sure his foot is higher than his hip. That'll help the swelling go down."

Digger repeated what he had said to Franklin, who was helping Josh lift his leg from the couch onto the stack of pillows. By the time they had accomplished that, Josh was white as a dogwood flower.

Digger retrieved the blue ice gel packs from the freezer and gently placed one on each side of the foot, with a couple kitchen towels draped over them. "When it gets really cold the pain will be somewhat better."

"The doctor gave me a pain pill and a prescription to get more tomorrow. Kind of feels like I might need it."

"Did you eat?" Digger asked.

He shook his head. "But I don't want to be any trouble."

Digger grinned. Franklin laughed and said, "You already are, but don't worry about it."

"I'll warm up a small piece of lasagna and put some stuff on the coffee table that you might need tonight. Flashlight, water, you have your phone." She headed for the kitchen.

While she heated the lasagna and took a bottle of water from the fridge, Digger thought about Bruno Sampson. What on earth made him shoot to ward off a stranger? It might be technically legal to protect his property, but with people looking to buy land for a campground and the possibility of naïve treasure hunters, it sure wasn't safe.

She wondered if his mother had kept in touch with him through the years. Uncle Benjamin had said Bruno's father died a number of years ago and was buried in the city cemetery. Digger would look him up on Ancestry or Find a Grave to learn more about him. Though she couldn't think why she should care.

It occurred to her to wonder how Marty had heard about the coins Bruno found. The man didn't sound like the type to look for attention. She'd have to ask Marty how he learned of the discovery.

Digger yawned. Almost ten o'clock.

Uncle Benjamin floated into the kitchen. *"Franklin put his number in the guy's phone so he can call Franklin if he needs something during the night."*

"Good idea. I hoped I didn't have to help him get into the bathroom later."

Franklin came into the kitchen. "I'll do it. You know you're talking to yourself again. You maybe spend too much time alone."

Irritated at herself for talking aloud, Digger simply smiled. "Or you could visit more often."

"I wish. I'm going up the back stairs. He can call me if he wants. Not to be overbearing, but I think you should leave him to me overnight."

"I heartily agree." Digger took the lasagna from the microwave. "You're the best."

Franklin grinned as he started for the stairs. "I won't tell Marty."

"I won't either," Uncle Benjamin said.

Ragdoll meowed from the doorway.

"Where have you been? I'll feed you soon." The cat looked at Uncle Benjamin as if expecting him to feed her.

Digger took a tray from the top of the refrigerator and put the lasagna, water, utensils, and an apple on it. She walked through the dining room and peered into the living room. For a moment she thought Josh was sleeping, but his eyes opened.

"Hey, brought you something to eat." She sat the tray on the coffee table and pulled it closer to the couch. "Franklin can move the coffee table if you need to get up during the night. Don't try to do it yourself."

Josh had been leaning into a couple pillows and sat up straighter. "I am so sorry…"

Digger waved away the apology. "It's a small town. People always do what needs to be done. Besides," she smiled. "Tomorrow we can talk more about what happened today and what the heck you were looking for up there."

He hung his head for a second. "I'm an idiot."

Ragdoll meowed from next to the coffee table, and Digger smiled. "I'll take the dog and cat upstairs with me tonight."

"I like animals. I guess not on my foot."

Digger returned to the kitchen and shut the door that separated it from the dining room. Uncle Benjamin sat in his usual cross-legged position on the Formica table.

As Digger placed cat food in a bowl, Ragdoll swatted her hand – no claws. "I'm sorry girl. Next time I'll put more food in your bowl if we go out. Or you could meow at Franklin."

"*Probably be a lot of people moving around up there the next few days. Bruno should keep his gun or rifle in his cabin.*"

"It's almost as if he's trying to protect something more than land and a couple old buildings."

Uncle Benjamin stared into the distance for a moment, then looked at Digger. "*Do we know whatever happened to his mother?*"

Digger shrugged. "I don't think so. Not likely she'd be up there with him."

"I wasn't thinking of her still walking around."

CHAPTER EIGHT

WHEN DIGGER WOKE UP Sunday morning, she couldn't remember what was different. She still hadn't replaced the beige curtains Uncle Benjamin had hung at the window many years ago, and the antique oak chest of drawers still sat opposite her bed.

Then she remembered. A man she barely knew slept in the living room last night because he'd hurt his foot going someplace even she wasn't nuts enough to wander to.

She'd slept until 7:30, which was late for her. From the first floor came the sound of low male voices. Either Josh talked to himself, or Franklin had already made it downstairs.

She dressed quickly in lightweight jeans and a t-shirt from the Garrett County Historical Society – "treasuring family above and below ground." By the time she took the back stairs, Franklin had bacon cooking in the kitchen.

He greeted Digger with, "Good morning, sleepy head."

"Morning to you, too. Hope you didn't have to get up a lot last night."

"Checked on him about six, my usual wake-up time." He lowered his voice. "He's hurting. When the pharmacy opens, I'll run into town and get his prescription filled." He nodded to the coffee pot.

Digger poured a cup and added cream. "I'll take him another ice gel pack and some Tylenol." She grabbed the bottle from a cupboard and poured two of the white pills into her hand.

Franklin stayed with the bacon and Digger walked through the dining room to the sunny living room. Bitsy lay on the floor by the couch and Ragdoll sat on Josh's chest. "Oh dear, I hope she didn't hurt you."

She placed the ice pack on his wrapped ankle, and Josh said, "Thanks much. She hid behind the lamp table in front of your window, and as soon as Franklin left, she jumped on my stomach." He petted the fluffy cat, who ignored him.

Bitsy's tail thumped and Digger looked down at him. "I'm sure Franklin let you out."

He barked once and stood to stretch, butt in the air.

"Okay, you can go out front, but stay out of the bushes." Digger let him out the front door and returned to sit on a stuffed chair across from Josh. "Are you up to telling me more about yesterday?"

"Yeah. I'm embarrassed about it." He took a breath. "I drove out of Maple Grove, up the west side of the mountain. There was this one house, about a mile up the road, with a white mailbox with tulips around it?"

"The Elders. Very nice couple."

He smiled. "I asked them where the Sampson property was. They said about three-quarters of a mile more, but it wasn't marked and didn't have a mailbox."

"That's all they told you?" Digger asked.

Josh flushed. "They said there was a narrow turnoff, more a lane, but not to turn in there unless Bruno Sampson had specifically invited me. The husband – I forget his name..."

"Maxwell. Max Elder."

"Right. He said this Bruno was a loner and didn't like strangers. He said I'd probably see No Trespassing signs."

"And you did?"

"Yeah, but I didn't see anyone around at all, so I parked on the lane and got out."

"Is there even a path?" Digger asked.

"If you look really closely, there's a pile of brush by the road, and a few feet behind it is a narrow path."

Digger shook her head, but smiled. "A true invitation to go no farther. What did you hope to find?"

"Sounds ludicrous now, but I thought if there were coins that had been my uncle's, maybe there were other things. I mean, he worked with metal. He made my grandmother a thin chain to put on her dog's collar. Maybe he carried an old skeleton key."

Digger nodded slowly. "I supposed those things might not be shiny enough to show easily. But after all these years, you'd probably need a metal detector."

Josh's face brightened. "What do they look like?"

"Not that I'm advocating that you look," Digger said, quickly. "Think of a golf club with a round, metal plate on the bottom."

He sighed. "I was stupid to try. I walked back maybe twenty or thirty yards and realized there was nothing to see. Heck, I don't even know if my great-uncle died there."

Digger thought trying would be okay in a location without a rage-man. "And then you ran into Bruno?"

"A man yelled I should 'get the hell out,' and I yelled back that I was looking for something, but I'd leave."

"And you turned to go?"

"Not for a couple minutes. I just stood there slowly turning, and about the time I moved toward the road somebody fired a gun. Sheriff told me later it was a shotgun."

"So, Sheriff Montgomery talked to Bruno?"

"Yeah. I started to run, but I fell really hard. I yelled that I broke my leg. This Bruno was decent enough to call for an ambulance, and he told the E-911 people to send a sheriff's deputy, too. He told them to look for a dark orange car. I guess he saw it on the road."

"What else did he say?"

"He told me to stay the hell off his property, and if I came back I'd have more than a sore leg. Then he turned around and walked away. He just left."

Franklin came in with three plates of bacon and buttered toast. "You wouldn't have had much to talk about anyway." He placed all the plates on the coffee table.

"You know Bruno Sampson?" Digger asked.

"He was a year ahead of me in school. Not that he came too often." He nodded to Josh. "I'm twelve years older than my dear cousin, who is twenty-six. Bruno's about thirty-eight or thirty-nine."

"I thought he was older, but I mostly saw a long beard and angry eyes," Josh said.

"The day we saw him in the diner, I thought he was probably early forties. I suppose you look older when you're outside all the time."

"I doubt he's the type to use sunscreen," Franklin said, dryly. He nodded to Josh. "The independent pharmacy we have here opens at nine. Give me your prescription and I'll take it down there."

"Thanks. It's the throbbing that bothers me most. I really appreciate it."

Franklin stood. "Dishes are yours, cuz."

MARTY SAT WITH MALCOLM and Maria in their usual pew – third back on the right in the Maple Grove Methodist Church. He didn't mind going with them every few weeks, largely because they so liked having him with them.

What he did mind was that every time he attended, the minister tried to get him to become an official member. Though he sometimes enjoyed Reverend Simon's sermons, regular church going wasn't his thing.

The minister discussed how people should rise above material goods. "And remember Luke 12:15, which tells us life is not measured by how much you own."

Marty chuckled to himself. Good thing he didn't measure that way. His small apartment was crammed with books and music, but not much else. When he'd left the *Baltimore Sun* to reinvent himself in a smaller town, he gave up aspirations of wealth. Not that writing made many people rich anyway.

The sermon ended, and soon he and his grandparents were on the lawn just outside the church door. They loved introducing him to any of their friends he hadn't yet met.

As they walked to the car, a man about fifty approached them. Marty thought he'd met him on an earlier Sunday.

The slightly balding, tall man held out a hand. "Marty Hofstedder, I think. I'm Lucas Heller."

Marty took the handshake. "Thanks for reminding me of your name." Then it hit him. Heller. The long-ago banker's family name. His expensive suit and almost regal bearing proclaimed either wealth or self-importance.

Heller greeted Malcolm and Maria, who clearly liked him. "May I borrow your grandson for five minutes?"

Malcolm said, "You can have him for ten." Maria gave her husband a teasing slap on the arm.

Marty moved toward the church parking lot. "Would you be related to the late banker, Robert Heller?"

"My great-grandfather. Said to be a very colorful fellow." He smiled. "I was never sure whether to believe family lore about him having gold coins that were stolen."

Marty nodded. "I can see how it would be pretty hard to know."

"Word around town is that Bruno Sampson is the one who found some coins on the mountain." He grinned. "Or word in the diner, anyway."

"Right. Another colorful fellow. And not anxious to make new friends."

Heller nodded. "I was curious if there were other things found with the coins."

"Bruno didn't mention anything. What are you thinking of?"

Heller leaned against a late model Volvo, which Marty figured was the only one in town. "Here's the thing. I'm not interested in coins, but Great Grandfather Robert said that my great-grandmother's engagement ring and a bag of dozens of old marbles were also taken."

"Must have been hard on your grandmother."

"Apparently she hadn't worn it for some time. You know how knuckles get bigger as people age. But she was supposed to have been angry that the drawer of Grandfather's desk had been left unlocked. Seems that's the only place the thief looked."

Marty hesitated. "On the cop shows, I think they would be suspicious that was an 'inside job.' Or at least someone who'd been in the house before."

Lucas Heller nodded. "Some people, my father Martin included, thought Great-Grandfather Robert had pawned or sold them. My father was most angry about the marbles. His father played with them and even as an adult he talked about how sad he was when they were stolen. Aside from that, some of them would be worth a lot."

"Marbles?"

Heller nodded. "Marble collectors, if you can believe it. My grandfather showed me pictures of some that were like his. I think of them as marbles with swirls, but some of the hand-blown ones are quite valuable."

"I heard a vague reference to your great-grandfather enjoying card games."

"And he didn't know how to quit when he was ahead in poker." Heller shook his head. "He gambled away a lot of money, if my great grandmother was to be believed."

Marty had one more question. "Though I don't think Bruno Sampson would ask me for advice, if he wants to know anyone who might want to buy what he finds, should I give him your name?"

Heller smiled broadly. "I'll give you my card and write the mobile number on back."

To be polite as Heller wrote, Marty asked, "What do you do? Work here in town?"

"I manage the mall in Frostburg. I thought about moving over there when I was younger, but I like the atmosphere here. I sit on the board for Maple Grove's Chamber of Commerce. That keeps me involved in town."

Marty looked up from the card. "Maybe you can help me out. I heard there's some interest in creating a campground on Meadow Mountain. Have you heard anything about it?"

Heller frowned and his shoulders sort of sagged. "There's a big push to get more tourists to this area, and that would require more places to sleep. I mentioned this, in general, to my sister Veronica, who lives in

Northern Virginia. She's decided we need a campground on the mountain."

"Huh. I guess there are some near Deep Creek Lake, but not so much up here."

"Prices for housing, everything really, have skyrocketed where Veronica lives, so she wants to move back here. There aren't many jobs, so she's announced she'll create her own opportunity."

"Should be..." Marty looked for a word.

"A challenge, possibly foolish?"

Marty grinned. "Does she already own the land?"

"Most land at higher altitudes is state-designated parkland. She thinks that property owners who've not built homes on any they own will welcome her offers."

"People could hold onto land for emotional reasons. She may be in for a surprise."

"And," Heller said, "she is not the most tactful person. Could be fireworks before the 4th of July."

JOSH WAS ABLE TO FIND two friends who were willing to take a long Sunday drive to Maple Grove. One would drive home in the car they rode up in, the other would drive Josh's BMW, with him in the back seat.

Digger began to clear away their lunch of grilled cheese and bacon sandwiches, the remnants of which lay scattered on the coffee table.

"Those are some good friends," Franklin said.

"*You know those sayings about house guests and day-old fish?*"

Digger ignored Uncle Benjamin.

"Those pain meds you picked up for me really help. Otherwise, I don't think I could tolerate the bumps."

Marty's Toyota beeped, and Digger walked to the front foyer to let him in. She'd given him a key, but for someone who was so organized in his writing, he amazed her with how often he forgot it.

He bounded up the steps. "I heard some interesting news at the Methodist Church."

Digger kissed him lightly. "Do tell. We're in the living room." She gestured in that direction.

"Oh, right." He moved from the foyer to the living room. "How are you doing, Josh?"

"He's experiencing the wonders of modern pharmaceuticals," Franklin said.

Josh did a thumbs up. "Not going to walk on that foot for a few days at least, but it's a lot more bearable."

Marty brought in a dining room chair, and Digger asked him if he wanted a sandwich.

"Are you kidding? My grandmother insisted I eat four pancakes."

Franklin picked up the lunch plates. "Tough duty."

"Do your parents live here, too?" Josh asked.

"No. Let me tell you what I heard at church today."

Digger knew nothing of Marty's family beyond his grandparents. The one or two times she'd asked a question – being conversational, not prying – he had eluded the query with as clipped an answer as he'd given Josh.

Marty looked at Digger. "Did you know there were Heller descendants still in town?"

"Obits I found on Ancestry.com mentioned survivors living elsewhere. A guy on the chamber's board is named Heller, but I don't know if he's related."

"Yep, that's Lucas Heller. I talked to him at church today. But he works at the Mall in Frostburg, so you wouldn't run into him much."

Franklin had come back into the room and leaned against the fireplace mantle. "I think I know who you mean. Don't think he and his wife had any kids, so he could be the last Heller around."

"He has a sister, Veronica, who wants to move back here." Marty launched into a description of the woman's idea for a campground and how unlikely it seemed she could acquire land. He nodded to Josh. "She lives in Northern Virginia, so not too far from Bethesda."

"Is her last name Heller?" Josh asked.

Marty thought for a minute. "I don't think that came up."

"Even if she did acquire land," Digger said, "there's no water up there except for one narrow creek and snow melt in the early spring. It would have to be primitive camping only."

"What's that mean?" Josh asked.

"*It means you take a leak in the woods,*" Uncle Benjamin said.

"It's generally tent-only camping. There'd be established campsites with fire pits, and maybe latrines. But not running water."

"Sometimes the people running a site like that have a big tank for drinking water, and they fill it periodically," Franklin said.

"You'd still want to boil it," Digger added.

"I think I'll pass," Marty said.

Franklin left the room. Digger figured he'd had enough latrine talk.

Josh furrowed his brow. "I don't know much about camping, but I have an MBA. I can't see how you could make much money from that. I mean, how many people think vacationing means sleeping on the ground and using a latrine?"

Digger shrugged. "I might be willing to do it to see the Grand Canyon, but not in the Maryland woods."

Marty laughed. "If she plans to offer Bruno Sampson money for his land, I think she can forget it."

"How did that guy come to own land up there?" Josh asked. "It's awfully lonely."

"It belonged to his parents, I think. All he'd have to do is pay taxes," Digger said.

Marty stared at something over Digger's shoulder.

"What?" she asked.

"Wonder if he's kept up his taxes," Uncle Benjamin said.

"Just thinking I might trace the lineage of that land," Marty said..

CHAPTER NINE

DIGGER HAD A BUSY week planned. She and Holly were going to visit several local restaurants with their menu ideas, and she wanted to spend time organizing the thousands of digital photos they had taken or scanned from other people's collections.

Though it could only be a sideline, they both thought that if they became the go-to people for current and past photographs of Garrett County, they might bring in a couple hundred dollars a month. And then grow it to more.

Some of the online services let photographers upload hundreds of digital photos. People from around the world could buy them by downloading copies. Holly had been hesitant, but Digger explained that to prevent pirating, the display photos had watermarks on them. If someone wanted to use one, they had to buy it and the watermark would be removed.

Keeping Digger from the photography was her home work, so to speak. The Ancestral Sanctuary always needed a lot of attention in the spring. It had been so dry she didn't want to burn brush and last fall's leaves, so she was considering buying a woodchipper and shredder to make mulch. Then she wouldn't have to buy mulch for the paths and gardens on the property.

She outlined her idea to Uncle Benjamin before she drove into work on Monday. "What do you think?"

"*I guess it makes sense. The last few years before I was pushing up daisies, I paid boys from the Scout troop to do a lot of spring clean-up. You think about that?*"

"I could, but I have more energy than you did when you were in your eighties. And I like the idea of turning downed limbs into something useful."

"*Did you see the movie Fargo?*"

Digger winced. A scene near the end had a gruesome use for a chipper. "Don't go there."

"*Just watch where you put your fingers and toes.*"

"If you're sure you want to stay home, I'll leave the TV on the Frostburg station. At least you can hear the news at noon."

"*I'll let you know who gets married on the soap operas.*"

HOLLY GREETED HER Monday morning with a bow. "At the Coffee Engine, I heard all about your rescue mission Saturday night. One of the EMTs who brought the guy down said his ankle was the size of a grapefruit."

"Yep. Dr. Webb wrapped it, so that helped."

"Is he still with you?"

"No, two of his friends came up Sunday. One drove him home and one his car."

"Those are some good friends," Holly said.

"Yep. They're talking about coming back up here and staying at one of the Deep Creek Lake lodges. At least the county will get some tourism revenue out of the deal."

Holly nodded at a note on Digger's desk at the same time she saw it. "The voicemail had a message from the woman who's thinking of developing a campground. I guess Grandmother Audrey heard right after all."

"What does she want from us?"

"Mostly you, as usual."

Digger wrinkled her nose at Holly. She glanced at the message Holly had transcribed. "Veronica – she didn't give her last name -- was at the historical society Sunday and learned that you had hundreds of Garrett County photographs. She's seen photos of kids splashing in ponds in the 1920s, with tents in the background. Did you know where prior camps were?"

Digger glanced up from the message. "I have some photos labeled for camping or vacation cabins. Now, the trick is to see if she'll pay for some access."

"How is that going to work? You aren't the original photographer."

"The pictures are long out of copyright, but I'll hold the copyright to the digital version, since I scanned them and cleaned them up a bit."

"Most came from the historical society, though," Holly said. "Won't they think they should own them?"

Digger shrugged. "They can scan copies, too. Anyway, a bunch came from Uncle Benjamin's albums, and a lot of those were in his family for generations."

She could sense the question reflected in Holly's furrowed brow. "If I'm contacted here or because of our other work, as this woman did, then the money comes to You Think, We Design. On my own time, for example if I do a pictorial history book for a specialty publisher, then it's my income."

Holly nodded "Sounds good. Call that lady. Charge her a lot."

Digger called Veronica and listened to an earful of her plans to provide a "rugged vacation experience" in the Maryland mountains.

She could finally get a word in. "Is that the kind of camping you enjoy, Ms...?" She let her question hang there.

After a pause, Veronica said, "Heller. I'm not much into camping. I figure other people are, and there aren't a lot of motels near Maple Grove."

This last point was true. "A lot of camping is down by Deep Creek Lake. People do water sports."

In a barely civil tone, Veronica asked, "What's your point?"

"Just kind of thinking out loud. Did you talk to people at the Chamber of Commerce in Maple Grove?"

"I told them my brother is on the board. But all that fat man did was suggest I talk to you about pictures."

So, she was Lucas Heller's sister. Even so, Digger didn't blame the Chamber's executive director for wanting to get rid of the unrealistic Veronica. Especially if she let him know what she thought of his appearance.

"Let me go through some files. You could maybe do a retro look in ads and show how your sites will be more…modern, or something."

"Ours will be better, "Veronica said.

Digger did a rotating motion with her forefinger and Holly grinned. "Our prices are reasonable…"

Veronica sort of sputtered. "Pay? You mean I have to pay!"

"For the kind of photos we're talking about, digital files would be ten dollars. Prints…"

"What? I need to think about that. Meanwhile, I have another question."

"Sure," Digger said.

"I read that article about a man finding gold coins. My great grandfather said some of his were stolen. Do you know who found those coins? Maybe some of them should belong to my family. I could sure use them."

"How would you prove it?"

"Who else would they belong to? Meanwhile, I thought I might look for more coins with a metal detector."

Digger shook her head in Holly's direction. "I think if you went looking for coins with a metal detector you'd likely be on private property. People aren't always too friendly with trespassers."

"I'm not saying I'd ask permission. Do you…?"

Digger had had enough of Veronica. "Listen I have a call on the other line. Get in touch if you'd like me to look for some photos for you." She depressed the button on the phone.

Holly nodded toward the receiver, still in Digger's hand. "She sounds like a real charmer."

"Marty said when he talked to her brother – who's Lucas Heller by the way -- at his grandparents' church, he didn't seem too thrilled with her idea for a campground. I wonder if she's even explored who owns the parcels of land on the east or west sides of Maple Grove?"

Holly shook her head. "If we're lucky, she won't call us back."

IN MID-AFTERNOON, DIGGER and Holly took the sample menus they (mostly Holly) had designed and headed for Maple Grove's six local restaurants.

They went first to the All Kinds Restaurant on Union Street, which had Mexican and American food. Holly had put chiles and sombreros in one margin and hamburgers and chickens on the other. They told the owner, Jose Gomez, they could use any artwork he liked, or put pictures of some menu items. They left him a few paper copies of the sample menu so he could think about how he wanted to arrange his offerings.

They waited until they were on the sidewalk and a couple of storefronts away before talking about Jose's reaction. "He'll use us, don't you think?" Holly asked.

"He sounded like he would. Especially because he kept asking if he could easily update it as prices increased." Digger glanced at the hardware store as they passed it. As she did so, Bruno Sampson emerged.

As his eyes adjusted to the sunlight, he spotted Digger. "Hey, you. Lady!"

"Is that the guy who yelled at you and Marty at the diner last week?"

"Bruno, yes." Digger raised her hand in greeting, but kept walking.

He walked toward them. "Hey, how come you told that guy to come to my land?"

Under her breath, Digger said, "Like I'd do that." She stopped walking. "I didn't tell anyone to go on your land."

Bruno had almost crossed the parking lot and stopped a few yards from them. "Yeah, you did. The idiot fell and hurt his leg so bad I had to call an ambulance."

"That was Josh Henry," Digger said, "and I specifically told him not to walk around at your place. He went on his own."

Bruno threw up his hands in exasperation. A few nails fell out of the brown paper sack he held, and he stooped to pick them up. "So, why'd he do it?"

"You know how Marty's article mentioned a blacksmith whose body was found on the mountain in 1910? Josh is that man's great-nephew. Or something like that."

"What, he thinks my old man did him in?"

Holly clutched the folder of samples to her chest. "I don't think your father would have been old enough."

He ignored Holly. "If that blacksmith was like this Josh guy, he probably tripped on his own feet and hit his head on a rock." Bruno turned and stomped toward his pickup truck.

Digger hung her head on her chest for a moment, then raised it. "I really don't like that guy."

"He seems sort of, I don't know, maybe dangerous," Holly said.

"I think he's a lout, but he wouldn't hurt me. And he could have gotten away with shooting Josh Saturday."

"Not a very high bar for 'not dangerous,'" Holly said, and they both laughed.

Digger's phone rang and she fished it from her pocket to glance at the caller ID. "Sheriff Montgomery." She pushed answer, said hello, and tilted the phone so Holly could hear him.

"Digger, I'm sorry to bother you, but I need a favor. I don't think it'll take a lot of time."

"Sure. What's up?"

"You know that article Hofstedder wrote about gold coins."

"I wish I didn't know."

"A couple of Robert Heller's descendants, or people who say they are, have called insisting if there's coins they should belong to Heller's family."

"How on earth could they prove where the coins came from?"

Montgomery grunted. "I'm not dealing with that right now. I don't even know if these people are descendants. Can you give me a list of Robert Heller's children and grandchildren?"

"Probably. You'll also want great-grandchildren. Send me an email with the names of the people who contacted you, and anything they said about how they were related."

"If you don't mind, I'd rather you just give me the information you find."

Digger felt irritated that he seemed to be keeping something helpful from her, but realized that there might be some privacy issues. "Sure."

"And I hate to rush you, but do you have time today?"

Holly said, "Hello, Sheriff. We can make time for Digger to do this, but remember who helped you." She said it in a playful tone, but Digger knew she'd feel free to call in a chit.

"Oh, uh, sure. Talk to you later." He hung up.

DIGGER FINISHED THE draft of the tourism brochure and opened Ancestry.com. To Holly, she said, "You think I should charge the sheriff anything?"

"We should probably consider it an in-kind contribution."

Digger grinned. "Or what goes around comes around." To refresh her memory, she pulled up the information she'd gathered last week.

Robert Heller (1857-1917) married Caroline Shaw (1867-1932) in 1887. Their children were:
> Robert Heller, Jr. 1889-1951
> Helen Heller 1891-1938
> Herbert Heller 1892-1943
> Herndon Heller 1895-1975

Now she needed to find spouses and their children. Since most of Robert and Caroline's grandchildren, and certainly great-grandchildren, would be alive, it would take quite a while, since Digger doubted most were in town or neatly buried in local cemeteries.

A quick check of the local phone book showed the only Heller in Maple Grove was Lucas, as she expected. She supposed it made sense. There weren't a lot of jobs in the area, unless you were in retail, teaching, or tourism. Some in health care. But after leaving for college or the military, not many young people returned.

She started with the only girl. Digger still couldn't believe her parents had named her Helen Heller, but then realized she was named long before Helen Keller was well known.

Helen did not appear to have married and died at only forty-seven. A brief obituary noted she had cared for her mother for many years and worked part-time at a dress shop. Neither vocation would have brought a lot of eligible men to the door.

Her staying single would make at least the grandchildren easy to identify, since all would have the name Heller.

Robert Heller, Jr., married Kathryn and had two boys and a girl. His obituary identified them and Digger added their dates of birth and death. They were Samuel (1915-1980), Eugene (1920-1965), and Alexis, known as Lexie (1925-2002). Digger had a jolt when she saw Eugene had been killed in Vietnam and was in the Rocky Gap Veterans Cemetery in Flintstone, Maryland, roughly fifty miles east of Maple Grove.

He seemed old to have been killed in that war. Cemetery records showed he'd been career Army, a lieutenant colonel. Eugene's wife was Carly, no maiden name given, and his obit said they had two daughters "of the home," which was near Fort Benning in Georgia. The girls were Hannah and Haley. They could have been college age when their father died in 1965, or younger if he and his wife had their kids in their thirties.

Digger let out a breath. Maybe she would get lucky and find an obituary for Carly, though that would be harder if she remarried. An obit could list the girls' married names, if any. She thought for a moment. If the girls had been born even in 1950 or 55, they'd be on Social Security by now and could have their own grandchildren.

Holly's voice interrupted her thoughts. "You're hunched over. That'll make your neck and shoulders hurt." She brought Digger a can of Dr. Pepper from their small fridge.

"Thanks. I should never have promised him anything today. I can do a couple generations and do more tomorrow."

"Lots of kids and grandkids?"

Digger nodded. "Looks like it. If I get him some information today, he can use it to ask questions to verify identities."

Sheriff Montgomery called at four-thirty. "How's it going?"

"I should have known it would take a while. I can give you his kids and their spouses and I think all of their kids, Robert Heller's grandchildren. I can do more tonight."

"Anything'll help. This one woman calls every hour."

"Yikes. Make her tell you how she fits in, and then compare it to what I send you in a few minutes. If she gives you a song and dance or tells you she was put up for adoption as a baby, that could be what you guys call a clue that she's feeding you a line."

"Very funny. Send your stuff soon if you can."

At five Digger sent him what she had.

Robert Heller (1857-1917) married Caroline Shaw (1867-1932) in 1887. Their children were:

Robert Heller, Jr. (1889-1995), married Kathryn and had three children.

- o Samuel (1915-1980) married Jean Marie and had Mark and Matthew.
- o Eugene (1920-1965) married Carly and had Hannah and Haley.
- o Alexis, known as Lexie, (1925-2002) whose obit named a son Nicholas Heller, which could mean she had not married. The article also mentioned three grandchildren but did not name them.

Helen Heller 1891-1938. Cared for her mother after her father's death. No marriage noted.

Herbert Heller (1892-1943) who married Annette Amos (1900-1960) in 1930. He was a World War II pilot who was killed over Germany, body never recovered.

Two children listed had a different last name. Could they be stepchildren?

Herndon Heller (1895-1975) who married Bridget (1900-1982) and had five children: Michael, Sean, Catherine, Colleen, and Patrick.

Herndon had married an Irish lass and was buried in a Catholic Cemetery near Pittsburgh. With five children, there would be lots of great-grandchildren from that family.

She sent what she had to Montgomery and he called immediately.

"I didn't fully realize how much work this would be."

"You want more? There could be at least two additional generations. Easily 100 descendants or more."

Montgomery sighed. "I know Lucas, he's Mark's son. Focus on Eugene's family for now, would you?"

"Sure. He was killed in Vietnam, but had those two daughters."

"Talk to you tomorrow." He hung up.

Digger had been about to ask him if he knew Lucas' newly divorced sister planned to relocate to Maple Grove. Montgomery wasn't usually so abrupt. Maybe he'd had a bad day.

Holly regarded her as she recradled the receiver. "You spent more than two hours on that. I wish we could bill him."

Digger grinned. "In fairness, he has bailed me out of a couple of jams."

Holly gave a ladylike snort. "More like saved your bacon."

CHAPTER TEN

MARTY PLANNED TO STAY at the courthouse in Oakland until almost closing time on Monday. Since the county seat was forty miles from Maple Grove, he usually only went there to look for information he couldn't find any other way. He'd never dealt with Garrett County land records, but he quickly learned that deeds were recorded in the Office of the Clerk of the County Circuit Court.

A staff member took pity on him and helped him figure out the plat listings for Bruno Sampson's land. Margo Johansson had worked for the clerk's office since high school graduation. "If there's a record here, I can find it even if no one else can."

"I really appreciate this," he told her. "I'm trying to get what I need in one trip. Gas prices, you know."

She nodded a riotous bunch of auburn curls that she had attempted to capture in a large barrette at the nape of her neck. Many had escaped. "Land on Meadow

Mountain doesn't change hands often, not outside of Maple Grove itself."

Marty agreed. "Lots of parkland. Keeps a good deal of development away."

"And jobs, and tourism." She winked at him. "When you get home, you can sign up for an account at Maryland Land Records. You can find a lot of information from your own computer. After the early 1980s." She wrote down a web address for him.

He wanted a lot earlier than that. He found the deed transfer to Bruno Sampson from his father, Silas Sampson Jr. in 1985. Because Silas Jr. had not had a will, the transfer was initiated through Probate Court.

Marty searched back a number of years and could not find records for Silas Jr. acquiring the parcel. Then an idea struck him, and he jumped back to 1910 land transfers. The 4.5 acres of woodland had been in arrears on taxes so had reverted to Garrett County. Abe Sampson bought it for $720 on August 31, 1910.

Abe Sampson was smart enough to have a will, and left it to his son Silas Sampson Sr. The land transfer was dated October 2, 1952. Silas Sampson Sr. left it to Silas Sampson Jr. and his wife Susannah, with the deed for the land transfer to them on March 22, 1972.

Marty checked back to when Bruno inherited the land in 1992. It mentioned that it came only from his father. That made sense, given that they had heard Bruno's mother left. But had Silas Jr. had her declared dead? Or could she be alive and living elsewhere?

He finished jotting his notes and reviewed them. Was it just coincidence that Abe Sampson had $720 in 1910, or had he come to it because of the death of one

Gerard D. Morton, whose body was found on Meadow Mountain in June 1910?

DIGGER HAD TAKEN spaghetti sauce from the freezer before she left for work and left Marty a text to ask if he would like to come to dinner. She wanted to talk to him about Veronica's call about campground photos.

"You should have told him to bring one of those frozen loaves of bread. I can almost smell those baking."

"I left him a message and haven't heard back. I don't even know if he's coming."

The wall phone rang as she put water on to boil for the noodles. "Digger here."

A hard-sounding woman's voice asked, "That's an odd name for a woman. Are you a grave digger?" She laughed at her own joke, a laugh that sounded half like a bark.

"Noooo. Who's this?"

"It's Veronica Glazer. I mean Heller. I took back my maiden name when I divorced a few months ago. I decided not to buy any pictures."

"That's fine." Digger hoped she wouldn't ask for anything else.

"A lady at the historical society said you know everything that's gone on in this county. What do you know about campgrounds on Meadow Mountain?"

Digger wished the woman hadn't called her at home. "There aren't any now..."

"I know. I mean a long time ago."

"I was about to talk about that."

"Sorry. People tell me I interrupt too much."

Digger reined in her irritation. "In rural areas, you'll sometimes find informal camping areas near creeks or springs. Before air conditioning, people had screened-in porches or sometimes set up tents outdoors when it was really hot. There isn't a lot of that now."

"Seems to me the east side up from Maple Grove has properties with houses on them, and then it's mostly parkland. If I do something it should be on the west side."

"You grew up here, Veronica?"

"I did. Got outta here as fast as I could after college. Been living in Northern Virginia."

"Did you know a lot of people who liked to camp? Is that what made you think of developing a campground?"

She said nothing for several seconds. "We mostly liked to borrow the folks' car and try to get into the bars over by Frostburg University."

Uncle Benjamin sat on the counter next to Digger. *"Ask her if she likes spiders."*

"Tourists come to this part of Maryland to boat on Deep Creek Lake or ski in the winter. You could certainly try a campground in an area without a lot of outdoor activities, but I don't know how much business you'd get."

She sighed. "Everything's so expensive and so crowded where I am. I quit my job so I have my retirement money and I could build a small cabin and then rent campsites nearby."

Digger was aghast at several levels. First that someone so inexperienced would take on any outdoor recreation project, but mostly because she spoke so candidly about her finances and personal life. And investing her retirement money in a cabin in the woods? Nuts. "I'm sure you've done a lot of planning. What makes you think this would be a good location?"

"I'm more of a shoot-from-the-hip type. And I've got family in Maple Grove. I figure I could stay with them while I build my cabin."

"Gee, I have food on the stove. Good luck with your project." Digger hung up without saying goodbye.

"*She sounds like a hothead.*"

"Or at least an impatient, impetuous person."

While she waited for the spaghetti noodles to boil, Digger looked up Eugene's children, Hannah and Haley Heller. Both could have married long ago and could have different names. Or they might have kept their maiden names.

She found nothing on quick Google searches, so went to the Rocky Gap Veterans Cemetery in Maryland and found Eugene Heller. Then she got lucky and found his wife Carly, who died in 1995, had apparently not remarried. She was buried as Carly Heller.

Digger quickly found her obituary at a newspaper archives site. She died in Quantico, Virginia. The cause of death was colon cancer. "Ouch," Digger said aloud.

Uncle Benjamin had been watching the news in the living room and floated in to look over her shoulder.

Digger pointed to the laptop screen. "When Sheriff Montgomery asked me to look up Robert Heller's descendants, he later said to focus on his son Eugene's family. This was his wife, who died thirty years after he did." Her finger moved down the screen. "Their two daughters were alive then, Hannah McKenzie lived in

Germantown, Maryland and Haley Nicholas lived in Denver, Colorado."

"They were obviously alive before 1965 when their father died, so they would be senior citizens now, too," Uncle Benjamin said.

Digger jotted notes on a pad. "One of them has apparently called Sheriff Montgomery. My money would be on the one who lives in Germantown, which is only about 120 miles from here."

The spaghetti water boiled vigorously, so Digger headed to the kitchen. She hesitated to add the noodles, and called Marty one more time.

He picked up right away. "Hey, I just got your message. I was down in Oakland. What time's dinner?"

"It can be twenty minutes or an hour."

"I'll be there in twenty. Can I bring anything?"

"Tell him the bread!"

"Nope." Digger smiled as she turned on the oven to preheat. "A ghost we know wants some special bread, but I have some hiding in my freezer. See you soon."

"You could've told me."

She smiled. "Now you know."

"I'm going out front to wait for Marty."

Ragdoll meowed.

Uncle Benjamin leaned down to pet the cat, who took no apparent notice. *"Get Digger to feed you and then you can come, too."*

AFTER DINNER, DIGGER outlined the family information she had gathered for Sheriff Montgomery and his instruction that she focus on Eugene's family. "One of the descendants is a woman who lives in

Germantown, Maryland. I would guess she's the one calling him."

Marty pointed to Robert Heller's children and grandchildren. See the name Mark? He's one of the banker's grandsons and he also happens to be Lucas and Veronica's father."

"I hadn't gotten that far. We certainly know Veronica's interested in the coins. Does he even know she's in town? I'll send him an email about the brochure and mention her."

"Okay, my turn." Marty spread his notes on the table as well as a couple pages he had photocopied from deed records in the clerk's office in Oakland. "This is the history of land transfers on the land Bruno Sampson lives on. See if something jumps out at you."

Digger started from Bruno being left the land by his father and worked her way back. When she got to Abe Sampson buying the land in 1910, she jerked her head up to look at Marty. "Abe Sampson bought it right after Gerard Morton's death?"

"He did. We'll have to see if we can find out more about Abe Sampson."

Uncle Benjamin said, "*See what he was worth on the 1900 and 1910 census records.*"

Digger tilted her head toward her laptop at the far end of the large table. "His lordship advises, and I agree, that we look at land valuation on census records and see when Abe first owned any."

"*His lordship. It's about time I get some respect around here.*"

"Good suggestion, Benjamin," Marty said. He pulled up a chair to sit next to Digger.

"Of course it is."

Digger went to Ancestry.com and searched for Abe Sampson and then Abraham Sampson by name in 1900. "They have to be here. Probably the name was misspelled."

"Now what?" Marty asked.

"Not many people lived in Maple Grove. We can skim through the pages for the town." She switched to the census files and after a couple of minutes drilled down to the Maple Grove portion of Garrett County.

She first started to look outside of town, but Uncle Benjamin said, *"He probably didn't own land outside of town in 1900. Look in town. Maybe in rooming houses. Unless you think you'll find him on the east side of town."*

Digger repeated what he said and went back a few pages.

"Why the east side?" Marty asked.

"A lot of those homes have been converted to apartments now, but in 1900, they were large, family homes. I believe my dear uncle is being facetious."

"Facetious how?"

"He doesn't expect us to find Abe Sampson in the well-to-do parts of town."

"Well put. Some of the stores on Main Street and other parts of the shopping area had apartments above them."

Digger nodded. "Stores did have living space above them. But it usually housed store owners. I'm going to rooming houses."

Marty smiled. "I take it you're ignoring your uncle's advice."

"At her peril."

Digger didn't look away from the computer screen. She sped through several pages that had few people in each household. "Not exactly ignoring, just...Hey, here he is." She glanced toward the opposite end of the table, where Uncle Benjamin sat in his usual cross-legged position. "With seven other men in a house on the edge of town."

Marty leaned toward the screen and Uncle Benjamin floated to stand behind Digger.

"But they spelled his name Abraham Simpson on the index." She squinted. "I can see why. There's a sort of smudge so the "y" in the name above the "a" in Sampson extends too far. It takes out the open space in the A so it could seem like an "i" to someone transcribing it."

"*Cut to the chase,*" Uncle Benjamin said. "*Does he own land?*"

"Put a cork in it," Digger said. She glanced at Marty. "Not you."

"I figured. What have you got?"

"You can see the place he lives has seven men and one woman." She pointed. "The woman owns the residence. Abe rents." She continued to stare at the page. "He's also illiterate. That's kind of odd for Maryland at that time."

Uncle Benjamin put his face close to the screen and Digger pulled back.

Marty laughed. "I love that I can tell what's he's doing."

"*If you look closely,*" Uncle Benjamin said, "*the handwriting is very uniform. It should all be in the census taker's own writing, but when it's uniform like this, it often* meant one person was dictating the information. Like this landlady, maybe. See, it says they all speak English, but they don't read or write it. That doesn't seem likely for all of them."

Digger repeated what he said. "I bet he's right."

"Of course I am."

She continued. "Two of them work in saloons, including Abe. Four of the others are railroad workers and the seventh man owns a general store. The landlady even said he didn't read or write English. They were all born in Maryland. That's ridiculous."

"Maybe they didn't pay their rent on time," Marty joked.

Uncle Benjamin shrugged. "Or a lazy census taker. Go to 1910."

"My uncle suggests we go to 1910, but I'm going to look first at 1920. I think the 1910 census was taken here before August when Abe Sampson bought the land."

"Shouldn't you check?" Marty asked.

She grinned. "The censuses have varying months, but it was as of April 15th in 1910."

"So even if the census taker got there later, the information was supposed to be as of that date?" Marty asked.

"Such a smart guy," Uncle Benjamin said.

"Is it still April 15th? That'd be an easy date to remember." Marty said.

"Nope, now it's as of April 1st. Anyway," she glanced at Uncle Benjamin, "we're going to 1920."

Neither man interrupted as Digger set up an entry in Ancestry.com for Abe Sampson, noting his month and year of birth as March 1878 and linked him to the 1900 census. That made hints for the 1910 and 1920 censuses pop up so she didn't have to search for him in those years.

Digger clicked on the 1920 reference and Marty pointed at the screen. "There he is. What's he doing?"

"It says he cuts timber. He's forty-two and married to Mary and they have a son, Silas, who is two years old."

"Hot damn," Marty said.

"He's not in town. Is he farther up on the mountain?" Uncle Benjamin asked.

"It'll take me a few minutes of comparing people around him in 1920 and who lived there in 1930 or 1910. That'll be the easiest way to see if it's the same area Bruno lives in now rather than looking the census tract up on a map. But he's definitely way outside of town."

Marty peered more closely. "He owns the land."

"He does." Digger saved the information to Abe's record in Ancestry and closed the 1920 census. She found him in 1910. "And he lived in town in April 1910, still single, and owned no land. We knew he acquired this property in August 1910. Now we know he wasn't trading up land, he was buying his first parcel."

"The hard part will be learning where he got the money," Marty said.

CHAPTER ELEVEN

DIGGER AWAKENED TUESDAY with a question she thought she should have asked a week ago. How did Marty learn that Bruno had found those coins?

Before she asked that, she texted Lucas Heller to say she was almost done with the revisions for the brochure and mentioned she had met his sister. She left off her opinion about the campground idea.

She then texted Marty about Bruno. The more she heard him described as a hermit the less likely it seemed he would want any mention in the paper.

As she approached the children's clothing store to talk about an ad she'd designed for them, Marty texted back. "Library. He went there to look up info on gold coins, and I heard him talking to the librarian."

Since Maple Grove no longer had its Card 'n Coin collectibles shop, it made sense Bruno would go to the library. Perhaps it was his first visit in years. Aloud, she said, "Be Kind."

"But why did he agree to have an article about the coins?"

He replied. "Yeah, I think he wanted to sell some coins. Don't think he knew people would come out of the woodwork looking for more."

Uncle Benjamin floated from inside the store, through the plate glass window. *"Manager's busy with a customer."*

Digger pretended to be interested in the display and spoke softly as she relayed where Bruno had sought information on antique coins.

He shrugged. *"You never know. He may read books all winter. Hard to get down the mountain into town some days."*

Somehow, she didn't see Bruno as a big reader.

Digger had her fingers on the store's glass door when her phone announced another text, this one from Josh.

"Thanks again for the hospitality. Made it home and feeling some better. Still hobbling. My cousin and I tried to find this Bruno's property in county records, and it looks as if it has a tax lien on it. Would you know if he's trying to sell it to pay off the lien?" Josh.

She stuffed the phone in a pocket of her slacks and entered the store. Brightly colored children's clothes were on every rack except a sale space in the back, which had the darker colors of winter garb. "Good morning, Judy. It looks as if you're ready for every kid in town to buy new shorts and bathing suits."

The forty-something woman flashed a toothy smile. "I'm hoping. How's the ad coming?"

Digger placed the eight-by-ten mock-up on the glass counter next to the cash register. "The top half stresses the brands and size range, and the bottom half lists the few specific items you wanted in the ad."

Uncle Benjamin floated behind the counter wearing children's clothes, albeit fitting his adult frame. Dark red shorts and a gray tee-shirt with a Baltimore Oriole's logo were topped by a backwards baseball cap. Digger winked, which seemed to startle him.

The woman studied the draft ad. "I like the drawings of shorts and tops And the bathing suits. I wouldn't have thought to put in the pool toys. That's good."

"Anything you want changed?"

She regarded the ad for a few more seconds and shook her head. "It's good. Do you take it to the paper?"

"We send them the file, they send us the insertion cost. I put that with our design fees and you pay only one bill."

"Okay." They discussed the cost of various size ads and the fact that Judy could modify the ad later for a small fee.

"I heard about that Bruno Sampson yelling at you and Marty in the diner. He's a very coarse man."

Digger shrugged. "He had wanted to stay anonymous, but I guess people who've lived here for years had heard stories about lost coins and knew about where they might be. Since he lives in that area, gossip went right to him."

She shook her head. "If he hadn't made a stink, not very many people would have guessed."

Digger picked up her folder. "And the man does not like visitors."

Back on the sidewalk, she reread Josh's text and replied. "I wouldn't know what Bruno wants to do. Haven't you had enough of him?" She added a smile emoji so her words didn't sound harsh.

She couldn't imagine why a city slicker would want to buy forest land in Garrett County. Maybe to look for more coins?

DIGGER GOT BACK TO You Think, We Design before lunch to find a woman in roughly her early fifties reading the sign Holly had left on the door.

The woman turned at the sound of Digger's footsteps, and Digger figured she was about to meet Veronica Heller in person. The brand new, boot-cut jeans screamed, "I want to look like a woman who lives in the mountains." The ankle-high, shiny boots and fancy chin-length haircut said she was more of an urbanite.

"I saw your picture online from that story about you finding an old body. You're Beth Browning, but everyone calls you Digger."

Digger couldn't help but wonder if the woman thought she was conveying novel facts. "I am. Are you Veronica Heller?"

"Yes. I want to put an ad in the paper, and the editor over there said you could design one for me cheaper than he could."

Digger unlocked the office door and gestured that Veronica could precede her. "Sure. I can outline our prices and you can decide on the size you want."

Unasked, Veronica settled in the client chair next to Digger's desk. "Smaller ads are cheaper, right?"

"The newspaper insertion fees would be less, but our design fees would be pretty much the same for most sizes." She held up a hand toward Veronica. "We have to do much the same work. In fact, a smaller ad could be more expensive if it takes more design time."

She pouted. "Everything costs money. I thought it would be cheaper up here."

"*She's a real tightwad.*" Uncle Benjamin apparently bored of the conversation, because he floated to the attic.

Digger forced a smile. "If you went to an advertising agency in DC or Northern Virginia it would be a lot more." She took a folder from a stand-up file holder on her desk and removed a price sheet for ads for the *Maple Grove News*.

They haggled for a couple of minutes. "If I could find some of those gold coins, I wouldn't have to worry about prices."

Digger did an inward eye roll. "You know, there are a lot of Heller descendants besides you and your brother. If you're ever able to prove coins you found came from your great-grandfather, you'd probably have to share them with a bunch of people."

She smiled slyly. "Who says I'd tell anyone?"

Digger was about to suggest Veronica find a firm closer to her home when she finally decided on a five-by-seven ad, which could be altered and reinserted later, for smaller fees.

"I want an ad that says I'm going to develop a campground and am looking for investors." Veronica handed Digger a folded piece of paper with the text she wanted.

Digger's eyes widened. "This is way too much writing. You want at most three or four bullet points, with room for how to contact you."

After several more minutes of discussion, Veronica rolled her eyes and stuffed the paper in her handbag. "Fine. I'll look at it more tonight and come back tomorrow. It has to be at the paper by late Wednesday for the Friday edition. Can you do it in a few hours?"

Digger certainly didn't want to. "Just this once. Usually we require five days."

Still complaining, Veronica left. Digger heard her talk to someone on the stairs, someone who spoke at a much lower volume.

The door opened and Holly entered. "I recognized that voice from the phone message. She's just as brash in person."

Digger outlined what she'd promised and Veronica's initial desire that the ad be more like a treatise on mountain camping. "She said all this stuff about lots of space for tents, social activities, star gazing. Nothing about wanting investors for a site without shower houses or even running water."

"She can't have it?" Holly asked.

"She might be able to have a well dug, but I doubt it. She could have water delivered and stored in a huge tank of some sort. Her camping fees would have to be really high."

Holly giggled. "Does she know how many trees she'll have to chop down for campsites, or even just to see the stars?"

"She knows nothing about anything. She thinks if she pushes enough people, she can get what she wants."

WEDNESDAY MORNING, DIGGER and Uncle Benjamin got to the office at eight-thirty. Bitsy accompanied them in case Digger had to work late on Veronica Heller's ad. She didn't want to run home to let the dog out.

Bitsy enjoyed occasional days in the second-floor office. They put a blanket on an old credenza that sat in front of the picture window. For an hour or so, Bitsy would bark once at each person that walked on the sidewalk below him, but then he tired of that and snoozed.

Today, Uncle Benjamin sat next to him in the window and stared at people below. He occasionally made comments on the foot traffic. *"That guy who bought my old hardware store is going by. He kind of leans forward when he walks, as if he sat on something stiff and couldn't get it out."*

He cast a glance at Digger, who ignored him.

A somewhat disheveled-looking Veronica Heller dropped off a more realistic draft of an ad about nine-thirty. She wore a different blouse, this one deep red with long sleeves, but Digger thought the jeans were the same, and her hair was tousled. The smart boots had a couple scuff marks on the toes, and Digger wondered who or what Veronica had kicked.

Digger studied the ad. "I can have a draft by about early afternoon. I might have to cut a word or two for space, but nothing substantive. Do you have any particular images you want depicted?"

Veronica stared at her as if she had two heads.

"I mean, drawings of tents, a campfire. That sort of thing."

Veronica made a dismissive gesture. "You pick. I'm done with it. I don't need to see the next draft."

Holly's eyes met Digger's across the desk, and she shook her head slightly.

"That's okay, but if you don't like something, no complaints."

"Yeah, yeah." Veronica turned to leave.

"Where do we send the bill? Are you staying at a particular hotel?"

That made her pause and she turned back. "Send it to my brother Lucas' house. You know the address?"

"I'll find it easily," Digger said.

She left without a goodbye and tromped loudly down the stairs and out the front door.

"I bet she gave you that address because she doesn't plan to pay," Holly said.

"And she thinks her brother will?"

Holly shrugged. "Maybe. She has a strong sense of, I don't know, entitlement."

"Just rudeness, I think."

Bitsy barked once, seemingly in agreement.

DIGGER AND BITSY MET Marty for lunch in the small corner park a block from her office. The hot dog stand that had occupied the bottom floor of an old frame building had burned in the 1980s. The owner eventually didn't pay taxes on it. When it reverted to the city, the city council turned it into a small park.

Local service clubs took turns mowing it, and the benches had been donated. Each bore a small brass plaque to recognize the donor organization or person.

"Pay once, get lifelong advertising," Uncle Benjamin said. He began to watch several boys, roughly middle school age, take turns throwing beanbags through the gaping mouth of a wooden wide-mouth bass. Below the mouth was an ad for a firm that rented boats on Deep Creek Lake.

"Not a bad idea. Maybe Holly and I can donate a bench one day."

Uncle Benjamin laid on one hip on the back of a bench, certainly not a position he could have maintained while alive. *"Can I sit with you and Marty?"*

"How about being elsewhere in the park for the first few minutes. Is that okay?"

"Sure. I'll stand in the street and pretend to direct traffic." He added a striped school patrol vest and a cardboard stop sign on a narrow piece of wood.

Marty came into view carrying a brown bag with the promised sandwiches from Subway. Digger opened the thermos of coffee she'd brought and pulled two slightly dented paper cups from her purse.

He sat the bags on the bench. "Great day for a park." He lowered his voice. "Are we alone?"

"He's gone into the street to play traffic cop. In front of the Ice Cream Shoppe."

Marty glanced in that direction. "If I were writing a movie script with a ghost only one person could see, I'd have him periodically be visible, just for a second. That'd get people's heart rates up."

"Warped thinking, Hofstedder." Digger described the ad she'd designed for Veronica and the woman's continuing inability to grasp how much work she'd have to do to open and run a campground. "Plus, she's talking about building a cabin. Imagine hauling all that lumber up there."

"That's crazy even to think of."

Digger nodded. "One creek runs down from the top of the mountain. In pioneer times there were more and people would dam them so they'd have enough water to operate a small mill. I think old census records showed Bruno's great grandfather, Abraham, worked in 'timber.' I bet he cut trees and sold the lumber to mills nearby."

"No Home Depot?"

"Not even a chain saw." Her phone rang and caller ID showed Josh Henry. "Second time he's contacted me today. Hello, Josh." She tilted the phone so Marty could hear.

"Hey, Digger. Sorry to bother you, but my cousin and I keep wondering if any of those coins belonged to our uncle. Can't prove anything, of course. We were thinking about asking Bruno if we could go up there with a metal detector."

"Did you want to sprain your other ankle? Or find out how shotgun pellets feel in your tailbone?"

"I could do without that. We thought we'd offer to look for metal and split what we find with Bruno."

Marty shook his head and made a gimme gesture. Digger handed him the phone.

"Hey, Josh. Marty here. You can try to talk Sampson into that, but I don't think he's looking to make friends." Marty listened for thirty seconds or so.

"The thing is, he'd eventually find any coins, and then he'd get to keep all of them."

Bitsy inserted his head between Digger's knees and she rubbed it. "Good boy."

Marty said, "Okay. Good luck. You want to talk to Digger again?" He ended the call and handed the phone to Digger.

"What do you think they're going to do?" she asked.

"He didn't say. Probably try to talk to Bruno."

After eating part of her sandwich, Digger put the leftovers in the bag it had come in and commended Marty on hitting the trash can with his wadded up wrapper. "Uh-oh. Bitsy's leaving a present." She stood and took a plastic bag from her pocket.

Marty grinned. "Make sure you don't mix up the bags."

DIGGER FINISHED VERONICA'S ad by mid-afternoon, so she and Bitsy left work a few minutes early on Wednesday so she could stop at the historical society and look at the county plat book. It was one of the few modern items on hand. Uncle Benjamin had started purchasing it for the society every few years so people who found their ancestors' lands on an older book could compare it to what sat on the property today.

She didn't think the relatively few privately-owned lots on that side of the mountain had changed hands much in the last few decades, but was curious about who Bruno's neighbors were besides Max and Sandy Elder. Theirs seemed to be the only property with relatively modern structures.

Bitsy was not allowed into the society, so Digger tied him to the tree outside and he introduced himself to all passers by in hope of a pet. He usually got one.

She stood for a few moments examining the large front window, with its local memorabilia and other artifacts. A coal miner's hat sat between a model of the first log cabin in Garrett County and a grouping of arrowheads. New in the window was a book on coin collecting, which lay flat with a page opened to "U.S. Gold Coins of the 17 and 1800s." Next to it was a neatly hand-printed note that said, "Come in to Learn More."

Holly's grandmother sat at the small desk just inside the society, which occupied the space of a recently closed antique store and a former print shop. The owner of the antique store had joined other businesses in a large building near Interstate 68. The print shop had gone belly up when every local business bought computers and laser printers.

Audrey almost jumped up to give Digger a hug. This usually meant she wanted someone to move books or something, but today what she wanted was information.

"Did that Bruno Sampson tell Marty how many coins he found all together? I heard hundreds were stolen from the bank in 1910. Maybe we should organize a search party."

Digger returned her hug. "It's private property and Bruno does not welcome guests."

Audrey frowned. "Most of the land up there is owned by the state, part of the hiking trails."

"True. I'm actually here to look at the plat books to see who owns nearby parcels." She hoped Audrey wouldn't offer to help.

Audrey opened her mouth to offer her services, but fortunately the front door opened. A woman with four bored-looking kids about age twelve entered. Audrey turned. "I bet you all have a history project for school."

Digger moved to the back of the large room, passing microfilm readers, shelves of history books, family Bibles, and scrapbooks the society created each year. She put her purse on the eight-foot wooden table researchers used and found the current book of plat maps on a shelf that held over-sized books.

She tuned out the exclamations of the kids when Audrey showed them the glass-enclosed case with a full Civil War uniform.

Digger always started with the four acres that comprised the Ancestral Sanctuary because she could get a better perspective on other properties if she looked at them in relation to her land.

She was surprised to see that her place on the east side of Meadow Mountain was almost a direct line to Bruno's on the west side. Not that it would be an easy trek between them. About two miles of dense brush separated them, without even a trail.

A few houses stood between the Ancestral Sanctuary and the top of the mountain, but on Bruno's side, everything above his land belonged to the state of Maryland. His land ended at Jessup Lane and went back several thousand feet. Two individual parcels abutted his to the south. Two and nine-tenth acres were owned by the estate of R. Bishop. That person must have died years ago, because Digger didn't recognize the name.

The second parcel was 6.2 acres, owned by M.A. Montgomery, who happened to be Sheriff Montgomery's grandmother. Funny he hadn't mentioned that the night Josh Henry tripped while avoiding Bruno's shotgun burst.

CHAPTER TWELVE

AS DIGGER STEPPED OUT of the historical society, a red Honda sedan sped past, then stopped. It reversed and backed up to where Digger stood. The driver's side window came down.

Without even a hello, Veronica Heller called, "Digger, do you know where I can get information on whether somebody paid their property taxes?"

Digger motioned that Veronica should pull to the curb. She did. "Do you know where? Are they open?"

Digger found herself more irritated with this woman all the time. She could easily have found the information online. "The Garrett County Collection Office is on 4th Street in Oakland."

"But there's an office up here, isn't there?" Veronica asked.

Digger shook her head. "Oakland is the county seat. The only government people up here are the sheriff's staff at a satellite office and a small maintenance building on the edge of Maple Grove. It's mostly not open except when snow is around."

Veronica pounded one fist on her steering wheel. "How do you ever get anything done around here?"

Digger stepped back from the car. "By planning ahead." She didn't add that Veronica should try it.

The woman's face broke into a smile. "I found a place I can buy these sheds you assemble. Some of them are as big as efficiency apartments."

"So, you can use it for an office for campers to check in and such?"

Veronica frowned. "I guess I probably do need something for that." She sped away.

Digger wished one of the sheriff's deputies would be sitting on a side street and pull her over.

That thought reminded her to call Maryann Stevens Montgomery at the senior apartments in town.

Her firm voice came through clearly. "Digger Browning. You haven't called me in weeks, you scoundrel."

Digger laughed, picturing the ninety-year-old woman with her straight posture sitting in a Queen Ann chair in her apartment. "I've been busy, but that's no excuse."

"Yes, my grandson told me you'd been harboring pests."

"Pests…Oh, you mean Josh Henry, the blacksmith's descendant."

"Yes. I'm glad he didn't get the stuffing beat out of him. If Bruno Sampson is anything like his father, he plays rough."

Digger beeped the lock on her Jeep. "That's sort of why I'm calling. The plat book I saw may be outdated, but it looks as if you own property that abuts Bruno Sampson's place."

"I do. You know my father used to deliver milk all over this part of the county."

"I remember you said you rode with him a few times."

"Yes, those were the days. Unpasteurized milk, bumpy roads, and humid summer weather with no air-conditioning."

"So, those fond memories led you to buy that land?"

Maryann laughed. "My father bought it. Since we had the farm, I have no idea why he wanted it. Probably to cut and sell some timber, but he never got around to it as far as I know."

Digger pointed Bitsy toward the back seat and the German Shepherd leapt into the Jeep. "None of my business, but why haven't you sold it?"

"At this point, laziness. It only costs me a few hundred in property taxes. If the land values go up much, then I would. Roger will get it when I go to the Great Tea Plantation in the sky."

"You know from Marty's article that someone found those coins."

"Bruno Sampson, I heard," Maryann said.

"Did Sheriff Montgomery tell you the so-called pest who stayed with me over the weekend descends from the family of the blacksmith whose body was found up that way?"

"No, he just said the young man was interested in the coins. Do you know for sure the blacksmith died on the Sampson property instead of mine?"

"Can't imagine there's any way to find out. Marty looked up land records, and it seems Bruno's great-grandfather, Abraham Sampson, bought that parcel in 1910 not long after Gerard Morton, the blacksmith, died."

"Ooh. Find some lawyer to tell you what happens if Abraham bought it with money he took from a dead man."

"You have a devious mind, Maryann. After more than 110 years, we'll never know more than we do now."

"An active brain is the key to long life."

"I have another question. Why do you say Bruno's father was rough?"

"All I remember is that he wanted to buy out my father. Even came to the house. I think Dad would have sold if the man, Silas Sampson, I think, had asked rather than demanded."

"I don't really know Bruno," Digger said. "He thinks Marty told people he found the coins, and he hollered at Marty in the diner last Friday."

"So, I heard. Sticks and stones and all that."

"Yeah, I think he's all talk." Digger slid into the driver's seat. "Did you ever hear anything about that 1910 bank robbery, or Robert Heller getting coins stolen?"

"I don't remember a Robert Heller."

"Now that I think of it, he would've died years before you were born. What about the robbery?"

Maryann said nothing for a few seconds. "That did get talked about some through the years. Banks weren't insured back then, but I don't know that people personally lost money. Do you think the coins were from that robbery?"

"I guess my personal thought would be they came from the blacksmith. He had money from selling his business in Baltimore."

"Marty's article said he was an itinerate blacksmith."

Digger outlined what they had learned about Gerard Morton through Josh Henry. "Marty's supposed to be writing a follow-up, to make it clear he had just sold his business and was venturing west with purpose."

"Okay, here's the $64,000 question, Maryann said.

"This should be fun."

Maryann laughed. "If this Bruno Sampson found coins on the mountain, they were probably on his land, which, of course abuts mine. What do you think the odds are of coins being on my property?"

Digger thought for several seconds. "It would go back to how the coins got there. If some hiker had a hole in his pocket, coins could be spread out."

"Not too likely," Maryann said.

"But maybe just as likely as coins coming from the bank robbery, the theft at the Heller house, or the deceased blacksmith."

"Hmmm. I'm thinking about something. I'll let you know if I decide to do it."

"What...?" Digger paused. "Wait. I don't want to know. It's probably something your grandson will be irritated about.

"I do like the way your mind works. Good night, Digger."

WHILE SHE FIXED DINNER on Wednesday, Digger thought about the color paint for the master bedroom and whether to buy blinds or pull shades. She was tired of thinking about gold coins and people murdered on the mountain long ago. And especially tired of thoughts about Bruno Sampson.

She carried a plate into the living room to eat the freshwater bass and broccoli. She had tuned the TV to local news so Uncle Benjamin could watch it. Before she sat down, the house phone rang and she walked to the kitchen to answer it. She didn't know the number, but it was local.

"Ms. Browning? This is Lucas Heller."

Digger couldn't imagine why anyone from the Chamber board would call her at home. "What can I do for you?"

"My sister, Veronica, whom I believe you've met, tells me you're advising her about buying some property on Meadow Mountain."

Digger felt her cheeks redden in anger. "I've met her. But have not talked to her about buying property. She talked to me about opening a campground and asked my firm to design an ad for her." She wondered if she should tell Heller that his sister wanted the bill for her ad to go to him.

Heller said nothing for several seconds. "You aren't advising her about buying property when the county has a lien on it for back taxes?"

"No. She stopped me on the street today to ask how to find the county office that deals with that, and I told her Oakland. That's it."

Heller cleared his throat, and his voice became tight. "I apologize for disturbing you."

"No problem at all. Have a good evening."

Digger wondered why Veronica would tell her brother that? Either she was a chronic liar, or she had learned he knew Digger and thought advice from her would make Lucas think more positively about Veronica's campground idea. Aloud, she said, "Don't try to interpret a fool's mind."

When Digger returned to the living room, Uncle Benjamin sat on the couch and pointed to the TV set. "*The Pittsburgh channel said there's a story about the gold coins coming up.*"

"Oh boy, that'll set off Bruno if people head his way. I wonder if he has a TV."

"*You don't need cable to get most local channels. I bet he does.*"

A female reporter began the story. "Way back in June 1910, Maple Grove, Maryland saw its version of a crime wave with a bank robbery, a home burglary, and discovery of the body of a former Baltimore blacksmith. That man had recently sold his business and was traveling west, supposedly with some of his money in gold. The victim of the home burglary, Robert Heller, also reported coins were stolen from his residence."

A male reporter continued. "Last week, the *Maple Grove News* reported that a local man had found some gold coins in an area on Meadow Mountain not far from where the blacksmith died. The value of the coins was not provided. We'll have more on this intriguing story during the 11 PM wrap-up."

"Sounds as if they did some of their own research after they read Marty's article. I don't recall Marty mentioning the bank robbery."

Digger's cell phone rang. "I know who that'll be." She punched the answer button. "Did you get scooped?"

Marty laughed. "No. About four this afternoon I posted a short feature about Gerard Morton. I didn't want to leave the 'itinerate blacksmith' description as it was."

"Good to know the Pittsburgh station reads your website."

Marty swallowed. "Sorry. I'm eating an apple. Yeah, they called and said they were going to use what I wrote. That should make Josh Henry happy."

"Do you think they know Bruno Sampson is the one who found the coins?"

"Not from me."

Uncle Benjamin grunted. *"Half the town knows. Somebody'll tell the station."*

"I learned two things today, one of them especially interesting," Digger said.

"I'll bite," Marty said.

Uncle Benjamin grinned. *"Me, too."*

"I looked at the current plat book at the historical society."

"I used to buy those for the society every year."

Digger nodded at him. To Marty, she said, "Guess who owns the undeveloped land next to Bruno's."

"Holly's grandmother," Marty said.

Uncle Benjamin muttered, "*That busybody.*"

"Nope. Maryann Montgomery."

Uncle Benjamin cackled and Marty said, "What the heck is she doing with a patch of forest land?"

Digger explained that Maryann's father had bought it, and since her brother had died, Maryann was the only child to inherit it."

"*I thought her parents owned a dairy farm,*" Uncle Benjamin said.

"Her parents did own a dairy farm. Her father wanted some timber, he didn't do much with it."

"So," Marty said, "are you going to suggest that Josh hunt for coins on her land?"

"I doubt there truly are more coins to be found. But Maryann said she's thinking about something to do with it, and she acknowledged her dear sheriff grandson might get irritated."

"Jeez. That's something to stay away from."

"Yep. I didn't tell her Lucas Heller's sister wants land for a campground. She sort of implied today she thinks Bruno might be late with his taxes and that'll be an incentive for him to sell."

"*Politicians hate to hassle people about taxes. Doubt anyone around here is in danger of having their property seized,*" Uncle Benjamin said.

Digger repeated Uncle Benjamin's point.

"Probably true," Marty said. "If I were a mean person, I'd say tell her to sell to Veronica and Bruno can have her for a neighbor."

GOLD WAS FAR FROM Digger's mind as she drove to work, alone, on Thursday. She and Holly had gotten their first order to design a menu. Fortunately, it was from the Ice Cream Shoppe, which had a more limited menu than the diner or even the Coffee Engine. It would be a good place to start.

Uncle Benjamin decided that if Digger would spend much of the day working with Holly, he'd have more fun prowling the Ancestral Sanctuary property. "*Maybe somebody left gold coins at our place.*"

It didn't hit her until she was looking down from the second-floor office window that the extra traffic in town had come because of the TV station story about gold coins found on the mountain.

Holly, coffee cup in hand, stood next to her. "This is ridiculous. I saw both those stories last night. They didn't offer any indication of where to look."

As they watched, a mini-van with what looked to be a mom and three kids younger than twelve pulled to the curb and the mom shouted at a man on the sidewalk. Digger recognized him as a co-owner of Suds n' Duds Laundry. He gestured west and pointed up.

"Oh, boy. He's telling them to go toward Bruno's place."

Holly grimaced. "They won't be up there long."

At their respective desks, each worked separately on a menu design. Holly thought it would be a good way to get their creative juices flowing.

Digger sketched what she wanted and then began working in her graphics software to do a professional rendition. "You think we should show all the ice cream in color, or do one side in black and white? In our draft, I mean."

"I think all color," Holly said. "Ultimately, it's up to them when they see the price difference between color and black and white."

The Ice Cream Shoppe operated on what Uncle Benjamin would call a shoestring budget. "Don't they have kids in grade school?" Digger asked.

"Middle school, I think. Why?"

Digger stared at her copy for several seconds. "If we do it in black and white, we could give them some of those washable markers and let the kids color in chocolate and strawberry. Or whatever."

"Probably end up with purple ice cream," Holly said.

Digger grinned. "We could make it like color by number. The kids would know that seven means strawberry or eight means chocolate."

"Not a bad idea, partner."

The phone rang and Digger picked it up.

"Hey, Digger, Josh here. I saw Marty's article on the web page. I really like it."

"Good. Did you let him know?"

"I sent him an email. I figured if the print edition comes out tomorrow he's pretty busy."

Holly shrugged her shoulders and Digger mouthed "Josh."

"How's your foot healing?"

"It's somewhat better. The doctor here gave me one of those boots so I can walk on it."

Digger wanted to tell him to get to the point so she could get back to work. But she didn't.

Josh cleared his throat. "I was thinking of coming up your way again."

"Trying to see if you can fall and break your arm?"

He laughed. "Nope. I'm ready for some R&R. I'm going to see if I can get a room at one of the B&Bs for a couple days. Will you and Marty be around this weekend?"

"We don't plan to be away. You can meet us for lunch at our favorite diner."

"That'd be great. I'll call you when I get in."

"Talk to you then." Digger hung up and half-frowned. "Why would a young guy want to spend a weekend up here?"

"Maybe he liked your sparkling personalities," Holly said.

BY LATE THURSDAY MORNING, they had two options to show to Serena and Bill at their shop. The main difference was one version had prices at the bottom left of a page and the other had them at the top right.

Digger volunteered to drop them at the Ice Cream Shoppe on the way to pick up lunch for herself and Holly at the diner. As she left the office, she stopped to answer the ringing phone. "Hel…"

"Where the hell is that reporter?"

Holly had heard the loud voice and frowned as Digger replied, "Marty is probably at the paper. Is this Bruno Sam…?"

"You know damn well who this is," Sampson hollered. "I got people trying to sneak onto my property all the damn time!"

CHAPTER THIRTEEN

JOSH PHONED ABOUT three-forty-five Thursday to say he was in Maple Grove. "Hey Digger. I decided to come up a day early. Could we meet for coffee? Marty too, if he'd like to. My treat."

She didn't dislike Josh. However, he seemed to have the same streak of impulsivity that Veronica had, though he was much smoother about it. But at the end of a workday, she wanted to get home.

"I'll tell you what. Why don't you have coffee with me at the office? I need to leave in a few minutes to let Bitsy out, so I don't have a lot of time."

"Uh, sure. I've seen your sign. Second floor, right?"

"Yep. See you soon."

Digger shrugged at Holly. "Our wounded treasure hunter. I figure you're about done today, so we won't bother you. Right?"

"I am, but I'll stay 'til he gets here. I'd like to meet the guy who had the nerve to trespass on Bruno Sampson's property."

Digger texted Marty that Josh was a day early and would stop by her office. "I'm not going to mention we're heading to Bruno's place later."

She was surprised when Marty texted that he'd be over. She glanced at Holly. "Did you see that newer article he did on Josh's uncle, the blacksmith?"

"I did. He could have gotten away with saying he was only quoting the 1910 piece when he called the man an itinerate blacksmith. It's classy that he wrote an article to counter the first one."

"If you tell him he's classy he'll probably ask if he can quote you."

Holly laughed, and then footsteps on the stairs drew their attention.

"Sounds like two people," Holly said.

"I think the extra thump is the big boot he's wearing." She opened the door before Josh could knock. "I'd recognize that swollen ankle anywhere."

Josh entered and pointed at the orthopedic boot, which almost reached to his knee. He had cut the inside seam on an older-looking pair of khakis. "Hairline fracture. Hard to see it on an x-ray at first."

Digger introduced Holly and pointed Josh to a client chair next to her desk. She opened the bottom drawer. "You can stick your foot in there if you need to elevate it."

As Josh settled himself, Holly asked, "What do you think of Maple Grove, aside from being a place where you can fall down on the mountain above it?"

"It's very friendly. If you bust up your foot, strangers will let you spend the night at their place."

Digger smiled. "Mountain hospitality. What's up today?"

"I saw Marty's story on my uncle. I texted him to say it was good and thank him."

"If he hasn't gotten back to you yet, he will. The day before the print version comes out is pretty busy."

There was a pause of several seconds and Josh said, "I made some calls and looked up information on Bruno's land and traced ownership back more than 100 years."

"What did you find?"

"I bet you looked, too. The first Sampson to buy the property was a man named Abraham in 1910. Just a few months after Gerard Morton died in the same area."

"I found it. I'm not sure what to think about it."

"Do you know if anyone has access to the coins Bruno found?" Josh asked.

"He showed Marty one and supposedly had a small bag of others."

"I keep telling myself to let go of this. Ten days ago, I didn't know Maple Grove existed. I'll never prove who took my great uncle's money."

"You mentioned that Gerard made some small items. I think you said a belt buckle, for example. Make a list of possible items and give it to Sheriff Montgomery."

"I don't understand," Josh said.

"It's not likely Abraham took anything from Gerard, or if he did that it's still in that cabin. But if he did keep something..."

"Oh, I get what you mean. Mmm. I think my grandmother kept a couple things he made for her. I'll have to see if my mother has them. Then we'd have samples of his work for comparison if there's anything in Bruno's cabin."

"Right," Digger said. "I don't know how that would help. But if he died without a will maybe, just maybe, a lawyer could argue you deserved the property."

"I don't want the property, but I'd like to be able to look for more coins up there."

Marty's familiar footfalls came up the staircase. Digger grinned at Josh. "We can tell when people we know climb the stairs. It's as good as a peephole."

Holly nodded toward Josh. "A peephole would still be good. Maybe when we get one more client."

Marty kissed Digger as he came in, then turned to Josh. "You up here to bang up the other leg?" He extended a hand and Josh, still sitting, shook it.

As Marty leaned against Holly's desk, Josh said, "I'd like to talk to Bruno Sampson again. He might have heard talk about exactly where my uncle's body was found. If one of those coins he found is from 1910, I'd offer to buy it for a decent sum."

"You're a brave man," Marty said.

"What do you do for a living?" Holly asked.

"I'm a tax accountant, but for businesses, not individuals."

"So, you don't do an all-nighter on April 14?" Marty asked.

"No, I deal more with strategies to lessen businesses' tax burdens. I don't do their filings."

"So, without being too personal, you could afford to pay a couple thousand dollars for a coin?" Digger asked.

"Yes, not every day, but sometimes."

She nodded. "Good for you." She glanced at Marty. "Do you have a thought on how to get Bruno to talk to Josh?"

Marty frowned slightly. "This is all still fresh, and Bruno has had to deal with tourists and treasure hunters ever since the TV news did a story on the coins."

Josh sat up straighter. "I didn't see that. Was there anything more on exactly where he found them?"

Marty shook his head slowly. "We're part of the Pittsburgh media market. I sure hope the Baltimore stations don't pick up on it. The thing is…" he paused.

Holly interjected. "You folks should make yourselves some coffee. I need to get home." She smiled broadly at Josh. "A pleasure to meet you."

He waved lightly. "I'd stand but I might take out Digger's desk drawer."

Holly picked up her purse and pointed a finger at Digger as she left. "Don't forget you have to let Bitsy out."

"I've got about ten more minutes," Digger said.

Holly blew Marty a kiss, and he grinned at her before turning back to Josh. "The thing is, I'm one of the few people who's visited Bruno at his cabin. With all that's happened the last week, I know he's unhappy he told me about those coins."

Josh's tone was almost pleading. "And he'd be annoyed to see me. But could you at least ask him if he wants $2,000?"

Digger noted Marty didn't mention he thought Bruno had agreed to an article because he might want to sell coins. As much as Bruno hadn't liked the attention, it sounded as if he might get what he wanted.

"I don't think..." Marty began.

The clomp, clomp of boots on the stairs sent a light shiver through the building.

"I know who that is," Digger said. "Veronica Heller."

"Isn't that the name of the banker who said he had gold coins stolen from his house?" Josh asked.

Digger stood to let her in. "Yes. She's thinking of opening a campground of some sort and is interested in Bruno's land. Supposedly."

Before the woman knocked, Digger opened the door. "Veronica. Looking for me?"

"Yes." She began to enter, but paused when she saw Marty and Josh. She pointed to Marty. "Him I recognize." Her eyes went to Josh. "Who are you?"

She was so brash Digger almost smiled. "This is Josh Henry. His great uncle was the blacksmith who died on the west side of Maple Grove, near or on what is now Bruno Sampson's property."

Veronica's stare in Josh's direction could have cut through the Death Star. He gave her a similar, though less deadly, appraisal. "I got here first," she said. "Those coins were taken from my great-grandfather's house."

Josh flushed. "More likely they were stolen from my uncle. Could even be why he was killed."

Veronica pointe a red fingernail at him. "I read those stories in the paper. It doesn't sound as if anyone ever saw your uncle with any coins."

"Doesn't prove your great-grandfather had a lot of them, either."

Digger had a sense he enjoyed goading Veronica.

"Well, well," she sputtered, "you're not from here. You just came to try to get gold coins."

"Now, hold on…" Marty began.

Veronica yelled, "You hold on!"

Digger took a dictionary off Holly's desk, held it above her head, and dropped it. The thunderous sound stopped all conversation. "Nobody's holding anything! Veronica, if you want to talk about your ad that ran today, fine. If not, head down the steps."

Marty, Veronica, and Josh didn't move. Only Marty had a hint of amusement in his eyes.

"Fine." Veronica sat an oversized purse on Holly's desk and began pulling out her checkbook, wallet, a long list of coupons that probably came from the Walgreens in Frostburg, a novel-size book on coin collecting and, finally, a photocopy of the ad that had appeared on the *Maple Grove News* website.

"You need to make some changes. I didn't have any calls today about people who wanted to invest money in my campground."

Under his breath, Josh said, "Imagine that."

Marty's lips twitched.

Calmly, Digger said, "You may get some calls when the print edition comes out tomorrow. If not, what changes would you like?"

"How would I know?" Veronica bared her teeth. She looked like a wild bat with an overbite. "You think of something. Just make it so people with money call me." She stuffed her belongings into her purse.

She looked at Josh. "I'm sorry I yelled. Maybe we can compare notes sometime." Veronica turned and stalked down the stairs.

When the door to the street slammed, Marty said, "Just make it so people with money call her?"

"She's off her rocker." Digger turned to see Josh smiling at her. "That was unprofessional of me."

"But spot on," he said. "Seriously, has she learned anything that would help me find out more about my uncle? Or the coins?"

Digger thought for a moment. "Without being overly disparaging, I don't think she's done a lot of research – either about campgrounds or how the coins got there."

Josh grinned. "I'm sort of a shoot-from-the-hip type, too."

Digger thought she'd heard Veronica use those same words. She spoke to Marty. "I need to let Bitsy out. You want to hang here with Josh for a few minutes?"

"You still have hot chocolate in the cabinet above the coffee maker?"

"Help yourself."

He held out a hand. "Give me a key and I'll lock up and head your way within the hour."

As she took a key off her ring, Digger turned to Josh. "I'm glad people now know more about your great uncle. The only way you'll see any gold, unless Bruno takes your $2,000, would be if Bruno dies with no heirs and you spend a lot of money on lawyers."

"You're probably right. Thanks for the hospitality -- again."

MARTY WAS ABLE TO ditch Josh and make it to the Ancestral Sanctuary just before five o'clock.

"What did you guys talk about?" Digger asked.

"I showed him Bruno's place on Google Maps. He said the forest all looks the same and he hadn't been able to pick it out on the Internet."

"Can you see the cabin through the trees?"

"Nope. But it gave him an idea of what four acres of woods look like. You could walk around for six weeks and not see something partially hidden in the soil."

"Are you going to ask Bruno if he's willing to sell a 1910 coin to Josh?"

"I left a voicemail for Bruno before Josh left for the B&B where he has a reservation. If Bruno's going to be mad about it, maybe he'll get it out of his system before we get there."

Uncle Benjamin was pleased to be included. *There are only so many books I can dive into in a day.*

Digger told him what had gone on at her office and why they were going to see Bruno. To Uncle Benjamin she added, "I'd say you can be a witness if Bruno gets mad enough to kill us. But who would you tell?"

"Not funny."

Bitsy begged to go for the ride, but the dog could easily get lost in unfamiliar woods. "I promise we'll go for a long walk later."

Ragdoll hissed as Uncle Benjamin walked out behind Digger.

Digger climbed into the Toyota's front seat and Marty started down the driveway. "I've been trying to guess what he wanted to show me."

"He was really mad when he called me earlier today."

"At first he was with me, too, but he calmed down. He said he had a secret, and he'd rather tell me about it than have, and I quote, 'one of the frickin' gold hunters,' stumble over it."

"*Is that some new kind of gold miner?*" Uncle Benjamin asked.

Digger ignored him. "Did any of the searchers come into the newspaper office?"

"One guy said he'd like to see where the coins were found, and I could honestly tell him I didn't know. Then he wanted to know who found them and I told him I keep my sources confidential." Marty grinned. "He said to get over myself, I wasn't protecting Deep Throat."

Digger laughed and Uncle Benjamin said, "*He'd have to be pretty old to know who that was.*"

Marty turned onto the state road that went up the west side of the mountain. "I hope this is quick. I haven't done laundry or even taken out the garbage for a week."

"Remind me not to come over until you have." She yawned. "It's been a tiring day."

"*I'll come over,*" Uncle Benjamin said. Digger repeated his comment.

"Thanks, Benjamin, but I prefer your niece."

"*Imagine that.*"

Marty turned onto Jessup Lane and parked a couple feet onto Bruno's property. "Not likely anyone else'll be up here at this time, but no point getting the car hit."

They got out and Marty called for Bruno. No response.

"Can't imagine he'd stand you up," Digger said.

"*I'll look around.*" Uncle Benjamin moved ahead of them.

Marty pointed. "You can just see his cabin in the clearing through there. The little building where he does his taxidermy work is behind it about thirty yards."

Digger squinted. "What's that box just to the right of the cabin door?"

Marty laughed. "A bird feeder. Go figure."

A very loud blue jay apparently didn't like them paying attention to the feeder. Digger tilted her neck and found him on a low branch in front of the cabin.

They reached the cabin and Digger took in the homemade door, but noted that he had a very modern draft blocker along the bottom. "Does he have electricity?"

Marty pointed to two small solar panels at the peak of the cabin. "He heats with wood, but the panels heat his water. Pretty cool, huh?"

"Very." Digger noted several small lights on the ground, each with tiny solar collection squares. Safety lights after dark. "He lives a more modern life than I expected."

"No point coming out here if we don't knock," Marty said. He pounded twice on the door.

Uncle Benjamin's voice cut through the trees. "*Oh, no! Hurry!*"

Digger turned sharply to the right and ran toward the sound. She couldn't see him in the dense foliage. "Where are you? Are you okay?"

Marty came more slowly. "I doubt ghosts can get hurt."

In a few more seconds, Digger could see Uncle Benjamin, who pointed to a spot on the ground.

Bruno Sampson lay sprawled, the eyes in his very white face open and staring skyward.

CHAPTER
FOURTEEN

AFTER SEVERAL SECONDS, Digger realized she had been holding her breath. She let it out in a whoosh and scanned the trees that surrounded them. She heard a car go by on the road well behind them, but saw no one. A single crow cawed and was answered by the angry blue jay.

Digger turned toward Marty. "He looks dead. I don't want to touch him."

"I don't think we need to check for a pulse. Did you hear anyone else since we've been here?"

"No, and there weren't any cars coming up from town when we did." She glanced behind her. "Let's walk back toward his cabin."

"Just a second." Marty stooped and, without staring at Bruno's face, took in the ground around the body. "I'm no detective, but the brush looks more trampled than it might if only one person had walked here."

Digger suddenly realized that Uncle Benjamin had called them to this spot, but she didn't see him. "Uncle Benjamin! Where are you?"

"Behind you. I sped all over to see if I could see anyone else."

"Is anyone else here?" she asked

"Not a soul. But something gives me the heebie jeebies."

Digger turned toward Marty. "He doesn't see anyone else. Something must have brought Bruno to this exact spot. There's no foot path, and the branches hang really low."

"Yeah, but I'd rather not hang around to figure it out. Let's get back to my car and call the sheriff."

Sheriff Montgomery didn't wonder why Bruno died where he did, but he questioned what had drawn Digger and Marty to the body. "Did you hear him yell? Hear someone running?"

"If I'd heard someone running, I'd have gone the other way." She glanced the short distance down Jessup Lane, where Marty stood talking to Deputy Sovern. Behind them was the medical examiner's private car as well as the two sheriff vehicles.

"Keep your focus here, Digger." Sheriff Montgomery gestured behind him where Medical Examiner Alex Cluster had set up a portable halogen light on a six-foot stand. "He was lying down. How did you find him?"

Digger racked her brain trying to remember the color clothes Bruno had been wearing. All some version of dull green or brown, with his usual camo jacket. She couldn't claim to have seen a spot of red. She wished she and Marty had talked about what to say about what led them to Bruno. She couldn't say a hollering ghost.

Uncle Benjamin appeared behind the sheriff. "*Tell him the crow cawed a lot.*"

Digger put on an expression of deep thought. "I guess it was that crow. Or maybe the blue jay. They made a lot of racket. When we didn't find Bruno, I started walking that way."

"And what did Marty do?"

"He was standing in one place, still looking around. Then he followed me. I guess."

Sheriff Montgomery glanced up from the notes he had jotted. "You guess?"

She shrugged. "I wasn't standing next to us observing us. I was just…moving around."

"And why did you two come up here?"

This she and Marty had discussed before the sheriff arrived. "Bruno called Marty to say he had to show him something. Something secret. He said he'd rather show it to Marty than have one of the frickin' gold hunters find it."

"That's all he said?"

"That's what Marty told me. He may remember something else if you badger him enough."

"Not funny," Montgomery snapped. "Now…"

Cluster called from near Bruno's body. "Looks like we found what he hit his head on."

"Stay here." Montgomery moved toward the ME, careful to tread the same ground he had previously walked.

Jim Sovern went that way, too, so Marty came to stand by Digger. He whispered, "Where's your uncle?"

Digger replied in a low voice. "He was here, but he's headed back toward Bruno." She rubbed her temples. "I told him what drew me to that spot was the crow cawing, and you sort of followed."

Marty's somber expression lightened. "Good. I told him I followed you but didn't think you had a clear idea of where you were going."

Digger grinned momentarily. "My life in a metaphor."

He grunted a short laugh. "I wish to heck we knew what he wanted to show me. It almost sounded like he thought someone would steal something from him."

"Did you see any blood?"

"I didn't look hard, but I don't think so. I was too focused on calling the sheriff and getting back to the car."

Digger hadn't planned on standing outside in temperatures that dropped after sunset. She shivered. "Do you have a travel blanket in the back of your car?"

Marty fished in his pocket and handed her his keys. "Always have one for my grandmother."

"Thanks. I'll be right back." She took out the blanket and peered through the trees. She could barely see Cluster and couldn't make out Sheriff Montgomery at all. But she could hear him.

"I need to know if this was a simple fall or if you find any markings on the body that indicate someone shoved him or struck him with something."

A sound like someone slapping a newspaper on a table reached her. Deputy Sovern had pulled crime scene tape from a roll and begun stretching it from tree to tree. She could barely see him.

What would anyone gain by killing Bruno? If someone like Josh wanted the land so he could search for more gold coins or Veronica wanted it to create a campground, Bruno's death – as opposed to purchasing the land – would only delay that. If he had a will, it could also put the land in someone else's hands.

She returned to where Marty stood just as he placed his phone in the pocket of his jeans. "Who were you calling?"

He spoke in a low voice. "My editor. I'll need to get this on the paper's website. I let him know I'd be sending him something as soon as I can. Maybe the printer can insert one line on the front page directing people to the website."

"That'll make Montgomery happy. It'll be hard to keep people away from here."

"They'd have to put roadblocks where the state road meets Jessup Lane."

HALF AN HOUR LATER, Deputy Medical Examiner Penelope Parker drove the ME van into the lane. In town it wouldn't have attracted much attention. In the woods, if anyone saw it, there would be many questions.

Three minutes later, a silver Toyota came toward Digger and Marty and stopped. She recognized Max and Sandy Elder from down the road.

Max put down the driver's side window. "What's going on? There's never much traffic here after dark."

Marty leaned toward them. "Bruno Sampson died."

"Good heavens," Sandy said. "We saw his pickup pass our place a couple hours ago."

Digger tilted her head toward the halogen light among the trees. "You should probably tell Sheriff Montgomery that."

Max raised his window and guided their car farther into narrow Jessup Lane and he and Sandy got out.

Digger walked to them. "If you saw Bruno, did you see anyone else?"

Max shook his head. "We were behind the house putting up a new bird feeder. We only saw Bruno out our front window because we went inside to get some iced tea."

Montgomery called from near Bruno's body. "Max, Sandy. Hang tight for a few minutes, would you?"

They both said, "Sure."

"Digger, Marty, head back near Marty's car, please."

Sandy's brows furrowed. "Why would he…"

Digger smiled as she moved away. "He has to interview people separately."

Max said, "We don't know anything."

"You saw Bruno two hours ago. That'll help a lot," Marty said.

They walked the twenty yards to Marty's Toyota in silence. Marty glanced in the direction of the body and back to Digger. "Do you think he really suspects us?"

Digger shook her head. "But he can't make any assumptions. I suppose we could have hurt Bruno and then called the sheriff."

"Damn, I wish we knew what they were talking about over there."

"Is your memory hiding?" Digger asked.

Marty stared at her.

Digger whispered, "Uncle Benjamin will tell us."

"Oh, right. He's over there?"

"I can't spot him, but he's somewhere nearby."

A couple minutes later, he peered out from behind Jim Sovern and waved. As Montgomery walked toward Max and Sandy, Uncle Benjamin sped toward Digger and Marty.

Digger turned her back to those surrounding Bruno's body and faced Marty. She listened to Uncle Benjamin without comment. Marty knew her well enough to know she was listening, and kept quiet.

"Montgomery and Cluster think there's enough disturbed vegetation that two or three people might have been standing in that spot. They can't figure out why they were there, though. There are a few narrow paths through the property; places Bruno walked most days. But no paths near there."

Digger repeated the gist of what Uncle Benjamin had said. "Any weapons?" she asked.

"He hit his head on a rock when he fell, but they think a bruise started to form along his forehead. Dr. Cluster won't know what killed him until he can do the autopsy."

Again, she repeated the information.

"Why do they think that?" Marty asked.

"Not sure. Cheez it, the fuzz!"

Digger looked over her shoulder and saw Montgomery approaching. She shrugged lightly at Marty and they both faced him.

"You can go in a minute. You be in town tonight and tomorrow?"

They nodded, and Digger asked, "Can you tell how he died?"

Sheriff Montgomery shook his head. "Have to wait for the autopsy. Go home."

They both started to go toward Marty's car, but Digger turned back. "Sheriff, was any of that Heller family material helpful? When I looked some more, I found a woman in Germantown."

"Yes, thanks. I'll be too preoccupied to look at it again real soon."

As they climbed into Marty's car, Digger thought about what a bruise might indicate. Did it mean someone had brought a weapon with them, intending to commit murder?

They started the drive to the Ancestral Sanctuary in silence. Uncle Benjamin broke it. *Do you know where Josh and the Heller woman were late this afternoon?*

Digger repeated the question to Marty. "I don't know, do you?"

"Nope, but I'll leave that to Montgomery."

CHAPTER FIFTEEN

DIGGER WOKE UP EARLY Friday morning with a sense of anticipation. But why? She decided it was because she still expected to find out whatever Bruno planned to tell Marty. Was he going to show him more coins?

She doubted that. He would have simply said that, or even brought the coins to Marty at the *Maple Grove News*.

Bruno's murder dominated the *Maple Grove News* website. With a jolt Digger realized Marty might mention their names as having discovered the body. However, he simply said "a local couple" found him and called the sheriff. She remembered the editor didn't like him to write a story if Marty was part of it. This must be his way around it.

She skimmed the piece. She knew the basic facts, and that Marty had tried to get comments from friends but hadn't found any. Bruno's neighbors, the Elders, said he was polite but kept to himself, and the school provided a yearbook picture from about twenty years ago.

She'd have to remind Marty he could check with the hardware store to see if they would download images from their security system. Bruno had to be on the system somewhere.

Uncle Benjamin read over her shoulder. "*Somebody had to see something.*"

Digger kept reading. The Elders didn't recall any odd cars on the road Friday afternoon, just the usual hikers. But they'd been on their back porch much of the afternoon. "We wouldn't have noticed unless somebody honked a lot," Max Elder said.

The Elders added that the day before there had been cars driving slowly by, looking for Bruno's property. He'd added more No Trespassing signs. "I expect," Max said, "that word got around that he could get real angry real fast."

Marty said that the medical examiner had not yet determined a cause of death. A quote from Sheriff Montgomery stated, "At this point I'd classify it as suspicious. He had spoken by phone to a local resident about an hour before he died, and did not indicate he felt ill. He did hit his head on a rock as he fell, but there are other contusions that may have caused the fall."

Whatever that meant. Marty must have talked to the sheriff later in the evening.

"*You ready to go to work?*"

"Yep. You coming?"

"*Can we go to Bruno's property first? I want to figure out why I have the heebie jeebies about that place.*"

DIGGER FIRST STOPPED at the Coffee Engine for morning fuel. She was surprised to see Josh Henry and Veronica Heller chatting as if they were old friends. They didn't notice her as she stood in line, so she kept observing them.

After another minute, she thought she detected that the friendliness was a thin veneer covering two strongly competitive spirits.

She paid Leslie for her cup of coffee and approached them. Would they look so casual if they knew about Bruno's murder? Had they not read the paper's website?

She stopped at their table. "Looks as if you two are buddies now."

Josh smiled, but he looked tense. "We ran into each other last night at the Mexican restaurant and decided we'd have better luck with Bruno Sampson if we approached him together."

"Are you going to head up to the property together?" Digger asked. She couldn't believe they hadn't heard the news about Bruno's death.

Veronica made no attempt to be friendly. "I think I should offer to buy his property, maybe for more than it's worth. I could get my brother to co-sign a loan."

Digger wasn't so sure. Not that it mattered at this point.

Josh stared at his cup of coffee.

Digger asked him, "Mr. Tax Advisor, would that be a good business deduction for Veronica?"

"Good question." He looked at Veronica. "If you use it for a campground, it likely would be."

Digger hesitated, but said, "I'm not sure Bruno has ever lived anywhere else. Money might not be a good motivator."

Veronica waved a hand. "Money is always a motivator. Speaking of which, I still haven't had any investors call me."

"I reread your ad last night," Digger said. "You probably need to tell potential investors what benefits would come to them."

"What do you mean?" Veronica asked.

"You know, when you invest in a stock you expect a certain rate of return. Would your investors own a portion of the campground, would they expect a percentage of your annual profits?"

Veronica stared at her blankly.

Digger nodded toward Josh. "Josh is a financial guru. He can explain."

Josh's smile became fixed.

"I'll see you later." Digger left before she could hear Veronica ask him to explain investment returns for her pie-in-the-sky campground. They'd find out about Bruno's death soon enough.

DIGGER PARKED ON THE narrow lane next to Bruno's property. She'd told Holly she'd be late, but hadn't said why. It occurred to her that if Bruno had been killed rather than simply fallen, she might run into his murderer checking out the property. No one would know where to look for her if she didn't make it to work.

She spoke to Uncle Benjamin's back as he led the way onto the property. "Maybe we should rethink this. We could get in trouble for returning to a crime scene."

"*You want to know what's going on as much as I do. You won't go behind Montgomery's yellow tape.*"

"I also don't want Sheriff Montgomery to haul me to his office for questioning."

"*Last time we were up here, I got the heebie jeebies. We're missing something.*"

Digger stepped over a log that had branches sticking out of it like spikes. If she hadn't had on hiking boots, she would have lost her footing. "The problem is, we don't know what *something* is, so it'll be hard to recognize it." She walked on the narrow path toward Bruno's cabin.

Now behind her, Uncle Benjamin called, "*There's lilies of the valley all over this one patch.*"

She glanced at her feet. "Poison ivy here. Damn it!"

From farther away, Uncle Benjamin called, "*Don't touch your boots when you take 'em off.*"

Digger stopped ten yards from the forlorn cabin. Police tape stretched across the door, as it did around the area where Bruno's body had been found.

His seemed such a pointless life. He was so angry the few times she talked to him, and the frown lines in his face made her think he rarely, if ever, felt happy.

As she turned toward where she thought Uncle Benjamin had headed, her phone rang. Caller ID said Marty, and she answered. "Hello from the woods."

"What? You're near Bruno's place? Why would you go up there?"

"Two guesses."

"Ah. Yesterday's feeling of heebie jeebies?"

"Are you with someone?" Digger asked. "You sound stiff."

"You could say that. I'm in Sheriff Montgomery's office in Oakland. Fortunately, not handcuffed."

"Why are you there? Did he ask you for help?"

"Nooo. Guess whose fingerprints were the only ones in the cabin besides Bruno's?"

"But you interviewed him there. They can't believe you killed him!"

Marty grunted. "Mostly they don't, I think. But my prints were on his kitchen counter and the coin he showed me."

Digger said nothing for several seconds. "Can't they tell it was a couple weeks ago?"

"According to our favorite sheriff, it's hard to put a date stamp on latent fingerprints."

"What do you want me to do? He isn't arresting you, is he?"

"I doubt it. Mostly I wanted you to know where I am. I have to figure out how to write about this."

Digger smiled to herself. "If you're thinking about what you'll say in the newspaper you must be pretty relaxed."

"Not the word I'd use, but…listen, I need to go." He hung up.

Digger put her phone back in the pocket of her jeans and stared at the cabin. She'd never been in it, but imagined it had one large room with maybe a small bedroom or curtained area for sleeping. Marty said he had been in there to interview Bruno, but not the smaller building behind it, where Bruno turned dead animals into hunters' trophies. The cabin and outbuilding now had padlocks on them.

Montgomery would never suspect Marty. Would he?

Uncle Benjamin's tone came through loud and urgent. "*Get over here!*"

She swung around. His voice came from east of her. She began to jog in that direction and jumped across the downed log. Absurdly, she called, "Are you hurt?"

He laughed, then spoke in a calmer voice. "*No. But hurry.*"

Digger peered between the dense brush and saw Uncle Benjamin's pale figure about twenty yards ahead of her, floating a foot off the ground. "It's hard to walk through all this. Can you come to me?"

"*There's something you have to see.*"

She pushed a low-hanging branch away from her face and swatted in the direction of a spider who hung on that branch. "This better be good."

"*Not good, but suspicious.*"

She reached him and raised her palms to her shoulders. "What?"

Uncle Benjamin pointed to the ground.

Digger wasn't sure what was significant. Amid the brush and groundcover there was a partially cleared area. Had an animal grazed here regularly? But the ground had a slight indentation, and near where Uncle Benjamin stood at one end of the small clearing was a batch of bell-shaped lilies of the valley.

She raised her head and met Uncle Benjamin's eyes. "What am I looking at besides pretty flowers?"

"*If I'm not mistaken, a grave.*"

Digger stepped back. The indentation was about six feet in length, two to three feet wide. "The dirt on top isn't packed down too much. You think someone added soil to make it less noticeable?"

"*That'd be smart. I suggest you turn around and walk back toward the cabin in almost the same steps you used to get over here.*"

She turned, intending to follow his instructions but not sure why it mattered. "I can't pretend we didn't find this. I don't need to cover my tracks."

Uncle Benjamin floated ahead of her. "*True, but you don't want to disturb signs of other people who may have been up here.*"

"Good point." When she again stood ten yards from the cabin, Digger turned toward the grave. "We know Gerard Morton was found in this general area, but his body was returned to his sisters. Are people sure Bruno's mother left here alive?"

Uncle Benjamin stood next to her as he stared at the cabin. "*The problem will be that the Sampsons didn't mingle. Bruno's father, Silas Junior, came into the hardware store now and again. They had to buy groceries, but there used to be three or four small stores, not the IGA we have now. I wouldn't know who to tell you to talk to.*"

"Maybe Marty's grandparents. And I could talk to Maryann Montgomery again."

Uncle Benjamin chuckled. "*I suppose the sheriff's grandmother would be a good start. But she lived away from here for a long time?*"

"True, and when she and her husband came back, she lived in Oakland until last year. But she was born about 1930. She would have been in town during the fifties and early sixties. She didn't move to Ohio until she had her kids. At least, that's what I remember."

"When did Bruno's father inherit this land?"

"Gee I think Bruno's grandfather left it to his parents in 1972. Maryann wouldn't have known Bruno's mother, I suppose. At least, not as Silas Sampson's wife."

"You've got some genealogy digging to do."

"But I have to talk to Sheriff Montgomery first."

AFTER HE GOT THROUGH lecturing Digger because she went to the Sampson property, Sheriff Montgomery said he would call the state police about exhuming a possibly decades-old body from an unmarked grave. "I got Marty with his prints in Sampson's cabin and you traipsing around a crime scene. What is it with you two?"

She was glad Montgomery was working in his Oakland office today. She could roll her eyes while she listened to him on the phone.

"That was not a rhetorical question," Montgomery said.

"Obviously, if I thought I'd find a grave I wouldn't have gone up there. When can Marty come back?"

"He left here fifteen minutes ago." Sheriff Montgomery hung up.

Deputy Jim Sovern sat across the table from Digger in the sheriff's small Maple Grove office, feet propped on the conference table. "I need you to take your time going through what you saw on the property. I don't need to know how many squirrels chattered at you, just what you did."

Digger blew out a breath. "It was mostly a blue jay. I don't know how much more I can tell you, Jim. I walked around. I'd been there maybe ten minutes when I saw the little clearing."

"Why'd you go back there, anyway?"

Uncle Benjamin spoke from his seat atop a tall file cabinet. *"Why don't you tell him your dead great uncle had the heebie jeebies?"*

"The whole thing felt odd to me. Bruno Sampson lived on that property all his life, could probably have drawn a map showing every stone or hole. How could he trip and hit his head on a rock?"

Sovern took his feet off the table and stood. "I tripped over a bag of fertilizer when I was working in my yard a couple weeks ago. Landed hard on my elbow. Damn near broke it."

"But the fertilizer didn't sit on that spot in your yard all the time. Bruno's rocks or whatever didn't move around."

"You don't know what goes on when you sleep," Uncle Benjamin said.

Sovern gestured toward the door. "Come back anytime you don't find a body, Digger."

Tired of being reprimanded, Digger left her Jeep in its spot two doors down from the sheriff's satellite office and walked toward the *Maple Grove News*. The warm late morning sun felt good. She wished it would carry into the spring evening, but it wouldn't.

Uncle Benjamin accompanied her, a shovel slung over his shoulder and worn bib overalls hiding his skinny legs. *"Are we going to get Marty to help us see who's in that grave?"*

"No. That's up to the sheriff."

"I can look a few inches under the soil. You think I could go down a few feet?"

"Would you want to come back up?"

From behind her, Abigail asked, "Who are you talking to, Digger?"

"Uh-oh." Uncle Benjamin sped toward the paper.

Digger turned and smiled at the Chamber of Commerce admin staffer. "I'm developing a terrible habit of talking to myself." She fell into step with Abigail.

"I've been worried about you, girl. Living all alone in that big house. When you had your house in town you were out and about."

"True. But it's a big job to keep that place in shape." She grinned. "I do have Bitsy and Ragdoll."

"I know that silly dog from when you brought him to work at the ad agency that one time."

"Right." Digger laughed. "The day we were supposed to get a foot of snow and Dale made us come into the office anyway."

"Good old Mr. Stufflebeam. I heard he's looking for jobs down in Hagerstown."

"Gee, he has such a nice place here. Anything there would cost at least twice as much."

They stopped in front of the paper and Abigail shrugged. "Looks like you're still dating Marty."

"Yep." Digger realized news of Bruno's death hadn't reached Abigail or she would have asked about it. Had she not seen the newspaper's web page? "Lucky me."

"He is a nice guy."

"I'm a nice guy. You know any lady ghosts?"

"He is. Keep me posted on Dale." Digger opened the glass door to the newspaper office and waited a second for her eyes to adjust to the dimmer light.

As usual, no worker sat behind the counter. Uncle Benjamin sat on it reading a note someone had left in an envelope on the desk.

"Don't be a busybody."

"I was hoping for a torrid tip. It's just a check for a subscription."

Digger could have let herself behind the counter and walked to Marty's office, but she didn't like to do that. She dinged the round bell.

From down the hall, Marty said, "Just a minute."

"It's just me," Digger called.

"Be right there."

Uncle Benjamin floated back to the newspaper morgue. He could amuse himself there for hours.

Marty came to the doorway of the hall that led to his office. "Besides calls about Bruno's murder, I've gotten a lot about the article on Gerard Morton. They saw the Pittsburgh story and then read my piece."

"Are they calling to say it was a titillating story?"

"Nope. Mostly people wanting to know where to look for coins."

She leaned on the counter and pictured the possible grave near Bruno's cabin. Could it be his mother? His father was in the town cemetery. It could be a pet. What did Bruno do with animal carcasses if he didn't sell them? One person could eat only so much deer meat in a year.

"What are you thinking, Digger?"

"Two things. The uninteresting one is since Bruno went to the hardware store and they have a security system, maybe they can isolate a picture of him you can use as a photo."

He grinned. "Good idea. Of course, it'll be blurry and taken from the rafters."

"Beggars can't be choosers."

"What was the other thing?" he asked.

Uncle Benjamin had come back to the lobby. "*It's a good one.*"

"I have some big news related to Bruno's place."

Marty raised his eyebrows. "You didn't find another body, did you?"

"Not quite. Uncle Benjamin saw a patch of lilies of the valley in the middle of the underbrush. Looks as if someone planted them near this indentation in the soil. We may have found a grave."

Incredulous, he asked. "How could the sheriff's deputies have missed that?"

"It was dark, and it's easily 100 yards from the cabin, not on any path." She lowered her voice. "You-know-who can float anywhere. Lots of dense brush, and then a small area that's clear except for lilies of the valley."

Marty leaned on his side of the counter. "You tell Montgomery?"

"Jim Sovern's at the office here. He put Montgomery on the phone. He's going to talk to state police or somebody."

"They'd have to try to exhume, don't you think? Or maybe they'd have dogs sniff around first."

Digger shrugged. "If someone's been in there for decades, would there be much scent?"

Marty picked up a pencil from the jar on the counter and took a three-by-five card from a stack to make a note. "I'm really glad I have a job where I don't have to know that."

CHAPTER SIXTEEN

DIGGER AND UNCLE Benjamin walked into You Think, We Design at nine-thirty Friday morning. "Sorry to be late."

Holly didn't glance up from her keyboard. "Find us any new clients?"

Holly was definitely annoyed. They'd talked a couple of times about how it couldn't be that Holly minded the office while Digger came and went as she pleased.

She wished she didn't have to tell her partner where she'd been, but if there were an unmarked grave it would be all over town by afternoon.

The phone rang and Holly picked it up. But before she finished their greeting, Sheriff Montgomery's voice barked, "Let me talk to Digger."

Digger picked up her extension. "Yes, sir."

"You've got to head up there to show me where this maybe grave is."

"Would you like to set a time for our date?"

"Quit fooling around. I'm on my way from Oakland. Meet me on Jessup Lane in forty-five minutes." He hung up.

Holly raised her eyebrows. "I didn't hear all his yelling, but it sounded as if he was talking about you finding a grave."

"Maybe." Digger flushed. "I felt like we missed something yesterday, so I went back to Bruno's property to…"

"Are you crazy? If he was murdered, his killer could have been up there!"

"Maybe not…"

Holly's deep brown eyes turned almost black with fury. "And what do you mean 'we' missed something. You aren't the sheriff!"

Digger sat heavily in her desk chair. "You're right."

Holly sat back in her own, as if she'd been expecting a strong argument and didn't know what to say when Digger agreed with her. "You won't involve yourself anymore?"

"I have to go up there to show him the indentation in the ground. Then I'll stay out of it."

"*I hope you don't mean that*," Uncle Benjamin said.

Holly's expression softened some. "You're my good friend and I love you. But we're also business partners. When people think of us, I want it to be in terms of our…" she smiled, "creative genius. Not your talent at finding dead people."

SHERIFF MONTGOMERY ARRIVED at Bruno's property soon after Digger did. As he got out of his car,

Digger saw signs of strain she hadn't noticed last night in the dark. His fifty-something face seemed more lined, and he moved his head from side to side for a moment, as if his neck was stiff. He also looked as if he'd lost a few pounds.

"Looking more svelte there, Sheriff."

"Don't try to butter me up, Digger." He smiled briefly and then reached into the car and pulled out a package of something yellow.

"Cluster and the state police crime guy told me we have to wear these yellow booties."

Digger walked to him and took a pair. "Did you tell them sometimes there's sharp stuff on the forest floor that'll tear these to shreds?"

"They know. I think somebody busts their chops if they don't have us take," he made an air quote, all precautions to preserve the scene."

Digger pointed in the direction of the cleared ground, which was perhaps 100 yards from the cabin, and they started walking. "Did you find out if Bruno died from a fall?"

"You remember that I ask most of the questions, don't you?"

Digger pushed a low-hanging branch away from her face. "I do. Did you find anything interesting in his cabin?"

"You mean like a note from somebody saying where I should look for a murder weapon?"

"So, he was killed?"

"Shut up, Digger."

He had spoken in an almost amiable tone, so Digger didn't take offense.

"*Tell him to stop and look around.*" Uncle Benjamin said.

"Stop for a second and look straight ahead," she said.

"What am I looking at, Digger?"

"See those spots of white? Those are lilies of the valley. There aren't any others around here, so they caught my eye."

The flowers were the best explanation Digger could come up with for walking so far into the brush.

"I see 'em." Montgomery walked closer. "They're grouped in a line."

Digger bent over to pull the bootie back over her hiking boots. "Sort of where a headstone might be."

They stopped about fifteen feet from the spot. Sheriff Montgomery sighed. "It would be about the right size for an adult, but why would someone who hid a body keep the area cleared? You'd think they'd want new foliage to cover the spot."

Digger smiled. "You do ask good questions."

"Smart aleck." He removed a radio from his belt. "Sovern, do you copy?"

"Right here, Sheriff."

"Tell the state folks it looks like we'll need help exhuming. I'll need Cluster and Parker, but not until we can give them something to work with."

"*I think he means some_one_ to work with,*" Uncle Benjamin said.

Digger winced. When Montgomery turned his head toward her, she said, "I wonder who it would be?"

Montgomery shrugged. "I checked about Silas Sampson's wife. He reported her for desertion about thirty years ago. He produced a note she supposedly left for him that talked about how depressed she was, how much she hated him. Told him to treat their son better than he treated her."

"Susannah, wasn't that her name?"

Uncle Benjamin straightened and moved toward the grave.

Sheriff Montgomery turned to fully face Digger. "Her name doesn't come up on legal documents except when she married Silas Jr."

"Marty went down to Oakland to research the transfers of this property."

"Ask him to send me that. Or drop off info." He stared ahead. "Going back how far?"

The single crow who had announced itself yesterday began to caw incessantly. A blue jay chattered just as loudly.

"To 1910. Abraham Sampson bought it a couple months after the body of the blacksmith, Gerard Morton's, body was found somewhere near here."

Montgomery shook his head. "The only records of that death are the newspaper articles."

"Not even a death certificate?"

"I'll send somebody to Vital Records in Baltimore on Monday. Even if they have one, it won't give a detailed cause of death. It'll be something like 'head wound' and may say it came from a fall."

Uncle Benjamin seemed to be talking to someone. He began to move toward the cabin.

"What is it, Digger?" Montgomery asked.

"I'm trying to remember. Census data show that Abraham Sampson was far from well-to-do. It's tempting to jump to the conclusion that he killed Morton, stole his money, and bought land."

"You can jump, but I can't. Doesn't seem to have been a very well-educated family, but if there's a diary in your historical society, it would likely say old Abraham came across a dead man and, finding no relatives, believed that the Good Lord had led him to the money so Abe Sampson could better provide for his family."

"There won't be anything. Certainly nothing that said who killed Morton." She paused. "So how did those gold coins suddenly show up in the dirt?"

"You gotta accept you'll never know that. Your folks live on the Texas Gulf Coast, right? Why don't you take a long weekend and visit them? Take your mind off dead bodies."

SINCE SHE HAD FOUND the seeming grave, Montgomery said Digger could be nearby when the person was exhumed. "But not Hofstedder."

Montgomery's face reddened as he talked to Marty on the phone. "I realize you were with Digger yesterday. But as soon as I let you up here, every TV station from 100 miles around will want to set up cameras."

Sheriff Montgomery sat in his car making phone calls and talking on the radio. Digger stood near hers, glad it was almost sixty degrees rather than the forty it could have been in March.

Twenty yards from her sat a small bobcat. The state diggers hadn't realized the dense tress and undergrowth would make it unusable. They resorted to hand tools.

Digger turned her eyes back to the three men who carefully wielded shovels and placed the dirt on a tarp a few feet from them. Every now and then they commented on something to each other, and twice they sifted through the soil and carefully removed a small item, which they then placed into a clear bag.

After about half an hour, the shorter of the three men called out, "We have a skull. Small amount of hair attached."

Digger felt a wave a nausea and managed to quell it. She turned away from the men and faced the lane. A couple of tears ran down her cheeks. She thought of Bruno Sampson as a bully, but at some point he was a little boy whose mother died. And he couldn't tell anyone.

Someone came behind her and she brushed away the tears and turned.

Sheriff Montgomery nodded toward her. "Sad day."

"Yes."

He held out three small plastic bags. One had a small toy horse, another a Matchbox car, and a third two marbles. "Must have been Bruno who..."

"Marbles!" Digger reached for that bag but Montgomery pulled it back. "Lucas Heller told Marty that marbles were stolen from his great-grandfather's house back in 1910. He said they'd be valuable today."

Montgomery looked at the items again. "Odd things to be in a grave."

Digger thought for a moment. "If they were near the surface, maybe Bruno, as a little boy, left gifts for his mom."

"Hard to think of a child in that situation," Montgomery said.

"You know, if those marbles were from the Heller home in 1910, it could mean Abraham Sampson was a one-man crime spree."

"I've thought of that. Of course, he could have worked with others." Montgomery stared ahead for a couple of moments. "I just can't think of one way to show who committed any of those three crimes."

"I'm sure anything would be long gone, but Josh said his uncle forged some small objects. He mentioned a belt buckle, and he said he'd talk to his mother to see if she heard of – or has – any other items."

Montgomery smiled. "A handmade belt buckle from 110 years ago would be a potential clue."

From a few hundred yards down the state road, in the direction of town, came angry voices. Digger had to strain to distinguish the words.

"But he's dead! He said I could look at the property." Veronica Heller's brash attitude came through clearly.

Montgomery spoke one word into his radio. "Status."

"Collins here," a man said. "Just turning around traffic."

To Digger, the sheriff said, "Sounds like someone doesn't want to go."

"I think it's Veronica Heller. She wanted to buy land up here to live on it and open some sort of campground."

"Lucas Heller's sister. I haven't met her, but Gene told me she really ticked him off at the Chamber the other day."

Digger grunted. "He sent her to me to prepare an ad for the paper."

Montgomery started to move toward his car.

"Lucas called me a couple nights ago and said his sister told him I was advising her about how to purchase land that had a tax lien on it."

"Are you?" Montgomery asked.

"Nope. I don't know how. But I wouldn't tell her if I did. She's rude." Digger explained how difficult Veronica was to work with on the ad.

Montgomery took his radio off his belt again. "Deputy Collins, hold that individual at your line. I'll be down to talk to her." He turned to Digger. "Go home, or go to the Coffee Engine or some place. I don't need to tell you not to talk about this."

DIGGER TEXTED MARTY before she went into her office. "The sheriff told me not to TALK about them finding a woman who was buried a long time ago. I don't know any more."

"I didn't hear it from you," he texted back.

AT YOU THINK, WE DESIGN, Holly grew sympathetic and then more curious after she heard about Digger's last few hours. "Don't you think if she died naturally or in an accident that Bruno's father would have gone with a funeral rather than burying her himself?"

"For sure. I guess the sheriff needs to be sure it's Susannah Sampson."

"Who else would it be?" Holly asked.

Digger shrugged. "Maybe she left on her own and this is an old girlfriend of Bruno's."

Holly's eyes widened. "You really think so?"

"No. Or, I don't know what I think." Digger headed to their coffeepot and turned on the warmer. "Maybe this'll help me function better."

She had just begun sorting through some historical photos when an irritable Veronica Heller called on her cell phone. "Were you even going to tell me Bruno Sampson is dead!?"

Holly whispered, "Just hang up."

Digger shrugged toward her. "Hello, Veronica. I guess you know I'm not the Sheriff Department Public Information Officer. Why don't you give them a call?"

Veronica's voice rose an octave. "I was going to make him sell me that property! I know you were up there yesterday to talk him out of it."

Digger tried to keep her voice even. "It's too bad if you lost a business deal. No doubt you can find other plots of land. Land with willing sellers."

Veronica had probably guessed Digger was about to hang up. "So, you know this fellow, Josh, who says he's descended from the blacksmith who was found on the mountain in 1910."

"Gerard Morton was his uncle."

"What's the diff...? Never mind, I don't care. What was I saying?"

Digger rolled her eyes toward Holly. "You mentioned descendants of the blacksmith."

"Oh, right. That Josh wants some of those gold coins. I figure if I buy the land, whatever's on it belongs to me."

"If you're asking me which interpretation is correct, I have no idea. You'd have to talk to a lawyer."

"I don't have money for that," she snapped.

More politely, Digger asked, "Would your brother pay for a session with an attorney?"

Veronica emitted an elongated sigh. "He's so, so, unimaginative. Also, kind of a jerk sometimes."

"Gee, he speaks so well of you. I have to get back to work." She grinned at Holly as she hung up.

"You found someone who speaks well of Veronica Heller?"

"Of course not. When one person badmouths another, if I say 'so-and-so speaks well of you,' the gossip shuts up for a second and I can exit the conversation."

As she turned on her computer, Digger realized Veronica thought Digger had been at Bruno's yesterday to talk him out of selling to her. The paper didn't say Digger had been one of the people to find the body. How did she know?

CHAPTER SEVENTEEN

MARTY HAD SPENT Friday night with Digger. Today he had a lot of leads to follow for the newspaper. "I hope I can get someone on the ME staff to tell me how they think Bruno died. I don't even know if they'll do the work on that poor woman or send it to Baltimore."

Digger drained her coffee. "I thought maybe you could talk to some people he went to high school with. Someone might have an idea for when his mother was last around."

"From what my grandparents said, she was gone long before high school."

"True, but he would have gone to school with the same kids all the way through. Someone might remember."

"It'll be all over town that we found his body and you – for some mysterious reason – went back the next morning and found the grave."

Digger grinned. "I can't exactly say 'the ghost made me do it.'"

"What time does Franklin get here?"

"Usually around ten. I have a lot of cleaning and laundry to do before then."

"Does he know what's gone on the last two days?"

"I sent him an email and the link to your article on the website. At least I wasn't by myself when we found Bruno. He always says I'm going to vanish one day, and he'll never find me."

"Did you tell him you were alone when you found what's probably Bruno's mom's grave?"

"I might have left that out."

AFTER THE WEEK SHE'D been through, Franklin thought Digger needed company on a Saturday trip to the hardware store. "If you decide to buy a chipper, you'll want help loading it."

She elbowed his arm as they walked into the store that had once belonged to Uncle Benjamin. "I think I have more muscles than a lawyer."

They both stopped to gawk at the new décor. Behind them, Uncle Benjamin hollered, "*What the hell did this new guy do?*" He scuttled toward the manager's office at the back of the store.

Digger didn't think the owner cared what a predecessor thought. But even she could give the guy some design advice.

Instead of grills or large tools or camping equipment, the front of the store was awash in pastels, mostly household items. Rows of enamel bakeware in varied colors competed for space with a tall cage of colorful balls for lawn play.

On the far left were large yard toys for toddlers, including a bright blue plastic slide and yellow faux log cabin with a bright green roof. Yellow? Everything screamed "Made in China." Although the rattan furniture on the right had an East Indies air.

"Good heavens," Franklin said, but in a low voice. "Dad'll be turning over in his grave."

Uncle Benjamin's bellow came from a few aisles over. "*I'll be putting this guy in one.*" He followed the new owner, himself a recent import, but from the Pittsburgh area. The second owner after Uncle Benjamin, he clearly felt no nostalgia for an old-fashioned hardware store motif.

The thirty-something man approached them wearing a canvas apron adorned with a buck with at least a ten-point rack. "Oh, good. Benjamin Browning's kids, right? What do you think of the revamp?"

Uncle Benjamin trailed him. "*Revamp? That sounds like a plumbing job!*"

Franklin and Digger made sure Greg Sondheim knew their names and relationship and continued to gaze around the large store.

"It's an amazing...modernization," Digger said.

Into Sondheim's ear, Uncle Benjamin yelled, "*An abomination.*"

"I bet it'll appeal to some of the families moving into the county from the DC metro area," Franklin added.

Sondheim beamed. "My precise target market. A lot of them have kids, and they won't just be remodeling houses, they'll be getting used to doing more outdoors."

Digger watched a young couple pull a couple of balls from the caged batch of them. Somehow, she didn't think of pink and bright blue as outdoorsy colors.

"*You want them throwing those balls all over the store?*"

If he hadn't been dead, Digger would worry Uncle Benjamin would have a stroke.

Sondheim held up one finger. "Look around. I'll find you."

"Sure," Franklin said.

They said nothing as they made their way toward the back of the store, where lawnmowers, barbeque supplies, and gas and electric-powered tools resided, as well as paint and other traditional hardware items.

"Did you want a yellow or pink woodchipper?" Franklin asked.

"I'll go with traditional green or orange, and I should probably get a shredder so I can make mulch."

"*Get something you can use to shred this place!*" Uncle Benjamin spoke next to Digger's head.

Digger waved a hand in front of her face, as if fanning.

"You hot?" Franklin asked.

"Thought I sensed a flying pest."

"*There's a walking pest up front.*" He zoomed toward the lawn furniture in the front of the store.

"Let's split up," Franklin said. He headed toward the lawn care aisle. His townhouse had a postage-stamp sized patch of grass and flowers.

Digger moved toward larger tools, glad to be thinking about something besides bodies in the woods and angry would-be campground owners. She soon located a shredder. Less expensive than a combination chipper and shredder, but it would still set her back a few hundred dollars. Would save a lot in mulch costs, though.

Uncle Benjamin appeared in front of her wearing a sulky expression.

"Don't do that," she hissed.

"Not like you'd trip over me. What do you think of this place?"

She kept walking toward an aisle with hiking and camping equipment. "There's some good things."

"I don't see a damn one."

She kept her voice low. "I like that there's more lawn furniture."

Franklin's voice came from the next aisle. "You should really only talk to yourself at home."

"You know what your dad said."

"You can talk to yourself," Franklin said.

"As long as you don't expect an answer," Digger finished.

"I give good answers."

Franklin met her at an end cap. "You found a shredder?"

Digger grinned. "Let's get home and start mulching."

FRANKLIN AND DIGGER set up the mulcher not far from the back porch and tentatively fed in branches no more than three inches thick. Bitsy assisted by staying about twenty feet away and barking every time the machine gurgled mulch.

"The mulch is great," Franklin said. He had placed a wheelbarrow a foot from where the machine spit its products, and a lot of it flew into it. The rest they periodically scooped from the ground.

"You should take some home," Digger said.

"I get it delivered every spring."

"But this comes from your ancestral home. How many other people on Dupont Circle can say some of their mulch came from trees hundreds of years old?"

He grinned and tilted his head. "I'll fill one trash bag. I'll go get some more long branches from that pile."

Uncle Benjamin continued to fume. "*I believe in progress, but that guy's…*"

"Greg Sondheim," Digger supplied.

"*That Sondheim fellow has turned that wonderful business into an ordinary, suburban knick-knack store.*"

"I saw no knick-knacks." Digger bent to collect more handsful of mulch from the ground.

"*Garden gnomes! With droopy hats.*"

"Garden gnomes are cute."

"*That's the point! Hardware stores don't do cute!*"

"It's competitive. People could go to Frostburg for a bigger selection. If Sondheim wants them to come to our hardware store, he has to jazz it up."

Franklin's voice came from behind her. "Digger, who are you talking to?"

"*Oh boy. I'm sorry, I shouldn't have…*"

Digger looked at Uncle Benjamin, who had moved away from Franklin. "It's okay. I need to tell him." Then she turned to her cousin. "Can we talk in the kitchen?"

He stared at her for several seconds. "Sure."

Digger turned off the mulcher and they turned without speaking and walked the short distance to the house.

LATE AFTERNOON LIGHT POURED through the kitchen window and spots of sunshine danced on the kitchen counter. They did not brighten Digger's mood.

She stole a look at her cousin as he took a sip of iced tea. She gathered her courage and took the plunge. "I have something important... actually unusual, to tell you."

Franklin grinned. "I'm not sure I've ever seen you tongue-tied before."

Digger looked above his head and finally met his gaze. Franklin frowned, though still seemed amused.

She drew a breath. "You remember what it was like when your dad died?"

Franklin frowned. "Hard to forget. Are you OK? You have a kind of weird expression."

Digger swallowed. "I am but, in a way, so is he. You see, the day of his funeral, the burial part, he sort of popped up."

Franklin gestured that Digger should sit. She kept standing, leaning against the kitchen counter.

Franklin's tone was gentle. "Digger, dead people don't pop up. They're gone."

She stretched her neck to try to loosen the tight muscles. "I know that's how it's supposed to work. But Uncle..."

Franklin's tone became abrupt. "That's how it always works."

Uncle Benjamin had been sitting cross-legged on the kitchen table, his eyes moving from one to the other. *"You can't just spring it on him!"*

Digger ignored Uncle Benjamin and focused on Franklin. "I was at the counter, almost where I am now, and he appeared on the kitchen table." She pointed to where Uncle Benjamin sat, not that Franklin could see him.

Uncle Benjamin raised his eyebrows. *"He'll hate me."*

Franklin's tone became soothing again. "Have you talked to a therapist, Cuz? You've been under a lot of stress. First you lost your job, then Dad died..."

Digger shook her head firmly. "I wanted to tell you, but I was worried you'd think I'm nuts, and..."

He smiled tightly. "Good thinking."

She plowed ahead. "I've been trying to figure out how to talk to you about it. I don't understand why I'm the only one who can see him. Maybe because I found..."

Franklin's tone returned to gentle. "The fact that only you can see him could be an indication that it's not something real."

Digger shook her head in frustration. If he would just be angry instead of compassionate. "It's really him. I know it. We don't just talk. Sometimes he tells me things I don't know."

"What do you mean?" Now he used the tone a parent might employ with a sick child.

"When Holly was trying to figure out who her great grandfather was, he told me a lot about Black families in Garrett County in the mid-1800s. I didn't know any of what he told me."

Uncle Benjamin nodded firmly. *"There's a lot more I could tell you, too."*

Franklin adopted a lawyerly voice. "Sometimes, we absorb information almost passively..." he began.

"No!" Digger surprised herself with her vehemence. She lowered her voice. "I have to convince you." She felt tears burn and turned her back to Franklin and drew a breath. She faced him again. He seemed almost smug as he was about to disavow what she knew to be true.

"OK, Digger, is he in the kitchen with us?"

"You bet your bottom dollar I am." Uncle Benjamin moved to stand in front of Franklin.

Digger nodded and felt her shoulders become less tense.

"Can you ask my father to do something to demonstrate he's here?"

Uncle Benjamin floated out of the kitchen at high speed.

Digger gave Franklin a blank look.

"Can he, I don't know, spill the saltshaker that's on the stove?"

Digger shrugged. "He can't move things. He tried a few times and he almost faded away."

Franklin tilted his head back and stared at the ceiling.

Uncle Benjamin floated through the ceiling from the floor above. Digger started and Franklin regarded her with a quizzical look.

"Sorry," Uncle Benjamin said. *"I tried to do the stairs, but this is faster."*

Digger stared at him but said nothing.

"Tell him I said he has two Snickers bars in his duffel bag. They're wrapped in plastic He's always so careful."

Digger grinned and faced Franklin. "Uncle Benjamin says to tell you there are two Snickers bars in your duffel."

Franklin opened and shut his mouth, words not coming.

"He can go anywhere I am, or he can stay here. He dives into books to read, and I guess he snooped in your bag."

"I didn't snoop. I was adding to the conversation."

Franklin groped the edge of the counter and almost staggered.

Uncle Benjamin tried to grab his elbow, but his hand floated through the arm. *"Don't let him fall!"*

Digger moved to Franklin and touched his elbow. "You're the one who should sit."

He patted her hand and Digger let go. Franklin sat, heavily, in a chair at the Formica-topped table.

Digger sat across from him. Her cousin had grown serious and pale. People turned whiter before they fainted, but she didn't sense that was coming. "Are you OK?"

"No. You just told me my father lets you see him but not me, and you've known about... whatever this is for a year and kept me in the dark."

"Tell him it's not my choice."

Digger stopped smiling. "I was afraid you would be mad." She repeated what Uncle Benjamin had just said.

Franklin stared at her and Digger shifted in her chair. Franklin stood. "I'm going upstairs for a few minutes." He turned and headed for the back staircase.

Stricken, Digger sat without moving. After about thirty seconds, she realized Uncle Benjamin had planted himself on the tabletop across from her.

"*Should I go with him?*" he asked.

"Only if you can comfort him," Digger said, dryly. But she smiled. "It's a lot to digest. Give him time."

Digger stood and walked to the living room. She stared out the front window, across the newly green grass, and down the driveway. The tulips that grew to the right of the long driveway were part-way up. The ones on the left were not yet visible.

Uncle Benjamin stood next to her. "*What made you decide to tell him now?*"

"Earlier, he asked me if Marty was coming over this evening. You probably figured out that we usually spend the night at his place when we want to sleep together."

"*Not too hard to figure that out.*"

"It would make sense for Marty to stay here tonight. He and Franklin like each other. Plus, I don't want Franklin to think that if he stays here then Marty won't. I wanted to explain it. Plus, he heard me talking to you again."

"*Maybe we should have rehearsed.*"

Digger smiled. "I'm not sure this is a conversation that would benefit from stage direction."

"*Are you going to tell him Marty knows?*"

"That won't be so hard. Marty doesn't really know, he's just seen enough to believe me."

From behind her, Franklin said, "What could Marty possibly know that lets him believe this?"

CHAPTER EIGHTEEN

DIGGER WHIRLED AROUND. "Actually, he thought I was nuts. He pretty much told me he didn't want to see me anymore. Although," she shrugged, "he also offered to help me get help. As in psychiatric assistance."

Franklin smiled grimly. "But really, what made him believe?"

"I told you Uncle Benjamin can't move things. A couple of times when he was upset, he did. But he almost faded away."

"And Marty saw one of these times?" he asked.

"Sort of. You no doubt remember when I was locked in the Halloway house last year."

"One of your escapades that I find hard to forget."

Digger grinned. "Me too. Marty didn't have a key, so he broke a window in the back door. He wanted to get into the house to see if I had left a note or something that would tell him where I was."

"But no note?"

"Correct. Uncle Benjamin managed to push an old newspaper article off the dining room table. The second time he did it, Marty realized Uncle Benjamin really did exist as a ghost and he was trying to tell Marty to look at the Halloway place."

Franklin spoke slowly. "I guess I thought you had told him where you'd be. So why not tell me right away?"

To give herself a few moments to think, Digger moved the crock pot from a spot at the back of the counter near the sink and plugged it in. She'd have to remember to add water and pork chops. "At first, it was really confusing for me. I was pretty sure he – or whatever he is –"

"*Hey.*"

"...was really here. But no one else seemed to hear or see him, and I had no idea how long he would be visible. A day, a month?"

Uncle Benjamin's tone was plaintive. "*Tell him I really want to talk to him. It's not up to me who sees me.*"

Digger had glanced at him and now looked back at Franklin.

"Is he talking to you?"

She repeated what Uncle Benjamin had said.

Franklin stared at a point over Digger's shoulder, then met her eyes again. "Is there anything besides Snickers? Does he follow you around the house?"

Digger grinned. "Sometimes I can ditch him by bringing library books home and he spends a lot of time reading them."

"*That's rude.*"

"Seriously, he acts like he did when he was alive. He doesn't walk into my room unless he calls to me and I say come in."

Franklin's tone became insistent. "Tell me something besides the Snickers bar."

"*Say please*," Uncle Benjamin said.

"That's not helpful."

"What?" Franklin asked.

"He's just being a smart aleck." She faced Uncle Benjamin. "It's not a joke. We need another example."

Uncle Benjamin floated to the kitchen counter and sat on the edge. "*Okay. Remember that 1964 silver dime you lost?*" Uncle Benjamin gestured to Digger. "*Ask him.*"

"Did you lose a 1964 silver dime?"

Franklin straightened. "I did. I was maybe twelve and took it to school to show it off. That's the last time the U.S. Mint made silver dimes. Somewhere between school and home, it vanished."

"*It's here,*" Uncle Benjamin said.

"Where?" Digger asked.

He pointed toward the front of the house. "*Follow me. We're going outside.*"

Digger looked at Franklin. "Are you up to following him outside?"

He smiled, tightly. "I'll follow you."

She grinned. "Right."

They walked onto the front porch, Bitsy squeezing out before Digger could shut the screen door. No sign of Uncle Benjamin.

His voice came from below the front steps. "*Down here.*"

Digger leaned over the porch rail and spotted Uncle Benjamin sitting cross-legged on the ground about a foot from the lattice work that hid the gaping space under the porch.

Uncle Benjamin glanced at her, seemingly pleased with himself. "*I found it not too long after I came back.*" He pointed to a spot next to one of the beams that supported the porch.

She started down the steps, Bitsy on her heels. "I don't see it."

"*If it was sitting on top of the flowers, even you would have spotted it. Uh, maybe I should have told you to wear gloves.*"

Franklin now stood next to her. "What?"

"He wants me to dig in the dirt a bit. He thinks it's there."

"*I know it's there.*"

"Okay, you know it. We corporeal beings need to see the damn coin."

Franklin nodded to the dirt. "You have on jeans."

Digger knelt and immediately felt the knees of her jeans become muddy and wet. "You could have picked a drier day."

"*You're the one who told him today.*"

"Yeah, yeah."

Somewhat sarcastically, Franklin asked, "Should I get you a trowel?"

Digger ignored him and began to move the softened dirt at a spot Uncle Benjamin pointed to. Bitsy tried to put her nose by her hands and she gently elbowed his head. "No bones here, Boy."

He lay down next to Digger and put his head on his paws.

"Great. Now you'll need a..." She frowned and began to probe with just the middle and index fingers of her right hand.

Franklin leaned down.

"*Can't you feel it yet?*" Uncle Benjamin asked.

Digger pulled something small and hard from the soil. A rock? Small and circular. She rubbed it with the fingers of her other hand and gasped. Wordlessly, she handed the dirty coin to Franklin. She thought it was a dime, but couldn't be sure.

He took it and rubbed it with the hem of his tee-shirt. Then he stood completely still and stared at the coin in the palm of his hand.

He raised his head. "It's my 1964 silver dime." He sat on the porch step that was second from the bottom. "How?"

Digger pointed to Uncle Benjamin. "You heard him."

"*See, I wanted to see if the roots of that small maple tree extended as far as the foundation.*"

"You can go underground?" Digger asked.

"*I can go anywhere on the property. You know that.*"

"What's he saying?" Franklin asked.

"You found it when you were looking for tree roots?" she asked.

Uncle Benjamin's tone implied she should understand. "*It was the only shiny thing down there.*"

"It isn't shiny..." she began.

More forcefully, Franklin asked, "What is he saying?"

Frustrated, Digger stood. "He wanted to see if the maple tree roots extended to the foundation. When he was prowling around, he saw the coin. He couldn't bring it up, of course."

Franklin glanced at the coin again and shook his head. "He was always looking for anything that could damage the foundation of this old house. Places water collected, tree roots that could burrow against the limestone."

Uncle Benjamin had an expression that Digger hadn't seen before. A mix of sadness and confusion, if she had to guess.

Franklin cleared his throat. "So, I'm sorry to ask this, Digger, but how do I know you didn't put this coin there so you could..."

Digger felt anger rising quickly. She patted her thigh. "Come on Bitsy. Let's take a walk." She started down the driveway toward the road.

Franklin didn't try to stop her, and Uncle Benjamin must have stayed near him because he didn't join Digger.

The temperature seemed to have risen twenty degrees. Or maybe it was anger seeping under her skin. Franklin's lack of faith hurt. No, not lack of faith. He thought she was a liar.

Digger had been walking fast and slowed as Bitsy stopped to inspect a daffodil and water it.

If Uncle Benjamin hadn't told her things she didn't – sometimes couldn't – know, she might have thought she was hallucinating. She had asked Franklin to accept the unbelievable. Yes, it was hard. But he knew her.

Her legs felt cold and she glanced at the muddy jeans. Too bad she had worn a good pair today, not ones she used for gardening.

Bitsy trotted next to her, a stick in his mouth.

Digger smiled. "Okay, Boy. I'll pay attention to you." She took the stick and lobbed it thirty feet ahead of them.

The German Shepard took off running and barking. Such an uncomplicated existence. Digger felt jealous.

She reached the end of the long driveway and stared at the road for a minute. A pink dogwood was just visible across the road, through taller trees. She turned and plodded back to the house.

"Come on, Boy."

Bitsy returned with the stick. Digger didn't want to bother with the slobbery thing, but realized if she kept tossing it toward the house she might not have to cajole her dog into going inside on such a nice day.

It worked. As Digger tromped up the front porch steps and into the foyer, her eyes adjusted to the dim light. As they began to, she took in Franklin's weekend duffle bag on the floor. Was he leaving?

In the kitchen, the coffeemaker purred. He always made a cup to take with him for the drive back to DC. He was definitely leaving.

Digger felt more angry than bereft. She had one foot on the main stairway to the second floor when he called from the kitchen. "Digger? I didn't want to leave without saying goodbye."

She didn't respond, but didn't climb the stairs either. Where was Uncle Benjamin?

Franklin came through the dining room, travel mug in hand. "I…it's a lot to take in. I thought I might drive back and think while I negotiated the mountain curves."

A lame attempt at humor, Digger thought. "Sure."

He stopped a few feet from her. "I'm sorry I'm having a hard time with this. I'm not mad." He paused. "It's more like I don't get Dad not insisting that you tell me."

Uncle Benjamin appeared behind him, looking morose. *I guess it's better that he's mad at me than you.*

"It is a lot. It seems like something you either believe or don't." She scowled. "I didn't bury the damn dime."

He smiled slightly. "I guess I know that." He picked up his duffel back and walked past her. "Tell Marty I said hi, and I'll be back."

Digger watched him drive away. For the first time in her life, she didn't care whether he came home again or not.

CHAPTER NINETEEN

DIGGER FELT ANGRY AND hurt, but also at loose ends. She and Franklin had been clearing old limbs and leaves from the family plot and then used the new shredder to grind up the branches. She could have continued alone, but didn't feel like it.

Uncle Benjamin roamed the Ancestral Sanctuary as a morose spirit, and nothing Digger said could cheer him up.

She did try. "Franklin has a lot to consider. I think he wants to believe me. Besides, this is his home, too. He isn't going to abandon us."

"*But when he's here, he'll always wonder if I'm following him around. I don't understand why he can't see me.*"

"I was in the kitchen when you popped up after your burial. Maybe if he had been there, then he'd be the one carting you around."

"*Would you have believed him?*"

She thought for a second. "Nope. I'd think he was off his rocker."

"*Digger!*"

"I'm trying to see this from his point of view. You always said when you don't understand someone you should walk a mile in their moccasins."

"*I've tried. It didn't help.*"

"Then we need to do something to distract ourselves. Let's head over to Bruno Sampson's property."

"*Why? There's police tape all over the place.*"

"True, but I know someone who can enter the cabin without being seen."

"*Oh, right. What do you hope to find?*"

"Maybe a motive for why Bruno was killed."

"*Not likely to be a billboard. It was probably somebody from outside of town who came to look for gold coins and they got in a fight. They don't have any ties to Bruno or this town, so it'll be impossible to identify them unless they left a fingerprint or something like that.*"

"Or it could be somebody from here and they may go back to see what they can find."

Uncle Benjamin tilted his head and pointed a bony finger at Digger. "*I'm willing to play detective.*" He now held an oversized magnifying glass and wore a deerstalker's cap, which looked a lot like the depictions of Sherlock Holmes' hat.

"*But we have to do some legwork first. Get some paper and a pen.*" He moved to sit in the middle of the dining room table.

Digger took paper and pen from a kitchen drawer. "What are we writing about?"

"Who stands to gain from Bruno's death?"

She shook her head. "We won't know that until we see a will."

"Not necessarily. Suppose there were proof that Abraham Sampson got the money to buy that land from either the bank robbery, stealing the blacksmith's money, or stealing coins and other items from Robert Heller's family?"

"What are you getting at?"

"Bruno has no relatives we know of. If he didn't have a will, an attorney could argue that the original purchase was from ill-gotten gains, meaning the property should go to the people he stole from."

"That's a stretch."

Uncle Benjamin shrugged. *"Sure, but if some third cousin twice removed would inherit, maybe he would say screw it and sign over the land to the people making the claim."*

"So, what are we writing about?"

He grinned. *"I was just trying to make you stop and think. Should we call Marty?"*

Digger thought for a moment. "No. I don't care if I get arrested for trespassing, but his editor might not take kindly if he did. Besides, he can't cover a story if he's in it."

"Go get your hiking boots."

DIGGER HADN'T THOUGHT about media still being near Bruno's property. She drove by the van filming for a Pittsburgh television station, as if she were just driving by.

"I'm going to look in the cabin." Uncle Benjamin floated out of the Jeep.

"Uncle..." Digger fumed. How would she get him back?

She drove for another quarter-mile and pulled into a trailhead that had a few parking spaces. She started to back out to return, but decided to wait a few minutes to give Uncle Benjamin more time to prowl. He wouldn't fade being away from her for such a short time.

Digger rolled down her windows even though the early spring air felt chilly. For ten minutes, she breathed deeply and studied the buds just appearing on the trees. Yesterday someone was killed and today she stared at new life.

Not a car passed her. One car sat in another of the five parking spaces, so there must be a hiker somewhere. She took in one more deep breath and a thought occurred to her.

The Elders had not noticed anyone, nor had Digger and Marty as they drove up to see Bruno yesterday.

Digger thought in terms of someone killing Bruno, accidentally or on purpose, and driving back to town. They could have gone farther up the mountain, maybe even pulled into the woods at some point and stayed there until things settled down. Did Sheriff Montgomery think about that?

Or they could have done as she just did, and pulled into one of the few parking spaces above Bruno's place and walked down to his property. But that would imply they didn't want to be seen. Did someone go there with intent to harm him?

Digger pulled back onto the state road and drove slowly toward town. She squinted as she neared Bruno's place. No sign of Uncle Benjamin. Then she saw him sitting atop the large television camera that was recording an interview with none other than Veronica Heller. She sped up, not wanting Veronica to recognize her Jeep.

She had reached the edge of Bruno's property line when Uncle Benjamin dove through the front passenger window. She jerked the Jeep to the left and then straightened it. "What are you doing?"

"*Practicing a swan dive. Keep driving.*"

"Are you afraid someone will recognize you?"

"*Not recognize, but maybe follow.*"

"What are you talking about?"

"*Remember I said I had the heebie jeebies?*"

"Yes. I figured it was because you could sense the grave nearby."

"*What I apparently sensed was a restless spirit. There's a very pale ghost, a woman, wandering around.*"

"Did you talk to her?"

"*I don't think she saw me. She stays near where she was buried. Seems very confused.*"

"I've never seen a picture of Susannah Sampson. Maybe we could find one."

"*Perhaps. It probably won't have the large bruise across her forehead.*"

Digger was silent for several seconds. "Poor woman."

"*Bruno was young when she supposedly left. I hope he didn't see her get killed.*"

After another brief silence, Digger asked, "Did you go in the cabin?"

"*Yes. There are a few black stains from where the cops pulled fingerprints.*"

"Including Marty's."

"Sparse furnishings. Usual stuff for cooking. He did have a TV, a lot of books. A bottom drawer had a few old toys, including marbles and a set of jacks. Not one thing that looked as if it belonged to either of his parents."

"What about the coins?" Digger asked.

"The gold coins were well hidden. He had a metal box for hot ashes next to the fireplace. Somebody would've looked in it eventually, but they wouldn't have noticed the false bottom too quickly. He had them wrapped in oilcloth so they didn't rattle."

"How many, and could you see denominations?"

"Mostly twenty-dollar coins. And, you'll love this, most between 1900 and 1909."

"I guess the dates are most important."

"Verifies what you knew, and then some. Did you see who that swanky TV guy was interviewing?"

"Veronica Heller. Did you hear any of it?"

"She was saying how sad it was, and how he'd just agreed to sell her the property."

Digger frowned. "That's baloney."

"You going to call Marty?"

"I'll tell him what..." Her phone rang and Digger pushed the answer button for hands-free calling. "Hello, Marty."

"Hey, I'm at your place. Thought you and Franklin would be here."

Digger winced. "He had to go back to DC. I'll be home in about ten minutes. You know where the spare key is in case you forgot yours."

"Your dopey dog barked so much I used it to let him out. I'm on the porch swing."

"You know you can go in. Give Ragdoll a treat. I don't pay enough attention to her."

What would she tell Marty about Franklin's reason for leaving? It didn't take long to decide. Everything. After all, Marty had been a skeptic – no, a disbeliever – until Uncle Benjamin managed to get a newspaper article from the tabletop to the floor. Maybe Marty could help Franklin.

WHEN DIGGER AND UNCLE Benjamin turned into the Ancestral Sanctuary driveway about six o'clock on Saturday, they saw Bitsy run across the lawn at high speed. In the fading light, Digger realized the dog was chasing his raunchy tennis ball. He must have taken it to Marty to throw.

Ragdoll sat on the porch railing. She didn't go outside a lot, which likely meant she was lonely when Digger and Uncle Benjamin left. She liked it when her human family was home on the weekends.

As Digger parked, Marty's next throw took the ball near the house. Ragdoll was off the porch like a rocket and got to it before Bitsy did. She put one paw on it, and Bitsy stayed several feet away.

"*Good for you, Ragdoll,*" Uncle Benjamin said.

Marty opened her car door and kissed Digger as she stood. She hugged him for several seconds.

"Good hug. You okay?"

"Sure, just been a weird day."

Bitsy barked once and danced around Ragdoll, who ignored him.

Marty asked, "Will she relinquish the ball to Bitsy?"

At almost the same time, Digger and Uncle Benjamin said, "When she's bored." Digger laughed and explained why to Marty.

"Why did Franklin have to go back to DC?"

Digger's smile faded. "Let's go inside. I'll tell you and maybe you can cheer up Uncle Benjamin. And me."

"*Especially me,*" Uncle Benjamin said.

Digger turned on the foyer lights and they walked past the living room and through to the dining room. She and Marty sat next to each other at the table and Marty listened without interrupting.

Digger relayed their trip to the hardware store and first efforts to use the shredder. She hesitated as she started to describe what she had told Franklin about his father's reappearance. Marty put his hand over hers and squeezed.

"I thought when Uncle Benjamin led us to the dime that it would make Franklin believe, but it didn't."

"Exactly what did he say?" Marty asked.

"He said he wasn't mad." She paused, thinking. "He didn't exactly call me a liar. Franklin said he didn't understand why Uncle Benjamin didn't insist that I tell him right away."

Uncle Benjamin had been sitting cross-legged on the table. He let out a howl and rocketed through the ceiling to an upper floor.

Digger stared at the ceiling, her mouth partially open. She looked at Marty and pointed. "He sort of howled and went up." Her eyes filled with tears. "I can't say anything to make him feel better."

Marty stood and half-lifted Digger to a standing position and held her close. "He will understand when he thinks more about it. Remember how hard a time I had? I almost broke up with you. Always talking to yourself and not willing to tell me what was going on."

Digger hiccupped. "You wanted me to see a shrink."

"And I'm still not opposed to it."

Digger pulled back and saw he was smiling. She stood on her toes and kissed him lightly before releasing herself from the hug. "My definition of crazy has definitely changed in the last year."

CHAPTER TWENTY

DIGGER TOLD MARTY about what Uncle Benjamin saw in the cabin and seeing Veronica do a television interview. "I think knowing the coins' years is important."

"Do you think it actually proves anything?"

"If he finds newer ones later, well...I don't know what the means, except later coins definitely wouldn't have been Morton's."

Marty thought for a moment. "Let's take another approach. Have you talked to Josh or Veronica since Bruno's murder?"

"Actually, I saw them in the Coffee Engine Friday, sitting together, but..."

"Together?"

Digger grinned. "I was surprised, too. They said they decided to pool their resources, or something like that. I don't think they'd read the paper's website yet, because they didn't mention Bruno's death."

"That doesn't seem realistic. If they were in the Coffee Engine, they would have overheard people talking about it."

"And what, they didn't want to talk to me about it?"

"Sure," Marty said. "You and I are the only two people who know they each wanted those coins. And they met in your office Thursday evening. Maybe they went up to Bruno's place together on Thursday."

"But how would that have led to Bruno's death? Josh was willing to offer him money for a coin. And $2,000 or so could have meant a lot to Bruno."

"Do you know…" Marty began.

Digger snapped her fingers. "I almost laughed at her when she said she wanted to buy his property and knew her brother would cosign a mortgage with her."

"Her brother?" Marty thought for a moment. "He doesn't strike me as a spur-of-the moment investor."

"I don't know Lucas well, only through the Chamber board. He did call to ask about whether I was advising her on buying properties with a tax lien. Which I'm not, of course."

"So, he caught her in a lie," Marty said.

"I suppose."

"On the Josh side of the equation, do you know which B&B he stayed in?" Marty asked. "He said he planned to spend the weekend here."

Digger shrugged. "Easy enough to find out." She took the small local phone directory from a kitchen drawer and first dialed Mountain View B&B."

Dottie Colby answered the phone, and Digger held it so Marty could hear. "Yes, Josh and his girlfriend are here. I think they're out. Would you like to leave a message?"

Marty's shocked expression probably mirrored her own. "No thanks. I left a message on his cell. They're probably hiking and out of range. He'll get back to me."

She disconnected and stared at Marty. "You want to bet where they are?"

"Yep. See if your uncle will come up to Bruno's place with us."

DIGGER FOUND UNCLE Benjamin in Franklin's third-floor apartment, sitting on the top of a bookshelf. "Why are you sitting so high?"

"I guess I do it a lot because I can. Things look different from up high." He regarded Digger. *"Did Marty go? I bet he thinks I'm an idiot for leaving the dining room like that."*

"He doesn't. He asked me to find you."

Uncle Benjamin arched an eyebrow. *"Why?"*

"We're thinking of going to Bruno's property to see if Josh and Veronica are there."

"You mean together?"

Digger repeated that she had seen them together in the Coffee Engine and they appeared to be staying together at Dottie's B&B. "We wonder if they might have visited Bruno together on Thursday afternoon."

"As in killed him?"

She shrugged. "We haven't gotten that far in our thinking. Just want to see if they're still looking for the coins."

"Sure," Uncle Benjamin said. *"Anything's better than sitting around here."*

THEY DECIDED TO DRIVE above Bruno's property and walk down. When they got to the trailhead, Josh's BMW took up two spaces, parked diagonally.

"When I was in high school," Marty said, "If somebody parked a fancy car that way in a mall parking lot, this guy I knew would key the passenger door."

"Why that door?" Digger asked.

Marty and Uncle Benjamin gave similar answers. Because the driver probably wouldn't notice it right away and thus would have a hard time pinpointing where the car was keyed.

"Sounds like a good friend," Digger said, sarcastically.

"Not my friend," Marty said, evenly. "Just a guy I knew."

They started the quarter-mile trek downhill, walking on the side facing cars driving up. Since it was late afternoon, the few cars that passed them were heading toward town.

"Benjamin," Marty said, "why don't you go ahead of us to see where Josh is."

A less morose Uncle Benjamin sped ahead. *"Don't go past that little bend in the road until I come back to tell you."*

"That was a good idea," Digger said. "Any plans for what to say to him, or both of them, if they're hunting for coins?"

"We can't exactly ask where they were Thursday about five-thirty PM, but I'd sure suggest that Sheriff Montgomery do it. I guess we just ask them if they've found anything."

Land rose from each side of the road, creating a small hill. When Digger and Marty got to the bend, they sat a couple feet up from the pavement. "Wonder what's taking him so long?" Digger asked.

"If they're having an interesting conversation, he might stick around to listen."

Uncle Benjamin appeared a minute later and gestured, rapidly, that they should climb the hill above where they sat. "*They're walking this way!*"

Digger asked, "Why does it matter they're coming?"

"What difference..." Marty began.

"*Just go!*" To emphasize his point, Uncle Benjamin sped ahead of them, up the small rise.

They quickly walked up twenty feet or so, and each stood behind the broad trunk of separate oak trees.

"This is ridiculous," Digger hissed.

Uncle Benjamin shook a finger at her. "*You'll hear why in a few seconds.*"

Two voices came into hearing range just before they could peer around a tree and see Josh and Veronica. Hers was higher-pitched. "I told you it would have been worth it to buy a better metal detector."

"And I told you the sporting goods store in Frostburg only had this one left," Josh said, clearly irritated.

"I bet the mall where my brother works in Frostburg has better ones."

"So, head up there tomorrow," Josh said.

They continued in that vein for another thirty seconds or so and were then out of earshot.

"We should probably stay here until they drive back down," Marty said.

"Good thing we took your car. Josh rode in my Jeep but I don't think he's seen your Toyota."

"*Tell Marty I'm going to talk for a minute, and you'll repeat it,*" Uncle Benjamin said.

Digger did.

"*They were out of water, so they'd probably been looking at least a couple hours. They hadn't found any coins. Veronica was all for trying to get into the cabin, but Josh told her she'd have to go by herself if she wanted to do that. Still has the police tape.*"

Digger relayed what he said to Marty, then stopped talking as the BMW sped down the road. "Is there a hole from when they exhumed the woman yesterday? Did they comment on that?"

Uncle Benjamin laughed. "*The fools think someone else was up there looking for coins. They didn't understand why they dug so deep.*"

Marty started down the small incline ahead of Digger and reached back to give her a hand as she got closer to the pavement.

"Veronica didn't have her own metal detector?" Digger asked.

"*Didn't see one,*" Uncle Benjamin said. "*She kept trying to grab Josh's and he said she should have hung onto hers. Whatever that means.*"

Digger told Marty what her uncle said. "That seems odd, if she was so intent on finding more coins."

Digger stared ahead of her for a moment. "Sheriff Montgomery said Bruno had a bruise on his face. I wonder if someone hit him with a metal detector?"

MARTY WANTED AN EXCUSE to talk to Lucas Heller again, so he volunteered to go to church with Malcolm and Maria the following day. They were thrilled, but he had to extract a promise that if their minister mentioned Marty becoming a member of the congregation, they were not to endorse the idea.

"What am I supposed to say?" Maria asked, as they rode together in Marty's car.

"I could mention the wanted posters in the Post Office," Malcolm offered.

"What wanted posters?" Maria asked.

"You walked into that one, Grandmother. Just don't encourage him, okay?"

As they entered, Marty saw not only Lucas Heller and his wife but also Veronica. They sat on the other side of the aisle and one row more to the front, so Marty could stare without being obvious. What interested him was that Veronica and her brother never looked at each other, even as people gathered for coffee in the back of the church.

Lucas wore a tailored sports coat with a shirt and tie, and the muted colors seemed to blend with his wife's taupe-colored dress with its cream-colored jacket. Both said expensive.

Marty positioned himself to be in Lucas' line of sight, then pretended to see him for the first time and nodded. He picked up a cup of coffee and headed to Lucas. As he got closer, Veronica, who'd been several feet from her brother, saw Marty, turned her back, and moved farther away.

Marty put his coffee in his left hand and held out his right. "Good to see you, Lucas."

"You, too. This is my wife, Mary Margaret. Honey, this is Marty Hofstedder, from the paper."

Her eyes brightened. "I read your piece about that blacksmith who died 110 years ago. The Internet gives us access to so much history. And that nephew. How good that he read your original story."

They spoke for a couple minutes. Then Mary Margaret saw a friend and excused herself.

Marty faced Lucas. He lowered his voice somewhat. "My friend Digger and I have run into your sister a couple of times this week. She's very focused on getting land for her campground and finding more gold coins."

Lucas shut his eyes for a second.

"She can be very…" he searched for a word.

"Intense." Marty smiled.

"Stubborn," Lucas said.

"You said you worked over in Frostburg and like it here. Did Veronica live here at all after college?"

Lucas shook his head. "Couldn't wait to leave. Frankly, I think she's only back here because cost of living is so high in Northern Virginia. She's tired of working hard enough to support a big mortgage. She thinks I'll open my checkbook and help her get settled the same way our dad spoiled her when she was a kid."

"That's an interesting expectation," Marty said.

"An incorrect one. My wife and I built our beautiful home with a lot of sweat equity. If my sister were the kind of person to repay a loan, I wouldn't hesitate. Unfortunately, she doesn't have a good track record."

Marty kept his tone noncommittal. "Sibling relationships can be a challenge."

As Lucas was about to say something else, Veronica walked toward them. "Do you know if that mom-and-pop drugstore is open on Sunday?"

"Yes," Lucas said. "It closes at two today, though."

"Good. I have bug bites to beat the band."

She ignored Marty and told her brother she'd be stopping by his place for dinner.

After an awkward few seconds as Veronica walked out, Marty said, "Family. What are you going to do?"

Heller shook his head. "Those damn coins. Money brings out the worst in people. My sister and I were never close, so at first I was pleased that she decided to move here for retirement. Now," he shrugged with a smile, "I remember why we never hung out together."

Heller's eyes shifted from his sister's retreating figure to Marty. "Do you have family here? I seem to recall you moved here only a few years ago."

"I've always been close to my grandparents, Malcolm and Maria Wilson. They're nearly eighty now. Reminded me time is precious."

Heller nodded.

"Listen," Marty hesitated, "you know I work for the paper. I always like to give people fair warning before I put on my reporter hat."

"Sure. How can I help you?"

"Did you know Veronica has become friendly with a man named Josh Henry? He's the great nephew of Gerard Morton, the blacksmith who was visiting here and died in 1910."

"I didn't realize the late Mr. Morton had family here."

"Josh lives in Bethesda. Mary Margaret referred to him reading my article about the coins being discovered, which referred to his uncle as an itinerate blacksmith and," he smiled, "he came to Maple Grove to defend his uncle's reputation."

"I see. How did he and Veronica meet?"

"In my friend Digger's office, about an hour before Bruno's murder. They both wanted Bruno to let them search his property for more coins, and I think Veronica was about to approach Bruno with a suggested price to buy his property. Josh intended to offer to buy one of the coins. They're worth a pretty penny today."

"Yes," Heller said, dryly. "I heard she mentioned that I'd be co-signing a loan. I've set her straight on that point. Now, what is your reporter-type question?"

"Would you know where Veronica was between about 4:15 and 5:30 this past Thursday?"

Heller raised his eyebrows and started to laugh, but realized Marty was serious. "No. She isn't staying with us, but she does drop by every day."

"So, she wasn't with you?"

Heller frowned and stood straighter. "This sounds more like a question the sheriff might ask, if, and it's a big if, he thought I would have a reason to suspect my sister of something."

"I'm not sure he knows how angry Veronica made Bruno."

"I certainly don't. If you'll excuse me." He walked to the other side of the room to join his wife.

CHAPTER TWENTY-ONE

MONDAY MORNING, SHERIFF Montgomery listened to Digger without comment as she described Josh and Veronica's desire to hunt for coins even when Bruno had made it clear they were not welcome.

"But that's not a motive for them to murder Bruno Sampson."

"No, of course not. But combine that with Veronica's lies about her brother co-signing a loan and how they buddied up pretty soon after meeting…"

Sheriff Montgomery's phone buzzed, and he picked it up and listened. "Did it already run?" He frowned. "Thanks for telling me."

He sighed. "You're friends with my grandmother. Do you have any idea why she does half the things she does?"

Digger grinned broadly. "She's an inspiration."

He glared at her. "She put a notice in the newsletter at the senior apartments announcing she owns the land next to Sampson's, and asking if anyone wanted to hunt for gold coins with her."

Digger threw back her head and laughed.

"I don't need a lot of people tromping around up there." Sheriff Montgomery pointed a finger toward his door.

"And another thing," Digger continued, "the fact that they're secretive about sleeping together. It should be enough to at least ask them where they were Thursday between four and five o'clock."

"I already have, both of them." He picked up his mug to take a sip of coffee.

"*He's smarter than I give him credit for,*" Uncle Benjamin said.

Digger sat back in her chair. "I hope Josh didn't say he was with Marty and me."

Montgomery sat his cup down. "Are you saying he wasn't?"

"He stopped by the office about 3:45, Marty came over and I left to take care of Bitsy. Marty stayed maybe fifteen minutes more with Josh. Then Marty came to the Ancestral Sanctuary to pick up me and...me to visit Bruno."

Montgomery called out, "Deputy Sovern. Give a call to Hofstedder and ask him exactly when he and Josh Henry parted company late Thursday afternoon."

"Sure thing, Sheriff."

Montgomery turned to Digger. "I'll check that again. Anything else?"

"Do you have any suspects?"

He fixed her with a noncommittal stare. "I'm sorry you had to find his body, Digger, but you aren't part of this investigation."

"So, nothing?"

He smiled. "I have one errant fingerprint from a button on Mr. Sampson's jacket, as if someone grabbed him. So far, it's not in any database in Maryland. We've sent it to the FBI's Integrated Automated Fingerprint Identification System. Are you happy now?"

"That's terrific," Digger said.

He shrugged. "I don't jump to conclusions. Bruno could have had his coat on the back of a chair in the diner, it fell to the floor, and someone picked it up for him."

Digger stood. "Thanks for telling me that."

Sheriff Montgomery frowned. "That's not for Hofstedder's consumption just yet."

DIGGER had finished reworking the tourism brochure by early Monday afternoon. The office phone rang. Holly answered and listened intently. "Okay, Grandmother. I'll tell her. Thanks for letting us know."

She did a thumbs up gesture to Digger. "Sheriff Montgomery is having a press conference at three o'clock today. Do you think they've found Bruno's killer?"

Digger's cell phone rang. As she picked it up, she said, "I'd be surprised. Pleasantly. Hey, Marty, bet I know why you're calling."

"How'd you find out?" he asked.

"Audrey called Holly." Digger held the phone so Holly could hear Marty's reply.

"Damn, she's good."

"*Some would say she's a gossip,*" Uncle Benjamin said.

"That's one way of looking at it," Holly said.

"I have a lot to do here, Marty. Can you let me know what he says?"

"Too bad. I'll call you as soon as I know something." He hung up.

Digger would love to be there and said as much in a quick email to Marty. "I've been away from the office too much. Holly's right. It's your job to find out, not mine."

A dejected Uncle Benjamin sat on the file cabinet. "*I wanted to go, but Holly can't do all the work.*"

Digger opened a new folder in her word processing program and typed. "All the work? Marty'll call us right away."

She deleted those words and went to her email to type a note to Lucas Heller. "I'm attaching a revised draft of the tourism brochure. I left a couple placeholders for photos. See what you think about the text." She attached the pdf file and hit send.

BY THREE-FIFTEEN, EVEN Holly was antsy. "Why haven't we heard from Marty?"

"The press conference is probably still going on. But he'll text me as soon as he knows something." She kept her phone on the desk to spot a new text.

At three-twenty-five, Marty's text read, "Sheriff asked for rush on DNA comparative analysis. The woman in the grave was Bruno's mother. They estimate she died almost thirty years ago."

Digger read it aloud to Holly even as the phone rang. "Your grandmother, no doubt."

Holly listened for about ten seconds. "Sure thing, Lucas. She's right here."

Digger picked up her extension. "What did you think?"

"I'll go over it carefully, probably tomorrow. Have you given any thought to photos?"

"Since you wanted to stress outdoor activities, I have several outside shots you can consider. Or you can tell me you want a certain photo and I'll take the picture."

"I may do that. I'll talk to you soon." He hung up.

Digger nodded to Holly. "No reaction yet. I hope he likes it. I'm tired of working on it."

"Not as much fun as menus?"

Digger nodded. "We won't have to check out a place for dinner. We'll already know the menu."

Digger's mind returned to the DNA results. "If it was roughly thirty years ago, Bruno would have been somewhere between nine and twelve."

"Think how sad he must've been."

"When Marty tried to find people to talk about him, there wasn't one person. He thought there might be a couple teachers, but I guess the ones who knew him retired."

Digger's cell phone rang and she answered.

Maryann Montgomery asked, "Did you hear they said the second body you found was poor Bruno Sampson's mother?"

Digger pointed to her phone and mouthed "Maryann" for Holly's benefit.

"I did. Such a shame."

"It kind of makes me feel bad about trying to get people to wander around my property. I thought that would annoy him. Now we know why he was so grouchy."

"If it makes you feel any better, I was with your grandson when he heard about your offer in the apartment newsletter. He's annoyed."

"Oh, good. He gives me too much advice these days."

"Did you get any takers on your offer to look for coins on your property?"

"There's an old man on the floor above me, but he just crushed another vertebra in his back. I think he's a fall risk."

Digger pictured the ninety-year-old Maryann. "Just out of curiosity, what do you consider old?"

"He'll be ninety-seven next month."

"Good genes."

"It's still light. You want to visit my property?"

"Gee, Maryann. I have work I have to finish today."

"Okay, pick me up at eleven-thirty tomorrow morning." She hung up.

Digger told Holly what Maryann wanted her to do. "If she falls, do you have any idea how much trouble I'll be in with Sheriff Montgomery?"

CHAPTER
TWENTY-TWO

TUESDAY MORNING, DIGGER left her office to drive the short distance to Maple Grove's senior apartments. She planned to be early so she could check out Maryann's choice of shoes. If she didn't have at least good athletic shoes, Digger wouldn't take her.

"*It's a darn shame she can't talk to me. We could be the Hiking Twins, or something like that,*" Uncle Benjamin said.

"Sure, I can see the headline. 'Hiking Twins Fall to Their Deaths on Meadow Mountain.'"

Maryann did not need to be tutored on what to wear. Her hiking boots looked well worn, which was a side of her Digger was unaware of. She also had a cane, but wasn't relying on it.

Instead, she lectured Digger. "Where is your hat?" She touched her own, a floppy canvas hat with an orange ribbon. "You have to wear a hat in the woods to keep the ticks off your scalp."

She made Digger stop at a dollar store to get an orange baseball cap. "Orange is the best color in the woods. You won't get shot."

Uncle Benjamin changed into full hunter regalia, complete with a new-looking rifle over his shoulder, Davy Crockett style.

"Did you tell the sheriff where we're going?" Digger asked.

"Did you tell Marty?"

"I sent him an email when I got to your place," Digger said.

"Clever. He wouldn't object to you going, certainly."

"Not at all. He'd say I was corrupting you."

Digger turned onto the state road that would take them to Maryann's property.

"I haven't driven in years," Maryann said. "There used to be an indentation off the road. You know, the same way hunters park in deer season."

Digger knew what she meant. In the fall, drivers had to be really careful because hunters would pull three-quarters of the way off the road if there weren't nearby parking spaces.

Maryann's four-acre parcel sat closer to town than the late Bruno's did. Digger drove the few hundred yards farther to show the orange cones that still blocked the entrance to Jessup Lane. "There aren't any houses past here, and the lane turns into a path and then ends. Bruno had a number of narrow paths he followed, especially near his cabin."

She turned partway into the lane, backed out, and started downhill. "There's a hill a few feet back from the road. It isn't big, but can you climb it?"

Maryann pointed to two dogwood trees that grew on the hill. "Park there. You get a grip on one tree, pull yourself up a couple of feet, and grip the next one."

"Very smart." Digger parked directly between the trees. That way, if Maryann fell on the way down, she'd run into the car rather than the road.

She put the car in park. "I'll open..." Maryann had already left the car, "your door."

"She's almost as spry as I am," Uncle Benjamin said.

Maryann reached for the first one of her "grips" and Digger hurried to get behind her. "Steady there."

Uncle Benjamin pretended to shove her buns. Digger shook a finger at him.

Maryann made it up the small hill in three quick steps. "I've been here a couple dozen times."

Digger followed her. "When was the last time?"

"Don't tell Roger, but not long after I moved back up here from Oakland. My grand-nephew, Brian, brought me. But when he figured out Roger wasn't keen on me walking in the woods, he didn't volunteer again."

The trees were even more dense than on Bruno's property. Digger figured he must have cut down a few of his own through the years, since he used wood to heat. The tree density on Maryann's property meant less light filtered through and the ground cover was more sparse. Walking was easier than on Bruno's property.

Uncle Benjamin had transformed himself into a Paul Bunyan character and pretended to chop a tree with a huge ax. *"Not bad for an old guy, is it?"*

He looked so comical Digger had to stifle a giggle.

Maryann did a slow 360-degree turn. "I love the smell of pine trees that mix with the oaks." She took several breaths with her eyes closed. She opened them and smiled at Digger.

"Are there lots of wildflowers in the summer?"

"Some near the edge of the trees," Maryann said. "I don't have my full bearings. Which way is Bruno's cabin?"

Digger pointed to Maryann's right, as she stood with the road behind her. "Walk another hundred yards or so and you'll see it. And you'll also see all the police tape."

Maryann walked using the cane. "This isn't because I need it, it's for balance."

"Of course," Digger said. She followed Maryann's slow pace.

She pointed with her cane. "Don't walk in that poison ivy."

"Thanks. I wasn't looking down."

They were aware of occasional cars passing on the state road. Eventually one could be heard coming to a stop.

Digger peered through the trees to see a royal blue sedan; she wasn't sure of the make. The driver had come to a spot near the orange cones that blocked entry to Jessup Lane. He or she must have moved the cones because the car drove down the lane and stopped.

Maryann looked at Digger and shrugged.

She couldn't see Uncle Benjamin. Then she realized he had moved to the street and stood near the car. She figured if he knew the person, he'd call to her.

Digger stood next to Maryann and whispered. "I'm sure it's fine, but if we have to talk, let's whisper."

Maryann whispered. "I have an odd feeling. Take off your orange hat."

Digger threw it on the ground behind a clump of bushes and Maryann dropped hers on top of it.

One car door opened and shut. In the quiet among the trees, the person's footsteps were clear as they walked through the brush.

Digger pointed that they should walk toward a spruce tree. No one could see behind it. Not that she expected anyone to look.

Maryann crooked her finger and Digger leaned down. "It can't be one of Roger's people. They'd be in a sheriff's car."

Eventually the walking stopped, and Digger heard the sound of metal on metal. Someone was sawing something. Since there wasn't much that was metal, it had to be the padlock the sheriff's staff had put on the cabin door.

Digger took her phone from her pocket. She whispered. "I'm going to try to get a picture of whoever's there."

"I'm coming," Maryann said.

Digger shook her head vigorously. "If I had to run, you'd slow me down." She blew her a kiss and began walking slowly toward Bruno's cabin. Why, she asked herself, do you keep calling it Bruno's cabin? He's dead.

When she was fifty yards closer, Digger realized the person, a man it seemed, was standing in front of the small building behind the cabin. Marty had said that's where Bruno did his taxidermy work

The blue jay, not accompanied by the crow, cawed and clucked at him.

"Shut up, bird," she whispered.

The man's full camo gear might be odd in the grocery store, but it was not out of place in the woods. The dull green hat covered a hood. When he briefly stood in profile, Digger saw wrap-around sunglasses, not something needed in the dense shade.

She had a gnawing feeling she was looking at Bruno's killer. What could be in that shed that he wanted? A dead fox? Hardly.

Uncle Benjamin hovered over the man's shoulder, but didn't look in Digger's direction.

The man had a familiar air, but he wasn't someone she knew well. He kept sawing on the padlock. Uncle Benjamin stood next to him, frowning as he watched.

After another minute, a male voice said, "Yes!" He removed the lock and reached into the wood building – little more than a shed – and extracted something long and thin. He placed it against the wall of the building, put the damaged padlock in one pocket, and pulled another out of a different pocket.

Very smart. Unless it looked quite different, a cursory glance from a deputy checking on the site would not indicate the original lock had been replaced.

A rustling near her announced Maryann. She stood behind a closer spruce tree. Digger put her finger on her lips, but screeching tires drowned out any sound. Uncle Benjamin sped toward Jessup Lane.

The bright red sedan announced Veronica, who shot out of the car and walked quickly toward the man in the hoodie. "Get away from there, Lucas!"

Maryann and Digger both said, "Lucas Heller!" Fortunately, the siblings' yelling drowned them out.

Lucas pulled his hood down, adjusted his hat, and took off the sunglasses. "Shut the hell up!"

She stopped a few feet from her brother. "Josh said we needed to stay away from here. The sheriff could have people watching this place."

Digger felt a chill. Josh. She would never have imagined him involved in something so nefarious.

The blue jay flew about eight feet above both siblings' heads, making the jeering sound jays used to warn other birds or predators.

Lucas shook the narrow pole at her. "The stupid metal detector has all of our fingerprints on it. It needs to vanish."

Veronica raised her hands in the air. "This isn't a true crime show. They probably think he died from hitting his head. Leave it alone!"

Digger put her hand on Maryann's shoulder. She moved slightly to be sure the two Hellers couldn't see her. But the fallen branch she stepped on cracked as loud as a rifle shot.

Lucas and Veronica turned quickly and looked in their direction. Digger stooped. Maryann was still largely blocked by the spruce. She took one step sideways so she'd be totally blocked.

"Who's there? I saw you." Lucas Heller yelled.

"I saw you first!" Veronica hollered.

"*I think they did,*" Uncle Benjamin called. "*I saw you duck. Run to your car!*"

But she couldn't of course. That would mean leaving Maryann, who could not move fast enough.

Lucas started toward her, taking long strides, even given the brush at his ankles. He didn't seem to notice that Veronica picked up the metal detector and started for her car.

To Maryann, Digger hissed, "Stay here!"

She walked toward the man. "What are you doing here, Lucas? Wanting to have a conversation with me about the brochure?"

He stopped about fifteen yards from her, clearly surprised. "Just checking the, uh, property. Since my sister is thinking of buying it."

Uncle Benjamin peered at the man's waistband at his back. "*He has some sort of a weapon.*"

Digger could hear her heart pounding in her ears. "You passed my car on the road. A friend owns this property. I'm checking something for her."

"This was Bruno Sampson's land."

She shook her head. "Where you are was his. Where I am belongs to someone else. What did you take out of that shed?"

"You and your friend Marty Hofstedder ask too many questions."

"*At least he gets paid for it,*" Uncle Benjamin said.

"He'll be here pretty soon," Digger said.

Heller laughed. "I don't think so. But I'm not some calculated killer. I think we can make a deal."

"What's that?"

"We just...walk away. You go back to your world of brochures and old photographs, and I'll return to my beautiful home and convince my annoying sister to leave town before I get the urge to kill her."

"Hey!" Veronica called.

"That's insulting. Your home is gorgeous," Uncle Benjamin said.

"Not helpful," Digger said.

"What's not helpful?"

"Any deal you could offer. Why did you kill Bruno Sampson?"

"You've no proof that I did."

Digger nodded toward the shed. "What you left propped against the shed must be something you don't want the sheriff to have."

"You should mind your own business."

"You know your sister took it, don't you?"

Lucas turned toward Jessup Lane. "Veronica!"

"The sheriff already has your fingerprint. It was on a button on Bruno's coat." Digger fervently hoped it belonged to one of the Hellers.

He took two quick steps toward Digger and a bright light flashed from behind her.

"What the hell was that?"

"Say cheese. Good job, Maryann!"

Digger smiled. "Just a friend."

"I don't believe you."

"If you want to think one of the dead spirits around here took a picture of you, feel free."

"I'm not falling for some trick."

Maryann's voice came from behind the spruce tree. "It's no trick, moron. I just texted your photo to my grandson."

If face color was an indication, Heller's rage continued to grow. He was an average guy who'd gotten in big trouble. He or Veronica may not have meant to kill Bruno Sampson. But that didn't make him any less dangerous to Digger and Maryann.

Uncle Benjamin switched to a boxing outfit and began dancing around Lucas Heller, throwing practice punches with oversize gloves.

"How old's your grandson, twelve? Maybe he's the only name in your contacts."

"He's around fifty. You know my Roger."

Digger smiled slightly. "You wouldn't want to harm Sheriff Montgomery's grandmother, would you?"

He took two more steps, but Digger backed up the same distance. "We could do this all day."

Ever so faint, the sound of a siren grew closer. The blue jay jeered more loudly.

"If you want to head out, now would be the time," Digger said.

Maryann stepped from behind the spruce tree. "My grandson is very fond of me."

"*But he'll still be royally peeved,*" Uncle Benjamin said. He turned toward Digger. "*Especially at you.*"

Heller looked from side to side, perhaps gauging where to run.

"If you have a gun, it doesn't make sense to use it," Digger said. "Sheriff Montgomery and his deputies would be better shots."

Heller's shoulders sagged and he turned to walk toward his car.

CHAPTER TWENTY-THREE

VERONICA HAD TURNED her car around and faced the state road. As she started to turn on it from Jessup Lane, a deputy's patrol car pulled up and blocked her.

She backed up again, this time into her brother's taillight, which crunched loudly.

Deputy Collins jumped from his car, pulling his gun from a holster as he did so. Lucas Heller was still twenty yards from the road. He stopped, and Digger wondered if he hoped Collins would shoot Veronica.

In the silence that followed, Digger could hear Veronica Heller lock her car doors. As if that would help. She couldn't go forward without plowing into the deputy. Backward would crunch her brother's car even more.

Collins called. "Mrs. Montgomery. Are you up here?"

"Yes dear. I'm with Digger Browning."

Collins muttered, "Figures." He raised his voice. "Sheriff's on his way."

Deputy Sovern's car careened to a stop and he exited, gun drawn."

"No one's going to shoot anyone," Lucas called.

"I think he has a gun in his waistband," Digger yelled.

In a lower voice, he said, "It's a BB gun."

"Put your gun on the ground, Heller. Very slowly," Sovern said.

Lucas pulled it out and dropped it, barrel first.

Sheriff Montgomery arrived. He got out of his car without drawing his gun. "Who's armed?" he asked.

"He put his down." Collins nodded to Lucas Heller.

"We don't know about her," Sovern said.

"She doesn't own one," Lucas said.

Maryann said, quietly, "He can't really know that."

Uncle Benjamin floated into her car and looked around. He pressed his face to the back passenger window and shook his head.

Montgomery walked to Veronica's car and motioned that she should put down her window.

She put it down, but Digger couldn't see how far. She held her breath. None of the sheriff's men had on bullet proof vests, including him.

"I'm meeting someone at Dottie's B&B. I need to be there."

"That's going to drop down on your to-do list," Montgomery said. "Get out of the car please."

For a tense five seconds, nothing happened. Then she popped her locks and Montgomery opened the car door for her.

"She doesn't have her seatbelt on. That's a ticket right there," Uncle Benjamin said.

As Veronica got out, the sheriff peered into her back seat. "That's a nice metal detector. Looks like the rounded edge might fit the bruise Bruno Sampson got right before he died."

Veronica stamped one foot. "It does not!"

Digger thought an innocent person wouldn't acknowledge they knew what the bruise looked like.

The blue jay began jeering and clucking. He dive-bombed Veronica so close that she screamed and the sheriff backed up.

Bruno fed the birds, Digger thought. Are they identifying his killer?

Perhaps to emphasize his point, the bird pooped on Veronica's head.

She reached up, felt it, and began to wring her hands and cry.

A FEW MINUTES LATER, after giving Veronica a wipe and handcuffing both Heller siblings, Montgomery walked to where Digger and Maryann stood.

Sheriff Montgomery said only, "Are you okay grandmother?"

"Better than okay," she replied.

He turned toward the small group of Sheriff Department cars without another word.

"Veronica's metal detector was in the shed. Lucas removed it," Digger called.

He raised and lowered his hand and kept walking.

Digger and Maryann watched as Lucas Heller spoke animatedly to Montgomery and Sovern. When Collins started walking toward the shed, Lucas pointed at Digger and Maryann. Perhaps trying to put some blame on them.

Digger leaned toward Maryann. "Can you surreptitiously take a couple more photos? Marty can use them for the paper."

"You don't want to?" she asked.

"The sheriff won't confiscate your phone."

"*Not if he knows what's good for him,*" Uncle Benjamin said.

When Maryann moved a few steps away, Digger mouthed to her uncle. "Is it a large metal detector?"

"*Looks fairly small. Do you suppose the Hellers came up here to look for coins, Bruno saw them, and they fought?*"

Digger wondered if Bruno had been using it when Lucas Heller came to pay him not to sell his land to his sister. Or had Veronica brought it with her? Did Veronica drive up after she left Digger's office and start a fight?

Uncle Benjamin sped over to where Heller was talking to the sheriff.

Bruno had called Marty at least an hour before she and Marty found his body. Plenty of time for Veronica – or someone -- to kill him and leave.

After a few minutes, Maryann said, "I need to sit down."

"Oh, sure. Let's walk to my car."

Maryann leaned more heavily on her cane.

"Where are you going?" Montgomery shouted.

"To sit in my car." Digger pointed to Maryann.

He made a shooing gesture. "Go down to my office."

They got to the small hill that led to the car. "I'm not so sure about you walking down there," Digger said.

"I'd probably do better scooting, but there'd be the issue of standing up."

Marty's car sped past, came to an abrupt halt, and backed up. He parked across from Digger's car. "What the hell is going on?"

"Can you help Maryann get in my car?" Digger asked.

That blunted any anger he displayed. He quickly climbed the small hill, and when Maryann started to take his arm, he scooped her up, in bridal carry form.

"Goodness, Marty. Is this a proposal?"

"Definitely not. I couldn't handle two of you." He trudged down the incline and deposited Maryann by the car door.

Digger came down after them. "Maryann took some pictures for you. I figured if I did, the sheriff would confiscate my camera."

Maryann settled in the front seat. "I'll text them."

"Jeez Louise." He turned to Digger. "Who is it?"

"Lucas and Veronica Heller. They came separately. Lucas took a metal detector from the shed over there." She gestured to the building behind the cabin. "It's in Veronica's car now."

Marty crossed the street, got back into his car, and drove the couple hundred feet to Jessup Lane.

SHERIFF MONTGOMERY'S STAFF made a fuss over Maryann. There were more than the usual two or three in the satellite office. He must have asked some to come up from Oakland.

Uncle Benjamin sat cross-legged on a credenza behind the small conference table. *"I want to tell you all of what I heard, but you won't be able to ask questions."*

Digger took a small notebook from her pocket. "Maryann, I'm going to jot some notes. Maybe it'll be a help to Marty when he writes his story."

"I have my hot tea. You go ahead."

"At first, he tried to pretend that he saw you two there and got out of his car thinking you might need help. Or Maryann might. But one of the deputies, Collins I think, noticed the padlock was different. Sheriff had Heller empty his pockets, and there was the sawed lock."

"Did anyone confess to killing Bruno?" she wrote.

"Not in so many words. He said something like he came up here yesterday to offer Bruno a couple thousand dollars not to sell land to his sister. Then Veronica and Josh showed up and they all started arguing."

"Montgomery asked him if he knew how Bruno got a bruise across his forehead. That's when Heller stopped talking and asked for a lawyer. All Veronica did was blubber."

Digger wasn't sure what to think. She could see Lucas coming to talk to Bruno. Did Veronica wait for Josh after she left Digger's office, or had he looked for her?

Who among the three would take a swing at Bruno with a metal detector – if that was what sent him to the ground? She herself would consider taking a whack at Veronica.

She wrote another note to Uncle Benjamin. "Who were you talking to?"

He shook his head. "*The very pale ghost of Susannah Sampson. She recognized the cabin, so we walked over there. I told her I'd be back, but I wouldn't be surprised if she totally fades before I get there.*"

A VERY ANGRY SHERIFF Montgomery returned to the office late Tuesday afternoon. Digger stood next to the conference room door and tried to make out the words, which seemed to be directed at his deputies. She heard the name Heller a couple of times.

Steps came toward the small conference room and Digger just made it back to her seat next to Maryann and her cup of tea.

"*None for me?*" Uncle Benjamin asked.

Sheriff Montgomery came in carrying a folder. "There's a gap between the door and the floor, Digger. I can see when you're standing there."

"Curses, foiled again," Maryann said.

He sat across from her and Digger. "Not funny grandmother." He opened his mouth to say something else, but Digger interrupted.

"Remember you were going to have someone look at Gerard Morton's death certificate, down in Baltimore?"

He rubbed his hand over his face and stared at Digger, who shrugged.

He looked at Maryann. "Grandmother, Mr. Heller said he stopped moving closer to you two because you waved something shiny at him. He thought it might be a hatchet."

Digger and Maryann laughed and Maryann reached into her purse and took out her phone, which had a silver back. "I couldn't even club a mouse to death with this."

"She took a picture of him, with the flash on. The flash surprised him and he stopped moving toward us," Digger said. "While he and I talked for a few more seconds, she texted it to you."

He jotted a note and tried to hide a smile. He looked up and met Maryann's gaze. "That was a good idea."

"Of course it was. Now, I want to know what's going on."

He regarded her with what Digger thought of as his impermeable stare. She'd been the recipient of it several times.

"Since you won't tell anyone," he stressed the last two words, "he said he went up there to ask Bruno not to sell the land to his sister. Mr. Sampson wouldn't say one way or the other, but Heller said their discussion was friendly."

Someone knocked on the door and Deputy Sovern stuck his head in. "Lucas Heller's lawyer wants to know if he can leave."

"I'll be out in five minutes." Montgomery gestured that Sovern should shut the door.

Sovern nodded and did so.

"Continue," Maryann said.

Digger covered her mouth with her hand so he didn't see her smile.

"Mr. Heller maintains that as he was leaving, Veronica and a man he did not know – but whom she called Josh – pulled up. She started screaming at Lucas, Josh started yelling at her to calm down, and eventually Sampson roared at all of them to leave. According to Heller, that's when he left."

"Do you believe him?" Digger asked.

Maryann turned to her. "He'll have to investigate more."

The sheriff stood. As he was about to close the door behind him, Digger thought she heard him mutter, "Too many cooks."

She turned to Maryann. "I've met Josh several times." She stopped. Digger had been about to say he was not the hothead Veronica was, but he had been the first few minutes she and Marty had talked to him.

"I guess," she continued more slowly, "I've seen him angry, but he isn't a perpetually bad-tempered person, which is what Veronica seems to be."

"How about Lucas?" Maryann asked.

She shrugged. "Like any good businessman. He's direct, but always seems calm. Although Veronica was really trying his patience, going around saying he'd co-sign a loan for a campground, telling him I was advising her on..."

The door opened and Deputy Collins stuck his head in. "Your buddy Marty is here." He glanced at Maryann. "He might be more irritated at you than Digger, for a change."

Maryann gave him a smile that would melt butter. "Thank you. I'll have my big knife ready."

His eyes widened, then he relaxed. "I'm kinda getting what the sheriff means when he talks about you."

Collins led them to the small waiting area, where Marty stood at the window looking out. In a forced tone, he said, "My two wandering souls." He faced them.

Maryann spoke before Digger could. "Now, Marty, Digger wanted you to come. But I said we mature women didn't need a male escort."

Marty turned toward Digger. "So, if I call you a mature woman, you won't take offense?"

"*I sure wouldn't do it,*" Uncle Benjamin said.

Marty looked at Maryann. "I heard about you saying people could hunt for gold on your land. What were you thinking?"

She frowned and raised both hands, one holding her cane. "That was before Bruno's death, of course. I told our town crier at the apartments to take it out of the newsletter."

Marty looked at Digger. "I need to go do an article for the website."

"Oh." Maryann pulled her phone from her purse. "Did you get the pictures?"

"You do get a couple good behavior points for that. I'll open them at the paper. I may I call you with questions."

"Of course."

Marty pointed a finger at Digger. "You, I know where to find. Usually."

Uncle Benjamin floated out the door after him. "*Hey, ask me some questions. Digger could answer for me.*"

CHAPTER
TWENTY-FOUR

AS SHE DROVE HOME Tuesday evening after dropping Maryann at her apartment, Digger called Holly on her cell. "I get caught up in the moment and I forget."

"I knew where you went. I called Marty when it seemed that you were gone too long, and he had just picked up something on the police scanner. It didn't sound as if you were hurt."

"Just stupid to go."

"*Not stupid, but you've had brighter moments*," Uncle Benjamin said.

"Blame Maryann." Holly was silent for several seconds. "The pancake place on the edge of town wants a menu."

"I'll be in at 8:30 Wednesday. And I'm sorry."

"We can talk more later. I'm not into funeral planning."

Digger smiled as she hung up. Ever since she'd been laid off from her job with Western Maryland Ad Agency, she seemed to walk into trouble's path every couple of months. Finding Uncle Benjamin's body was the worst, and hardly her fault.

But could she have avoided discoveries at the old train depot and the Halloway place? She couldn't think of how, but she was going to have to start wearing a better danger detection antenna.

Digger could hear Bitsy's barks when she was still hundreds of yards from the house. She hoped the dog hadn't soiled on the carpet. The foyer was so much…"Franklin!"

As she said it, Uncle Benjamin bolted out of the Jeep and rocketed toward the Volvo. He looked inside and then zoomed into the house.

The screen door opened and Franklin let Bitsy out. He waved lightly and stepped back into the house.

It's a Tuesday, Digger thought. It must be important. He has to believe!

She parked in front of Franklin's car and jogged up the steps, well behind Uncle Benjamin. She opened the screen door and almost tripped over Ragdoll. "Careful cat."

Franklin stood in the hall. He took a small ceramic ghost from his pocket and held it out. "On Dupont Circle, we really decorate for Halloween."

Digger took two steps and hugged him. Tears formed and she stepped back and brushed them away. She accepted the ghost.

Franklin gestured to the living room and then the couch.

Uncle Benjamin already sat on it. *"He told me to sit here."* He beamed.

"I don't want to sit on him," Franklin said.

"Sit closer to the opening to the foyer," Digger said. She sat on the other end of the couch, with Uncle Benjamin between them. "He's in the middle."

"I owe you an apology, Digger. I just couldn't wrap my head around it. Especially…"

"Because I didn't tell you right away."

Franklin nodded.

"After he popped up, I walked to where you were in the living room, with the funeral guests. You didn't see him. At that point, I thought I was losing it."

"And I was so frustrated that he couldn't," Uncle Benjamin said.

Digger repeated this.

"I understand a little better now. How do we proceed? I don't want Digger to have to interpret the whole time I'm here."

Uncle Benjamin said, *"I've thought a lot about that. I'd like to hear what you're up to. Just talk sometimes, I'll listen. Digger doesn't have to be in the room. If you want to ask me something, go find her."*

Digger recited this. "He shows up if I call him. If you want to know if he's around, you can ask me. If he's with you and leaves or goes to another room, I'll tell you so you aren't talking to the walls."

Uncle Benjamin shook his head. *"Sadly, it's almost the same thing."*

"We'll have a learning curve," Digger said.

Headlights turned into the driveway. Bitsy barked from the front porch.

"I forgot he was out there. Probably Marty. It's been a sort of weird day."

"How do you differentiate?" Franklin asked.

Digger laughed. "In a way, Marty will be able to explain more to you than I can, since he can't see or hear Uncle Benjamin either." She paused. "He gets your dad's humor."

Ragdoll jumped onto the sofa as Digger stood. She pointed to the cat. "I can't be sure, but I think she sees him. She's sitting right next to him."

Franklin petted the cat. "Tell me your secrets." He stood.

"*I wish she could,*" Uncle Benjamin petted her and his hand fell through Franklin's.

Marty let himself in and walked quickly to Franklin, hand extended. "I hope this is good news."

Franklin grasped it. "I'm sure you helped her after I left. When I found out, I didn't know what to do."

"I'm right here," Digger said.

"*Now you know how I feel,*" Uncle Benjamin said.

Franklin smiled. "I put on the tea kettle. Let's sit at the kitchen table for a few minutes, then I have to get to bed early."

"Going to work tomorrow?" Marty asked.

Franklin nodded as Digger led them to the kitchen. "Have to. Big case. Three-and-a-half hour drive. I didn't want this to wait for the weekend."

Digger glanced at Uncle Benjamin. He had positioned himself in his favorite spot on the Formica-topped table. He only had eyes for Franklin.

Franklin looked at her. She pointed to the table. "He sits on it cross-legged a lot. Now he'll feel like his minions are giving him his due."

"*As they should. Tell Franklin and Marty I'll just listen.*"

She did so as she poured.

When they were settled with tea, Franklin spoke. "I know we have a lot to figure out, but I think it will be more awkward if we're all sitting around wondering who's where."

"Story of my life," Digger muttered.

Marty grinned. "Double that for me."

"Last weekend...only last weekend," Franklin said. "We talked about learning bridge. Let's do something like that. Bridge, Scrabble, pinochle, something with more friends. Invite Holly."

"*Not Audrey,*" Uncle Benjamin said. He pointed to Franklin. "*You could bring a friend up. I suppose you'd rather not tell him about me.*"

Digger repeated it. "In some ways, be glad you can't see him. He can change clothes on a whim, just thinks of them and he has new ones.

"*Heck of a lot of fun.*"

"Today, somebody was bothering me and he switched to boxing shorts and gloves and started dancing around."

"Count me out," Marty said.

Franklin looked to the center of the table. "I never once saw you in shorts."

Uncle Benjamin did a 'yes' sign. "*He's talking to me.*"

Digger smiled. "He likes that you spoke to him."

"We'll get it figured out," Franklin looked at Marty. "Did you have a story to tell about today?"

"Take too long. Sheriff Montgomery's going to talk to me at nine-thirty tonight. I need to get to the paper so I can do that and finish writing a story for the newspaper's web page." He yawned.

"Can't stay here?" Digger wiggled her eyebrows.

"This is also a little weird. Marty, I'll look for your article tomorrow night." Franklin stood and bent to kiss Digger on the cheek. "Come on Dad, before I go to sleep I'll tell you about the case I'm working on."

Uncle Benjamin did a summersault over all of them to get off the table and made for the back stairs.

Marty's eyes followed Franklin and came back to Digger. "Your uncle's excited?"

"Beyond words." She paused. "I thought we were going on a short walk on Maryann's property."

"When you get with Maryann, it's always something." He paused. "Why not leave me a note somewhere, so if you vanish I don't need to rely on Uncle Benjamin pushing paper off the table?"

"I'll email or call you if you won't try to talk me out of something."

Marty glanced out the kitchen window and back at Digger. "I can't always keep that promise, but nobody makes you take my advice."

"Maryann certainly wouldn't." She stood and moved to Marty's lap, sitting sidesaddle with her arm around his shoulders. "I'm glad we met."

"Me too. If you think about it, if Uncle Benjamin hadn't died, I wouldn't have come out here to talk to you that day. Remember, you were weeding in the family plot, before his funeral?"

"I hadn't thought of it that way. One more thing I can credit to Uncle Benjamin."

CHAPTER
TWENTY-FIVE

DIGGER DIGGER LOOKED FOR MARTY'S article on the paper's website as she ate her corn flakes Wednesday morning, and once more before she left for work. She figured he must have a couple more things to find out.

She wore a dressier blazer in case people from the Pittsburgh television station read something Marty wrote and asked for an in-person interview. He might be able to leave her name off a discussion about discovering the body (at least for now), but her visit to Maryann's property and the after-effects would require identification.

"*You look nice.*" Uncle Benjamin said. "*Auditioning for a TV show?*"

"It's a 'just in case I'm interviewed' outfit," Digger said. "You coming to work?"

"*Probably be the best place to get the news today.*"

As she fed Bitsy and Ragdoll, Digger figured Sheriff Montgomery would be far from thrilled that his grandmother would be mentioned. Since they'd gone to her property, perhaps that would take some focus off Digger.

No such luck. When she reached We Think, You Design, Holly had printed out the *Maple Grove News* web article for her. "Quite the day you had yesterday."

"One I hope never to repeat. Thanks for printing this." Digger picked up the copy, very aware that Uncle Benjamin was as anxious to read as she was.

Suspects Emerge in Sampson Murder
Marty Hofstedder

On March 24th, the body of Bruno Sampson was found on his property on the west side of Meadow Mountain. He had recently let it be known that he had found gold coins, though he didn't provide a location when interviewed for the May 18th edition of the *Maple Grove News.*

Theories as to where the coins came from were rampant, and after a television story on a Pittsburgh station, other treasure seekers sought to search for coins. He added more No Trespassing signs to his property and assured them they were not welcome.

The couple who found Sampson's body had received a call from him saying that they could come to the property because he had a secret to show them. Sheriff Roger Montgomery believes that Mr. Sampson wanted to show them the hidden grave of his mother, Susannah Sampson, who died about thirty years ago.

(See the article on page 3 on Sheriff Montgomery's press conference about the discovery.)

Mr. Sampson indicated he did not want a "frickin' coin hunter" to discover his secret. He had apparently decided to be the one to announce the grave. Sampson would likely have been a pre-teen when his mother died, and is not considered a suspect. Montgomery believes it is reasonable to suspect Silas Sampson, Jr., Bruno's father, but forensic information may be sparse.

Garrett County Medical Examiner Alex Cluster has said he will provide information on the recent death as it becomes available. At this point, he is able to confirm that Bruno Sampson was hit in the forehead with likely a smooth metal object.

When he fell to the ground, he hit his head on a protruding, sharp rock. Cluster believes that while the rock dealt the death blow, it would not have occurred without the blow to the forehead.

Mrs. Maryann Stevens Montgomery owns land that abuts the Sampson property. Her father purchased it more than fifty years ago, thinking he might supplement income from his dairy farm by selling timber. She inherited the property from him.

On Tuesday, March 29th, Mrs. Montgomery asked a friend, Digger Browning, to take her to visit her property. They made a disturbing discovery with the arrival first of Lucas and then Veronica Heller. Veronica had previously let it be known that she wanted to find some of the gold coins and buy property to open a primitive campground.

Late in the afternoon the day Sampson was killed, Veronica Heller came to his property ostensibly to offer to buy his land. However, she had an unfounded expectation that her brother Lucas would co-sign a loan for the land.

With Veronica Heller was Josh Henry, the great-nephew of blacksmith Gerard Morton, who died somewhere in the vicinity of what had become Sampson's property.

Henry was interested in the coins. He thought if they were dated 1910 or earlier, they could have belonged to Morton. This could show that Abraham Sampson, Bruno's great-grandfather, killed Morton and used money he had with him to purchase the property. Sheriff Montgomery doubts this could be proven today.

At some point, Lucas Heller arrived and he and his sister argued together and with Sampson. It is believed when Sampson insisted they leave, that Veronica Heller hit Sampson with the round end of a metal detector she had brought to search for coins.

Mrs. Montgomery and Ms. Browning were on Montgomery's property when Lucas Heller returned on March 29th to remove the metal detector from a shed on Sampson's property, where he had hidden it.

When asked why, he said that after Veronica Heller struck Sampson, she threw the detector into the brush and left. Lucas Heller did not want the metal detector to be found so near Sampson's body, nor did he want to take it with him. He hid it in what was then the unlocked shed where Sampson did taxidermy projects.

Correctly assuming that Sheriff Montgomery would have had the shed locked, he returned the next day with a replacement padlock. He planned to take the detector and replace the lock that deputies had installed.

After he removed the metal detector from the shed, Lucas Heller became aware that the women had seen him do it. He offered Ms. Browning a "deal" in the form of a suggestion that she and he simply walk away.

The ninety-year-old Mrs. Montgomery, hidden behind a spruce tree, distracted Heller by taking a flash photo of him. While he continued to talk to Browning, Mrs. Montgomery texted the photo to her grandson, Sheriff Roger Montgomery, who ordered Deputies Collins and Sovern to speed to the property. He later joined them.

There are more details to be sorted through. Sheriff Montgomery has had help in this from Josh Henry. Henry spent time with Veronica Heller on March 24th and went to Sampson's property with her. He is believed to have witnessed the killing, but says he immediately fled the vicinity. This left Veronica Heller with her brother.

Veronica and Lucas Heller will be in court Friday for pending bond hearings. Both have been taken to the Maple Grove Urgent Care Clinic for treatment of poison ivy acquired on Sampson's property.

This article will be updated.

Digger looked up when she finished reading. "He packed a lot of information in that article."

Holly nodded. "It makes me feel really sorry for Bruno Sampson. Can you imagine probably seeing your mother killed, and then tending her grave for perhaps thirty years? And not being able to tell anyone."

"*I wonder why he didn't call the sheriff after his father died?*" Uncle Benjamin asked.

Digger almost answered him. Instead, she spoke to Holly. "So much bottled up pain." She paused. "I can't help but think if Marty hadn't run into Sampson in the library, there would have been no newspaper article to attract coin hunters. Maybe he wouldn't have been killed."

Holly nodded. "Just goes to show that even small actions can have consequences. Oh, you should look at the article on the website. Marty found a newer photo of Bruno."

Digger turned on her computer and went to the *Maple Grove News* site. In the middle of the article was a photo of Bruno from the hardware store's security system. He had a large bag of birdseed over his right shoulder and looked to the left.

"What's in that bag?" Holly asked. "I couldn't make it out."

"Birdseed," Digger said, quietly. "I guess they kept him company."

Someone came up the steps slowly, with an odd thumping sound. "Josh Henry," Digger said. She stood to open the door.

Josh faced her. "May I come in?"

Digger nodded and stood aside. She hadn't seen him since running into him and Veronica at the Coffee Engine the morning after Bruno's death. She had thought him merely distracted, or sorry to be dealing with Veronica. The latter was probably a given.

How would she feel if she witnessed a murder? He hadn't immediately gone to the sheriff.

Josh nodded to Holly and Digger gestured to a chair by her desk. "Did you have something to say, Josh?"

He took a breath. "Mostly that I'm truly sorry I didn't speak up earlier. I stayed in town. I kept thinking I'd get up the nerve to talk to the sheriff."

"I saw you at the Coffee Engine the next day."

He nodded. "Veronica and Lucas thought if we pretended we hadn't read the article the morning after, it would seem we knew nothing about the murder."

Digger didn't change her expression. "Marty and I were near Sampson's place after he died. You and Veronica went there."

He buried his face in his hands. "So stupid. She was looking for...something she threw away. A metal detector."

"The one Lucas took from the shed," Digger said.

He raised his head. "I don't know why I wanted any coins. I truly thought if they were all 1910 or earlier that they would prove they were my uncle's. That Bruno's ancestor killed him."

He spread his hands. "I didn't want the money. I was willing to buy a coin or two."

"So why not speak up?" Holly asked, softly.

"Scared. More scared than I've ever been. And Lucas said if we didn't say anything no one would find out he and I were there when she hit him. I'm not blaming Lucas. It was my choice not to say anything until after," he nodded to Digger, "you and the older woman saw Lucas get the metal detector."

Digger nodded slowly. "Will you be charged with anything?"

"Maybe, maybe not. I've given Sheriff Montgomery any information I can think of. I had a lawyer with me yesterday when we talked about all of it. He told the sheriff and someone from a prosecutor's office that we were speaking freely in hope of getting 'some consideration.'"

Digger let those words hang in the air for several moments. "Thanks for coming by."

He nodded and put his hands on the arm of the chair as if he were about to stand, then sat back down. "You know what's funny? I really like it up here. I'm my own boss, I can work from anywhere."

Digger shook her head slightly. "Heck of a way to meet everybody, be named in the paper as a witness to a murder."

He grunted and stood. "Yeah, when the song says you want to go to a place where everybody knows your name, I don't think this is what it meant."

Holly and Digger smiled at him, and she said, "Good luck, whatever you do."

"Ditto," Holly said.

"Thanks." Josh left.

Uncle Benjamin had been uncharacteristically quiet. Digger glanced at him, sitting cross-legged on the tallest file cabinet. He stared out the window.

She stood and stretched. "Holly, do you mind if I take a short walk? I need to clear my head."

"Sure." She grinned. "Two more menu orders. We'll be busy."

"Busy is good," Digger said, and walked down the steps to the street. As she expected, Uncle Benjamin followed her. With few people on the street, she muttered, "Are you okay?"

"*Bruno's murder and all that aside, it's been an...eventful week.*"

"Some good parts," Digger said. "We can be ourselves around Franklin."

"*Yes. It all sort of makes me realize I'm really dead. Why did I come back like this and most others don't?*"

"Too ornery to die?" Digger asked.

He grunted a laugh. "*Probably.*" He didn't speak for a minute. "*I think I helped Bruno's mother cross over. I would never have expected to do that.*"

"I'm sorry I didn't ask more about that. What exactly did you say to her?"

"*Not too much, really. I reminded her who she was. She said she wanted to see her son. I told her he was grown up, and I thought if she let herself sleep, she'd probably see him.*"

"And did she? Sleep, I mean."

"*I think so. She headed into the cabin, said she was going to sleep. I suppose we should go back up there sometime.*"

"Are you sad?" Digger asked.

"*Kind of melancholy. I'll be fine.*" He grinned. "*We make a good team, don't you think?*"

"Yes, we do. I'm glad we have Franklin and Marty on our team, too."

"*When Holly comes over to play cards, are we going to tell her?*"

"I...don't think I'm ready for that. She's on our team. She just doesn't know it."

They had reached the small corner park when Marty's voice drifted across the street. "Digger. Wait up."

"You should probably marry that guy."

"You should probably shut up."

"Is that any way to talk to your elders?"

"It is today."

Marty came up to them and gave Digger a quick hug. "I don't think we've ever hugged in public."

Digger smiled. "Lots of things to try for the first time."

THE END

Other Books by Elaine L. Orr

The Jolie Gentil Cozy Mystery Series.
Appraisal for Murder
Rekindling Motives
When the Carny Comes to Town
Any Port in a Storm
Trouble on the Doorstep
Behind the Walls
Vague Images
Ground to a Halt
Holidays in Ocean Alley
The Unexpected Resolution
The Twain Does Meet (novella)
Underground in Ocean Alley
Aunt Madge and the Civil Election (long short story)
Sticky Fingered Books
Jolie and Scoobie High School Misadventures (prequel)

River's Edge Mystery Series
From Newsprint to Footprints
Demise of a Devious Neighbor
Demise of a Devious Suspect

Logland Mystery Series
Tip a Hat to Murder
Final Cycle
Final Operation

Family History Mystery Series
Least Trodden Ground
The Unscheduled Murder Trip
Mountain Rails of Old
Gilded Path to Nowhere

Bio for Elaine L. Orr

Elaine L. Orr authors four mystery series, including the eleven-book Jolie Gentil cozy mystery series, set at the Jersey shore. *Behind the Walls* was a finalist for the 2014 Chanticleer Mystery and Mayhem Awards. The three-book River's Edge cozy mystery series is set in Iowa, and *Demise of a Devious Neighbor* was a 2017 Chanticleer finalist. The three-book Logland series takes place in small-town Illinois. Elaine also writes plays and novellas, including the one-act, *Common Ground*, and novellas *Falling Into Place* and *In the Shadow of Light*. A novella, *Biding Time*, was one of five finalists in the National Press Club's first fiction contest, in 1993. Nonfiction includes *Monett* and *Writing When Time is Scarce*.

Elaine conducts presentations on publishing and other writing-related topics. She also blogs on writing and publishing and presents her musings at *Irish Roots Author* (found at htttp://elaineorr.blogspot.com). A member of Sisters in Crime, Elaine grew up in Maryland and moved to the Midwest in 1994.

http://www.elaineorr.com
For Elaine's monthly newsletter go to
http://eepurl.com/crf3F1

For articles on reading, writing, and publishing, check out http://elaineorr.blogspot.com

Made in the USA
Middletown, DE
23 November 2022

Contemporary Chinese Politics

fifth edition

Contemporary Chinese Politics

An Introduction

JAMES C.F. WANG
University of Hawaii at Hilo

PRENTICE HALL, Englewood Cliffs, New Jersey 07632

Library of Congress Cataloging-in-Publication Data
WANG, JAMES C.F.
    Contemporary Chinese politics: an introduction/James C.F. Wang.
    —5th ed.
        p.   cm.
    Includes bibliographical references and index.
    ISBN 0-13-059198-X
    1. China—Politics and government—1976-   I. Title.
DS779.26.W365   1995
320.951—dc20   94-5934
                                                              CIP

Editorial director: Charlyce Jones Owen
Assistant editor: Jennie Katsaros
Copy editor: Virginia Rubens
Cover design: Wendy Alling Judy
Production coordinator: Mary Ann Gloriande
Editorial assistant: Nicole Signoretti
Editorial/production supervision
    and interior design: Rob DeGeorge

Printed in the United States of America

10   9   8   7   6   5   4   3   2

ISBN 0-13-059198-X

PRENTICE-HALL INTERNATIONAL (UK) LIMITED, *London*
PRENTICE-HALL OF AUSTRALIA PTY. LIMITED, *Sydney*
PRENTICE-HALL CANADA INC., *Toronto*
PRENTICE-HALL HISPANOAMERICANA, S.A., *Mexico*
PRENTICE-HALL OF INDIA PRIVATE LIMITED, *New Delhi*
PRENTICE-HALL OF JAPAN, INC., *Tokyo*
SIMON & SCHUSTER ASIA PTE. LTD., *Singapore*
EDITORA PRENTICE-HALL DO BRASIL, LTDA., *Rio de Janeiro*

To Sally, my wife,
and to my children, Sarah and Eric,
for their tolerance, patience, and assistance.

Contents

Preface

This fifth edition of *Contemporary Chinese Politics: An Introduction*, originally published in 1980 and revised in 1985, 1989, and 1992, is designed for both undergraduate and graduate students. The publisher and author have striven to make the text as current and as comprehensive as possible by revising and updating its content and substance periodically. The events rapidly unfolding in China necessitate such revision and updating.

The fifth edition contains several major changes. One is a new introductory chapter that briefly reviews China's past history and cultural heritage. Several reviewers who have used the textbook for their classes have pointed out the need to provide historical perspective for those students who have not been exposed to Chinese history and cultural traditions. The new Chapter 2 is devoted to the rise of the Chinese communist movement, China under Mao Zedong, the Cultural Revolution, and the return to power by Deng Xiaoping in 1977–78.

The text dealing with the Chinese Communist Party as a basic political organization, and with the central government structure, has been reorganized into three separate chapters. A new Chapter 4 focuses on the party and the government as political institutions, the structural issues, and the policy process. The new Chapter 5 deals with the Chinese elites and their recruitment, elite characteristics and factionalism, and the succession problem after Deng Xiaoping. Brief biographical sketches are presented on the probable successor(s) to paramount leader Deng among the new top leadership elected at the conclusion of the Fourteenth Party Congress in October

1992. The new Chapter 6 focuses on the Chinese legal system, with discussion of the need for new civil laws following China's decision in 1992–1993 to move full speed ahead to a socialist market economy.

Some new material has been added to Chapter 7, on provincial and local politics: a discussion of the new coastal development strategy that has created persistent conflicts between the central government and coastal provinces, such as Guangdong in the south, over economic growth and investment. As the central government under economic reform has transferred power to local governments, the processes of decentralization and local autonomy have become more entrenched. Also added to Chapter 7 is a discussion of the planned future status of Hong Kong as a special administrative region (SAR) when the colony reverts to China in 1997. The section on Hong Kong centers on a description of the Basic Law to be implemented after 1997. In addition, new material is presented on Tibet's position in Chinese history as a background to understanding its present relationship with China.

Added to Chapter 8, on the military's role in Chinese politics, is a discussion of the controversial issue of Chinese arms sales abroad and the almost autonomous defense industries operated and controlled in the main by the People's Liberation Army (PLA). Included in Chapter 10, on democracy, dissent, and the Tiananmen mass movement, is a new section on dissent in China in the 1990s. Chapter 11, on rural and urban economic reform, is now introduced by a brief discussion on modernization as a development concept. In addition, the revised Chapter 11 now includes sections on the declining influence of large-scale state-owned enterprises, peasant discontent and riots in the countryside, and the present state of China's economy. This chapter also includes a discussion of Dengism or "the Theory of Deng"— its meaning and its implications for China's future development.

The fifth edition contains the same informative features found in previous editions. The source material cited in the chapter notes provides rich and up-to-date references so that students can explore topics of interest in depth. Although the text is comprehensive, with facts and information interspersed with pertinent analysis, it leaves ample room for instructors to use the material flexibly in order to meet their own specific needs for a course in Chinese politics or a general comparative politics course. As supplements to the text, charts and tables have been updated to make them more current. For easy reference, the appendices contain two basic documents: the Constitution of the People's Republic of China (1982) and the Constitution of the Communist Party of China (1982) and its 1987 revisions. As a unique teaching aid, a guide to romanization of the Chinese Pinyin system used in the text, with notations on the Wade-Gile system, has been preserved in this edition.

The preparation of this new revision would not have been possible without the help of a number of persons. Many colleagues from a large number of universities and colleges have made useful comments and suggestions. To all of them I owe a debt of gratitude. Once again I must acknowledge my great indebtedness to the China scholars whose work is cited in this edition. I especially want to thank my colleague and close friend, Professor Louis P. Warsh, formerly at this university, for his careful reading of the manuscript for style and his editorial suggestions; and Edith Worsencroft, for typing and some editing of the revised manuscript. Karen Horton and Julie Berrisford, former editors for political science at Prentice Hall, were indispensable in launching this project. Many thanks also to Jennie Katsaros, assistant editor for social sciences at Prentice Hall, for providing the continuity and supervision for this revision. Many thanks to Rob DeGeorge for supervising the editorial production of this edition. Lastly, special thanks to my daughter, Sarah O. Wang at Virginia Law School, for her editorial assistance.

The following provided valuable assistance in reviewing the manuscript for the fifth edition of this book: Peter Kim at Westminster College, and Lowell Dittmer at the University of California at Berkeley.

Romanization of Chinese Names of Persons and Places*

CHINESE PHONETIC ALPHABET, OR THE PINYIN SYSTEM

How to Pronounce

Following is a Chinese phonetic alphabet table showing alphabet pronunciation, with approximate English equivalents. Spelling in the Wade system is in parentheses for reference.

"a"   (a), a vowel, as in *far*

"b"   (p), a consonant, as in *be*

"c"   (ts), a consonant, as "ts" in *its*; and

"ch"   (ch), a consonant, as "ch" in *church*, strongly aspirated

"d"   (t), a consonant, as in *do*

"e"   (e), a vowel, as "er" in *her*, the "r" being silent; but "ie," a diphthong, as in *yes* and "ei," a diphthong, as in *way*

"f"   (f), a consonant, as in *foot*

"g"   (k), a consonant, as in *go*

"h"   (h), a consonant, as in *her*, strongly aspirated

---

*Based on official version published in *Beijing Review*, 1 (January 5, 1979), 18–20. A specific rule requires that the traditional spelling of historical places and persons such as Confucius and Sun Yat-sen need not be changed.

xv

"i"   (i), a vowel, two pronunciations:
         1) as in *eat*
         2) as in *sir* in syllables beginning with the consonants, *c, ch, r, s, sh, z,* and, *zh*
"j"   (ch), a consonant, as in *jeep*
"k"   (k), a consonant, as in *kind*, strongly aspirated
"l"   (l), a consonant, as in *land*
"m"   (m), a consonant, as in *me*
"n"   (n), a consonant, as in *no*
"o"   (o), a vowel, as "aw" in *law*
"p"   (p), a consonant, as in *par*, strongly aspirated
"q"   (ch), a consonant, as "ch" in *cheek*
"r"   (j), a consonant, pronounced as "r" but not rolled, or like "z" in *azure*
"s"   (s, ss, sz), a consonant, as in *sister*; and
"sh"   (sh), a consonant, as "sh" in *shore*
"t"   (t), a consonant, as in *top*, strongly aspirated
"u"   (u), a vowel, as in *too*, also as in the French "u" in *tu* or the German umlauted "ü" in *Müenchen*
"v"   (v), is used only to produce foreign and national minority words, and local dialects
"w"   (w), used as a semivowel in syllables beginning with "u" when not preceded by consonants, pronounced as in *want*
"x"   (hs), a consonant, as "sh" in *she*
"y"   used as a semivowel in syllables beginning with "i" or "u" when not preceded by consonants, pronounced as in *yet*
"z"   (ts, tz), a consonant, as in *zero*; and
"zh"   (ch), a consonant, as "j" in *jump*"

Spelling of Chinese Names of Persons

In accordance with the Chinese phonetic alphabet, the late Chairman Mao Tsetung's name will be spelled "Mao Zedong"; the late Premier Chou Enlai's name will be "Zhou Enlai"; and the late Chairman of the Standing Committee of the National People's Congress, Chu Teh, will be "Zhu De."

Following are names of party leaders of China, romanized according to the Chinese phonetic alphabet. The old spelling is in parentheses for reference.

Chairman of the Central Committee of the Chinese Communist Party:
   Hua Guofeng (Hua Kuo-feng)
Vice-Chairmen of the Party Central Committee:
   Ye Jianying (Yeh Chien-ying)
   Deng Xiaoping (Teng Hsiao-ping)
   Li Xiannian (Li Hsien-nien)
   Chen Yun (Chen Yun)
   Wang Dongxing (Wang Tung-hsing)
Members of the Political Bureau of the Party Central Committee:
   Hua Guofeng (Hua Kuo-feng)

(The following are listed in the order of the number of strokes in their surnames.)

   Wang Zhen (Wang Chen)
   Wei Guoqing (Wei Kuo-ching)

Ulanhu (Ulanfu)
Fang Yi (Fang Yi)
Deng Xiaoping (Teng Hsiao-ping)
Deng Yingchao (Teng Ying-chao)
Ye Jianying (Yeh Chien-ying)
Liu Bocheng (Liu Po-cheng)
Xu Shiyou (Hsu Shih-yu)
Ji Dengkui (Chi Teng-kuei)
Su Zhenhua (Su Chen-hua)
Li Xiannian (Li Hsien-nien)
Li Desheng (Li Teh-sheng)
Wu De (Wu Teh)
Yu Qiuli (Yu Chiu-li)
Wang Dongxing (Wang Tung-hsing)
Zhang Tingfa (Chang Ting-fa)
Chen Yun (Chen Yun)
Chen Yonggui (Chen Yung-Kuei)
Chen Xilian (Chen Hsi-lien)
Hu Yaobang (Hu Yao-pang)
Geng Biao (Keng Piao)
Nie Rongzhen (Nieh Jung-chen)
Ni Zhifu (Ni Chih-fu)
Xu Xianqian (Hsu Hsiang-chien)
Peng Chong (Pen Chung)

(The following are listed in the order of the number of strokes in their surnames.)

Alternate Members of the Political Bureau of the Party Central Committee:
Chen Muhua (Chen Mu-hua)
Zhao Ziyang (Chao Tsu-yang)
Seypidin (Saifudin)

Spelling of Chinese Place Names

Names of well-known places in China are listed as follows. The old spelling is in parentheses for reference.

Municipalities directly under the central authorities:
Beijing (Peking)
Shanghai (Shanghai)
Tianjin (Tientsin)

Ningxia Hui (Ningsia Hui) Autonomous Region
Yinchuan (Yinchuan)

Qinghai (Chinghai) Province
Xining (Sining)

Shaanxi (Shensi) Province
Xian (Sian)
Yanan (Yenan)

Shandong (Shantung) Province
Jinan (Tsinan)

Qingdao (Tsingtao)
Yantai (Yentai)

Shanxi (Shansi) Province
Taiyuan (Taiyuan)
Dazhai (Tachai)

Sichuan (Szechuan) Province
Chengdu (Chengtu)
Chongqing (Chungking)

Taiwan (Taiwan) Province
Taibei (Taipei)

Xinjiang Uygur (Singkiang Uighur) Autonomous Region
Urumqi (Urumchi)

Xizang (Tibet) Autonomous Region
Lhasa (Lhasa)

Yunnan (Yunnan) Province
Kunming (Kunming)
Dali (Tali)

Zhejiang (Chekiang) Province
Hangzhou (Hangchow)

ABBREVIATIONS

APC	Agricultural Producers' Cooperatives
CCP	Chinese Communist Party
Comintern	Communist Third International
CPPCC	Chinese People's Political Consultative Conference
CYL	Communist Youth League
MAC	Military Affairs Committee
NCNA	New China News Agency
NPC	National People's Congress
PLA	People's Liberation Army

Contemporary Chinese Politics

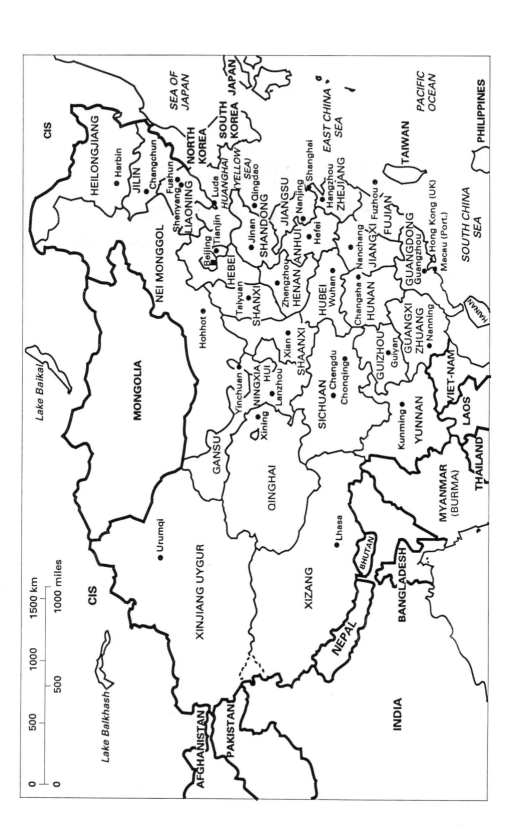

chapter one

Introduction
Historical and Cultural Perspectives

China has one of the most ancient and continuous civilizations in the world. Its recorded history is about 3,000 years old. For instance, the beginning date of the Shang dynasty was probably around 1700 B.C. Obviously, it is not possible for us even to summarize China's long history as part of the introduction to an understanding of the Chinese political system. Particularly for those who have not been exposed to a study of Chinese civilization and history, what is proposed here instead is to provide a broad historical background by focusing on some important stages in China's historical development.

Before sketching a broad outline of Chinese history, it is necessary to point out the crucial importance of the relationship between the land and the people.

THE LAND AND THE PEOPLE*

A fundamental prerequisite for understanding China is understanding the relationship between the land and its people. China's total land area is about 3.7 million square miles, slightly greater than that of the United States. However, about 85 to 90 per-

*Grateful acknowledgment is hereby given for permission to use material from James C. F. Wang, *Contemporary Chinese Politics: An Introduction*, 4th ed. (Englewood Cliffs, N.J.: Prentice-Hall, Inc., 1991); and James C. F. Wang, "Section 5: The People's Republic of China," in Rolf H. W. Theen and Frank L. Wilson, *Comparative Politics: An Introduction to Six Countries* (Englewood Cliffs, N.J.: Prentice-Hall, Inc., 1986).

1

cent of China's more than one billion people live and work on only one-sixth of this area. The remaining land is mostly hilly and mountainous. Unlike the United States, only 15 to 20 percent of China's land area is cultivable, and much of this land has been used intensively for centuries.

In addition to the limited land area available for cultivation, the climatic conditions compound the problem of food production for a vast population. The uneven rate of precipitation is one example. Rainfall comes to most parts of China in the spring and summer, usually in torrential downpours. It decreases from south to north. Average annual rainfall is about 60 to 80 inches for south China and less than 10 inches for the northwest. The fertile Yangtze River valley receives about 40 to 60 inches, while most of northern China receives about 25 inches annually.

If the torrential downpours during the rainy season are not channeled into reservoirs, a serious water shortage may result that can ultimately affect the livelihood of millions of people. The successive downpours during the rainy season can cause flooding in China's two major river systems, the Changjiang (Yangtze) (3,900 miles) and the Huanghe (Yellow) (3,600 miles) and their tributaries. The Yellow River, known as "China's Sorrow" for centuries, has caused devastating floods. It has flooded fifteen hundred times in a period of two thousand years. Its silt-laden waters have changed course at least 26 times. The Yellow River normally carries 57 pounds of mud per cubic yard; but when it rises after a torrential downpour, its mud-carrying capacity can reach as much as 900 pounds per cubic yard.[1] In one flood, the Yellow River overflowed its banks in a northern province, inundating towns and cities, with a loss of life estimated at close to one million. In 1981, heavy rains in late July and August caused the Yangtze River to flood over 65 percent of the counties in the southwestern province of Sichuan, leaving 1,500,000 people homeless. Chinese scientists estimate that each year 250 million tons of earth are washed into the Yangtze's three main tributaries.[2] One study showed that during the period between 206 B.C. and 1911 A.D. there were a total of 1,621 floods and 1,392 droughts, bringing endless sorrow to the Chinese people.[3]

With the factor of limited land for cultivation and the frequency of flood and drought added to the enormous population—over one billion by the official census—one can readily understand that China's primary problem is to mobilize its productive forces to feed its burgeoning population. This basic problem of population pressure on the limited land available for cultivation has plagued China throughout its history. The functions of government, and in many respects the very performance of government, have involved what John Fairbank described as the control of "the land, the manpower, and the water supply" for this agrarian society.[4]

GLIMPSE OF CHINA'S EARLY HISTORY[5]

Inscriptions on oracle bones and tortoise shells discovered in northern China in the past century provide a well-established list of rulers for the Shang dynasty; the dates for the rulers of the feudal principality are established at about 1766–1122 B.C. The feudal agrarian society, basically growing millet or rice in the Yellow River valley, was rather advanced: in addition to writing inscriptions on oracle bones, people used cowry shells in exchange for goods, and there is evidence of the presence of domestic animals. The society was organized on a patriarchal basis, but was controlled by a ruling aristocracy, which had a standing army of cavalry and chariots. Religion took the form of ancestor worship. Rulers performed both civil and religious duties.

The Kingdom of Shang was overthrown by the ruler of Zhou (Chou), a principality located in the Wei River valley, then China's western frontier. Subsequent rulers of Zhou extended the domain into the northwest. The Zhou kingdom then endured a state of decline, so that from the eighth century B.C. to the middle of the third century B.C. China was fragmented into unstable but separate principalities or fiefdoms resembling those of Europe in the Middle Ages. It was during this period that Chinese civilization grew and expanded, aided by the development of written characters, the original ideographs. Using these characters, scribes wrote books with ink on tablets of wood or bamboo. Soon anthologies of ancient verse, the classics of poetry called *Shih Ching*, and the classics of history called *Shu Ching*, were compiled by the scribes, forming the basis of early Chinese literature.

In many respects the Zhou period represented a period of intellectual growth, particularly in the area of philosophy, which concerned itself with explanations of spirits, including those of ancestors, of earth, and of heaven. During the latter reign of the Zhou Kingdom, these interpretations eventually developed into schools of philosophy. Common threads woven through these deliberations concerned the creation of an ideal society and the question of society's preservation. Among the schools of thought that flourished during this time was that of Confucianism; the sage Confucius (*c.* 551–*c.* 479 B.C.) was primarily interested in the creation of a government of goodness administered by virtuous rulers.

As the Zhou Kingdom disintegrated there arose a ruthless revolutionary ruler who built a united Chinese empire known in history as the Qin-Shih-Huang-Di (221–210 B.C.). In addition to being a ruthless ruler, the "Founder of the Empire," Qin-Shih-Huang-Di, built the Great Wall, burned books, issued death sentences for some scholars, and organized an effective, efficient administrative state, introducing an elaborate bureaucracy system with grades and honorific titles under the ultimate central direction of an emperor. He built a national capital at Sian and created an imperial force for suppressing domestic discontent and for keeping the barbarians, or those outside the Great Wall, at bay. He promulgated harsh laws and demanded absolute obedience to the emperor—the autocrat—in accordance with the precepts of the Legalists, a short-lived school of philosophy competing with Confucianism. Whereas Confucianism placed emphasis on the goodness and virtuosity of people, the Legalists denied the validity of such an assumption by insisting that there was no way to be sure that the ruler would be virtuous and morally good at all times. Therefore, the Legalists argued, there must be laws that would be fixed but impartial in their administration. Humans, as imperfect beings, must be restrained and guided by law, which in turn had been formulated by study and rectification in order to meet changing conditions.

It is perhaps interesting to note that the anti-Confucius campaign launched by Cultural Revolution radicals in 1973–74 not only criticized Confucius as a conservative reactionary for advocating the rule of a slave-owning society, but also praised the Legalist teachings. Thus, Chairman Mao was identified, by implication, with Qin-Shih-Huang-Di, the ruthless autocrat.

It was this rudimentary form of centralized civil administration, as fashioned originally by Qin-Shih-Huang-Di, that was adapted and perfected by subsequent rulers, including the alien conquerors known as Mongols (1279–1368 A.D.) and the

Manchus (1644–1911 A.D.). As the people of central Asia began to have contact with the Chinese under Qin's empire, the name for the country in the east was designated as "China" by the non-Chinese.

The unified Qin Empire was one of the shortest-lived dynasties. It was succeeded by the Han Dynasty in 206 B.C., concurrent with the rise of the Roman Empire in the Mediterranean region. The Han Empire extended the boundaries of China to the Tarim basin, the Ili valley in the northwest, Manchuria and Korea in the northeast, and Annam in the south. It further refined the centralized bureaucracy by introducing a competitive system of examination as a basis for recruitment to the civil service. It was under Han-Wu-Di (140 B.C.–87 B.C.) that Confucianism (to be discussed in a separate section) became the official ideology of the state. Han deliberately selected those who were proficient in the classics to be members of the civil administration—a tradition that prevailed until the 1911 revolution. Under the Han, as Chinese territory expanded, commerce and trade beyond the border also flourished, for by then commercial and cultural contacts had been established with India and extended as far as the Indian Ocean. Silk from China reached central Asia and Rome by the first century A.D. As early as 190 A.D., Buddhism, which stressed the inevitability of suffering in life and escape from it only by eliminating desire and the need for material well-being, came to China under Han by way of India.

The collapse of the Han Dynasty was followed by a dynamic empire, the Tang (618–907 A.D.). Instead of centralized rule, the Tang rulers opted for decentralization by granting more autonomy to the provinces. Some of the Tang rulers engaged in court extravagances that brought widespread discontent to the country. Soon rebellions arose, which the Tang military force suppressed only with great difficulty. Gradually the dynasty collapsed. However, Tang was noted for the cultural enrichment it brought to Chinese civilization. Under Tang rule there was a golden age of poetry and painting amidst a life of economic prosperity and order. With cross-cultural influences from the Greco-Roman and Indo-European civilizations, sculpture reached its height during Tang rule in the seventh and eighth centuries A.D. The printing of Buddhist sutra using wooden blocks as an art form originally appeared in 868 A.D., along with large quantities of block-printed books produced under Tang.

Under the Sung Dynasty (960–1279 A.D.) the empire extended its jurisdiction to the west (Sichuan) and south China. (Gunpowder probably originated during this period, in about 1000 A.D.) But the rulers had difficulty enforcing effective control over the north, which was in effect ruled by rivals from Manchuria. By 1211–15, the Mongols had invaded the north, and their mighty cavalry, led by Genghis Khan and Kublai Khan, had swept across China, Korea, parts of central Asia, and into Austria and Hungary in Europe. China under the Sung Dynasty was noted for a number of cultural developments. From a modern political science viewpoint, there were the political reforms introduced by Wang An-Shih, who advocated appointment of a commission of experts to draft a state budget, a state monopoly of commerce, loans by the state to farmers, the abolition of state conscription of labor, and demobilization of the military—all in all a program of paternalism and state responsibility in many aspects of civil life. These reform programs generated heated debate and were eventually abandoned. The Sung Dynasty's most enduring contribution to Chinese civilization was in the development of neo-Confucianism, a blending or synthesis of Buddhism, Taoism, and Confucianism. Briefly, the synthesis represents a school of thought that implies that the essence of humanity, the *Li*, is always good and never changes. Thus, the goodness of humanity must be nurtured or cultivated through "formal education" and "self-enlightenment."[6] A government of goodness is possible only if the ruler is enlightened and virtuous.

The Mongols who ruled China from 1279–1368 kept the system of government intact even though its rulers, such as Kublai Khan, embarked on military conquests of Asia and parts of Europe. In China the Mongols pursued a policy of conciliation and tolerance toward the Chinese. Kublai Khan saw to it that food was plentiful in public granaries and took care of scholars, whom he relied on to continue the governmental administration developed by previous dynasties, even though few Chinese were entrusted with the highest levels of office. He encouraged and promoted trade and contact with Europeans, notably through the Venetian explorer Marco Polo. The less-than-ninety-year Mongol rule was overthrown by a successful peasant rebellion that established the Ming Dynasty from 1368–1643.

Under Ming rule, China established extensive commercial contacts with the southern and southeastern Asian nations of India, Ceylon, Siam, Java, and Sumatra. There was trade with Japan. The Portuguese were the first Europeans to arrive in the southern ports of China, in 1514 A.D. The Dutch followed in 1622, forcefully occupying the enclave of Macao, and later the islands of Formosa (Taiwan) and Pescadores. In the late sixteenth century, through the Europeans, the Chinese under the Ming regime imported tobacco, sweet potatoes, and corn, which have constituted major agricultural products for China ever since. Printing, both with wooden blocks and with movable type, enriched the literary life. There were government presses as well as flourishing private (family) presses. The Ming period was not noted for its brilliance in either political thought or art, but it was a regime that maintained economic prosperity.

THE MANCHUS: THE LAST IMPERIAL RULERS OF CHINA

For a second time China was overrun by "barbarians" from outside the Great Wall: the Manchus invaded from the northeast and established an empire known as the Qing Dynasty, which ruled China for over 268 years, from 1644 to 1911 A.D. At the height of Manchu rule, China had extended its boundaries not only to Manchuria, but also to Mongolia, Xingjiang, Xizang (Tibet), and the far eastern portion of Russia. The Manchu court in Beijing established China's suzerainty—claiming sovereign rights, but not direct administration—over Nepal, Siam, Annam, and Korea. As alien rulers the Manchu Dynasty maintained intact the traditional Chinese political system, continuing recruitment by examination for the services of Confucian scholars as civil administrators for a vast empire. One Manchu ruler, Qian Lung, reigned for over six decades, from 1736 until 1796 A.D., at which time he was 86 years old. For its first 150 years the Qing Dynasty provided internal order and prosperity amidst a rapidly rising population. China's population stood at 60 million in 1650, but it multiplied to over 143 million in 1740 and to 265 million in 1775.

China, the "Middle Kingdom," the center of the universe, had long been admired by the Europeans for its silk products, its tea, and its art treasures. The Europeans' eagerness for trade with China, coupled with their zeal for missionary work in "heathen" China, produced a substantial amount of cultural misunderstanding. This was compounded by the demand for an "open door" trade and commerce policy, leading to the granting of territorial concessions to Europeans on Chinese soil. These pressures from abroad, plus gradual internal decay in the dynastic cycle, served as contributing factors to the decline of the Manchu empire in modern times. It is to the topic of Western impact that we must now turn in our continued discussion of Chinese history.

The first major clash between the West and China was over the importation of opium by the British for Chinese consumption. Prior to the British discovery of opium as a lucrative trade item, the Europeans, particularly the British, had an unfavorable balance of trade with China; the Chinese acquired little from the "inferior" West, but exported large quantities of Chinese tea, art objects, and porcelain to the West. As a result, the British had a trade deficit with China—until they discovered opium as an addictive drug desired by the Chinese for analgesic purposes. The importation of opium from British India turned around the Sino–British trade balance in favor of the British. Worse still, not only were the Chinese now in a terrible trade deficit situation, but opium addiction had become a serious national health problem. The imperial order to ban and confiscate opium importation was the spark that ignited the confrontation.

Complicating Sino–British relations, and Sino–European relations in general, was the Chinese practice of confining or restricting foreigners with trade and missionary objectives to one designated place in a southern port. The first Jesuits came to China in 1552 A.D.; they were followed by Mathew Ricci, who began successful missionary work in China in 1582. British envoys were subjected to the Chinese custom of bowing to the emperor whenever an imperial audience was granted. It was a humiliation and an insult to the British, who subscribed to the recognized principle of equality of status between nations. The twin pressures of trade and sovereign equality status between nations became underlying causes for the war with Great Britain that resulted in the signing of the unequal treaty of Nanking on August 24, 1842—the first severe blow dealt to an already weakening Qing empire. China was forced to open up five coastal ports where the British could reside and trade under European laws and customs, in addition to ceding Hong Kong and agreeing to treat the British on an equal basis. The treaty of Nanking was followed by a succession of treaties imposed on the Chinese by other European powers. By the time Japan defeated China in 1895, the prestige of the Qing Dynasty had reached its lowest ebb.

Let us now pause for a moment prior to our discussion of the Revolution of 1911, which brought down the imperial dynasty of Qing. It is perhaps appropriate to take a closer look now at the traditional Chinese political system that prevailed on the eve of the revolution.

THE TRADITIONAL CHINESE POLITICAL SYSTEM

To understand contemporary China, we must first look at the historical background and at the traditional political system that existed prior to the Revolution of 1911. The traditional Chinese political system was based upon a predominantly agrarian society. It was administered by an officialdom of scholars and was controlled, theoretically, by an authoritarian emperor. Although the Chinese empire was centralized, there was a great deal of regional and local autonomy. In the following pages we will examine some of the major characteristics of the traditional Chinese political system: the emperor, Confucian ideology, the gentry-officialdom, and the nature of local autonomy.

The Emperor: Mandate of Heaven and Dynastic Cycle

The Chinese emperor ruled with unlimited power over his subjects. His legitimacy and power to rule the vast empire derived from the belief that he was the "Son of Heaven" with a mandate to rule on earth. The mandate of heaven was legitimate as long as the emperor ruled in a righteous way and maintained harmony within the Chinese society and between the society and nature. A corollary to the mandate of heaven theory was the right to rebel if the emperor failed to maintain harmony. It was, therefore, an ancient tradition providing for rebellion as a means of deposing an intolerable imperial ruler—but rebellion was legitimate only if it succeeded.

Rebellions in Chinese history fall into two general patterns: peasant uprisings with religious overtones, and military insurrections. The peasant uprisings, such as the Taiping Rebellion of 1850, while at times widespread, only once led directly to the founding of a new imperial dynasty. The Ming Dynasty, which succeeded that of the Mongols in the fourteenth century, was founded by a laborer.[7] Peasant unrest and rebellions did, however, contribute indirectly to new dynasties by further weakening declining reigns and providing evidence of the loss of the mandate of heaven. These new dynasties, with the exception of the Ming, were founded either through a takeover by a powerful Chinese military figure, who had exploited peasant discontent and obtained the support of the scholars, or by foreign invasion.

While dynastic changes were effected through rebellion or invasion, the form and substance of government remained essentially unchanged. Each new emperor accepted the Confucian ideology, claiming the mandate of heaven for himself by virtue of success. He governed the empire through an established bureaucratic machinery administered by career officials. Each ruler was dependent upon these officials to administer the vast, populous empire. Dynasties rose and fell, but officialdom remained intact. Each of the twenty-four historic dynasties followed a common pattern of development, the dynastic cycle. At the beginning of a new dynasty, a period of national unity under virtuous and benevolent rule flourished and usually was accompanied by intellectual excitement and ferment; then, midway in the cycle, there emerged a period of mediocre rule, accompanied by signs of corruption and unrest. Finally, natural disasters occurred for which the ruler was unable to provide workable remedies, and a successful rebellion or invasion was mounted. A new dynasty was born, and the cycle repeated itself.[8]

Confucian Ideology

Confucianism, which permeated traditional Chinese society, was basically conservative and establishment-oriented. The central concepts stressed the need to achieve harmony in society through moral conduct in all relationships. The mandate of heaven implied explicit adherence to the Confucian theory of "government by goodness."[9] This code of proper behavior for the emperor and all government officials was prescribed in detail in the writings of Confucius and his disciples. Officials were recruited on the basis of competitive examinations designed to test mastery of the Confucian classics. It was assumed that once the Confucian ethic was mastered and internalized by the scholar-officials, a just and benevolent government would result. Since the government was administered by those who possessed the required ethics and code of conduct, there was really little need for either the promulgation of laws or the formal structuring of government institutions.

As the officially sanctioned political ideology, Confucianism conditioned and controlled the minds of rulers and subjects alike; it became the undisputed "orthodox doctrine of the imperial state."[10] It was perpetuated by the scholars as the basic foundation for the education of young men of means. Traditional Confucian ideology made its greatest impact on the wealthy elite. Confucianism as a humanistic philosophy served for thousands of years as a set of moral and ethical codes for correct behavior for the leaders or rulers. It left an ideological vacuum among the peasantry—the bulk of the population then, as now—who were more concerned with the burden of taxes and the hardships of life than with theories of government.[11] In later chapters we will discuss in detail how the Chinese Communist Party purposefully molded the minds of the Chinese people to conform to a different, but equally orthodox, political ideology. It is sufficient to note here the central role of political ideology in both the imperial and communist Chinese systems.

It must also be pointed out that Confucianism contained some elements of religious rites and beliefs—ancient rituals observed by the imperial officialdom. In fact, Confucianism promulgated the concept that the emperor was the "Son of Heaven" and that he not only had the mandate to rule on earth, but as political head of the state must perform certain prescribed ceremonies necessary for order and harmony among men and in the universe. The circular marble structure of the Altar of Heaven in the Forbidden City in Beijing was one of the places where the "Son of Heaven" conducted the ceremonies. The Confucian classics also contained references to ceremonies in honor of ancestors, though some of the ceremonial practices were influenced by Buddhism and Taoism.

The Gentry-Officialdom

Under the imperial system, the government officials—the mandarins—dominated the political and economic life of China. The mandarins were those individuals who held office by virtue of imperial degrees obtained by passing the civil service examinations. They came almost solely from the wealthy landholding class with resources to provide extended education for their sons. Because of the status and the power of the office, the mandarin officials were able to acquire fortunes in landholdings for themselves and their families. They constituted the small, privileged upper class of the Chinese agrarian society. Under the imperial civil service for the Manchu Dynasty—the last dynasty before the revolution of 1911—these officials were estimated to total not more than 40,000, or one one-hundredth of 1 percent of the population.[12] The officials of the imperial civil service wielded complete and arbitrary power over their subjects, the vast majority of whom were peasants living in the countryside. A typical magistrate for a Chinese county, according to one study, was responsible for the lives and well-being of about a quarter of a million subjects.[13] The magistrate, therefore, had to seek the cooperation and support of the large landholders to administer the county on behalf of the emperor and the central administration in Beijing. This administrative setup illustrates the gulf that existed between the educated elite and the illiterate peasants, and indicates the hierarchical structure of Chinese imperial rule.

The Chinese bureaucracy was classified into ranks and grades, each with a special set of privileges and a compensation scale. A voluminous flow of official documents and memoranda moved up and down the hierarchical ladder. At each level of the hierarchy, a certain prescribed form and literary style had to be observed—a multiplication of bureaucratic jargon. To control the huge bureaucracy, the emperor designated special censors at the various levels of government to report on the conduct of public officials. The provincial governor or the top man in a branch of the central bureaucracy in Beijing could become a bottleneck in the policy initiation and implementation process. At the lowest level of administration—the Chinese county—all important decisions affecting the community were made by the elites with the blessings of the magistrate. These decisions often disregarded, or were contrary to, the wishes of the earthbound peasants, who constituted the majority. Arbitrary decision making, unresponsive to the uneducated masses in the villages, remains to this day a basic problem in the relationship between the leaders and the led in China. In traditional Chinese politics, as in modern China, the elites or officials exercised control over the mass of peasants.

Local Autonomy

While the Chinese imperial government was centralized at the court in Beijing and was hierarchical in structure, the system did permit some degree of autonomy at the local level, provided that this did not interfere with the absolute authority of the emperor. A magistrate for a county, the lowest administrative unit in traditional China, could not possibly carry out his duties without working with and through the "local power structure."[14] While this power structure was headed by the large landowners, it also included merchants, artisans, and other persons of wealth and power in the community. As a convenient administrative arrangement, these groups were permitted by the magistrate to manage their own affairs within their own established confines. The magistrate naturally reserved the right to intervene if he deemed it necessary. Under this pragmatic arrangement, spokesmen for special interest groups in the community, such as the clans, the merchants' guilds, and the secret societies, often articulated their views and positions before the magistrate by informal and unofficial means, but never by overt pressure. It was considered an unforgivable sin for officials to organize themselves into factions that advocated competing interests of groups in the community. But articulation of group interests was often carried out by officials within the bureaucratic framework.[15] Thus, there was keen competition and maneuvering by officials within the bureaucratic setup to gain favorable decisions on a particular matter. In all instances, politics of this sort was conducted in secrecy and was influenced by the personal ties that competing officials might have with the local power structure, by their own rank within the bureaucratic hierarchy, and by their finesse in these maneuverings.

ATTEMPTS AT REFORM AND MODERNIZATION

One must keep in mind that long before the upheavals of the twentieth century—the Revolution of 1911, the Nationalist era that followed, and the rise of Chinese communism in the 1930s and 1940s—Chinese scholars, as reformers, had begun the search for a modernized China by exploring Western political, economic, and social ideas and institutions. Long before the Manchu Dynasty reached its lowest ebb, reform efforts were made to prevent further decay. Reformers basically sought remedial measures to abolish an inefficient and corrupt bureaucracy. They attempted to strengthen the imperial government's ability to meet unrest and rebellion in the countryside—the source of China's manpower, food supply, and government revenues. Unrest and rebellion were triggered by the demands of an increased population on the limited supplies the land could produce, and by the perennial recurrence of drought, flood, and famine. Reformers then sought to strengthen the old Chinese empire by making changes in such traditional institutions as the examination system and the military establishment. For instance, in the 1860s a group of provincial leaders came out openly for the need to acquire Western scientific and technological knowledge, particularly in areas related to the development of military science (arsenal manufacturing and shipbuilding for a navy). The leading advocates of these limited reforms of learning from the West were Zeng Guofan and Li Hongzhang. However, these attempts at modernization did not take root, as they were basically experimental projects undertaken on a personal level with limited resources. Led by a number of prominent scholars, a wave of reforms surfaced again in the decade of the 1890s. One reformer, Zhang Jitong, a viceroy, advocated the adoption of Western methods in order to preserve the dynasty. Another group of scholar-reformers, led by Kang Youwei and his student Liang Qichao, proposed reform measures such as popular election of officials, public care of the aged and children, and abolition of the family. Kang Youwei and Liang Qichao even opened a school in southern China that taught students mathematics and military drills, in addition to the classics. As justification for his reform efforts, Kang advocated the theory that Confucius encouraged political and social reform.

In 1895 Kang and Liang organized a reform movement known as the Society for the Study of National Self-Strengthening. Kang Youwei and his supporters were able to enlist the endorsement of Emperor Kuang Shu for the reform. Kuang Shu issued imperial edicts calling for changes in the archaic examination system, which had by now degenerated into pure memorization of the classics and clever juxtaposition of words and phrases. Having evidently read Kang's works, the emperor called for modern schools, including an imperial university for the study of Western ideas and methods; railroad building; and military reform. These efforts were collectively known as the One-Hundred-Day Reform. Nevertheless, in September 1898 they were crushed by the empress dowager, who imprisoned the emperor in his own palace chambers. (Guides now show tourists the prison grounds at the Forbidden City in Beijing.) Reformers were either arrested or exiled, and the empress dowager declared the reform edicts null and void.

A direct reaction to the reform movement of 1898 was the outbreak of the Boxer Rebellion of 1900, blessed and encouraged by the empress dowager and the conservative elements in power. This was a last desperate effort to "protect the nation, destroy foreigners" (the slogan and battle cry for the campaign against all foreigners). The upheaval was quelled by the dispatch to Beijing of a joint military force from eleven nations, including the United States and Japan. This action resulted in China's signing another humiliating treaty in 1901 under which China was to pay an indemnity of over U.S. $300 million, plus 4 percent interest, for missionary lives lost and properties damaged.

The Boxer Rebellion and the defeat by Japan in 1895 convinced some that reform alone could not possibly save the empire; this gave rise to the idea that a radical revolution might be necessary to overthrow the traditional imperial system. More importantly, some felt that a revolution must also advocate abandonment of traditional thinking and ideology.

THE CHINESE NATIONALIST REVOLUTION, 1911–1937

The Revolution of 1911

One leader who advocated revolutionary change was Dr. Sun Yatsen. In 1894 he founded a small secret society among overseas Chinese for the purpose of overthrowing the decaying Manchu Dynasty. As a revolutionary with a price on his head, much of the time Dr. Sun was forced to operate and organize abroad. After many years of hard work in southeast Asia, Japan, and Hawaii, Dr. Sun's movement took hold among educated young Chinese abroad. In 1905, 400 of Dr. Sun's followers gathered in Japan to form the first viable revolutionary movement, the Tung Meng Hui.[16] Its members took a solemn oath to bring down the alien Manchu empire and to replace it with a Chinese republic. Ten different attempts were organized and financed by the group, headquartered variously in Tokyo and Hanoi, to strike down the vulnerable Manchu rule by assassinating imperial officials. As these revolutionary attempts failed one by one, and more revolutionaries lost their lives, the movement became demoralized and ran low on funds. On October 10, 1911, an eleventh attempt was made. It resulted in a successful uprising by discontented and dissatisfied provincial officials, merchants, and imperial army commanders. The Manchu emperor abdicated, and shortly thereafter the Chinese imperial dynastic system was ended.

While Dr. Sun's revolutionary movement, comprised largely of students, youths, and overseas Chinese, gave impetus and momentum to the revolution, it was not the force that brought down the empire. It was the new imperial army, headed by Yuan Shihkai, that forced the abdication of the emperor. Under an agreement with Dr. Sun, who had little bargaining power, Yuan Shihkai assumed the powers of government immediately after the abdication and stayed on to become the first president of the Chinese republic. The new republic floundered from the start. Very few Chinese had any real understanding of Western democracy. All Chinese political traditions and institutions were designed for imperial rule and, therefore, were ill-suited for constitutional democracy. Yuan Shihkai increasingly disregarded the constitution, and finally attempted to establish himself as emperor. The Chinese nation disintegrated as the new government proved incapable of commanding allegiance from the people in the midst of mounting domestic problems and the constant meddling in Chinese internal affairs by European powers and Japan. Yuan's death in 1916 marked the final collapse of the central government's effective authority.[17]

Warlordism, the May Fourth Movement, and the Nationalist Revolution

The disintegration of the Chinese nation led to the emergence of a warlord period, which prevailed for two decades, from 1916 to 1936. At Yuan's death some of his officers—and others with sufficient power—seized control of various regions. These territories were controlled by the warlords, who maintained private armies manned with conscripted peasants, to protect and extend their provincial domains.

Even Sun Yatsen and his followers had to seek refuge under the protection of the warlord in Canton. Dr. Sun's revolutionary program now called for the eventual establishment of constitutional government in three stages: (1) unification of the nation through elimination of warlordism by military force and termination of foreign intervention in China; (2) a period of political tutelage to prepare the people for democratic government; and (3) the enactment of a constitution by the people. Neither the European powers nor the warlords paid any attention to the disillusioned Dr. Sun, who was now desperate for a way to save China from further disintegration.

The immediate aftermath of the Revolution of 1911 was a period of utter chaos for China. Having brought down the pillars and support system for imperial rule, the revolution provided only an unworkable paper constitution, unfamiliar to and untried by the Chinese. In the midst of chaos and disintegration, there was a revival of the call by the early reformers, such as Kang Youwei and Liang Qichao, for the study of Western ideas for the purpose of building a new nation and "a new society." This was the underlying reason for the intellectual enlightenment movement called the May Fourth era, 1919–29. The movement began as a Beijing student protest against the humiliation China had suffered at the hands of the victorious Allied powers in the Versailles Treaty negotiations, the demands and pressure by the Japanese over Chinese territorial integrity, and the spread of warlords in the provinces in China. Thousands of students marched in protest on May 4, 1919, carrying banners and shouting slogans calling for national awakening and survival. The intellectuals were joined and supported by merchants and workers, not only in Beijing, but in many major cities throughout China. The themes for this intellectual enlightenment movement were nationalism, anti-imperialism, anti-warlordism, and the call for a "new society" that could embrace "democracy and science." While thousands of students were jailed, the movement nevertheless forged on to create a lasting national ferment that formed the genesis of the subsequent Nationalist and communist revolutions in China. From then on, Chinese intellectuals served as the harbingers of change. The May Fourth Movement led to reform in the written Chinese language, from the archaic classical style to use of the vernacular, or everyday spoken form. It also introduced the study of Western science, technology, and political ideologies, including Marxism. The movement was closely tied in with demonstrations by university students against foreign intervention in Chinese affairs and against warlordism. These activities gave impetus to a new nationalist and patriotic feeling emerging among the general population.

It was in this atmosphere—one of anger, humiliation, and disillusionment—that the Nationalist revolution took place. In 1922, Dr. Sun was forced to flee Canton for Shanghai in order to escape from the southern warlords. While in Shanghai, he was contacted by an agent of the Communist Third International (Comintern), who offered to assist the Chinese revolutionary movement by providing Soviet personnel. Dr. Sun accepted the offer and signed an agreement that reorganized his hitherto ineffective political party into a Chinese counterpart of the Soviet Union's communist party. Dr. Sun's party became the Nationalist Party (the Nationalists), the Guomindang, and formed an alliance with the newly formed Chinese Communist Party. Another agreement provided limited support in terms of arms and military training in the Soviet Union for members of Dr. Sun's revolutionary army. Although Dr. Sun died in 1925, a military expedition was launched in 1926 to unify China by defeating the warlords. News of the expedition both inspired the people with nationalist feelings and aroused the populace against foreign imperialism.

The expedition was launched under an uneasy all[...]
lowers, who were receiving financial backing from merc[...]
from large landowners in the countryside, and the members[...]
nist Party, controlled by the Comintern. By March 1927 the n[...]
ment was dominated by the left-wing elements of the Guomind[...]
nists with headquarters in Wuhan in central China. When the [...]
control of eastern China on its push north, Chiang Kaishek, comman[...]
lutionary armies and successor to Sun Yatsen, decided to end the i[...]
between the left and the right by first eliminating members of the Chine[...]
nist Party within the revolutionary movement. In April 1927 a lightning s[...]
sacred communists in the cities under Chiang's control. The surprise blow, kn[...]
the "Shanghai Massacre," was so effective that it practically decimated the co[...]
nist ranks. Chiang also expelled Soviet advisers from China. He then established[...]
Nationalist government in Nanjing, and this was recognized by most nations as th[...]
legitimate government of China in the 1940s. The remaining Chinese communists[...]
sought refuge in the mountainous regions in central China after 1930.

China under the Nationalists, 1927–1937

During the decade of Guomindang rule, from 1927 to 1937, modest progress was made in many areas of modernization, initiated by the Nationalists under the leadership of Chiang Kaishek and his Western-trained advisers and administrators. For the first time, China had a modern governmental structure. As soon as major provincial warlords were eliminated or co-opted into the system, the transportation and industrial facilities were improved and expanded in the area. Earnest attempts were made to expand elementary school education and to provide political indoctrination for the young. Most important from Chiang's point of view was the building of a more efficient and dedicated modern army for a host of purposes—including the eventual elimination of warlords and communist guerrillas in mountainous areas of central China, as well as protection of China's borders from foreign attack.

There were glaring negative features in the Nationalist balance sheet. First, no real efforts were made to provide progressive economic and social programs to improve the lot of the people. Land reform measures were few. Second, the regime alienated the intellectuals by its repressive measures against them in the guise of purging any elements of communist influence from their ranks. Third, enormous expenditures from the national treasury were devoted to the "extermination" of the Chinese communists operating in remote mountain regions. The Nationalists steadfastly refused to seek a nonmilitary solution to the problem of insurrection by the communists. Nor were they willing to seek consultation with other political groups, let alone share political power with other elements of society. The Guomindang's modest accomplishments in nation building were soon obliterated by its obsession with eliminating all opposition.

The Chinese Nationalist Revolution (1927–37), or the Nanjing Decade, has been analyzed by various China scholars. In one early work the revolution was labeled a tragedy.[18] Another scholar characterized it as an abortive revolution, implying that the successors to Dr. Sun's revolution had lost their "revolutionary momentum" and that the Nationalist regime had deteriorated into a "military dictatorship."[19] One China scholar has called the Nationalist Revolution "the misconceived revolution" because of its belief that by terminating warlord rule and foreign imperialism

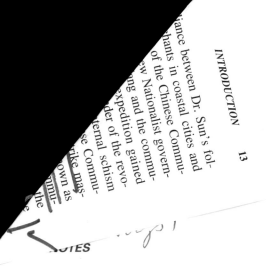

livided in accordance with "sectorial

ts. In 1931, when they had achieved
nization while waging encirclement
ces, Japanese militarists annexed
 northern China, inside the Great
in allocating its limited resources
st insurgents. In the early 1930s,
nmunist guerilla forces and then
entiment, expressed in frequent
further territorial losses to the
ioin in a united front with the
⌐apan was waging full-scale war

NOTES

1. *Hawaii Tribune-Herald* (October 4, 1981), p. 9.
2. *Beijing Review*, 31 (August 3, 1981), 4–5.
3. Shan-yu Yao, "The Chronological and Seasonal Distribution of Flood and Droughts in Chinese History, 206 B.C.–A.D. 1911," *Harvard Journal of Asiatic Studies*, 7 (1942), 275.
4. John King Fairbank, *The United States and China*, rev. ed. (New York: Viking Press, 1962), p. 48.
5. For early Chinese history the following are recommended readings: Kenneth Scott Latourette, *The Chinese: Their History and Culture*, 3rd ed. rev. (New York: Macmillan, 1946); John K. Fairbank and Edwin O. Reischauer, eds., *The Cambridge History of China*, vol. X (Cambridge, England: Cambridge University Press, 1978); Bai Shouyi, ed., *An Outline History of China* (Beijing: Foreign Language Press, 1982); and Ranbir Vohra, *China's Path to Modernization: A Historical Review From 1800 to the Present* (Englewood Cliffs, N.J.: Prentice Hall, 1987).
6. Lawrence Ziring and C. I. Eugene Kim, *The Asian Political Dictionary* (Santa Barbara, Calif.: ABC-CLIO, 1985), p. 105.
7. Charles P. Fitzgerald, *Revolution in China* (New York: Holt, Rinehart & Winston, 1952), pp. 12–16.
8. John King Fairbank, *The United States and China*, 3rd ed. (Cambridge, Mass.: Harvard University Press, 1971), pp. 90–95.
9. Fairbank, *The United States and China*, Third Edition (A Hard Paper Back, 1971), p. 55.
10. Fitzgerald, *Revolution in China*, p. 23.
11. Kung-chuan Hsiao, *Rural China: Imperial Control in the Nineteenth Century* (Seattle, Wash.: University of Washington Press, 1960), pp. 253–54.
12. Fairbank, *The United States and China*, pp. 20–34.
13. Ibid., p. 103.
14. Ibid., and James Townsend, *Politics in China* (Boston: Little, Brown, 1974), pp. 35–36.
15. Townsend, *Politics in China*, p. 37.
16. Fairbank, *The United States and China*, p. 191. Also see Sterling Seagrave, *The Soong Dynasty* (New York: Harper and Row, 1985), pp. 76–79 and 92–94.
17. Fitzgerald, *Revolution in China*, p. 38; and Fairbank, *The United States and China*, pp. 197–98.
18. Harold Robert Isaac, *Tragedy of the Chinese Revolution* (Stanford, Calif.: Stanford University Press, 1951).
19. See Lloyd E. Eastman, *The Abortive Revolution: China under Nationalist Rule, 1927–1937* (Cambridge, Mass.: Council on East Asian Studies, Harvard University Press, 1990).
20. See John Fitzgerald, ed., *The Nationalists and Chinese Society, 1923–1937: A Symposium* (Melbourne, Australia: University of Melbourne History Monographs No. 4, 1989).

chapter two

The Origin and Rise of the Chinese Communist Movement

From Military Communism to Deng's Reforms

THE EARLY YEARS

Although Marxism was introduced in China about the time of World War I, this ideology, which called for revolution by an urban proletariat under mature capitalism, elicited little attention. Fabian socialism—progressive and social change through gradual constitutional means, developed in England in 1884—became the most popular liberal ideology imported from the West. For example, Dr. Sun's program incorporated socialist planks, including nationalization of land, a welfare state, and a planned economy. Interest in Marxism suddenly flowered among Chinese intellectuals after the 1917 Bolshevik Revolution in Russia. They saw in Lenin's revolution a relevant solution to China's political and economic problems. The keen interest in Bolshevism also reflected disillusionment with Western democracy as a model for Chinese development. In addition, it expressed Chinese bitterness over the imperialist activities of the Western democracies in China.

The early Chinese Marxists and the founders of the Chinese Communist Party were leading intellectuals in the Beijing National University (Beida). In 1918 Li Dazhao, the university's head librarian, formed a Marxist study group to which many young students, including a library assistant named Mao Zedong, were attracted. These young students were more interested in learning how to make a revolution than in theorizing about Marxism. With some urging from Comintern agents, the Chinese Communist Party (CCP) was formed on July 1, 1921. The group of thirteen intellectuals and revolutionaries, representing a total of fifty-seven members, were called together by Chen Duxiu, who became the first secretary general. Meetings for the first two party congresses were held secretly in the French concession in Shanghai to prevent harassment by the police. This was the very modest beginning of the party, and of the movement that took root in later years.

The CCP, the Comintern, and the First United Front (1922–1927)

For the first six years of the CCP's existence, 1921–27, the movement was under the control and direction of the Third International, or the Comintern. The Comintern was formed in 1919 at the insistence of Lenin, who wanted a new international organization, controlled by Moscow, to provide direction for all proletariat parties and to promote anti-imperialist revolutions throughout the world. Moscow directed and controlled the CCP and its leadership through Soviet Comintern agents who came to China with financial aid and military materiel. The leadership of the CCP before 1934, with few exceptions, was in the hands of the "returned Chinese Bolsheviks," trained for party work in Moscow under the sponsorship of the Comintern.

The Comintern's doctrine insisted that revolutions in colonial areas be based on industrial workers. Its strategy called for the participation of nonproletariat elements, such as the bourgeoisie, in a united front alliance to lead national revolutions. The manifestos adopted by four consecutive CCP congresses, from 1922 to 1925, echoed the Comintern line, calling for a revolutionary alliance with the landlord-merchant-based Guomindang, Dr. Sun's Nationalist Party. This Comintern strategy, which limited the communist base to urban industrial workers and called for individual communists to join the Guomindang under a united front, enhanced the CCP's growth as a viable political party during its early years.

The first alliance or honeymoon between the Nationalists and members of the Chinese Communist Party occurred in May 1922 at the latter's Second Party Congress in the lake region of Hangchow. Realizing the growing strength and support for the Nationalists, the party congress delegates were encouraged to ally with them by Comintern agent Maring (alias Sneevliet), a Dutch communist with organizational experience in the Dutch East Indies (now Indonesia). Maring's persuasive argument was that the weak Chinese Communist Party would be able to grow if its members joined the Guomindang (the Nationalists) as individuals and then infiltrated the latter's organizational apparatus as the instrument for a socialist revolution.

The resulting First United Front, pressured by Comintern agents, created tension within the Chinese Communist organization in its relations with Stalinist Moscow. The tension was further aggravated by the rift between Stalin and Trotsky. The Chinese communists who went to Moscow for training under the auspices of the Comintern returned to China and increasingly assumed leadership of the party. They came into conflict with those Chinese communists who all along had been questioning continued alliance with the Nationalists as a possible reversal of the proletarian nature of the socialist revolutionary movement; Comintern agents assigned to China had demanded this maneuver. In fact, there were two distinct factions that surfaced at the CCP's Fifth Party Congress in April 1927. One faction, mostly Moscow-trained returnees, supported the Comintern's continued policy of cooperating with the leftist elements of the Nationalists in Wuhan in central China, with the goal of eventually seizing control of the entire Nationalist movement. The other faction, led by Mao, gradually expressed the need to introduce land reform by working with the peasants in the countryside as a basis for revolution. Confusing and contradictory instructions from the Moscow Comintern only sharpened the schism within the party. Parenthetically, it was this rift that served as the original basis for subsequent inner party struggles, purges, and rectification campaigns.

By 1927 the united front alliance had become unworkable. Chiang Kaishek's power as commander in chief and head of the Guomindang was threatened by leftist elements in control of the revolutionary government, which was supported by the communists. As pointed out earlier, Chiang decided to purge the communists from his organization and to set up a rival government in Nanjing. Not long after, the leftist-dominated Wuhan government also turned on the communists when it became known that the Comintern, acting under direct orders from Stalin, had instructed the CCP to eliminate the landlord elements and militarists in order to transform the alliance into a new revolutionary force. The result was a bloody mass execution of the communists who were caught.

Instead of admitting the mistake in his China policy, Stalin blamed the CCP leaders for their failure to prepare the workers in Wuhan for action.[1] Partly as a rebuttal to criticism raised by Leon Trotsky, Stalin ordered the Comintern agents in China to plan a series of armed insurrections. He hoped that quick victories would silence critics of his unsuccessful united front policy.[2] On August 1, 1927, now celebrated as the founding day of the People's Liberation Army, Zhou Enlai and Zhu De led a mutiny of communist troops within the Guomindang forces in Nanchang in central China. After occupying the city briefly, the communists were forced to seek refuge as guerrillas in the hills of eastern Guangdong province. The CCP also authorized a number of "Autumn Harvest Uprisings" in the fall of 1927 in central and southern China. One of these was led by Mao Zedong in his home province of Hunan. These uprisings were ill-fated misadventures that ended in defeat and brought heavy losses to the already-decimated CCP ranks. When Mao and his group sought refuge in the mountain stronghold of Jinggangshan on the Hunan–Jiangxi border in central China, he repudiated the Comintern-inspired strategy. As a reprimand, Mao briefly lost his membership on the Politburo, the executive and policy-making body of the party.

After the rupture of the united front between the CCP and the Guomindang, the Chinese communist movement fragmented into two areas of operation: one in the cities, as an underground movement, with close links to the Comintern; the other in rural areas, as experimental soviets, operating almost autonomously and feuding constantly with the Comintern advisers. By the end of 1930, the party had been driven out of the cities, and only pockets of guerrilla bands operated in remote mountain regions of central and southern China and northern Shaanxi. The plight of the CCP was evidenced by the fact that its Central Committee had to operate underground in Shanghai's foreign concessions, and the Sixth Party Congress had to meet in Moscow in 1928. The leadership of the party was still in the hands of the returned Bolsheviks, who adhered to the Comintern policies. In a last attempt to recapture an urban base for a proletarian revolution in the summer of 1930, the CCP leadership, under Li Lisan, launched an attack from rural bases with the objective of capturing a number of cities on the Changjiang (Yangtse) River. Like previous Comintern-instigated misadventures, this one also ended in failure, with the small bases in rural mountain regions under blockage by Chiang Kaishek's forces. The Chinese communists' future at this juncture seemed bleak.

The Rise of Mao Zedong, the Second United Front, and Military Communism (1936–1946)

The future of the Chinese communist movement hinged on the survival of the small pockets of experimental soviets in the remote rural areas, mostly in central and southern China. The CCP's decision, in the fall of 1931, to establish a Chinese Soviet Republic—which would unite the scattered bases—was both a political necessity and an admission that a revolution based on an urban proletariat was no longer possible in China. Thus, by 1931, when the CCP's Central Committee moved from urban Shanghai to the rural Jiangxi soviet, a decade-long quarrel within the Chinese communist movement—regarding the theoretical correctness of a revolutionary strategy based on the peasants—officially ended. The foremost proponent of a peasant base was the leader of the Jiangxi soviet, Mao Zedong. Mao had developed a strategy for victory during the six years he operated the Jiangxi guerrilla base. Besides the need for a highly disciplined united party, Mao's strategy contained three indispensable ingredients: (1) the development of a strong and mobile peasant-based Red Army for a protracted armed struggle; (2) the selection of a strategic terrain for military operations; and (3) the establishment of a self-sufficient economic base in the Red Army-controlled soviet areas to provide personnel and supplies for the armed struggle.[3] Mao believed that a highly disciplined party could only be built by a recruitment policy that would draw in the tough and dedicated guerrilla soldiers of the Red Army, who were predominantly poor peasants. The party became "militarized" as Mao began to build a new base for revolution.[4]

The Guomindang intensified its attack against the guerrilla base in its fifth and most extensive military campaign, which included an effective blockade that deprived the guerrilla base of outside supplies, particularly salt. By 1934 the guerrilla base had to be abandoned. The communists broke out of the Guomindang encirclement and moved the surviving forces, numbering not more than 150,000 westward and then north to the Great Wall. This was the legendary Long March of more than 6,000 miles over treacherous terrain of high mountains and rivers, amidst ambushes from warlords, Guomindang troops, and hostile minorities.[5] In October 1935, after almost a year's march, the greatly reduced forces of about 20,000 survivors arrived in Yanan in the northwestern province of Shaanxi and established a new base for guerrilla operations. By this time, the stormy Politburo meeting—held at Zunyi in southwest Guizhou Province in January 1935—had selected Mao as the undisputed leader of the CCP, including the cells operating mainly in industrial centers such as Shanghai and Wuhan. This marked the end of Comintern dominance and the beginning of Mao's supremacy as the CCP's political and military leader. This supremacy lasted until his death in 1976, forty years later.

Expansion of Communism under Mao and Final Victory

When Chiang Kaishek learned that the communists had established a base in Yanan, he sent his crack troops to Shaanxi. The Guomindang force included soldiers who had been driven from Manchuria by the Japanese army in 1931. The Manchurian troops showed signs of low morale and a reluctance to fight the communists. This was largely due to effective political propaganda by the communists, which stressed the urgent need for a united front against Japan. In an effort to step up the offensive, Chiang Kaishek went to Xian in Shaanxi to direct the campaign personally. The mutinous Manchurian troops seized Chiang as a hostage in order to force him to agree to a united front policy. The Chinese communists by then had established contact with the Manchurian troops. Both Mao Zedong and Zhou Enlai served as mediators for the release of Chiang Kaishek under an agreement for a united front to fight the Japanese. This was the Xian Agreement, which temporarily terminated the civil war and marked the beginning of a second alliance between the CCP and the Guomindang.

The 1936 Xian Agreement between the CCP and the Guomindang (Nationalists) was not finally implemented until July 1937. Under the terms of the agreement, the CCP was to terminate its policy of armed insurrection against the Guomindang government in Nanking; this in effect terminated, officially at least, the state of civil war. The Chinese communist forces were to be "integrated" into the Nationalist military setup—although in practice they never adhered to the Guomindang jurisdiction, except that the official designation of the Red Army became the Eighth Route Army. And Mao promised not to continue his land confiscation policy in rural areas. In effect, both sides were very distrustful of each other's motives and intentions.

When Japan attacked northern China in the summer of 1937, the Red Army was slowly brought into action under the united front agreement. The cessation of the civil war gave the CCP the needed respite to expand its base of operations and to strengthen its military forces for the eventual showdown with the Guomindang.[6] As China suffered repeated military defeats by the Japanese, the CCP-controlled Red Army expanded its guerrilla operations behind enemy lines. Party membership grew rapidly, from a little over 20,000 at the end of the Long March in 1935, to over 800,000 in 1939, and to about 1.2 million at the end of the war in 1945. Of this enlarged party membership, perhaps a million were party members of the "military supply system," peasants and patriotic students who served the Red Army without salary but under strict military discipline.[7] They were the backbone of the leadership, not only for the communist guerrilla forces but also for the militarized border-region governments established in the areas under Red Army control. In each of these border regions, experiments in mild land reform and self-government by popular election were introduced. It was during this period that many of the practices and experiences became revolutionary traditions that persist today under the overall label "Yanan spirit."

When the Japanese surrendered in 1945, open clashes occurred between the Guomindang and the communist forces in many parts of China. China was once again engulfed in civil war, but this time the communists were in a much stronger position in terms of discipline, numerical strength, and the will to combat—not to mention having the support of the intellectuals and a large segment of the rural population. The policy of President Truman of the United States was to bring the parties together for a political settlement. A series of cease-fire agreements were reached under American supervision. The mediation efforts by General Marshall for the United States soon deteriorated. Neither side had any intention of observing the truce and settling the future of China by political means. As the strength and morale of the Guomindang forces ebbed, the People's Liberation Army won victories over the Nationalist troops equipped and supplied by the United States. By the summer and fall of 1948, The People's Liberation Army had overrun Manchuria and most of northern China. Guomindang forces were surrendering in divisional strength. With captured American military hardware, a large-scale military offensive was launched by the communists in the spring of 1949 against the remaining Guomindang forces in central and southern China. Although the Nationalists did not flee to the island of Taiwan until December 1949, the communists convened the People's Political Consultative Conference on October 1, to establish a new People's Republic of China in Beijing. At last the Chinese communist movement, which had begun as a Marxist study group, had seized power in China. A new search now began to find a suitable model to follow in building an industrially powerful China.

CHINA'S SEARCH FOR A DEVELOPMENT MODEL

After almost eight years of war with Japan and four years of civil war, the initial years of the new republic were preoccupied with the immediate problems of consolidation and reconstruction. In the beginning, the CCP formed a coalition government, applying the tenets first formulated by Mao Zedong in his "New Democracy" (1940) and "On Coalition Government" (1945).[8] In this pragmatic way, twenty-three other political groups were permitted a partial share of political authority. The central government in Beijing proliferated with ministries on economic affairs. More than 55 percent of the top national administrative posts were reserved for leaders of the CCP; the remainder were distributed among experienced and talented liberal noncommunist intellectuals. During these early years, the new regime also relied heavily on the regional pattern of government to superintend the provinces. The regional government was, in turn, bolstered by the military field armies that had conquered and had remained in these regions after the civil war.

The enormous task of reconstruction called first of all for a solution to the problem of mounting inflation. During the last few months of the Nationalist regime, prices had risen 85,000 percent.[9] Inflation abated somewhat when the new regime came to power, but with huge budget deficits from increased governmental expenditures, it still remained a serious problem. By a variety of fiscal and monetary devices, including the central control of local taxes, and the measuring of prices and wages in terms of commodity units, prices were finally stabilized by the summer of 1950.

Private industry and commerce, while restricted, were rehabilitated and developed along with the socialistic national economy. National ministries of economic production saw to it that the privately owned industries obtained needed raw materials to make their products, and that they received orders from private or state-owned enterprises for these goods and services. Rapid economic recovery was made, and by 1952 production had reached China's peak pre-1949 levels. This rapid recovery was attributable to the policy of gradualism in nationalization, with no outright confiscation of private industry. Privately owned industries were eventually transformed into joint state and private enterprises and finally into completely state-owned operations through the "buying-off" policy, under which former owners of private enterprises were paid interest on their shares at a rate fixed by the state.[10]

Land Reform: Transformation of the Countryside

The most important program enacted by the new regime from 1950 to 1953 was agrarian reform. Land redistribution, a basic plank in the CCP program, had been carried out in the early soviet phase in the Jiangxi border areas, and later in the northwest, with varying degrees of intensity. In 1949, when the CCP took over the country, some 500 million people were living in the rural villages. The land tenure system was such that "half the cultivated land was owned by less than one-tenth of the farm population, while two-thirds of the population owned less than one-fifth."[11] This serious problem of uneven land distribution was further aggravated by the large number of landless tenants who had to pay exorbitant annual rents, as high as 60 percent of their production. The 1950 Agrarian Reform Law was basically a mild reform measure that permitted rich peasants to retain their land and property (Article 6), and landlords to retain the land for their own use (Article 10). The later harsh treatment of landlords, which accompanied the implementation of land redistribution through the "struggle meetings" and the "people's tribunals" to settle accounts by the peasants, was attributable to the speedy implementation needed to prevent "foot dragging" by cadres and activists assigned to do the job and by the peasants themselves.[12] The Korean War also generated some fear on the part of the peasants of the possible return of the Nationalists.[13] Land redistribution was completed in 1952, when 113 million acres—plus draft animals and farm implements—were distributed to over 300 million landless peasants.[14]

It soon became obvious that land redistribution was only a step toward collectivizing the countryside. The millions of new landowning peasants realized very quickly that their small plots of land were too small to produce enough even to feed their own families. The individual peasants simply did not have the means to acquire modern tools, much less to build irrigation projects. Having committed themselves to the party's cause by participating in land redistribution, the peasants had to accept the party's new appeal for mutual aid teams and for the pooling together of draft animals, implements, and shared labor. In 1953–54, the mutual aid teams gave way to larger and more complicated cooperative ventures—the mandatory agricultural producers' cooperatives (APCs). An agricultural producers' cooperative was, in essence, a unified management system of farm production. The individual peasants pooled their land, draft animals, implements, and houses in return for shares in the enterprise. Detailed accounting was kept, and after deductions were made for expenses incurred and taxes to be paid, income was distributed to the members on the basis of their contributions, stated in terms of shares. While the movement was voluntary, the party conducted massive campaigns to persuade and sometimes to coerce peasants to join the APCs. Although an overwhelming majority of the peasants had joined the cooperatives by 1957, official accounts showed resistance to the program. In some parts of the country, peasants deliberately consumed what they produced to avoid forced delivery to government purchasing agencies.[15]

The APCs enabled the peasants to better utilize resources and labor. During the slack seasons, surplus labor could be mobilized easily to carry on small-scale irrigation works, such as making ditches, ponds, and dams. Combined surplus labor could reclaim land through irrigation and reforestation. The APCs certainly allowed the peasants to realize greater savings and investment. Even more important was the sharing of the risks of crop failure. Individual peasants no longer had to face the possibility of bankruptcy if crops failed. But there were also many problems inherent in the APCs: many peasants were too poor to contribute funds to the cooperatives; there was a lack of qualified technical personnel such as accountants among the illiterate peasantry to provide efficient management; and peasants were frequently unhappy when centralized purchasing and marketing operations were imposed on the cooperatives by the state, leading to intensified animosity toward the party, and a reluctance to cooperate.[16]

The First Five-Year Plan (1953–1957) and the Soviet Model

By 1953 the regime had completed the immediate tasks of rehabilitating the war-torn economy and consolidating its control over the nation. With the end of the Korean War, the regime was confident enough to embark on a rapid industrialization program. The approach selected was the Stalinist strategy of long-term centralized planning, a proven socialistic model that had enabled the Soviet Union to emerge from World War II as the second most powerful nation in the world. For ideological reasons it was the only logical strategy comprehensible to the Chinese communists at the time, particularly in view of the emerging bipolarization of the world into Soviet and Western orbits. The pragmatic Chinese were aware of the benefits of Soviet aid, in terms of both financial credit and technical assistance, which would be forthcoming to promote this model.[17]

Fundamental to the Stalinist model was the rapid buildup in the heavy industry sector through the concentrated allocation of investment into capital goods industries. The model also called for highly centralized decision making at the top to determine targets and quotas to be fulfilled by the various economic sectors.[18] In many ways, this strategy required basic structural change in the agricultural sector, from which the bulk of savings for investment must come. The introduction of agricultural producers' cooperatives was needed in order to accumulate savings through increased agricultural production and controlled consumption. The First Five-Year Plan allocated 58 percent of the 20-billion-dollar investment fund to capital goods for heavy industries.[19] The bulk of these investment funds was financed by the Chinese themselves. The Soviet Union made considerable contributions in the form of technical assistance, construction, and equipment for 154 modern industrial plants that were paid for by the Chinese, and the training of Chinese technicians. In June 1960, when Soviet-trained Chinese technicians numbered about 10,000, Soviet aid was suddenly withdrawn. By 1957, when the First Five-Year Plan was completed, an annual growth rate of 8 percent had been added to China's economic growth,[20] an impressive achievement by any standard. In addition, the First Five-Year Plan made a lasting investment in education (130,000 engineers graduated) and public health (control of such communicable diseases as cholera and typhus, which formerly had plagued the Chinese people).[21]

The First Five-Year Plan had a number of drawbacks, however. First, the plan was rather costly when one considers that the bulk of the 20 million dollars in investments came from the Chinese. Second, the plan required large forced savings from the agricultural sector. Third, the Stalinist model placed undue concentration of investment in such heavy industries as steel, at the expense, not only of agriculture, but also of light and consumer goods industries. Fourth, the model required a high degree of centralization and the development of an elaborate bureaucratic structure to implement, control, and monitor the plan according to fixed targets and quotas. Fifth, since planning and implementation of the model emphasized the roles of technocrats, engineers, and plant managers, it thus neglected the need to involve politically the millions of uneducated and tradition-oriented peasants in the rapid construction of an industrial socialistic state. After an agonizing reappraisal of the First Five-Year Plan,

Mao and his followers launched the Great Leap F<
faster rate of growth and to develop a socialist eco<
na's conditions and needs.

The Great Leap Forward and Communizati<

Under the Great Leap Forward, the regime r
of the Chinese masses for economic growth and in
had mobilized them for the communist revolution.[2]
China's most plentiful resource, manpower, for capital goods, in the same way it had
successfully substituted committed men for modern weapons during the guerrilla and
civil war days. The unemployed were to be put to work, and the employed were to
work much harder, under military discipline, so that China could make the gigantic
leap required to become an industrial power through the widespread use of labor-
intensive, small-scale production. The emphasis was placed on the techniques of
mass mobilization.

The program called for use of "dual technology." The Chinese economy at the
end of the First Five-Year Plan consisted of a mixture of modern sectors (capital-
intensive and large-scale) and traditional sectors (labor-intensive and small-scale).
These two types of economic sectors in a typical developing country (like China) are
more or less independent of each other. In the modern sectors, goods produced are
mostly exported to earn foreign exchange to pay for the imported machines. In the
traditional sectors, small-scale industries in villages are self-sufficient, providing virtually all their own consumption and production needs. Under the Great Leap strategy, the modern sector would not need to supply capital goods for the traditional sector, but the traditional sector would increase its flow of food and raw materials to
build up the industrial sector. This was the meaning of the Chinese slogans so familiar during the Great Leap period: "walking on two legs" and "self-reliance in the
simultaneous development of industry and agriculture." Land was to be reclaimed,
and irrigation systems were to be built by the peasants, using simple tools at their
disposal. Rural communities were to build "backyard furnaces" to produce enough
pig iron to allow China to surpass Great Britain in steel production. Other popular
small-scale projects were electric power generators and chemical fertilizer plants.

Conceptually, the Great Leap model was not only rational but had some economic validity.[23] However, there were unrealistic expectations and an overzealous
implementation of the program. In an effort to fulfill the required quotas, workers
often sacrificed quality for quantity. Quality also suffered from the lack of technical
knowledge among the peasants. Some statistics on increased production were based
on exaggeration and fabrication. Millions of tons of pig iron, much substandard and
all a long way from being steel, were produced by backyard furnaces. Pig iron accumulated along railways, which could not possibly handle its movement, causing a
serious bottleneck in the entire transport system.[24]

The merging of cooperatives into people's communes was an integral part of
the Great Leap program. The communes were, in essence, devices to collectivize
agricultural production on a scale much larger than that of the cooperatives. Unlike
the APC, the commune became a local government, performing a multiplicity of
functions in agriculture, industry, education, social welfare, public health, public
works, and military defense. The peasants turned over to the collective entity their

nd, tools, draft animals, houses, and shares in the cooperatives. They members of a commune, of which they claimed collective ownership. hey were to receive five guarantees: food, clothing, housing, medical care, cation. During the early stage of commune development (1958), communal ens were installed to free more women for production. In some extreme cases, n and women lived in segregated communal dormitories, with their children in communal nurseries. The people's communes were hailed with great fanfare as the ideal collective life described by classical Marxism: "From each according to his abilities, to each according to his needs."

By the spring of 1959, there were 26,000 communes. Although there was no uniform size, an average commune consisted of about 2,000 households, or about 10,000 peasants. Within each commune, peasants were organized into production brigades and production teams, the basic unit of the commune. This radical experiment encountered a host of problems. For instance, the peasants could not adjust to communal kitchens and dormitories. The demands imposed by the cadres—those selected for leadership positions—for long hours of work at a feverish pace, sapped the peasants' energy and enthusiasm. Without their tiny private plots to grow vegetables to supplement their meager diet, the peasants' general health declined. Initially, the peasants were neither willing nor able to make decisions under the commune setup, which required their participation. Their inexperience in the management of complex production activities also made them reluctant to assume responsibilities. In 1959 some corrective measures were implemented: Private garden plots were permitted, forced communal living was halted, and commune members were given adequate time for rest and recreation.

The numerous problems implicit in the Great Leap and communization, accompanied by the natural disasters of flood and drought, should have doomed the program. In 1958, when the Great Leap and commune programs were launched, there was a good harvest. In 1959 heavy floods and drought laid waste almost half the cultivable land. Then, in 1960, floods, drought, and pests ravaged millions of acres. To make matters worse, the Soviets withdrew all their technicians and advisers from China in June 1960 because of a disagreement over development strategy. The drastic reduction in agricultural production stalled the drive for rapid development of industry. Famine occurred and rationing was imposed in the communes. There were large purchases of grain from abroad. China's experience was typical of an agricultural setback in developing nations: Scarce foreign exchange had to be diverted from capital goods to food imports. A new policy had to be adopted to give first priority to a minimally sufficient food supply rather than to industrialization.

Post-Great Leap: Leadership Dissension and Economic Recovery

The failure of the Great Leap brought to a head growing division within the Chinese leadership, not only over development strategy but also over the ideological implications of the strategy. This division is frequently referred to as the "red" (politics) versus "expert" (technology) controversy. Mao later made a self-criticism for the errors committed in the Great Leap. Mao's most outspoken critic was Marshal Peng Dehuai, the defense minister and a Politburo member.[25] Peng's criticism focused on three effects of the Great Leap: (1) the damage to the long-term economic development of China, which must rely on technical proficiency rather than on sheer mobilization of the masses; (2) rejection of the Soviet development model, which caused a deterioration in Sino–Soviet relations; and (3) the obvious decline in morale and efficiency he had observed in his inspection of the armed forces. Marshal Peng's central concern seemed to be that China needed a modern army, which must rest on the development of heavy industries and technical skills to produce and operate advanced weapons, including nuclear weapons. Peng delivered his criticisms at an enlarged meeting at the Politburo in Lushan in July and August of 1959. Red Guard pamphlets, circulated later during the Cultural Revolution, revealed that Mao admitted some mistakes in the implementation of the Great Leap; but in the main, he vigorously defended his role and the policies associated with the program. He demanded a showdown at a subsequent enlarged meeting of the Central Committee, and won. After these Lushan meetings, Marshal Peng was purged. Mao later was criticized for the purge of Peng. As planned before the Lushan meetings, Mao stepped down as the president of the People's Republic and handed the powerful position over to Liu Shaoqi, a leading party theoretician and an able administrator.[26]

The policies initiated by Liu Shaoqi reversed and corrected the Great Leap programs. It should be noted that before Liu assumed office, the Central Committee and its Politburo, in close consultation with the party's provincial secretaries, had already made a number of recommendations to correct the mistakes of the Great Leap. Some of these measures are given here as background to the policy dissension that came into full bloom during the Cultural Revolution. First, Liu called for a reintroduction of material incentives, such as private plots and free markets, to spur agricultural production. Second, he issued directives to those who managed state enterprises to pay strict attention to profits and losses: all enterprises must be managed and evaluated in terms of efficiency. Third, Liu insisted that technical "expertise" must command ideological "redness": managers must have more authority in their plants than the ideologues. Fourth, he declared a relaxation of centralized planning by giving local units more freedom in setting their production quotas and targets. Fifth, he demanded that basic-level cadres observe strict discipline and report accurate statistics. Sixth, Liu introduced measures to reorganize the party by placing more emphasis on party discipline and institutional control mechanisms; these measures helped him consolidate his power and place his supporters in key positions.

The economic recovery soon took shape under Liu Shaoqi's direction.[27] Agricultural development was now the top economic priority. With the introduction of material incentives and a good harvest in 1962, economic conditions improved in the countryside. With hard work and an end to constant ideological and political interference, many of the industrial projects were completed and new ones were initiated, despite the withdrawal of Soviet technical assistance. The new economic policy continued to encourage the development of medium- and small-sized industries in the countryside, such as farm equipment factories and rural electrification plants. In order to reduce China's dependence on Soviet imports, self-reliance was stressed by encouraging technological innovation and exploration for such new resources as petroleum, found in Daqing. By 1964 Premier Zhou Enlai announced that the recovery was complete, and a Third Five-Year Plan was ready for implementation in 1966. The Chinese had learned that with some realistic adjustment to suit Chinese conditions, a centralized, planned economy, based on the Stalinist model, worked for China.

The Socialist Education Campaign, 1962–1965

The Socialist Education Campaign was the prelude to the Cultural Revolution.[28] It was a campaign of ideological education and of rectification of cadre behavior (which requires honest, hard-working leadership qualities). The main theme of the campaign was class struggle, a theme for which Mao fought hard when he resumed an active political role in the party at the tenth session of the Eighth Central Committee in 1962. Mao and other top leaders had become alarmed at reports of widespread corruption among the rural cadres. They feared that the free markets and private vegetable plots were fostering the growth of economic individualism, which posed a serious threat to the collective economy. The Socialist Education Movement consisted of three interrelated mass campaigns: (1) an educational campaign to assist the formation of poor and lower-middle-class peasant associations in order to prevent the rise of a class of well-to-do middle-class peasants; (2) a rectification campaign aimed at eliminating the corrupt practices of rural cadres, such as embezzlement, large wedding parties, and misuse of public property; and (3) a purification movement for the nation—with the People's Liberation Army (PLA) heroes as models—which stressed the virtues of self-sacrifice, the collective good, and endurance of hardship.

There was a great deal of controversy with respect to the directives and guidelines issued by the Central Committee. Mao's original instructions, the "earlier ten points," were altered by the Central Secretariat on instructions from Liu Shaoqi and Deng Xiaoping, who were then responsible for the day-to-day operation of the party. There were debates and quarrels among the top leaders, primarily between Mao and Liu, on methods of investigating corrupt cadres in rural communes.[29] Mao advocated open investigation in the communes by work teams of top cadres from the center; Liu wanted in-depth investigation by covert infiltration among the peasants, both to gather true information and to ferret out the corrupt cadres.[30] There was also divergence between Mao and Liu in terms of the role of the party and its leaders in the Socialist Education Movement. Mao intended it to be a mass education movement. Liu wanted a party-controlled rectification operation, with emphasis on corrective and remedial measures, in accordance with established norms within the party organization.

The entire Socialist Education Movement was carried out under a cloud of uncertainty and contradictory instructions. The local cadres, most of them recruited after land reform in the early 1950s, had developed strategies for survival; they knew how to play the game and how to protect themselves against outside investigations by work teams dispatched from far-away Beijing or from provincial capitals. If necessary, these bureaucratized cadres would withhold information or intimidate poor peasants. By 1965 most of the Socialist Education Movement had ended in failure, mainly because of disagreements over its implementation.

Only the campaign to emulate PLA heroes was a success. It began in the military, where the soldiers were required to form small groups to systematically study Mao's writings, particularly three essays on self-sacrifice and self-negation, written for the cadres during the Yanan days. Exemplary PLA companies were formed to demonstrate their living application of the thought of Mao. This ideological education campaign within the PLA was personally supervised by the new defense minister, Lin Biao. With the campaign's success in the military, a nationwide movement to emulate the PLA was launched.

The battle lines for the Cultural Revolution were now clearly drawn. Although the party apparatus under Liu Shaoqi and Deng Xiaoping had shown its disdain for Mao's mass mobilization approach (seeing it as disruptive to the routine operation of the party and government), the PLA, under Lin Biao, had not only embraced Mao's style but applied Mao's teachings to their activities. Mao now saw that the cadres who monopolized the party apparatus, and the career-oriented status seekers, had become resistant to change and were reluctant to accept the new socialist values. The party could no longer be considered an effective instrument for the revolutionary change Mao so desired.

THE CULTURAL REVOLUTION

Before describing the events of the Cultural Revolution, let us look briefly at some of the issues underlying this great upheaval. If we survey the voluminous literature about the Cultural Revolution, we find several basic themes that serve to explain the causes of the upheaval.[31] One popular view depicted the Cultural Revolution as an "ideological crusade" aimed at preventing gradual erosion of the revolutionary spirit fostered by the early guerrilla experience of reliance on the masses and egalitarianism. Closely related to this was the idea that a thorough rectification campaign had to be waged in order to halt further growth of bureaucratic tendencies within the party and government. Another approach contended that as the regime moved toward further development, its leaders inevitably would reach a point where resolution of policy differences regarding strategy and priority would become more difficult. Prolonged dissension among the top leadership generally resulted in a power struggle between contending groups, with each jockeying for position and eventual vindication of its views. Thus, policy differences and power struggles among a divided leadership became intertwined. In addition, the contest for power among the top leadership in China probably was intensified by the question of who would succeed Mao as leader of the party.

There is some evidence that the launching of the Cultural Revolution coincided with the deterioration of Sino–Soviet relations and the escalation of the Vietnam War by the United States. Some scholars contend that the Soviet Union's offer to China in 1965 of a joint action to counteract the United States' escalation in Vietnam served as the catalyst that triggered the policy debate among China's top leaders.[32]

Events of the Cultural Revolution

The Cultural Revolution was officially launched on August 8, 1966, when the eleventh session of the Eighth Central Committee approved a sixteen-point guideline for conducting a thorough revolution. The revolution was to be concerned not only with the economic base (the socialist collectivized economy) but also with the superstructures (education, the arts, literature, and institutional arrangements).

Some nine or ten months before the Central Committee approved the guidelines, the battle had actually begun with a controversy over the political implications of a play by a historian and playwright, Wu Han. Wu Han, who was also deputy mayor of Beijing, and his superior, Peng Zhen, mayor of Beijing and a member of the Politburo, were politically allied with Liu Shaoqi. The play, *Hai Rui's Dismissal from Office*, was a historical allegory about a Ming official's final vindication after dismissal from office. Mao and his supporters charged that the purpose of the play was to vindicate Marshal Peng Dehuai, who had been purged for his 1959 criticism of Mao and the Great Leap program. When a lengthy critique of the play by Yao Wenyuan, a radical writer from Shanghai and a supporter of Mao, was refused publication in the party press, Lin Biao had it published in the PLA paper, the *Liberation Army Daily*. This action forced publication in the leading party paper, the *People's Daily*, for nationwide circulation. At first the party leaders refused to admit the political implications of the play, saying it was a purely academic matter. After Mao's supporters intensified their attack, Liu Shaoqi and Peng Zhen appointed a team to investigate the matter. The team's final report, known as the "February Outline Report," written under the direct supervision of Peng Zhen and subsequently approved by the Politburo under the acting leadership of Liu Shaoqi, called for toleration of ideas within the party, less stress on the class struggle in academic and literary fields, and a rectification campaign against the radical left. Mao rebuked the "February Report" and asked for mass criticism of art and literature.

The literary debate was followed by mass criticism, which led to purges of top party and military leaders. The purged party leaders included Beijing municipal party committee members Peng Zhen and Wu Han. General Lo Ruiqing, the chief of staff for the PLA, was also purged because of his advocacy of military professionalism and his reluctance to implement the Socialist Education Movement in the army. The attack then spread to the party committees in China's two leading universities, Beida and Qinghua. The university students organized themselves as Red Guards, Mao's "revolutionary successors."[33]

Some high school and university students throughout China formed their own Red Guard groups to investigate cadres' behavior and attitudes.[34] This gave the students an opportunity not only to air their grievances against school officials and teachers but also to vent their frustrations with the system's inability to absorb the large number of graduating youths into appropriate jobs and to provide advancement opportunities.[35] By the autumn of 1966, the Red Guard movement had grown to such proportions that normal schooling had to be abandoned. Mass criticism, led by Red Guards against the party leaders and their apparatus, became an everyday occurrence. Party leaders were dragged out into the street for failing to provide the answers the students wanted to hear. To counter the roaming Red Guards organized by university students, party leaders in many localities formed their own Red Guards. This was a period of chaos and violence as factional Red Guard groups feuded endlessly with each other. All functions of the party and some activities of government came to a standstill. The only organization that was intact was the military. The Red Guard movement was supported by the radical leaders loyal to Mao and was fueled by access to confidential information about the leaders and their policy differences. From this movement the tabloid Red Guard wall posters became a major source of insight for the outside world into the policy debates. The Central Committee and its secretariat had by now ceased to function. In its place a Central Cultural Revolution Group—dominated by the radicals, with shifting membership—now served as the party's most authoritative spokespersons, with direct lines of communication to Mao.[36]

To outside observers, China in January and February 1967 was a gigantic spectacle of big-character posters, slogans, and endless processions and meetings in a sea of banners and portraits of Mao. Factionalized Red Guard groups openly employed physical force in their frequent skirmishes against each other all over China after the party machinery had been effectively paralyzed. The established party authorities, in some cases with the active support of the local PLA commands, mounted a counterattack against the radical Red Guards, which resulted in more bloodshed. The chaos and violence reached such alarming proportions that the only remaining alternative was to call in the military to restore order and to prevent any more violence. The PLA was ordered by Mao to intervene in this domestic turmoil in January 1967. The main tasks of the military were to fill the power vacuum created by the dismantled party and government organizations in the provinces, to supervise economic production, and to prevent violence by the rampaging Red Guards. The PLA was also to provide ideological training in universities and schools and thereby to exercise control over the students after their return to campus. Military control commissions, a device that had been employed for control and consolidation of the country in the early 1950s, reappeared in order to provide supervision and control in industries and many other institutions of the party and government. By the end of 1967, the military effectively controlled China and began rather uneasily to govern.[37]

Once in control, the military intervened in provincial politics to establish provincial revolutionary committees—a new power structure to temporarily replace the provincial party committees. The provincial revolutionary committees were made up of representatives of the PLA commands, the Red Guards as a mass organization, and the repentant veteran cadres—the "three-way alliance." With the inception of the revolutionary committees, the military became the real power. The success of the revolutionary committees was dependent upon the PLA's active intervention on behalf of Mao's supporters in Beijing. Order was gradually restored in the provinces as new revolutionary committees were formed to operate as party committees, purged and cleansed of "revisionist" tendencies, at least for the moment.

The Ninth Party Congress in Beijing in April 1969 declared the end of the Cultural Revolution and the reestablishment of the party structure. The party congress, dominated by Lin Biao and his military supporters, sanctioned "a revolutionary seizure of power," as described by Edgar Snow.[38] Unity, proclaimed by Lin Biao, was the major, but short-lived, theme of the Ninth Party Congress.

Effects of the Cultural Revolution

Although the effects of the Cultural Revolution on the Chinese political system will be discussed in later chapters, it may be helpful to outline here some of the long-term effects the upheaval had on the Chinese political scene.

One direct and far-reaching effect of the Cultural Revolution was the change it brought about in the relationship between the power center in Beijing and the provinces. Beginning in 1969 there was a steady increase in the representation of the provinces at the central decision-making level, as evidenced by the number of provincial party secretaries elected to the party's Central Committee (see Table 7.1 in Chapter 7). Second, the political prominence of the military at both the central and provincial levels was more apparent during and immediately after the Cultural Revolution. The increased involvement of provincial and military authorities in decision making, both at the center and in the provinces, benefited the more pragmatic veteran administrators (who had been allies of the regional and provincial military powers) in their conflict with the more radicalized party ideologues. This rise in political influence by the provincial leaders, many of whom had their power base in the military establishment, certainly must be attributed to the military intervention in the Cultural Revolution.[39] Third, the greatest impact of the Cultural Revolution was on education.[40] As we shall see in later chapters, not only were curriculum content and teaching methods reorganized, but educational opportunities were opened up for those of rural, nonelite background. However, abolition of the examination system for university entrance and for measuring competence at the higher educational levels contributed to low academic quality in students and, in the long run, impeded the country's advanced scientific and technological development and research. Fourth, the Cultural Revolution's stress on decentralization in decision making and on mass participation in economic development programs called attention to the evils of bureaucratization, so common in all planned economic systems. To some analysts, participation in economic decision making contributed both to more institutional responsiveness and to more institutional accountability to the masses.[41]

What final assessment can one make regarding the Cultural Revolution? In its official evaluation in 1981, the Chinese Communist Party admitted that the launching of the upheaval[42] by Mao was a serious mistake, in that it was responsible for "the most severe setback" and "the heaviest losses suffered by the party.[43] Party general secretary Hu Yaobang called the decade between 1966 and 1976 an economic, cultural, and educational "catastrophe" for China.[44] Perhaps the gravest indictment that can be leveled against the Cultural Revolution is that great human suffering was caused by the radicals' witch-hunting escapades and the breakdown of regular party authority.[45] Prior to the trial of the "Gang of Four," the Chinese media published reports of one episode after another of the maltreatment and persecution of cadres and intellectuals.

No one knows exactly how many party members and intellectuals were persecuted and tortured by the Red Guards and radicals. In many cases it was sufficient merely for the accused to be labeled "rightist" or "counterrevolutionary." The denounced and their relatives were subjected to beatings, imprisonment, loss of jobs, and banishment to rural areas to do menial labor. During the 1981 trial of the Gang of Four, it was revealed that 729,511 people had been persecuted, including a number of high-ranking party and state officials. Of that group, about 34,000 died.[46] Other official figures indicated that political persecution was even more widespread. In 1978 more than 300,000 victims of false accusations and persecution were rehabilitated and exonerated.[47] In 1980 some 13,000 overseas Chinese were found to have been wrongly accused of "crimes against the state."[48] At the same time, Deng Xiaoping was personally convinced that as many as 2.9 million people had been victims of persecution during the decade of the Cultural Revolution.[49]

There seems to be no question that the Cultural Revolution was not only a gross policy error in the name of ideological purity but was also a dark page in the CCP's history. In his interview with Oriana Fallaci, Deng Xiaoping emphasized that it actually had been a civil war that decimated the ranks of the experienced veteran cadres.[50] Further, a large percentage of China's intellectuals—educators, scholars, teachers, and scientists—were uprooted from their institutions, with their talents wasted in menial work in the countryside. Finally, the Cultural Revolution failed to produce any long-term fundamental institutional changes. Most of the institutional changes actually accomplished were either abandoned or have undergone drastic alterations.

THE "GANG OF FOUR" AND THE TRIAL[51]

The top radical leaders, later known as the "Gang of Four," included Jiang Qing, Zhang Chunqiao, Yao Wenyuan, and Wang Hongwen. Jiang Qing, Mao's wife, had been a member of the Central Committee's Cultural Revolution Group, which directed the Red Guards and the upheaval, and a vice-chairperson of the Cultural Revolution Committee in the PLA under Lin Biao. Zhang Chunqiao and Yao Wenyuan were active in the Shanghai Municipal Party Committee and had used Shanghai as a base for Mao's counterattacks against Liu Shaoqi's forces during the Cultural Revolution. It was Yao who wrote the first critique of the play *Hai Rui's Dismissal from Office*, which served as the first salvo against Liu Shaoqi at the beginning of the Cultural Revolution. Both Yao and Zhang, along with Jiang Qing, subsequently became key members of the Central Committee's Cultural Revolution Group. Wang Hongwen was a young leader of the Shanghai Congress of Revolutionary Workers Rebels, a workers' group that supported the radical activities in Shanghai during the Cultural Revolution.

The radicals were a minority group within the party and advocated continuous class struggle under the dictatorship of the proletariat. Their greatest strength came from activists and young university students. As a group, the radicals had little institutional support within the society. Their survival after the Cultural Revolution was dependent upon two factors: personal support from Chairman Mao, and their fragile alliances, first with Lin Biao and then with Zhou Enlai's forces. The fact that they served as Mao's spokespersons on ideological matters during and after the Cultural Revolution gave the radicals an aura of strength. While Mao remained mentally alert, few dared to oppose his views openly for fear of incurring his wrath. The radicals' control over the mass media and over the fields of art, literature, and drama added to their strength. Hua Guofeng later charged that they had "spread a host of revisionist fallacies" and that "metaphysics" ran wild and "idealism went rampant." The radicals' base of operation was limited to a few urban centers, primarily the municipalities under the direct administration of the central government: Beijing, Shanghai, and Tianjin. Their activities were mainly concentrated in the trade union federations in these cities.

Realizing their weakness in case of a showdown, the radicals helped build an urban militia in an attempt to secure a countervailing force to the PLA. The urban militia, which was organized and controlled by the various trade union federations and municipal party committees allied with the radicals, appeared to be a potentially powerful political instrument for the radical elements within the party.[52]

During and after the Cultural Revolution, the top radical leaders acquired influence and position in the party. The Ninth Party Congress in 1969 elected all four radical leaders members of the Central Committee. Zhang Chunqiao, as first secretary of the party's Shanghai Municipal Committee, was also elected to the Politburo. With the demise of Lin Biao, the four leaders were elected to the Politburo of the Tenth Central Committee in August 1973. In addition, Wang was said to have been Mao's personal choice for vice-chairman of the party, the post previously held by Lin Biao.

When the much-delayed Fourth National People's Congress, China's equivalent to parliament, convened in January 1975, it presented an appearance of surface unity. However, behind the scenes, the radicals, led by Jiang Qing, jockeyed for power against the moderates, who supported Premier Zhou Enlai. At first Zhou made some compromises with the radicals. Zhang Chunqiao was made a vice-premier and a director of the PLA's General Political Department, responsible for the political and ideological education of the troops. But at Zhou's insistence, Deng Xiaoping was brought back and rehabilitated as a vice-premier and as the chief of staff for the PLA. Deng, considered a chief villain by the radicals, had been purged along with Liu Shaoqi during the Cultural Revolution. Zhou, in failing health, wanted Deng, who was a capable and trusted colleague, to provide the needed leadership and experience in the central government.

The Fourth National People's Congress was dominated by Zhou and his party and government veterans. Zhou made it clear at the session that in order to speed up development and modernization of the economy, it was necessary to make changes, including implementing wage differentials to spur production, placing decision making in factories in the hands of plant managers and experts, and emphasizing scientific research through the upgrading of university education. Zhou even invoked one of Mao's statements on the need for a technical-revolution and for borrowing scientific and technical know-how from abroad.[53] These changes were viewed by the radicals as reversing the gains of the Cultural Revolution.

The radicals' offensives soon converged on the individual whom they considered most vulnerable in the Zhou Enlai group, the rehabilitated Deng Xiaoping, who had been designated by Zhou to implement the economic acceleration and modernization. As Zhou became increasingly incapacitated by cancer (and was hospitalized most of the time in 1975), the attacks against him and Deng intensified in the radical-controlled media. The radicals were very much concerned about who would take over the premiership in the event of Zhou's death. Wang Hongwen was said to have been dispatched on several occasions to see Chairman Mao, to persuade him to designate either Zhang Chunqiao or Jiang Qing to succeed Zhou.[54] Their aim was to at least prevent Deng Xiaoping from assuming the premiership in case Zhou should die in office. In the radicals' eyes, Deng was the "capitalist roader" who had long advocated that hard work, not politics in command, was what really mattered: "Never mind about the color of the cat as long as it catches mice." In January 1976 Zhou Enlai died. There was a genuine outpouring of affection and respect by the masses for Zhou. But as soon as the nation had paid final tribute to the leader, the battle for succession began in earnest. Wall posters in the streets of Beijing demanded that Deng Xiaoping be purged again for his efforts to restore "bourgeois rights." The campaign of vilification against Deng culminated in the April 1976 Tiananmen incident.

The entire incident at Tiananmen Square was a large, spontaneous demonstration during the traditional festival in honor of the dead. The crowd, reportedly more than 100,000 at its height, was angered by the removal of flower wreaths placed in the square to honor the late Premier Zhou. The demonstrators created disturbances and damaged property belonging to the public security units stationed at public buildings on the square. The incident was a spontaneous show of support for the late premier's policies on material development and incentives. It could also be considered a show of support for Deng Xiaoping, who was a major target for attack by the radical leaders. Toward the end of the demonstration, the radicals entered this round-of-power contest by dispatching some units of the urban militia, presumably to quell the riots. By all accounts, this show of strength by the urban militia was rather feeble and unimpressive.[55]

While the urban militia did not prevent the mass riot at Tiananmen in April 1976, an estimated 3,000 to 4,000 demonstrators were arrested by the public security forces with the assistance of the urban militia.[56] Among those arrested were workers, cadres, and intellectuals.[57] The CCP subsequently declared the demonstration "a revolutionary mass action against the radicals."[58]

The radicals used the incident for their own purposes. They labeled the disorderly conduct of the demonstrators in support of Zhou and Deng as "counterrevolutionary" and blamed Deng for instigating the incident. The radicals at this time had the support of Mao and enough Politburo members to have Deng dismissed from all positions of power and, thereby, to remove him as a candidate to succeed Zhou Enlai for the premiership. The spontaneous outburst of the huge crowd in the Tiananmen Square incident demonstrated the radicals' alienation from the masses. The radicals, nevertheless, won the first round of the succession struggle by removing Deng Xiaoping from the seat of power for the second time. The compromise choice of Hua Guofeng as first vice-chairman of the CCP, a newly designated position, and as acting premier may have been made personally by Mao, who surely by then had realized the danger of a split within the top echelons of the party. While Mao lived, he somehow kept the factions in balance—even, at times, tipping the balance slightly in favor of his radical disciples.

The campaign to criticize Deng Xiaoping sputtered forward, without arousing any genuine mass support or enthusiasm, from April through July, ending in August when a series of major earthquakes shook the Beijing area. The ancient Chinese saying that unusual natural phenomena generally precede some earth-shaking event seemed prophetic: Chairman Mao died on September 9, 1976, at the age of eighty-two. While the nation again mourned the loss of a great leader, political maneuvering for the succession contest reached its peak. At first the open dispute revolved around Mao's will. The radicals claimed that the will called for the gains and values of the Cultural Revolution to be upheld by Mao's successors. The moderates, now a close alliance of party, government, and veteran military cadres, claimed that Mao had designated in writing that Hua Guofeng be named his successor: "With you in charge, I am at ease."[59] These were merely skirmishes of the pen. The real combat took place from the end of September to the first week of October at Politburo meetings, which included some heated debates. Reportedly, the radical leaders proposed that Jiang Qing be named the new party chairperson, and Zhang Chunqiao the new premier. It has also since been reported that the radical leaders mapped out a military coup to be staged in Shanghai as a last resort in the contest for power.[60]

The final decision of the Central Committee on October 7 was firm and direct: Hua Guofeng was to succeed Mao as chairman of the party, and all opposition to this decision had to be silenced. Almost simultaneously, the four radical leaders were placed under arrest by the special security force No. 8341, directly under the supervision of the Central Committee and the Politburo and under the personal command of Politburo member Wang Dongxing. Swiftly, regular PLA units, all under the command of Politburo members, moved into Beijing, Shanghai, and other cities to disarm the urban militia. The PLA placed these cities under temporary military control to prevent any disturbances. By October 24 Hua's successful move against the radicals was complete, and an estimated 1 million Chinese gathered in Tiananmen Square to cheer a new leader and to celebrate the dawn of a new era for China.

The Gang of Four, along with twelve other principal defendants (all former ranking military officers closely associated with Lin Biao), were tried during

November and December 1980 under the recently enacted criminal code. The trial was open to selected observers and was televised in order to demonstrate the need for a return to law and order. The pragmatic leaders hoped that by using the legal process, rather than summary execution, public confidence and respect for socialist legality would be restored. Nonetheless, the staging of the trial by the pragmatic leaders served to vindicate the position they took during the Cultural Revolution.

The new leadership also wanted to tie the Gang of Four to Lin Biao's attempted assassination of Mao and the abortive coup d'état, even though each faction had its own goals. This linkage was designed to achieve two objectives. First, it attempted to protect Mao's reputation and to downplay his close relationship with the radicals on trial. Second, the strategy was also intended to shield Hua Guofeng. An agreement reportedly was worked out to delete any reference to Hua's association with the radicals—particularly his role in suppressing the 1976 Tiananmen demonstration.[61]

The radical leaders and the former top military brass under Lin Biao were convicted of persecuting veteran party leaders, of plotting to assassinate Mao, and of organizing a secret armed rebellion. All but two of the defendants received sentences ranging from sixteen to twenty years in prison. Jiang Qing and Zhang Chunqiao were sentenced to death, with a two-year stay of execution.[62] In January 1983 the Supreme People's Court ruled that since both Jiang and Zhang had shown "sufficient repentance" and "had not resisted reform in a flagrant way" during the two-year reprieve period, the execution would not be carried out in 1983. (Jiang Qing died in May 1991 by committing suicide while under house arrest.)

The trial of the radical leaders seems to have been successful not only in repudiating the Cultural Revolution but also in meting out punishment through the judicial process. The trial represented a victory for the pragmatic leaders who were themselves victims of the Cultural Revolution. However, for cynics inside and outside of China, the trial was just another episode in the grand tradition of the Beijing opera.

The arrest of the radicals in 1976 paved the way for the twice-purged Deng Xiaoping to return to power. Gradually, Deng was able to outmaneuver the conservative hard-liners within the party. By the beginning months of 1979 he was finally able to pack the party congress with his supporters, who in turn elected Deng's hand-picked leaders to control the party's Central Committee and its Politburo. The stage was now set for launching Deng's reform program, which had been dominating Chinese politics for the past decade. Deng's pragmatic reform has been called "China's Second Revolution."[63]

NOTES

1. For a detailed account of the events in 1927, see Franklin Houn, *A Short History of Chinese Communism* (Englewood Cliffs, N.J.: Prentice-Hall, 1967), pp. 21–33.
2. Ibid., pp. 35–38. Also see Sterling Seagrave, *The Soong Dynasty* (New York: Harper and Row, 1985), pp. 239–46.
3. Hsiung, *Ideology and Practice: The Evolution of Chinese Communism* (New York: Praeger, 1970), pp. 61–62. Also see Edgar Snow, *Red Star Over China* (New York: Grove Press, 1961).
4. John M. H. Lindbeck, "Transformation in the Chinese Communist Party," in *Soviet and Chinese Communist: Similarities and Differences*, ed. Donald Treadgold (Seattle: University of Washington Press, 1967), p. 76; and Stuart Schram, "Mao Tse-tung and the Chinese Political Equilibrium," *Government and Opposition*, vol. 4, no. 1 (Winter 1969), 141–42.

5. Hsiung, *Ideology and Practice*, pp. 45–46; and Dick Wilson, *The Long March 1935: The Epic of Chinese Communism's Survival* (New York: Avon Books, First Discus Printing, 1973). Also see Edward E. Rice, *Mao's Way* (Berkeley, Calif.: University of California Press, 1972), pp. 83–88. Also see Harrison E. Salisbury, *The Long March: The Untold Story* (New York: Harper and Row, Basic, 1985) and Zhou Zheng, "Long March 50th Anniversary: General Looks Back," *Beijing Review*, 40 (October 6, 1986), 19–25.

6. Hsiung, *Ideology and Practice*, pp. 52–53; and Fairbank, *The United States and China*, pp. 269–70.

7. John Lindbeck, "Transformation in the Chinese Communist Party," p. 76.

8. See *The Selected Works of Mao Tse-tung* (Peking: Foreign Language press, 1967, II, 339–84; III, 205–70.

9. John King Fairbank, *The United States and China*, 3rd ed. (Cambridge, Mass.: Harvard University Press, 1971), p. 313.

10. Houn, *A Short History of Chinese Communism*, pp. 173–77.

11. E. Stuart Kirby, "Agrarian Problems and Peasantry," in *Communist China, 1949–1969: A Twenty Year Appraisal*, eds. Frank N. Trager and William Henderson (New York: New York University Press, 1970), p. 160.

12. Ezra Vogel, "Land Reform in Kwangtung 1951–1953: Central Control and Localism," *The China Quarterly*, 38 (April–June 1969), 27–62.

13. Ibid., 27–62.

14. Houn, *A Short History of Chinese Communism*, p. 159.

15. Ibid., p. 164; and Kirby, "Agrarian Problems and Peasantry," p. 162.

16. See the official documents dealing with the debate over the cooperatives. The texts of these documents are in Robert R. Bowie and John K. Fairbank, *Communist China, 1955–1959: Policy Documents With Analysis* (Cambridge, Mass.: Harvard University Press, 1965), pp. 92–126.

17. Discussion on the First Five-Year Plan was based on the following sources: Alexander Eckstein, *China's Economic Revolution* (London and New York: Cambridge University Press, 1977), pp. 31–66; E. L. Wheelwright and Bruce McFarlane, *The Chinese Road to Socialism: Economics of the Cultural Revolution* (New York: Monthly Review Press, 1970), pp. 31–65; and Houn, *A Short History of Chinese Communism*, pp. 177–85.

18. Houn, *A Short History of Chinese Communism*, pp. 178–79; Wheelwright and McFarlane, *The Chinese Road to Socialism*, p. 35.

19. Houn, *A Short History of Chinese Communism*, pp. 178–79.

20. Ibid., pp. 178–79.

21. Wheelwright and McFarlane, *The Chinese Road to Socialism*, p. 36.

22. Discussion in this section on the Great Leap program is based on these sources: Houn, *A Short History of Chinese Communism*, pp. 181–82; Fairbank, *The United States and China*, pp. 369–75; Eckstein, *China's Economic Revolution*, pp. 54–65; Roderick MacFarquhar, *The Origin of the Cultural Revolution: The Contradictions among the People, 1956–1957* (New York: Columbia University Press, 1974), pp. 57–74; Hsiung, *Ideology and Practice*, pp. 185–99.

23. Eckstein, *China's Economic Revolution*, p. 59.

24. Byung-joon Ahn, *Chinese Politics and the Cultural Revolution: Dynamics of Policy Processes* (Seattle, Wash. and London: University of Washington Press, 1976), pp. 31–47.

25. *The Case of Peng Teh-huai* (Hong Kong: Union Research Institute; 1968); and J. D. Simmons, "Peng Teh-huai: A Chronological Re-examination," *The China Quarterly*, 37 (January–March 1968), 120–38. Also see Jurgen Domes, *Peng Te-Huai: The Man and the Image* (Palo Alto, Calif.: Stanford University Press, 1986).

26. There are many accounts of the Lushan decision. The latest is in Ahn, *Chinese Politics and the Cultural Revolution*, pp. 38–44.

27. The brief survey here is based on Eckstein, *China's Economic Revolution*, pp. 202–5, and on Houn, *A Short History of Chinese Communism*, pp. 182–85. Also see Ahn, *Chinese Politics and the Cultural Revolution*, pp. 48–86, for a more detailed account of the recovery for the period 1962–65.

28. Discussion of the Socialist Education Campaign is drawn from these sources: Hsiung, *Ideology and Practice*, pp. 200–16; Richard Baum and Frederick C. Teiwes, *Ssu-Ch'ing: The Socialist Educational Movement of 1962–1966* (Berkeley, Calif.: Center for Chinese Studies, University of California, 1968); Ahn, *Chinese Politics and the Cultural Revolution*, pp. 89–122; Philip Bridgham, "Mao's 'Cultural Revolution': Origin and Development," *The China Quarterly*, 29 (January–March 1967), 1–35; Richard Baum and Frederick Teiwes, "Liu Shao-chi and the Cadres Question," *Asian Survey*, vol. viii, no. 4 (April 1968), 323–45; and Richard Baum, *Prelude to Revolution: Mao, the Party and the Peasant Question, 1962–1966* (New York: Columbia University Press, 1975).

29. C. S. Chen, ed., *Rural People's Communes in Lien-chiang*, trans. Charles P. Ridley (Stanford, Calif.:

Hoover Institution, 1969); Baum and Teiwes, "Liu Shao-chi and the Cadres Question"; and Ahn, *Chinese Politics and the Cultural Revolution*, pp. 99–108. Also see Hsiung, *Ideology and Practice*, pp. 206–8.

30. Ahn, *Chinese Politics and the Cultural Revolution*, p. 103; and for an insight into the interpersonal behavior of the cadres, see Michel Oksenberg, "The Institutionalization of the Chinese Communist Revolution: The Ladder of Success on the Eve of the Cultural Revolution," *The China Quarterly*, 36 (October–December 1968), 61–92.

31. For a bibliography on the subject, see James C. F. Wang, *The Cultural Revolution in China: An Annotated Bibliography* (New York and London: Garland Publishing, Inc., 1976). Also see the following books on the Cultural Revolution: Goo Yuan, *Born Red: A Chronicle of the Cultural Revolution* (Stanford, Calif.: Stanford University Press, 1987); Yang Jiang, *Six Chapters from My Life "Down Under,"* translated by Howard Goldblat (Hong Kong: The Chinese University Press, 1983); and Judith Shapiro and Liang Heng, *Cold Winds, Warm Winds: Intellectual Life in China Today* (Middletown, Conn.: Wesleyan University Press, 1986).

32. See Donald Zagoria, *Vietnam Triangle: Moscow, Peking, Hanoi* (New York: Pegasus, 1967); Uri Ra'amam, "Peking's Foreign Policy 'Debate,' 1965–1966," in *China's Policies in Asia and America's Alternatives*, ed. Tang Tsou (Chicago: University of Chicago Press, 1968), pp. 23–71; Robert Scalapino, "The Cultural Revolution and Chinese Foreign Policy," in *The Cultural Revolution: 1967 in Review* (Ann Arbor, Mich.: Michigan Papers in Michigan Studies No. 2, Center for Chinese Studies, University of Michigan, 1968), pp. 1–15.

33. For an account of the struggle at these two universities during the Cultural Revolution, see Victor Nee, *The Cultural Revolution at Peking University* (New York: Monthly Review Press, 1969); and William Hinton, *Hundred Day War: The Cultural Revolution at Tsinghua* (New York and London: Monthly Review Press, 1972).

34. See Gordon Bennett and Ronald N. Montaperto, *Red Guard: The Political Bibliography of Dai Hsiao-ai* (New York: Anchor Books, Doubleday, 1972).

35. See Michel Oksenberg, "China: Forcing the Revolution to a New Stage," *Asian Survey*, vol. vii, no. 1 (January 1967), 1–15; and John Israel, "The Red Guards in Historical Perspective: Continuity and Change in Chinese Youth Movement," *The China Quarterly*, 30 (April–June 1967), 1–32.

36. See Lowell Dittmer, "The Cultural Revolution and the Fall of Liu Shao-chi," *Current Scene*, vol. xi, no. 1 (January 1973), 1–13; Israel, "The Red Guards in Historical Perspective," 1–32.

37. Philip Bridgham, "Mao's Cultural Revolution in 1967: The Struggle to Seize Power," *The China Quarterly*, 34 (April–June 1968), 6–36; Ellis Joffe, "The Chinese Army in the Cultural Revolution: The Politics of Intervention," *The Current Scene*, vol. ii, no. 18 (December 7, 1970), 1–25; William Whitson, *The Chinese Communist High Command: A History of Military Politics, 1927–69* (New York: Holt, Rinehart & Winston, 1971); Jean Esmein, *The Chinese Cultural Revolution* (Garden City, N.Y.: Anchor Books, Doubleday, 1973); Stanley Karnow, *Mao and China: From Revolution to Revolution* (New York: Viking, 1972), pp. 276–316.

38. Edgar Snow, "Mao and the New Mandate," *The World Today*, vol. 25, no. 7 (July 1969), 290.

39. Parris H. Chang, "Regional Military Power: The Aftermath of the Cultural Revolution," *Asian Survey*, vol. xii, no. 12 (December 1972), 999–1013, and "The Revolutionary Committee and the Party in the Aftermath of the Cultural Revolution," *Current Scene*, vol. viii, no. 8 (April 15, 1970), 1–10.

40. "Recent Development in Chinese Education," *Current Scene*, vol. x, no. 1 (July 1972), 1–6.

41. See Richard M. Pfeffer, "Serving the People and Continuing the Revolution," *The China Quarterly*, 52 (October–December 1972), 620–53.

42. "On Questions of Party History—Resolution on Certain Questions in the History of Our Party Since the Founding of the People's Republic of China" (adopted by the Sixth Plenary Session of the Eleventh Central Committee of the CPC on June 27, 1981), *Beijing Review*, 27 (July 6, 1981), 20.

43. Ibid.

44. Summary of an interview with the visiting editor of the Greek communist party newspaper, reported in *Ta Kung Pao Weekly Supplement* (Hong Kong) (December 8, 1980), p. 3.

45. For a series of articles assessing the impact of the Cultural Revolution, see *Asian Survey*, vol. xii, no. 12 (December 1972). Also see Maurice Meisner, *Mao's China: A History of the People's Republic* (New York: The Free Press, 1977), pp. 340–59; and David Bonavia, "The Fate of the 'New-Born Things' of China's Cultural Revolution," *Pacific Affairs*, vol. 51, no. 2 (Summer 1981), 177–94. Also see William Hinton, *Shenfan: The Cultural Revolution in a Chinese Village* (New York: Random House, 1983).

46. *A Great Trial in Chinese History* (New York: Pergamon Press, 1981), pp. 20–21.

47. Jiang Hua, president of the Supreme People's Court, recently reported that 326,000 people framed or falsely imprisoned had been exonerated after investigation by the court. See Michael Weisskopf,

"China Reports End of Trials," Washington Post Service, as reprinted in *Honolulu Advertiser* (January 28, 1983), p. A-18.

48. *People's Daily* (July 16, 1980), p. 1. Also see Nien Cheng, *Life and Death in Shanghai* (New York: Grove Press, 1987). The personal account was excerpted in *Time* (June 8, 1987), pp. 42–56.

49. Fox Butterfield, *China: Alive in the Bitter Sea* (New York: Times Books, 1982), p. 349.

50. "Cleaning Up Mao's Feudal Mistakes," *The Guardian* (September 21, 1980), p. 16.

51. Suggested readings about the downfall of the Gang of Four include Jurgen Domes, "China in 1976: Tremors of Transition," *Asian Survey*, vol. xiii, no. 1 (January 1977), 1–17; Peter R. Moody, Jr., "The Fall of the Gang of Four: Background Notes on the Chinese Counterrevolution," *Asian Survey*, vol. xvii, no. 8 (August 1977), 711–23; Jurgen Domes, "The 'Gang of Four' and Hua Kuo-feng: Analysis of Political Events in 1976–76," *The China Quarterly*, 71 (September 1977), 473–97; James C. F. Wang, "The Urban Militia as a Political Instrument in the Power Contest in China in 1976," *Asian Survey*, vol. xviii, no. 6 (June 1978), 541–59; and Andres D. Onate, "Hua Kuo-feng and the Arrest of 'Gang of Four,' " *The China Quarterly*, 75 (September 1978), 540–65. For coverage at the trial by the Chinese press, see "Written Judgment of the Special Court Under the Supreme People's Court of the PRC," *Beijing Review*, 5 (February 2, 1981), 13–28; "Trial of Lin Biao and Jiang Qing Cliques— Major Points of the Indictment," *Beijing Review*, 47 (November 24, 1980), 12–17; "Trial of Lin-Jiang Cliques: Indictment of the Special Procuratorate," *Beijing Review*, 48 (December 1, 1980), 9–28. For Chinese public reaction to the trial, see Butterfield, *China: Alive in the Bitter Sea*, pp. 357–61; Richard Bernstein, *From the Center of the Earth: The Search for the Truth About China* (Boston and Toronto: Little, Brown, 1982), pp. 107–8; Frank Ching, "Mao's Widow Finally Finds Her Place in the Spotlight," *The Asian Wall Street Journal Weekly* (December 22, 1980), p. 6.

52. Wang, "The Urban Militia in China," p. 550.

53. Chou En-lai, "Report on the Work of the Government," *Peking Review*, 4 (January 24, 1975), 24.

54. "The Crux of 'Gang of Four's' Crimes to Usurp Party and State Power," *Peking Review*, 2 (January 7, 1977), 30.

55. Wang, "Urban Militia in China," pp. 552–53.

56. For an eyewitness account, see Roger Garside, *Coming Alive: China After Mao* (New York: McGraw-Hill, 1981), pp. 114–41. For the current status of those who were still under detention, see *Ming Pao* (Hong Kong) (April 9, 1981), p. 1.

57. *Beijing Review*, 46 (November 17, 1978), 13.

58. "Communiqué of the Third Plenary Session of the Eleventh Central Committee," *Beijing Review*, 52 (December 29, 1978) 14. Also see "Carry Forward the Revolutionary Tiananmen Spirit," editorial of *Renmin Ribao*, reprinted in *Beijing Review*, 15 (April 13, 1979), 9–13; *Ming Pao* (Hong Kong) (April 8 and 9, 1981), p. 1; Garside, *Coming Alive: China After Mao*, pp. 114–41; *Beijing Review*, 46 to 48 (November 17–December 1, 1978).

59. See "Chairman Mao Will Live For Ever in Our Hearts," *Peking Review*, 39 (September 24, 1976), 35; and "Comrade Wu Teh's Speech at the Celebration Rally in the Capitol," *Peking Review*, 44 (October 29, 1976), 12.

60. Wang, "Urban Militia in China," pp. 555–58.

61. See Lowell Dittmer, "China in 1981: Reform, Readjustment, Rectification," *Asian Survey*, xxii, 5 (January 1982), 33–34. Also see Ching, "Mao's Widow Finally Finds Her Place in the Spotlight," *The Asian Wall Street Journal Weekly* (December 22, 1980), p. 6; and David Bonavia, "Exit Jiang left With Hua Not Far Behind," *Far Eastern Economic Review* (January 2, 1981), 12.

62. For analyses of Hua Guofeng's problems, see Parris Chang, "Chinese Politics: Deng's Turbulent Quest," *Problems of Communism*, vol. xxx (January–February 1981), 1–21, and "The Last Stand of Deng's Revolution," 3–19; Lowell Dittmer, "China in 1980: Modernization and Its Discontents," *Asian Survey*, vol. xxi, no. 1 (January 1981), 36–42, and "China in 1981: Reform, Readjustment, Rectification," 33–35, 42–43; Xu Sangu, "Starting with Hua Guofeng's Resignation of Premiership," *Perspective* (Hong Kong), 557 (September 16, 1980), 4–6; Frank Ching, "Central Committee Said to Plan Consideration of Hua's Resignation Soon," *The Asian Wall Street Journal Weekly* (December 29, 1980), p. 2; Yen Qing, "What Happened to Hua Guofeng," *Ming Pao* (Hong Kong) (January 22, 23, and 24, 1981); Dorothy Grouse Fontana, "Background to the Fall of Hua Guofeng," *Asian Survey*, vol. xxii, no. 3, (March 1983), 237–60; "Hua Guofeng's Political Fate," *Issues and Studies*, vol. xviii, no. 2 (February 1981), 4–6; "The Two Whatevers and Discussions on Criteria for Truth," *Beijing Review*, 44 (November 2, 1981), 24–25, 28; "Document of the CCP's Central Committee, Chung-fa, 1981, No. 23," *Issues and Studies*, vol. xcii, no. 12 (December 1981) 71–78.

63. Harry Harding, *China's Second Revolution: Reform after Mao* (Washington, D.C.: The Brookings Institution, 1987).

chapter three

The Erosion of Chinese Communist Ideology
Marxism-Leninism, Mao's Thought, De-Maoization

Let us begin by defining the term *ideology*. It may be defined as the manner in which an individual or a group thinks. Ideology is a set of political values, feelings, and ideas that guides individuals to act or behave in a certain manner for the purpose of achieving a particular goal. It has been said that the success of the Chinese communist movement rests on two basic elements: an effective set of organizations, guided by a set of clearly stated principles.[1] Schurmann differentiates among ideologies in terms of the consequences the ideas may generate. If an idea leads to the formulation of a policy or an action, it is a "practical" ideology; but if an idea is employed for the sole purpose of molding the thinking of the individual, it is a "pure" ideology.[2] Pure ideology is a set of theories; practical ideology is based on experiences and practices. The Chinese make a clear distinction between these two sets of ideologies in their political communication. To the Chinese, the ideas of Karl Marx and of Lenin are pure ideology that have universal application. In the Chinese language, pure ideology is called *lilun* or *chuyi*, and practical ideology is *suxiang*.

The Chinese communist ideology consists of three basic elements: (1) the influence of the Chinese revolution, particularly the intellectual ferment of the May Fourth Movement; (2) the ideas of Marxism-Leninism; and (3) the thought of Mao Zedong. Let us keep in mind that while the thought of Mao constitutes a major portion of the Chinese communist ideology, it is by no means the only element. In the sections that follow, we shall briefly discuss the origin and the nature of the main elements of Chinese communist ideology today.

PREAMBLE

China is one of the countries with the longest histories in the world. The people of all nationalities in China have jointly created a splendid culture and have a glorious revolutionary tradition.

Feudal China was gradually reduced after 1840 to a semi-colonial and semi-feudal country. The Chinese people waged wave upon wave of heroic struggles for national independence and liberation and for democracy and freedom.

Great and earth-shaking historical changes have taken place in China in the 20th century.

The Revolution of 1911, led by Dr. Sun Yat-sen, abolished the feudal monarchy and gave birth to the Republic of China. But the Chinese people had yet to fulfill their historical task of overthrowing imperialism and feudalism.

After waging hard, protracted and tortuous struggles, armed and otherwise, the Chinese people of all nationalities led by the Communist Party of China with Chairman Mao Zedong as its leader ultimately, in 1949, overthrew the rule of imperialism, feudalism and bureaucrat-capitalism, won the great victory of the new-democratic revolution and founded the People's Republic of China. Thereupon the Chinese people took state power into their own hands and became masters of the country.

After the founding of the People's Republic, the transition of Chinese society from a new-democratic to a socialist society was effected step by step. The socialist transformation of the private ownership of the means of production was completed, the system of exploitation of man by man eliminated and the socialist system established. The people's democratic dicta-

However, it is important to note that some Chinese intellectuals, including Mao, were influenced by the ideas of anarchism that were a part of modern Chinese thought. As explained by Peter Zattow, Chinese anarchists drew their inspiration from the belief in human goodness associated with Confucianism, the egalitarianism of Daoism, and the selflessness of Buddhism;[3] and beginning with the May Fourth Movement they merged these traditional thoughts with Western ideas such as Marxism.

MARXISM-LENINISM

The theoretical foundation of the Chinese communist ideology is Marxism-Leninism. It is the guiding principle for both the party and the state. It is pure theory with universal applications. Let us examine briefly the essential features of Marxism.

The first key Marxist concept is historical materialism. Karl Marx began with the assertion that the character of any society is determined by the manner or the mode of production by which people make their living. The mode of production determines social structure and political order; it also determines social ideas and customs. Therefore, to change the minds of people, it is necessary to change the mode of production or the economic system. This, Marx said, is the universal truth and the "evolutionary law of human history." Every human society has at its foundation an economic base, the mode of production that produces goods and services to support human life. This economic basis, in turn, is supported by superstructures of culture, law, courts, and governmental instututions.

Having asserted that materialism determines the nature of society, Marx described how human history evolves in a predictable pattern. This is dialectical materialism. For this, Marx borrowed the theory of the dialectical development of history from the German philosopher Hegel. Hegel proposed that every idea or thesis, once started, goes too far and becomes exaggerated or false. When this inevitably happens, the thesis is met with an opposing idea, the antithesis. These two opposing ideas clash, and out of the conflict comes the synthesis, an entirely new idea that contains the essential truths of both opposing ideas. Soon this synthesis becomes a thesis, and the process of change continues, ad infinitum. Marx used Hegelian dialectics to predict that a communist society would inevitably result from this historical process after society had passed through certain stages: first, the primitive communal society, with no class differentiation; then the slave society, with the concept of ownership and with caste status separating the slaves and the masters; next, feudal society, with pronounced class distinctions between the lord and his serfs; and the fourth stage of development, the capitalistic society, with the owners of the means of production pitted against the impoverished workers, who lead a meager existence, suffering exploitation by the capitalists. Marx predicted that this struggle between the capitalists and the working class would result in a communist society where there would be no class distinctions. The economy would be operated under Marx's dictum: "From each according to his abilities, to each according to his needs." Finally, the state, with its coercive instruments, would no longer be needed and would wither away.

Marx believed that the course of human history must pass through these stages; but before the arrival of the communist stage, there must be intense class struggle. In fact, Marx maintained that human history is a history of class warfare. As long as property or the means of production is owned by private individuals for the purpose of exploiting the work of others, there will always be a struggle between the two classes. It is an unfair struggle, since all the superstructures of society—laws, police, courts, and other political institutions—support the property-owning class. The property-owning class has all the privileges, sanctioned by social customs and mores. Marx argued that this situation cannot endure long; the working class has no alternative except to forcefully overthrow the existing social order. He concludes the Communist Manifesto with a call for revolution: "Workers of the world, unite! You have nothing to lose but your chains."

It is not the purpose of this section to engage in a critique of Marxism. However, we need to keep in mind that two basic responses to this doctrine have developed under different sets of circumstances, in answer to the appalling conditions of the early industrialization Marx criticized. One was the evolution of social democracy in the West, which brought changes through constitutional reform and progressive social legislation. The other was the Russian Bolshevik Revolution, which brought change through violent revolution.

Lenin made two basic modifications to Marxism. One was his treatise on imperialism, published in 1916. Marx had predicted that a forceful but spontaneous workers' revolution would descend upon the capitalistic European societies, such as England, France, and Germany. But for over seventy years, no revolution by the working class occurred in continental Europe. When the revolution came, it came to Russia, an industrially backward country. Even more significant was the fact that the lot of workers in the advanced capitalist countries had improved through progressive social legislation. How could the disciples of Marx explain this phenomenon? Lenin answered this question in his treatise, *Imperialism*. Lenin argued that capitalism had broken away from the cycle of contradiction as prescribed by Marx in his dialectical materialism theory. Capitalism had expanded and grown by seeking new sources of raw materials abroad, in undeveloped parts of the world, and by setting up factories with cheap labor in colonies, which in turn became the ready markets for the manufactured goods. Lenin rationalized the situation by claiming that the capitalist nations had developed a monopoly that accumulated enormous profits from the backward areas of the world and then rewarded labor at home with better wages and working conditions from those profits. By making concessions to labor at home, the capitalists were able to maintain the status quo, preventing a workers' revolution. Therefore, the imperialists' exploitation of the backward areas of the world had sustained capitalism. Capitalism would not collapse as long as colonial power and monopolistic capitalism could successfully exploit the backward areas of Russia, China, India, and Africa. From this analysis Lenin concluded that the first blow of the revolution must be dealt to the weakest part in the system, the colonial complex in Asia and Africa. The Bolshevik Revolution and Lenin's treatise on imperialism made sense to the Chinese intellectuals, who were frustrated by their previous efforts in revolution making. Now there was a meaningful and emotional link between nationalism on one hand and anti-imperialism on the other.

Lenin's second major modification of Marxism was in regard to organization for the revolution, which Marx had not discussed beyond saying that it would be spontaneous. In *What's To Be Done?* Lenin outlined his strategy for the working class to achieve and to maintain political power. His first key principle was that a revolutionary party was needed, led by a highly disciplined and dedicated corps of professional revolutionaries, to serve as the vanguard of the proletariat. Lenin insisted on professionalism and self-discipline in this vanguard. Another key organizational principle was the doctrine of "democratic centralism." This called for centralized decision making, with free discussion at the policy formulation level. Once a decision was made at the top, however, all must abide by it without dissent. Lenin insisted on strict discipline within a "single, unified party." The Leninist organizational model was hierarchical and pyramidal, with the supreme power vested in the hands of a few at the apex. At the base of the pyramid was the level of primary organizations—units or cells. Between the base and the apex were a myriad of intermediary organizations (see Chapter 4).

A few remarks on the current state of Marxism-Leninism in China after Mao may be in order. First, there is rising doubt about the validity of Marxism-Leninism among the young. American journalists stationed in China have reported an increasing lack of interest among China's youth in the compulsory study of Marxism.[4] Reportedly, a survey taken at Fudan University in Shanghai revealed that only 30 percent of the students polled believed in communism.[5] Disillusionment about communism, and the dissidents' campaign for democracy and human rights, prompted Deng Xiaoping in 1979 to insist that the party adopt some basic guidelines within which criticism about the communist system could be tolerated. These guidelines directed that no one should speak against the socialist road, the dictatorship of the proletariat, the leadership of the party, Marxism-Leninism, and Mao's thought.[6] Presumably, these guidelines were intended to put a stop to the rising tide of dissent against communism.

In 1979, propaganda efforts were mounted to reiterate the applicability of Marxism-Leninism and to reinterpret its meaning in the light of the aberration of the Cultural Revolution and the liberal reforms introduced in the economic system. In July 1981, in his maiden speech as the new party chief, Hu Yaobang called Marxism the "crystallization of scientific thinking" and theory verified in practice. Hu then cautioned that Marxism was only a guide to action; as a theory it should neither be looked upon as a "rigid dogma to be followed unthinkingly" nor viewed as comprising "all the truth in the unending course of human history."[7] In answer to those who advocated the abandonment of socialism in China, numerous theoretical studies were published in the media to justify the socialist nature of Chinese society. For instance, in a theoretical essay, the vice-president of the CCP's party school stated that socialism is basically public ownership of the means of production and the principle of "to each according to his work."[8] These two fundamental principles are the only way to judge the socialist nature of a society, and China—the theoreticians now argued—had completed the transfer of agriculture, handicrafts, industry, and commerce to public ownership.[9] The Chinese leaders seemed to argue that the concepts of Marxism-Leninism must go through stages of modification as dictated by new concrete conditions.[10] Now that China is a socialist society in accordance with Marxism, Hu Yaobang stressed, all Marxists must make sure that "it does not become divorced from social life and does not stagnate, wither or ossify; they must enrich it with fresh revolutionary experiences so that it will remain full of vitality."[11] The new party chief urged that the application of Marxism-Leninism be integrated with the "concrete practice of China's realities."[12]

We must now turn to a discussion of the thought of Mao Zedong.

THE THOUGHT OF MAO ZEDONG

Mao Zedong, The Man

Wind and thunder are stirring.
Flags and banners are flying
Wherever men live.
Thirty-eight years are fled
With a mere snap of the fingers
We can clasp the moon in the Ninth Heaven
And seize turtles deep down in the Five Seas;
We'll return amid triumphant song and laughter.
Nothing is hard in this world.
If you dare to scale the heights.[13]

This is the second stanza of a poem written by Mao in May 1965 when he revisited Jinggangshan, the mountain retreat where he had gathered the remnants of the defeated and disillusioned urban revolutionaries in 1927 before reorganizing them into a fighting guerrilla force. This poem shows a familiar image of Mao: a man with infinite faith in the ability of human beings to accomplish any task, no matter how difficult. Mao Zedong was a much more complex person than has commonly been portrayed. In this section we will look at Mao, the man, by focusing on his background.

Mao was born in 1893 to a middle-class, not poor, peasant family in the village of Shaoshan, Hunan Province, in central China. He was brought up in a traditional Chinese family environment, where the father exercised almost dictatorial power over the family. As a boy he learned the value of hard labor by helping his father on the farm. His primary school curriculum centered on recitation of the Confucian classics, but he enjoyed reading popular romantic literature depicting heroic adventures, peasant rebellions, and the contests of empires. At the time of the 1911 revolution, Mao was 18, a fledgling youth, not too sure of what was happening to China. His social awakening did not begin until he went to the provincial capital of Changsha for his secondary education in 1912. In Changsha he learned from the newspapers about the various revolutionary activities of Sun Yatsen and others. Excited by these events, Mao wrote his first wall poster—already a popular medium for expressing political opinions. Following local uprisings in Changsha and Wuhan, he joined the revolutionary army. Military life with its regimentation and authoritarianism did not suit young Mao, who was alert and impatient with the world around him. For some months after his short sojourn in the army, Mao toyed with the idea of becoming a lawyer. Finally, in 1918, at the age of 25, he settled for a teaching career and obtained a degree from a teacher training school. Stuart Schram, an authoritative biographer of Mao, views the five years in teacher training school as an important landmark in the shaping of Mao's future.[14] The greatest and perhaps most successful role that Mao played was as a teacher to his people: he showed them how to learn by themselves and how to learn together.[15] In later years schoolmates described the Mao of this period as a loner, but a well-behaved person.[16]

The most important change that occurred in Mao's life was the move from his native province of Hunan to Beijing, the center of political and intellectual ferment.

Toward the end of World War I, Mao went to Beijing with some thirty fellow-Hunanese as members of a society to study new ideas. Through his former teacher in Changsha, Mao obtained a menial job as a librarian's assistant at Beijing National University to support himself. Although he shared a room with seven other students from Hunan, Mao was lonely. As a means of meeting people, he joined the Marxist Study Group, organized by Li Dazhao, founder of the Chinese communist movement. As Mao later admitted to Edgar Snow, at that time he was rather confused by the new ideas proliferating like mushrooms at Beijing National University, and he leaned toward anarchism while "looking for a road."[17] Before becoming a Marxist in the summer of 1920, Mao had read only three Chinese translations of major works on Marxism: *The Communist Manifesto*, by Marx, *Class Struggle* by Kautsky, and *History of Socialism* by Kirkupp. A year later Mao was a delegate to the founding of the Chinese Communist Party in Shanghai. From 1921 until 1927, he was an obedient Chinese communist, following the orders of the Comintern. From 1927 to 1935, he began to shape a different movement, with reliance on the peasantry as a base. Mao's rise to leadership of the Chinese Communist Party, and his maintenance of that position until his death in 1976, are discussed in chapter 2 and in other parts of this book.

As Lucian Pye has pointed out, Mao must be seen at various times and under various conditions.[18] In his youth he was a loner and exhibited signs of "aloofness and solitariness."[19] When he went into the field as an organizer among the workers and peasants, Mao not only dressed but acted like them. As Mao gained power and grew as a leader, he was distinguished as a "man of decisive action, great energy, and increasing aloofness."[20] He developed his maturity as a student of Marxism-Leninism and as a theoretician of guerrilla warfare during the Yanan years of 1935 to 1940, when he wrote and lectured to the soldiers and cadres. He was then looked upon by his followers as a scholar, a teacher, and a man of wisdom—an image that remained with him long after the establishment of the People's Republic in 1949. This image of a scholar and of a man with answers to problems became veiled in an aura of mysticism and magic—the image of a charismatic leader. But the private Mao remained a Chinese scholar, reading books and reports or writing poetry in the traditional style. As many foreigners who interviewed him testified, he was a good conversationalist and was remarkably well-informed. Interestingly, he engaged in philosophic conversations about the existence of a god or gods with the late Edgar Snow.[21] Mao personally seemed to have detested the campaigns to build an image of him as a god or an emperor, to be worshipped by the people. The epithet that Mao preferred was that of a "great teacher."[22] There is really no appropriate epithet to describe so complex a man as Mao. The recent attempt to measure Mao in the scale of history has produced a number of themes on major areas of Mao's public life: philosopher, Marxist, theorist, political leader, soldier, teacher, economist, patriot, statesman, and innovator.[23] Mao's contribution to the development of the Chinese communist ideology is truly enormous. The following discussion represents only some of the salient aspects of his thought.

Before examining Mao's thought, the importance of the Yanan years in the development of Mao's thinking must be stressed. About half the articles in the first four volumes of the *Selected Works of Mao Tse-tung* were written during this period. Mao, as leader of the communist movement, was under great pressure in 1939 and 1940 to develop ideas and to provide leadership not only for the communists but also for all Chinese who would listen.[24] The fifth volume of Mao's collected works, covering the period 1949–57, was published in April 1977. It was edited mainly under the direction of Hua Guofeng and Wang Dongxing, leaders of the "Whatever" faction. Apparently, the new pragmatic leaders felt that it was sufficiently radical to merit reediting.

Peasantry as the Base for Revolution

In 1927 Mao reported on his investigation of the peasant movement in Hunan province. In the report Mao made a strong appeal to the party, then dominated by the Comintern, to exploit discontent in the countryside and to organize peasant associations as a vanguard for the revolution.[25] Mao noted that poor peasants had been fighting the landlords and feudal rule, and that the countryside was on the verge of an agrarian revolution. Mao urged that "a revolutionary tidal wave" must be generated in the countryside to mobilize the masses and to "weld them into this great force" for revolution.

The thrust of Mao's guerrilla efforts in the 1930s and 1940s was the mobilization and welding of the peasants into a formidable revolutionary force for the CCP in its quest for eventual control of the nation. This concept and practice of mobilizing the peasantry as a revolutionary base has created some controversy among scholars as to whether Mao was a heretic or an original thinker and contributor to communist theory.[26] We may attribute the origin of the idea not to Mao but to Lenin, who recognized the potential of the Russian peasants as a revolutionary force in 1905. We may also say that Mao probably was influenced by Li Dazhao, who saw the peasantry as a possible base for the revolution. The importance of Mao's contribution, as some scholars have noted, was the timing. Mao was the first orthodox Marxist-Leninist to advocate using the peasantry as a major rather than a secondary force, and he made his appeal at the time when the CCP leadership had committed the party to relying on the urban proletariat.[27] With the benefit of hindsight, we might argue that reliance on the peasants was not a conceptual contribution but rather the only practical revolutionary strategy that could be effective. Practical ideas based on experience were the keynote of Mao's practical ideology.

Mass Line and Populism

At the heart of Mao's political philosophy was the concept of "from the masses, to the masses," commonly known as the mass line. Briefly stated, the concept of the mass line specifies that a party policy is good only if the ideas of that policy come originally from the masses—the peasants and the workers—and only if the interests and wishes of the people are taken into account and incorporated into the policy. The implementation of a policy, no matter how good it is, must have the wholehearted support of the masses. The mass line concept is applied in several stages to achieve the enthusiastic support of the masses for its implementation. These stages have been described by John W. Lewis as "perception, summarization, authorization, and implementation."[28] First, the party cadres list the "scattered and unsystematic" views of the masses. Second, the cadres study these ideas and put them into systematic and summary form in their reports to higher authorities. Third, the higher authorities make comments or give instructions based on these systematic ideas and return them to the masses. During the stage, political education or propaganda is carried on by the cadres among the masses, not only to explain the ideas but also to test their correctness. Finally, when the masses have embraced the ideas as their own, the ideas are translated into concrete action.[29] According to Mao, this is not the end; the proper application of the mass line must repeat the process several times "so that each time these ideas emerge with greater correctness and become more vital and meaningful."[30]

The mass line concept, formulated during the Jiangxi soviet days of the 1930s, was an effective method for securing the support of the masses. The application of the mass line required that both the leaders and the masses go through an educational process, learning from and supporting each other. It provided for a continuous dialogue between the leaders and the led. In going through the various stages of the mass line process, the masses were given ample opportunity to participate in the decision-making process, and the leaders were able to obtain popular commitment for policies and programs.

While Mao had immense respect for the virtues of the masses, this did not mean that there were not limits to what the masses could do. The Red Guards' demonstrations and big-character posters during the Cultural Revolution were applications of the mass line.[31] As we saw in Chapter 2, however, when the fighting between the various factions of Red Guards reached a state of anarchy, Mao did not hesitate to call in the army to restore order in the tradition of Lenin's democratic centralism. Stuart Schram writes that Mao, who clearly opposed unrestricted mass rule, prevented the Shanghai radicals from organizing leaderless people's committees.[32] Within limits, the concept of mass line does provide a monitoring device on the bureaucratic elite and their tendency to rule the inarticulate masses by party and governmental sanction.[33]

Mass line is considered Mao's theoretical contribution to populism.[34] At the root of this concept is the assertion that simple people—peasants and workers—possess virtue and wisdom. Mao again seems to agree with Li Dazhao, who once said that one becomes more humanistic as one gets closer to the soil. The methods of mass campaigns and small study groups, developed for applying the mass line, have been what Townsend terms "the primary institutions of Mao's populism."[35]

Closely associated with the mass line is Mao's belief in the intellectual tradition of voluntarism: human will and determination will, in the end, remove all obstacles to making a better world. To Mao, it is this human will—diligence, hard work, and self-reliance—that must be inculcated into the minds of China's impoverished masses, whose potential had been inhibited by centuries of ignorance and superstition. Before and particularly during the Cultural Revolution, repeated references were made to Mao's favorite folk tale about a foolish old man who was able to move mountains through faith and perseverance. The tale, or parable, conveys the idea that it is necessary to rely on one's strength and to have faith in one's own ability to accomplish revolutionary tasks in building a new society.[36]

Theory and Practice

"We should not study the words of Marxism-Leninism, but study their standpoint and approach in viewing problems and solving them," Mao wrote in a theoretical essay in 1943.[37] He warned that too much reliance on purely abstract ideas or theory yields nothing but dogmatism, for theory is of no value if it does not involve practice. For Mao, the process of cognition involved more than merely what one observes and conceptualizes from observations. There was a third element—action or practice for the purpose of making changes in the material world. Knowledge cannot be separated from practice, since it begins with our experience. For example, Mao wrote that Marxism as a theory did not experience imperialism, and therefore, it was good only up to a point. When Lenin, who had perceived and experienced imperialism, added imperialism to the body of Marxist theory, it became meaningful to the Chinese situation. Theory must be subject to modification as changes occur and as new experiences enter into the situation. Marxism, according to Mao, must take into account both the historic experience and the characteristics of China in order to discover solutions to that country's problems. If one compares Mao's essay to practice with the writings of American pragmatists, such as John Dewey and William James, one finds many interesting parallels. As John Bryan Starr has noted, the philosophy of American pragmatists suggested not only that we discover the world around us but that we "know how to remake it."[38]

An example of the application of theory and practice can be seen in Chinese education during the 1950s and the Cultural Revolution, when students split their time between study and work in rural areas. Another example was revealed in Mao's attitude toward student participation in the Cultural Revolution. He would fondly tell the millions of students that they were the "revolutionary successors" and that the only way they could learn about revolution was to dare to make revolution in the streets. Perhaps the most important point to remember about Mao's treatise on practice is that Mao thought that one can discover knowledge and truth only through practice, which must become an integral part of theory, or conceptual knowledge. This conceptual knowledge will be changed by additional experiences and practices. If knowledge comes from practice, as Mao argued, then practice means action, or at the very least, an orientation toward action.

Contradiction

Mao's theory of contraction, which may have been formulated in collaboration with others, begins with the assertion that society has always been full of contradictions: life–death, sun–moon, darkness–lightness, black–white, individual–collective, and red (meaning politically correct)–expert. It is from the juxtaposition of these contradictions that changes can take place in society. Change takes place because there is a tendency for one aspect of the contradiction "to transfer itself to the position of its opposite" through some type of struggle between the two opposites. Adhering to Marxist theory, Mao said that all conflicts are class conflicts between social groups: prior to socialism, peasants versus landlords; now, proletariat versus bourgeoisie. The origin of this theory, sometimes known as the "law of unity of opposites," can be traced to Hegelian dialectics and Marxian dialectical materialism. As others have noted, Mao probably was also influenced by the traditional concept of opposites, yin and yang.[39] The idea that conflict and change are normal was certainly revolutionary. As was said in Chapter 1, the traditional Chinese society, under Confucianism, had been told to strive for harmony and to maintain the status quo. The theory of contradictions is considered by many to be the core of the thought of Mao Zedong.

Mao felt that the interplay of contradictions would continue even though society had advanced into the higher level of socialism. In 1957 Mao said that none of the socialist countries, including China and the Soviet Union, could transcend the contradictions of social classes by forgetting the class struggle. In an essay entitled "On the Correct Handling of Contradictions Among the People,"[40] Mao advanced the idea that class struggle would continue for an indefinite period of time. It would no longer be in regard to the contradictions between "friends" and "enemies" but rather would apply to those between proletarian and bourgeois thinking and behavior. In 1957 Mao explained that there are two types of contradictions: "antagonistic contradiction" between ourselves and the enemy; and "nonantagonistic contradiction" among working people, between peasants and workers, or between cadres and the masses. The nonantagonistic contradictions are essentially matters of ideological and political right and wrong. Since there are two different types of contradictions, Mao proposed two different methods of resolving these conflicts. For antagonistic contradictions, the proletariat dictatorship must suppress the reactionary elements in society; but for the nonantagonistic contradictions among the people, a continuous process of struggle and criticism must be employed to "raise the level of consciousness" and to correct erroneous thinking and behavior of the people. It is through this continuous process of struggle and criticism that unity can be achieved. The key objective of struggle and criticism is to proletarianize the behavior and thinking of the individual, no matter what economic background he or she may possess. It is the "proletarian consciousness" that is important in the final determination of one's class status.[41] Mao defined several major nonantagonistic contradictions or problems that the Chinese must resolve: (1) those between heavy industry and agriculture; (2) those between central and local authorities; (3) those between urban and rural; (4) those between national minorities and the Han Chinese over pluralism or radical assimilation.[42]

Mao made it clear that there were bound to be conflicts and struggles to resolve issues within the party:

> Opposition and struggle between different ideas constantly occur within the Party, reflecting contradictions between the classes and between the old and new in society. If in the Party there were no contradictions and no ideological struggles to solve them, the life of the Party would come to an end.[43]

The intraparty disputes, which have beset the party since the 1930s, usually are to be resolved by rectification campaigns; but when the contradictions within the party are so severe that they cause a serious "cleavage of opinion" among the members of the Politburo, the contradictions must be resolved by some type of mass campaign.

The Cultural Revolution has been viewed both as a rectification campaign and as a mass campaign for class struggle to resolve the contradictions between the proletariat and the bourgeoisie. It was called a "Cultural Revolution" because, according to both Marx and Mao, the construction of a socialist society demands transformation in the superstructure of culture, customs, and habits to eliminate the contradictions between proletariat collectivism and bourgeois individualism.[44]

Most Americans tend to be very skeptical about the utility of Mao's theory on contradiction, treating it as a piece of incomprehensible diatribe. It is very difficult for our highly technological and analytical minds to understand why, for instance, the workers and staff in a blast furnace attribute their higher output to simply studying the dialectics on contradiction. Still, the theory of contradiction was said to have helped the peasants and workers develop "a habit of analysis." Take, for instance, the case of the blast furnace. The workers and staff sat down and analyzed why the conventional way of increasing the temperature of the furnace brought about an increase in output only up to a certain level. By altering the structure of the layers of the furnace through analysis, they were able to control the flow of coal gas and to realize a greater yield after the standard level of pressure had been applied.[45] Another example is of peasants who have just been thrust into a position of leadership in their village and are daily confronted by a host of conflict-of-interest situations for which they must provide resolution. By studying the theory of contradiction, they are able to carry on some analyses of their own and to feel more confident in providing resolution to the conflicts.[46] In addition, the theory of contradiction is useful, as pointed out by Schurmann, in a struggle-and-criticism session, where the deviant individual's erroneous thinking is brought into sharp focus to facilitate correction through thought reform.[47] Finally, the theory of contradiction, by focusing on the law of unity of opposites, compels those involved in a conflict situation to agree on the proper means for resolving the conflict. Schurmann describes how discussion of a controversial issue at the Politburo level first produces two opposite sets of opinions and then results in the adoption of one set of opinions as a majority view and the other set as a minority view. Before a decision is reached, however, there must be what Schurmann calls the "juxtaposition" or polarization of opinion as a logical consequence of the application of the theory of contradiction.[48]

Permanent Revolution[49]

The ideas about change and struggle contained in Mao's essays on practice and contradictions logically lead to his concept of a permanent, or continuous, revolution: if society is rampant with contradictions, then "ceaseless change and upheaval" must be the normal condition to enable the society to reach a higher level of proletarian consciousness. The continuous class struggle is therefore necessary to create the "new socialist man."

Mao emphasized that his concept of the permanent revolution was different from Leon Trotsky's, a point that Khrushchev seemed to have missed. In 1959 Khrushchev compared two concepts, labeling Mao's concept of a permanent revolution a mixture of anarchism, Trotskyism, and adventurism. One essential difference was that Trotsky was merely concerned about "the transition from the democratic to the socialistic stage of the revolution," while Mao was concerned about "a separate stage of social transformation" during which the revolutionary environment must be maintained to eliminate all bourgeois influences and tendencies and to rebuild the superstructures.[50] Another difference was that Trotsky and Stalin would permit a new class of technocrats to emerge in order to establish a new economic base. Mao, on the other hand, argued that a new economic base does not necessarily bring about a new superstructure; class struggle must continue from the beginning to the end and while the society is undergoing transformation. Mao believed that "politics must take command so that the elites understand the correct ideological line." The contradictions must be solved by continuous struggle or revolution. Mao would insist: "We must destroy the old basis for unity, pass through a struggle, and unite on a new basis." Viewed from this perspective, both the Socialist Education Movement and the Cultural Revolution were important examples of the theory of permanent revolution. At the heart of Mao's theory of permanent revolution is the thesis that even after the establishment of a new economic base, both individuals and institutions can acquire bourgeois tendencies and thus change the color of the revolution.

In light of the events since Mao's death and the pragmatic leaders' quest for political and economic reform, how have the basic tenets of Mao's thought come to be viewed in China? To what extent has there been modification of Mao's thought?

First, efforts were made by pragmatic leaders to demolish the myth that Mao was the only contributor to the thought of Mao. The party's assessment of its history clearly stated that Mao's thought was "a summary of the experiences that have been confirmed in the practice of the Chinese revolution." In other words, it was the product of "collective wisdom," since "many outstanding leaders of our party made important contributions to the formulation and development of Mao Zedong Thought."[51] The new leaders took the position that Mao's thought had been contaminated by the erroneous "ultra-Left" ideas of the radicals. The 1981 party assessment maintained that Mao's thought must continue to play the guiding role in China's revolution; it should not be discarded "just because Comrade Mao Zedong made mistakes in his later years."[52] The party document went on to point out that "it is likewise entirely wrong to adopt a dogmatic attitude toward the sayings of Mao Zedong, to regard whatever he said as the immutable truth which must be mechanically applied everywhere, and to be unwilling to admit honestly that he made mistakes in his later years."[53]

Second, major modifications have been made with regard to Mao's concepts and ideas of class struggle, continued revolution, and contradiction.[54] The Cultural Revolution, the party now said, conformed neither to Marxism-Leninism nor to Chinese reality: "They represent an entirely erroneous appraisal of the prevailing class relations."[55] The actual targets of the upheaval were neither "revisionist" nor "capitalist" but instead were Marxist and socialist principles.[56] The 1981 party document declared that "class struggle no longer constitutes the principal contradiction after the exploiters have been eliminated as classes in socialist society."[57] While there would be class struggles in the future, they would differ in terms of scale, targets, and methods. Large-scale class struggle, such as that of the Cultural Revolution, which stressed the overthrow of one class by another, was no longer to be tolerated.[58] The targets for future class struggle would be counterrevolutionaries; enemy agents; criminals who engage in economic crimes such as bribery, embezzlement, and profiteering; and the remnants of the Gang of Four.[59] Since class struggle was no longer the principal contradiction in Chinese society, "tempestuous mass movement" was no longer the appropriate method to be employed. Instead, legal procedures embodied in the state constitution and party rules ought to be prescribed as the proper way for handling different types of contradictions in society.[60] Thus, the theory of contradiction must be discarded because it is not only wrong but "runs counter to Marxism-Leninism and Chinese conditions."[61]

The party's assessment went on to say that labeling party leaders as "capitalist roaders" failed to distinguish the people from the enemy.[62] The reinterpretation then invoked Mao by saying that class struggle between antagonistic classes was eliminated when landlords and rich peasants were eliminated in the 1950s. Moreover, to differentiate among classes according to people's political attitudes, as the radicals had done in the Cultural Revolution, was fallacious because "it is impossible to make scientific judgment of class by using people's thinking as a yardstick."[63] The principal contradiction, it argued, was no longer between the proletariat and the bourgeoisie but between the need of the people for more and better material well-being and the present low level of economic development.[64] Since the downfall of the radicals, certain "social contradictions" had surfaced—for example, the craving for Western-type individual freedom and decadent lifestyle versus the socialist system and the people's interest.[65] The method for resolving these new "social contradictions" should be that of criticism, not of physical struggle.

MAO'S LEGACY AND DE-MAOIZATION

Something unusual has happened to China: the present leadership moved to deemphasize the "personality cult" of Mao. On July 1, 1978, the fifth-eighth anniversary of the founding of the Chinese Communist Party, the major mass media published the text of Chairman Mao's 1962 talk to some 7,000 cadres at an enlarged central work conference.[66] What was so significant about the publication of the talk was that it was at that 1962 gathering that Mao admitted he had made serious mistakes and should be criticized for the ill-fated Great Leap programs. Mao admitted frankly that he knew very little about "economic construction" or about industry and commerce. Some of the policies of the Great Leap, Mao confessed, had been mistakes on his part, and he took full responsibility for them. There were many other small signs or signals of the downgrading of some of Mao's teachings: For instance, the *People's Daily* stopped carrying Mao's quotations on the front page.

But there is also continued veneration for Mao as a great leader. One need only look at the thousands of people who have filed silently into the memorial hall in the Tiananmen Square in Beijing every day since it opened in 1977 to realize the profound affection the people had for Mao. None of China's new leaders ever makes a speech without quoting a line or two from Mao, either to illustrate or to justify his or her own position. In the post-Mao era, as well as in those periods when he was alive and active, Mao has been a unifying symbol for the Chinese. More than any other leader in modern China, Mao has left an enormous legacy for his people.

The thinking of Mao was very complex, as we have pointed out. His ideas had their roots in the Chinese intellectual tradition, particularly in the May Fourth Movement, in the Marxist-Leninist tradition, and in the revolutionary experiences of the Chinese Communist Party. Yet Mao's populist approach, contained in the concept of the mass line, was distinct and went beyond Marx, Lenin, and the Chinese tradition. The vision that the semiliterate peasants and workers—collectively, the masses—could be the source of ideas and inspiration for the leaders was truly revolutionary. The application of this core concept enabled the CCP to secure popular support from the period of guerrilla operations in the 1930s and 1940s through the land reform and communization movements in the 1950s and 1960s. The failure of the Great Leap, and the questions raised about the results of the Cultural Revolution, make it appear doubtful that Mao's concept has been realized. Yet in spite of the dampening effect of the Great Leap and the Cultural Revolution, Mao's prescription for a proper relationship between the leaders and the led in the mass line formula remain a fundamental work style for the Chinese leaders. The state constitution of 1982 and the party charter of 1982 enshrine this Maoist vision of relying on the masses for inspiration, support, and implementation of policies and programs. It is the mass line as an ideological concept that has given the Chinese their national identity.[67]

Mao's practical ideology also has functioned as a guide, if not as a basis, on which individuals in Chinese society shape their attitudes and regulate their behavior. These ideas serve as a set of preferred societal values against which actions and thoughts are judged. Mao's philosophical ideas and teachings, such as human will and determination, self-sacrifice, and service to the people, have become an integral part of today's value system, governing behavior. To many Americans, and to some of Mao's own colleagues, the idea of a permanent revolution and of ceaseless change may be too unsettling, bordering on anarchy; but in Mao's vision, the revolution is like a pair of straw sandals that have no definite pattern but rather "shape themselves in the making." Stuart Schram's tribute to Mao is worth quoting: "Mao has left the sandal of the Chinese revolution unfinished, but it has already begun to take shape, and for a long time to come it can scarcely fail to bear his stamp."[68]

Ideology alone could not have had such a great impact on China. In the final analysis, it took a man like Mao, with exceptional skill and acumen as a political leader, to translate ideas into concrete actions and to make people do over a long period of time what the leader wanted. No other Chinese leader in modern times was involved directly in so many important issues over such a long period of time as was Mao Zedong.[69]

It has been fashionable since Mao's death and since the arrest of the radical leaders in October 1976 to detect signs of the deemphasis of Mao's ideology and of the programs he supported during the Cultural Revolution. The term *de-Maoization* has come into vogue.[70] There is even some debunking of "Maoism," which has been termed a "myth"—too abstract to be understood.[71] However, we must use caution in assessing Mao's ideas and programs. First, the function of a political ideology is to serve a unifying purpose, and the thought of Mao, perhaps more than anything else, has done just that. Mao's ideas have given the Chinese people the hope that they can do something about their lives using their own initiative and hard work. The accomplishments of the Chinese during the past forty years in finding solutions to some of the most pressing and difficult problems of humankind cannot be dissociated from Mao's ideology and the organizations he established for translating these ideas into concrete programs. Second, because of the enormity of these human problems for so large a populace—who for centuries lived in stagnation, inertia, and pessimism— Mao's ideas offered the message that the people must constantly experiment, think afresh, and be willing to take risks.

Mao, however, has been subjected to intensive criticism since 1978. One of the first such criticisms appeared in the publication of a speech made by Zhou Enlai to the First All-China Youth Congress in 1949, in which Zhou warned young people not to look upon Mao as a demigod.[72] Zhou related a story about how unhappy Mao was when he learned that a school textbook had said that he had been opposed to superstition when he was a boy of ten. On the contrary, Zhou explained, Mao believed in gods when he was a little boy and "prayed to Buddha for help" at one time when his mother became ill.[73] Zhou's message to youth in 1949 was twofold: they should not regard Mao as an infallible leader, and they should seek truth from facts. It is this blind worship of Mao that has been deemphasized. Truth, including Mao's thought, as the leaders now insist, must eventually be tested by practice—this is the major theme in China's policy of moderation.

After a lengthy debate at the Third Plenary Session of the Eleventh Central Committee meeting (December 18–22, 1978), China's new leadership agreed that the time had come for the people to "emancipate their thinking, dedicate themselves to the study of new circumstances, things, and questions, and uphold the principle of seeking truth from facts." [74] While paying tribute to Mao's "outstanding leadership," the party's Central Committee nevertheless found that Mao had made mistakes: "It would not be Marxist to demand that a revolutionary leader be free of all shortcomings and errors." [75] This was the beginning of the drive to deemphasize Mao and to dispel the myth of his infallibility, which had been built up over the years by the radicals. Anti-Mao posters appeared in Beijing in late 1978 and early 1979, along with the party's admission of "erroneous" action in the Tiananmen Square incident in April 1976 and its reexamination of the events of the Cultural Revolution. In December 1978 the Central Committee exonerated and rehabilitated a host of top leaders purged in 1959 and during the Cultural Revolution for opposing Mao or his policies, including Pen Dehuai, Peng Zhen, Bo Yibo, and Tao Zhu. Deng Xiaoping, who repeatedly endured Mao's wrath, has been quoted as saying that Mao was perhaps "seventy percent correct and thirty percent wrong." [76]

The Central Committee's final assessment of Mao came at its June 1981 session when it approved the report on the party history. [77] The document represented a culmination of intensive discussion and debate about Mao's role in the party. The report was initiated by the pragmatic leaders under Deng Xiaoping. It may be instructive for us to find out how these leaders evaluated Mao and what they considered to be Mao's mistakes.

First, an agonizing attempt had been made by the pragmatic leaders to distinguish between Mao as leader and the body of ideas collectively known as the thought of Mao Zedong. Deng Xiaoping repeatedly emphasized that Mao's contribution to the Chinese communist revolution could not possibly be "obliterated" and that "the Chinese people will always cherish his memory." [78] In the party document, Mao's thought was considered "a correct theory" and "a body of correct principles and a summary of practical experience." [79] It went on to point out that it would be wrong to deny its guiding role in the Chinese revolution "just because Comrade Mao Zedong made mistakes in his later years." [80]

One may ask why they insisted on such a distinction. One possible reason may be that this was a necessary political compromise to placate opposition within the party and the army. The army in particular still found it difficult to denounce Mao's leadership after years of religious adherence to his ideology. [81] Chinese leaders now argued that Mao made a "tremendous contribution" in the formation of his thought. But that did not imply that "every word Mao uttered and every article he wrote, much less his personal mistakes, belong to the Mao Zedong Thought." [82] It was obvious that the party was not prepared to completely denounce Mao, as Khrushchev had denounced Stalin in 1956. Chinese theoreticians and propagandists adhered to the line that "under no circumstance should one confuse a leader's mistakes with the scientific ideological system named after him or describe the mistakes as a component part of the scientific system." [83] To either abandon Mao's thought [84] or reject Mao's correct ideas would "lead China along a dangerous path, bring a great loss to us and court disaster." [85] During the top leaders' debate in 1978, the venerable Marshal Ye emphasized that "we cannot negate entirely Mao Zedong Thought." Ye expressed the fear that if the party lost its theoretical and ideological base, China would regress to its position prior to 1949. [86]

What mistakes had Mao committed in his later years? The party's official assessment identified five major political errors that were largely attributed to Mao.

First, the 1957 "rightist" rectification campaign launched after the "Hundred Flowers Bloom" movement was misdirected. Instead of criticizing "a handful of bourgeois rightists," the class struggle was extended in scope and intensity so that it eventually engulfed a substantial segment of the population. The intellectuals particularly were branded unfairly as "rightists," and were purged. Some leaders now in power admitted that Mao was not the only one responsible for the large-scale purge of the intellectuals in 1957; other senior party officials had supported the ill-considered policy at the time.[87]

Second, Mao was responsible for mistakes committed in the 1958 Great Leap Forward and the commune programs. He was blamed for the "Leftist" errors in promoting "excessive targets" and issuing "arbitrary decisions." The party assessment charged that Mao violated his own principles by initiating the Great Leap and the commune programs without thorough investigation, study, and experimentation. He was criticized for "smugness" and "arrogance" and charged with being impatient— looking for "quick results" and ignoring economic realities. One senior party leader extended the blame to the entire Central Committee that had endorsed the Great Leap decision in 1958.[88] While the party assessment noted that Mao had made self-criticism in 1962 for his mistakes in the 1958 Great Leap, this did not exonerate him from the error.

Third, Mao erred in forcing the Eighth Central Committee in 1959 to launch a vicious campaign to discredit and vilify a number of senior party leaders, including Marshal Peng Dehui, the defense minister at the time, for disagreeing with Mao over the Great Leap policies. Mao was condemned for launching a struggle within the top party leadership that "gravely undermined inner-party democracy" at all levels.[89]

Fourth, Mao was blamed for widening the erroneous policy of class struggle and mistakenly applying the theory of contradiction in another mass campaign, the Socialist Education Campaign, in 1963. Here Mao was blamed for insisting that the contradiction between the proletariat and the bourgeoisie was the main contradiction and for proclaiming that the bourgeoisie class continued to exist under socialism. The 1963 Socialist Education Campaign focused on party leaders who had taken "the capitalist road." Mao, the party assessment in 1981 pointed out, had contradicted himself—treating contradiction among the people as contradiction with the enemy. The 1963 mass campaign unjustly purged a large number of party cadres and plunged China once again into confusion and chaos.

Finally, according to the party assessment, the greatest mistake Mao made was the Great Proletarian Cultural Revolution in 1966. The new pragmatic leaders viewed this upheaval as an extreme expansion of Mao's "ultra-Left" ideas of class struggle and continued revolution.[90] The party declared that the theses of the Cultural Revolution were not only erroneous but inconsistent with Mao's thought, for these ideas misinterpreted the class relations that existed in China at that time. The very things the Cultural Revolution denounced were, in fact, Marxist and socialist principles. To insist on continued revolution, Deng now pointed out, was to make a "wrong judgment of the Chinese reality." The gravest of all Mao's mistakes, in Deng's view, was the attack launched during the Cultural Revolution on veteran party leaders with years of dedicated revolutionary service and administrative experience.[92] Deng revealed that Mao himself admitted a year or two before his death that the Cultural Revolution had been wrong because it had resulted in the "decimation"

of experienced cadres through purge and physical abuse and, in effect, had constituted a nationwide "civil war." [92]

The party's assessment charged that in the Cultural Revolution—where "one
class overthrows the other"—Mao had violated his own mass line principles. The
upheaval was "divorced both from the party organization and from the masses." [93] It
involved masses but was "devoid of mass support" because, the new leaders now
argued, it was launched by Mao personally with the knowledge that "the majority of
the people were opposed to the 'ultra-Left' ideas." [94] The party assessment concluded
that the Cultural Revolution was initiated by one leader, Mao, who labored under
"misapprehension" and was taken advantage of by the radicals. The final result of the
Cultural Revolution was "catastrophe to the party, the state, and the whole people." [95]

The new leaders also made remarks about Mao as a leader and about his personal character. Deng found Mao's "patriarchal behavior" to be a major shortcom-
ing, an "unhealthy style of work": "He acted as a patriarch. He never wanted to
know the ideas of others, no matter how right they could be; he never wanted to
hear opinions different from his." [96] Associated with this behavior was Mao's
"smugness" about his early success, which led to his "overindulgence" of ultra-
Left ideas in his later years. He became "overconfident" and "arrogant." [97] He also
was accused of "feudal practice," a disparaging remark used by Deng to describe
Mao as a leader and as a person. To Deng, the manner in which Mao chose Lin
Biao as his successor in 1969 clearly illustrated Mao's feudal practice—he
behaved as though he were the emperor who could pass on the reign to his chosen
successor.

Perhaps the most damaging condemnation of Mao was for his promotion of the
"personality cult" that viewed him as a demigod and treated his thought as "infinite
and boundless." [98] The party assessment concluded that Mao had gradually isolated
himself from the masses and the party, he had "acted more and more arbitrarily and
subjectively, and increasingly put himself above the Central Committee of the party."
Thus, he had become less "democratic." [99] With Mao's image reduced to that of a
Marxist mortal, Hu Yaobang, the party's new general secretary, declared at the 1982
party congress that "personality cult" must henceforth be forbidden. [100] Further, the
new leaders abolished the practice of life-long tenure for leaders. [101]

In effect, what the Chinese said in their reevaluation was that there were really two Mao Zedongs: a good Mao and a bad Mao. The serious mistakes of his later
years must be renounced; but his thought, ideas, and practice—as reinterpreted and
modified by the pragmatists now in power—must be preserved and enshrined. Was
this a true and accurate assessment of Mao, or was it some sort of "convoluted
logic"? [102] Can we really separate the man from his ideas? Was the Mao of the Great
Leap and the Cultural Revolution really different from the Mao that existed before
1957? Was Mao more innovative and less arrogant before 1957? Can we really say
in the same breath that Mao violated his own principles and practices but was also
"the spiritual asset of the party"? It may also be argued that Mao had always been
an innovator who preferred an "alternative model of development for China." [103] Perhaps the Great Leap and the Cultural Revolution were actually symbols of Mao's
constant search for a new lifestyle. [104]

Certainly, the process of assessing Mao is by no means complete. We have
not exhausted our study of Mao the man nor of his role in Chinese history. [105] Nev-

ertheless, the reevaluation of Mao has yielded and will continue to yield important facts—as well as varied perspectives—on his role in the Chinese revolution and his legacy to the people. Meantime, Mao, who has been dead for nineteen years, has not been rejected by the Chinese people altogether. Judging by the hundreds of books on Mao that have appeared in bookstores in China in the past few years, his image has made a comeback—not as a feared, ruthless, godless dead leader, but as a folk god. His laminated portrait has been displayed on trucks, taxicabs, and walls of rural homes as an omen or good luck charm to fend off evils and misfortunes. The new deification of Mao may have begun in Guangzhou in South China as a fad; it spread nationwide by 1992. The cult of Mao worship may simply be the manifestation of a recurring need for the Chinese to look for a folk deity in hard as well as good times under economic reform. From that perspective, the appearance of Mao portraits may be to some Chinese another way of criticizing the current leadership by showing nostalgia for more stable times when there was no inflation and there was guaranteed job security—the "iron rice bowl." According to a survey conducted in 1992 by a research group at the People's University in Beijing, four in ten out of a sample of over 3,000 said they were not entirely satisfied with political an economic conditions; but six in ten gave their approval. Nevertheless, on the 100th anniversary of Mao's birth on December 26, 1993, party chief Jiang Zemin claimed that Deng's reform ideas are rooted in Mao's thought despite their inherent contradictions.

The most revealing recent biography about Mao and Deng Xiaoping has been the book written by an old China hand, the late Harrison E. Salisbury.[106] Mao is portrayed in this book as a decadent, traditional emperor surrounded by young dancing girls. According to Salisbury he embarked on ruinous adventures during his rule, in addition to pursuing the destruction of his colleagues with demonic zeal.

IDEOLOGY IN FLUX: RESURGENCE AND REDEFINITION

Is Marxism still applicable for solving China's problems today? The debate on this question began in December 1984 when there appeared in the *People's Daily* an unsigned commentary that expressed the view that orthodox Marxist theory was obsolete and its rigid application could no longer solve China's problems.[107] A correction was made the very next day by inserting a word in the original text that read: "We cannot expect the writings of Marx and Lenin written in their time to solve *all* (italics are author's) of our present problems."[108] (The original version was said to have been based on comments made by the then-party chief Hu Yaobang.) The suggestion that Marxism-Leninism was perhaps no longer applicable to today's China opened up a debate between orthodox hard-liners and pragmatic reformers. The latter held the view that Marxism-Leninism was somewhat outdated in China's search for practical solutions to her economic ills. The orthodox hard-liners took the position that to deny the validity of Marxism-Leninism in today's world would be tantamount to committing ideological heresy. The current debate stresses three interrelated ideological problems facing China's leaders today. First, there seems to be a need to justify or "legitimize," to use one China scholar's phrase,[109] the economic reforms and the open door policy through which capitalistic techniques had been imported into China since 1978. (These reform measures will be discussed in Chapters 11 and 12.) The second question concerns how far China can go in adapting techniques and still call itself socialist.[110] Finally, there is the problem of how to uphold socialist ethics and morality and prevent the corrosive influence of bourgeois tendencies.[111]

Problem No. 1: Has China Rejected Marxism?

One of the underlying reasons for sacking former party chief Hu Yaobang in January 1987 was his outspoken views about the need to adapt Marxism to China's conditions. When addressing a group of visiting Italian Communist Party officials in June 1985, Hu said that in order to develop Marxism, its "outdated theories must be rejected," and "the latest achievements of all humanity must be incorporated into it."[112] Hu asserted that Marxism could be developed and enriched by practice. He emphasized, as Mao had done in the Yanan days, that "Marxism is not an immutable rigid dogma."[113] A communist, according to Hu, "must be good at rejecting or replacing individual Marxist concepts that are outdated or proved through practice to be inapplicable."[114]

It must then be remembered that the views expressed by Hu in 1985–86 were no different from what he said in 1981 after assuming the party's chief position. In his maiden speech, Hu issued a note cautioning that Marxism was only a guide to action, not "rigid dogma."[115] On the issue of Marxism's validity in today's China, Hu had support from some of the more liberally inclined theorists within the party. Ma Ding, a pseudonym for a lecturer at Nanjing University, wrote an article in November 1985 in which he argued that the works of Marx were more of a critique of capitalism than a blueprint for building socialism. Moreover, Ma argued that he found no ready answers in Marxism to existing problems in China today. Ma went a step further by pointing out that even Marx had given credit to some "bourgeois economic theories." As a Marxist economist, Ma Ding not only took the position that Marxist classics offered no ready answers to the problems of China's new socialist world, but advocated the study of bourgeois economic theories such as monetarism and Keynesian economics to take the place of Marxist classics.[116] In addition to the questioning of Marxism's continued relevance to a changing world, there were also criticisms raised by those who were more reform-minded that the very method of studying Marxism needed reform. They argued that the "dogmatic and repetitive teaching methods" must be changed at the universities and in the high schools.[117] They called attention to the indifference and apathy among high school and university students to Marxist studies, and attributed this growing attitude to the repetitious and boring methods used to teach the subject. Some universities, like the prestigious Beida, had decided to reduce study time on Marxist classics by as much as 30 percent in classrooms.[118] (In the aftermath of the 1987 and 1989 student demonstrations, however, an increase in the ideological study had been urged for most universities.)

By 1986 a discernible shift had taken place on the issue of Marxism's relevance to present-day China. This shift may have been influenced by the inner party debate between orthodox hard-liners and the pragmatic reformers, which eventually culminated in the sacking of Hu Yaobang. In early January a commentary appeared in the mass media that repudiated the assertion that Marxism was outdated; instead it argued that such views were "inaccurate" and represented "a distortion."[119] While admitting that Marxism was only a guide to action, the commentator reiterated that the party had always considered the study of Marxism "an unshirkable duty" for its members.[120]

Partly as a defense and partly as a way of placating the orthodox hard-liners, Tian Jiyun, the Politburo member and vice premier in charge of economic reforms and the protégé of premier Zhao, presented the reformers' views in January 1986 when he addressed the state cadres in the central government. Tian told the state bureaucrats that the economic reforms so far introduced in China would not deviate from socialism if the following principles were upheld: public ownership of means of production; "to each according to his work"; and a socialist planned economy for the production of the nation's major commodities.[121]

But Tian's defense on behalf of the reformers paled in comparison with the rebuke by Peng Zhen, a leading voice from the orthodox hard-liners' faction, in a lecture to students at Zhejiang University in eastern China. Peng raised the rhetorical question: in what direction would China carry out its various reforms without using Marxism-Leninism as a guide? He also expressed his annoyance over accusations that labeled him "conservative" in this thinking. He then told the students that "Marxism-Leninism is revolutionary and not conservative, and that it can develop; it is not fossilized," for that was how socialist China was founded.[122]

While serving as chairman of the NPC's standing committee, Peng also seemed to have aimed his criticism at Hu Yaobang. In a stinging statement before that committee, Peng lashed out at those who proclaim the inferiority of socialism and who seemed to have forgotten their vow as party members to carry out faithfully the communist ideal.[123] Peng also attacked Deng Xiaoping for confusing the issue when Deng told the visiting Polish delegation in September 1986 that China had yet to prove that socialism was better than capitalism. Peng made a defense of the superiority of social democracy already evolving in China.[124] Other attacks on the reformers also surfaced. An editorial appeared in the *Workers Daily* that asserted (1) that Marxism is a science; (2) that Marxism constantly opens new avenues to truth; and (3) that the basic tenets of Marxism "have been proved correct in practice many times and must remain true for all times," including what was happening at that time in China.[125]

The ideological debate became even more pronounced after the removal of Hu Yaobang as party chief, a temporary victory for the orthodox hard-liners. Then Deng Xiaoping made a hasty tactical retreat. In his meeting with U.S. Secretary of State George Shultz in early March 1987, Deng made these points for both domestic and foreign consumption: First, he declared that he could not see a populous nation like China going capitalistic; and second, that China must modernize socialism in order to enable it to break away from its backwardness.[126] However, prior to Deng's now modulated view of socialism, the aged orthodox hard-liners such as President Li Xiannian and Bo Ibo had peppered their speeches with the old Maoist slogans such as "self-reliance" and "austerity," while urging the party cadres to be more diligent in the study of Marxism-Leninism.[127] Hu Sheng, president of the Chinese Academy of Social Sciences, lent his position and prestige to the argument by stating that the roots of socialism had been firmly planted in China, that what had come out of the roots was a youthful but vibrant growth, and that what was needed now was to "nurture" this "socialist plant" to enable it to grow into a strong tree that "would reach the sky."[128]

Problem No. 2: How to Redefine Socialism

The debate on the validity of Marxism in present-day China led to the second ideological problem: how to redefine socialism in light of what has happened in China since 1978.

In an interview by American business leaders and reporters from *Time* in the fall of 1985, the first question put to Deng Xiaoping was whether it was possible to have a free-market economy coexisting with a socialist state.[129] Deng's answer was that there was no contradiction between the two: "So if we can combine the planning and the market economy, then I think it will help to emancipate the forces of social production and help accelerate them."[130] Market economy experiments in China did not violate socialist principles, Deng asserted emphatically at that interview. "To Get Rich Is Glorious," a popular slogan in China in the 1980s, was no sin because the major objective of socialism was to improve people's livelihood and society's wealth.

So even if China's economic reforms deviated here and there from classical Marxism, it should not be labeled as a "betrayal" of Marxist principles, wrote one reform-minded theorist in the leading liberal economic journal in Shanghai.[131] After all, the article continued, neither Lenin's Bolshevik Revolution (1917) nor Mao's guerrilla strategy to win political power was to be found in the works of Marx and Lenin. Marxism, as it was now defined by the reform-minded theorist, was a science but needed "constant revision in order to enrich itself and retain its vitality."[132]

In surveying the numerous pronouncements by the pragmatic leaders and the reform-minded theorists, there emerged a set of redefinitions, known as "socialism with Chinese characters."[133] What follows is a brief summary of what that term implied as defined by the reformers.

The reformers consistently held the view that there was no change in the economic base—that is, the public ownership of the means of production. To the reformers that was the single most fundamental requirement for socialism. To Deng Xiaoping, so long as public ownership played a dominant role, it must be considered as upholding socialism.[134] Individualized economy and joint ventures with foreign capitalist investors could be justified because these experiments were considered "necessary supplements to the socialist economy.[135] Deng was firm in his view that socialism could be preserved in China if "public ownership plays the dominant role in our economy."[136]

To reinforce Deng's assertion that these reforms had not endangered the basic precepts of socialism, Vice Premier Tian Jiyun, an economist, pointed out that the reform experiments with individualized economy and the joint ventures with foreign investors constituted less than 1 percent of the total industrial output in China, thus implying that China was far from being capitalistic.[137] Reformers also seemed to have taken the position that not only had the state continued to own the major means of production, but that there was still no deviation from socialism even if the government ceased to directly manage the state-owned enterprises, so long as it continued its ownership.[138] They pointed out to their critics that so long as the land was still collectively owned, the responsibility system introduced in the rural areas after 1978 would not lead to exploitation. Reformers argued that in socialist China the principles of "each according to his work" or "to teach according to the means of production contracted" was still very much emphasized under the rural responsibility system.[139] They charged that Mao was wrong in insisting on implementing concepts such as "absolute egalitarianism" or the "iron rice bowl," for these ideas stifled "people's enthusiasm for work" and sanctioned "laziness and shoddy work."[140] Deng Xiaoping told Mike Wallace of CBS News that "to get rich in a socialist society means prosperity for the entire people" and that common prosperity would not lead to polarization with the rich pitted against the poor.[141] (Parenthetically, William Hinton, author of the classic work on the land reform entitled *Fanshen*, felt that it was difficult to justify ideologically the assertion that there was no polarization when a peasant contracted land from his collective and then began to hire extra farm hands to help in the field. Hinton took the position that there was already polarization under the rural responsibility system simply because the peasant who contracted land was going to reap "a lion's share of profit" and that the hired hand received only a wage comparable to that existing before the 1953 land reform.)[142] As soon as rural reform became successful, party propaganda publicized those peasants who suddenly became affluent, the so-called "ten-thousand yuan" (about $3,000), rural rich. Then when criticisms began to mount about how to justify the basic principles of socialism, a propaganda shift took place that pointed out that there were only a handful of those rich households in the rural areas and that they must face many business risks, plus the added burden of no longer being eligible for collective welfare.[143] Nonetheless, even Vice Premier Tian had to admit that there was "the problem of wide income gap among wage-earners working in different trades" in urban areas.

Problem No. 3: How to Prevent the Corrosive Influence of Bourgeois Tendencies and the 1986 Policy on Culture and Ideology

For reasons of party unity and political stability, pragmatic reformers reached a compromise with the orthodox hard-liners by adopting the party's resolution on culture and ideology at the Sixth Plenum of the Twelfth Central Committee on September 28, 1986.[144] Deng Liquan, the former propaganda chief who lost his position for pushing the "Spiritual Pollution" campaign in 1983 (see Chapter 9), revealed that the 1986 party resolution on culture and ideology produced intense debate within the party hierarchy, so much so that the original text went through eight or nine different drafts.[145] Let us now summarize briefly the key points in the 1986 party document on culture and ideology.

First, the party resolution admitted that the economic reforms had produced changes in people's outlook and orientation toward ideology. It asked the key question: "Will we be able to resist the decadent bourgeois and feudal ideologies and avoid the danger of deviating from the right direction?"[146] Evidently as a concession to the reformers, the resolution then stated that China must keep its door open and continue the reforms, so long as the Four Basic Principles (socialist road, people's dictatorship, party leadership, and Marxism-Leninism-Mao's thought) were to be upheld.

Second, the resolution condemned the "capitalist ideology and social system ... and the ugly and decadent aspects of capitalism" but, on the other hand, encouraged learning from "developing capitalist countries the advanced science, technology, and applicable expertise and economic management."[147] In other words, the party resolution, as a compromise between two contending factions, wanted to have the best of both worlds. In case there was any doubt or confusion as to which direction China was headed, the document stated that "the ultimate ideal of our party is to build a communist society that applies the principle, 'from each according to his needs.' " [148] Third, as a concession to the orthodox hard-liners, who had criticized the reformers and those intellectuals who openly questioned the validity of Marxism, the 1986 party resolution on culture and ideology reiterated that "Marxism is the theoretical basis of socialism" and that "we have to depend on Marxism as our guiding theory." But, as a rebuke to Hu Yaobang and perhaps Deng Xiaoping to some extent, the orthodox hard-liners had their last word on Marxism's validity: "It is wrong to regard Marxism as a rigid dogma. It is also wrong to negate its basic tenets, view it as an outdated theory and blindly worship bourgeois philosophies and social doctrines." [149] Although it condemned bourgeois liberalization as "negating the socialist system in favor of capitalism," the 1986 party document tiptoed cautiously about academic freedom, of "creative writing," and freedom of discussion—all these could be permitted if "Marxism is to serve as a guide in academic work and the arts." [150] Fourth, perhaps in deference to Chen Yun and other orthodox hard-liners for their concern about the need to combat "the corrosive ethics" brought on by the open door policy, the 1986 party document spoke of "socialist ethics" and "socialist morality." Socialist ethics must reject "both the idea and the practice of pursuing personal interests at the expense of others . . . putting money above all else, abusing power for personal gains, cheating and extortion." [151]

The compromise on culture and ideology reached between the orthodox hard-liners and the pragmatic reformers, as reflected in the party document, was short-lived. The promise of academic freedom, freedom for creative writing, and freedom of discussion by the intellectuals under the slogan of "let a hundred flowers bloom" (a revival of the 1957 slogan) was discarded instantly when university students' demonstrations erupted in December 1986. Once again the pendulum seemed to have swung slightly to the left and the party intensified the campaign against "bourgeois liberalization." (See Chapter 9.) Within a week the *People's Daily* issued two front-page editorials urging the eradication of bourgeois liberalization that "poisons our youth, is harmful to socialist stability, disrupts our reform and open door policy." [152] Bourgeois liberalization was now defined as "an idea negating the socialist system in favor of capitalism." [153] Newspaper editorials charged that there were a few people who advocated "the capitalist road" and "capitalist practices." Then on January 12, a *People's Daily* commentator lashed out against those who advocated "complete Westernization"—meaning "learning from Western science, technology, culture, politics, ideology, and ethics"—and against those who held that socialism had failed in the last thirty years. [154] Obviously these comments were aimed at intellectuals like Fang Lizhi and Liu Binghua who had already been expelled from the party. The commentator made a convoluted argument that the open door policy and "complete Westernization" were two different things: it was possible to master advanced science and technology from capitalist countries but to discard at the same time "the capitalist ideology and social system which safeguard exploitation and oppression, as well as its evil and corrupt aspects." [155] Du Yun, vice minister of the State Education Commission, charged that the December 1986 student demonstrations reflected the influence of bourgeois liberalization that had appeared in the last few years. [156]

Thus China is now facing an ideological dilemma: how to adhere to the ide-

ological rigidity of Marxism-Leninism
desire of the intellectuals for thinking an
possible for China's leaders to make a
niques on the one hand, and the capitalis
advanced scientific developments, on th
for people to demand more freedom an
are introduced into the economic system
la argues that in essence "capitalist te
from the pluralistic system from which
that economic reforms will most likely
more liberties and prosperity, there is a
of more freedom and more free choices
validity of socialism and Marxism.[158] Deng Xiaoping,
the gap between the two contending factions, argued that there was a need to modernize, but not to "derevolutionize," to make the socialist system work, but not to "negate" it in favor of capitalism. But the ultimate question remains: how is this to be done?

An answer to which the party leaders agreed in the aftermath of the December 1986 student demonstrations was to reiterate and reinstitute the "Four Basic Principles" laid down by Deng in 1978–79 when the "Democracy Wall" movement was crushed. Zhao Ziyang, then the new party chief, ruled out a political campaign against the intellectuals, but reaffirmed that the party leadership must adhere to these basic principles.[159] In a lengthy talk on January 20, 1987 in the Great Hall of the People in Beijing, Zhao proposed that if party members follow the "Four Basic Principles," it would be possible to keep bourgeois liberalization in check. Zhao insisted that the battle against bourgeois liberalization must be limited to remaining within the party as "an inner party issue."[160] Zhao then indicated that to build socialism with Chinese characters required "the integration of the universal truth of Marxism-Leninism with the practice of China's development and reform."[161] On the importance of adherence to the "Four Basic Principles," the pragmatic reformers now had the support of the orthodox hard-liners. Peng Zhen told the NPC standing committee on January 21, 1987 that these principles were the result of China's socialist revolution and an integral part of its constitutional makeup.[162] Peng said that it was the historic conclusion that "if there were no CCP, there would be no new China; only socialism can save China."[163] In other words, the "bird" of economic reform must be caged— to use octogenarian Chen Yun's famous metaphor—by Deng's "Four Basic Principles," in which the party leadership was paramount. Zhao made it clear that "anyone who departs from Marxism on so serious a question will be censured by the party and the masses."[164] A number of dissenters within the party who raised questions about the party's continued dominance and control had been asked to resign from the party or face expulsion.[165] But in the end, Zhao was sacked during the 1989 Tiananmen protest on the charge that he was not too keen on the anti-bourgeois-liberalization campaign. (See Chapter 10.)

Since the June 1989 Tiananmen crackdown, not only have Deng's "Four Basic Principles" been reemphasized, but old slogans laden with heavy ideological content have been revived. In Li Peng's report on the work of the government to the NPC on March 20, 1990, he declared that adherence to the "Four Basic Principles" must cies of reform and opening to the outside world. He cau-

political propositions in contravention of the Constitution put forward by
g to negate the socialist system in China and leadership by the Chinese
st Party under the banners of freedom, democracy, and human rights.[166]

proposed in one breath that

We should conduct intensive education in the need to uphold the Four Cardinal Principles and oppose bourgeois liberalization and in patriotism, collectivism, socialism, communism, self-reliance, hard work, revolutionary traditions and professional ethics.[167]

One of the great revolutionary traditions was revived—the Lei Feng campaign of the
Cultural Revolution days.[168] Revolutionary outlook, not competence (the old "red"
versus "expert" theme), was prerequisite in promotion and advancement in a cadre's
career.[169]

Recently, the traditional revolutionary greeting of "Comrade" replaced "Good
evening" in news broadcasts for the first time in years, for the term "Comrade" represents revolutionary tradition and is "a glorious title." The transitional leadership
under Jiang Zemin and Li Peng named bourgeois liberalization as a "major root
cause" of the Tiananmen upheaval. In the words of Jiang, agreed to and supported by
Li Peng, the ideological task is that "We must enhance socialist ideology while carrying out to the end the struggle against bourgeois liberalization."[170]

It remains to be seen how successful these efforts will be in reeducating the
populace to accept traditional revolutionary values and concepts, for the intellectuals
and China's youth, who comprise three-quarters of the population, no longer accept
the validity of socialism. (For a discussion of Dengism, market socialism, or the
Theory of Deng, see Chapter 11.)

NOTES

1. Franz Schurmann, *Ideology and Organization in Communist China* (Berkeley, Calif.: University of
   California Press, 1966).
2. Ibid., pp. 21–22.
3. Peter Zattow, *Anarchism and Chinese Political Culture* (New York: Columbia University Press,
   1990).
4. *China: Alive in the Bitter Sea* (New York: Times Books, 1982), pp. 300, 417; and Richard Bernstein, *From the Center of the Earth*, pp. 104–5.
5. Richard Bernstein, *From the Center of the Earth: The Search for the Truth about China* (Boston and
   Toronto: Little, Brown, 1982), p. 104.
6. "Recognize Correctly the Situation and Policy by Upholding the Four Guidelines," *Hongqi*, 5
   (March 1, 1981), 2–11; "Overcoming Two Erroneous Trends of Thought," *Beijing Review*, 24 (June
   8, 1979), 3.
7. "Hu Yaobang's Speech," *Beijing Review*, 28 (July 13, 1981), 20.
8. Feng Wenbin, "Following the Party Line Laid Down by the Third Plenum, Resolutely March Forward on the Socialist Road," *Hongqi*, 10 (May 16, 1981), 2–12. Also see *Beijing Review*, 23, 25, and
   26 (June 8, 22, and 29, 1981).
9. "Nature of Chinese Society," *Beijing Review*, 23 (June 8, 1981), 22.
10. Ibid., pp. 7–8.

11. "Hu Yaobang's Speech," p. 20.
12. Ibid., p. 20.
13. Mao-Tse-tung, "Ching Kanshan Revisited," *Peking Review*, 1 (January 2, 1976), 5.
14. Stuart Schram, *Mao Tse-tung* (London: Penguin, 1970), p. 36.
15. See Enrica Collotti Pischel, "The Teacher," in *Mao Tse-tung in the Scale of History*, ed. Dick Wilson (London: Cambridge University Press, 1977), pp. 144–73.
16. Lucian Pye, *Mao-Tse-tung, the Man in the Leader* (New York: Basic Books, 1976), pp. 20–21.
17. Edgar Snow, *Red Star Over China* (New York: Grove Press, 1961), p. 151.
18. Pye, *Mao Tse-tung, the Man in the Leader*, pp. 17–38.
19. Ibid., pp. 17–38.
20. Ibid., p. 23.
21. Edgar Snow, *The Long Revolution* (New York: Vintage Books, 1973), pp. 170–71.
22. Snow, *The Long Revolution*, p. 169.
23. Wilson, ed., *Mao Tse-tung in the Scale of History*.
24. Hsiung, *Ideology and Practice: The Evolution of Chinese Communism*, p. 67.
25. Mao Tse-tung, "Report on an Investigation of the Peasant Movement in Hunan," in *Selected Works of Mao Tse-tung* (Peking: Foreign Language Press, 1967), vol. i, pp. 23–59.
26. Benjamin I. Schwartz, *Communism and China: Ideology in Flux* (Cambridge, Mass.: Harvard University Press, 1968), p. 41; Hsiung, *Ideology and Practice*, pp. 61–62; and Chester C. Tan, *Chinese Political Thought in the Twentieth Century* (Garden City, N.Y.: Doubleday, 1971), pp. 345–46.
27. James C. Hsiung, *Ideology and Practice*: The Evolution of Chinese Communism (New York: Holt, Rinehart and Winston, 1970) p. 67; and Conrad Brandt, Benjamin Schwartz, and John Fairbank, *A Documentary History of Chinese Communism* (New York: Atheneum, 1966), pp. 80–93.
28. John W. Lewis, *Leadership in Communist China* (Ithaca, N.Y.: Cornell University Press, 1963), p. 72.
29. Mao Tse-tung, "Some Questions Concerning Methods of Leadership," in *Selected Works of Mao Tse-tung* (Peking: Foreign Language Press, 1967), vol. iii, pp. 117–22.
30. Ibid., p. 113.
31. See Lowell Ditmer, "Mas Line and Mass Criticism in China: An Analysis of the Fall of Liu Shao-chi," *Asian Survey*, vol. xiii, no. 8, (August 1973), 772–92.
32. Schram, "The Marxist," in *Mao Tse-tung in the Scale of History*, p. 48. Also in Lewis, *Leadership in Communist China*, p. 79.
33. Lewis, *Leadership in Communist China*, pp. 84–86.
34. James R. Townsend, "Chinese Populism and the Legacy of Mao Tse-tung," *Asian Survey*, vol. xviii, no. 11 (November 1977), 1006–11.
35. Ibid., p. 1009.
36. See James C. F. Wang, "Values of the Cultural Revolution," in the *Journal of Communication*, vol. 27, no. 3 (Summer 1977), 41–46. Also see Maurice Meisner, "Utopian Goals and Ascetic Values in Chinese Communist Ideology," *Journal of Asian Studies*, vol. 28, no. 1 (November 1968), 101–10.
37. Mao Tse-tung, "On Practice," *Selected Works of Mao Tse-tung* (Peking: Foreign Language Press, 1967), vol. i, pp. 295–309.
38. Starr, *Ideology and Culture: An Introduction to the Dialectic of Contemporary Chinese Politics* (New York: Harper and Row, 1973), p. 30.
39. Hsiung, *Ideology and Practice*, pp. 102–3; Pye, *Mao Tse-tung: the Man in the Leader*, p. 45; Schram, "The Marxist," in *Mao Tse-tung in the Scale of History*, p. 60.
40. *Selected Works of Mao Tse-tung* (Peking: Foreign Language Press, 1977), vol. v, pp. 384–421.
41. Starr, *Ideology and Culture*, p. 128.
42. Mao Tse-tung, "On the Ten Major Relationships, April 25, 1956," *Peking Review*, 1 (January 1, 1977), 10–25.
43. Mao Tse-tung, "On Contradiction," in *Selected Works of Mao Tse-tung* (Peking: Foreign Language Press 1967), vol. i, p. 517.
44. William Hinton, *Turning Point in China: An Essay on the Cultural Revolution* (New York: Monthly Review Press, 1972).
45. Shih Kang, "Dialectics in Blast Furnaces," *Peking Review*, 41 (October 12, 1973), 19–20.
46. The illustration is given by Gray and Cavendish, *Chinese Communism in Crisis* (New York and London: Holt, Rinehart & Winston, 1968), pp. 59–60.
47. Schurmann, *Ideology and Organization*, p. 54.

48. Ibid., p. 55.
49. "Talks at the Chengtu Conference, March 1958" in Stuart Schram, ed., *Chairman Mao Talks to the People, Talks and Letters, 1956–1971* (New York: The Pantheon Asia Library, 1974), p. 108. For further insights into the concept, see Stuart Schram's two articles, "Mao Tse-tung and the Theory of Permanent Revolution," *The China Quarterly*, 46 (April–June 1971), 221–44, and "The Marxist," *Mao Tse-tung in the Scale of History*, pp. 56–62. Also, see John Bryan Starr, "Conceptual Foundations of Mao Tse-tung's Theory of Continuing Revolution," *Asian Survey*, vol. xi, no. 6 (June 1971), 610–28.
50. Starr, "Conceptual Foundations of Mao Tse-tung's Theory of Continuing Revolution," p. 612.
51. "On Questions of Party History," p. 29.
52. "How to Define Mao Zedong Thought," *Beijing Review*, 1 (January 7, 1980), 5–6. Also see Deng Xiaoping's interview with Oriana Fallaci, *The Guardian Weekly* (September 21, 1980), p. 17.
53. "On Questions of Party History," p. 35.
54. Ibid. On the matter of class struggle, see the following issues of *Beijing Review*: 7 (February 18, 1980), 6; 20 (May 19, 1980), 24; 22 (June 2, 1980), 24; 34 (August 24, 1981), 3; 44 (November 2, 1981), 20; 17 (April 26, 1982), 3; 33 (August 16, 1982), 17; 49 (December 6, 1982), 16.
55. "On Questions of Party History," p. 21.
56. Ibid.
57. Ibid., p. 37.
58. See editorial in the *People's Daily* (November 6, 1982), p. 1; and Xi Xuan, "Why Should a Theory be Discarded?" *Beijing Review*, 44 (November 2, 1981), 20.
59. *People's Daily* (November 6, 1982), p. 1.
60. "Communiqué of the Third Plenary Session of the Eleventh Central Committee, Adopted on December 22, 1978," *Peking Review*, 52 (December 29, 1978), 19.
61. Ibid., p. 11; and *Beijing Review*, 7 (December 18, 1980), 6.
62. "Why Should a Theory be Discarded?" p. 20.
63. Ibid., pp. 21–22.
64. "Current Class Struggle," *Beijing Review*, 17 (April 26, 1982), 3.
65. Ibid.
66. Mao Tse-tung, "Talk at an Enlarged Working Conference Convened by the Central Committee of the CCP," *Peking Review*, 27 (July 7, 1978), 6–22. The version has been, however, included in translation form in Schram, *Chairman Mao Talks to the People*, pp. 158–87.
67. Townsend, "Chinese Populism and the Legacy of Mao Tse-tung," p. 1011.
68. Schram, "The Marxist," in *Mao Tse-tung in the Scale of History*, p. 69.
69. Mike Oksenberg, "Mao's Policy Commitments, 1921–1976," *Problems of Communism*, vol. xxv, no. 6 (November–December 1976), 19–26. Also see his article "The Political Leader," in *Mao Tse-tung in the Scale of History*, pp. 88–98.
70. Fox Butterfield, "China Disputes Legacy of Mao More Directly," *The New York Times* (May 17, 1978), pp. 1–2; Linda Mathews, "Demaoization' Extends to People's Daily," Los Angeles Times Service, reprinted in *Honolulu Advertiser* (January 13, 1978), E-15; and David Bonavia, "Dismantling Parts of Maoism—But Not Mao," *Far Eastern Economic Review* (October 7, 1977), 39–41.
71. Simon Leys, *Chinese Shadows* (Middlesex, England: Penguin, 1978).
72. Chou En-lai, "Learn from Mao Tse-tung," *Peking Review*, 43 (October 27, 1978), 7.
73. Ibid., p. 8.
74. Communiqué of the Third Plenary Session of the Eleventh Central Committee of the Communist Party of China, pp. 14–15.
75. Ibid., p. 15.
76. *Ming Pao* (Hong Kong) (November 30, 1978), p. 1.
77. "On Questions of Party History," pp. 8–39.
78. Deng Xiaoping's interview with Oriana Fallaci in "Deng: Cleaning Up Mao's Feudal Mistakes," p. 16.
79. "On Questions of Party History," p. 29.
80. Ibid., p. 35.
81. See Dittmer, "China in 1981: Reform, Readjustment, and Rectification," pp. 34, 42.
82. "Differentiations Are Necessary," *Beijing Review*, 38 (September 21, 1982), 17.
83. "On Questions of Party History," p. 35; and "Differentiations Are Necessary," p. 17.
84. Huang Kecheng, "How to Assess Chairman Mao and Mao Zedong Thought," *Beijing Review*, 17 (April 17, 1981), 22.

85. Ibid.
86. See text of document entitled "Senior Cadres' Appraisal of Mao Zedong," in *Issues and Studies*, vol. xvi, no. 5 (May 1980), 77.
87. Huang Kecheng "How to Assess Chairman Mao and Mao Zedong Thought." Also see "Deng: Cleaning Up Mao's Feudal Mistakes," p. 17.
88. Huang Kecheng, "How to Assess Chairman Mao and Mao Zedong Thought."
89. "On Questions of Party History," p. 19.
90. Huang Kecheng "How to Assess Chairman Mao and Mao Zedong Thought," p. 21; and "Deng: Cleaning Up Mao's Feudal Mistakes," p. 16.
91. "Deng: Cleaning Up Mao's Feudal Mistakes," p. 16.
92. Ibid., p. 16.
93. "Had 'Cultural Revolution' Mass Support?" *Beijing Review*, 47 (November 23, 1981), 20–21.
94. "On Questions of Party History," p. 22.
95. Ibid.
96. "Deng: Cleaning up Mao's Feudal Mistakes," pp. 7, 18.
97. "On Questions of Party History," pp. 19, 25. Also see "Hu Yaobang's Speech," p. 12.
98. "The Correct Concept of Individual Role in History," *People's Daily*, (July 4, 1980), p. 1. Also see "On Questions of Party History," p. 25.
99. "On Questions of Party History," p. 25.
100. Ibid.
101. *People's Daily* (August 14, 1981), p. 1.
102. Krishna P. Gupta, "Mao's Uncertain Legacy," *Problems of Communism*, xxxi (January–February 1982), 45. One China scholar felt the Mao assessment in the early 1980s was not really "de-Maoism," but a Dengist effort to "use Mao's charism." See Jean C. Robinson, "Mao after Death: Charisma and Political Legitimacy," *Asian Survey*, vol. xxviii, no. 3 (March 1988), 353–68.
103. Gupta, "Mao's Uncertain Legacy," 50.
104. Ibid.
105. For scholarship on Mao, see Ross Terrill, *Mao: A Biography* (New York: Harper and Row, 1980); Dick Wilson, *The People's Emperor Mao: A Biography of Mao Tse-tung* (New York: Doubleday, 1980); Maurice Meisner, "Most of Maoism's Gone, But Mao's Shadow Isn't," *Sunday New York Times* (July 5, 1981), E-15; Raymond F. Wylie, *The Emergence of Maoism* (Stanford, Calif.: Stanford University Press, 1980).
106. Harrison E. Salisbury: *The New Emperors: China in the Era of Mao and Deng* (Boston: Little, Brown, 1992).
107. *People's Daily* (December 7, 1984), p. 1.
108. *People's Daily* (December 8, 1984), p. 1.
109. Hong Yung Lee, "The Implication of Reform for Ideology, State and Society in China," in "China In Transition," *Journal of International Affairs* (Winter 1986), 87.
110. *Beijing Review*, 2 (January 13, 1986), 4.
111. *Beijing Review*, 49 (December 8, 1986), 14–15.
112. *Beijing Review*, 26 (August 30, 1985), 26.
113. Ibid.
114. Ibid.
115. *Beijing Review*, 28 (July 13, 1981), 20.
116. Ibid.
117. *People's Daily* (February 17, 1986).
118. Ibid.
119. *Beijing Review*, 2 (January 13, 1986), 4.
120. Ibid.
121. *Beijing Review*, 5 (February 3, 1986), 16–17.
122. *Beijing Review*, 20 (May 19, 1986), 23.
123. *Far Eastern Economic Review* (February 11, 1986), 5.
124. Ibid.
125. *Beijing Review*, 48 (December 1, 1986), 26.
126. *Ming Pao Daily* (Hong Kong) (March 5, 1987), p. 1.
127. *Ming Pao Daily* (Hong Kong) (February 17, 1987), p. 1.
128. *Ming Pao Daily* (Hong Kong) (March 9, 1987), p. 2.
129. *Time* (November 15, 1985), pp. 39–40.

130. Ibid., p. 39.
131. *World Economic Herald* (Shanghai) (November 3, 1986), as translated in *Ta Kung Pao Weekly Supplement* (Hong Kong) (November 27, 1986), p. 10.
132. Ibid.
133. For discussion of the term "Socialism with Chinese Characters," see the following articles from *Beijing Review*; 5 (February 3, 1986), 15–17; 25 (June 23, 1986), 14–15; 38 (September 22, 1986), 4–7; 49 (December 8, 1986), 4–5; 3 (January 29, 1987), 14–15; 4 (February 26, 1987), 14–18. Also see *China Trade Report* (May 1983), 5; and John Bryan Starr, "Redefinition of Chinese Socialism," *Current History* (September 1984), 265–68 and 275–80. An earlier discussion on the term by the Chinese was found in *Beijing Review*, 47 (November 19, 1984), 18–19.
134. *Time* (November 4, 1985), p. 39.
135. *Beijing Review*, 49 (December 8, 1986), 14.
136. *Time*, op. cit.
137. *Beijing Review*, 5 (February 3, 1986), 17.
138. Ibid.
139. *Beijing Review*, 49 (December 8, 1986), 14.
140. Ibid. Also see Liu Guoguang, "Socialism Is Not Egalitarianism," *Beijing Review*, 39 (September 28, 1987), 16–18.
141. *Beijing Review*, 38 (September 22, 1986), 6.
142. William Hinton, "Transformation in the Countryside: Part I—From the Communes to the Responsibility System," *US-China Review*, viii, no. 3 (May–June, 1984), 9.
143. *Beijing Review*, 5 (February 3, 1986), 15.
144. See *Beijing Review*, 40 (October 6, 1986), i–viii.
145. *Zhengming*, 109 (November 1986), 30.
146. *Beijing Review*, 40 (October 6, 1986), ii.
147. Ibid., iii.
148. Ibid.
149. Ibid., vii.
150. Ibid.
151. Ibid., iv.
152. See *Beijing Review*, 3 (January 19, 1987), 15.
153. Ibid.
154. *People's Daily*, (January 12, 1987), p. 1.
155. *Beijing Review*, 3 (January 19, 1987), 16.
156. *Beijing Review*, 8 (February 23, 1987), 14; and *New York Times* (January 19, 1987), p. 1.
157. Jan S. Prybyla, "China's Economic Experiment: From Mao to Market," *Problems of Communism* (January–February, 1986), 23.
158. *Wall Street Journal* (February 2, 1987), p. 19.
159. *Beijing Review*, 5 and 6 (February 9, 1987), 26–29.
160. Ibid., p. 28.
161. Ibid., p. 30.
162. *People's Daily* (January 22, 1987), p. 1.
163. Ibid.
164. *Beijing Review*, 5 and 6 (February 9, 1987), 29–36. Also see these issues in *People's Daily*: (January 15, 1987), p. 1 and p. 4; (January 29, 1987), p. 1; (January 30, 1987), p. 1; (February 2, 1987), p. 1; and (February 22, 1987), p. 1.
165. See *Zhengming*, 119 (September 1987), 13–14.
166. *Beijing Review* (April 4–22, 1990), 11.
167. Ibid., xviii.
168. *China News Analysis*, no. 1411 (June 1, 1990), pp. 7–8.
169. *The New York Times* (January 25, 1990), A-10.
170. *Beijing Review* (July 31–August 6, 1989), 6.

chapter four

Political Institutions of the Party-State
Structural Issues and the Policy Process

Most of us who are familiar with democratic political systems tend to think of political institutions in terms of the different functions they must perform: executive (administrative), legislative, and judicial. In democratic societies these functions or powers are generally defined by state constitutions. Constitutions in democratic societies do not undergo drastic changes due to periodic upheavals. For China, because of its revolutionary nature as a state, there have been changes and upheavals, as discussed in Chapter 2, particularly during the Cultural Revolution decade (1966–76), when the goal of the upheaval, as instigated by Mao, was to "revolutionize" the established institutions. However, taking contemporary political developments in the People's Republic of China as a whole, we see that the basic structure of political institutions remains the same as that existing prior to the Cultural Revolution in terms of (1) continued party control or monopoly, (2) the hierarchical pattern, (3) methods by which party control is exercised, and (4) the highly bureaucratic nature of the political system.

In this chapter we will look more closely at two areas: first, the party as a basic political institution; second, the central government as an entrenched, cumbersome, bureaucratic machine in need of structural reform.

The Chinese Communist Party (CCP) is the source of all political power and has the exclusive right to legitimize and control all other political organizations. The CCP alone determines the social, economic, and political goals for society. The attainment of these goals is pursued through careful recruitment of members and their placement in party organs that supervise and control all other institutions and groups in society. All other institutions in China are controlled by the elites, who are themselves leaders of the party hierarchy.

HIERARCHICAL STRUCTURE OF THE PARTY

The salient characteristics of the party as an organization are that it is hierarchical, pyramidal, and centralist in nature. A simplified representation of the structure of the CCP is shown in Figure 4.1. The pyramidal structure of the CCP has four main levels of organizations: (1) the central organizations; (2) the provincial organizations; (3) the xian (county) or district organizations; and (4) the basic and primary organizations—party branches in schools, factories, and villages.

CENTRAL-LEVEL PARTY ORGANS AND FUNCTIONS

In this section the central level of the party structure will be discussed in some detail. As we study the highest level of the party's organizations, we need to bear in mind that it is this network of overcentralized organizations that initiates, at the Politburo and Central Committee levels, or at the apex, policy decisions that are perfunctorily approved by the Central Committee. As we look at the overall organizational chart for the party in Figure 4.1, we see that the emphasis is on the flow of authority from top to bottom in accordance with the Leninist organizational concept of centralism. China, North Korea, and Vietnam have the only Leninist parties remaining after the collapse of the Soviet Union bloc in 1990–91.

FIGURE 4.1   Simplified Model of CCP Organizational Pyramid. *Source:* **Modified version of Joseph L. LaPalombara,** *Politics within Nations* **(Englewood Cliffs, N.J.: Prentice Hall, 1974), p. 527. By permission of publisher.**

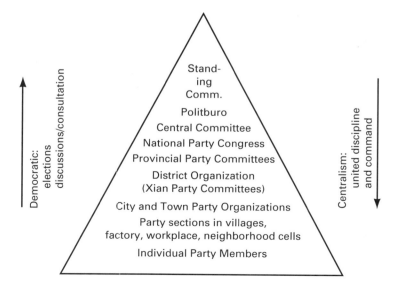

National Party Congress

In conformity with the tradition of a Leninist party, the CCP vests its supreme authority, at least nominally, in the National Party Congress. During its seventy-three year history, fourteen National Party Congresses have convened. The 1969, 1973, 1977, and 1982 party constitutions all stipulated that a congress must meet every five years. The two longest intervals between congresses were eleven years and thirteen years, between the Seventh Congress in 1945 and the Eighth Congress in 1956, and between the Eighth Congress and the Ninth Congress in 1969. The party constitutions of 1956, 1969, 1973, 1977, and 1982 contain a proviso, an escape clause, which states that "under special circumstances, it [the National Party Congress] may be convened before its due date or postponed" by the Central Committee. The 1982 party constitution also stipulated that the party congress may be convened if more than one-third of the provincial party organizations so request. Since the party congress generally meets in a perfunctory manner to approve policy changes recommended by the Central Committee, generally its sessions have been short, a week or two in duration.

We do not know how the delegates are chosen. The procedures for selection are generally determined by the Central Committee. Presumably, delegates are selected at the provincial and district levels to reflect the "constellation of power" at the central level. It is also possible for the power at the center to engage in slate making. The process of packing the congress at various levels of the party organization to represent factionalized leaders also may be in operation. Wang Hongwen, a radical leader from Shanghai, had been accused of pressuring his close supporters to run for the position of delegate for the Tenth Party Congress.[1] However, it was revealed in 1968 by Xie Fuzhi, the minister for public security, that delegates to the Second through the Seventh Party Congresses had been appointed.[2] The Central Committee instructed that delegates to the 1982 party congress be elected "by secret ballot after full consultation at party congresses" at every level of the party structure. For the first time, the instructions stipulated that "the number of candidates shall be greater than the number of delegates to be elected."[3] This was an attempt to democratize the party's election process. In addition, the Central Committee urged election to the party congress of experts in economics, science, and technology, and of women and minorities.

The sheer size of the party congress—1,545 delegates for the Twelfth Congress (1982) and 1,510 for the Eleventh Congress (1977)—makes it too unwieldy a body to be truly deliberative. However, the party congress does have certain basic functions to perform. Generally speaking, each session of the party congress has three standard items that constitute the entire agenda: a political report by the party chairperson or the chairperson's designee, a report on the revision of the party constitution, and the election of the Central Committee and its Standing Committee.

In 1980 some modification was made to the party congress agenda. The Central Committee in its February 1982 resolution set five agenda items:[4] report of the Central Committee, report by the party's discipline inspection commission, revision of the party constitution, outline of the long-term economic development plan, and election of a new Central Committee and Politburo.

A major task of the National Party Congress is to select the new Central Committee. Perhaps selection is not the proper term to describe the actual process involved: a preliminary list of those to become members of the Central Committee is usually drawn up by the key leaders in the hierarchy, and then the list is presented to the party congress for formal ratification. For instance, the draft list for members of the Eighth Central Committee (1956) was prepared by Liu Shaoqi supporters—Peng Zhen and An Ziwens.[5] At the Twelfth Party Congress (1982), delegates were given colored computer cards listing the names of all nominees for the Central Committee and for Central Advisory Commission membership. It was reported that during the balloting, delegates were permitted to delete any names on the list, as was the practice of the Seventh Party Congress (1945). Another feature introduced at the 1982 party congress, presumably a measure designed to democratize the party, gave delegates the right to "write up" names not on the nominations list.[6]

The party constitution adopted by the 1982 party congress was said to have been initiated by Deng Xiaoping, Hu Yaobang, and Hu Qiaomu, a key member of the Central Secretariat before he was elevated to the Politburo, and a former president of the Chinese Academy of Sciences. Hu Qiaomu and Peng Zhen presided over the drafting of the 1982 party constitution. The draft was circulated for discussion and comment at the Fifth Plenum of the Eleventh Central Committee in February.[7] After further revision by the Politburo and the Central Secretariat, it was sent to all levels of the party apparatus for discussion. While the 1977 party constitution was influenced by the remnants of the Left led by Hua Guofeng and Wang Dongxing, the 1982 party constitution represented the influence and power of Deng Xiaoping. The preparation of the 1982 party constitution was actually carried out in the winter of 1979 by the leaders associated with Deng. It went through four drafts before being introduced at the last session of the Eleventh Central Committee for adoption. The 1982 party constitution was as lengthy and detailed as the 1956 party constitution.

Some students of Chinese politics have pointed out that in addition to the important tasks of ratification of the party constitution and election of the Central Committee, the party congress accepts and reviews political reports from party leaders.[8] Reports presented at the National Party Congress have been published, and one can infer policy shifts and program emphasis from them. Since the Central Committee debates are never published except for occasional communiqués summarizing policy formulations and personnel changes, reports of the National Party Congress provide a unique source of information about the issues and programs of concern to the party. For example, at the party's Fourteenth Congress, held in October 1992, 2,000 delegates approved the party line for the next five years, or until 1997. It was outlined in the general secretary's lengthy speech that China must embrace the reform known as "socialist market economy," which was initiated by the 89-year-old paramount leader, Deng Xiaoping.[9]

Finally, there has always been a great deal of fanfare and publicity focused on the party congress. This is more than mere public relations work by the party. The convocation of the congress serves as a rallying point for the party members and for the populace in general. It creates a feeling of participation in the important decisions of the party among the delegates themselves, many of whom come from very humble backgrounds and remote regions of China. It instills in them the "sense of commitment" to and unity with their leaders and the party.[10] In 1982, for the first time, television programs focused on the proceedings of the 1982 party congress. Provincial and local stations broadcast many features about the party, including new songs composed for the occasion.

In view of the limited duration and agenda of the party congress, the question arises as to how preparations for it are made. Technically, the outgoing Central Committee is responsible for preparing the forthcoming congress. In practice, however, the Politburo or the Standing Committee of the Politburo prepares the agenda and designates members to draft the political reports and work on the new party constitution under its supervision. We probably can assume that political reports from the Seventh Party Congress (1945) through the Tenth Party Congress (1973) received personal approval from Mao. There have been admissions of hasty preparation for the proceedings of the party congress. Mrs. Liu Shaoqi (Wang Guangmei) admitted, under Red Guard interrogation during the Cultural Revolution, that "everything was done in a hurry" in preparation for the Eighth Party Congress (1956).[11]

Evidently, this was not the case when preparations for the 1982 party congress were initiated in the winter of 1979. The agenda for the 1982 party congress was not approved until February 1980 at the Central Committee's sixth plenary session.[12] The date for convening the party congress was not set by the Politburo until the spring of 1982, a delay of more than two years—yet within the five-year interval prescribed by the previous 1977 constitution. There were several reasons for the long delay in convening the party congress: (1) Deng Xiaoping needed time to consolidate his power by first installing Hu Yaobang and Zhao Ziyang in key party and governmental positions; (2) the vestiges of the "Whatever" faction had to be removed from the center of power; and (3) the issue of how to assess Mao needed to be decided before delegate selection to the new party congress could take place. Thus, disunity and disagreement had to be minimized or eliminated. In short, Deng needed time to arrange matters so that his control over delegate selection would be assured.

Preparation for the Thirteenth Party Congress began on September 25, 1986 when the Central Committee announced its decision to convene the congress in the fall of 1987. Provincial and local congresses were held in the summer months to elect delegates to the Thirteenth Congress. A total of 1,936 delegates were elected by 46 million party members, at least in theory. In practice, disproportionate allocations were made to allow special or "electoral units" to provide a fixed number of delegates. Thus, the military was represented by a total of 279 delegates, more than 14 percent of the total delegates to the congress. Another block of delegates—about 300, or over 16 percent of the total—came from the central party and governmental units. Delegates elected from the provinces represented the remaining two-thirds of the total delegates to the congress, which was unique in at least two respects. One, it provided a smooth transition of power from "the Long March generation" of old party veterans who joined the party in the 1930s to a younger but better educated group of technocrats who were groomed and promoted by the paramount leader Deng Xiaoping, who also stepped down from the top leadership rank and semiretired after the congress. Two, the importance of the congress went beyond the changing of the guard. It reaffirmed the correctness of Deng's economic reform measures and the open door policy with the outside world. The 1987 congress represented a decisive victory for Deng Xiaoping, the architect of a modernized post-Mao China.

The Fourteenth Party Congress, convened in October 1992, represented the final triumph of Deng Xiaoping when it endorsed wholeheartedly his "socialist market economy," or "building socialism under Chinese characteristics"—the official party acceptance of capitalist tools as "magic weapons" for a prosperous China (see the section on Dengism in Chapter 11).

Central Committee

The party constitution vests in the Central Committee the supreme power to govern party affairs and to enact party policies when the party congress is not in session. The large size of the Central Committee makes it an unwieldy body for policy making. Although the Central Committee as a collective body rarely initiates party policy, it must approve or endorse policies, programs, and major changes in membership of leading central organs. Thus, with a few exceptions, the Central Committee usually holds annual plenary sessions, either with its own full membership and alternate membership in attendance, or with non-Central Committee members as well in enlarged sessions. The few deviations from the norm occurred during the Korean War (1950–53), during the turbulent period prior to the Cultural Revolution (1962–66), and during the Lin Biao affair (1971–73). These regularized plenums of the Central Committee are the forums through which party and state policies and programs are discussed and ratified. On at least two occasions—the October 1955 plenum (enlarged), and the August 1959 plenum (enlarged)—the Central Committee became the "ultimate" body in deciding which agricultural policies were to be implemented. This occurred as a result of dissension among top leaders of the party.[13]

There has been a steady increase in the size of the Central Committee. The first session of the Eighth Party Congress (1956) expanded the full membership of the Central Committee from 44 to 97; the Ninth Party Congress (1969) almost doubled the size to a cumbersome 170; the Eleventh Party Congress (1977) elected 201 full and 132 alternate members of the Central Committee, for a total of 333; the Twelfth Party Congress (1982) elected 210 full and 138 alternate members, making the size (348 members) of the Twelfth Central Committee the largest to date. The Thirteenth Party Congress (1987) reduced the size to a total of 285 members (175 full and 110 alternate). The Fourteenth Central Committee, elected in October 1992, has a total membership of 317 (188 full and 129 alternate members).

There are several reasons why the membership of the Central Committee has increased its size. First, increased membership in the Central Committee reflects the phenomenal growth of the party membership as a whole since the Cultural Revolution, from approximately 17 million in 1961, to over 28 million at the time of the Tenth Party Congress in August 1973, to 53 million when the Fourteenth Party Congress convened in 1992. Second, as in the former Soviet Union, membership in the Central Committee has been used as a reward for loyal service to the party and to the government. Preeminent scholars and scientists have been elevated to Central Committee membership. Third, the Ninth and Tenth Party Congresses expanded Central Committee membership in order to make it reflect post-Cultural Revolution party leadership recruitment policy—increased representation by workers and peasants who have rendered significant political service to the party.

In order to provide solid support for Deng Xiaoping's economic reform policies, the top leadership was reshuffled in the fall of 1985. A total of 64 members of the Twelfth Central Committee, roughly 18 percent of the total membership of 210 full members, were retired to make way for a younger generation of leaders. By the time the Thirteenth Party Congress elected its new Central Committee, about 150, or 43 percent, of the aged Twelfth Central Committee members failed to be reelected. For the 1987 Thirteenth Central Committee, 95, or 54.2 percent, of the reduced 175 full membership were elected for the first time. The average age for the full Thirteenth Central Committee was 55, four years younger than the previous Twelfth Central Committee (1982). The educational level for the 175 full and 110 alternate members of the Thirteenth Central Committee had also been increased so that 209, or 73.3 percent, had some college-level education and about 57, or 20 percent, had specialized training in institutions of higher learning. In terms of organizational affiliation, the Thirteenth Central Committee's total 285 full and alternate membership was distributed as follows: 122 members, or 43 percent, came from the provincial and local government units; 98, or 31.4 percent, came from the central government and party departments; 53, or about 19 percent, represented the military establishment; and only 12, or 4.2 percent, represented personnel from the scientific and technological fields.

Almost half of the total 317 full and alternate members of the Fourteenth Central Committee elected in October 1992 were new faces representing young and middle-aged technocrats, and those provincial party secretaries, a dominant group, who were supportive of economic reform. The average age of the Fourteenth Central Committee members was 56.3 years. About 84 percent of the new members have advanced degrees.

The Politburo and Its Standing Committee: The Apex of Power

The principle of Lenin's democratic centralism calls for decision-making power within the party to be vested in a small number of key leaders who occupy positions at the apex of the power structure, the Political Bureau (Politburo). The formal language in the party constitution does not reveal the actual power of this top command of the CCP. The party constitutions of 1969, 1973, 1977, and 1982 simply stipulate that the Politburo shall be elected by the Central Committee in full session and shall act on its behalf when the Central Committee is not in session. The day-to-day work of the Politburo is carried out by its Standing Committee, the apex of the pyramidal structure of the party.[14] In essence, it is the Politburo and its Standing Committee that possess "boundless" power over the general policies of the party and all important matters of the regime that affect the government organs.[15] It is the Politburo that selects top personnel to direct the vast apparatus of the party, the government, and the military.

The Politburo holds frequent meetings; discussion is said to be frank and unrestrained. It has been compared to a corporate board of directors.[16] Decisions of the Politburo are generally reached by consensus after thorough discussion of the available alternatives.

When the party took power in 1949, the CCP Politburo consisted of eleven members, and its operation very closely resembled that of Lenin's inner circle of key leaders who made all the important decisions for the Soviet party, government, and the state.[17] By 1956 the CCP Politburo membership had increased to seventeen full and six alternate members, paralleling the enlargement of the party congress and the Central Committee. With fluctuations—as a result of deaths and purges—its membership rose to over twenty full members in later years. The Twelfth Party Congress (1982) elected twenty-eight members to the Politburo: twenty-five full and three alternate members. As we have seen with the party congress and the Central Committee, enlargement reflected a shift in function. The 1956 party constitution introduced the concept of the "apex of the apex": the formation of the Standing Committee of the Politburo, which became the top ruling clique. The membership of the

Standing Committee has varied from five to nine. The 1982 party congress elected a six-member Standing Committee. In many instances the Standing Committee makes decisions without even consulting the Politburo.[18]

It should be noted that prior to the Cultural Revolution, the decision-making process was institutionalized to a large extent by the frequent use of work conferences under the sponsorship of the Politburo of the Central Committee.[19] Since the purge of the radical leaders in October 1976, this institutionalized device for policy formulation has been revived, so that at least several dozen national conferences have been convened to develop national policies on various matters, including modernizing agriculture and industry, national defense, and science and technology.

According to the party constitution, the Central Committee elects members to the Politburo and its Standing Committee, but between 1935 and 1975 the actual selection rested in the hands of Chairman Mao. In fact, the determination of which Central Committee members were to sit on the powerful Politburo had been termed Mao's "personal prerogative."[20] Franklin Houn points out that Mao followed a general set of guidelines in his selection of candidates to Politburo membership: seniority in the party, contributions made to Mao's own rise to power, and loyalty and usefulness to Mao and to the party.[21]

At the first session of the Fourteenth Central Committee, held in October 1992, election of the twenty-member Politburo was done by secret ballot. However, there had been reports of behind-the-scenes "intervention" by Deng Xiaoping.[22] The elected twenty-member Politburo did not really elect the seven-member Standing Committee in October 1992. The list of seven names was nominated by the party's general secretary and approved by a show of hands in the twenty-member Politburo.[23]

Of the seven-members of the Standing Committee of the Politburo (featured on the cover of this book), the apex of the apex of the party, five are holdovers: Jiang Zeming (66), general secretary; Li Peng (64), the premier; Qiao Shi (68), the party's security chief; Li Ruihuan (58), the "manager of ideology"; and Zhu Rongji (63), an engineer by training, the economic chief. The two new Standing Committee members are Liu Huaqing (76), a naval commander who has been brought in at Deng's insistence to be a neutral or swing vote in future power contests between the reformists and conservatives within the apex of the apex; and Hu Jintao (49), the youngest new member of the Politburo and its Standing Committee, who has been engaged mostly in youth work and has been a party secretary in the Tibetan regions.

The average age for the present Politburo's Standing Committee is about 63, a comparatively younger crop of top leaders. About half of the current Standing Committee members have had formal education up to the university level, or have studied abroad. The other half had their training in party organization work and/or as carpenters, peasants, and soldiers in their earlier lives.

Other Principal Organs of the Central Committee

The Central Committee and its Politburo are serviced by a host of centralized organs, responsible for executing party policies and managing party affairs. Some of this machinery deals with the routine matters of party organization, propaganda, and united front work. However, four principal central party organs need to be briefly mentioned here: the Central Secretariat, the Military Affairs Committee, the Central Commission for Discipline Inspection, and the Central Advisory Commission.

The Central Secretariat. The Central Secretariat, as it existed from 1956–66, was the administrative and staff agency that supervised the party's numerous functional departments, paralleling the functional ministries of the central government. The total number of these central party functional departments may once have reached more than eighteen. Membership of the Central Secretariat was not fixed: it ranged from six or seven to ten or eleven top-ranking Central Committee members. For over a decade, the Central Secretariat was under the control of Deng Xiaoping, who served as its general secretary. Deng and the members of the Central Secretariat used the machinery to make or influence many important party decisions without even consulting Mao, the chairman of the party.[24] In the aftermath of the Cultural Revolution, the Central Secretariat, as a formal unit, was abandoned, probably at the insistence of Mao, who felt that it had overstepped its authority. From then until 1977 or 1978, the administrative functions of the party secretariat were absorbed by the General Office for the Politburo, headed by Politburo member Wang Dongxing. In the winter of 1978, Wang was replaced by Yao Yilin. At the same time, newly elected Politburo member Hu Yaobang, a trusted protégé of Deng Xiaoping, was appointed secretary-general of the Central Secretariat, which has been reestablished in its pre-Cultural Revolution form.

The reinstitution of a general secretariat and the abolition of the post of party chairperson must be viewed as an obvious rejection of Mao's practice of "overconcentration of personal power" in the party. The daily work of the party or of the Central Committee was now to be supervised by the Central Secretariat headed by Hu Yaobang, who in turn was assisted by eleven other members (one died in January 1983), four of whom were concurrently members of the Politburo. The 1982 party constitution makes it clear that the daily work of the Central Committee is to be carried out by the Central Secretariat under the overall direction of the Politburo and its Standing Committee. Article 21 of the 1982 party constitution stipulates that the general secretary must be a member of the Standing Committee of the Politburo and that it is his or her responsibility to convene its meetings.

The Central Secretariat now consists of seven major departments:[25] organization, propaganda, united front work, liaison office with the fraternal parties abroad, publication office of the *People's Daily*, a policy research office, and an office of party schools. Each of the eleven secretaries elected in 1982 to the Central Secretariat was to be chiefly responsible for a particular aspect of the party's activities. For instance, Wan Li had been in charge of agricultural polices and was credited with implementing rural reform. Yao Yilin, another member of the Central Secretariat, was in charge of economic reforms. Both Wan Li and Yao Yilin served concurrently as vice premiers on the State Council or the central government administration. Hu Qili was in charge of the party's organizations, including the activities of the Communist Youth League, of which he was once director.

We now know that the Central Secretariat meets twice a week behind the red walls of Zhongnanhai, a part of the former imperial palace and now both party headquarters and the seat of the central government, the State Council. Members of the Central Secretariat, elected by the National Party Congress, can initiate and formulate policies on anything they wish. The Central Secretariat has invited leaders in industry, commerce, agriculture, science, and education to Zhongnanhai to brief its members on current developments or problems. In addition, it processes a large volume of mail received from party cells and branches, as well as from the public.

Significant changes had been made by the Thirteenth Party Congress on membership election to and the role of the Central Secretariat. The Central Committee no longer elects the Central Secretariat members under the revision of the party charter (see second paragraph under Section 4 in Appendix B-1). Members of the Central Secretariat are now appointed by the Politburo, subject to approval or endorsement of the Central Committee; and it is now the working body of the Standing Committee and the Politburo.

The Military Affairs Committee.   Although the Military Affairs Committee (MAC) is a subunit of the Central Committee of the CCP, it reports directly to the Politburo and its Standing Committee. The MAC supervises the administration of the armed forces and makes policies in national defense. The MAC directly controls the General Political Department (GPD), the party's political agent within the PLA, which is in theory a branch of the Ministry of Defense but in practice operates independently of it. The GPD is responsible for the political education of the troops and publishes the *Liberation Army Daily*, the military's own daily newspaper.

The basic function of the MAC has been its exclusive responsibility in directing the party's military activities, including the power to appoint and remove military personnel. As a subunit of the Central Committee, with responsibility for strategy and tactics of the Chinese army, it can be traced back to the guerrilla days of the early 1930s.[26] After the 1935 Zunyi Conference, Mao assumed the chair of the Revolutionary Military Committee, the predecessor of the present MAC. By that time the committee had assumed the responsibilities of educating the troops in political matters and of approving the party's political commisars assigned to the various armies. The MAC operates through a standing committee; the members of that committee regularly conduct inspection trips to the thirteen regional military commands and submit reports directly to the Politburo. Throughout the years the MAC has held periodic special work conferences for military leaders from all regions and provinces on military and political–ideological topics. New policies and directives are explained at these conferences to ensure proper implementation. From around 1954 on, the MAC has also been responsible for conducting numerous political training schools for army officers. Ralph Powell points out that MAC supervision of the PLA is extensive and direct, covering even the most routine matters.[27]

A longstanding practice, instituted by Mao, was to have the party chairperson automatically serve as the chairperson of the MAC. That practice was abandoned by the 1982 party constitution, which stipulates only that the chairperson of the MAC must be a member of the Standing Committee of the Politburo (see Article 21 in Appendix B). In 1978 Deng Xiaoping assumed the chairmanship of the MAC, assisted by a permanent vice-chairman, Yang Shangkun, a trusted Deng associate. The three military marshals—Ye Jiangying, Xu Xiangqian, and Nie Rongzhen—served as nominal vice-chairmen of the commission by tradition.

Since his ascension to power in the 1980s, Deng has been the top party cadre whom the military could trust as the chairman of the MAC. At one time Deng was trying unsuccessfully to persuade the military to accept the late Hu Yaobang, then the party chief, as his successor to the chairmanship of the MAC.[28]

Deng submitted his resignation as the MAC chairman to the CCP Politburo on September 4, 1989, thus ending his reign of more than a decade over the military. After endorsing Deng's resignation, the CCP Central Committee elected as the new

MAC chairman Jiang Zemin, the new party chief in the aftermath of the Tiananmen crackdown. Now the Maoist tradition had been restored—that the party chairman concurrently holds the MAC chairmanship.

Although no official list of MAC members has been published, two general guidelines seem to determine its composition: (1) members include most of the senior military figures, particularly the PLA marshals; and (2) members usually reflect the composition of the Politburo. The size of the MAC ranges from at least ten members to perhaps nineteen or twenty. Traditionally, the first vice-chair of the MAC concurrently serves as the minister of defense. By 1982 that tradition, too, was abandoned. One recent defense minister, Zhang Aiping, age 72, was elevated from the position of deputy chief of staff in the military's senior command. Zhang was not, at the time of his appointment as defense chief, a vice-chairman of the MAC. The chief of staff for the PLA is usually a member of the Standing Committee of the MAC. There is also an interlocking membership situation existing among the MAC, the Politburo, and in Central Committee. The high degree of interlocking membership between the MAC and the Politburo is such that at least nine members of the Politburo elected by the Eleventh Central Committee (1977) had been members of the MAC. Similarly, at least ten members of the Politburo elected in 1982 have been members of the MAC, including Deng and Yang Shangkun.

Officially the Fourteenth Central Committee in October 1992 listed Jiang Zemin, Liu Huaqing, Zhang Zhen, Chi Haotian, Zhang Wannian, Yu Yongbo, and Fu Quanyou as members of the MAC. In order to accommodate Deng, who was no longer a member of the Central Committee or the Politburo in 1987, the party charter had to be amended. Article 21 now reads that "The members of the Military Affairs Committee of the Central Committee are decided on by the Central Committee" (see Section 4 in Appendix B-1), instead of the requirement that the MAC chairman must be a member of the Politburo's Standing Committee.

The Central Commission for Discipline Inspection. The true functions of the original party discipline control commission had not been spelled out anywhere, not even in the informative party constitution of 1956, which gave the hierarchical structure of the original Control Commission. However, based on recent revelations, the reestablished party control mechanism seems to have the following main functions: (1) maintenance of party morale and discipline; (2) control over the performance of party organizations; and (3) investigation of breaches of party discipline.[29]

As the party's internal rectification campaigns became more numerous and intensified in the late 1950s and 1960s, the Control Commission at all levels became more active in conducting investigations. This was particularly true on the eve of the Cultural Revolution, when a disunited party at the center caused confusion about the direction of party policies for the lower-level organizations. By the time the Cultural Revolution was in full swing in 1966, the entire party control mechanism simply fell apart. The end result was the abolition of the old Control Commission by the Ninth Party Congress. Both the 1969 and 1973 party constitutions directed that the masses, not the party control machinery, must provide overall supervision and control over matters of party discipline and the correctness of party policy or line. At least three forms of mass supervision over party discipline and unity were provided: (1) direct contact between the party cadres and the masses when investigation was required; (2) mass criticisms when policy was being implemented; and (3) mass participation in the management of party affairs through their representation in the revolutionary committee.

The party constitution of 1977 created a new control device—the Central Commission for Discipline Inspection—to strengthen party discipline and internal party democracy in the aftermath of the abusive practices instituted during the Cultural Revolution by the radical leaders. The new commission for party discipline is charged with the task of enforcing party rules and regulations, as well as with the development of sound party style, including the inculcation of all the requisite party virtues. In 1978 the third plenary session of the Eleventh Central Committee elected the first hundred-member Central Commission for Discipline Inspection, headed by veteran party administrator Chen Yun.[30] Prior to the Cultural Revolution, the sixty-member Control Commission operated through a standing committee of nine or ten members.[31] The standing committee for the newly formed Central Commission for Discipline Inspection consists of twenty-four party veterans, all purged or mistreated during the Cultural Revolution. In its first report, published in March 1979, the party's inspection commission urged that any false charges, wrong punishments, and frame-ups leveled against any party member be corrected and the victims rehabilitated. Thus, a first step was taken to tighten the slackened party discipline and to restore internal party democracy.

The Central Commission for Discipline Inspection was given considerable power and jurisdiction by the 1982 party constitution to monitor party rules and regulations; it reports directly to the Central Committee on violations of party discipline and on the implementation of party policies and decisions. An elaborate system of local commissions for inspecting party discipline was also established at the various party levels. The commission and its subsidiary bodies were now also made responsible for providing education among party members about party discipline and work style.

The Central Commission for Discipline Inspection is authorized to receive appeals and complaints from any party members and cadres who can prove that they were framed and charged by the radicals with false evidence. Xinhua News Agency reported in September 1979 that there were 150,000 letters of appeal addressed to the commission between December 1978 and August 1979.[32] Lower-level investigation of inner party discipline and breach of party rules from seventeen provinces, municipalities (Shanghai and Beijing), and autonomous regions processed 3.8 million cases of appeals and complaints.[33] The statistics provide us with some idea as to the number of verdicts reversed from 1979 to 1980.[34] The officially published statistics also seem to indicate the widespread ferreting out from the party ranks of those who evidently blindly followed the orders of the radicals during the decade of the Cultural Revolution. In one province, Fujian, the commission's investigation resulted in 1,560 cases of expulsion from party membership for violating party discipline.[35] The pingfan (reinstatement and exoneration) campaign was followed in January 1981 by another inner party review, ostensibly of all 38 million party members, but in actuality aimed at the rapid expulsion of the undesirables among the 15 million who became party members during the Cultural Revolution.[36] This inner party membership-cleansing campaign was preceded by the commission's investigation and expulsion posthumously of two leading party veterans of the Cultural Revolution: Kang Sheng, Politburo member and close advisor of Mao, and Xie Fuzhi, another Politburo member and public security minister and the height of the Cultural Revolution.

They were charged with participating in the plots of the Gang of Four to "usurp the supreme leadership of the party" and other grave crimes.[37]

If correct party style is a matter of life and death for the Central party, to use the words of Chen Yun (the first secretary for the Commission for Discipline Inspection), then some serious efforts must be made to rebuild the party on the basis of discipline and rules that will regulate and govern the behavior of party members. From this perspective, the guidelines for inner party political life must be considered a major accomplishment of the commission. Upon recommendation of the commission, the Central Committee in March 1980 adopted a set of twelve guidelines, or guiding principles, for inner party political life.[38] These general guidelines correct the abuses, anarchy, and laxity in party discipline that prevailed during the Cultural Revolution. Collectively, these guidelines tell us clearly what happened to the party when Mao permitted radical ideologues to seize the party machinery and disrupt inner party life. These rules may be read as a catalog of indictments against Mao's personal arbitrary rule and the ills of the party. For instance, one of the guidelines is to uphold the collective leadership of the party, not individual, arbitrary decision making. On important issues the guidelines now provide for collective discussion by the rank and file of the party and for decision making by the party committee. The fostering of a "personality cult" is now strictly prohibited: there may be no celebration of leaders' birthdays, no gifts, and no congratulatory messages. Henceforth, no memorial hall shall be erected for any living person, nor shall a street, place, or school be named after a party leader.

The new inner party political life guidelines demand tolerance for dissenting views at the discussion stage of policy making. No punishment is to be given for erroneous statements by a party member—so long as these dissenting opinions do not advocate factional activities or divulge party and state secrets. It is a criminal act to organize secret groups within the party. Party members are to speak the truth and to be honest in words and deeds. There shall be no abridgment of a party member's right to participate in meetings or to criticize any party organization or individual at party meetings. All party committees are to hold regular meetings and elections. Erroneous tendencies and evil deeds such as graft, embezzlement, factionalism, anarchism, extreme individualism, bureaucraticism, and special privileges are to be opposed at all times. In inner party struggles, a correct attitude must be adopted toward those who make mistakes, but "it is prohibited to wage ruthless struggle against those erring party members." Everyone is equal within the party and before party rules and regulations. No party member is permitted to show favoritism toward family or relatives. Finally, all party members must be reviewed and rewarded in accordance with their ability and competence. Hu Yaobang, the new party general secretary, argued that life-long tenure in a leadership position should be abolished, and that emphasis should be placed on promoting those capable party cadres who are in their prime.

Preliminary review of the work of the Central Commission for Discipline Inspection indicates clearly that the CCP has revived the pre-1956 concept of a central party organ to serve as a "party court" or "ecclesiastical court," for governing not only party discipline but also the inner party political life. It has also performed the task of "judicial review"—overruling a previous Central Committee decision by declaring a decision on Liu Shaoqi to be "unconstitutional" in accordance with party rules and discipline. As a kind of party court, the commission has also cleared the names of millions of party members and cadres who were unjustly accused of wrongdoing during the Cultural Revolution.

The commission may have been given another role when it was assigned the task of drafting the document on guidelines for inner party political life and shepherding its passage through the Central Committee: that of serving as a central organ for supervising the implementation of the guidelines. The commission is encountering difficulties and resistance among party members and cadres as regards this new role. A proper attitude toward good work style and party life, notwithstanding the promulgation of the guidelines, is still lacking.

In recent years an important area of the commission's task has been its investigation of violations of party discipline committed by party members. The crackdown on party cadres who engaged in corrupt practices became urgent as the number of cases mounted nationwide. Some party cadres took advantage of their position and power by engaging in bribery, smuggling, and embezzlement as economic reform took shape and as the open door policy to the outside world widened. In its first nationwide conference, held in 1983, the Discipline Inspection Commission revealed that the number of cases investigated for discipline violations committed by party cadres was a staggering 380,000.[39] In the southern province of Guangdon alone, over 500 party members were expelled in one year as a result of the commission's investigation into various "economic crimes" such as smuggling and embezzlement of public funds.[40]

The commission identified three main problems in its work: party cadres' refusal to reveal their wrongdoing; party leaders' reluctance to report their subordinates, friends, and family members for wrongdoing; and party leaders' habit of providing cover for their shady operations.[41] Further, there were reports that the commission itself had developed a lenient attitude toward some offending party cadres.[42] The convening of a special conference of 8,000 party officials in January 1986 marked in intensification of the anticorruption campaign aimed at party cadres,[43] particularly those in positions of power. To curb the commission's power, the reformers established the "Central Party Working Leadership Group," headed jointly by Central Secretariat members Qiao Shi and Wang Zhaoguo, a close colleague of Hu Yaobang, the party chief.[44] It was Qiao Shi and Wang Zhaoguo who conducted an on-the-spot investigation of the infamous scandal of the massive purchase of cars imported from Japan to Hainan Island on the South China Sea. Officials of the island then diverted the cars to island party cadres for resale at a profit.[45] The pragmatic reformers felt that Chen Yun had used the Central Commission for Discipline Inspection as an instrument to embarrass them. As evidence, they pointed out that in his criticism of corrupt practices, Chen Yun linked "economic crimes" with the open door policy.[46] The commission often painted a picture of rampant corruption brought on as a direct result of economic reform. Deng and his reformers saw this linkage as something that might jeopardize the effectiveness of the reform policies. In order to dilute Chen Yun's power in the Central Commission for Discipline Inspection, the new central party working leadership group within the Central Secretariat wanted to shift the target for rectification from the narrow issues of corruption and party discipline to the broader issue of party–government relations and the locus of power for dealing with the "economic crimes."[47] At a June 1986 Politburo standing committee meeting, Deng Xiaoping observed obliquely that he was concerned about Chen Yun's commission overreaching its authority.[48] Chen was said to have insisted on his exclusive responsibility for monitoring any offenders in accordance with party rules of discipline and work style.[49] Thus, inner party factional disputes most likely would affect the party's control of discipline and the elimination of corruption among entrenched party members in the long run. The Thirteenth Party Congress elected Qiao Shi to head the commission.

There is widespread violation of party discipline. During the Fourteenth Party Congress, which convened in October 1992, it was revealed that there were over 870,000 party discipline violation investigations of corruption, and that 154,000 members had been expelled during the period from 1987 to 1992.

The Central Advisory Commission. Another new central-level body established by the 1982 party constitution was the Central Advisory Commission, designed to serve as "political assistance and consultant to the Central Committee" (see Article 22 of the 1982 constitution in Appendix B). Membership on the commission was limited to party elders with at least forty years of party service. This was mainly a device to permit party elders to vacate their long-held positions so as to provide some upward mobility for younger members. Also, the Central Advisory Commission was intended to do away with the tradition of providing life tenure for top leaders in the party. As consultants, commission members could attend plenary meetings of the Central Committee without a vote. The Advisory Commission's vice-chairperson was also permitted to attend Politburo meetings ex-officio, if necessary. The Advisory Commission could make recommendations to the Central Committee, at least on paper, on party policy formulation or on tasks assigned by the Central Committee. Initially, the commission had 172 members and was presided over by Deng Xiaoping. Roughly 50 members, or over one-third of the membership of the Eleventh Central Committee, were forced to become Advisory Commission members. The Advisory Commission also included elderly senior military officers and provincial and local party chiefs. A vast majority of the Advisory Commission members were over seventy years of age. Some were under seventy but evidently were forced to join the group because of their past political mistakes—former Politburo members Wu De, Chen Xilian, and Xu Shiyou were forced to retire from the Politburo when Deng Xiaoping consolidated his power.

The original purpose of the Central Advisory Commission was twofold: to provide a means by which the aged party veterans, the Long March generation, or simply the "Gang of Elders," could retire from active service; and to enable the younger leaders to tap the experience and wisdom of the veterans. The original intention certainly was not to endow the commission with any real political power to influence the inner party decision-making process. The "Gang of Elders," presumably retired from active politics, demonstrated considerable residual power, however, particularly in the inner party debate that forced Hu Yaobang to resign. The Central Advisory Commission members attended and perhaps voted to accept Hu's resignation as party chief at an enlarged session of the Politburo in mid-January 1987. If, in fact, they did take part in the voting at the enlarged Politburo meeting, then they violated the party constitution, which granted no such power (Article 22 of the 1982 party constitution stated that members of the Central Advisory Commission could attend Politburo meetings as nonvoting participants). As it turned out, there were as many Central Advisory Commission members as there were members of the Politburo at that crucial meeting when Hu Yaobang resigned and Zhao Ziyang was made the acting party chief. Even before that fateful enlarged Politburo meeting, a number of the Central Advisory Commission members had played a key role in speaking out on party matters.[50] The unexpected role of members of the Central Advisory Commission caused some party members to question whether the retired veterans were fronting for some members of the Central Committee who chose to remain silent and invisible on so important an issue as the resignation of the party's general secretary.[51] The events surrounding Hu's forced resignation seemed to indicate that the Central Advisory Commission had gradually evolved into a political force representing the views of the orthodox hard-liners in the never-ending contest for political succession. It was finally abolished by the Fourteenth Party Congress in October 1992.

PROVINCIAL PARTY ORGANS AND FUNCTIONS

Theoretically speaking, provincial party committees derive their power from the party congresses at the provincial level. The 1982 party constitution (Article 24, see Appendix B) mandates that party congresses at the provincial level and in autonomous regions, in municipalities under the central government, and in cities with districts be held at least once every three years. Each provincial party committee is generally run by a standing committee consisting of the first secretary and a number of subordinate secretaries within the hierarchy of the provincial party structure.

The provincial party committee is responsible for supervision and provides direction over five basic areas: organization and control of the party; economic activities in agriculture, industry, finance, and trade; capital construction; mobilization of women and youth; and research for policy development. Initially, the provincial party committees played a subordinate role in supervising provincial economic development. This was more pronounced during the period of high centralization of the First Five-Year Plan (1953–56), when the national functional ministries had a great deal of authority and control over the provincial party activities. During and after the Great Leap Forward (1957–59), there was a period of decentralization; the provincial party committees were given greater responsibility and more power in managing economic activities in the provinces. In many respects the provincial party committees behaved as though they were "underdeveloped nations" in bidding for resources to develop economic and productive activities.[52]

Since the provincial party committees and their subordinate primary party organs within the provinces are responsible for implementing party policies, they hold a unique position within the party structure. The first secretary of the provincial party committee wields an enormous amount of power. Provincial party secretaries, as pointed out by one study, on occasion have deliberately refused to carry out directives from the center.[53] This power is reflected in and enhanced by the provincial party secretaries' participation in central party affairs (see Chapter 7).

PRIMARY PARTY ORGANS AND FUNCTIONS

Below the provincial party committees are the primary units at the county level and below. They are the "fighting bastions" (to use the phraseology in the 1982 party constitution) for carrying out the party policies and line. It is here that the party makes its immediate contact with the rest of the society. Like the provincial party structure, all basic units of the party are headed by a party secretary, who in turn is guided by a party committee. Party units at the primary level never contest policies and programs imposed from above. However, honest and vigorous discussion often prevails at these lower-level party meetings.

The lowest level of party organization, the so-called primary party units or cells, are party branches formed in "factories, shops, schools, city neighborhoods, co-operatives, farms, townships, towns, villages, companies of the People's Liberation Army and other basic units, where there are three or more full party members," in accordance with Article 30 of the 1982 party constitution, as amended in 1987. While there are no official figures on the total number of party branches at the lowest level, one source estimated the total number in 1982 at 2.5 million.[54] It is at this level that the organizational functions of the party are carried out: membership recruitment, political and ideological education about the party line, exercise of party discipline, and maintenance of "close ties with the masses." It is generally the party branch in a given enterprise, or office that provides leadership, supervision, and guidance in party affairs. Like the first secretaries in the higher party organizations, the party branch secretary exercises overall leadership. In addition, a party branch secretary also serves as a "friend, counselor, and guardian of all the people under his [or her] jurisdiction."[55] Popular literature and drama often depict the party branch secretary as one who is always fearless, fair, firm, and devoted to the welfare of his or her people in the unit.

The party committee is the leading organizational unit, providing leadership, supervision, and management of all political and economic activities in the countryside. But as party discipline slackened, and as opportunities arose for persons with special privileges to use their office for personal gain, it was not uncommon to find the corrupt practices of party secretaries exposed. There were also a number of cases of commandism (communist work style characterized by dictating or ordering) and incompetence found within the ranks of party secretaries.[56] The party committee at the basic level directs party organizational work and is responsible for general policy. It also controls the assignment of personnel at the local level.

We can summarize by saying that the party was highly institutionalized from the 1950s to the early 1960s. This was interrupted during the turbulent years 1966 to 1976 by the Cultural Revolution. The process of reinstitutionalization now appears to be accelerating. This process can be expected to lead to a period of stability and moderation, for China is again under the leadership and control of professionally oriented, veteran party administrators.

THE GOVERNMENT AND THE PARTY: INTERLOCKING STRUCTURE AND DECISION MAKING

In this section we shall examine the structure of the Chinese central government by focusing on the central government complex. Subjects to be discussed include constitutions, the National People's Congress (NPC), and the State Council and its multifarious agencies. Before we take up these topics, two general comments must be made about the Chinese national government. First, as discussed in the previous section, the Chinese Communist Party controls and directs the complex system of government machinery. It is through the agencies of the government that the policies and programs approved by the party are implemented. The CCP closely monitors how the government executes its directives. Second, the People's Republic of China is a unitary state. In a federated system, such as that of the United States or the former Soviet Union, certain governmental powers and responsibilities are reserved for local governments. Under a unitary system, all powers theoretically are vested in the central government and must be specifically delegated to local governments by the central authority. This centralization of power in the national government has led to perennial debate in China over the degree and nature of power to be allocated to local governments. The governments in the provinces and local units generate constant pressure for decentralization by seeking to increase their discretional power over such local affairs as finances and allocation of resources. The topics of provincial and local politics and government will be discussed in detail in Chapter 7.

The 1982 Constitution[57]

The 1982 constitution is China's fourth state constitution (see Appendix A). The 1978 constitution was said to have become obsolete, in that it "no longer conforms to present realities or needs of the life of the state."[58] The 1978 constitution had been drafted when the "Whatever" group still commanded some influence in Chinese politics; it had to be revised to reflect the thinking of the new leaders under Deng and Hu Yaobang. We must remember that in China the state constitution has never been regarded as a sacred document meant to be permanent and inviolable.

We are told that the 1982 constitution was the product of more than two years of work by the Committee for Revision of the Constitution, which was established in September 1980 by the Fifth NPC. The revised draft of this constitution was circulated within party and government circles for debate and discussion. Reportedly, 7.3 million speakers commented on the draft constitution at millions of meetings held across the nation. The review produced over a million suggestions for revision.[59] The final version of the draft was adopted by the Fifth NPC at its session on December 4, 1982. The Sixth NPC, which met in June 1983, was elected, organized, and conducted under the provisions of the 1982 constitution.

One major change in the 1982 constitution was deletion of lavish praise for Mao and of reference to the Cultural Revolution in the preamble. In its place the new constitution affirms adherence to the four fundamental principles of socialism: the socialist road, the people's dictatorship, the leadership of the CCP, and Marxism-Leninsim and Mao Zedong Thought.

Articles 79–81 provide for the election of a president of the republic—a position the 1975 and 1978 constitutions failed to provide for, presumably in deference to Mao's long opposition to Liu Shaoqi, the president under the 1954 constitution who subsequently was purged in 1966 and died while under house arrest. Another new feature was the establishment of the State Military Council to provide direction for the armed forces (see Articles 93–94 in Appendix A). As will be discussed in Chapter 7, the 1982 constitution restricts the role of rural people's communes to economic management in rural areas; they no longer have responsibilities in local government and administration.

A provision in the 1982 constitution that aroused a flurry of speculation was

Article 31, which authorizes the NPC to establish "special administrative regions." To many, this provision opened the way for the return of Hong Kong, Macao, or even Taiwan to China as "special administrative regions." Thus, two recent agreements[60]—the 1984 Sino–British Joint Agreement on Hong Kong's reversion to China in 1997 and the 1987 Sino–Portuguese Declaration on Macao's return in 1999—invoked Article 31 for establishing the two territories as "special administrative regions" that would enjoy "a higher degree of autonomy."

The area of ambiguous change concerns the control of China's armed forces. While the 1978 constitution, in Article 19, stated specifically that the chairman of the party's Central Committee commands the nation's armed forces, the 1982 constitution, in Articles 93 and 94, places the armed forces under the command of the chairman of the Central Military Commission—which is theoretically responsible to the National People's Congress. However, there is some confusion as to whether the party's powerful committee on military affairs supersedes the constitutional provision stated here. There is really no clear delineation of the two organs in terms of their respective power, except the vague explanation that

> The draft of the revised Constitution not only confirms the leading role of the Chinese Communist Party in state political life but also stipulates that the Party must carry out activities within the extent of the Constitution and the Law. . . . Therefore, the Party's leadership over the armed forces could not be taken to mean that the armed forces do not belong to the state.[61]

The 1982 constitution contains twenty-two articles dealing with fundamental rights and duties of citizens, such as the equality of all citizens before the law, inviolability of the dignity of the person, and prohibition of extralegal detention of citizens. Article 35 briefly states that "Citizens of the People's Republic of China enjoy freedom of speech, of the press, of assembly, of association, of procession and of demonstration." This new article was a revised version of Article 45 of the 1978 constitution, which provided citizens the right to "speak out freely, air their views fully, hold great debates, and write big-character posters." After a short flurry of wall posters put up by the young dissidents during the "democracy wall" movement in 1978–79 under the guarantees of the 1978 constitution, China's pragmatic reformers led by Deng Xiaoping saw these rights being used as weapons by ultra-leftists to advance their aims. The wall posters are viewed by the present leaders as instruments that may be used by dissenters to incite "anarchism" and "factionalism." Thus, the rights to "speak out freely, air their views fully, hold great debates, and write big-character posters" were deleted from the 1982 constitution.

Theoretically, Article 35 of the 1982 constitution guarantees citizens the right "to enjoy freedom of speech, of the press, of assembly, of association, of procession and of demonstration." The extent to which these rights can be exercised is, in fact, limited by Article 54. That provision lays down a set of conditions under which citizens have the duty and responsibility "to safeguard the security, honor and interest of the motherland; they must not commit acts detrimental to the security, honor and interests of the motherland." Moreover, Article 51 states that the rights guaranteed by Article 35 "may not infringe upon the interests of the state, of society and of the collective, or upon the lawful freedoms and rights of other citizens." This means that stern and repressive measures may be taken by the state to suppress any dissident engaging in "counterrevolutionary activities."

NATIONAL PEOPLE'S CONGRESS

The NPC is the highest government organ and has constitutional duties similar to those of many parliamentary bodies in other nations. It is empowered to amend the constitution, to make laws, and to supervise their enforcement. Upon recommendation of the President of the People's Republic, the NPC designates, and may remove, the premier and other members of the State Council and can elect the president of the Supreme People's Court and the Chief Procurator of the Supreme People's Procuratorate. These structural relationships are reflected in Figure 4.2.

Since 1954, eight National People's Congresses have been convened, as shown in Table 4.1. The first three congresses, which then were elected to four-year terms rather than the present five-year terms, met annually from 1954 through 1964. After 1964 the regular annual meetings were interrupted first by the Cultural Revolution and then by the Lin Biao affair. The Third NPC was not replaced by the Fourth NPC until 1975. After the Fourth NPC promulgated the 1975 constitution, the work of the

FIGURE 4.2   Governmental Structure of People's Republic of China (1982 Constitution).
Source: **A modified version based on Kim and Ziring,** *An Introduction to Asian Politics* **(Englewood Cliffs, N.J.: Prentice-Hall, 1977), p. 74. By permission of the publisher.**

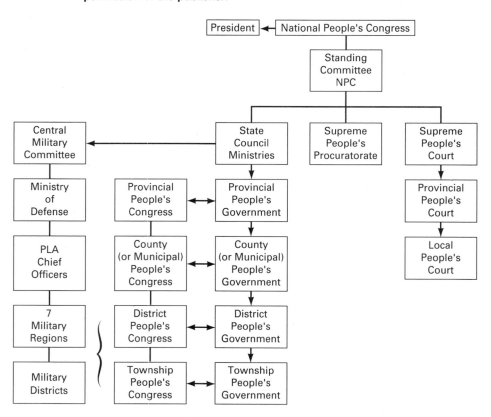

TABLE 4.1   The National People's Congress, 1956–1988

NPC	YEAR CONVENED	NUMBER OF DELEGATES	CHIEF OF STATE	CONSTITUTION PROMULGATED
1st	1954	1,226	Mao Zedong	Constitution of 1954
2nd	1959	1,226	Liu Shaoqi	
3rd	1964 (Dec.)			
	1965 (Jan.)	3,040	Liu Shaoqi	
4th	1975	2,885	—	Revised, 1975
5th	1978	3,459	—	Revised, 1978
6th	1983	2,978	Li Xiannian*	Revised, 1982
7th	1988 (March)	2,978	Yang Sangkun**	Revised, 1987
8th	1993 (March)	2,903	Jiang Zemin***	Revised, 1987

*Elected by the Sixth NPC on June 18, 1993.
**Elected by the Seventh NPC on April 8, 1988.
***Elected by the Eighth NPC March 1993.
Source: Delegate number is based on "Brief Notes about the People's Congresses," in *Renmin Ribao* (February 27, 1978), 2. For delegates to the Sixth NPC, see "Sixth NPC Meets in Beijing," *Beijing Review,* 24 (June 13, 1983), 5. For the Seventh NPC, see *The New York Times*, March 26, 1988, p. 3. For delegates to the Eighth NPC see *Beijing Review* (April 12–18, 1993), 5.

congress was again interrupted by the radicals' attack on the Zhou Enlai-dominated government. In accordance with the election law adopted by the Fifth NPC in December 1982, the Sixth NPC, convened in June 1983, had a ratio of one deputy, or delegate, for every 1.04 million people in rural areas, and one for every 130,000 people in the urban areas. Sparsely populated provinces and autonomous regions, however, were entitled to no less than fifteen delegates each. The Sixth NPC, dominated by Deng Xiaoping and his reform-minded supporters, seemed to have achieved some degree of stability under a moderate and pragmatic program. Deng and his reformers were able to control the Seventh NPC, held in 1988, and the Eighth NPC, which convened in March 1993.

Working Sessions of the NPC

A session of the NPC generally meets for a period of about two weeks. During that period only a handful of full plenary meetings are convened to discuss and approve reports of the central government. Delegates or deputies are divided into groups, according to regions, which meet constantly throughout the two-week period when the NPC is in session. It is at these group meetings that one can find occasional spirited discussions on matters of national concern. It is there that the delegates can exercise their oversight functions by submitting motions or inquiries on the performance of the various administrative bodies in the central government. At these sessions vice-ministers representing the central government usually are present on the floor either to answer questions or to provide information about governmental affairs. It has been revealed that during the Sixth NPC (1983–88), deputies raised 830 motions and 14,215 suggestions, criticisms, and opinions to the congress on a variety of subjects. The ad hoc committee served as a clearinghouse, referring these motions to the various governmental agencies concerned for comment.[62]

It was reported that at the end of the Third Plenum, Sixth NPC, delegates made a total of 2,832 recommendations, criticisms, and suggestions.[63] About 744, or 26.3 percent of the total, were resolved or had action taken on them by the governmental units concerned. A large majority, about 73 percent, were either being processed or were shelved for further study.[64]

Recently there has been criticism about the caliber of delegates selected to the NPC. Qian Jiaju, a noted economist, pointed out that the practice of selecting NPC delegates from model workers in industries and trades did not provide the NPC with the qualified delegates it needed for policy making.[65] He revealed with some candor that most members on the NPC finance committee could neither follow the discussion at the sessions nor comprehend the process of budget making. This view was contradicted by a Chinese TV reporter, who followed the NPC debate on the proposed bankruptcy law by pointing out that there was heated debate and that the NPC was no longer a "rubber stamp." [66]

Standing Committee of the NPC

When the NPC is not in session, its Standing Committee serves as the executive body to act on behalf of the congress. While the Standing Committee is elected by the NPC, it is this committee that has the power to conduct elections of the deputies of the NPC and to convene the NPC sessions. Since the NPC meets once a year at most, the Standing Committee controls a great deal of that body's powers.

The 1982 constitution gives the Standing Committee the power to enforce martial law in the event of domestic disturbance. Article 67(20) (see Appendix A) states that the NPC's Standing Committee can declare martial law either for the country as a whole or for a particular province, autonomous region, or municipality directly under the central government. Hypothetically, measures for suppression of domestic disturbance can now be constitutionally instituted and enforced. Presumably the NPC, through its Standing Committee, could suppress upheavals similar to the Cultural Revolution, if it wants to exert its constitutional prerogatives in the event of a national crisis situation. On the other hand, this provision may provide an avenue through which factional groups within the party and government leadership could very well seize power by suppressing the opposition forces in a power contest.

On May 20, 1989, at the height of the student demonstration in Tiananmen Square, the promulgation of martial law in the capital city of Beijing by the republic's president and premier raised a constitutional controversy, for there was no formal involvement by the Standing Committee in the issuance of the martial law order. (Wan Li, then chairman of the Standing Committee, was traveling in the United States.)

Also, the 1982 constitution gives the Standing Committee the powers and functions normally possessed by the NPC itself, to serve as an interim national congress when the NPC is not in session. The Standing Committee now supervises a new system of parliamentary committees on nationalities, law, finance and economics, public health, education, foreign affairs, overseas Chinese, and any other areas deemed necessary (Article 70, Appendix A). As an interim NPC, the Standing Committee can enact and amend decrees and laws in civil and criminal affairs, including those affecting the structure of the central government. It can annul any administrative regulations and decisions of the central government, and it has the power to interpret the constitution. In order that the Standing Committee be an independent body, its members are not permitted to hold posts in any branch of the central government concurrently.

NPC's Potential as a Creditable Legislative Institution

As seen in Table 4.1, The Eighth National People's Congress convened in March 1993. Since 1983 the NPC has consisted of about 3,000 delegates—a rather cumbersome body for deliberative purposes. Apparently the size of the NPC has been expanded to broaden representation and to allow greater participation in national government.

In drafting the 1982 constitution, the question was raised as to whether the size of the NPC should be reduced to a more manageable level. The suggestion evidently was rejected on the grounds that it was necessary to have "every class, every social strata, every nationality, every locality, and every field of work" represented. The size of the 1993 NPC—2,903 deputies—remained cumbersome.

The enormous size of the NPC raises the question of whether this institution was ever intended to be a genuinely deliberative body. The argument can be made that if the NPC was intended to be a "rubber stamp" for the CCP, then it might as well be very large and representative. However, the NPC cannot be totally dismissed as a rubber stamp. Under the leadership of Liu Shaoqi, the NPC at times did scrutinize proposals on economic development programs before giving its approval. On at least one occasion, at the 1957 session, NPC delegates attacked Mao in relation to the antirightist campaign and the party's meddling in the affairs of a Shanghai university.[67] Delegates to the third session of the Fifth NPC (September 1980) demanded information from officials of the Ministry of Petroleum Industry about the 1979 capsizing of the offshore oil rig Bohai No. 2, which cost more than seventy lives. The disaster was the result of many years of management neglect and disregard for safety measures in offshore oil drilling.[68] However, the fact remains that generally the NPC enacts legislation of importance only after the CCP has made its wishes known within the party hierarchy.

There is some evidence to indicate that Peng Zhen, former chairman of the NPC's Standing Committee, not only used that body as a platform for launching the orthodox hard-liners' criticism of Deng's reforms, but also turned it into a political and institutional base for building a formidable opposition to the reformers. Peng was vocal on issues concerning the need for waging an "anti-bourgeois liberalization" campaign. He said sarcastically that the reformers wanted to learn from abroad "as if the moonlight of capitalist society were brighter than our sun." [69] By using the NPC as his base for criticizing some of the reform measures, Peng Zhen was said to have blocked the passage of the legislation that would grant the factory manager the sole power to make decisions without any interference from the party secretary. Peng, however, explained in a press interview that the proposed law on factory directors' responsibilities needed further investigation because there were differences within the Standing Committee.[70] Peng had strong views with respect to the NPC Standing Committee's constitutional power in providing supervision for the State Council. He, in fact, wanted to strengthen further the Standing Committee so that it would serve as a check to the reformer-dominated State Council.[71] As chairman of the Standing Committee, Peng had been successful in persuading the NPC to permit the Standing Committee to supervise all provincial people's congresses. As it was constituted before March 1988, Peng's NPC Standing Committee might have been used as a second power center and a strong voice in defense of the orthodox ideology. Peng, one of the first party leaders purged during the Cultural Revolution, now defended Mao by saying that "Mao's theory was an important contribution to Marxism-Leninism," which was "revolutionary and not conservative," and that "Marxism can develop; it is not fossilized."[72]

Prior to the convening of the Thirteenth Party Congress, Peng was reported to covet a seat on the Politburo; he later denied this in a press interview. The final lineup for the Politburo elected by the Thirteenth Central Committee showed that Peng had retired for good—he was not elected to any of the central party organs. In March 1988 the Seventh NPC elected Wan Li, a trusted Dengist, the new chairman for its Standing Committee.

Another piece of evidence indicating that the NPC behaved contrary to popular expectations that it would be the "rubber stamp" for the party was the approval in the 1992 session of the controversial Three Gorges Dam Project on the Yangtzee River.[73] The huge 2,000-meter-long hydroelectric dam would cost $12 billion, with two dozen hydroelectric generators producing 17,680 megawatts of electricity per year. The construction of the gigantic project would force as many as one million residents to move their farms and houses to make room for the 370-mile reservoir. In defiance of the party leadership, a number of deputies of the 1992 NPC session raised objections to the project. When the final vote was called there were 1,767 for, 77 against, and 664 abstentions. The debate on the Three Gorges Project contained criticism of Premier Li Peng. At the Eighth NPC in March 1993 as many as 11 percent of the 2,960 deputies either cast negative votes against Li Peng's reelection for the premiership or abstained.

There is also a strong indication that the newly elected chairman of the Eighth NPC Standing Committee, Qiao Shi, may seek to strengthen the NPC's lawmaking ability. He has reportedly recruited legal experts from abroad to reorganize the NPC's Legislative Commission,[74] which drafts many of China's economic laws (to be discussed in Chapter 6), because the NPC has now embraced "socialist market economy" laws and regulations needed for opening up opportunities and making use of capitalistic tools.

For instance, new laws are needed to prevent "the blooming Chinese stock markets" from getting out of hand. Foreign contract laws need to be written to reflect acceptable practices in the rest of the world. In addition, political reforms amidst economic prosperity in Taiwan in recent years, and Singapore's stability and economic miracle, may be possible "models" for China. Deng Xiaoping is said to have made a remark to that effect in his 1992 tour of southern China.[75] As pointed out by Brantly Womack, in both Singapore and Taiwan "it is possible to have a party-state democracy dominated by a single political party."[76]

THE STATE COUNCIL

The State Council, the nation's highest executive organ, administers the government through functional ministries and commissions, as indicated in Table 4.2. The constitution stipulates that the State Council be comprised of a premier, vice-premiers, and heads of national ministries and commissions. The State Council may also

TABLE 4.2   Composition of the State Council, 1988 and 1993

	STATE COUNCIL MINISTERS APPOINTED BY	
	7TH NPC (1988)	8TH NPC (1993)
Premier	1	1
Vice-Premiers	3	4
Ministers	86	59
Secretary-General	1	1
	91	65

Source: For 1988, see Ming Pao Daily (Hong Kong) (30 March 1988), p. 12. For 1993, see Beijing Review, 29 (March–4 April 1993), 8.

include others, such as vice-ministers. The membership of the State Council has ranged from a low of thirty to over one hundred members. As the government expanded over the years, the number of ministries and commissions expanded to a peak of forty-nine just prior to the Cultural Revolution.

To streamline the ministerial structure within the State Council, the total number of ministries and commissions was reduced in 1981–82, from ninety-eight to forty-one, mainly through the merging of functions and staff. As of March 1993 there was a total of 59 ministries and commissions. The composition of the State Council is shown in Table 4.2.

Since the full State Council is too large for effective decision making, in practice this role has been assumed by an inner cabinet of the premier and his vice-premiers.[77] In 1982–83 the inner cabinet consisted of a premier, four vice-premiers, ten State Council senior counselors, and a secretary-general for the Office of the State Council. The personnel of the State Council has remained relatively stable over the years. During the Cultural Revolution this body suffered much less than the party apparatus, largely due to the leadership of Zhou Enlai, who was premier from 1949 until his death in 1976. Zhou stayed away from the debates during the initial stage of the revolution but joined Mao and Lin Biao when he realized their faction would emerge dominant. For Zhou's support, concessions were made for the State Council, including exemption from participation in the upheaval by scientists and technicians. As Thomas Robinson points out, Zhou was Mao and Lin's "chief problem solver, troubleshooter, negotiator, organizer, administrator, guide-advisor to revolutionary groups, and local enforcer of Central Committee policy."[78] It has been estimated that between one-half and two-thirds of the 366 ministers, vice-ministers, commissioners, and vice-commissioners kept their posts during the turbulent period from 1966 to 1968.[79] Another reason for the stability of the State Council, whose members represented a concentration of administrative and technical expertise, was the need for production to continue unimpeded. The ability of the State Council to issue directives, often jointly with the party's leading committees, is evidence that the central civil bureaucracy was quite institutionalized and functionally effective in spite of the turmoil during the Cultural Revolution.

Doak Barnett has described the State Council aptly as the "command headquarters" for a network of bureaus and agencies staffed by cadres who administer and coordinate the government's programs at the provincial and local levels.[80] The degree of centralization of authority has fluctuated over the regime's history. During the First Five-Year Plan, from 1953 to 1957, the ministries had enormous power over the provincial authorities in terms of quota fulfillment, allocation of resources, and management of such enterprises as factories and mines. The increasing complexity of coordinating the economy and the gravitation of power to the individual ministries, the "ministerial autarky," led to numerous problems and a continuing debate over centralization versus decentralization.[81] In 1957, during the Great Leap, decentralization was instituted by giving the provinces authority to administer and coordinate consumer-goods-oriented industries. The decentralization of the Great Leap hampered central planning and resulted in inefficiency. Following the failure of the Great Leap, a modified version of centralization was adopted until the Cultural Revolution ushered in another period of decentralization.[82] With the reestablishment of planning operations and the emphasis on research and development under the Sixth Five-Year Plan (1981–85), approved by the Fifth NPC in December 1982, the pendulum once again has swung back to more centralization. In his report to the Fifth NPC, Premier Zhao Ziyang indicated that to execute the Sixth Five-Year Plan, it was necessary for the State Planning Commission to exercise strict control over the volume of total investment in fixed assets. Investments in capital construction were to be placed under the control of the Bank of Construction of China.[83] Most ministries under the State Council are concerned with economic affairs; a minority deal with matters such as defense, foreign relations, public security, civil and minority affairs, education, and public health. The ministries on economic matters in early 1980 can be grouped into the categories shown in Table 4.3.

Several new features were added to the State Council by the 1982 constitution. First, a group of ten senior administrators were designated as advisors to the State Council. These senior advisors were retired veteran administrators such as Bo Yibo, age 75, who had been a vice-premier and minister for machine building, and Geng Biao, age 74, former Politburo member and defense minister. Second, tenure for the premiership was now limited to two consecutive five-year terms. Finally, the 1982 constitution mandated the establishment within the State Council of an independent audit agency, under the supervision of the premier, for the purpose of auditing the revenues and expenditures of the various ministries both at the central and provincial levels. The power of audit may eventually become an effective instrument in monitoring and checking the vast Chinese bureaucracy.[84] A majority of the twenty-three new ministers and vice-ministers appointed in 1993 were in their fifties and early sixties, slightly younger than their predecessors.

In another State Council personnel reshuffle that occurred in the fall of 1985, five new ministers were appointed to head the following ministries: public security, state security, labor and personnel, metallurgical, and geology and mineral resources. All five new appointees were younger men whose age ranged from 47 to 59. In June 1987, another new ministry was established, the Ministry of Supervision, for the purposes of overseeing the execution of laws and regulations in the government and of serving as a watchdog of bureaucratism.

PROBLEMS IN CHINA'S POLITICAL INSTITUTIONS

Three key problems can be identified in the Chinese political institutions that have been discussed so far. One is the issue of party–government separation. Solving this interlocking problem at one time as an institutional reform goal, but interlocking now

TABLE 4.3   Ministries on the Economic Functions of the State Council, 1982–83

PLANNING	ECONOMIC/FINANCE	SPECIAL INDUSTRIES
State Planning Commission	State Economic Commission	Machine Building[a]
Scientific/Technological Commission	Urban and Rural Construction	Nuclear[b]
Statistical Commission	Foreign Economic Relations and Trade	Aviation[c]
Restructuring Economic System	Agriculture	Electronics[d]
Family Planning	Forestry	Ordinance[a]
	Railways	Space
	Communications	Power
	Post and Telecommunications	Metallurgical
	Finance	Water Power
	People's Bank	Coal
	Commerce	Chemical
		Petroleum
		Textile
		Light
		Geology and Minerals

[a]Formerly the First Ministry of Machine Building
[b]Formerly the Second Ministry of Machine Building
[c]Formerly the Third Ministry of Machine Building
[d]Formerly the Fourth Ministry of Machine Building
[e]Formerly the Fifth Ministry of Machine Building
[f]Formerly the Seventh Ministry of Machine Building (The former Sixth Ministry of Machine Building was abrogated).

Sources: "Explanations on the Draft of the Revised Constitution of the PRC," *Beijing Review*, 19 (Mary 10, 1982), 4; and *China Trade Report* (June 1982), p. 12.

is intensified more than ever at the top echelon. The second problem is the need for streamlining the bureaucracy to eliminate the overstaffing of the national government. The third issue is the problem of political structure reform.

Interlocking Structure of the Government and Party

To students who are familiar with Western constitutions, it is often a surprise to read in the Chinese constitution the stipulation that the party is "the core of leadership of the whole Chinese people," and that "the working class exercises leadership over the state through its vanguard, the Communist Party of China." This, of course, means that the governmental institutions in China exist to serve the party.

The Chinese Communist Party controls and directs the machinery of state through an interlocking system of party personnel and a structure parallel to that of the state government. Fewer high party leaders held high government positions concurrently in 1982–83 than at any previous time. The 1977–78 period represented a heightened state of interlocking between the party and government hierarchy. The best example was Hua Guofeng, who was chairman of the CCP, premier of the central government, and chairman of the party's Military Affairs Commission. Of the thirteen vice-premiers of the State Council elected by the Fifth NPC in 1978, nine were members of the powerful CCP Politburo, and all were members of the CCP Central Committee elected in 1977. Of the thirty-six ministers in charge of various governmental agencies, twenty-nine, or 81 percent, were members of the Central Committee. All major economic ministries, including economic planning, capital construction, research and development, foreign trade, and heavy and light industries, were in the hands of ministers who were members of either the Politburo or the Central Committee. In fact, the party's highest policymaking body, the Politburo, is functionally organized to parallel the government ministries, with members specializing in the various governmental activities. In each state bureaucracy, there is always the presence of the party cell of leading CCP members who provide direction for the state organ. The party has always been able to exercise its control in a state bureaucracy by supervising its personnel. Thus, the state structure and the party are not truly parallel entities, since they interlock from top to bottom.

The party control over the state bureaucracy has been the subject of much discussion among scholars. Too often students of Chinese politics look at the bureaucracy under the State Council as if it were an independent power base competing with the party. The fact that all the forty-five ministers approved by the Eighth NPC were members of the CCP's Central Committee demonstrates that the State Council is not only interlocked with the party but is controlled by it. Conflicts that do occur are not primarily between the government and the party but rather are intraparty conflicts between high-ranking party members.

Interlocking Relationships of Politburo Members.   The interlocking relationships of the members of the Politburo, the highest decision-making body of the party, not only demonstrate how the party exercises its control over the central government but also give an indication of possible areas of speciality and of power bases for the top elites who are members of the Politburo. Several questions need to be posed here about the State Council, an enormous national administration comprised of more than forty bureaucratic departments and commissions, which in turn are staffed by more than forty thousand bureaucrats. First, what is the premier's "span of control" over the multitude of administrative units? As mentioned earlier, there was an inner cabinet within the State Council for policy formulation and problem-solving. This inner cabinet was formally established in 1982–83 to constitute a standing committee, consisting of the premier, the five vice-premiers, the secretary-general for the State Council or the premier's office, plus ten senior advisors or counselors. Second, how often does the premier hold his cabinet meetings? According to a study by Michel Oksenberg, the inner cabinet meets regularly each week to discuss policy issues.[85] There is obviously elaborate staff work involved in the management of the State Council office: the setting of agenda for meetings, and the preparation of documents and background analysis, which is often generated by the research institutes associated with the Chinese Academy of Social Sciences.[86] Since the State Council is generally preoccupied with the implementation and the monitoring of the multifarious economic programs, research (or think tank) institutes became increasingly influential in policy formulation. For instance, the Economic Reform Research Center (affiliated with the Chinese Academy of Social Sciences) has made heavy inputs to reform policies and strategies for the reform-oriented leaders in the State Council. It is probably accurate to say that the "control span" for Premier Li Peng is manageable and that he is able to devote time to policy development. It is likely that no more than fifteen key officers in the inner cabinet make daily or weekly reports to him. No doubt he delegates responsibilities for supervising a number of ministries to his five vice-premiers and the ten counselors. We know, for instance, that vice-premier Zhu Rongji, an economist, is mainly responsible for matters concerning economic reforms. Li Peng, then a vice-premier, was in charge of scientific, educational, and energy development. A study by Professor Oksenberg points out that the inner cabinet has been overburdened by "interagency and interprovincial disputes" and that the vice-premiers must spend an inordinate amount of time and energy in solving the disputes.[87]

The interlocking system that existed in 1987 after the Thirteenth Party Congress and before the convening of the Seventh National People's Congress, scheduled for March 1988, was still very visible. Four of the vice-premiers of the State Council were elected to the new Politburo, and Li Peng, the premier, was also a member of the Politburo's Standing Committee along with two other vice-premiers (Hu Qili and Yao Yilin). Zhao admitted in his report to the Thirteenth Party Congress that the lack of distinction between the function of the party and of the government continued to be one of the outstanding problems to be resolved. He outlined four specific steps to be taken in this area of separation of party and government functions: no full-time party secretary at a given level should hold a government post or take charge of government work; no more overlap of party departments with counterpart governmental departments; leading party groups in a government department must be held accountable at the same level for which it was established; and party discipline inspections must not deal with law violation or infractions of administrative regulations. Zhao wanted the party to handle party affairs.

Since the political demise of Zhao in May 1989, not only has there been no implementation of Zhao's reform measures for breaking up the interlocking and parallel nature of the party and government discussed above; on the contrary, the degree of interlocking has intensified at the hierarchical level. For instance, Jiang Zemin, the reelected general secretary of the party, member of the Standing Committee of the powerful Politburo, and chairman of the Military Affairs Commission of the party's Central Committee, was elected in March 1993 as president of the People's Republic of China. Jiang is in effect the head of the party, the government, and the military. Li Peng, the premier since 1988 for the State Council, was reelected as a member of the Politburo in April 1993. Qiao Shi, a long-time member of the Politburo, was elected in March 1993 as chairman of the Standing Committee of the Eighth National People's Congress.

The Overstaffing Problem

The overstaffing problem in the Chinese government is nothing new; overstaffing has been going on since the early 1950s. During the Eighth NPC session, held in March 1993, a proposal for reducing the number of employees by 20 percent was approved. Loa Gan, secretary-general for the NPC, revealed that seven existing ministries would be phased out and six small ones instituted.[88] This was said to be contrary to what vice-premier and Politburo member Zhu Rongji (Deng's choice responsible for economic reforms) preferred: a two-thirds across-the-board reduction.[89] What can't be ascertained is whether the 20 percent or two-thirds across-the-board cut applied to the 40,000 employees referred to by the 1988 NPC, or to all 4.2 million central government employees. There were 55,000 more central government units in 1990 than in 1984, and the number of "superfluous" personnel in government departments has reached over 500,000.[90] Premier Li Peng reported to the Eighth NPC delegates that he would like to devote the next three years to streamlining the national government functions by reducing the pre-1993 total of 86 ministries to 59, and then to 41.[91]

Political Structure Reform

We shall discuss the issue of political reform by examining these questions: Why must there be political reform? What does it mean? What specific problems are the advocates of reform trying to solve? Who opposes political reform? And, finally, how soon can one expect political reform?

It was known that a number of pragmatic reformers from Deng Xiaoping on down had at one time or another advocated the need for reform in the political system. They and several scholars in the Chinese Academy of Social Sciences had been issuing warnings to the country that it would not be possible to carry out economic reforms successfully without political reform. Discussion and debate about political reform reached a peak in the summer of 1986 when the Central Party School held a seminar to address the issue. As late as November 1986, Deng had told the visiting Italian Prime Minister Bettino Craxi that the purpose of political reform in China was to "stamp out red tape, and bring the initiative of the grassroots and the people into full play."[92]

In August 1980, long before the reforms launched the ambitious urban reform in 1984 (see Chapter 11), Deng Xiaoping broached the topic of reforming the party and government leadership system at an enlarged meeting of the Politburo. Deng bemoaned the fact that the party and government institutions were plagued by problems that seriously hindered the final realization of "a superior socialism."[93] Deng itemized the bureaucratic evils in much the same way as Mao had done some fourteen years earlier at the beginning of the Cultural Revolution. Deng charged that cadres were:

> . . . indulging in empty talk; sticking to rigid ways of thinking; being hidebound by convention; overstaffing administrative organs . . . circulating documents endlessly without solving problems; shifting responsibility to others . . . being arbitrary and despotic; practicing favoritism; participating in corrupt practices in violation of the law and so on.[94]

Deng also pointed out that there was a close relationship between bureaucratism and the "highly centralized management in economic, political, cultural and social fields." He observed that when the entire decision-making process is highly individualized in the hands of a few, the results are inefficiency and inability to make decisions.[95]

As discussion on political reform expanded, and was encouraged by the party leaders favoring reform, the term political reform implied more than just personnel management changes. In surveying the speeches and documents for 1985 and 1986, one finds that the term political reform referred to concepts in policy science, democratization of the NPC, the separation of power between the party and government, and the strengthening of the legal system. One case in point involved reform in the policy-making process. Wan Li, a vice-premier and Politburo member, favored the system approach in policy making. Wan Li seemed to advocate policy making based on "computerized quantitative input–output analysis, rather than on an individual leader's subjective judgment."[96] He deplored the fact that China had not yet established a policy-making procedure that included research support, consultation with experts, evaluation, and feedback before a policy was adopted. Instead, Wan pointed out, China had a system of policy making by intuition or osmosis. As a first step, Wan proposed the creation of "a political climate of democracy, equality and consultation." [97] He argued that policy issues must go through three stages or processes: research, decision, and implementation. [98] He seemed to stress the need at the research stage to permit free airing of views "within certain limits." He also carefully pointed out that these free discussions could not be permitted to deviate from the ideological guidance of Marxism. [99]

The movement for studies on political reform gained increased recognition in July 1986 when Zhu Houze, then the party's propaganda chief, organized a conference of scholars and political thinkers in Beijing to establish a distinct political science in "Chinese characters" to conduct research on reform measures in the political system. [100] (Zhu Houze was fired soon after the January 1987 student demonstrations were put down and Hu Yaobang resigned.)

Another specific issue in the debate on political reform was the question of the plant manager's autonomy in decision making in the factory. As discussed earlier, there was strong opposition on these issues from party branch secretaries, who feared the loss of party power and who had the backing of the orthodox hard-liners at the top leadership level[101] (see Chapter 11). The orthodox hard-liners won a temporary victory in the aftermath of Hu Yaobang's ouster and obtained a concession from the reformers to restore the veto power to the local party secretary in some 28,000 state-owned factories. [102]

Deng Xiaoping revealed his thoughts on the meaning of political reform when Stefan Korosec, a presidium member of the League of Communists of Yugoslavia, visited China in June 1987. Deng seemed to have ruled out abandoning centralized decision making in favor of "a system of multi-party elections and a balance of the three powers"—referring to the American system of government. [103] He argued that the present system of centralized decision making was more efficient than the proposals: "The efficiency I am talking about is not efficiency of administration or economic management, but overall efficiency. We have superiority in this respect, and we should keep it." [104] Deng listed three basic areas that required "political restructuring"[105] (1) the revitalization of the party—the problem of replacing aging leaders by younger cadres (he described the old leaders as "conservative" and as having the common tendency of looking at problems "in the light of their personal experience"); (2) the elimination of bureaucratism by instituting administrative efficiency; and (3) decentralization in decision making, or "delegating power to lower levels."

When the Thirteenth Party Congress met in late October 1987, political reform was said to be an important item for discussion. One of the major items covered in Zhao Ziyang's report to this congress on October 25, 1987 was entitled "Reforming the political structure." [106] What Zhao reported at the opening session of the congress must be viewed as representing the party consensus. (Zhao's report had gone through seven revisions, the last in mid-October 1987, and was approved by the outgoing Central Committee.)[107] In the report Zhao pointed out briefly the defects of the political system as being overconcentration of power, rampant bureaucratism, and feudal influences. He then offered seven measures as keys to political reform. [108] One, as discussed earlier, is the separation of party and government functions. Two, the delegation of powers to lower levels. Local matters must be handled by local authorities. Three, Zhao asked for efficiency by merging departments and their functions; he also wanted the Seventh NPC to make more laws and regulations that would govern administrative organs. Four, he wanted to establish "a system of public service" to replace the cadre system so that "public servants" are to be classified into political affairs and professional categories.[109] Five, Zhao embraced the Wan Li appeal, discussed earlier, for consultation and dialogue in decision making. In August 1993 the Politburo finally embraced Wan Li's idea for the establishment of a new "central policy consultation group" under its control for making advisory input on major policy issues. Six, improvement in the work of the NPC with younger delegates and more working rules, as well as more elections with more candidates than posts. And, lastly, Zhao asked for improved legislation by the NPC on legal procedures, law enforcement procedures, and the development "of judicial organs to exercise independent authority" as prescribed by law.[110] These measures do pinpoint some of the basic problems in Chinese bureaucracy.

One of the basic weaknesses of the party–government bureaucratic machine has been the party's control and "intervention" in matters of government policy. But also there is lack of discipline in the party itself. It has become increasingly more corrupt, and its members too often subvert party directives.[111] In a case study of China's energy policy, Kenneth Lieberthal and Michel Oksenberg detailed the massive and fragmented party–state bureaucratic structure that relies on "consensus decision making" through bargaining and negotiation between competing bureaucracies.[112] Parris H. Chang points out that the Chinese policy-making process at times involves "honest disagreement" among party leaders, but at other times, reflects the results of power struggles.[113] Once the leaders agree on a policy it is the party–state bureaucracies that must thrash out the concrete details.[114] Parris Chang paints a picture of many participants in the policy-making process, each with political resources at his or her command.[115]

A "Multi-Party" System for China?   From 1986 to 1988 there was some discussion by Chinese intellectuals of the possibility of instituting a multi-party system as an integral part of political reform. In the aftermath of the Tiananmen crackdown a symbolic gesture has been made in the area of political structure reform: the guidelines proposed by the CCP Central Committee on December 30, 1989 for improving the system of multi-party cooperation and political consultation.[116] There are at present eight so-called "democratic parties" in China that exist under the leadership of the CCP. The proposed guidelines call for an invitation by the CCP Central Committee to the principal leaders of the "democratic parties" to meet for consultation on major policies, as well as meetings for the purpose of briefing or informing these leaders on specific policy matters. The proposed guidelines also call for "an appropriate proportion" of NPC deputies to be elected and represented at the NPC Standing Committee level and other special committees. The guidelines suggest that members of the "democratic parties" be selected for government positions in the State Council, as well as selected for leading positions in the judicial organs as supervisors, procurators, auditors, and educational inspectors. Thus, it would not be surprising to see ministerial appointments in the foreseeable future given to those leaders who are not CCP members. Press reports indicated that leaders of the "democratic parties" in China expressed their readiness to participate in the proposed system of multi-party consultation and cooperation.[117]

Some leaders of the "democratic parties" are well-known Chinese intellectuals and academicians—men such as Professor Fei Xiatong, China's famed anthropologist and chairman of the China Democratic League, and the late Zhou Peiyuan, former president of Beijing University and a well-known scientist, chairman of the Jiusan Society of Scientists, Technocrats and Educators.

NOTES

1. *Renmin Ribao* (March 1, 1977); and *Ming Pao* (Hong Kong) (March 3, 1977), p. 3.
2. *Survey of Chinese Mainland Press*, 4097 (January 11, 1968), 1–4.
3. "Resolution of the Convening of the Twelfth Party Congress," *Beijing Review*, 10 (March 10, 1980), 11.
4. Ibid.
5. Roderick MacFarquhar, *The Origins of the Cultural Revolution, Vol. 1: Contradictions Among the People, 1957–1967* (New York: Columbia University Press, 1974), p. 144.
6. Lo Bing, "Inside View of the Elections at the Twelfth Party Congress," *Zhengming* (Hong Kong), 60 (October 1982), 7.
7. "Communiqué on the Fifth Plenary Session of the Eleventh Central Committee of the CCP," p. 8. Also see Lowell Dittmer, "The Twelfth Congress of the Communist Party of China," *The China Quarterly*, 93 (March 1983), pp. 112–13.
8. William Brugger, "The Ninth National Congress of the CCP," *The World Today*, vol. 25, no. 7 (July 1969), 297–305; Roderick MacFarquhar, "China After the 10th Congress," *The World Today*, vol. 29, no. 12 (December 1973), 514–26; Richard Wich, "The Tenth Party Congress: The Power Structure and the Succession Question," *The China Quarterly*, 58 (April–May 1974), 231–48.
9. Jiang Zemin, "Accelerating Reform and Opening Up," *Beijing Review* (October 26–November 1, 1992), 16.
10. Houn, *A Short History of Chinese Communism*, p. 87.
11. MacFarquhar, *The Origins of the Cultural Revolution*, p. 101.
12. "Resolution on the Convening of the Twelfth Party Congress," p. 11.
13. Parris Chang, *Power and Policy in China* (University Park, Pa. and London: The Pennsylvania State University Press, 1974), p. 184.
14. "Constitution of the Communist Party of China, Adopted by the Eleventh National Congress on August 18, 1977," in *Peking Review*, 36 (September 2, 1977) 21–22.
15. Franklin W. Houn, *A Short History of Chinese Communism*, (Englewood Cliffs, N.J.: Prentice Hall, Inc., 1967), p. 87.
16. "Board of Directors, China, Inc.," *Far Eastern Economic Review* (September 2, 1977), 9.
17. Robert J. Osborn, *The Evolution of Soviet Politics* (New York: The Dorsey Press, 1974), pp. 213–14.
18. Houn, *A Short History of Chinese Communism*, p. 93.
19. Chang, *Power and Policy in China*, p. 184.
20. Houn, *A Short History of Chinese Communism*, p. 91–92.
21. Ibid., p. 89.
22. See *Zhengming*, 181 (November 1991), 11; and *Far Eastern Economic Review* (October 29, 1992), 11.
23. See *Zhengming*, 181 (November 1992), 11.
24. "Talk at the Report Meeting, 24 October 1966," in *Chairman Mao Talks to the People*, pp. 266–67.
25. "The Central Committee's Secretariat and Its Work," *Beijing Review* 19 (May 11, 1981), 21.
26. Gittings' notes on the formation of this organ in 1931 by the First All-China Soviet Congress; see John Gittings, *The Role of the Chinese Red Army* (London: Oxford University Press, 1967), pp. 263–65.
27. Ralph Powell, "Politico-Military Relationships in Communist China," External Research Staff, Bureau of Intelligence and Research, Department of State, October 1963.
28. *Far Eastern Economic Review* (February 5, 1987), 34.
29. Yeh Chien-ying, "Report on the Revision of the Party Constitution," *Peking Review*, 36 (September 2, 1977), 32. For a detailed discussion of the party's control organ prior to 1982, see Graham Young,

"Control and Style: Discipline Inspection Commission since the 11th Congress," *The China Quarterly* 97 (March 1984), 24–30. Also, for a more detailed study of the new party control organ see Lawrence R. Sullivan, "The Role of the Control Organs in the CCP, 1977–83," *Asian Survey*, xxiv, 6 (June 1984), 597–615.

30. Yeh Chien-ying, "Report on the Revision of the Party Constitution"; and "Communiqué of the Third Plenary Session of the Eleventh Central Committee," *Peking Review*, 52 (December 29, 1978), 6, 16.
31. John W. Lewis, *Leadership in Communist China*, (Ithaca, N.Y.: Cornell University Press, 1963), p. 134.
32. *Ming Pao* (Hong Kong), (September 2, 1979), p. 3.
33. Ibid.
34. See *Renmin Ribao* editorial, "Earnestly Strengthening Party's Discipline Investigation Work" (March 25, 1978), p. 1.
35. Ibid.
36. *Renmin Ribao* (December 5, 1980), p. 1; and *Min Pao Daily* (Hong Kong) (December 17, 1980), p. 1.
37. "Chinese Communist Party Expels Kang Sheng and Xie Fuzhi," *Beijing Review*, 45 (November 10, 1980), 3.
38. English translation of the text can be found in "Guiding Principles for Inner Party Political Life," *Beijing Review*, 15 (April 14, 1980), 11–19. For the original text see *Hongqi*, 6 (March 16, 1980), 2–11.
39. Xinhua New Agency release as reprinted in *Ming Pao Daily* (Hong Kong) (August 14, 1983), p. 1.
40. *Ming Pao Daily* (Hong Kong) (August 8, 1983), p. 3.
41. *Ming Pao Daily* (Hong Kong) (July 5, 1983), p. 1.
42. *Ming Pao Daily* (Hong Kong) (March 19, 1983), p. 1.
43. *Far Eastern Economic Review* (January 23, March 6, and May 9, 1986) and *Zhengming*, 101 (March 1986), 14–15.
44. *Zhengming*, 101 (March 1986), 15.
45. Ibid.
46. *Zhengming*, 108 (October 1986), 15.
47. Ibid.
48. Ibid.
49. See Stanley Rosen, "China in 1986: A Year of Consolidation," *Asian Survey* (January 1987), 37.
50. *Zhengming*, 114 (April 1987), 15.
51. Ibid., p. 15.
52. Franz Schurmann, *Ideology and Organizations*, (Berkeley, Calif.: University of California Press, 1956), p. 210.
53. Chang, "Provincial Party Leaders' Strategies for Survival During the Cultural Revolution," in *Elites in the People's Republic of China*, ed. Robert A. Scalapino (Seattle, Wash. and London: University of Washington Press, 1972), pp. 501–39.
54. "Decision of the Central Committee of the CCP on Party Consolidation's," *Beijing Review*, 42 (October 17, 1983), vi.
55. Houn, *A Short History of Chinese Communism*, p. 106.
56. *People's Daily* (June 27, 1982), p. 1.
57. See Appendix A for the text of the 1982 constitution. See also Byron Weng, "Some Key Aspects of the 1982 Draft Constitution of the People's Republic of China," *The China Quarterly*, 91 (September 1982), 492–506.
58. "Report on the Draft of the Revised Constitution of the People's Republic of China," *Beijing Review*, 50 (December 13, 1982), 9.
59. *Ta Kung Pao Weekly Supplement* (June 3, 1982), p. 10.
60. *Beijing Review*, 40 (October 1, 1984), i–xx and *Beijing Review*, 14 (April 6, 1987), iii–iv.
61. *Beijing Review*, 18 (May 3, 1982), 16.
62. Ibid., p. 3; and *China Trade Report* (June 1982, p. 12. Also see Dorothy J. Sollinger, "The Fifth NPC and the Process of Policy-Making: Reform, Readjustment, and the Opposition," *Asian Survey*, vol. xxii, no. 12 (December 1982), 1239–76.
63. *People's Daily* (Overseas Edition) (January 28, 1986), p. 1.
64. Ibid.
65. *Ta Kung Pao Weekly Supplement* (Hong Kong) (September 4, 1986), p. 15.
66. See Ji Sanmeng, "A Functioning Legislature?" *Xexus: China in Focus* (Spring 1987), 2–6.

67. See MacFarquhar, *The Origins of the Cultural Revolution*, pp. 273–78.
68. "Investigating the Causes of the Oil Rig Accident," *Beijing Review*, 31 (August 4, 1980), 7.
69. *Far Eastern Economic Review* (December 11, 1986), 51.
70. *Beijing Review*, 17 (April 27, 1987), 15, and *The New York Times*, March 29, 1987, p. 4.
71. *Beijing Review*, 17 (April 27, 1987), 15, and *Far Eastern Economic Review* (June 28, 1984), 38. Also see a recent discussion on the extent of the NPC's conservatism: Kevin O'Brien, "Is China's National People's Congress a 'Conservative' Legislature?" *Asian Survey*, vol. xxx, no. 8 (August 1990), 782–94.
72. *Beijing Review*, 20 (May 19, 1986), 23.
73. See *Asian Wall Street Journal* (6 April 1992), p. 1; and *The Christian Science Monitor* (3 April 1992), p. 1.
74. See *Asian Wall Street Journal* (30 March 1993), p. 6.
75. See *The New York Times* (9 August 1992), E-4.
76. King-Yuh Chang, ed., *Mainland China after the Thirteenth Party Congress* (Boulder, Colo.: Westview Press, 1990).
77. Donald Klein, "The State Council and the Cultural Revolution," *The China Quarterly*, 35 (July–September 1968), 78–95.
78. "Chou En-lai and the Cultural Revolution in China," *The Cultural Revolution in China* (Berkeley: University of California Press, 1971), p. 279.
79. Klein, "The State Council," p. 81.
80. See Doak Barnett, *Cadres, Bureaucracy, and Political Power in Communist China* (New York: Columbia University Press, 1967), pp. 3–17.
81. Chang, *Power and Policy in China*, p. 50.
82. Ibid., pp. 63–64, 106–108; also see Barnett, *Uncertain Passage*, pp. 136–43.
83. "Report on the Sixth Five-Year Plan," p. 24.
84. Weng, "Some Key Aspects of the 1982 Draft Constitution of the PRC."
85. See Michael Oksenberg, "China's Economic Bureaucracy," *China Business Review* (May–June 1982), 23–24. Also see John P. Burns, "Reforming China's Bureaucracy, 1979–82," *Asian Survey*, xvii, 6 (June 1983), 707–714.
86. "China's Economic Bureaucracy," pp. 23–24.
87. Ibid., p. 24.
88. See *Beijing Review* (29 March–4 April 1993), 8.
89. See *Far Eastern Economic Review* (1 April 1993), 13.
90. *Beijing Review* (25–31 May 1993), 21.
91. "Report on the Work of the Government," *Beijing Review* (12–18 April 1993), xi.
92. Xinhua News Agency release reprinted in *Ta Kung Pao Weekly Supplement* (Hong Kong) (November 6, 1986), p. 3.
93. *Beijing Review*, 32 (August 11, 1986), 15. Also see *Selected Works of Deng Xiaoping* (Chinese language edition), People's Publishing House, 1983, pp. 280–302 and the English translation in *Beijing Review*, 41 (October 10, 1983), 18–22.
94. *Beijing Review*, 32 (August 11, 1986), 15.
95. Ibid.
96. See *People's Daily* (August 15, 1986), pp. 1–2. Also see *Beijing Review*, 32 (August 11, 1986), 5–6, and *China Daily* (August 23, 1986), p. 1. Also see an editorial in *China Daily* (August 9, 1986), p. 4.
97. *China Daily* (August 23, 1986), p. 1.
98. Ibid.
99. Ibid.
100. *People's Daily* (Overseas Edition) (August 16, 1986), p. 3; and *China Daily* (July 22, 1986), p. 1.
101. See *Far Eastern Economic Review* (February 5, 1987), 12. Also see *Zhengming*, 112 (February 1987), 7, and *The Wall Street Journal* (February 2, 1987), p. 19.
102. See *Far Eastern Economic Review* (February 5, 1987), 13, and *Ta Kung Pao Weekly Supplement* (Hong Kong) (November 6, 1986), p. 2.
103. See "Deng Calls for Speedup in Reform," *Beijing Review*, 34 (August 24, 1987), 15.
104. Ibid.
105. Ibid., 15–16.
106. "Advance Along the Road to Socialism with Chinese Characteristics," *Beijing Review*, 45 (November 9–15, 1987), 37–42.

107. *Ming Pao Daily* (Hong Kong) (November 6, 1987), p. 1. Also see Joseph Fewsmith, "China's 13th Party Congress: Explicating the Theoretical Bases of Reform," *Journal of Northeast Asian Studies*, vol. vii, no. 2 (Summer 1988), 56.
108. "Advance Along the Road to Socialism," pp. 37–43.
109. Ibid., pp. 40–41. For a background study on a proposal to reform the cadre system by making changes in the nomenklatura system in China, see John P. Burns, "China's Nomenklatura System," *Problems of Communism* (September–October, 1987), 36–51.
110. "Advance Along the Road to Socialism," p. 43.
111. See Kenneth Lieberthal, "China's Political System in the 1990s," *Journal of Northeast Asian Studies*, vol. x, no. 1 (Spring 1991), 73–74. Also see *China News Analysis*, 1407 (April 1, 1990), 1–9.
112. See Kenneth Lieberthal and Michel Oksenberg, *Policy-Making in China: Leaders, Structures and Process* (Princeton, N.J.: Princeton University Press, 19880.
113. See Parris Chang, *Power and Policy in China*, 2nd and enlarged ed. (University Park, Pa. and London: The Pennsylvania State University Press, 1978), pp. 178–81.
114. Ibid., p. 180.
115. Ibid., p. 181.
116. For the proposal, see *Beijing Review* (March 5–11, 1990), 18–22.
117. See *Beijing Review* (February 26–March 4, 1990), 18–22.

Elite⸴
Cad⸍

Leadership ꜱtyᷚᷤ,
Succession, and Recruitᴍᷤᷚᷤ

ELITES AND THE CADRE SYST

104

charismatic leader is one who
mand the devotion and loyal
ble.³ Charismatic leadership
sonal leadership. Both ᴺ
Salisbury as China's "
The Fourteen
the Central Advis
nated by what ᵃ
been made uₚ
cy making
over, grₑ
Commᵢ
in 1⁹
Aₛ

This chapter is concerned with China's elites—the political leaders who make policies and the organizational–institutional cadres at the various levels of the party and government who implement, and sometimes attempt to influence, policy making. An examination of China's elites and cadres logically follows our study of China's political institutions in the previous chapter.

The conceptual framework for elite study and recruitment is that the selection of political and administrative–managerial leaders in any political structure is an essential system function. Gabriel A. Almond and G. Bingham Powell refer to the selection of political elites as "recruitment structure—the way by which the political system selects policy makers and executives."[1] In the case of China, the "recruitment structure" includes, first and foremost, those leaders in the top echelon of the party's hierarchy, as well as some 4.2 million cadres who manage the government units.[2]

CHARACTERISTICS OF THE RULING ELITE

As pointed out earlier, the Leninist organizational structure is hierarchical and pyramidal in that decisions are made at the top by a few party leaders: in this case the members of the Standing Committee of the Politburo—the apex of the apex in decision making. However, for decades the top leadership has been dominated first by a charismatic leader, Mao Zedong (1935–76), and then by a paramount leader, Deng Xiaoping. According to Max Weber, the classical social organization theorist, a

possesses the exceptional ability or charisma to com-
of the people and whose views are considered infalli-
such as that exercised by Mao is also very much a per-
ao and Deng have been portrayed by the late Harrison E.
New Emperors."

Party Congress, which convened in October 1992, abolished
ory Committee. Until then, the Chinese top elite had been domi-
s known as a gerontocracy. The Central Advisory Committee had
of aged party veterans who were permitted to provide input into poli-
at the top. Then by the early 1990s several aged leaders, mostly 80 and
dually passed away. The average age of the current Politburo Standing
ttee is about 63. Half of the Fourteenth Central Committee members elected
92 were young and middle-aged technocrats—their average age was 56.3 years.
more aged veteran leaders at the top, including Deng Xiaoping, pass away from
he scene, the problem of gerontocratic rule will tend to fade. However, one serious
problem will continue to trouble the top elites in China: elite cleavage or strife and
the related succession problem.

ELITE STRIFE AND FACTIONALISM

Lowell Dittmer points out that "elite strife is the Achilles heel of the Chinese political system."[4] Dittmer argues that major past crises of the regime can be attributed to
"severe elite conflict" at the top.[5] Mao's Cultural Revolution represented a violent
pattern of elite strife or power struggle, while elite conflicts under Deng's reform
measures have been "institutionalized" and have been "less disruptive."[6] By analyzing the four major power struggles—the "Gang of Four" (1976), the removal of Hua
Guofeng from power (1980), the dismissal of Hu Yaobang (1987), and the removal
of Zhao Ziyang (1989)—Dittmer formulated the concept of the elite conflict cycle:
from "open and legitimate disagreement," to "impersonal discussion of problems," to
"destruction of the target's political base," and finally to "formal disposition of the
case" by an official party meeting convened to legitimatize the disposal.[7] Political
maneuvers among the top leaders in China were factional and did not necessarily follow ideological lines. The factions were based on personal relationships and associations. Several China scholars have studied factionalism in Chinese politics.[8] For
instance, Parris Chang comments on the emergence of two major coalitions, or
groupings, among top leaders since the arrest of the Gang of Four in 1976.[9] One
coalition, the "Whatever" group, consisted of Politburo members who were Mao loy-
alists and who collaborated with the Gang of Four during the Cultural Revolution.
Included in the "Whatever" coalition was the so-called "petroleum" or "oil" faction,
a group of veteran economists and technocrats who directed the economy. Hua
Guofeng became the "Whatever" coalitions's symbolic leader. The pragmatists of the
second coalition, led by Deng Xiaoping, consisted mainly of Politburo members who
were veteran party leaders and northern military leaders. Most of the Deng group
had been victims of purges during the Cultural Revolution. Allied with the Deng
pragmatists were (1) the Chen Yun economic planners, (2) elder statesmen (Ye
Jianying), and (3) so-called "independents."

Another commentator, Dorothy Fontana, has constructed a factional model utilizing the familiar radical-left, left-of-center, and political-right spectrum.[10] She believes that the radical left was made up of the Gang of Four and the "Whatever" group, joined earlier by the Lin Biao supporters. The left-of-center faction included the Long March military leaders and the "oil" or "petroleum" group of central economic administrators. The political-right faction included the late Zhou Enlai, the purged party victims of the Cultural Revolution, such as Deng, and the southern military leaders who later split with the Deng group.

In 1978 Deng began taking steps to consolidate his power and control over the party. A campaign was first launched against party officials who had collaborated with the Gang of Four and were now supporters of the "Whatever" faction. The campaign soon focused on the Politburo members who were led by Hua Guofeng and Wang Dongxing and who opposed Deng's reform policies. Hua's group appealed for reconciliation with those who had made serious mistakes during and after the Cultural Revolution. Marshal Ye, Hua's mentor on the Politburo, intervened by calling for "stability and unity" in order to mitigate the leadership purge that was about to begin and perhaps save something for those Politburo members who were known to have collaborated with the Gang of Four in the past.

At the Third Plenum of the Eleventh Central Committee (December 1978), Deng made some important gains as well as some concessions. The most important gain was the designation of Deng's protégé, Hu Yaobang, as the CCP general secretary to supervise the daily administration of the party affairs in an effort to dilute Chairman Hua's power. Deng gained another victory when the Central Committee agreed to elect four of his supporters as additional members of the Politburo. Those named were Chen Yun, Deng Yingchao (widow of Zhou Enlai), Hu Yaobang, and Wang Zhen. Chen Yun's elevation to Politburo membership was owed primarily to his reputation as a realistic economic planner. Chen was also made a vice-chairman of the Politburo's Standing Committee as a way of obtaining the support of the "independents," of whom he was a leading spokesperson. In addition, nine veteran party officials purged during the Cultural Revolution were elected as additional Central Committee members. Thus, Parris Chang developed a Chinese leadership factional scheme to show the dominance of the Deng group in coalition with the groups associated with the "Elder Statesmen" group of septuagenarians.[11] As pointed out in Chapter 2, by 1982 Deng and his close associates had emerged as the dominant faction in Chinese politics.

In 1978 Deng, as a leader of what has become the "grand coalition" of pragmatic reformers, orthodox hard-liners (conservatives, or ideological left), and the professional military, began taking steps to consolidate his power and control over the party. The "grand coalition" that Deng forged has many power centers revolving around personal ties within the party hierarchy. It is dependent on power sharing, not only with the young reformers but with the military and many aged veteran leaders, whose party experience dates as far back as the Long March in the 1930s. Deng serves as a power broker for a variety of viewpoints coming from the many power centers. Because Deng shares the early communist experience of the Long March and the purges of the Cultural Revolution, as well as personal friendship with the veteran cadres, he has been able to serve as a "bridge" between the aged orthodox hard-liners (conservatives) and the younger pragmatic reformers.[12] Parris Chang has portrayed Deng as a leader who, lacking Mao's charismatic power, has had to "rely on a skillful mix of cajolery, compromise, and threat to keep the coalition together."[13] Like Mao, Deng is considered a master in the game of politics—at present he has been able to balance power by playing one group against another to remain in power as the paramount leader of the "grand coalition."[14] The forced resignation of Hu Yaobang in January 1987 is evidence of continuing differences within the "grand coalition." The orthodox hard-liners tried to create the impression that Deng was in their camp when it was shown that Deng had criticized Hu for his indecisiveness in carrying out the party directives.[15] On the other hand, Deng's decision to let Hu go might be interpreted as a move "to placate the conservatives" in order to protect the reforms introduced after 1978.[16] Or, we may view Deng's action to remove Hu as a tactical move to "preempt his adversaries' attack" by upstaging them.[17] Parris Chang thinks that the firing of Hu, Deng's closest protégé and carefully groomed successor, "reflected Deng's poor political judgment and exposed his political weakness."[18] Another China watcher thought that Deng was simply a master tactician: having realized that it was not possible to yield to the students' demand for real democracy, Deng merely took "two steps forward and one step backward," rather than sacrificing or scrapping the reform measures altogether.[19]

The factional model, described above, has been supplemented by a bureaucratic politics model developed by Susan Shirk in her analysis of conflicts in Chinese society that were brought on by economic reform. In Shirk's analysis the vast and powerful central and regional bureaucracies in China constitute a "communist coalition," dominated by the planning agencies, heavy industries, and the vertically organized state-owned enterprises. This bureaucratic politics model postulates that known personalities within the party's hierarchy, because of their past long association with the bureaucratic entities, became the "high-level patrons" for the complex of powerful but entrenched bureaucracies and the vested interests they represent.[20] (Interest group theory and bureaucratic politics as an approach to the study of the communist system only recently gained recognition in the literature for comparative study of communism.)

The top party leadership lineup that emerged from the Thirteenth Party Congress reflected and retained the essential features of Deng's "grand coalition": a mixture of pragmatic reformers (in dominance), orthodox hard-liners' views (represented by Yao Yilin and Li Peng or Qiao Shi, whose views came closer to those of Peng Zhen), the PLA representation (reduced significantly), and the regional or provincial/municipal representation that seems to be on the rise. In addition, the powerful party provincial secretary from Sichuan in the southwest (Yang Rudai), mayors of the three municipalities of Shanghai (Jiang Zemin), Beijing (Li Ximing), and Tianjin (Li Ruihuan) were also elected to the new Politburo.

The top party leadership lineup that emerged after the 1976 Tiananmen repression was on the surface in favor of the hard-line conservatives. However, on close examination, the lineup still reflected and retained the essential features of Deng's "grand coalition": a mixture of orthodox hard-liners, represented by Li Peng, Yao Yilin and Qiao Shi (who followed generally the views of Chen Yun), the moderate reform-oriented Jiang Zemin (the new party chief), Li Ruihuan (former mayor of Tianjin), and possibly Song Ping (the party's head for organization).

While the military leadership is divided (see Chapter 8), it has strong influence in the inner-party struggle. Until the aged leaders, who constitute a powerful clique, pass from the scene and there emerges a new leadership lineup, three factions may remain locked in a power struggle.[21] One faction of younger leaders, more reform and open-door-oriented, is led by Jiang Zemin and Zhu Rongji with support from a provincial and regional power base.[22] Li Ruihuan has been more critical of the policies of the hard-liners.[23] The second faction is represented by Li Peng and Yao Yilin, whose mentor has been the 86-year-old Chen Yun, China's leading advocate of centralized planning and a critic of Deng Xiaoping's economic reform measures.[24] The Li Peng faction also has the support of the aged conservative party leaders and some segments of the central bureaucracy. This faction has basic differences with the moderate reform-oriented group led by Jiang and Zhu Rongji over the unsettled question of economic reform, converging on the extent of return to more centralized control over the economy, as well as the question of the long-run status of socialism impacted by changes in Eastern Europe and the former Soviet Union under Gorbachev. The third faction consists of the so-called "leftist" or "whatever" group led by Deng Liqun and a few like-minded party elders who are opposed to Deng Xiaoping's reforms and proclaimed "undying support" for whatever policy or program Mao had endorsed in the past. The factions have been marking time, apparently awaiting the death of one or more of their mentors and powers behind the scenes (particularly the aged Deng Xiaoping and Chen Yun) before launching any open power struggle or drive for consolidation. Until then the factions have made efforts to maintain surface "unity" and "stability." The political future of China is unpredictable because of the factionalism and divisions in its political leadership and the uncertain role of the military in any future power struggle.[25]

COLLECTIVE LEADERSHIP UNDER DENG XIAOPING AND THE CONTENDERS FOR SUCCESSION

From 1980 to the end of 1986; on the surface, China was under the collective leadership of three key leaders: Deng Xiaoping, Hu Yaobang, and Zhao Ziyang. This triumvirate controlled three main pillars of the Chinese political system: the military, the party, and the central government. However, some analysts held the view that the triumvirate was merely a facade to disguise Deng Xiaoping's role as the paramount leader. Power in China became consolidated under Deng beginning in 1978. The pragmatic reform measures launched since 1978 might be called Dengism (see Chapter 11).

The student demonstrations of 1986–87 and 1989, to be discussed in Chapter 10, had shaken the reform-oriented triumvirate that paramount leader Deng had installed. Within two and one-half years, Deng and his fellow octogenarians were twice required to remove their choice to head the party. In other words, the political leadership situation in China for the 1990s is anything but stable. In the pages that follow, brief sketches are presented of the top leaders who have ruled China from 1980 until today.

Deng Xiaoping: Architect of the Power Transition and the Succession

In 1979 Americans had a chance to observe at first hand China's new strongman, Deng Xiaoping, when he visited the United States at the invitation of President Carter. For eight days Deng traveled from Washington to Atlanta, Houston, and

Seattle, accompanied by members of Congress and the Carter cabinet. He was interviewed by the press at each stop; he mingled with the crowd in Atlanta; and he donned a ten-gallon hat at a Texas rodeo. His tour included visits to the space technology complex and oil-drilling-machine plants in Houston, and to the Boeing plant in Seattle.

What type of person is China's paramount leader, and what are his views? Although a dedicated communist and Leninist, Deng has never been dogmatic. When China was experiencing economic recovery during the early 1960s following the disastrous Great Leap, Deng said, "It makes no difference if a cat is black or white—so long as it catches the mice." In 1975 he expressed his disdain for a requirement that everyone spend long hours after work studying correct political thought. He called the practice "social oppression." A pragmatist, Deng has advocated the line of profit-in-command, rather than Mao's dictum of politics-in-command.

Deng was born in Sichuan province in 1904. He was an early organizer for the Chinese communist movement when both he and the late Zhou Enlai were students in France under a work-study program.[26] Before returning to China in 1927 to work in an underground party cell in Shanghai, Deng studied briefly in Moscow. He joined Mao's guerilla movement during the early 1930s and took part in the Long March. His rise in the party hierarchy was rapid, and by 1955 Deng was elected to the powerful Politburo and held the position of general secretary to the party. He remained the party's general secretary until 1966, when he was purged by the radicals during the Cultural Revolution.[27] In 1974 he returned to power at the request of the then ailing Zhou Enlai and Mao to introduce reforms that would enable China to modernize its industry, agriculture, sciences, and military defense. When the Tiananmen riot erupted in 1976, Deng was again purged. Following the arrest of the Gang of Four, Deng was once more returned to power to oversee China's modernization program as a deputy premier and vice-chairman of the party.[28] The twice-purged Deng realized that to fulfill his task as chief architect of modernization, he must consolidate his power by replacing the remnants of Mao's followers with his own people.[29]

The party's declaration at the Third Plenum that the 1976 Tiananmen demonstration was an "entirely revolutionary mass movement" must be viewed as a personal vindication for Deng.[30] It was also a blow to those Politburo members who, sooner or later, would have to criticize themselves about their role in support of the Gang of Four in that riot which caused Deng's second purge. Finally, after some heated discussion, the party adopted Deng's view that practice was to be the sole criterion for testing truth, and that things did not have to be done according to books or to "ossified thinking." This was a direct refutation of the "Whatever" faction's stand. Deng was not yet strong enough to demand the immediate ouster of his opponents still sitting on the Politburo. Actually, Deng had to agree to shelve for the time being any further discussion on the sensitive, divisive issue of assessing Mao's role in the Cultural Revolution.

During 1979 Deng made little headway in instituting organizational reforms because of resistance from his adversaries. However, he prevailed upon the party at its Fourth Plenum in September 1979 to add twelve new members to the Central Committee. These new members included veteran leaders Peng Zhen, Bo Yibo, and Yang Shangkun. Deng was able to install Peng Zhen and Zhao Ziyang as alternate members of the Politburo and thus further improve his numerical strength on that body.

In February 1980 Deng's final move came at the party's Fifth Plenum. Key Deng supporters Hu Yaobang and Zhao Ziyang were elevated to membership on the Politburo's Standing Committee, the apex of the apex in decision making in the party hierarchy.[31] Their elevation was preceded by the removal of four Politburo members (Wang Dongxing, Ji Dengkui, Wu De, and Chen Xilian) who were held to be collaborators of the Gang of Four and critics of Deng's policies. While Hua Guofeng remained as the nominal party chairman, his power and influence by this time were those of a mere figurehead, for it was at the Fifth Plenum that the Central Secretariat was reestablished to manage and oversee the day-to-day work of the party, presided over by Hu Yaobang, the general secretary. By September 1980 Hua also had been replaced as premier of the State Council by Zhao Ziyang at a session of the NPC. Having removed his critics from the Politburo, Deng now was in a firmer position to issue a party communiqué calling for the implementation of the modernization program. By the end of 1980, he controlled the party, government, and military. But the new era in Chinese politics was not ushered in until some time later in September 1982, when the Twelfth Party Congress was convened under the complete control and domination of China's paramount leader, Deng Xiaoping, and his supporters.

Deng Xiaoping had said that he did not want to be honored for his accomplishments,[32] and had accepted responsibility for any mistakes made under his leadership in the thirty years prior to the 1966 Cultural Revolution.[33] However, Deng Xiaoping most likely will be accorded a unique place in history as the man who engineered the "Second Revolution" in China during the decade after Mao's death, a period that ushered China into the era of economic and political reforms. Deng was the chief architect for change and the one who dared to make significant modification in China's experiment with socialism. He opened China's door to foreign investment and transfer of technology—thus ending its long isolation from the rest of the world, an isolation imposed mainly by Mao's ideological rigidity. (Detailed discussion on these topics is included in Chapters 3 and 11). Deng and his pragmatic reformers also introduced agricultural reform in the countryside: a profit-incentive or responsibility system that replaced the egalitarian commune system. While the final verdict is not yet in, Deng's image has been damaged considerably as a result of his order and support for the military crackdown on the students in Tiananmen on June 4, 1989 (see Chapter 10). While he resigned from the only official post he held after his semiretirement at the end of 1987—that of the chairmanship of the powerful Military Affairs Committee—in the aftermath of the Tiananmen massacre, Deng still makes important decisions as China's paramount leader.

Succession to paramount leader Deng Xiaoping is a serious problem, and possibly disruptive for the Chinese political system because of two institutional characteristics inherent in a Leninist party: the overconcentration of power in one leader, and the lack of a procedure or process by which political leadership can be transferred smoothly and with legitimacy. When Mao was alive he tried to handpick his successors, but he failed at both attempts: Liu Shaoqi was purged at the beginning of the Cultural Revolution, and Lin Biao was purged in 1972. After consolidating his power in 1978–80, Deng, too, failed in his attempts to place his handpicked colleagues at the top to succeed him: his protégé Hu Yaobang was forced to resign in 1987, and Zhao Ziyang was removed for his handling of the student protests at Tiananmen in May 1989.

As Deng approaches the age of 90, the following five Politburo members elected by the Fourteenth Party Congress in 1992 may be considered as possible successors to Deng when he passes away.

Li Peng, the New Premier: A Compromise Choice of a Soviet-Trained Technocrat

Li Peng is one of the many symbolically adopted children of the late Premier Zhou Enlai and his wife. An electrical engineer trained in the Soviet Union, Li speaks fluent Russian and some English. Before he became prominent, Li, at the age of 54, was in charge of China's hydroelectric and nuclear energy development. In 1983, Li was elevated to be one of the five vice-premiers under Zhao Ziyang. Long before he was appointed as acting premier at the end of the Thirteenth Party Congress in November 1987, Li was considered by many as the likely successor to Zhao because of his training, education, and executive experience, in addition to his good connections with the old veterans by virtue of being an adopted son of Zhou Enlai.

Li's father, an upper-middle-level party cadre, was captured and put to death by the Nationalists in 1937. Li went to Hong Kong as a youngster to live with his mother, who was then a party member working underground. In 1939 Li returned to wartime Sichuan, his native province. He became a party member in 1945 and was one of the privileged few to go to the Soviet Union for further training. Li attended the Moscow Power Institute from 1948 to 1954 and graduated with an electrical engineering degree. Until recently most of Li's work was concerned with the technical aspects of electrical power and hydroelectric development projects in Beijing. He became concurrently the minister for the State Education Commission before he was promoted to the post of vice-premier in the State Council in 1983. In the 1985 reshuffle of top echelon leaders, Li was elected to the Politburo.

When Li was designated in late November 1987 as the acting premier, several questions were raised about his elevation to succeed Zhao at the State Council.[34] These questions or concerns seem to fall into two major areas. One is his Soviet connection. His training as an engineer from the Moscow Power Institute in the 1950s placed him in the "pro-Soviet" camp. At an unusual press conference of China's vice-premiers in April 1987, Li defended his position by saying that "The second question seems to ask whether I favor a pro-Soviet policy. Here I formally declare that I am a member of the Chinese government, and also a new young member of the Communist party's Central Committee. I'll faithfully carry out the policies of the Central Committee and the government."[35] Thus it may not be fair to have labeled Li as "pro-Soviet" on the ground that he received technical training in the Soviet Union. A number of Soviet-trained technocrats, now members of the new Politburo, have supported Deng Xiaoping and Zhao Ziyang and the reform programs; they have been given important positions in the party and government.

A second question raised about Li concerns the degree of his support for economic reforms, particularly urban reform and the open door policy. Li is said to be under the influence of Chen Yun, who championed centralized planning and issued cautions on current economic reforms. Li's selection to succeed Zhao as premier was one of the compromises struck just prior to the Thirteenth Party Congress between Deng and the conservative hard-liners at Beidaihe in the summer of 1987. Apparently Zhao's opposition to Li was based on two main considerations: their disagreements on some reform measures, and Zhao's fear that Li's elevation to the premiership in time could lead to a takeover by the conservative hard-liners. There is little evidence to document Li's open opposition to any of the economic reforms. On the day when he was designated the acting premier, Li pledged to carry on both the economic reform and the open-door policies. However, at a general staff meeting of the State Council, he stated that the speed of economic reform might be "too fast."[36] For the foreseeable future Li seems to be committed to the reform policies.[37] But, in the long run, he may advance his own ideas, influenced perhaps by his Soviet training and the advice of his more conservative mentors.

Li disagreed with Zhao over the issue of how to handle the Tiananmen student demonstrations. By allying himself with the hard-liners on the Politburo and Yang Shangkun, the People's Republic of China president and the then-permanent secretary for the Military Affairs Committee, Li proclaimed martial law on May 20, 1989. Since then, Li has emerged as one of the spokesmen for the hard-liners and as a target of attack and criticism by students, intellectuals, and those who have been sympathetic toward political and economic reforms. Li Peng suffered humiliation at the 1993 NPC session when more than 11 percent of the deputies voted against or abstained from his reelection as premier. Li Peng's power has been weakened considerably since 1993, and there have been signs suggesting his gradual political decline.

Jiang Zemin: His Precarious Position in the Power Struggles[38] as Deng's Designated Successor

Jiang Zemin was 63 years old in June 1989 when he was selected to replace Zhao Ziyang as the third party chief since Mao's death in 1976. His earlier work with the party was mostly in Shanghai factories manufacturing foodstuffs, soap, and electrical machinery. In 1955 he went to Moscow as a trainee at the Stalin Automobile Factory, where he studied Russian. He returned after one year and was placed as deputy engineer at an auto plant in the northeast; in 1970 he rose to become the director of foreign affairs for the machine building ministry. In 1982 he was a vice-minister for the Ministry of Electronics Industry. In 1985 he became the Mayor of Shanghai and its party chief; two years later he was elevated to membership in the Politburo, the apex of the party's decision-making hierarchy. By then he had established wide contacts with diplomats and was able to speak several languages, including English, French, and Russian.

Jiang was obviously the personal choice of Deng Xiaoping, who selected the former to succeed the deposed Zhao as an acceptable compromise to the octogenarians in order to avoid a factional fight among the divided top leadership.[39] Other plausible reasons for Deng's backing of Jiang might be Jiang's handling of student protests in 1986–87 when he skillfully, but peacefully, terminated an otherwise dangerous situation. Deng also might have been impressed by Jiang's plans for developing Shanghai as the premier industrial giant—the two had a secret meeting in the spring of 1989 in Shanghai.[40] During the Tiananmen demonstration, Jiang acted decisively in support of the Center's desire to curb intellectual dissent and criticism by firing the chief editor of an outspoken Shanghai liberal economic journal. However, to some, Jiang's record in Shanghai was not by any means a distinguished one.

It is doubtful that Jiang is to be the successor to Deng, even though the latter proclaimed that the newly appointed party chief must be "the core of the third generation of leaders."[41] Jiang lacks some essential factors to survive and ultimately win the inner party factional struggles. First, he does not have any previous military association or connection to inspire the military's support. He was recently appointed chairman of the powerful Military Affairs Committee after Deng stepped down in September 1990. China's military establishment had been under the control of Yang Shangkun and his brother Yang Baibing until they were purged in 1992. As an outsider, it will take Jiang time to build up support and confidence among the military officers to counteract the power of the Yang brothers. Second, it is also doubtful that Jiang, as the party chief, possesses the real authority, in spite of Deng's backing, because collectively and individually the octogenarians exercise the real power. In this context, Jiang may be regarded as a figurehead, or a caretaker, until the next power struggle surfaces, and when some of the leading octogenarians pass away. If Deng dies before Chen Yun, Jiang may not survive, since Chen's faction most likely would back Li Peng as the ultimate leader. Third, while the waiting game or the wake is in progress, Jiang needs to cultivate a support base, not only in the military but also in the party and central government bureaucracy, which is the domain of Li, the premier. On the eve of convening the much-delayed seventh plenary session of the Thirteenth Party Congress, originally scheduled for October or November 1990, there seemed to be clear evidence that there was already some opposition building up against Jiang.[42] However, at the Fourteenth Party Congress (1992) and the Eighth National People's Congress (1993), Deng promoted the party chief, Jiang Zemin, to be his successor. By the spring of 1993 Jiang had become not only the party chief and the chairman of the party's powerful Military Affairs Committee, but the president of the Republic—the first leader since Mao to control the party, the government, and the military. Jiang has been busy in building the military's support by promoting top military officers to generalships.

Liu Binyan, a dissident leader now in exile at Princeton University, writes that Deng's choice of Jiang as his successor may be another one of Deng's power-balancing acts among other contending members of the Politburo's Standing Committee.[43] Jiang's purging of the Yang brothers in September 1992, at the urging of Deng, may have alienated the military officers' support for Jiang, for the PLA officer corps is close to the Yang brothers, and some of them may be resentful of the dismissals and transfers.[44] So who else, besides Jiang, are the possible contenders for succession? With Li Peng's tarnished image and his heart ailments, the following three Politburo members may be the possible or probable contenders.

Qiao Shi: The Security Enforcer and His Independent Base at the NPC

Before his elevation to the Politburo's Standing Committee in 1987, Qiao Shi was for some time the shadowy figure behind the party's security apparatus—China's equivalent to Lavrenti Beria under Stalin. In 1986 Qiao was the top leader in charge of correcting corruption and security-related problems within the party.[45] He was said to be tough and firm. He was born in 1925 in the coastal province of Zhejiang and joined the party at the age of 16, a mere teenager. In 1945 he was operating underground as a deputy party secretary in Shanghai and was soon promoted to party secretary in North Shanghai as an organizer for the student movement. When the war with Japan ended, Qiao returned to his native province of Zhejiang to continue in party work, holding a position as leader in charge of youth work for the East

China Bureau of the Central Committee. In 1954 he shifted to industrial work as the technical division chief for Anshan Iron and Steel, one of the largest state-owned enterprises in China. In 1962 Qiao was enrolled in the party school of the Central Committee, and a year later he established his organizational reputation as a leader and as head of the party's international liaison (security) department with other fraternal communist parties of the world. He also headed the Central Party School, a base for recruitment of party leaders.

Qiao is a serious contender for succession because of concurrent or interlocking positions he holds in the Politburo's Standing Committee and his elevation as chairman of the NPC Standing Committee, plus his many years of organizational and security work within the party and behind the scenes. Qiao's task now is to prepare the NPC to enact more economic laws.[46] He could use the NPC as a power base in the succession contest.[47] What Qiao lacks is a close working relationship with the military—the final arbiter in the power competition. But Qiao is a careful manipulator in inner party struggles—for instance, he chose to abstain from the vote at the May 1989 meeting of the Standing Committee of the Politburo on martial law declaration.

Zhu Rongji: The Economic Czar in the "Jiang–Zhu System" of Power Control

Li Peng's illness and unpopularity provided the opportunity for Jiang Zemin—with the consent and support of Deng and perhaps of Chen Yun, the other powerful octogenarian—to elevate Zhu Rongji, the vice-premier, to acting premier. Then in July 1993 Zhu was concurrently named the governor for the central bank, replacing Li Peng's appointee, who was deemed unable to provide effective leadership in curbing the overheated economy. Zhu Rongji's star is on the rise and he most probably will replace Li Peng as premier if and when the latter steps down or is eased out of power.

Zhu Rongji is 63 years old and a graduate of China's prestigious Qinghua University, where he majored in electrical engineering. Zhu has been associated closely with the State Planning Commission. In addition, he was appointed vice-minister in charge of the State Economic Commission in 1983, before he succeeded Jiang as mayor and party chief for Shanghai in 1985. While Jiang lacks a working knowledge of the intricacies of economics and trade, Zhu is very well versed in these matters. It is this combined "Jiang–Zhu tixi (system)" that would be the center of attention and power for China as Deng fades out of the picture and eventually dies. The Jiang–Zhu combination's most immediate problem is to consolidate and reinforce central control in cooling down growth and to check the provincial and local governments' unrestrained expansion, which contributed to the overheated economy.

Li Ruihuan: The Wildcard in the Succession Contest

Deng Xiaoping elevated Li Ruihuan to the Politburo in August 1987, not only because he was at age 53 a relatively young leader, but also because of the reforms he had introduced while serving as mayor of Tianjin, an industrial city. Li was born of a peasant background and trained as an expert carpenter at a construction company in Beijing in the early 1950s. In 1958 he had the opportunity to study at Beijing Civil Engineering Institute. He joined the party in 1959, and by the 1960s was serving as a party secretary in the building material trade. He was purged during the early part of the Cultural Revolution. In 1971 he came to Beijing and engaged in party organizational work in the lumber and building material industries. He was also active in the trade union federation in Beijing, having served as a member of the executive committee for the All China Federation of Trade Unions, a mass organization.

In 1981 Li Ruihuan became the mayor of Tianjin. As mayor he introduced significant reform work in urban housing; he insisted on work efficiency. He is reform-minded and a key supporter of Deng's reforms. He is a crowd pleaser, speaking in a plain and clear manner with humor.

He is a wildcard in the serious game of power struggle and succession if there is a deadlock among Jiang Zemin, Zhu Rongji, and Qiao Shi. Li Ruihuan can use his new state responsibility, as the chairman of the National Committee of the Chinese People's Political Consultative Conference (CPPCC), as a base for his succession contest. He has many friends in China's minor political parties and is acceptable to many intellectuals and industrial units without party affiliation. Also, he has wide support from overseas Chinese, particularly in Hong Kong and Macao, the economically booming areas crucial to economic development and investment in China.

RECRUITMENT OF PARTY MEMBERS

When the Eleventh Party Congress convened in August 1977, almost a year after the downfall of the Gang of Four, it was announced that the party had a membership of more than 35 million. In his speech, Ye Jianying pointed out that 7 million of the 35 million party members had been recruited since the last party congress in 1973, and about one-half of the total party membership had been recruited since the Cultural Revolution.[48] He admitted that there was a serious problem in party organization and discipline, which resulted from the rapid recruitment of so many party members by the Gang of Four. The old soldier, then a vice-chairperson of the party, bluntly indicated that the radicals had recruited a large number of new party members in accordance with their own standards. What Ye was demanding was tighter requirements for party membership. What he failed to mention was that the Chinese Communist Party (see Table 5.1) membership had been steadily increasing since the party came to power in 1949, and that the party had not always insisted on ideological purity and correctness as the most important criteria for membership. Let us now discuss the factors that contributed to the expansion of party membership.

Factors in Party Membership Expansion

Several general remarks may be made with respect to the growth of the CCP membership. First, for the period from 1920 to 1927, from the party's First Congress to its Fifth Congress, members of the party were primarily urban intellectuals, intermixed with some members of the proletariat from coastal cities and from mines in the inland provinces. When the Sixth Party Congress convened in 1928, most of its members had been driven underground by the Nationalists. There was a significant reduction in membership, by as much as 17,900, between the Fifth Party Congress in 1927 and the Sixth Party Congress in 1928. This reduction can be attributed to the slaughter by the Nationalists in the 1927 coup and to the subsequent defections.

Second, from the Sixth Congress in 1928 to the Seventh Congress in 1945, the

TABLE 5.1 CCP Membership Growth Pattern

PARTY CONGRESS	YEAR	NUMBER OF MEMBERS
1st Congress	1921	57
2nd Congress	1922	123
3rd Congress	1923	432
4th Congress	1925	950
5th Congress	1927	57,967
6th Congress	1928	40,000
7th Congress	1945	1,211,128
8th Congress	1956	10,734,384
	1961	17,000,000
9th Congress	1969	20,000,000
10th Congress	1973	28,000,000
11th Congress	1977	35,000,000
12th Congress	1982	39,650,000
13th Congress	1987	46,000,000
14th Congress	1992	52,000,000

Sources: Figures from 1921 to 1961 are based on John W. Lewis, *Leadership in Communist China* (Ithaca, N.Y.: Cornell University Press, 1963), pp. 108–20. The 1969 party membership figure is an estimate calculated on the basis of about 40 percent increase in 1973 over 1969 given by Jurgen Domes, "A Rift in the New Course," *Far Eastern Economic Review* (October 1, 1973), 3. The 1973 total and membership figure is taken from Zhou Enlai's "Report to the Tenth National Congress of the CCP," *Beijing Review*, 35–26 (September 7, 1973), 18.
   The 1977 party membership figure is based on Ye Jianying, "Report on the Revision of the Party Constitution to the Eleventh Party Congress, August 13–18, 1977," *Beijing Review*, 36 (September 2, 1977), 36. The 1982 figure was based on *Beijing Review*, 36 (September 6, 1982), 6. Also see New China News Agency release of August 18, 1982, as printed in *Ming Pao* (Hong Kong) (August 21, 1982), p. 1, and *The New York Times*, (September 6, 1982), A-2. The 1987 party membership figure is based on *Renmin Ribao* (Overseas Edition) (September 30, 1987), p. 1. Party membership for 1992 is based on *Renmin Ribao* (October 21, 1992), p. 4.

primary membership recruitment shifted from intellectuals to peasants, who became the mainstay of the guerilla armies. In fact, beginning in 1939, the CCP, under the firm leadership of Mao, undertook to militarize the party membership. The 1.2 million members reached by the Seventh Congress in 1945, at the termination of the war with Japan, largely operated under the appropriate description "military communism." Party members essentially were recruited from the famed Eighth Route and from the New Fourth Armies. The late John Lindbeck noted the profound impact of the recruitment pattern in the character-building of the party membership:

> The result of the militarization policy was that dedication, fighting spirit, and responsiveness to discipline and orders became the hallmark of Communist Party members, as well as the harsher virtues of a soldier—ruthlessness, toughness, and a will to override and subdue other people. They held the guns out of which Mao's political power and everything else grew. By the time the party had conquered China, the bulk of its membership was made up of triumphant warriors.[49]

Lindbeck also pointed out that the militarization of the party membership created many problems that have continued to beset Chinese party politics. These problems—concerning the army as a special political power and as an independent interest group—will be discussed in later chapters. What we need to point out here is that the army has always been the model emulated by the CCP in organizational disciplinary matters.

Third, the period from 1945 to 1956, or from the Seventh to the Eighth Party Congress, represented the most rapid growth period in the party's history: from a little over 1.2 million members to just under 11 million members, or approximately an 886 percent increase. The years 1955–56 saw another sudden rise in membership recruitment, followed by a temporary lull and then a gigantic rise in 1956–57, when party organizational work was intensified in all rural areas of China. This was the period preceding the Great Leap Forward, launched in 1958. Although party recruitment took some great strides quantitatively—by 1961, some 90 percent of the 17 million party members had been recruited after 1949—the ideological purity of the new party recruits was questionable.

Fourth, during the period from the Eighth Party Congress in 1956 to 1961, recruitment of party members became institutionalized to ensure that party members possessed both ideological redness and technical expertise. Membership expansion during 1954 and in 1956–57 was designed to recruit personnel needed to direct and manage the nation's extensive political and economic activities. The rapid recruitment of those who possessed the needed technical skill resulted in a shift in the recruitment pattern of new party members in terms of social background.

Following this changed pattern of recruitment, the party cadre system was institutionalized to make it more attractive to intellectuals who were being co-opted into the party. By 1955 a rank system for cadres' work assignments had been instituted, based on the acquisition of technical skills. In addition, a salary scale system was promulgated along with the rank system for cadres. Recruitment and promotion rules were also instituted in the late 1950s. Recent studies point out the bureaucratization of the party. One study concludes that by 1965 China was no longer a revolutionary society because, by initial contact with the political system and a careful selection of education and occupation, a careerist could very well predict the outcome of his or her life.[50] Another study points out that one inevitable result of the institutionalization of the party in the late 1950s and the 1960s was bureaucratization, which stressed order, discipline, and routine as organizational virtues.[51] While no detailed official statistics on party membership have been released since 1961, when membership stood at 17 million, the general level of party membership has been indicated, as shown in Table 5.1. During the Cultural Revolution, aggregate membership remained at around 17 million, virtually unchanged from 1961. Membership for 1969 was approximately 20 million, a net increase of only 3 million from 1961. However, after 1969 party membership resumed its rapid rise, with the addition of 8 million members from 1969 to 1973, when the total stood at 28 million, and the addition of 7 million from 1973 to 1977, when the total stood at 35 million. This means, as Marshal Ye has indicated, that over half the 35 million party members in 1977 were recruited after the Cultural Revolution.[52] For the four-year period from 1978 to 1982, another 4 million new members were added, for a grand total of 39 million. The rate of increase has been six million party members from 1982 to 1987 and another six million from 1987 to 1992.

Without detailed data, we cannot be sure of the backgrounds of the new members recruited since the Cultural Revolution. However, fragmentary official figures showing the characteristics and social composition of new party members have been reported.[53] The party membership for the Beijing municipality may be used here as an illustration. From the Cultural Revolution to 1973, some 60,000 new members were added to the party membership roster for Beijing. Of these, about 75 percent were "workers, former poor and lower-middle peasants or children of such families," and just under 5 percent were "revolutionary intellectuals working in the fields of culture, health, science and education." The overwhelming majority of these new Beijing municipality party members were under thirty-five years of age, and women constituted 25 percent of the total.

Another important element in the recruitment pattern following the Cultural Revolution was the effort made to recruit members of the minority groups in the autonomous regions. Apparently, 143,000 new members from minority nationalities were admitted to party membership from 1969 to 1973. Although we do not have comprehensive official statistics for the entire CCP membership from 1961 to 1976, we may surmise, based on fragmentary data, that the new membership recruitment pattern placed greater emphasis on (1) industrial workers of urban areas, (2) women, (3) minority nationalities, and (4) youths. Since 1978 there has been a sharp increase in recruitment of party members from among intellectuals, particularly scientists and persons with technical knowledge, who in the past have been discriminated against either for being politically unreliable or for having complex social backgrounds. If the above conclusion is correct, and I believe it is not too far off target, then the CCP has greatly broadened its base, regardless of the shifting recruitment requirements.

Membership Requirements: Changing Emphasis

There is a marked difference between the party constitutions of the Eighth Congress (1956), and those of the subsequent congresses (1969, 1973, 1977, and 1982) with regard to eligibility for party membership. The 1956 constitution stipulated no class basis or origin for party membership: It was open to "all Chinese citizens" who qualified. The party constitution approved in 1969 by the Ninth Party Congress, at the end of the Cultural Revolution, and the ones adopted by the Tenth and Eleventh Party Congresses in 1973 and 1977, required that only those who are "workers, poor peasants, or lower-middle peasants" were eligible to become members of the CCP. In addition, PLA soldiers and "other revolutionary elements" might also be eligible for membership. The 1982 party constitution is less restrictive, providing that any worker, peasant, member of the armed forces, and—more significantly—intellectual may be eligible for party membership (see Article 1 in Appendix B). All recent party constitutions—1973, 1977, and 1982—prescribed four sequential requirements that an applicant for party membership must satisfy: (1) recommendation by two party members, after filing the application individually; (2) examination of the application by a party branch that solicits opinions about the applicant from both inside and outside the party; (3) acceptance of the application by the party branch at its general membership meeting; and (4) approval of the party branch's acceptance of membership by the next higher party committee. It has been a frequent practice, dating back to the late 1940s, for an applicant to be admitted to party membership solely upon the recommendation of top party leaders.[54]

All party members were obligated by both the 1969 and 1973 party constitutions to live up to the five requirements that Chairman Mao advanced for worthy revolutionary successors: to conscientiously study the works of Marx, Lenin, and Mao; to always serve the collective interests of the people and never work for private gain; to strive for united front work; to consult the masses; and to be willing to engage in criticism and self-criticism. The 1977 party constitution added three more requirements: never to engage in factional activities to split the party; to observe party discipline; and always to perform well tasks assigned by the party and to set examples as a vanguard. The added demands were designed to strengthen the standards for recruitment of party members and to tighten admission policy, in order to avoid the "crash admittance" program allegedly practiced by the purged radical leaders. In his report on the need to tighten requirements for party members, Marshal Ye said in 1977: "In recent years the Gang of Four set their own standards for party membership and practiced 'crash admittance' and as a result some political speculators and bad types have sneaked into the party." [55] The fact that the provisions for "purification of the ranks" and strict party discipline, as well as for tightening admission standards, were written into the 1977 and 1982 party constitutions illustrates the importance of the recruitment process to the party leaders and their awareness that the pattern of recruitment has great influence on the character of the party.

The 1982 constitutional requirements for party membership are almost identical to the provisions of the 1977 party constitution. However, the 1982 version stresses in Article 3 the responsibilities of party members to work "selflessly" and "absolutely never to use public office for personal gain or benefits." This provision certainly expresses the party's concern for the outbreak of widespread corruption among party members in recent years.

Party recruitment in the 1980s was still beset with problems, despite the crackdown on "crash admittance," widely practiced during the Cultural Revolution and immediately afterwards. Two of these problems were how to weed out unfit or unqualified party members, and how to upgrade party members' professionalism and competence as China moved toward modernization. In a speech to a conference of party cadres in January 1980, Deng Xiaoping stressed the fact that too many party members were simply unqualified. [56] He deplored their preoccupation with acquiring special privileges instead of serving the people.

Although no attempts have been made to implicate all those party members admitted during the Cultural Revolution, 17 million (about 40 percent of the 1982 total membership of 39 million) had been targeted for the first phase of the party rectification campaign. [57] Hu Yaobang told the 1982 party congress that beginning in mid-1983, for a period of three years until 1986, concerted efforts would be made to weed out undesirable and unqualified party members. The method used for the second stage of the housecleaning was the reregistration of all party members by national-, provincial-, and basic-level party organizations. The specific steps involved in the internal housecleaning campaign were comprehensive study of party documents, particularly those decisions endorsed by the party's Third Plenum in 1978 (including *Selected Works of Deng Xiaoping*); careful examination of party members' records; and reregistration on the new party membership roll. Special teams of investigators were dispatched by the party organizations at the central and provincial levels to lower levels—the investigations were to be supervised by a "Central Party Rectification Working Leadership Commission" under the joint leadership of Qiao Shi, a young Politburo and Central Secretariat member, and Po Ibo, a retired old guard serving as the vice-chairman for the Central Advisory Commission.[58] The requirements for membership stated in the new party constitution would be applied against party members who had been "rabble-rousers" during the Cultural Revolution or who had practiced factionalism or instigated armed violence. Hu Yaobang indicated that "those who failed to meet the requirements for membership after education shall be expelled from the party or asked to withdraw from it."[59] Also targeted for expulsion from party membership were those who had committed economic crimes, such as bribery, embezzlement, or smuggling. Originally the number targeted for expulsion by 1986 was estimated at as high as two million.[60] In 1987, at the end of the party purge, it was reported that some six million rural party members had been either transferred or simply expelled for being exposed to the "ultra-leftists" and for committing "economic crimes," but the latest official word is that only 150,000 were expelled because of the resistance.[61]

Upgrading the competence and professionalism of party members is a much harder task to accomplish. Since a majority of government leaders are party members, the problem centers on the educational level of the party cadres. The 1982 party constitution contains a special chapter on party cadres. Article 34 states that party cadres (leaders) must possess both political integrity and professional competence. But the fact remains that perhaps as many as 50 percent of the 20 million state cadres have a minimal education, equivalent to an American junior high school level. One Western source estimated that in 1985, 10 percent of the 40 million party members were illiterate and perhaps only 4 percent had any college level education.[62] A Chinese source was quoted as stating that in 1985 as many as 15 million of the 40 million party members were illiterate or poorly educated peasants.[63] An article in the *China Daily* attributed the high level of illiteracy within the party membership to Mao's dictum that the poor and uneducated peasants were the most reliable party members.[64] This is probably true among cadres at the party's basic organizational level in the countryside. Even at the party's central and provincial organizational levels, there is a dire need for trained and skilled administrators and managers. Some efforts have been made to upgrade party cadres' professional competence. Cadres younger than 40 with only a junior middle school education (the equivalent of an American eighth-grade education) have been sent to specialized party schools for three years on a rotation basis.[65] The ultimate goal in upgrading party cadres is to provide leaders at every level of the party who are "revolutionized, youthful, intellectualized, and expert."[66] The task is enormous, considering the sheer number of party cadres who are undereducated and in need of professional training.

THE DEVELOPMENT OF THE CHINESE
BUREAUCRACY: THE CADRE SYSTEM

A government's policies and programs are generally carried out by the functionaries who staff the administrative agencies. In the noncommunist world, we call these people bureaucrats, the "vast impenetrable and well-paid" corps of paper-shufflers.[67] The Chinese call these bureaucrats "cadres" or "ganbu," denoting leadership skill and capability in an organizational setup. Thus, we may refer to Zhou Enlai, Hu

Yaobang, or Deng Xiaoping as the party and central government's leading cadres. The intermediate layer of bureaucrats is the middle-level cadres; and those on the bottom layer, who must deal directly with the masses, are the basic-level cadres.

It should be kept in mind that not every cadre is a party member, nor is every party member a cadre. In short, cadres are the functionaries who staff the various party and government bureaucracies and who have authority to conduct party or government business. When we use the term "elite" in discussing Chinese politics, we are generally referring to the cadres at various levels.

On the basis of their employment, the cadres are divided into three general broad categories: state, local, and military. Each group has its own salary classification system with ranks and grades, similar to civil service systems in noncommunist countries. Urban state cadres have a system with twenty-four grades, while local cadres have twenty-six grades. Local cadres at the commune level or below are paid directly by the organizations they work for. This ranking system is also associated with status, privileges, and the degree of upward mobility in the career ladder. A cadre's rank, particularly at the state level, is determined not necessarily by length of service or seniority but frequently by educational background, expertise, or technical competence. Those cadres who have served the party since the days of the Long March and the war against Japan naturally command more prestige than those who joined after the liberation in 1949. During the Cultural Revolution, the term *veteran cadres* was widely used to denote cadres who had acquired administrative experience in managing party and government affairs prior to the Cultural Revolution.

It is difficult to obtain precise figures for the total number of state, local, and military cadres in China today. We know that in 1958 there were about 8 million state cadres, or one state leader for every eighty persons in China. If we use the ratio of 1:80 as a basis for a rough estimate, the total number of state cadres in 1982 was over 27 million.[68] This figure does not include the millions of cadres at the local level and in the military, and it includes only some of the thirty-nine million party members, many of whom are cadres. The leadership nucleus in China as of 1982 may well have totaled fifty and sixty million cadres. This is the Chinese elite that must provide leadership for the masses.

Development of the Cadre System

In the early days, when the Chinese communist movement was engaged in guerrilla activities, the vast majority of the cadres were basic level. They were the link between the party and the masses, the go-betweens in the execution of party directives. They were expected, then as now, to conscientiously apply the principle "from the masses, to the masses" and to always be attentive and responsive to the wishes of the masses. Most of these basic-level cadres were peasants with experience mainly in managing governmental affairs of a rural nature. Because of the guerrilla operations, it was necessary to require all cadres to be dedicated party members and to adhere strictly to the party principle of democratic centralism. In implementing policies, these cadres supervised the tasks called for by the policies. They were required, from time to time, to conduct investigations into the results of programs and to make reports to the party. The ideal cadre during the guerrilla days was also a combat leader who lived among the masses and exemplified the traits of modesty and prudence.

After the communist takeover in 1949, a new type of cadre was needed to manage the complex social and economic affairs of the vast nation. This required persons with administrative skills and experience not possessed by the cadres who came from the rural environment and guerrilla background. A massive infusion of both party members and government cadres took place from 1949 into the early 1950s. As a stopgap measure, party membership and loyalty were no longer required for the government cadres. Instead, education, technical skill, and experience became the prerequisites for cadre rank. The cadres from the guerrilla experience were placed in special training programs to prepare them for work in complex governmental agencies. By 1953 about 59 percent of the 2.7 million cadre force were graduates of either regular or people's universities; the remaining 41 percent had attended special training courses to prepare for their work in various government agencies.[69]

The transformation of cadres from revolutionary leaders, engaged in guerrilla warfare, to government bureaucrats, concerned largely with paperwork, became formally institutionalized in 1955, when the State Council promulgated a rank classification system for the cadres.[70] Rank within the system was based on acquisition of technical skills and on when the cadre had joined the revolution. As the need for manpower in government service grew, a salary system with a promotional ladder was also established to attract career-oriented young people.[71] It has been said that by this time a cadre could predict with some accuracy future promotions and status.[72] These developments in the bureaucracy presented a host of problems for a society dedicated both to egalitarian principles and to modernization, with its concomitant requirement for specialization and expertise, which could only be administered in a complex hierarchical structure. In an effort to maintain the egalitarian society and to correct various abuses, the regime developed three major strategies, aside from the use of persuasion through education and the dispatch of special work teams, to correct specific local abuses. These strategies were rectification campaigns, the xiafang movement, and May Seventh cadre schools.

Rectification Campaigns

Rectification campaigns have been used to correct deviant behavior of both party and government cadres. The campaigns generally have involved education, reform, and purge. These campaigns have been undertaken periodically to strengthen the cadres' discipline, to raise their political and ideological awareness, and to combat corruption and inefficient work performance.[73]

The first rectification campaign, conducted by Mao from 1942 to 1944, following his selection as party chairperson, was designed to remove lingering opposition to his strategy for revolution. This was followed by the 1950 rectification campaign, aimed at correcting deviant attitudes among party cadres at all levels. The party cadres were criticized for "commandism," or issuing orders without proper consultation with the masses; tendencies of bureaucraticism, including excessive paper shuffling; distrusting the masses; and lack of direction and coordination in their work. The campaign was also an attempt to resolve differences between cadres from the guerrilla days and those recruited after 1949, which had created friction and tensions within the party. The 1950 campaign required the cadres to study, in a systematic way, selected key party documents, to analyze China's situation, and to participate in self-criticism during small-group discussions. These two campaigns were followed by at least six more rectification campaigns, including the Socialist Education Campaign in 1963, prior to the Cultural Revolution. As Frederick C. Teiwes has pointed out, the measures used in these successive rectification campaigns ranged from educational persuasion, to reduction of rank and pay, to punishment by purge or even death.[74]

Despite these rectification campaigns, on the eve of the Cultural Revolution, problems still existed with the cadres—as bureaucrats and administrators—because they were committed more to efficiency and orderly completion of tasks than to revolutionary enthusiasm and vision.[75] As careerists, the cadres as a whole had established political power, comfortable income, and security as life goals.[76] There were particular problems that included difficulties in actual implementation of the mass line principle, deviant behavior, acquisition of special privileges, declining morale, and increased tensions.[77] The Cultural Revolution can be considered both a gigantic rectification campaign and a mass campaign aimed to a large extent at these bureaucratic problems. The numerous rectification campaigns have created fear and uncertainty among the cadres and have led to administrative chaos and waste in the management of government activities.

The Xiafang, or "Downward Transfer" Movement, and the May Seventh Cadre Schools

The temporary transfer of party cadres down to a lower-level assignment or to a rural village or factory was introduced in the 1940s. Originally, the primary purpose of the movement was to reduce bureaucratic machinery and to strengthen the basic-level leadership. The system of temporary downward transfer of party and government cadres became institutionalized in 1957, when the movement's primary purpose shifted to the "education and reform of cadres through labor." From 1961 to 1963, as many as 20 million education cadres, a large number with technical skills, were sent to work in villages with the peasants.[78] The movement was intensified during the Cultural Revolution, when it became fashionable for cadres to opt for downward transfer to rural villages and communes. The major objective then was twofold: (1) to combat the cadres' bureaucratic tendencies through physical labor in the fields, alongside the peasants; and (2) to develop the mass line by enabling the cadres to understand the masses' problems and aspirations through living and working among them. The program resulted in a marked change in the cadres' attitudes toward the masses. Interestingly, the manual labor also improved the participating cadres' health.[79] While the downward transfer of skilled cadres must be considered an underemployment of resources, the xiafang movement represents an innovative technique to check the perennial problem of elitism in China. However, one must also point out that when the concept is carried to its extreme, as it was during the Cultural Revolution, human resources are wasted. Further, doubts and disillusionment arise about a system that sanctions such widespread waste.

One of the devices that came out of the Cultural Revolution was the May Seventh cadre schools for the reeducation and rehabilitation of incorrect attitudes and ideological thoughts. Thousands of these cadre schools were formed under a directive—issued by Mao on May 7, 1966—that emphasized the need to reeducate and to rusticate cadres for ideological remolding. The schools' curriculum consisted of manual labor, including working in the fields with commune production teams, performing duties required to run the school, and theoretical studies of works by Mao, Marx, and Lenin. Life at the May Seventh cadre schools was initially spartan, and provisions for daily living had to be obtained by the participants through their own labor. A cadre was usually sent to a school for three, six, or twelve months. Occasionally their stay was for more than a year. Some Westerners and Chinese considered these schools innovative because they provided the opportunity to engage in both physical exercise and ideological study, all aimed at curbing tendencies toward bureaucratic elitism.[80] To many Chinese who endured the ordeal at the May Seventh cadre schools, it was simply a waste of time.

Trends in the Cadre System: Reforms and Problems

Over the past two decades, life for a cadre as an intermediary has not been easy. The cadre was not able to please either those at the top of the party or the masses at the bottom. Since all decisions were subject to criticism from many directions, frequently the wisest choice was to make no decision at all. The cadres who came from the intellectual class but who possessed technical expertise were subject to special abuse as China's privileged "new class."[81] To redeem themselves, cadres opted for physical labor in the countryside, putting aside their professional development, at least temporarily.

The pendulum has now swung back to the moderation of the mid-1950s, when China's economic development demanded the rapid recruitment of capable, skilled persons as cadres to manage the nation's complex economic activities. The attacks against the new "bourgeois right" of elites and intellectuals were silenced with the downfall of the radical Gang of Four. Recently, deliberate attempts have been made to reform the cadre system. One key reform measure has been to place leadership positions in the hands of cadres who are "staunch revolutionaries, younger in age, better educated, and technically competent."[82] Hu Yaobang called for greater emphasis on cadre utilization and promotion according to education and skills: "We must work strenuously to strengthen the education and training of cadres in order to prepare personnel needed for socialist modernization."[83] To implement this directive, a rotation system for further education and training has been instituted for government cadres whose educational attainment is below the secondary level. But the task of upgrading cadres' competence seems formidable indeed when one considers the fact that a large number of cadres, both at the center and in the provinces, have only the equivalent of a primary school education.[84]

Introduction of Nomenclature. As a part of the cadre management reform, the party's organizational department published a detailed organizational management handbook setting forth guidelines, policies, and regulations for cadre management.[85] The 1983 handbook also established a Soviet-type *nomenklatura*, a comprehensive list of offices for party and state leaders in state enterprises and institutions, including scientists, professors, and even athletes. However, a study by Melanie Manion, reveals that the 1983 handbook led to very little progress since 1983 to improve the cadre management system because the party leadership lacks "an emancipated outlook and boldness in innovation."[86] In 1986, however, a set of rigid rules for cadre promotion were issued.[87] To curb the widespread abuse of nepotism, the rules called for a system of secret ballots to nominate capable cadres for promotion in work units, the danwei.[88] One rule stated that no candidate who received less than a majority vote was to be nominated for promotion. The rules also prohibited senior officials from attending meetings at which promotion decisions were to be made. The criteria for promotion evaluation were to be on the basis of candidates' "political awareness," ability, diligence, and merits—particularly their recent achievements.[89]

Aged Cadres.   Closely related to the upgrading of cadres' competence is the problem of upward mobility for the middle-aged cadres. Prior to 1986, about 2 million of the 27 million cadres working for the Central Committee and the State Council were considered veteran cadres, having been recruited before 1949.[90] These veteran cadres, advanced in age, had clung to their posts in the party and government. A retirement system was instituted to provide turnover in personnel. During 1981 and 1982, there were massive resignations of older cadres. In one machine-building industry ministry, the 13 vice-ministers and 269 cadres resigned or retired at the bureau level.[91] In 1981 some 20,000 aged cadres retired in one province.[92] By early 1986 more than half of the then 2.1 million aged cadres had been retired.[93]

Corruption and Bureaucratism.   There are two other serious problems in the Chinese cadre system. One is corruption, and the other is bureaucratism. Corruption is not a new problem, but since 1978 its scope and intensity have reached an unprecedented level. The mass media have been saturated with exposés of so-called "economic crimes" committed by cadres at all levels. Premier Zhao Ziyang has called these corrupt practices "obnoxious," citing lavish dinner parties with presents to the bosses, influence peddling for personal gain, and graft.

The use of bribery or favoritism to get scarce goods or to get things done by way of "back-door" dealings have been common practices.[94] The offspring of higher party and government cadres in Hong Kong have often served as "connections" for foreign merchants who desire to establish contacts for trade with China.[95] Also widespread is the practice of gift-giving and wining and dining by cadres who do business with each other—Beijing municipal authorities have imposed a new prohibition against such practices.[96] In April 1982 the party Central Committee, the State Council, and the NPC Standing Committee enacted an order that demanded life sentences or death by execution for those cadres who were involved in graft or similar corrupt practices.[97] The party's theoretical journal, the *Red Flag*, called economic crimes such as embezzlement of public funds and smuggling new elements in the class struggle.[98] The number of economic crimes committed by the offspring of senior cadres also has been on the rise; one senior army officer agreed that his son should be punished for graft in an illegal timber sale scheme.[99] For the first six months of 1986, a total of 27,000 cases of economic crimes were investigated, an increase of 130 percent over the same period for 1985. Well over 31 percent of the total were considered "serious economic crimes, cases involving more than 10,000 yuan (about U.S. $2,700)."[100]

Since 1980, bureaucratic practices have been under constant attack in China. One manifestation of bureaucratism is inertia and the inability to make decisions. This foot-dragging is more evident at the middle and lower levels of the party organization and government structure. Deng Yingchao, a member of the Commission for

Discipline Inspection, made a lengthy speech at one of the
charging that a few cadres have adopted a bureaucratic work sty
a bad image for the party.[101] She characterized the bureaucratic wo
"When there is a problem, they suppress it; when it is not possib
they push the problem aside; when it cannot be pushed aside, they
nate."[102] Foreign businessmen stationed in China have given vivid p
cadres' bureaucratic work style.[103] Deng Xiaoping charged that cadres se
devoted to rules and regulations and to exhibit obstinacy, timidity, and
infallibility; they spent an enormous amount of time reading the interminable
documents and directives.[104]

Special Privileges.   Cadres are a special class in Chinese society. Like th
counterparts in the former Soviet Union, they enjoy special privileges. The acquisi
tion of these special privileges sets them apart from the masses. The problem of special privileges and material comfort for party and government cadres can best be
seen by Chen Yun's talk at a high-level work conference:

> For transportation, we travel by car and do not have to walk; for housing, we have lux-
> urious Western-style buildings. . . . Who among you comrades present here does not
> have an air conditioner, a washing machine, and a refrigerator in your house? Take the
> TV set for example, please raise your hand if the one in your house is not imported
> from some foreign country.[105]

High cadres and members of their families not only have access to goods and
services not available to ordinary citizens but also have access to foreign magazines
and movies. Chen Yun also indicated that the children of higher cadres were the first
ones to go abroad to study once the door was opened to the West in 1977. As a special privileged class, party and government cadres have been reluctant to give up any
of these prerogatives.

At first the campaign against official corruption and the extravagant lifestyle of
high party and government cadres seemed to coincide with Deng's attempt to oust
the "Whatever" faction within the Politburo. However, subsequent campaign efforts
indicated a genuine desire on the part of the leaders to make the party more creditable.[106] The general public has maintained its usual skepticism about the party and
the government's ability to eventually correct such undesirable bureaucratic behavior.

From the foregoing discussion, it seems obvious that one key to Chinese
bureaucratic reform lies in personnel management. During the Cultural Revolution,
Mao included incompetence, corruption, favoritism, and nepotism in his often quoted indictment of the "evils of bureaucratism." Harry Harding provides the following
"organizational pathologies" of personnel management in the Chinese bureaucracy:
"lack of commitment to goals and values," "lack of zeal and enthusiasm attributable
to low pay," "low morale brought on by erratic changes," and "lack of skills and
training."[107] Programs to retire aged bureaucrats and replace them with younger, bet-
ter-educated cadres certainly represented a positive step forward. John Burns notes
that the problem is further complicated by the party's long-held view that any
attempt to reform the personnel system challenges or interferes with party prerogatives.[108] As long as "political considerations" are the key criteria in cadres' recruit-

s than positions, the personnel system is sub-
'oor" favoritism and rampant nepotism. The
bureaucracy are intimately tied to "the per-
ks of personal relations (guanxi), and fac-
l analysis, as was admitted in an inner
ystem's overconcentration of power in
tence and the inability, or unwilling-
r levels of cadres in the vast bureau-
al solutions to the endemic bureaucrat-
e perspective of China's overconcentrated
m, as well as the insistence that the party must
supervision over economic planning and management.[111]
ecent years prompted the pragmatic reformers to institute
y in the economic system (structure), but in the political system as

Civil service revision had been a dominant reform item for the Thirteenth Party Congress in 1987. The improvement focused on an emphasis on recruitment of technical specialists or experts and reduction of the party's role in personnel management.[112] Civil service reform was interrupted by the June 1989 Tiananmen protests. However, a China scholar takes the view that with stepped-up emphasis on economic reform, cadre management efficiency will have to be improved to meet the new demands and changes.[113] On October 1, 1993, China promulgated temporary national civil service regulations that include among other reforms the requirement that open competitive examinations be held to recruit the best and most able cadres for government service.[114]

NOTES

1. *Comparative Politics Today: A World View* (Boston and Toronto: Little, Brown, 1980), p. 62.
2. The figure comes from John P. Burns, "Chinese Civil Service Reform: The 13th Party Congress Proposals," *The China Quarterly*, 120 (December 1989), 740.
3. Max Weber, *The Theory of Social and Economic Organizations* (New York: Free Press, 1947), pp. 324–26.
4. Lowell Dittmer, "Pattern of Elite Strife and Sucession in Chinese Politics," *The China Quarterly*, 123 (September 1990), 405.
5. Ibid.
6. Ibid.
7. Ibid, 414–19.
8. For a more detailed study of factionalism in China, see Lucian Pye, *The Dynamics of Factions and Consensus in Chinese Politics: A Model and Some Propositions* (Santa Monica, Calif.: The Rand Corporation, July 1980). Also see Dorothy Grouse Fontana, "Background to the Fall of Hua Guofeng," pp. 237–60, and Richard D. Nethercut, "Leadership in China: Rivalry, Reform, and Renewal," in *Problems of Communism*, xxxiii (March–April 1983), 30–32. Also see a more recent study by Lowell Dittmer, "Patterns of Elite Strife and Succession in Chinese Politics," *China Quarterly*, 123 (September 1990), 405–30.
9. Parris Chang, "The Last Stand of Deng's Revolution," Journal of Northeast Asian Studies, Vol. 1, no. 2, June 1982, pp. 3–19.
10. Fontana, "Background to the Fall of Hua Guofeng."
11. "Deng's Turbulent Quest," *Problems of Communism*, vol. xxx (January–February, 1981), 8.
12. See "How the Power Structure Works," *Far Eastern Economic Review* (March 19, 1987), 60–61.
13. *Far Eastern Economic Review* (February 5, 1987), 12.

14. See "How the Power Structure Works," 60, and *The Los Angeles Times* (February 9, 1987), p. 10. Also see David M. Lampton, "Chinese Politics: The Bargaining Treadmill," *Issues and Studies*, vol. 23, 3 (March 1987), 11–45.

15. *Asian Wall Street Journal* (March 17, 1987), p. 1, and *Far Eastern Economic Review* (February 26, 1987), 9.

16. *The New York Times* (January 30, 1987), p. 22.

17. *Far Eastern Economic Review* (January 29, 1987), 12.

18. *Far Eastern Economic Review* (February 5, 1987), 35.

19. *The New York Times* (January 30, 1987), p. 22.

20. "The Politics of Industrial Reform" in Elizabeth J. Perry and Christian Wong, eds., *The Political Economy of Reform in Post-Mao China* (Cambridge, Mass.: Harvard Contemporary China Series 2, 1985), pp. 197–98. Also see a recent article by a Chinese scholar studying in the United States on interest groups in China, Li Fan, "The Question of Interests in the Chinese Policy-Making Process," *The China Quarterly*, 109 (March 1987), 64–71. Also see Shaochuan Leng, ed. *Changes in China: Party, State, and Society* (Lanham, Md.: University Press of America, 1989); and Andrew G. Walder, "Beyond the Deng Era: China's Political Dilemma," *Asian Affairs: An American Review*, vol. 16, no. 2 (Summer 1989). Also see Ian Wilson and You Ji, "Leadership by 'Lines': China's Unresolved Succession," *Problems of Communism*, vol. xxxix, no. 1 (January–February 1990), 28–44.

21. See *Zhengming* (Hong Kong), 157 (November 1990), 16–17 and 20–21; *Far Eastern Economic Review* (August 23, 1990), 29–31; (May 10, 1990), 8–9; (November 8, 1990), 19–20; David Bachman, "Retrogression in Chinese Politics," *Current History* (September 1990), 249–52 and 273–74; *The New York Times* (July 17, 1990), A-2; and L. La Dang, "China's Hodgepodge of Leadership," *The Wall Street Journal* (July 5, 1989), A-13. Also see *The Christian Science Monitor* (July 18, 1990), p. 3.

22. *Far Eastern Economic Review* (August 23, 1990), 34 and 38.

23. See *Far Eastern Economic Review* (August 23, 1990), 34.

24. See *Zhengming* (Hong Kong), 156 (October 1990), 6–7; and *Far Eastern Economic Review* (May 10, 1990), 8–9.

25. For some recent studies on party leaders as individuals and the party-state, see Marcia R. Ristaino, "China's Leaders: Individuals or Party Spokesmen?" *Problems of Communism*, vol. xxxix, no. 4 (July–August 1990), 100–106; and Brantly Womack, "The Chinese Party-State," *Problems of Communism*, vol. xxxix, no. 5 (September–October, 1990), 84–92.

26. See Nora Wang, "Deng Xiaoping: The Years in France," *The China Quarterly*, 92 (December 1982), 698–705. Also see the unauthorized biography by Uli Franz, *Deng Xiaoping* (Boston and New York: Harcourt Brace Jovanovich, 1988).

27. Deng once told Oriana Fallaci that he was purged for the first time in 1932 for lending his support to Mao in the inner party struggle against the Moscow-trained returned Chinese group led at that time by Wang Ming. See Ariana Fallaci, "Deng: Cleaning Up Mao's Feudal Mistakes," *The Guardian*, September 21, 1980, p. 16.

28. Parris Chang, "The Last Stand of Deng's Revolution," pp. 5–6. Also see Michael Ng-Quinn, "Deng Xiaoping's Political Reform and Political Order," *Asian Survey*, vol. xxii, no. 12 (December 1982), 1187–1205. Also see "Man of the Year: the Comeback Comrade," *Time* (January 6, 1986), pp. 42–45; and Harrison E. Salisbury, "The Little Man Who Could Never Be Put Down," *Time* (September 30, 1985), pp. 54–57.

29. See Chang, "Chinese Politics: Deng's Turbulent Quest," and "The Last of Deng's Revolution"; "A Speech at the Enlarged Meeting of the Politburo of the Central Committee" in *Issues and Studies*, vol. xvii, no. 3 (March 1981), 81–103; "Important Speech by Deng Xiaoping to the 1980 December 25 Central Work Conference" printed in *Ming Pao* (Hong Kong) (May 3–8, 1981); and "Text of Deng Xiaoping's Speech at the Great Hall of People on January 16, 1980," *Ming Pao* (Hong Kong) (March 2–4, 1980). Also see Suzanne Pepper, "Can the House that Deng Built Endure?" *Asian Wall Street Journal Weekly* (August 10, 1981), p. 10; Fox Butterfield, "The Pragmatists Take China's Helm," *The New York Times Magazine* (December 28, 1980), pp. 22–31; and Lowell Dittmer, "China in 1980: Modernization and Its Discontents," pp. 31–42, and "China in 1981," pp. 33–45.

30. "Communiqué of the Third Plenary Session of the Eleventh Central Committee of the CCP."

31. Christopher Wren, "Deng Opens Drive on His Leftist Foes," *The New York Times* (October 3, 1982), p. 3. Also see Frank Ching, "The Chinese Party Shuffle Bolsters Deng As Pragmatists Gain Over Ideologues," *Asian Wall Street Journal Weekly* (July 13, 1981), p. 7.

32. "An Interview with Deng Xiaoping," *Time* (November 4, 1985), p. 40.

33. Ibid.
34. Information on criticism about Li Peng is culled from the following: *Zhengming* (Hong Kong), 105 (July 1986), 9–10, and 123 (January 1988), 6–10; *Christian Science Monitor* (November 25, 1987), pp. 7–8; *Asian Wall Street Journal* (November 25, 1987), p. 1 and p. 13; *Ming Pao Daily* (Hong Kong) (November 16, 1987), p. 1 and (November 7, 1987), p. 12; and *Far Eastern Economic Review* (September 10, 1987), 46–47.
35. See *Beijing Review*, 14 (April 6, 1987), 14.
36. See *Ming Pao Daily* (Hong Kong) (January 2, 1988), p. 1.
37. See *Renmin Ribao* (overseas edition) (November 25, 1987), p. 1.
38. Information about Jiang is culled from *Zhengming* (Hong Kong), 141 (July 1989), 6–7; 142 (August 1989), 9–10; 148 (February 1989), 10; 155 (September 1990), 8–9; *Far Eastern Economic Review* (November 23, 1989), 10–11; *Beijing Review* (July 10–16, 1989), 21–22; *The New York Times* (June 25, 1989), A4–6; (June 30, 1989), A-4; *The Wall Street Journal* (June 26, 1989), A-7; *China News Analysis*, 1394 (October 1, 1989), 1–9; and *Wen Hai Pao* (Hong Kong) (July 4, 1989), p. 1.
39. *Zhengming* (Hong Kong), 142 (August 1989), 10.
40. *Zhengming* (Hong Kong), 141 (July 1989), 7.
41. *Zhengming* (Hong Kong) (June 28, 1989), 1.
42. *Zhengming* (Hong Kong), 155 (September 1990), 8–9.
43. See Liu Binyan, "After Deng Xiaoping: How Long Can Jiang Zemin Remain on Top?" *China Focus*, vol. 1, no. 3 (30 April 1993), 3.
44. Ibid.
45. See *Beijing Review* (5–11 April 1993), 7.
46. See *Asian Wall Street Journal* (30 March 1993), A-1.
47. Ibid., A-6.
48. Ye Jianyin, "Report on the Revision of the Party Constitution," *Beijing Review*, vol. 36 (September 2, 1977), p. 36.
49. John M. L. Lindbeck, "Transformation in the Chinese Communist Party," *Soviet and Chinese Communism: Similarities and Differences*, Donald Tread, ed. (Seattle: University of Washington Press, 1967), p. 76.
50. Ezra Vogel, "From Revolutionary to Semi-Bureaucrat: The 'Regularization' of Cadres," *The China Quarterly*, 29 (January–March 1967), 36–40; Michel Oksenberg, "Institutionalization of the Chinese Communist Revolution: The Ladder of Success on the Eve of the Cultural Revolution," *The China Quarterly*, 36 (October–December 1968), 61–92.
51. Charles Neuhauser, "The Chinese Communist Party in the 1960s: Prelude to the Cultural Revolution," *The China Quarterly*, 32 (October–December 1967), 3–36.
52. See Ye Jianyin, "Report on the Revision of the Party Constitution," p. 36.
53. "New Party Members—A Dynamic Force," *Peking Review*, 27 (July 6, 1973), 6–7; "Millions of New Cadres Maturing," *Peking Review*, 52 (December 1973), 3; "Commemorating the 10th Anniversary of the CPC Central Committee's May 16 'Circular,' " *Peking Review*, 21 (May 21, 1976), 3.
54. Red Guard interrogation of Wang Guangmei, wife of Liu Shaoqi, revealed the practice of admission to party membership by recommendation by top party leaders. See Chao Tsung, *An Account of the Great Proletarian Cultural Revolution*, vol. ii (Hong Kong: Union Research Institute, 1974), pp. 836–39.
55. Ye Jianyin, "Report on the Revision of the Party Constitution," p. 36.
56. "Important Talk by Deng Xiaoping," *Ming Pao* (Hong Kong) (March 5, 1980), p. 1.
57. Song Renqiong, "Use the New Party Constitution to Educate New Members," *Hongqi (Red Flag)*, 24 (December 16, 1982), 15. For current status, see *Ming Pao Daily* (Hong Kong) (July 9, 1984), p. 2; and *Far Eastern Economic Review* (November 3, 1983), 43–44.
58. *People's Daily* (Overseas Edition) (February 7, 1986), p. 1. Also see *China Daily* (January 21, 1986), p. 1. For a discussion of the recent party rectification campaign, see Bruce J. Dickson, "Conflict and Non-Compliance in Chinese Politics: Party Rectification, 1983–87," *Pacific Affairs*, vol. 63, no. 2 (Summer 1990), 170–190.
59. "Create a New Situation in All Fields of Socialist Modernization," *Beijing Review*, 27 (July 6, 1973), p. 38.
60. *Ming Pao* (Hong Kong) (October 7, 1982), p. 1. Also see Dittmer, "The Twelfth Congress of the CCP," p. 120.
61. See *Honolulu Advertiser's* section on Asian/Pacific column (November 5, 1987), D-1.
62. *Asian Wall Street Journal* (September 15, 1985), p. 1.
63. *People's Daily* (September 25, 1981), p. 1.

64. *China Daily* (December 3, 1985), p. 1.
65. *Ming Pao* (Hong Kong) (October 16, 19, and 20, 1982). Also see Song Renqiong, "Building the Revolutionized, Youthful, Intellectualized and Specialized Cadre Forces," *Hongqi (Red Flag),* 19 (October 1, 1982), 14.
66. Song Renqiong, "Building the Revolutionized, Youthful, Intellectualized and Specialized Cadre Forces," 14. For a related analysis see Stanley Rosen, "The Chinese Communist Party and Chinese Society: Popular Attitudes Toward Party Membership and the Party's Image," *Australian Journal of Chinese Affairs,* 24 (July 1990), 51–92.
67. Robert Sherrill, *Governing America: An Introduction* (New York: Harcourt Brace Jovanovich, 1978), p. 412.
68. See Hong-Yung Lee, "Deng Xiaoping's Reform of the Chinese Bureaucracy," *Journal of Northeast Asian Studies,* vol. 1, no. 2 (June 1982), 21–35. The ratio for the number of people per cadre has been estimated by Lee as 1:50 for a total of 18 million state cadres.
69. See Vogel, "From Revolutionary to Semi-Bureaucrat," p. 45.
70. Ibid.
71. Oksenberg, "Institutionalization of the Chinese Communist Revolution," 61–92.
72. Ibid.
73. For a fuller discussion of the rectification campaigns, see Frederick C. Teiwes, "Rectification Campaigns and Purges in Communist China, 1950–61," unpublished doctoral dissertation, Columbia University, 1971, in University Microfilms, Ann Arbor, Michigan. Also see S.J. Noumoff, "China's Cultural Revolution as a Rectification Movement," *Pacific Affairs,* vol. xi, nos. 3 and 4 (Fall and Winter 1967–68), 221–33.
74. Teiwes, "Rectification Campaigns and Purges in Communist China," pp. 150–61.
75. Vogel, "From Revolutionary to Semi-Bureaucrat."
76. Oksenberg, "Institutionalization of the Chinese Communist Revolution."
77. See Richard Baum, *Prelude to Revolution: Mao, the Party, and the Peasant Question, 1962–66* (New York and London: Columbia University Press, 1975); and Richard Baum and Frederick Teiwes, "Liu Shao-chi and the Cadres Question," *Asian Survey,* vol. viii, no. 4 (April 1968), 323–45.
78. See Jan S. Prybyla, "Hsia-fang: The Economics and Politics of Rustication in China," *Pacific Affairs,* vol. 48, no. 2 (Summer 1975), 153. Also see Paul E. Ivory and William R. Lanely, "Rustication, Demography Change, and Development in Shanghai," *Asian Survey,* vol. xvii, no. 5 (May 1977), 440–55.
79. Notes of conversation with cadres in Peking during my visit in 1973.
80. See James C.F. Wang, "The May Seventh Cadre School for Eastern Peking," *The China Quarterly,* 63 (September 1975), 522–27. Also see Yang Chiang, *Six Chapters of Life in a Cadre School: Memoirs from China's Cultural Revolution,* translated by Djang Chu (Boulder, Colo.: Westview Press, 1986).
81. *Ming Pao Daily* (Hong Kong) (July 7, 1981), p. 1.
82. "Create a New Situation in All Fields of Socialist Modernization," p. 36.
83. Ibid.
84. Peng Zhen, "Report on Work of NPC Standing Committee," *Beijing Review,* 39 (September 29, 1980), 24–25.
85. See Melanie Manion, "The Cadres Management System, Post-Mao: The Appointment, Promotion, Transfer and Removal of Party and State Leaders," *China Quarterly,* 102 (January 1985), 203–233.
86. Ibid., p. 233.
87. *People's Daily* (Overseas Edition) (February 3, 1986), p. 1.
88. Ibid.
89. Ibid.
90. "Reforming the Cadres System," *Beijing Review,* 9 (March 1, 1982), 3.
91. "Veteran Cadres Retire," *Beijing Review,* 7 (February 15, 1982), 5.
92. Ibid.
93. *People's Daily* (Overseas Edition) (February 19, 1986), p. 1.
94. See editorial *Renmin Ribao* (August 7, 1980).
95. *Ming Pao Daily* (Hong Kong) (August 14, 1981), p. 3.
96. *Ming Pao Daily* (Hong Kong) (August 18, 1981), p. 1.
97. "Economic Criminals Surrender," *Beijing Review,* 17 (April 19, 1982), 7–8.
98. "Decision on Combating Economic Crimes," *Beijing Review,* 17 (April 26, 1982), 7; and *Hongqi,* 4 (February 16, 1982), 8.
99. "Senior Cadres Support Sentences on Their Criminal Sons," *Beijing Review,* 20 (May 17, 1982), 5.

100. See *China Daily* (July 31, 1986), p. 1. Also see an earlier report from *China Daily* (July 10, 1986), p. 2.
101. *Ming Pao Daily* (Hong Kong) (April 6, 1980), p. 3.
102. Ibid. Translation is by this author.
103. Fox Butterfield, *China: Alive in the Bitter Sea*, (New York: Time Book, 1982), pp. 217, 288; and Richard Bernstein, *From the Center of the Earth*, (Boston and Toronto: Little, Brown and Co., 1982), pp. 104, 131, 134, 136–137, and 140 for anecdotes to illustrate how Chinese bureaucracy works.
104. "A Speech at the Enlarged Meeting of the Politburo, August 18, 1980," in *Issues and Studies*, vol. xxiii, no. 3 (March 1981), 88; also see *Ming Pao Daily* (Hong Kong) (February 14, 1982), p. 3.
105. For text of Chen Yun's speech at the CCP Central Committee Work Conference, see *Issues and Studies*, vol. xvi, no. 4 (April 1980), 82.
106. Deng Xiaoping, "A Speech at the Enlarged Meeting of the Politburo of the Central Committee, August 31, 1980," *Issues and Studies*, vol. xvii, no. 3 (March 1981), 88. Also see *Ming Pao Daily* (Hong Kong) (February 14, 1982), p. 3.
107. See Harry Harding, *Organizing China: The Problems of Bureaucracy, 1949–1976* (Stanford, Calif.: Stanford University Press, 1981), p. 3 and p. 281.
108. John P. Burns "Reforming China's Bureaucracy 1979–82," *Asian Survey*, xvii, 6 (June 1983), p. 715.
109. Ibid.
110. See *Ming Pao Daily* (Hong Kong) (July 7, 1984), p. 8. Also see Huang Chi, "Why Deng Stresses Political Restructuring," *Beijing Review*, 38 (September 21, 1987), 14–16, and *People's Daily*, (June 19, 1987), p. 1.
111. *Organizing China*, p. 353.
112. See John P. Burns, "Chinese Civil Service Reform: The 13th Party Congress Proposals," pp. 739–770.
113. Ibid., pp. 769–770.
114. See *Wenhui Pao* (Hong Kong) (August 30, 1993), p. 2 and p. 11.

chapter six

Reform for a Creditable Socialist Legal System

THE CHINESE LEGAL SYSTEM

We begin this chapter on the Chinese legal system with two case studies: one, a criminal case of deviance; the other, a civil case of divorce. The purpose of these case illustrations is to enable those who are not familiar with the Chinese concept of law to have some understanding of how it works and why. Outsiders looking in at Chinese legal institutions and proceedings may get the impression that either the Chinese legal system today is nonexistent or there is no need for law at all, since there are few—if any—criminals in their society. Both of these impressions are, of course, misconceptions. The Chinese legal system is quite different from that in the West, and the manner in which deviance and disputes are handled has been shaped to a large extent by China's own revolutionary experiences of past decades, as well as by the communist political ideology.

In the criminal case,[1] a worker had stolen about $250 worth of material and equipment from his factory. A colleague and neighbor reported his deviant behavior to the factory revolutionary committee, which referred the matter to the public security unit. An investigation was made by a procurator, who—in accordance with Chinese legal practice—served as both prosecuting attorney and public defender. The procurator then presented a dossier of the case to an intermediate court. The court ordered an open trial to be held in the factory so that other factory workers could participate in the proceedings. At the trial the judge, with the help of two community-elected lay assessors, examined the charges and the evidence as presented by the procurator. A trade union leader who personally knew the defendant testified about the defendant's good character and appealed for leniency. After the defendant made a confession about his crime, the judge solicited the opinion of the masses, the workers in the factory. The consensus of the masses in attendance at the trial was that the defendant was a good worker but that his crime must be punished. Upon the suggestion of the masses, the judge sentenced the defendant to two years of labor with pay in the factory under the supervision of his fellow workers.

The civil case[2] is a divorce case. While divorce cases are not frequent, they represent 60 percent of all civil cases in China. The case came to trial in a lower court after reconciliation attempts had been made, first by the committee that handles misdemeanors, then by the procurator, and finally by the judge's department. The hearings were held in a storefront and included a judge, two lay assessors, and a procurator. The judge heard arguments from both the husband and the wife, and then retired for an hour with the two assessors to reach a decision. The verdict was that a final reconciliation attempt was to be made over forty-eight hours, and that a divorce would be granted if this last effort failed.

The Chinese legal system utilizes two basic approaches: one, the formal set of structures and procedures seen in the two cases summarized above; the other, a set of what Professor Jerome Cohen calls "extrajudicial" structures and practices, which generally emphasize continuous education on acceptable social norms, peer pressure dynamics, and persuasion to correct deviant behavior. These two approaches, or "models," interact and coexist within the Chinese legal system.[3] From 1954 to 1956, the formalized legal structures and procedures were dominant. From the Great Leap in 1958 through the Cultural Revolution, the extrajudicial structures and practices increased in importance. Following the convocation of the Fifth NPC and the promulgation of the 1978 constitution, there has been a reversion to more formalized structures and procedures, including the revising of civil and criminal codes by a group of experts headed by Peng Zhen, a former Politburo member purged during the Cultural Revolution but now rehabilitated.[4] That modest beginning at modernization of the legal code has now come to be a "growth industry" dictated by economic reform and the rise of contracts with foreign investors and joint ventures.

The Courts: Formal Structure and Functions

The 1982 constitution provides that judicial authority for the state be exercised by three judicial organs: the people's courts, the people's procuratorates, and the public security bureaus. The Supreme People's Court is responsible and accountable to the NPC and its Standing Committee. It supervises the administration of justice of the local people's courts. The local people's courts operate at the provincial, county, and district levels. The local people's courts at the higher levels supervise the administration of justice of the people's courts at lower levels. The local people's courts are responsible and accountable to the local people's congresses at the various levels of local government. Article 125 of the 1982 constitution stipulates that all cases handled by the people's courts must be open and that the accused has the right to a defense.

When legal reforms were introduced in 1978, 3,100 local people's courts were established at four levels: basic people's courts at the district and county level, intermediate people's courts at the municipal level, higher people's courts at the provincial and autonomous region level, and the Supreme People's Court at the national level. Each of the basic people's courts has a civil and criminal division presided over by a judge. An economic division has been added at the intermediate and higher levels to help process cases that involve economics and finance.

Alongside the court system is a parallel system of people's procuratorates, headed by the Supreme People's Procuratorate, which is responsible to the NPC and supervises the local procuratorates at the various levels. The system of procuracy is rooted both in Chinese imperial practices and in the Napoleonic civil code, which was used in part by the Soviets and many other continental European nations in their legal systems.[5] As was mentioned earlier, the procurator serves as both prosecuting attorney and public defender during a trial. The procurator is also responsible for monitoring and reviewing the government organs, including the courts, to provide a legal check on the civil bureaucracy.[6] Further, the procuratorate is responsible for authorizing the arrests of criminals and counterrevolutionaries. In other words, the procuratorate examines charges brought by the public security bureau (the police) and decides whether to bring the case before a court for trial.

The 1954 constitution provided for independence, under the law, of the courts and procuratorates. These provisions were eliminated by both the 1975 and 1978 constitutions. The period between 1954 and 1957 witnessed the strong development of judicial independence. Judges frequently made their own decisions, disregarding the views and wishes of the party in important cases. This independence elicited much criticism from the party and resulted in increased tension between the courts and the party.[7] Coupled with the development of judicial independence was a movement to develop legal professionalism and expertise. Law schools were established, and offices of "people's lawyers" were formed in cities to provide legal aid to citizens. In 1957 the party countered judicial independence with a two-pronged attack: first, it purged or transferred to other branches of government those court cadres who advocated strengthening judicial independence and professionalism; and second, it introduced many of the extrajudicial institutions and practices for handling cases, in order to bypass the formal court system. In addition, in 1959 the functions of the local procuratorates were merged into the party's political and legal departments at the local level. Thus, for all practical purposes, local procuratorates disappeared during the Cultural Revolution, and the Supreme People's Procuratorate existed in name only.[8] As mentioned earlier, the 1982 constitution restored the 1954 constitutional provision concerning judicial integrity. Article 126 declares that all China's courts shall exercise judicial power independently without interference from "administrative organs, public organizations or individuals." To what extent this provision will be applied in practice remains to be seen.[9]

At its fourth session in April 1985, the Sixth NPC enacted the new Civil Law's General Rules, a set of general principles to serve temporarily as a civil code; it became effective in 1987.[10] Because of the rapid development in rural and urban reforms (see Chapter 11), it became necessary to replace the inadequate ad hoc administrative rules and regulations with some general principles for regulating civil disputes. The temporary civil code contains 156 articles in nine chapters that define legal principles regarding citizenship, legal entities with the rights of a person, civil rights, civil responsibilities, and legal practices in relation to foreign firms doing business in China.[11] It is important to realize that while the legal concept of a business corporation as an "artificial person" endowed with the rights of a person to sue or be sued is commonly recognized in the Western democracies, the concept is difficult for a socialist nation like China to accept. This is because under socialism the interests of a business concern and the interests of the people traditionally have been considered one and the same. The practice in China, as determined by political and administrative fiat,[12] was to hold the individual leader, not the social organization, solely responsible for any wrongdoing.

The New Criminal and Civil Procedures

To restore law and order after the Cultural Revolution, a set of criminal and civil procedures was drafted in 1978. The astonishing fact was that since its founding in 1949, the People's Republic had had no criminal code. At its second session in July 1979, the Fifth NPC adopted the first criminal code and procedure, which came into effect in January 1980. The code contained some 192 articles in eight major areas. These covered offenses concerning counterrevolutionary activity, public security, socialist economic order, rights of citizens, property, public order, marriage and the family, and malfeasance. Principal penalties for offenses included public surveillance, detention, fixed term of imprisonment, and death. The death sentence was reserved for adults who committed the most heinous crimes, and an exception was made for pregnant women. Productive labor and reeducation were to be stressed for detainees and prisoners.[13]

Although the new criminal code represented China's effort to develop "a more predictable and equitable" criminal justice system,[14] the inclusion of "counterrevolutionary" activity as a criminal offense was reminiscent of the Cultural Revolution. The code defined the term *counterrevolutionary* so that an "overt act"—not merely a thought a person might have at a given moment against the socialist system—must be involved. It must be pointed out that a large number of those placed under detention during the Cultural Revolution were accused of committing "counterrevolutionary" offenses under a law enacted in 1951 that remains in force today.[15]

In summary, Chinese criminal procedure now calls for presentment of charges by the public security bureau after an investigation has been made. The procuratorate must then examine the charges and evidence submitted by the police; and if it determines that a criminal offense has indeed been committed, it approves the arrest. Before a trial is held, the procuratorate must file an indictment against the accused. All trials must be open to the public, except when a case deals with state secrets, private lives of persons, or a minor below the age of 18.[16] A trial must be presided over by a judge, assisted by two assessors. Together they must render a decision on the accused, who now can be defended by a court-appointed lawyer.

The civil procedure, which came into effect in October 1982, permits persons to bring a suit to a people's court in a dispute regarding infringement of rights. The court must then conduct an investigation and gather evidence on the suit. Once the court has decided when and where a trial on the civil case will take place, litigants in the case may gather facts and witnesses for the trial. The new civil procedure stresses mediation for solving disputes rather than a formal court trial. Because of increased contact and investment with foreigners, a section in the civil procedure deals with cases involving disputes with foreigners (persons, enterprises, or organizations). In these civil disputes, the court must apply the Chinese law, as well as treaties and international conventions. When there is a difference between the Chinese law and a treaty, the treaty must prevail. Foreigners may engage Chinese lawyers to file a suit or to defend them in a contractual dispute. The new civil procedure also provides for arbitration to settle disputes arising from contractual arrangements between China and foreign corporations.[17]

In both the criminal and civil procedures, provisions are made for the services of lawyers. For instance, Article 26 of the criminal code states that the accused not only has the right to defend himself or herself but also can obtain legal counsel from a lawyer or from citizens recommended by a people's organization in which the accused works or has close relatives. The court must assign a lawyer for the accused if he or she has none (Article 27).

A lawyer's position in China is very different from that in the West. In the first place, lawyers in China are organized to practice law collectively. They must work for state-supported legal advisory offices that assign them cases; they cannot engage in private practice. They are, in fact, "state legal workers," semiprofessional at best. The role of these legal advisors is rather limited; they are not advocates or adversaries in the Western sense. They act, when requested, as legal advisors to governmental units, state economic enterprises, and people's communes on property disputes or contract disagreements with foreign firms. They also dispense legal information to the public. In the streets of Guangzhou (Canton), lawyers set up street-corner stands to answer questions on rent disputes, property inheritance, and domestic quarrels.[18] Their role is not to protect their clients but merely to advise them as to what the law says. In fact, their first duty is "to safeguard the interests of the state."[19]

Lawyers' organizations known as "legal advisors' offices" existed prior to 1957 in many cities. These legal service organizations—which then numbered approximately 800, with about 2,500 full-time lawyers—disappeared in 1957 and were not revived until 1979, when the Fifth NPC enacted regulations for lawyers' services.[20] In 1979 there were 5,500 full-time and 1,300 part-time paid lawyers in some 1,500 law advisory offices in twenty-five provinces.[21] In 1983 there were about 8,000 lawyers in China, about one lawyer for every 300,000 people. This compares with 350,000 lawyers in the much less populous United States. By 1984 Beijing, the capital city, had 400 lawyers, or one for every 10,000 residents.[22] The total number of lawyers in China in 1987 has been estimated at 20,000 for a total population of over one billion.[23] As of August 1993 there were over 40,000 attorneys' offices staffed by 50,000 licensed lawyers. The shortage of legal services has become more acute as the role of lawyers has expanded with the new criminal and civil codes and as economic activities have proliferated. The Ministry of Justice had plans to augment the number of legal service personnel to include one lawyer for every 10,000 persons in the cities and one for every 50,000 peasants in the rural areas by 1985.[24] Thus, China must train as many as 200,000 qualified legal personnel by the next decade. The rate at which universities turn out law graduates certainly has not been adequate. Beida, the Beijing National University, produced only between eighty to one hundred law graduates a year in the early 1980s.[25] Some provinces have resorted to short-term professional training on legal affairs to provide the needed personnel.[26] Many industrial cities experienced a critical shortage of lawyers as economic activities boomed and disputes mushroomed under urban reform. For example, in 1983 only 275 professional lawyers were practicing in Shanghai, a city with a population of 12 million, and 70 percent of them were nearing retirement age.[27] According to reports of a survey conducted by Shanghai Lawyers' Association, some 6,200 additional lawyers would be needed if all 20,000 enterprises in that city were to retain their own legal advisors.[28]

The urgent need for trained legal professionals may be seen by the steadily rising rate of contract disputes that have been brought to the courts for settlement as the result of decentralization and rural specialized household diversification. A typical local government unit, such as a county government, might sign as many as 400,000 contracts per year.[29] For a three-year period, from 1980 to 1983, the Chinese courts handled more than 89,000 contract disputes, involving millions of yuan.[30] Because of the shortage of trained professional lawyers, the common practice for a group of enterprises, usually not more than one hundred, is to retain one lawyer.[31] These lawyers carry a heavy caseload—several hundred cases per year. Chinese lawyers, as state employees, are not well paid. In fact, in the 1980s, most of them were paid at the scale of a junior bureaucrat, about 60–80 yuan or the equivalent of U.S. $20–30, per month. In addition, numerous cases of harassment and persecution against lawyers by government and party cadres have been revealed by the Chinese media.[32] In one case a judge ordered a lawyer handcuffed to a tree for more than an hour for making persistent demands that the judge take up a case.[33] These incidents of mistreatment of the lawyers prompted Qiao Shi, Politburo member and vice-premier, to demand that all party personnel respect the rights of lawyers in his talk to the 1986 conference of lawyers. The conference established, for the first time, a new professional organization, the All-China Lawyers' Association.[34]

CIVIL LAW AND ECONOMIC REFORM

The change from a planned economy to Deng Xiaoping's socialist market economy requires not only a redefinition of the functions of China's enterprises and economic organizations, but also a host of legal frameworks and bases for legal meanings of ownership and management, or simply "the establishment of the legal person system" as a standard practice commonly accepted in most capitalistic market economies. This had been clearly pointed out by one expert from China at the Sino-American Economic and Civil Law Conference held in Honolulu in June 1989.[35] Legislatively, the state must sponsor new laws to regulate enterprise registration and verification of enterprise assets, and to establish a limited liability system, procedures for repayment of loans to state banks, contract responsibilities, requirements and rules for the merger of enterprises, rules on joint partnership operations, a set of investment laws, and a taxation scheme.[36] As noted by Marshall S. Shapo, in the 1980s China's NPC enacted the Civil Code, drafted in broad and general language that "presents complex legal problems."[37] Anthony Dicks noted that recent economic changes, and changes in the laws, particularly contract laws and laws on arbitration of trade disputes, involve more than "a matter of mere legal technicality," for these inevitably imply "political controversy."[38]

Such drastic reform would require Chinese leaders to discard altogether the Marxist-Leninist theory, which does not place much importance on the role of law in social and economic development; in the Chinese view, law serves merely "as a means to promote economic change," but "not as something that develops as a result of change elsewhere."[39] However, one cannot expect laws in today's China to be developed independent of the party. For the Chinese, as pointed out by James Feinerman, laws and legal procedures are only instruments for implementing party policies.[40] As the Chinese would say, "Policy is the soul of law." This is a basic point that foreign investors must understand in dealing with the Chinese.

INFORMAL PRACTICES AND COMMUNITY MEDIATION

The party cadres who came from a guerrilla background acquired a set of legal experiences that relied heavily on the use of reeducation, persuasion, and social group pressure. As Victor Li has pointed out, the informal handling of deviance by guerrillas had its roots in traditional China.[41] Except for very serious cases, the traditional settlement of a dispute was one of informality, compromise, and facesaving for everyone involved. Disputes were settled largely through mediation by elders in a family, clan, or village, with consultation all around. In China today we see similar mediation roles assigned to organizations, such as street or neighborhood committees, in settlement of disputes or in cases concerning deviant behavior. For instance, if a person steals a bicycle, the family is notified, and the family elders impose minor disciplinary action. If the person refuses to admit his or her wrongdoing or refuses to accept the sanction from the family, the neighborhood committee becomes involved. The leaders of the neighborhood committee then guide a group of neighbors in attempts to reeducate the offender. If the person is a first-time offender and confesses to the wrongdoing, the action is usually forgiven, and the individual is given a chance to amend his or her behavior under the supervision of the group. If the person repeats the deviant act, the public security unit is called in. The public security, or police, do not jail the individual but instead attempt reeducation. Only the incorrigibles are incarcerated in labor reform camps.[42] In a more serious criminal case, such as the one illustrated at the beginning of this chapter, the judicial proceedings are informal and emphasize mass participation in reaching a verdict. In fact, the illustration points out that the judge's sentence was handed out after the view of the masses—the fellow workers in the factory of the defendant—had been solicited.

A large percentage of both civil and criminal cases are settled in China by this type of informal method, without going through a court trial. In 1980 China institutionalized the informal method of mediation for settlement of disputes as an important feature in the new civil code and procedure. Mediation as a method for dispute settlement can now be conducted by a people's court or by people's mediation committees. As of 1982 there were about one million people's mediation committees, which are basically grassroots mass organizations. The primary role of the committees is "to mediate between the two parties by persuasion and education on a voluntary basis."[43] The process operates on the premise that conflicts or disputes are usually quarrels in a family or between neighbors, and that such conflicts can be settled most speedily and equitably by those who live within the community and act as mediators. These grassroots mass organizations exist within production brigades in communes, within neighborhoods in cities, and even in some workshops and units of industrial enterprises. As of 1982 close to 6 million mediators had been elected at the various basic levels with the responsibility of settling civil and minor criminal cases on the spot.[44] It has been reported that in 1980 alone the mediators handled over 6 million cases.[45] In Beijing 81 percent of the civil cases reportedly ended in court mediation.[46] One Western source estimated that up to 90 percent of all civil and minor criminal cases have been handled by the mediation committees.[47]

A study of mediation for the five-year period from 1980 to 1985 (see Table 6.1) shows that the total number of cases mediated has declined slightly since 1982, but the total number of mediation committees has increased steadily throughout the

TABLE 6.1   People's Mediation, 1980–1985

	MEDIATION COMMITTEES	MEDIATORS (MILLION)	CASES (MILLION)
1980[a]	810,000	5.7	6.1
1981	n.a.	—	—
1982[b]	860,000	5.3	8.17
1983[b]	930,000	5.56	6.98
1984[b]	940,000	4.38	6.75
1985[c]	977,499	4.7	6.3

[a]China Facts and Figures Annual (1982)
[b]China Statistical Annual (1985)
[c]People's Mediation (1986), vol. 2

Sources: These figures were originally prepared by Edward J. Epstein, Hong Kong, 1987, and then organized in table form by Andy Tang as printed in *Far Eastern Economic Review*, "China '87: The Door Shuts?" (March 19, 1987), 107. By permission of the publisher.

period, to just below one million.[48] It is safe to say that China is firmly committed to the mediation process for dispute settlement.

THE PUBLIC SECURITY BUREAU: LAW ENFORCEMENT

The public security bureau performs all the police tasks in China (national, provincial, and local) and is responsible for maintaining law and order. The operation of public security is headed by a national Ministry of State Security Affairs and has local branches in cities, towns, and villages. Its responsibilities include surveillance of the movements of citizens and foreigners and the investigation of all criminal cases. Since 1957 it has been empowered to pronounce sentence in criminal cases, including internment in labor reform camps under its control. The power of the public security bureau to sentence is another major type of extrajudicial practice, instituted in 1957, to bypass the courts. Local public security personnel are usually all members of the party or of the Communist Youth League.[49] At times public security offices have even been operated as organizations of the local party apparatus. Because of close ties with the party, the public security bureaus usually reflect the view of the party leaders in control.

Just prior to the Cultural Revolution, the procuratorate functions were carried out by the public security units. During the upheaval the attacks by Red Guards on the party frequently focused on the public security bureaus, disrupting—if not paralyzing—their functions. When the People's Liberation Army intervened in January 1967, the functions of the public security bureaus were placed under military control. During this period it became a common practice for the PLA to perform police work: arresting criminals, stopping riots, supervising prisons and labor reform camps, and even directing traffic.[50] In January 1982 the PLA's internal security units were transferred back to the Ministry of Public Security to serve as their own armed police units. This was done in an attempt to strengthen provincial and local public security power and to safeguard people's life and property.[51] The various provincial and local headquarters of the armed police were made subject to the command and direction of the party units within the Ministry of Public Security. The 1975 constitution again placed the procuratorate functions and powers in the local public security units. That constitution also prescribed that citizens could be arrested either by a decision of the courts or "by sanction of the public security organ." The constitution of 1978 restored to the people's procuratorate the sanction of arrest of criminal offenders, but assigned the duty of arrest to the public security unit. This fine distinction may not mean very much, since at the local levels, both the public security units and the procuratorate operate from the same administrative office of the party. In June 1979 the second session of the Fifth NPC enacted the new organic laws for the courts as well as a criminal procedure that delineated the relationship between public security organs and the courts as follows: the public security organ is responsible for investigation of crimes and detention of criminals; the procuratorate has the power of approving arrests and prosecuting criminal cases; the people's court is to try cases.

The restoration of the procuratorate and the enunciation of citizens' fundamental rights and duties in the 1978 constitution seemed to have provided a new framework of law and justice in post-Mao China. A campaign for human rights and equal justice for all was launched soon after the promulgation of the 1978 constitution; it reached its height in the winter of 1978, just prior to the convening of the third plenary session of the Eleventh Central Committee. Meanwhile, the Central Committee reevaluated the events of the Cultural Revolution and corrected erroneous decisions with respect to the purge of a number of top leaders. Special articles in the mass media, and wall posters in Beijing, focused on human rights and injustices to those who had been arbitrarily arrested and mistreated from the days of the Cultural Revolution to the time of the arrest of the Gang of Four. A special group of legal specialists was formed to undertake the major task of codifying and revising some thirty codes and regulations, including criminal and civil justice procedures, as mentioned earlier. The release and rehabilitation of over 100,000 "right deviationists" (a convenient label used by the radicals for those who were tagged as such in the antirightist campaign of 1957, for having attacked the party during the Hundred Flowers Bloom movement) demonstrated the new leadership's intention to observe and enforce "socialist legality and democracy." The many exposés appearing in the mass media in 1978 and 1979 pointed out clearly how widespread were the abuses sanctioned and practiced by the radicals in arbitrarily arresting and detaining cadres and masses alike. From this campaign for law and justice came the approval of regulations governing the arrest and detention of persons. The specific prohibitions contained in the new law on arrest and detention, promulgated by the second session of the Fifth NPC in June 1979, give us some idea of the state of lawlessness that had existed in China for some time. The new law provides that no person shall be arrested without a specific decision of a people's court or the approval of the procuratorate. Within three days of detention or arrest, the police (public security bureau) must submit the evidence to the procuratorate or make formal charges for the detention. The new law requires that interrogation of the detainee must commence within twenty-four hours of the arrest and that persons detained must be released immediately if there is no evidence against them. Notification must be made within 24 hours to the kin of the person under arrest.

The public security bureau maintains correctional labor camps for those who have committed serious crimes, including political ones. Irrespective of the 1988 government report entitled "Criminal Reform in China," which whitewashed the brutal conditions inside the prisons, there is considerable secrecy surrounding the prison labor system—the Chinese "gulag"—where torture and slave labor have been common occurrences.[52] Under U.S. pressure, China signed an agreement in August 1992 on goods made by prison labor, in order to gain U.S. congressional approval for most-favored-nation trade status. This agreement allows reimportation inspection by the United States of exportable Chinese goods that are suspected of being made by prison slave labor.[53] The public security units are also involved in criminal reform through education and hard labor for the incarcerated. For instance, minor criminals in the city of Beijing are sent to reformatories by decision of the Beijing municipal government's reformatory committee, headed by a deputy mayor, who is assisted by a deputy director of the city's public security bureau.[54] Public security bureaus are also actively involved in the campaign to apprehend persons who engage in the "economic crimes" of smuggling, profiteering, and bribery.

THE NEW NATIONAL SECURITY AGENCY AND STATE SECURITY

In June 1983 the Sixth NPC approved a new Ministry of State Security, modeled on the former Soviet Union's Committee on National Security, commonly known as the KGB. This national security agency was established because of the expressed need to protect the state security and to strengthen China's counterespionage work. Premier Zhao reported to the NPC that the new ministry was to combine the work of the public security units, the people's armed police force, border guards, and counterintelligence organs. Apparently, China wanted to intensify its domestic surveillance to prevent "leaks" of "state secrets," particularly to foreigners. In a number of cases, party cadres with overseas connections were sentenced to prison for writing articles for Hong Kong journals under pseudonyms. In at least one case, an American scholar conducting research in China was expelled for allegedly obtaining "state secrets." (The Chinese classify information on routine matters as confidential, or secret.) The establishment of the new national security ministry led, in addition to the vast social control mechanisms already present in Chinese society, to the growth of a monstrous security bureaucracy staffed by secret agents who spy on both Chinese and foreigners.

There was a marked increase in surveillance of foreigners in China following the student demonstrations during the winter of 1986–87. Guards were augmented at the compounds where foreign diplomats and reporters lived to monitor movements of foreigners, and, most importantly, to control contact between foreigners and students. A number of foreign reporters were expelled on the grounds that they acquired so-called "illicit" internal party information on debates about the removal of Hu Yaobang. Then in April 1987 the minister for public security, Yuan Chongwu, was removed from office, ostensibly for his more liberal attitude toward the student demonstrations, and/or for his close relationship with the ousted Hu.[55] The ministry of public security took a much harsher stand against disturbances that affected public order in the aftermath of the student demonstrations. The new minister for public security, Wang Fang, who has since been removed, was considered an "insider"; he had worked within the public security ministry for years. This contrasts to the background and training of Yuan Chongwu, the ousted minister for public security. Yuan, trained in the Soviet Union as an urban planner, had a reputation for wanting to curb the police abuses and for making himself accessible to the press. At a press conference when he assumed his post in September 1985, Yuan answered a wide range of questions on student demonstrations, police behavior, and crime.[56] Under Yuan's leadership, China's national police became a member of the Interpol.

In September 1988, the NPC approved a new secrecy law to safeguard national security. The law obligates all state units, the PLA, economic enterprises, and citizens "to keep state secrets" by not disclosing to any publications any information considered confidential or secret.

There are three compelling reasons for what the Chinese term "new beginnings" in restoring and strengthening the legal system, particularly in providing some protection for the cadres and the masses against arbitrary arrest and detention. One is the new regime's desire to create some order out of the anarchical conditions created and fostered by the radicals. Hu Yaobang told the 1982 party congress that there must be a close link between socialist democracy and the legal system "so that socialist democracy is institutionalized and codified into laws."[57] In addition to order and stability, which are necessary conditions for China's modernization, an atmosphere free from fear of arbitrary arrest and detention must be created so that China's intellectuals can dare to think, explore, and make innovations. Finally, if it is to be successful in efforts to encourage foreign trade and investment, China must demonstrate that it has a creditable legal system and that Chinese justice is workable and predictable.

The legal reforms introduced by the pragmatic leaders represent an attempt to establish a creditable legal system in order to restore the people's respect for law after more than a decade of lawlessness. However, there is still some doubt about the new regime's willingness to observe the legal procedures formulated in the criminal code enacted by the NPC in 1979. Mass executions conducted by the police throughout China in August and September 1983 have created a chilling effect on China's legal reforms and have raised serious questions about human rights. For a period of two months in 1983 more than 600 executions were carried out in twenty cities in China in an attempt to crack down on the rising wave of crimes, such as murder, rape, and robbery. By spring 1984 there had been more than 6,000 executions. Moreover, the police extended their dragnet to ensnare as many as 50,000 criminals and then banished them to labor camps in remote regions of Xingjiang and Qinghai. In these mass arrests and executions, no pretense was made of applying the new criminal code procedure. This flagrant disregard of the criminal code procedure indicates to the rest of the world that perhaps China has a long way to go toward the establishment of a creditable legal system.

Another development that needs to be commented on briefly is the formation in 1983 of a public security force of more than a half million, known as the Chinese People's Armed Police Force. Originally a part of the regular PLA, it was placed under the direction of the Public Security Ministry.[58] Peng Zhen, a leader of the orthodox hard-liners, was said to have played a major role in the formation of this armed national police force.[59] Its political commissar said that although the Chinese

People's Armed Police Force lacked legal education in law enforcement work, it nevertheless was "an armed force of the party and the State." [60] Possibly this new armed national police force could play an influential role in competition with the regular PLA as the drama for political succession unfolds in the future.

NOTES

1. Franklin P. Lamb, "An Interview with Chinese Legal Officials," *The China Quarterly*, 66 (June 1976), 323–37.
2. Frank Pestana, "Law in the People's Republic of China," *Asian Studies Occasional Report*, no. 1 (Arizona State University, June 1975).
3. J. Cohen, "The Party and the Courts: 1949–1959," *The China Quarterly*, 38 (April–June 1969), 131–40. Discussion of "models" in the Chinese approach to the legal system is based on Victor Li's article "The Role of Law in Communist China," *The China Quarterly*, 44 (October–December 1970), 72–110.
4. See "Socialist Legal System Must Not Be Played Around With," *Peking Review*, 24 (June 16, 1978), 28; and "Discussion on Strengthening China's Legal System," *Peking Review*, 45 (November 10, 1978), 5–6. Also see "Speeding the Work of Law-making," *Peking Review*, 9 (March 2, 1979), 3.
5. Pestana, "Law in the PRC," p. 2. Also see Li, "The Role of Law," p. 78; and George Ginsburgs and Arthur Stahnake, "The People's Procuratorate in Communist China: The Institution Ascendant, 1954–1957," *The China Quarterly*, 34 (April–June 1968), 82–132.
6. Ginsburgs and Stahnake, "The People's Procuratorate in Communist China," pp. 90–91.
7. For an account of these tensions and criticisms, see Cohen, "The Party and the Courts: 1949–1959," pp. 131–40.
8. Gerd Ruge, "An Interview with Chinese Legal Officials," *The China Quarterly*, 61 (March 1975), 118–26. Also see Lamb, "Interview with Chinese Legal Officials," 324–25.
9. "China's Criminal Law and Law of Criminal Procedure," *Beijing Review*, 23 (June 9, 1980), 17–26.
10. See "The Civil Law's General Rules," *China News Analysis*, no. 1312 (June 15, 1986), 1–8.
11. Ibid., p. 5.
12. Ibid., p. 6.
13. For more information about China's criminal code and procedure, see *Beijing Review*, 33 (August 17, 1979), 16–27; *Beijing Review*, 23 (June 9, 1980), 17–26; *Beijing Review*, 44 (November 3, 1980), 17–28; Hungdah Chiu, "China's New Legal System," *Current History*, 459 (September 1980), 29–32; Fox Butterfield, "China's New Criminal Code," New York Times Service, as reprinted in *Honolulu Star-Bulletin* (July 20, 1979), A-19; Takashi Oka, "China's Penchant for a Penal Code," *The Christian Science Monitor* (September 3, 1980), p. 3; and Stanley B. Lubman, "Emerging Functions of Normal Legal Institutions in China's Modernization," *China Under the Four Modernizations, Part 2: Selected Papers*, Joint Economic Committee, Congress of the United States (Washington, D.C.: Government Printing Office, December 30, 1982), pp. 235–85.
14. Hungdah Chiu, "China's New Legal System," p. 32.
15. Ibid., p. 31.
16. Ronald C. Keith, "Transcript of Discussion with Wu Daying and Zhang Zhonglin Concerning Legal Change and Civil Rights," *The China Quarterly*, 81 (March 1981), 115.
17. Cheng Yanling, "China's Law of Civil Procedure," *Beijing Review*, 33 (August 16, 1982), 20–23.
18. *Ming Pao Daily* (Hong Kong) (January 6, 1983), p. 3.
19. HeBian, "China's Lawyers," *Beijing Review*, 23 (June 7, 1982), 14.
20. Li Yun Chang, "The Role of Chinese Lawyers," *Beijing Review*, 46 (November 17, 1980), 24. Also see Lubman, "Emerging Functions of Formal Legal Institutions," pp. 251–54.
21. Li Yun Chang, "The Role of Chinese Lawyers," p. 9.
22. *China Trade Report* (March 1981), p. 6, and *The Christian Science Monitor* (July 11, 1984), p. 1.
23. See *The Wall Street Journal* (April 14, 1987), p. 31.
24. "The Need for More Lawyers," *Beijing Review*, 49 (December 8, 1980), 3.
25. *The Christian Science Monitor* (February 10, 1983), p. 11. Also see *The New York Times* (December 5, 1982), p. 22.
26. *Ming Pao Daily* (Hong Kong) (February 7, 1983), p. 3.
27. *China Daily* (February 14, 1983), p. 3.

28. Ibid.
29. *Ta Kung Pao Weekly Supplement* (Hong Kong) (April 12, 1984), p.
30. Ibid.
31. *China Trade Report* (April 1986), p. 6.
32. *The Wall Street Journal* (April 14, 1987), p. 31.
33. Ibid. Also see *People's Daily* (July 6, 1987), p. 1.
34. *People's Daily* (Overseas Edition) (July 6, 1986), p. 1.
35. Jiang Ping, "The Historic Role of Civil and Economic Law during Economic R
    can Economic and Civil Law Conference, vol. i (29 May–2 June 1989), East–West
    Hawaii, p. 51. Also see Thomas Chiu, Ian Dobinson, and Mark Findlay, *Legal Sys*
    (Hong Kong: Longman Group [Far East] Ltd., 1991).
36. Ibid., pp. 52–62.
37. Marshall S. Shapo, "Comments on the Civil Responsibility Provisions of the Chinese C
    Sino-American Economic and Civil Law Conference, vol. iii (29 May–2 June 1989), East–W
    ter, Honolulu, Hawaii, p. 5.
38. Anthony Dicks, "The Chinese Legal System: Reforms in the Balance," *The China Quarterly*, no
    (September 1989), 555–56.
39. James V. Feinerman, "Economic and Legal Reform in China, 1978–91," *Problems of Communism*, x
    5 (September–October 1991), 66.
40. Ibid., 70.
41. Li, "The Role of Law," p. 92.
42. Martin King Whyte, "Corrective Labor Camps in China," *Asian Survey*, vol. xiii, no. 3 (March 11,
    1973), 253–69.
43. Chen Yanling, "China's Law of Civil Procedure," p. 21.
44. "The Xiebeijiao Neighborhood Mediation Committee," *Beijing Review*, 47 (November 23, 1981),
    24–28.
45. "Mediation Committees," *Beijing Review*, 41 (October 12, 1981), 8–9; and "China's System of Com-
    munity Mediation," *Beijing Review*. Also see Lubman, "Emerging Functions of Formal Legal Institu-
    tions," pp. 257–59.
46. Chen Yanling, "China's Law of Civil Procedure," p. 21.
47. *The New York Times* (December 5, 1982), p. 22.
48. *Far Eastern Economic Review* (March 10, 1987), 107.
49. Doak Barnett, *Cadres, Bureaucracy, and Political Power in Communist China*, (New York: Columbia
    University Press, 1967), p. 227; and Ralph Powell and Chong-kun Yoon, "Public Security and the
    PLA," in *Asian Survey*, vol. xii, no. 12 (December 1972), 1082–1100.
50. Barnett, *Cadres, Bureaucracy, and Political Power in Communist China*, p. 227; and Powell and
    Yoon, "Public Security and the PLA," pp. 1082–1100.
51. *Ming Pao Daily* (Hong Kong) (July 31, 1981), p. 1.
52. See *The New York Times* (12 August 1992), A-5; *Asian Wall Street Journal* (31 January–1 February
    1992), p. 6; *Asian Wall Street Journal* (3 September 1992), p. 6; and *The Christian Science Monitor*
    (8 April 1992), p. 19.
53. *The New York Times* (8 August 1992), p. 3.
54. "Reforming Criminals: Interviewing Deputy Director of Public Security Bureau," *Beijing Review*, 8
    (February 23, 1981), 24.
55. See Daniel Southerland, "Chinese Hike Surveillance of Foreigners," Washington Post Service reprint-
    ed in *Honolulu Advertiser* (April 9, 1987), A-14. Also see *The New York Times* (April 12, 1987),
    p. 3.
56. *Beijing Review*, 52 (December 30, 1985), 15–18.
57. "Creating a New Situation in All Fields of Socialist Modernization," *Beijing Review*, 23 (June 6,
    1980), p. 1.
58. See "Reforming the Public Security Forces," *China News Analysis*, 1318 (September 15, 1986), 1–9.
59. LaDany, "China's New Power Center?" *Far Eastern Economic Review* (June 28, 1984), 39.
60. *Ming Pao Daily* (Hong Kong) (September 15, 1984), p. 8, and "Reforming China's Public Security
    Forces," pp. 1–9.

ial

'olitics

...ı versus Regionalism,

ᴐ∧ʀs, and National Minorities

OVERVIEW OF PROVINCIAL AND LOCAL GOVERNMENT

The government of China is administered through twenty-one provinces, five autonomous regions, and three municipalities—Beijing, Shanghai, and Tianjin. The five autonomous regions of Inner Mongolia, Ningxia, Xinjiang, Guangxi, and Xizang (Tibet) are located on China's borders with neighboring countries and are inhabited by minority groups. (A proposal to make Hainan Island the twenty-second province was approved at the August 1987 meeting of the Sixth NPC's Standing Committee—it has been ratified by the Seventh NPC.)

The Constitution of 1982 specifies three layers of local political power: provinces and autonomous regions, cities and counties, and townships. The source of constitutional power at these levels is the people's congress. We must keep in mind that deputies to the provincial people's congresses are elected indirectly. The 1982 constitution states that the deputies to these congresses are to be elected by the people's congresses at the next lower level. Eligible voters at the lower level of government (in this case, the counties and townships) directly elect deputies to their own people's congresses. The electoral law now provides that election for the county people's congress is carried out by dividing the county into electoral districts, each of which elects delegates to the county people's congress. A simple chart of the provincial and local government is shown in Figure 7.1. Deputies to the provincial congress

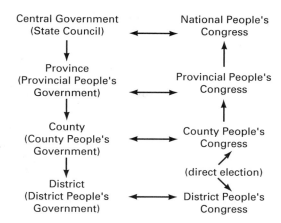

FIGURE 7.1
Provincial and Local Government Structure. *Source: Constitution of the People's Republic of China, adopted by the Fifth NPC on December 4, 1982. See Appendix A.*

are elected for five-year terms; deputies to the township and county congresses are elected for three-year terms.

It would be wrong to assume that the people's congresses at the various local levels are legislative bodies. However, Article 99 of the 1982 constitution authorizes the local people's congresses to "adopt and issue resolutions." These bodies have six main responsibilities: (1) to enact local statutes according to local conditions (authorized by the Organic Law of Local People's Congresses and Local Government in July 1979); (2) to ensure the observance and implementation of the state constitution, the statutes, and administrative rules; (3) to approve plans for economic development and budgets at the county level and above; (4) to elect or recall governors, mayors, and chiefs for the counties and townships; (5) to elect and recall judges and procurators; and (6) to maintain public order.

Theoretically, the deputies are not subject to the influence of local party committees—a political reform imposed under the 1982 constitution. In 1982 Peng Zhen reported that the organs at the grassroots level must be strengthened in order to serve as the basic organization of state power: "These organs must really be in the hands of the people, elected, supervised, and removed by them."[1] The party, the pragmatic leaders now maintained, neither replaces the government nor gives orders to organs of government.[2] (We need to keep in mind that these statements were based on assumptions at the time when the 1982 constitution was enacted.)

In June 1979 the Fifth NPC at its second session abolished the revolutionary committees as administrative organs of local government. They were replaced by the people's governments at all levels.[3] This action removed one of the last vestiges of the Cultural Revolution. The rationale for abolishing the revolutionary committees was that they no longer could meet the needs of socialist modernization and that their elimination would "strengthen democracy and the legal system."[4] With the abolition of the revolutionary committees, the positions and titles of governor (for the provinces), mayor (for the cities and counties), and chief (for the townships) were restored.[5] These changes regarding local people's congresses and governments were incorporated into the 1982 constitution (see Section V, Articles 95–110, in Appendix A).

ISSUES IN PROVINCIAL POLITICS

Chinese provincial politics is a complex subject. Three interrelated issues that have dominated provincial politics in China are discussed in this section.

Regionalism, Provincialism, Localism

We have noted that China is a unitary state with political power concentrated at the central government level, and that throughout China's long history there were many incidents in which centrifugal forces pulled away from the center because of geographical and sectional interests. The warlord period from 1916 to 1926 epitomizes this aspect of regional separation in recent history. Another general characteristic of Chinese politics has been the trend toward local initiative and self-government. In this section we will briefly examine the development of regionalism in provincial politics.

The terms *provincialism*, *regionalism*, and *localism* have been used to describe the problems of regions versus the center, or the central authority in Beijing. These terms are used here somewhat interchangeably because they all denote the centrifugal force constantly at play in Chinese politics. Regionalism has been defined as "the phenomenon whereby distinct groups, living in discrete territorial enclaves within larger political communities, exert pressures for recognition of their differences."[6]

The presence of regional forces that tend to pull away from the center in Chinese politics may be accounted for, to a large extent, by China's vast size and by the various cultures represented in her different geographic areas. It is common to speak of China as divided into the north, south, central, east, west, and the Asian portions of Inner Mongolia, Xinjiang, and Xizang.[7] Each of these regions may be considered an entity dominated by features of climate, drainage systems, soil composition, or dialect variations. A visitor who enters China by train from Hong Kong will notice the subtropical climate of southern China, which permits the harvest of two rice crops each year. The rugged hills and mountains of the south tend to foster a variety of dialects among the inhabitants. A visitor arriving at Beijing in the north sees an entirely different China in terms of climate, which is temperate and thus cold in the winter, and soil formation, which is the dry powdery loess of the Huanghe (Yellow) River basin. Wheat, millet, and cotton are the main crops grown in the north and northeast. Central and east China are watered by the Changjiang (Yangtse) River, whose vast plains permit the cultivation of rice and other crops that support a large population. The mountainous west and southwest are sparsely populated, except for the fertile valley of Sichuan, one of the richest but most difficult provinces to govern because of its geographic isolation and its relative economic self-sufficiency. These geographic and topographic variations are primary factors that have contributed to the feelings of sectional independence.

New Economic Regions and Regional Conflicts.[8]   As an integral part of economic reform, an effort has been made since 1984 to promote the growth of lateral, or horizontal, economic relations between geographic regions. This was advocated by the CCP decision on October 29, 1984 on economic structural reform: "We must . . . strive to develop lateral economic relations among enterprises and regions, promote appropriate exchanges of funds, equipment, technology and qualified personnel."[9] The detailed plan for promoting these lateral regional economic relations was presented to the Fourth Plenum of the Sixth NPC in March 1986.[10] The goal was to remove barriers between central departments and regions.[11]

Regional conflict discussed here focuses on inland versus coastal areas in the share of resources allocated for economic development.[12] To gain support from the peasantry and to have a more equitable economic distribution, China initiated in the 1950s a deliberate policy of avoiding concentration of industrial development in the coastal areas. Instead, industrial plants, resources, and skilled manpower were redistributed to scattered inland provinces. Susan Shirk's study indicated that before 1978 the inland regions received a much larger share of capital investment and fiscal subsidies from the central government.[13] Then in 1978 a shift in development strategy took place. Central control over investment and allocation of resources for coastal regions was modified to accommodate the open door policy. The coastal areas with their easy access for foreigners and "good economic foundations" (availability of factories, skilled labor, and port facilities)[14] were given higher priorities to attract foreign investors. These coastal regions had a broad history of industrialization and commerce prior to 1949 and were more receptive to investment. Further, many overseas Chinese had their roots there. Thus, it was logical to designate the first special economic zones in the coastal provinces of Guangdong and Fujian (see Chapter 12).

New Coastal Development Strategy.   In February 1988 the party's Politburo approved the Coastal Development Strategy (CDS), which aimed at expanding the export capacity of the coastal regions by linking them with the inland areas adjacent to the coast.[15] Under the plan some 284 cities and counties in some fourteen coastal regions were opened for trade and foreign investment. In many respects these cities and counties became foreign trade zones where raw materials could be processed and assembled as unfinished or industrial goods for export. These coastal areas reached from the Liaodong and Shandong peninsulas in the northeast and north to the central coastal regions of the Changjiang (Yangtze) River, which included Shanghai, to Zhejiang, southern Fujian, and the Zhujiang (Pearl) River delta in Guangdong in the south.

As pointed out in a study by Fuh-wen Tzeng, one of the problems in the strategy for developing the coastal regions has been persistent conflicts between the central government and provincial and local governments over control of trade and investment.[16] To the annoyance of the central government's Ministry of Foreign Economic Relations, there has also been cutthroat competition among the provincial and local authorities in bidding on foreign capital and equipment.[17] In these instances the local authorities demanded autonomy from Beijing's control and allocation of funds for infrastructure. Take, for example, the case of Guangdong. Guangdong province is China's "Gold Coast" today, with the fastest-growing economy anywhere in the world; in 1991 its annual growth rate was 27 percent. (In conversations with some provincial officials during my 1993 visit, I was repeatedly told that Guangdong points the way for China's future; its current per capita income is about $500 per year, the highest in China.) Guangdong Investment Ltd., one of China's biggest conglomerates, is an investment arm of the provincial government and is listed on the Hong Kong stock exchange.[18] In 1992 Guangdong won the central government's approval for greater economic autonomy in launching large-scale projects—such as power plants—as well as authorization for local initiative in wage setting and loan and bond issuance. (These grants of local autonomy in economic matters were originally approved by the State Council in 1988, but implementation was blocked by the conservative hard-liners.)[19] In 1992 it was reported that the local municipalities on the Pearl River delta, close to Hong Kong and Guangzhou, had formed a consortium that had invested in a prime real estate property in central Hong Kong for U.S. $490 million.[20]

As coastal provinces gained the center's attention and received more autonomy, inland areas began to feel what Susan Shirk termed a "competitive disadvantage."[21] Soon the hinterland provinces demanded that the center reinstitute centralization to safeguard their vested economic interests.[22] Provincial officials in the inland areas mapped out strategies to "sabotage the economic reforms."[23] They intensified the 1983–84 "spiritual pollution" campaign that was aimed largely at the coastal provinces (see Chapter 9). When the "spiritual pollution" campaign failed to gain sufficient support, provincial officials began openly opposing Deng's open door policy. To mitigate opposition to Deng's reforms and the open door policy from the inland provinces, the central government embarked on a new strategy of "interprovincial cooperation" to allow the inland regions and the coastal areas to participate in joint ventures and trade with each other.[24] Moreover, the central government even allowed a coastal enterprise to invest its retained profits in inland mines and factories.[25] In short, economic reform since 1978 has seen the rise of regional interests and of regional influence on policy making.

Centralization versus Decentralization

In a continuous search for an appropriate administrative formula, China has alternated between emphases on decentralization and centralization since 1949. When the communists took over in 1949, the provincial and local governments were built upon the base of the guerilla army and governments, which by their very nature operated with a great deal of autonomy in implementing government policies and programs. These new governments were staffed largely by local residents, both for convenience and to avoid accusations of a takeover by outsiders. To aid the central government's administration in Beijing and the coordination of the provinces, the six regional districts (government bureaus) were established. Each region was governed by both a military and an administrative committee. A corps of veteran party military leaders headed these committees with considerable authority and flexibility. A good deal of local autonomy was permitted under this regional arrangement while the regime consolidated its rule. The communists had neither the administrative personnel nor the experience to mount a tight central administration over the vast population and area. Under these conditions the ever-present local tendencies exerted themselves, frequently resulting in political factions at the local level.[26] Local officials often manipulated party officials at the regional level.

The conflict between the central and regional power structures came to a head with the introduction of the First Five-Year Plan. Centralized planning—with allocated resources, production quotas, forced savings, and formation of the voluntary agricultural producers' cooperatives (APCs)—required strong central control. Gao Gang, chairperson of the Northeast Military and Administrative Committee as well as the area's party chief, was purged for opposing the APCs and for disagreeing with the party over allocation of investment funds for Manchuria. Similarly, Rao Xuzhi, chairperson of the East China Military and Administrative Committee and party chief, was purged for demanding a slower-paced introduction of the APCs into his area. It was alleged that both powerful regional leaders had attempted to solicit support from the military stationed in their respective areas. The six regional government bureaus and the six party bureaus were abolished following these purges.[27] The 1954 constitution specifically stipulated that China was to have a single form of government, with headquarters in Beijing. Under the constitution the provincial authorities were the agents of the central government, with limited power to implement and execute the plans and directives from the center.

The years from 1953 to 1957 turned out to be a period of overcentralization, with excessive control over the provinces by the central authority in Beijing, particularly by those central functional ministries that proliferated under the First Five-Year Plan. All economic enterprises were placed under the direct control and management of the central ministries. Regulatory control devices were promulgated at the center, and all important decisions had to be made in Beijing. Even the acquisition of fixed property worth about one hundred dollars needed specific permission from the central ministry concerned.[28] This frequently resulted in delay and frustration in decision making. Even worse, the centralization of decision making resulted in ministerial autarky. A ministry became an independent economic system that tightly controlled the supply of materials and the allocation of resources under its jurisdiction. Instead of regional, independent fiefdoms, there were centralized, ministerial, independent kingdoms that interfered with provincial and local administration, drew up ill-conceived plans, and made repeated revisions of the plans. This resulted in the neglect of priorities and the waste of raw materials.[29]

At the end of the First Five-Year Plan, the Chinese leaders made an agonizing reappraisal of their experience with the Stalinist model of development. In advocating the return to decentralization, Mao spoke out openly for the extension of power in the regions. In his 1956 speech on the ten major relations or contradictions, Mao criticized the central functional ministries' habit of issuing orders directly to their counterparts at the provincial and municipal levels without even consulting the State Council and the party's Central Committee. He pointed out that local interests must be given due consideration if the central authority is to be respected and strengthened at the provincial and local levels.[30]

While Mao was genuinely concerned about the excess of centralization and the loss of local and provincial initiative, he may have been motivated also by purely political considerations. Centralism had placed tremendous power in the centralized ministries and with the members of the State Council, who, from time to time, challenged Mao's policies and who were opposed to rapid collectivization. By advocating the return of power to the provinces, Mao would receive support from the provincially based political forces, which could serve as a counterweight in a showdown with the top party-government officials at the center.[31] Mao's view on the return to decentralization was evidently accepted by the party leadership: in the fall of 1956, it met to endorse the Second Five-Year Plan, which provided for local initiative and administration that would be appropriate to local needs and interests.

The Great Leap of 1958 marked the beginning of real efforts at decentralization. Under the decentralization policy, the provincial and local authorities were granted a variety of powers in the administration and management of economic enterprises. Control of enterprises in consumer goods industries was transferred from the Ministry of Light Industry to provincial authorities. While certain basic industries of economic importance, such as oil refining and mining, were still controlled by the central ministries, the provincial authorities were given some say in their operations. In the area of finances, the provincial and local governments gained considerable power. Under the decentralization plan of 1957, provincial and local authorities were granted their own sources of revenues from profits of local enterprises and taxes, freeing them from complete dependence on central government grants for their budgets. The provincial authorities were to retain 20 percent of the profits from the enterprises transferred to the local authorities and a share of local taxes on commodities, commercial transactions, and agriculture. The provinces were even allowed to levy new taxes and to issue bonds, as long as the methods were approved by the center. Even more important for the initiative and growth of the provinces, local authorities were allowed to rearrange or adjust production targets within the framework of the targets of the overall state plan.[32] Thus, in the latter part of the 1950s, the top leaders, including Mao, recognized that the provinces had a definite role to play in the top-level decision-making process. By 1956 Mao had formulated a set of guidelines to be applied in the debates over central versus local issues. A key provision of these guidelines was Mao's insistence that the center must consult the provinces: "It is the practice of the Central Committee of the Party to consult the local authorities; it never hastily issues orders without prior consultation."[33]

A direct consequence of the 1957 decentralization under the Great Leap was the emergence of the provinces as independent entities. The provinces behaved as though they were little "underdeveloped nations"; each wanted to build its own self-sufficient industrial complex.[34] The inevitable result of the weakened centralized ministerial supervision over economic activities in the provinces was the rapid growth of localism, with provincial leaders acquiring an economic power base that challenged the center on policies and programs. In addition to being the agents of the party at the center, the provincial party secretaries also became spokespersons for the particular interests of their own provinces.

With the failure of the Great Leap in 1959, the Central Committee enacted a recentralization program to strengthen the leadership of the center over the provincial leaders. In 1961 the regional bureaus were reestablished to supervise the provinces and to control their tendencies to become "subnational administrations."[35] These regional bureaus also were mandated to supervise the rectification campaign launched by the Liu Shaoqi group to purge the radicalized provincial party leaders who supported the Great Leap program.[36] The recentralization in the early 1960s did not return the center–local relationship to the pre-1957 status of overcentralization. Many of the powers granted to the provincial and local authorities during the Great Leap remained intact. However, the crucial functions of economic planning and coordination were largely returned to the central authority.[37] Provincial politics remained a very important force during the early 1960s. During the period from the end of the Great Leap in 1961 to the eve of the Cultural Revolution in 1966, the provincial leaders were active participants at regularized central work conferences— a form of enlarged meetings of the Politburo or the Central Committee. These meetings also included selected party leaders who were not members of the highest decision-making body.

During the initial period of economic readjustment from 1979 to 1980 (to be discussed in Chapter 11), the provinces were given considerable autonomy in foreign trade matters. Provinces were encouraged to expand their foreign trade by obtaining from Beijing the right to import from or export to foreign countries directly. It was common for trading corporations to be formed at the provincial level to participate in foreign trade. A number of provinces—Guangdong and Fujian in particular—were designated as special economic zones (SEZs) for foreign trade and were encouraged to enter into joint investment ventures with foreign concerns. This policy led to a scramble to export provincial products in many inland localities. Decentralization also gave rise to price-cutting, bureaucratic game playing, and overlapping of responsibilities between and among provincial and local enterprises. Finally, the central authorities in Beijing had to revert to the policy of "balancing decentralization with unified planning,"[38] meaning more centralized control over provincial activities.

The 1984 urban economic reform promoted decentralized decision making at the local level.[39] Local governments under the reform had become "primary economic agents" for their own investment and production.[40] Decentralization created serious problems of "excessive and redundant investment."[41] Christine Wong gives an example from Henan province to illustrate the problem: to bolster Henan's economic development and profits, Henan officials fought to set up their own tobacco processing facilities rather than send their crop to an established processing center like Shanghai on the east coast.[42] In 1983 the central government initiated policies to reshape the local governments' pattern of profit-retention and investment in order to reduce capital construction outlays. These policies, especially a 10–15 percent surtax on state-owned enterprises in the provinces imposed to help reduce construction or fixed asset accumulation, were met with some local resistance.[43] The 1984 urban reform promoted decision making at the local level; while this "enhanced local power," it "exacerbated problems of localism."[44] It became a common practice in the 1980s for provincial and local governments to band together as "lobbying groups" to protect their interests and resist changes that would restrict benefits to their localities.[45] Thus, a new center versus regional/local relationship has evolved in the ever-changing political scene in China.

In a recent study of provincial elites,[46] Xiaowei Zang points out that the average age of current provincial elites—governors and party secretaries—is 55 years, and about 47 percent of the 274 provincial leaders included in the study have had a college education. However, over 70 percent of the provincial elites devote their careers to serving as provincial party-government workers. In that sense they tend to be advocates of localism.[47]

Tensions in Provincial–Center Relations

On the eve of the Cultural Revolution, the new center–provincial relationship showed signs of uneasiness as dissension within the top leadership deepened. Two major areas of tension were the allocation of resources and the types of economic activities to be carried on in the various provinces. For example, the party leader in the southern province of Guangdong was accused of promoting the development of a complete industrial complex for his province rather than concentrating on the development of light industries as dictated by the center.[48] On occasion, particular local conditions were used by provincial leaders as justification for resisting certain economic programs initiated by the center. Ganshu province used its backwardness as justification for not embarking on a rapid program of economic development.[49]

The degree of provincial autonomy or independence from the center varied according to the province's share of China's total industrial and agricultural resources and the stature of the provincial leaders in the hierarchy of the party and the central government. The provinces of the northeast—the massive industrial base in Manchuria—and the provinces of eastern and central China, with their commanding share of the resources, were in a better bargaining position when it came to allocation and distribution of these resources. The southwestern province of Sichuan traditionally has been known as a difficult province for the center to govern because of its rich resources and its remoteness from Beijing. Li Qingchuan, the party leader in Sichuan before the Cultural Revolution, was an old revolutionary veteran with close supporters at the center. He was also the party secretary for the southwest region before the Cultural Revolution. He enjoyed considerable autonomy and independence in governing the province of Sichuan and the southwest region.[50] Ulanhu, a powerful member of the Politburo at the beginning of the Cultural Revolution who had long governed the affairs of Inner Mongolia, could be described as an overlord for the autonomous region. Ulanhu not only identified himself with, but banked on, local nationalism to provide local resistance to orders from the center during the Cultural Revolution.[51] Prior to their purges during the Cultural Revolution, both Li Qingchuan and Ulanhu had been brought into the decision-making process at the Central Committee level. After 1978 many provinces formed their own independent shipping services to Hong Kong, Japan, and Southeast Asia in order to avoid domestic transportation bottlenecks. One province in southwest China offered preferential tax incentives in order to attract contracts from foreign investors for exploration of the province's hydroelectric power resources and ore mines.[52] Provincial autonomy was also reflected in the language, messages, and issues articulated in political communications between the center at Beijing and the provinces.[53]

In the 1980s, tensions between the center and the provinces developed in two areas. One, as pointed out earlier, was the local resistance to those economic reform measures that aimed at curbing the increased power of the local governments in making their own economic decisions. The other was the decision made by the party to replace aged and less-educated provincial leaders with younger Deng supporters. During the first six months of 1983, according to one calculation, "some 950 of China's 1,350 top provincial leaders were retired and replaced by about 160 new officials."[54] In addition, provincial leadership bodies, such as party secretaries, governors, and members of the standing committees for provincial NPCs, were reduced by as much as 38 percent, from a total of 1,082 to only 669.[55] The average age for provincial top leaders after 1983 was about 56, and one-third of them had college educations.[56] Despite widespread press reports of deliberate obstruction of reforms by local government organizations, the center won the fight for personnel changes at the provincial leadership level through a combination of actions: moving aged veteran leaders to advisory bodies so that they could still keep their salaries and privileges; demoting leaders considered unsuitable; and retaining those who pledged support to Deng and his reform policies.[57]

Provincial Representation at the Center

The turmoil of the Cultural Revolution created the need for an extensive "cooperative and consultative style of policy making" between the provinces and the center, to restore order as well as to reduce tensions.[58] The cooperative role played by the provincial leaders during the Cultural Revolution had enhanced their position in relation to the center. By the time the Ninth Central Committee was formed in 1969, a significant percentage of provincial party secretaries had been elected to that body.

As Table 7.1 shows, the provincial leaders' link with the center was strengthened further by their increased representation as full members on the Eleventh Central Committee (1977)—from 36 percent to 43 percent. When Hua Guofeng was the new party chief and premier of the central government, he sought a balance in the relationship between the provinces and the center. He cautioned about the tendency of the central departments and ministries to hamper local initiatives, but at the same time warned against the tendency of the provinces and regions to "attend only to their own individual interests to the neglect of the unified state plan."[59]

The power of provincial representatives on the Twelfth Central Committee (1982) decreased. While the number of provincial secretaries serving as alternate members rose 10 percent (from thirty-one to forty-six), the number serving as full members declined 9 percent (from eighty-six to seventy-two). The actual number of provincial representatives remained essentially the same, but more members were relegated to alternate membership. The decline of provincial party secretaries serving as full Central Committee members perhaps can be explained by the larger percentage of central party-governmental administrators, technical specialists, and academicians, who comprised 46 percent of the total full membership of the Central Committee elected in 1982. However, it should be noted that the provincial party secretaries and governors represented the single largest group of the Twelfth Central Committee.

There was a slight increase in the percentage distribution of the total number

TABLE 7.1 Provincial and Municipal Party Secretaries Serving on the Eleventh Through Thirteenth Central Committees

POSITION IN PROVINCIAL/ MUNICIPAL PARTY COMMITTEES	CENTRAL COMMITTEE					
	FULL MEMBERS			ALTERNATE MEMBERS		
	11th (201)	12th (210)	13th (175)	11th (132)	12th (138)	13th (110)
Provincial First Secretaries	24	42	30	0	0	0
Lesser Provincial Secretaries	62	30	35	31	46	30
Total Provincial Secretaries	86	72	65	31	46	30
Provincial Secretaries Percent of Total	43%	34%	38%	23%	33%	33%

Sources: *Beijing Review*, 14 (April 4, 1969), 9; *Beijing Review*, 35 and 36 (September 7, 1973), 9–10; and *Beijing Review*, 35 (August 26, 1977), 14–16. Figures for the Twelfth Central Committee are culled from *Issues and Studies*, vol. xviii, no. 11 (November 1982), 26–45. For the Thirteenth Party Congress, see *China News Analysis*, No. 1347 (November 15, 1987), p. 3.

of provincial party secretaries on the Thirteenth Central Committee, from 34 percent in the Twelfth Central Committee to 38 percent in the Thirteenth Central Committee. The percentage of provincial party secretaries elected to the Thirteenth Central Committee was about the same as in the Twelfth Central Committee. In short, the provinces continue to play an important role at the center.

Finally, as argued by Christine Wong,[60] with the continuance of Deng's economic reforms, as approved by the Fourteenth Party Congress in 1992 and enshrined in the constitution by the NPC in the spring of 1993, local governments will reap more benefits and power. This consequence is considered "detrimental to central objectives." Since the reform measures were essentially "administrative decentralization," a process by which "the central government transferred significant economic power to local governments,"[61] it is expected that local bureaucrats and enterprise managers will prefer the decentralized system rather than recentralization.[62]

CENTER–PROVINCIAL RELATIONS
AFTER TIANANMEN

There have been two parallel developments in center–provincial relations since the Tiananmen crackdown on June 4, 1989. First, there has been a resurgence of centrifugal forces as the central government has tightened its control over the allocation of credits, resources, and market-oriented reforms introduced during the reform decade. In fact, there has been some recentralization over the provincial autonomy in economic development since the launching of the austerity program in October 1988, as discussed in Chapter 11. After the 1989 Tiananmen crackdown the hard-liners imposed more measures for centralization by reducing the scale of government investment, requiring state approval of major construction projects, and checking any "excessive rise in consumer demands." One outcome of the central government's efforts in depressing retail markets, and a second development since the Tiananmen crackdown, has been an outbreak of "regional trade protectionism," or trade wars waged by provinces against each other's products.[63] Roadblocks have been erected by local authorities to prevent or curtail incoming goods desired by local consumers. This has recently led to a decision by the central government to impose controls over production of textiles, electronics, and light industrial goods, in addition to reinstituting a state monopoly over cotton and grain distribution.[64] Regional and local authorities seem to have determined to maintain their local autonomy enjoyed under the reform decade.

As one province that most enjoyed the local autonomy in economic development, the southern province of Guangdong has become targeted for resurgence of central control.[65] In a bargaining session on the budget and finance with the center, Guangdong must turn over to the central government a fixed amount, about 1.4 to 1.7 billion yuan, from its annual earnings. The central government has also taken over many commodities in the foreign trade sector for the province and has thus restricted its provincial exports.[66] Since 1988, when the austerity strategy was launched, the province has faced many problems, which include shortage of capital, a sluggish market for both capital and consumer goods, and widespread individual business failures that have caused unemployment in the province. In addition, there were then uncertainties in foreign trade caused by the Tiananmen crackdown that affected one-fourth of the provincial income as foreign investment and earnings from tourism have declined.

Unlike Guangdong, Shanghai's economic development receives no such restrictions imposed by the center. For 1990, a list of four construction projects for urban infrastructure, including the ambitious Huangpu River bridge, have been issued, plus investment for energy, steel (at Baoshan), and modernization of textile, electric, and machine tool development projects.[67] One may read the developments in Guangdong and Shanghai as a reflection of the prevailing political climate since Tianamen: Guangdong had been considered the reformer's showcase under Zhao Ziyang, and Shanghai is the metropolis once run by Jiang Zemin, former mayor and now the new party chief.

In the 1990 winter debate, the provincial leaders and the reformers seemed to have won the argument that there be no alteration in the contract system for revenue-sharing between the center and the provinces. One of Zhao Ziyang's key reform measures had been permission for the provincial government and state enterprises to retain profits above and beyond the contracted amount instead of turning them over to the central authorities. The result has been a reduction of central government revenue and an increase of decision-making power in the hands of the provincial, township, and village enterprises.

HONG KONG AS A SPECIAL ADMINISTRATIVE REGION (SAR)

With the ninety-nine-year New Territories (across from Hong Kong island) lease due to expire in 1997, Prime Minister Margaret Thatcher's September 1982 visit to China ushered in a series of negotiations between the PRC and Great Britain over the future status of Hong Kong. In December 1982 China's National People's Congress promulgated a new constitution, drafted under the direction of Deng Xiaoping, in which Article 31 provides a legal device to allow Taiwan or Hong Kong to be reunited with China as a special administrative region (SAR). The idea that Hong Kong, if reverted to China, could have its own constitution and administration as a special region was conveyed repeatedly to visiting Hong Kong delegations by Chinese officials.

The two years of negotiation produced the 1984 Joint Declaration of Great Britain and the PRC on Hong Kong, which was signed by Prime Minister Thatcher and Chinese Premier Zhao Ziyang on December 19, 1984. Key provisions of the joint agreement were the following:[68] (1) China is to resume its sovereignty over Hong Kong effective July 1, 1997; (2) in accordance with Article 31 of the PRC constitution, Hong Kong will become a special administrative region under the authority of the PRC central government, but will enjoy a high degree of autonomy except in areas of foreign affairs and defense; (3) laws in force in Hong Kong will remain unchanged; (4) current social and economic systems, as well as lifestyle, in Hong Kong will also remain unchanged; and (5) as an SAR Hong Kong may establish its own economic and cultural relations and conclude agreements with other nations, regions, or relevant international organizations.

While the Joint Declaration does not provide a time limit for Hong Kong's autonomy as an SAR, China's paramount leader, Deng Xiaoping, has stated repeatedly that the social and economic systems would not change for as long as fifty years, operating under Deng's concept of "one country, two systems." Until Hong Kong is reverted to China in 1997, the Joint Declaration also entrusted Great Britain to continue administering Hong Kong. The implementation of the agreement and the actual transfer of sovereignty are to be consulted upon by a Joint Liaison Group of PRC and British representatives during the interim.

By decree on April 4, 1990, the PRC president promulgated the Basic Law of the Hong Kong Special Administrative Region as the post-1997 constitution for Hong Kong, prepared for approval by the Chinese National People's Congress by a fifteen-member Drafting Committee for the Basic Law. The draft was the result of four and one half years of work. Details on the political structure of the future Hong Kong government and its power as an SAR under China will be discussed in the pertinent sections to follow.

Hong Kong under Basic Law from 1997 On[69]

The future political structure of Hong Kong as provided by the Basic Law of the Hong Kong Special Administrative Region (hereafter referred to as the Basic Law) approved by China's Seventh National People's Congress on April 4, 1990, consists of four institutions: the chief executive, the legislature, the judiciary, and the district organizations.[70]

The Chief Executive.   The chief executive for the Hong Kong SAR is accountable to the Chinese central government and the provisions of the Basic Law. The central government here refers to the State Council, headed by a premier who is appointed by the PRC president, based on prior arrangement by the Chinese Communist Party (CCP) Politburo, of which the premier and the PRC president are members. The reading of Article 43 leaves little doubt that the Hong Kong SAR has the same status as any other Chinese province or autonomous region. If there is any difference, the Basic Law has not defined it clearly or singled out a differentiation.

Under Article 48, the powers and authorities of the chief executive include the following: to lead the government and to implement laws applicable to the Hong Kong SAR; to sign and promulgate laws enacted by the Legislative Council; to approve budgets and decide on policies; to implement directives issued by the Chinese central government; to conduct external relations on behalf of Hong Kong as authorized by the Chinese government; and, finally, to appoint and remove judges and other public office holders. The text of the Basic Law provisions on the powers of the chief executive for the Hong Kong SAR leaves no doubt that the office is designed to be that of a strong and powerful executive, restrained in only a rather vague way by accountability to the Chinese central government and the Basic Law.

The qualifications, term of office, and method of selecting the chief executive are laid down in Articles 44, 45 and Annex I, 46, and 47. He or she is to be a Chinese citizen, not less than 40 years of age, a permanent resident, with no right of abode in any other country; must have resided continuously in Hong Kong for at least 20 years; and must be a person of integrity, dedicated to his or her duties. The term of office (Article 46) provides for a five-year term, but limited to not more than two consecutive terms.

While Article 45 states that the chief executive will ultimately be selected by universal suffrage upon nomination by a broadly representative nomination committee, in the meantime the selection of the first chief executive is governed by Annex I to the Basic Law. Annex I provides for an Election Committee, a sort of electoral college, of 800 members to represent basically the "functional constituencies" of occupational and professional groups, distributed as follows: 200 for the industrial, commercial, and financial sectors; 200 for the professions; 200 for labor, social services, and religious groups; and 200 for members of the Legislative Council and district-based organizations plus representatives from Hong Kong to the National People's Congress and to the Chinese People's Political Consultative Conference (a CCP-manipulated and controlled rubber-stamp body for the Chinese NPC). This 800-member Election Committee shall serve for a five-year term and vote by secret ballot in their individual capacities. However, the most important aspect of the selection process is the veto power over the appointment that may be exercised by the Chinese central government, in this case the State Council. Article 45 states clearly that "the Chief Executive shall be selected by election or through consultations held locally and be appointed by the Central Government."[71] As indicated by a Chinese official, the requirement that the appointment be approved by the Chinese central government is not "a mere formality" but is a rather "substantial one."[72] As argued by a Hong Kong scholar, there would be "a constitutional crisis" that would affect Hong Kong's "stability and prosperity" if an impasse developed in the future in which selection by universal suffrage was not accepted by the Chinese central government.[73]

There is also to be established under Article 54 of the Basic Law an Executive Council to assist the chief executive in policy making. Under Article 55, the chief executive appoints an unspecified number of persons to the Executive Council, which functions in much the same manner as the pre-1997 Executive Council, except that the Basic Law now stipulates that members must be Chinese citizens.

The Legislature. Legislative powers rest with the Legislative Council of sixty members, as stipulated in Annex II on the method for formation of the body for the Hong Kong SAR. Under Article 67, membership is divided into two categories: Chinese citizens with permanent residence, but with no right of abode in any foreign country; and non-Chinese permanent residents who have the right of abode in foreign countries—the total for this category must not exceed 20 percent of the total Legislative Council membership. Members are to serve for a term of four years, except those elected for the first term, which is limited to two years.

In accordance with Annex II and the decision by the Chinese National People's Congress on the first term of the first Legislative Council, there shall be a 60-member Legislative Council distributed as follows: 20 members by geographic constituencies through direct election, 10 by the Election Committee, and 30 by functional constituencies (occupational and professional groups). For the second term, membership composition for the Legislative Council will be as follows: 30 by functional constituencies, 6 by the Election Committee, 24 by geographical constituencies through direct election. For the third term: 30 by functional constituencies and 30 by geographical constituencies through direct election.

As provided by Article 73, powers and functions of the Legislative Council include the following: to enact laws; to approve budgets and public expenditures; to debate on public issues and to raise questions on the work of the government; to appoint or remove judges on the Court of Final Appeal and the chief judge for the High Court. A bill so enacted by the Legislative Council cannot take effect unless it is signed and promulgated by the chief executive (Article 76).

Another form of check and balance is provided under Article 73(9), which grants the Legislative Council the power of impeachment of the chief executive on a motion passed by a two-thirds majority vote, or forty members of the entire body. However, impeachment of the chief executive must be based on an investigation by an independent committee headed by the chief justice of the Court of Final Appeal. This impeachment provision may be interpreted as a needed safeguard to protect Hong Kong against a chief executive who is too subservient to the officials of the central government in opposition to the expressed wishes of the people of Hong Kong. Or it may be seen as a mere facade in view of the overall power of the Chinese central government, for the action—the impeachment—must be reported to the Chinese State Council for a final decision.

Executive–legislative relations for the Hong Kong SAR are governed by Articles 49–52 in the Basic Law. If the Legislative Council passes a law that in the view of the chief executive is not compatible with Hong Kong's interests, he or she must return it to the Legislative Council for reconsideration within three months. If the original bill is passed for the second time by a two-thirds majority vote, the chief executive must sign and promulgate it within a month. If he or she refuses to sign it, then Article 50 comes into play: the Legislative Council is to be dissolved by the chief executive after consultation with the Executive Council. The Legislative Council can also be dissolved if it refuses to enact a budget or any other important bill introduced by the government. However, the chief executive may dissolve the Legislative Council only once in each term of his or her office.

As a means of resolving a possible legislative impasse or refusal to act on the budget, Article 51 allows the chief executive to apply to the Legislative Council for a provisional appropriation. If such an appropriation is not possible because the Legislative Council is already dissolved, then prior to the election of the new Legislative Council, the chief executive merely approves on his or her own the provisional short-term appropriation at the level of the previous year.

Article 52 also states that the chief executive must resign if, after having dissolved the old Legislative Council, the new Legislative Council again passes by a two-thirds majority vote the disputed original budget bill that has still been refused by the chief executive. Or the chief executive must resign if the new Legislative Council still refuses to enact the original bill in dispute.

According to one Hong Kong scholar, the above procedural provisions to resolve executive–legislative conflict over the budget or any other key bills may not even be necessary, since the chief executive "controls" the budget submission process in the first place. He or she can alter the bill to meet any objections from the Legislative Council, so as to ensure final passage and thus make it unnecessary to be forced to resign.[74] Or, after a Legislative Council has been dissolved and a new one formed, the chief executive can make concessions or seek compromises on the disputed bill to such an extent that it is guaranteed passage, and thus can avoid the necessity for resigning from the office.[75]

The Judiciary.   Under Articles 8 and 18 of the Basic Law for the Hong Kong SAR, the laws previously in force in Hong Kong and the laws that may be enacted by the Legislative Council shall be applicable. Article 8 specifies the previous laws enforceable for the Hong Kong SAR as follows: the common law, rules of equity, ordinances, subordinate legislation, and customary law, except those that may contradict the Basic Law.

Under Article 81, the court structure consists of the Court of Final Appeal, the High Court (Court of Appeals and the Court of First Instance), district courts, and magistrate courts. Article 85 states that the courts must exercise independent judicial power and must be free from any interference. The principle of jury trial shall be maintained, and the principles previously applied to Hong Kong and the rights previously enjoyed by parties to criminal and civil proceedings shall also remain intact under the provision in Article 86.

Judges are appointed by the chief executive for the Hong Kong SAR based on recommendations of an independent commission made up of local judges, the legal profession, and other eminent persons. They can be removed only for inability to discharge their duties; dismissal is by the chief executive upon recommendation from a tribunal of at least three local judges appointed by the chief justice of the Court of Final Appeal (Article 89). All judges must be Chinese citizens who are permanent residents with no right of abode in any foreign country (Article 90).

A most controversial aspect in the Basic Law on the judicial system for the Hong Kong SAR has been the changes made dealing with the Court of Final Appeal. As stated in Article 82, the final adjudication power rests with the Court of Final Appeal, composed of five judges, some of them invited judges from other common law jurisdictions. This final appellate court will replace the old system of appeal to the British Privy Council sitting in London. A point of dispute or controversy has been that perhaps two out of the five sitting judges for the Court of Final Appeal should be invited judges from other common law jurisdictions. But at the September 1991 meeting in London of the Chinese–British Joint Liaison Group for Hong Kong, agreement was reached to establish such a court of final appeal in 1993, to be composed of a chief justice, three Hong Kong local judges, and a fifth invited member from two alternate panels: Panel A from retired Hong Kong judges, and Panel B from retired judges from other common law jurisdictions so as to ensure the presence of a foreign judge for only half of its sessions.[76] The presently constituted Hong Kong Legislative Council by a vote of 34–11 rejected the agreement described above, but the rejection was ignored by both the British and Chinese authorities.[77]

LOCAL GOVERNMENTS IN CHINA

The County Government[78]

Below the province is the administrative unit called the county, or xien. There are approximately 2,000 counties in China; each has a population of about half a million or less. The people's government is elected by the people's congress and supervised by the standing committee at the county level, which administers a host of local government activities. First, the county government exercises control over the personnel assignments for the entire county. In this manner the party manages to keep an eye on all the cadres working for the various units of county government. It is at the county seat that a people's court hears and handles serious cases of deviance. It is at the county level that we find the procuratorate operating when serious crimes are to be prosecuted. It is also at the county level that the public security bureau maintains a station for the surveillance of the county populace and for arresting criminals and counterrevolutionaries. Militia activities and relations with the regular PLA are handled at the county level.

The Township as a Local Government Unit[79]

The lowest level of government used to be the commune. In China there were about 75,000 communes, varying in number of households and the total farm acreage under production. Each commune was organized into production brigades and teams.

A typical production team had from 100 to 200 members and was subdivided into work groups. The work groups were led by team cadres, who were seldom members of the party. The team members elected a committee to conduct the team's affairs. Frequently, group leaders were placed on the nomination slate and elected to the committee. We should note that the slate of candidates for the committee election must be approved by the party cell. The team served as the basic accounting unit on the commune. Team committee members were assigned specific jobs, such as treasurer, accountant, work-points recorder, or security officer. The most important were the accountant and work-points recorder, who must keep detailed books on expenditures and income and on team members' earned work points, respectively. The work points usually ranged from zero to ten, with an able-bodied adult earning between eight and nine points per unit of time worked. The number of work points earned by a team member for a unit of time worked was determined at the beginning of each year by a meeting of all team members. Each member made a claim to this worth. This claim was evaluated by the assembled team members and a decision was reached on the points to be earned for each member for the coming year.

An average production brigade consisted of five or six production teams—over 1,000 people. Each production brigade had an elected people's congress, whose main responsibility was to elect a brigade chief and a revolutionary committee to assist the chief in administering the brigade's daily affairs. Frequently, the brigade chief was also chairperson of the revolutionary committee as well as the party secretary. The revolutionary committee and its staff were responsible for managing economic and financial affairs, including planning, budgeting, record keeping, and accounting. The committee was also in charge of providing social welfare, and medical and educational services. Brigades using agricultural machinery also maintained repair service units. In a number of communes visited by the author, a small-scale research and development unit was attached to the brigade's revolutionary committee.

From 1958 until 1982, the commune officially served two functions: it was the grassroots government below the county level, and the collective economic management unit. This combination of government administrative and economic management functions created a number of problems.[80] Many of the problems stemmed from the overconcentration of decision-making powers in the hands of a few commune leaders. Particularly troublesome was the interference of the commune, in its role as governmental administrator, in the activities of the production teams. Zhao Ziyang's experiments with local government in three counties in Sichuan province indicated that the separation of government administration from economic management in communes improved both economic activity and "the people's democratic life."[81]

Specifically, the new local structure for the rural areas permitted a greater degree of independent management of the rural economy. Formerly, the cadres at the commune centers held too many positions; it was practically impossible for them to devote much of their limited energy to economic activities. Too often these commune cadres had to spend most of their time supervising governmental affairs—such as planning, finances, and taxation for the communes—with insufficient time left to supervise production. In addition, there was a pressing need for a separate and more effective local government organization to discharge responsibilities in the areas of dispute mediation, public security maintenance, tax collection, and welfare distribution in rural areas.

The 1982 constitution reestablished the township government that existed before 1958 as the local grassroots government and limited the commune system to the status of an economic management unit. Under the new local government arrangement, the township people's congress elects the township people's government. Administration of law, education, public health, and family planning are the exclusive responsibilities of the township people's government.

With the introduction of the rural responsibility system as the first of a series of economic reforms, the commune system was more or less dismantled. In 1983 it was replaced by the "Township-Collective-Household System" with five distinct separate entities:[82] (1) local government; (2) the party committee; (3) state owned and managed units; (4) collective economic organizations (such as brigades, teams, supply and marketing); and (5) households (both contract and specialized). The township is also responsible for military affairs, public security, and statistics-gathering.

As of 1990 there were a total of 18 million township enterprises employing about 95 million workers who constituted 24 percent of the total agricultural labor force and earned $8 billion in foreign currency.

Village Committees[83]

Article 111 of the 1982 constitution also provided a grassroots level of local self-government below the township structure in rural areas. While this unit, the village committee, initially was not recognized formally as a local government unit, it undertook a number of administrative tasks in areas such as water conservation, village welfare programs, mediation of civil disputes, public order, and rules governing villagers' conduct. At the end of 1986, there were 948,600 village committees in rural areas. From 1986 to 1987, the NPC's Standing Committee debated questions concerning the relation between the village committee and township government, as well as administrative expenses incurred by the village committees.[84] The NPC's aim was to prepare a draft organic law that would stipulate the specific responsibilities of the village committees and their relationship with the township local government. Two major issues arose: the role of the village committee to serve as "a bridge" between the villagers and local township authorities, and the question of the direct election of committee members by the villagers even though village committees were not a governmental organ but a mass organization.[85] The Fifth Plenum of the Sixth NPC, held in April 1987, did not take up the draft law on village committees, but postponed it for further study and investigation by the Standing Committee. Peng Zhen, chairman of the Standing Committee, explained that the proposed draft law on village committees was "a big issue" because it would allow peasants to "exercise autonomy over their own affairs." Peng believed that the proposed law could provide an opportunity for the 800 million peasants to learn and "practice democracy" through election of village committees.[86]

The Standing Committee of the Sixth NPC eventually approved the Village Committee Law for some 900,000 rural villages in China. Responsibilities of the village committees are now defined as follows: road and bridge repairs; nurseries and homes for the aged; cultural and recreational activities; public order and security; and serving as a channel between the government and the masses. Any villager over age 18 can participate in village conferences to discuss and decide village affairs. Village committees are responsible to the village conference, the highest power in the village.

Local Government in the Urban Areas

There are two types of municipalities in China. One type includes the important urban centers—Beijing, Shanghai, and Tianjin—administered directly by the central government. The other type includes subdivisions of the provincial governments.

The municipal government of both types of cities—for example Beijing and Guangzhou—are administered by a municipal people's government, elected by the municipal people's congress. As a municipal government, the people's government for the city must supervise a large number of functional departments or bureaus dealing with law and order, finance, trade, economic enterprises, and industries located within the city limits. We also find in these cities subdivisions of state organs, such as the people's court, the procuratorate, and the public security bureau for social control and law and order. Because of the size of some of the larger municipalities, the administration of the municipal government is subdivided into districts. The municipality of Beijing, with a total population of more than seven million, is divided into ten districts as administrative subunits. Each district has a district people's congress, which elects a district people's government as the executive organ for district affairs.

Within each district of a city are numerous neighborhood committees, which are—in the words of the 1982 constitution—"mass organizations of self-management at the grassroots level" (Article 111, Appendix A). More than 1,794 neighborhood committees in Beijing city serve as arms of district government within the city. Each neighborhood committee has a staff of trained cadres whose work is to mobilize and provide political education for the residents in the area. Generally, a neighborhood committee has 2,500 to 3,000 residents.

The neighborhood committees perform a variety of functions, including organizing workers, teachers, and students in the neighborhood for political study and work; organizing and managing small factories in the neighborhood; providing social welfare services, such as nurseries and dining halls, to supplement those provided by the cities; and administering health, educational, and cultural programs. They also perform surveillance activities in cooperation with the public security units in the area.[87]

Neighborhood committees are the self-governing units organized and staffed voluntarily by the residents. A typical neighborhood committee has about twenty families, or approximately one hundred persons. It is generally headed by an elderly or retired woman, and it can deal with any matter of concern to the residents. It is common in the cities to find that a neighborhood committee is linked to a city hospital for family planning or birth control: the neighborhood committee disseminates information about the need for family planning. Meetings of all residents decide how to allocate the allowable births and who may have them.

Since 1954 there have been nearly 100,000 neighborhood committees established in China's urban areas, thus placing a total of more than 200 million urban residents under control and surveillance. The January 1990 Organic Law of the Urban Neighborhood Committees formally entrusted the following tasks to them: publicize state law and policy; protect residents' legal rights and interests; administer public welfare; mediate civil disputes; maintain social order and security; and serve as the "transmission belt" by channeling citizens' opinions and needs to the government.

ETHNIC POLITICS: AUTONOMOUS REGIONS AND NATIONAL MINORITIES

One of the interesting things about China is that it too has a minority problem. Like many of China's policies on major political, economic, and social matters, policies toward ethnic minorities have been subject to the periodic pendulum swings of the past two decades. This section will discuss the development of China's policies on national minorities and the reasons for policy changes, the status of autonomous regions, and minority group representation in party and government.

First, a few essential facts about China's national minorities are in order. There are about 91 million people in China who are considered to be national minorities. The largest of the fifty-six minority groups are the Zhuangs (13.3 million), Hui or Chinese Muslims (7.2 million), Uygur (5.9 million), Yi (5.4 million), Tibetans (3.8 million), Miao (5.0 million), Manchus (4.3 million), Mongols (3.4 million), Bouyei (2.1 million), and Koreans (1.7 million).[88] Although these minority groups—the non-Han people—total only 91 million, or 8 percent of China's population, they inhabit almost 60 percent of China's territory, covering sixteen different provinces. In two autonomous regions, Xizang (Tibet) and Inner Mongolia, the minority people constitute the majority. An extremely important element in understanding China's policies toward minorities is that over 90 percent of China's border areas with neighboring countries are inhabited by these minority people. When we discuss the border dispute between China and the Soviet Union, we inevitably are reminded that the disputed areas are inhabited by the Manchus, Mongolians, Uygurs, Kazakh, and Koreans. China's relations with Laos, Cambodia, and Vietnam bring to mind the minority people of Zhuang, Yi, Miao, and Bouyei in the autonomous region of Guangxi and the provinces of Yunnan and Guizhou. The border dispute between India and China involves the Tibetans living in Chinese territory in Xizang, Sichuan, and Qinghai. Changes in China's minority policies in recent years have been influenced to a large extent by concern for the security of her border areas.[89]

When the Chinese People's Republic was established in October 1949, the regime followed a policy that can best be described as one of gradualism and pluralism. Primarily for the purpose of a united front to consolidate control of the nation immediately after the civil war, minority customs and habits were tolerated in regions inhabited by minorities. Compromises were made to include as political leaders prominent minority elites of feudal origin in the newly formed autonomous areas for the minority nationalities. At the same time, modern transportation and communication networks were constructed to link the autonomous regions with the adjacent centers of political and economic power populated by the Chinese. The nomadic Mongols in pastoral areas were exempt from the application of land reform measures. The concept and practices of class struggle, so prevalent in other parts of China, were purposefully muted when applied to minority regions. However, no serious attempts were made to assimilate the national minorities into the mainstream of the revolutionary movement in other parts of China.

The period of the Great Leap ushered in a rapid change in policies toward the national minorities. From 1956 to 1968, the policy shifted from gradualism and pluralism to one of radical assimilation. For the first time, the Chinese spoken language was introduced in the minority areas. Training of minority cadres was intensified. More important, socialist reforms such as cooperatives and communization were introduced. The campaign against the rightists was also extended in the minority areas, aimed at those who advocated local nationalism. These policies of assimilation resulted in tension and violent clashes in the early 1960s between the Hans (Chinese) and the minority groups, particularly in Xizang and Xinjiang. It was precisely because of these disturbances in the minority areas that the assimilation programs were relaxed in the mid-1960s, prior to the Cultural Revolution. Radicalized communization programs in certain minority areas were disbanded. The slowdown did not last long, however. The Cultural Revolution brought back the radical line of assimilation for minority groups. Many prominent minority leaders in the border areas were subject to purges and vilification by the Red Guards, who were encouraged by the radicals. Ulanhu, of Inner Mongolia; Li Qingchuan, of Xizang; and Wang Enmao, of Xinjiang, were purged by the time the Cultural Revolution ran its full course (1966–76).[90] But the Sino–Soviet border dispute, according to Lucian Pye, made the Chinese realize the necessity of winning over the minority groups for reasons of national security.[91] The policy of assimilation was again modified to provide for diversity. In addition to having minority nationalities learn Chinese, the Chinese cadres were asked to learn the minority languages. Minority customs, dress, music, and dance were encouraged as expressions of ethnic diversity. It was within this policy of pluralism and diversity in the post-Cultural Revolution era that we began to see an increase in the representation of China's minority groups in party and government organs.

The constitutions of 1954, 1978, and 1982 provided identical detailed provisions for self-government in autonomous regions, in marked contrast to the brevity of such provisions in the 1975 constitution. This can be interpreted as a return to the policy of pluralism and gradualism. The people's congresses, as local organs of self-government for the autonomous regions, can make specific regulations in light of the special characteristics of the national minorities in these areas. This concept of diversity and pluralism was not mentioned in the 1975 constitution. In addition, the 1954, 1978, and 1982 constitutions mandated that local organs of self-government in these minority areas employ their own ethnic language in the performance of their duties. This represents a marked departure from past policies of assimilation, which urged the use of the Chinese language, both written and spoken, as the official medium of communication.

There has been increased recognition of minority groups in both the party and the government. Special efforts evidently were made to recruit new party members from the minority regions. We have figures that show that from 1964 to 1973, over 140,000 new members from the minority areas were admitted into the party.[92] There is no precise breakdown of party membership distribution over the various autonomous regions, but there appears to have been a steady increase in party membership. Three minority leaders (Wei Guoqing, a Zhuang; Seypidin, an Uygur; and Ulanhu, a Mongol) were elected to the presidium of the Eleventh Party Congress, and thirteen minority representatives were elected to the Eleventh Central Committee (seven full and six alternate members). Thirteen national minority leaders representing eight national minority groups were elected to full membership of the Twelfth Central Committee in 1982. Sixteen other minority leaders were elected to alternate membership. National minority leaders have held key government positions in various autonomous regions. For example, the chairpersons of the standing committees of the people's congresses for the autonomous regions of Xinjiang, Xizang(Tibet), Guangxi, and Ningxia were leading cadres of national minorities.[93] At the national level, Ulanhu, a Mongol, was elected to the vice-presidency of the republic in June 1983. Similarly, the Fifth National People's Congress, which promulgated the 1978 constitution, had 11 percent of its deputies drawn from the fifty-five national minority groups. At least four of the minority leaders (Wei Guoqing, Ulanhu, Seypidin, and Ngapo Ngawang-jigme) were elected as vice-chairpersons of the congress. Thus, after more than two decades of policy vacillation in search of an appropriate formula for dealing with the minority groups in the border areas, China seems to have found a solution that stresses the preservation of the cultural diversity of the 91 million national minority peoples and at the same time opens up channels for minority participation in decision making at the highest levels in the Chinese political process.

Muslim revolt in the border area of Xinjiang resurfaced in early April 1990. The armed revolt, in the form of jihad or "holy war," organized by the Islamic Party of East Turkistan, occurred near the city of Kashgar on the ancient Silk Road. Suppression of the revolt by the Chinese army involved more than twenty-two deaths. The revolt was triggered by the issuance of new identity cards to Kirghiz and Uighurs and restrictions on building a mosque. The recent rebellion in Xinjiang is only one of the continued challenges by the Muslim population to Chinese rule.

TIBET: A CASE STUDY

Tibet—Xizang in Chinese—is known as the "Roof of the World." It includes Mount Everest at 29,028 feet and it has an average elevation of 16,000 feet. Lying in the southwest part of China, it is dominated by the awesome Himalayas, which ring the southern part of the Tibetan plateau. The two million Tibetans who inhabit the region are devoted to Lamaism, a branch of Mahayana Buddhism. The lamas are the monks, "teachers or masters," who once controlled some 1,300 monasteries. Traditionally the monasteries serve as the main source of political, economic, and spiritual power. The Dalai Lama (meaning the "Ocean of Wisdom") is the temporal and spiritual leader of Lamaism in Tibet. The present Dalai Lama, who has been in exile in India since 1959, is the fourteenth reincarnation of the founder of the "Yellow-Head" sect, who was proclaimed the first Dalai Lama by the Mongols in 1570–1580.

The Dalai Lama is more than the Tibetans' spiritual leader, for in their traditional theocracy he is the ruler of the land and of the people for all of Tibet.

Tibet was an independent kingdom by the seventh century. But by the time of the Yuan Dynasty (1279–1368) under the Mongol conquest, Tibet was controlled nominally by Mongol rulers such as Kublai Khan, who had become a convert to Lamaism. This system of nominal control by China over Tibet, known as suzerainty—sovereignty in internal affairs, but control over external affairs by a stronger outside power—continued during the Qing Dynasty (1644–1911) under the Manchus.

With the eruption of the 1911 revolution, which brought down the Manchu empire, Tibet declared its independence. However, in 1886, the British in India had established trade relations with Tibet by consent of Chinese officials. In fact, the lamas had protested the signing of subsequent British trade treaties negotiated by the Chinese. Then through the influence of a converted Russian lama who came to Lhasa in 1880, Russia had become interested in Tibet. Because of Russian influence on the Dalai Lama at that time, Tibet was about to obtain czarist Russia's pledge of aid to eliminate the British influence, in view of China's repeated humiliation at the hands of the European powers (see Chapter 1).

With the specific objective of bringing Tibet under exclusive British control, in 1903–04 the British overlord in India decided to send military expeditions to Tibet from next-door Sikkim, then a British protectorate. The Tibetans mounted military opposition to the British expeditions. The British, with Chinese consent, in September 1904 were able to force Tibet to sign a treaty granting territorial and trade concessions, in addition to a Tibetan pledge to keep all other foreign powers out of Tibet.

In 1907 a treaty was concluded between the British and the Russians that recognized Chinese suzerainty over Tibet and internal territorial and administrative integrity for Tibet. In 1908 the Dalai Lama was received by the Chinese emperor, who then granted his holiness the authority to resume internal autonomous administration of Tibet. But in 1909 Chinese troops arrived to quell a rebellion by insurgent lamas; this military action forced the Dalai Lama to flee to China. In an attempt to make Tibet a buffer zone between China and India, in 1913 the British convened the Simla Conference in India to include three powers: China, Tibet, and Great Britain. The conference divided Tibet into an inner portion comprising the southwestern provinces of China, and an outer portion that was to be fully autonomous. The Chinese refused to ratify the convention.

In 1950, the Chinese communist government sent its PLA troops to Tibet for the purpose of reclaiming Tibet as an integral part of China and ending Tibet's declaration of independence, which dated back to 1911. The Tibetans initially resisted, but finally capitulated, signing an agreement on May 23, 1951 under which Tibet was to have nominal autonomy but China was to exercise full control as a sovereign power. Tibet was to be governed internally by a committee headed by the Dalai Lama. This 1951 agreement raised the international legal status of Tibet. Despite the settlement, there were widespread uprisings against the Chinese garrisons, particularly by the militant Khamba tribe. In March 1959 the Chinese authorities in Tibet summoned the Dalai Lama to military garrison command headquarters in Lhasa and requested that he use his temporal power to suppress the uprisings. This precipitated uprisings all over Lhasa; but the Chinese were able to restore order in a short time by brutally crushing the rebel forces. Meanwhile secret plans were made for the fourteenth Dalai Lama to escape from Chinese oppression. On March 31, 1959 the Dalai Lama led a detachment of followers in escaping from Tibet into India.[94] In Dharmsla, a hill station in North India, the Dalai Lama and his 10,000 followers established the Tibetan exile government, which has been sustained for more than thirty years. The question of Tibet was placed on the 1960 U.N. General Assembly agenda for discussion. The United Nation addressed only the human rights issue, expressing its concern in a resolution, but recognized the prevailing international stance that the Chinese maintained sovereignty over Tibet.

In recent years a great amount of world attention has been focused on Tibet as one of China's most troubled autonomous regions.[95] In 1980 Hu Yaobang, the party chief, and Wan Li, a member of the party's Central Secretariat, made an inspection tour of Tibet. Then, in the summer of 1982, the Chinese announced that 11,000 Chinese (Han) cadres would be withdrawn gradually from Tibet to permit the native Tibetans to take over and manage their own affairs. The immediate objective of this new self-government policy for Tibet was to replace more than two-thirds of Tibet's governmental functionaries with native Tibetans by 1983.[96] Ngapo Ngawang-jigme, chairman of the Tibetan Autonomous Regional Government, indicated that more than 12,000 Tibetans were being trained to take over the administration of Tibetan affairs from the Chinese cadres.[97] As of 1981 there were 29,400 Tibetan cadres in the autonomous regional government, comprising 54 percent of the total.[98] Other changes for Tibet included the abrogation of certain regulations imposed on the region that were deemed unsuitable to Tibetan conditions. In addition, farm and animal products were to be exempt from taxation for two years. More state funds were to be allocated for Tibet to improve the economy and living conditions in the region.[99]

The policy changes in Tibet must be viewed in the context of China's continuing attempt to persuade the Dalai Lama to return to Lhasa after more than thirty years of exile in India.[100] Since his escape to India, the Dalai Lama has been joined by over 100,000 Tibetan refugees who refused to live under Chinese rule. The Dalai Lama's exile and his continuing criticism of Chinese misrule in Tibet have been an embarrassment for Beijing. Since 1978 the Chinese official position has been to relax its control over Tibet with the hope that the Dalai Lama might be persuaded to return. However, his holiness has shrewdly used the Chinese desire to seek reconciliation, manipulating it as a bargaining chip to obtain concessions for his people. He has remained abroad to speak out against Chinese rule in Tibet and has delivered lectures in numerous countries to arouse world opinion in favor of Tibetan causes.[101] In 1982 a three-member delegation was dispatched by the Dalai Lama to Beijing, after the 1980 visit by the Dalai Lama's sister, to negotiate possible terms of reconciliation with China's new leaders. So far no tangible progress has been made in these negotiations. The Dalai Lama was reported to have proposed (1) that Tibet should not be treated as an autonomous region but should be given a special status with complete autonomy; and (2) that a larger Tibet should be created to include Tibetans now living in southeast China.[102] The Chinese did not accept these proposals, and the impasse continued. In the meantime, the Chinese have made further concessions by allowing pilgrimages to the lamaseries (monasteries) and the use of the Tibetan language in schools. In 1983, the Dalai Lama told Western reporters that he would like to pay a visit to Tibet by 1985.[103]

In 1985 the Chinese banned a visit to Tibet by a delegation organized by the exiled Dalai Lama. The Chinese maintain the policy that they would welcome the

Dalai Lama's return to Tibet only if he abandons the idea of an "independent Tibet" and accepts Tibet as an integral part of China.[104] In his 1987 visit to the United States, the Dalai Lama not only repeated his rejection of the Chinese offer to return to Tibet, but proposed a five-point peace plan for a future Tibet[105]: (1) demilitarize Tibet as a zone of "peace and nonviolence"; (2) curb further immigration of Chinese into Tibet; (3) initiate respect for human rights of Tibetans; (4) cease nuclear weapons production in eastern Tibet; and (5) conduct negotiations with the Chinese on the future status of Tibet.

The Dalai Lama's appeal to the United States for support for Tibetan independence provided the impetus for a protest rally in late September 1987 in Lhasa, Tibet's capital, staged and led by some two dozen Tibetan monks.[106] On October 1 more than 2,000 Tibetans demonstrated against Chinese rule by stoning police vehicles.[107] Chinese authorities in Tibet responded by arresting the monks who led the protest and by calling in reinforcements to quell the riot that resulted in six people killed and a dozen officers of the People's Armed Police injured.[108] For several days, Tibetan riots continued and the Chinese arrested more than sixty Tibetan protesters.[109] By then a curfew was declared for the capital city of Lhasa and foreigners were kept from entering Tibet.

The Chinese blamed the Dalai Lama for inciting the riots in Tibet, pointing out that he had advocated an "independent Tibet" during his ten-day tour of the United States.[110] The Chinese also opposed the Dalai Lama's "political activities" in other countries and condemned his repeated call for a separate Tibet as "detrimental" to achieving unity among national minority groups in China.[111] However, the riots in Lhasa clearly showed Tibetan dissatisfaction with Chinese rule in Tibet.

In an attempt to make up for neglecting Tibet's economic development, the Chinese launched in 1985 a package of forty-three development projects costing about $140 million. These projects, designed to woo support and allegiance from rebellious Tibetans, included tax exemptions for Tibetans for fifteen years, the right to own private farm land, and a 30-year lease on grazing land and livestock.[112] A number of these projects were for the development of infrastructure (sewer systems, transportation facilities, and two tourist hotels) for Lhasa. The Chinese also claimed that the percentage of Tibetan cadres to Chinese (Han) cadres had been significantly increased, to 70 percent Tibetans and 30 percent Chinese.[113] The fact remains, however, that no Tibetan had been appointed as the party's first secretary for the autonomous region. Worse still, a 1985 report by an economic research team from Beijing painted a rather gloomy picture of an almost bankrupt Tibetan economy.[114] The Tibetan Development Fund, a nongovernmental and nonprofit organization, was formed in July 1990 in Beijing to raise money from private and public sources to provide for more schools, homes for the aged, orphanages, and repairs of temples and monasteries.[115]

On March 8, 1989, after three days of rioting in Lhasa, the Chinese authorities imposed martial law on Tibet. The anti-Chinese riot resulted in at least thirty dead and marked the fourth time since 1987 that the 100,000 Chinese soldiers stationed in Tibet had crushed anti-Chinese uprisings. Under martial law Chinese soldiers raided lamaseries in and around the capital city of Lhasa and arrested monks suspected of being loyal to the Dalai Lama. Most monasteries in Lhasa were empty as monks fled to the countryside to hide.

The Dalai Lama has campaigned vigorously against the Chinese suppression. His worldwide influence increased considerably when the Nobel Peace Prize Committee named him the recipient of its 1989 award. In Oslo, in December 1989, as he had done in Strasbourg, France before the Council of Europe on June 15, 1988, the Dalai Lama proposed that Tibet be recognized as an independent country, thus becoming a "self-governing democratic political entity." He argued that independence for Tibet must be the basis for negotiation with the Chinese. The latter, of course, rejected the idea of an independent Tibet by unequivocally declaring that "China's sovereignty over Tibet is undeniable" and that "independence, semi-independence in a disguised form, is unacceptable."[116]

As a gesture intended both to mitigate criticism of human rights violations and to improve China's tarnished international image, China announced, effective May 1, 1990, the end of martial law in Lhasa. In lifting martial law for Tibet, Chinese premier Li Peng declared that the capital city had become stable and order had returned to normal.[117] The Dalai Lama viewed the lifting of martial law as "a public relations exercise" by the Chinese, since suppression and intimidation against the Tibetans continued unabated. In short, Tibetan protests and demonstrations are also indicative of a failed ethnic policy toward that troubled region.

As discussed in the prior section, China's policy toward its national minorities has been to a large extent dictated by the strategic considerations vis-à-vis its relations with neighboring countries. China's policy toward Tibet must be viewed in the context of its strategic importance in China's relations with the former Soviet Union and India.[118] (In 1962 China and India engaged in an armed conflict along the southern sections of their 700-mile-long joint border in the Himalayas. A cease-fire was accepted by both sides after the armed clash. But no progress has been made to negotiate the demarcation of their boundaries in almost inaccessible mountain ranges, even though the two neighboring nations have met seven times since 1981.)

While in 1991–92 there were continued Tibetan protests in Lhasa, the capital of Tibet, the issue of human rights violations against Tibetans by the Chinese has won significant international attention. First, the Tibetan human rights issue became a part of the conditions attached to the United States' extension of the most-favored-nation trade agreement to China. The U.S. Congress has inserted tough language into the trade extension bill to the effect that if the Chinese do not stop migration of Han Chinese into Tibet within a year, China's free trade status will be terminated. Asia Watch, the human rights monitoring group, reported the continued deterioration of human rights conditions in Tibet. To the chagrin of the Beijing government, President Clinton received the Dalai Lama in the White House in the spring of 1993. This was a high point in the Dalai Lama's continuing campaign abroad to call attention to the plight of the Tibetans under Chinese rule. However, China won a victory in March 1992 when the U.N. Human Rights Commission in Geneva supported a motion, sponsored by European nations, to end debate on condemning China's human rights abuses in Tibet. The United States opposed the resolution on the grounds that the UN must uphold the human rights of all citizens under Beijing's control, not just Tibetans.

For over a decade there has been a dialogue and negotiation process going on between Beijing and the Dalai Lama in exile, as discussed earlier.[119] The Dalai Lama is said to be increasingly conciliatory and willing to compromise with the Chinese, as evidenced by his Strasbourg speech in 1988 recognizing China's security interest and sovereignty. The Chinese have shown no willingness to compromise on the issue of Tibetan independence, but they are under increasing pressure from abroad to resolve the Tibetan issue by at least granting Tibet a higher degree of autonomy. In July 1993 the Dalai Lama sent his first official delegation to Beijing in about ten years, led by his older brother, Gyalo Thondup, for talks with Chinese officials. These talks were probably designed to build mutual trust and confidence without getting into the contentious issue of Tibetan independence.

NOTES

1. Peng Zhen, "Explanations on the Draft of the Revised Constitution of the PRC," *Beijing Review*, 19 (May 10, 1982) 25–26.
2. Feng Wenbin, "Reforming the Political Structure," *Beijing Review*, 4 (January 26, 1981), 18.
3. Hua Guofeng, "Report on the Work of the Government," *Beijing Review*, 4 (January 26, 1981), 23–24. Also see "Amendments to the Constitution," *Beijing Review*, 28 (July 13, 1979), 10.
4. "Amendments to the Constitution," *Beijing Review*, 28 (July 13, 1979) p. 10.
5. Peng Zhen, "Explanations on Seven Laws," *Beijing Review*, 28 (July 13, 1979), 9.
6. See Dorothy J. Solinger, *Regional Government and Political Integration in Southwest China, 1949–1954: A Case Study* (Berkeley: University of California Press, 1977), p. vii. Also see "Politics in Yunnan Province in the Decade of Disorder: Elite Factional Strategies and Central–Local Relations, 1967–1980," *The China Quarterly*, 92 (December 1982), 628–62.

   For a recent study of regional development see David S. G. Goodman, *China's Regional Development* (Routledge, N.Y.: Royal Institute of International Affairs, 1989). Also see Joseph W. Esherick and Mary Backus Rankin, eds., *Chinese Local Elites and Patterns of Dominance* (Berkeley, Calif.: University of California Press, 1989).
7. George Cressey, *Asia's Lands and Peoples* (New York: McGraw-Hill, 1951), pp. 96–165.
8. See the following issues of *People's Daily*: (March 13, 1986), p. 1; (March 17, 1986), p. 1; and (March 24, 1986), p. 1 and p. 2. Also see *China News Analysis*, 1311 (June 1, 1986), 1–9.
9. "Decision of the Central Committee of the CCP on Reform of the Economic Structure," *Beijing Review*, 44 (October 29, 1984), xiv. Also see *People's Daily* (October 21, 1984), p. 3.
10. "Decision on Some Questions Relating to Lateral Economic Ties," *People's Daily* (March 24, 1986), pp. 1–2.
11. Ibid.
12. *People's Daily* (April 15, 1986), p. 1.
13. "The Politics of Industrial Reform," in Elizabeth J. Perry and Christine Wong, *The Political Economy of Reform in Post-Mao China*, Harvard Contemporary China Series: 2 (Cambridge, Mass.: Harvard University Press, 1985), p. 210.
14. Ibid., p. 211.
15. See Fuh-wen Tzeng, "The Political Economy of China's Coastal Development Strategy," *Asian Survey*, xxxi, 3 (March 1991), 270–84. Also see *Beijing Review* (25 April, 1988), 35–37 for background of the strategy as outlined by Li Peng at the NPC session.
16. Ibid., 279.
17. Ibid., 279–80.
18. See *The Wall Street Journal* (January 10, 1992), A-7A.
19. *The Christian Science Monitor* (April 3, 1992), p. 6.
20. See *Asian Wall Street Journal* (March 17, 1992), p. 6. Also see Chen Zhen Xiong, "Foreign Direct Investment in Guangdong," paper presented at the 34th International Congress on Asian Studies held in Hong Kong, August 1993.
21. "The Politics of Industrial Reform," p. 211.
22. Ibid.
23. Ibid.
24. Ibid.
25. Ibid.

26. Schurmann, *Ideology and Organization*, (Berkeley and Los Angeles, University of California Press, 1966) p. 214.

27. For an account of the purge of Gao and Rao, see Jurgen Domes, "Party Politics and the Cultural Revolution," pp. 64–65; Edward E. Rice, *Mao's Way* (Berkeley, Calif.: University of California Press, 1972), pp. 130–32; Albert Ravenholt, "Feud Among the Red Mandarins," American University Field Service, East Asia Series (February 1954); Parris Chang, *Power and Policy in China*, (University Park and London: The Pennsylvania State University Press, 1978) pp. 47–48; Jurgen Domes, *The Internal Politics of China* (New York: Holt, Rinehart & Winston, 1973), pp. 24–25.

28. Chang, *Power and Policy in China*, p. 50.

29. Chang, *Power and Policy in China*, p. 51; and Audrey Donnithorne, *China's Economic System* (London: Allen and Unwin, 1967), p. 460.

30. The text of "On the Ten Major Relations" is to be found in *Peking Review*, 1 (January 1, 1977), 16, and *Selected Works of Mao Tse-tung*, vol. v (Peking: Foreign Language Press, 1977), p. 293.

31. Chang, *Power and Policy in China*, pp. 52–53.

32. For a detailed discussion on the powers granted to the provinces, see Chang, *Power and Policy in China*, pp. 55–61; and Victor C. Falkenheim, "Decentralization Revisited: A Maoist Perspective," *Current Scene*, vol. xvi, no. 1 (January 1978), 1–5.

33. "On the Ten Major Relations," in *Selected Works of Mao Tse-tung*, vol. v, p. 293.

34. Schurmann, *Ideology and Organization*, p. 210.

35. Ibid.

36. See Chang, *Power and Policy in China*, pp. 129–30.

37. Ibid., pp. 144–45.

38. *China Trade Report* (March 1981), p. 8.

39. See Barry Naughton, "False Starts and Second Wind; Financial Reforms in China's Industrial System" in Perry and Wong's *The Political Economy of Reforms in Post-Mao China*, (Cambridge and London: The Council on East Asian Studies, Harvard University Press, 1985) pp. 234–235 and pp. 251–252.

40. Christine Wong, "Material Allocation and Decentralization: Impact of Local Sector on Industrial Reform," ibid., pp. 268–278.

41. Ibid., pp. 224.

42. Ibid.

43. *Far Eastern Economic Review* (June 23, 1983), 57–58.

44. Wong, "Material Allocation and Decentralization," p. 224.

45. Ibid.

46. Xiaowei Zang, "Provincial Elite In Post-Mao China," *Asian Survey*, xxxi, 6 (June 1991), 512–25.

47. Ibid., 524.

48. See Frederick C. Teiwes, "Provincial Politics in China: Themes and Variations," in John Lindbeck, ed., *Management of a Revolutionary Society* (Seattle, Wash.: University of Washington Press, 1971), pp. 126–27.

49. Ibid.

50. See Thomas Jay Mathews, "The Cultural Revolution in Szechwan," in *The Cultural Revolution in the Provinces* (Cambridge, Mass.: Harvard University Press, 1971), pp. 94–146.

51. See Paul Hyer and William Heaton, "The Cultural Revolution in Inner Mongolia," *The China Quarterly*, 36 (October–December 1968), 114–28.

52. Vigor Keung Fang, "Chinese Region Offers Lures to Foreign Investors," *Asian Wall Street Journal Weekly* (December 21, 1981), p. 6.

53. Lewis M. Stern, "Politics Without Consensus: Center–Province Relations and Political Communication in China, January 1976–January 1977," *Asian Survey*, vol. xix, no. 3 (March 1979), 260–80.

54. William deB. Mills, "Leadership Change in China's Provinces," *Problems of Communism*, xxxiv, 3 (May–June 1985), 24.

55. Ibid., p. 27.

56. Ibid., p. 29.

57. Ibid., pp. 31–40.

58. Falkenheim, "Decentralization Revisited: A Maoist Perspective," p. 7.

59. Hua Kuo-feng, "Unite and Strive to Build a Modern, Powerful Socialist Country!" *Peking Review*, 10 (March 10, 1978), 25.

60. Christine F. W. Wong, "Between Plan and Market: The Role of the Local Sector in Post-Mao China," *Journal of Comparative Economics*, 11 (1987), 385–98.

61. Hunag Yasheng, "Web of Interests and Pattern of Behavior of Chinese Local Economic Bureaucracies," *The China Quarterly*, 123, (September 1990), 456.
62. Ibid., 458.
63. See *The Christian Science Monitor* (October 18, 1990), p. 5.
64. Ibid.
65. See *China News Analysis*, 1404 (February 15, 1990), 1–9. For an in-depth treatment, see Ezra F. Vogel, *One Step Ahead in China: Guangdong under Reform* (Cambridge, Mass.: Harvard University Press, 1989). Also see *Far Eastern Economic Review* (April 4, 1991), 21–28.
66. *China News Analysis*, 1404 (February 15, 1990), 2.
67. See *China News Analysis*, 1409 (May 1, 1990), 5. Also see *Far Eastern Economic Review* (April 4, 1991), 24.
68. Text of the Joint Declaration and Annexes are found in Ian Scott, *Political Change and the Crisis of Legitimacy in Hong Kong*, (Honolulu: University of Hawaii Press, 1989), pp. 353–85.
69. In addition to the text of the Basic Law as approved by the Chinese National People's Congress on April 4, 1990, the following contain discussion, analysis and criticism of the Basic Law, both in draft form and in the approved version: Ian Scott, *Political Change and the Crisis of Legitimacy in Hong Kong* (Honolulu: University of Hawaii Press, 1989); Jungen Domes and Yu-Ming Shaw, *Hong Kong: A Chinese and International Concern*, (Boulder, CO. and London: Westview Press, 1988) particularly the chapter by George L. Hicks, "Hong Kong after the Sino-British Agreement: The Illusion of Stability," pp. 231–45; Joseph Y.S. Cheng, "The Post-1997 Government of Hong Kong: Toward a Stronger Legislature," *Asian Survey*, xxix, 8 (August 1989), 731–48; "The Basic Law and Hong Kong's Future," *Asian Wall Street Journal* (5 April 1990), A-8; *The New York Times* (17 February 1990), A-3; Daniel R. Fung, "The Basic Law of the Hong Kong Special Administrative Region of the People's Republic of China: Problems of Interpretation," *International and Comparative Law Quarterly*, 37 (July 1988), 701–14; and Hungdah Chiu, ed., *The Draft Basic Law of Hong Kong: Analysis and Documents*, occasional papers/reprint series in Contemporary Asian Studies, no. 5, 1988, School of Law, University of Maryland; and *Ming Pao Daily* (Hong Kong) (14 December 1987), p. 2.
70. Text is found in *Beijing Review* (30 April–6 May 1990), entitled "The Basic Law of the Hong Kong Special Administrative Region of the People's Republic of China," pp. ii–xxiv, as approved by the Chinese Seventh National People's Congress at its Third Session on April 4, 1990 and put into effect as of July 1, 1997.
71. Ibid, p. vii.
72. As reported by Joseph Y.S. Cheng, "The Post-1997 Government of Hong Kong," 734.
73. Ibid.
74. Ibid, p. 737.
75. Ibid.
76. *Far Eastern Economic Review* (11 October 1991), 12.
77. *Far Eastern Economic Review* (19 September 1991), 10.
78. Information on the local government structure and functions is based on Doak Barnett, *Cadres, Bureaucracy, and Political Power in Communist China* (New York: Columbia University Press, 1967), Chu Li and Tien Chien-yun, *Inside a People's Commune* (Peking: Foreign Language Press, 1975); personal notes of my visits to China in 1972–73 and 1978; and "Our Neighborhood Revolutionary Committee," *China Reconstructs*, vol. xxii, no. 8 (August 1973), 2–3.
79. Barnett, *Cadres, Bureaucracy, and Political Power in Communist China*; Li and Chien-yun, *Inside a People's Commune*; personal notes of my visits to China; and "Our Neighborhood Revolutionary Committee." Also see footnotes 67, 78 and 81.
80. "Important Changes in the System of People's Communes," *Beijing Review*, 29 (April 19, 1982), 13–15.
81. Ibid.; also see *Ta Kung Pao Weekly Supplement* (Hong Kong) (June 17, 1982), p. 2.
82. For township structure see Frederick W. Crook, "The Rise of the Commune-Household System," *China's Economy Looks Toward the Year 2000*, Joint Economic Committee, U.S. Congress, vol. 1: The Four Modernizations (Washington, D.C.: U.S. Printing Office, May 21, 1986), pp. 360–361.
83. *Beijing Review*, 16 (April 20, 1987), 6.
84. Ibid.
85. *Beijing Review*, 15 (April 13, 1987), 5.
86. *Beijing Review*, 17 (April 28, 1987), 15.
87. "Our Neighborhood Revolutionary Committee," p. 3; "City Dwellers and the Neighborhood Com-

mittee," *Beijing Review*, 44 (November 3, 1980), 19–25; and John Roderick, "Kunming Housewife Helps Govern China," reprinted in *Honolulu Star Bulletin*, (October 29, 1981), p. 8

88. Figures here are based on *Beijing Review*, 21 (May 23, 1983), 19–20. Also see "China's Minority Peoples," *Beijing Review*, 6 (February 9, 1979), 17–21. The State Council in June 1979 recognized the Jinuo people, numbering over 10,000 in Yunnan province in the southwest, as the 55th national minority. See *Beijing Review*, 25 (June 22, 1979), 5–6.

89. Lucian W. Pye, "China: Ethnic Minorities and National Security," *Current Scene: Developments in the People's Republic of China*, vol. xiv, no. 12 (December 1976), 7–10.

90. For an account of the change of policies toward the minority groups from 1957–69, see Dreyer, *China's Forty Millions* (Cambridge, Mass.: Harvard University Press, 1976), pp. 140–259; "China's Quest for a Socialist Solution," *Problems of Communism*, xxiv (September–October 1975), 49–62; Pye, "China: Ethnic Minorities," pp. 5–11; and Hung-mao Tien, "Sinoization of National Minorities in China," *Current Scene*, vol. xii, no. 11 (November 1974), 1–14.

91. Pye, "China: Ethnic Minorities," pp. 9–10.

92. "New Party Members—A Dynamic Force," *Peking Review*, 27 (July 6, 1973), 6–7.

93. "Minority Leader Cadres in Various Provinces and Autonomous Regions," *Beijing Review*, 10 (March 10, 1980), 23.

94. See two recent works on the Dalai Lama's exile: *Freedom in Exile: The Autobiography of the Dalai Lama* (New York: A Cornelia and Michael Bessie Book/Harper Collins, 1990); and *My Tibet: Text By His Holiness The Fourteenth Dalai Lama of Tibet* (Berkeley, Calif.: Mountain Light Press and University of California Press, 1990). For related works see Melvyn C. Goldstein, *A History of Modern Tibet* (Berkeley, Calif. University of California Press, 1989); and Tom Grunfeld, *The Making of Modern Tibet* (Bombay, India: Oxford University Press, 1988).

95. For earlier discussion about Tibet, see the following issues of the *Beijing Review*: 40 (October 4, 1982), 5–7; 46 (November 15, 1982), 3–4; 47 (November 22, 1982), 15–18; 48 (November 29, 1982), 14–17; 49 (December 6, 1982), 21–24; 50 (December 13, 1982), 28–29; and 51 (December 20, 1982), 37–38.

96. "New Principles for Building up Tibet," *Beijing Review*, 24 (June 16, 1980), 3.

97. "Latest Development in Tibet," *Beijing Review*, 25 (June 21, 1982), 19.

98. "Tibet: An Inside View II," *Beijing Review*, 48 (November 29, 1982), 14.

99. "New Economic Policy for Tibet," *Beijing Review*, 27 (July 7, 1980), 4; and Ngapoi Jigme, "Great Historical Changes in Tibet," *Beijing Review*, 22 (June 1, 1981), 17–19.

100. "Situation in Tibet," *Beijing Review*, 31 (August 2, 1982), 6. Also see Harrison E. Salisbury, "Return of Dalai Lama to Tibet is Expected Soon," *The New York Times* (August 31, 1980), p. 11; Liu Heung Shing, "China Pulling Officials from Tibet," Associated Press, reprinted in *Honolulu Star-Bulletin* (August 12, 1982), C-5; and David Chen, "Dalai Lama Team Plans Visit to Tibet," *South China Morning Post* (Hong Kong) (April 24, 1982), p. 1; Christopher S. Wren, "Chinese Trying to Undo Damage in Tibet," *The New York Times* (May 31, 1983), A-1, A-8.

101. This was made very clear to the author in a rare luncheon meeting with the Dalai Lama when he came to Hawaii to dedicate a Tibetan temple in Woods Valley on October 28, 1980.

102. "Policy Towards Dalai Lama," *Beijing Review*, 46 (November 15, 1982), 3.

103. See Michael Ross, "Tibet's Dalai Lama Ponders Return," United Press International, as reprinted in *Honolulu Advertiser* (August 18, 1983), A-19.

104. *Beijing Review*, 16 (April 21, 1986), 9, and "Question and Answers on Tibet," *Beijing Review*, 28 (July 13, 1987), 16.

105. See Gene Kramer, "Dalai Lama Rejects Offer by China to Repatriate," Associated Press as reprinted in *Honolulu Star-Bulletin* (September 22, 1987), A-12.

106. *The New York Times* (October 3, 1987), p. 1.

107. *The New York Times* (October 4, 1987), p. 1.

108. *The Christian Science Monitor* (October 5, 1987), p. 9.

109. *The New York Times* (October 4, 1987), p. 1, and *Asian Wall Street Journal* (October 5, 1987), p. 1 and p. 6.

110. *Beijing Review*, 41 (October 12, 1987), 4.

111. *Beijing Review*, 42 (October 19, 1987), 15.

112. *Far Eastern Economic Review* (July 1, 1985), 20.

113. *Ta Kung Pao Weekly Supplement* (Hong Kong) (May 3, 1984), p. 3.

114. *Far Eastern Economic Review* (July 1, 1985), 21–22.

115. "Questions and Answers on Tibet," pp. 14–15.

116. See *Beijing Review* (February 19–25, 1990), p. 22.
117. See *The New York Times* (May 1, 1990), A-6; *Beijing Review* (April 16–22, 1990), 7; and *Hong Kong Sunday Standard* (May 20, 1990), p. 8.
118. Dawa Norbu, "Strategic Development in Tibet: Implications for Its Neighbors," *Asian Survey*, v. xix, n. 3 (March 1979), 245–59.
119. See Dawa Norbu, "China's Dialogue with the Dalai Lama 1978–90: Prenegotiation Stage or Dead End?" *Pacific Affairs*, vol. 64, no. 3 (Fall 1991), 367 and 371.

chapter

The Mili
in Chin

THE MILITARY'S ROLE

176

Military Commission,
explained to the New
military commission
chairperson of the
party's Military
der for the ar
Council and
minister i
responsi
vices
cur
ar

Chinese politics has been complicated by the participation of the military establishment at both the central and the provincial levels. In fact, following the Cultural Revolution, the military assumed the dominant political role at the local levels of government. In this chapter we shall examine first the structure of the PLA, focusing on the regional and provincial military commands as important factors in China's provincial politics; and second, the military's political role, from the Cultural Revolution to the Tiananmen protest.

THE PEOPLE'S LIBERATION ARMY (PLA): AN OVERVIEW

The 1975 and 1978 constitutions stipulated that the chairperson of the CCP was to be commander-in-chief of the armed forces, and that this individual would control the military through the CCP's Military Affairs Committee (MAC). The 1982 constitution provided a new Central Military Commission—responsible only to the National People's Congress—to direct the country's armed forces (see Articles 93–94 in Appendix A). This was a significant departure from the past in that the Chinese armed forces had always been under the control of the party. The 1982 constitution seemed to say that the armed forces now belonged to the nation, even though the party continued to exercise its leadership over the military.[1] The respective jurisdictions of the party's Military Affairs Committee and the new state Central however, are not clear. Politburo member Hu Qiaomu China News Agency that there would be no parallel central s.[2] At the Sixth NPC (June 1983), Deng Xiaoping was elected new Central Military Commission; he concurrently chaired the Affairs Committee. In effect, he became China's supreme comman- ned forces. The minister of defense, who operates under the State the premier, is the administrative head of the PLA. Under the defense the chief of staff for the PLA General Headquarters in Beijing, who is ble for the execution and coordination of combat operations of all the ser- nd commands. The PLA General Headquarters has a general logistics and pro- ment service. The party exercises its ideological and political control over the ned forces through the General Political Department (GPD), which is responsible for the party cells within the PLA and for propaganda, education, and cultural activities of the troops. Under the General Staff Office, the various service arms, such as the air force, naval headquarters, engineer corps, railway corps, armored command, and artillery, maintain their central headquarters for supervision of the armed forces.

At the regional level, the approximately 3.5 million troops are organized under the seven military regions, twenty-three provincial military districts, and nine garrison commands for principal population centers (See Table 8.1.) Elements of the PLA are assigned to these regions and districts on an almost permanent basis. For instance, troops for the Shenyang Military Region are stationed almost permanently in the northeast and are responsible for the defense of the northeastern provinces of Jilin, Liaoning, and Heilongjiang—each of the three is a military district by itself. In addition, the most heavily populated city in the northeast—Shenyang—is a garrison command, which is in charge of all ground, air, and naval forces in the area. The Shenyang Garrison Command reports directly to the Shengyang Military Region. The autonomous region of Inner Mongolia, like Xizang and Xinjiang, is a military region. Because of the tension and open clashes along the Ussuri and Amur Rivers

TABLE 8.1   Distribution of Personnel in the Chinese Army, 1984

UNIT	NUMBER	NUMBER OF TROOPS PER UNIT	TOTAL MANPOWER	PERCENTAGE GROUND FORCES
Main Forces (Field Army)				
Infantry divisions	118	13,300	1,569,400	49.8
Armored divisions	13	9,900	128,700	4.1
Artillery divisions	33	5,800	191,400	6.1
Regional Forces				
Divisions	73	7,500	547,500	17.4
Regiments	140	2,200	308,000	9.8

Sources: Defense Intelligence Agency, *Handbook of the Chinese People's Liberation Army*, Washington, D.C.: U.S. Department of Defense, November 1984.
John Frankenstein, "Military Cuts in China," *Problems of Communism*, xxxiv, 4 (July–August, 1985), 58. By permission of the publisher.

on the Sino–Soviet border, the Inner Mongolian Military Region was under the direct jurisdiction of the Beijing Garrison Command. Recently the Inner Mongolian Military Region at Urumqi was merged with the Lanzhou Military Region. Increased importance has been attached to the Inner Mongolian Military Region for the defense and security of western and northwestern China. So long as Sino–Soviet border disputes remain unresolved, and so long as Muslim unrest in Xinjiang continues,[3] The Inner Mongolian Military Region and the Shengyang Military region will remain crucial in China's national defense and security.

Under Deng Xiaoping's military reorganization, the eleven military regions were merged into seven: Shenyang, Beijing, Jinan-Wuhan, Nanjing-Fuzhou, Guangzhou, Kumming-Chengdu, and Lanzhou-Inner Mongolian Military Region. Each military region has a regional military commander and at least a political commissar. Sometimes the military commander for the region simultaneously holds the post of political commissar. Regional military commanders and commissars can be shifted from region to region or can be promoted up to the central headquarters in Beijing. Provincial military district commanders report to their respective regional commands, which in turn delegate responsibilities for local administrative, logistical, recruitment, and mobilization matters to the districts. In addition, the military commands in the provinces and garrison commands in large cities are responsible for maintaining law and order, as was so vividly demonstrated during the Cultural Revolution.

A close relationship between the regional military commands and the civil authorities in the provinces dates back to the days of the civil war against the Guomindang, when the armies operated in specific regions of the country. During the guerrilla days, the field armies were divided into five major groupings to provide civil and military administration for the regions they occupied: the First Field Army under the command of Marshal Peng Dehuai in the northwest region; the Second Field Army under Marshal Liu Bocheng in the southwest region; the Third Field Army under Marshal Chen Yi in east China; the Fourth Field Army under Marshal Lin Biao in the central and southern regions; and the Fifth Field Army under Marshal Nie Rongzhen in the north and northeast regions.[4]

The close link between the military and civil authorities in the provinces was cemented by the use of the military control commission.[5] The military control commission was a device used to take over administrative functions from the defeated Guomindang government during the gradual transition from civil war to normalcy. Each liberated town, county, and city was placed under a military control commission, established by the commanders of the newly arrived field army units. The ranking military officer for a particular locality held concurrently the leading position in the military control commission and the top political administrative post for the local government. Local administrative machinery, schools, factories, economic enterprises, and communications were placed under the jurisdiction of the military control commission. At the regional level, congruent with the six major administrative regions, were the six military regions under the control of the field armies. The highest organ of government in these regions was the regional military control commission. The chairperson of the regional military control commission was the senior military officer in charge of the military region and the field army headquarters.

While dissolution of military control began in 1953 and was completed in 1954, the close link between the military and the regional, provincial, and local authorities continued. To a large extent, these field army units remained stationed mostly in these areas, although after the Lin Biao affair in 1973, there was a reshuffling of some officers. Following the Korean War, most units sent to the front were reassigned to the regions from which they had been recruited.[6] Today local military commands still maintain local ties and concerns that have been established through the years with the local civil authorities.

The field army system has been seen by some scholars as a partial explanation for factionalism in the military. They see the elite field army systems competing with each other for power and for representation of their regions.[7] Other scholars have found very little evidence, within the field army system, of political power plays or of competition for assignments to the various military regions.[8] However, some China scholars still adhere to the "Whitson Thesis," that each of the five army systems plays a role in China's civil–military relations and that much of the internal military factionalism can be traced to the lineage of the original field armies.[9] At any event, it must be kept in mind that the Military Affairs Committee directly controls a main or central force, as distinct from regional forces, of about sixteen army corps. These units can be employed under direct orders from the central authorities in Beijing.

THE PEOPLE'S MILITIA

The militia was founded during the Jiangxi soviet days as an elitist organization to augment the Red Army and guerrilla units. During the civil war period, the militia's strength was not more than 8 or 10 percent of the total population under communist control. The people's militia has undergone six distinct stages of development since the establishment of the People's Republic in 1949.[10]

After liberation and during the Korean War, the activities of the militia were expanded to include maintenance of law and order, participation in joint defense measures with the PLA forces in border areas, and the spearheading of land reform activities.[11] This expansion of militia activities in no way altered its basic character as an elite force subordinated to the PLA command and discipline.

The people's militia acquired a new role with increased status when the people's commune and the Great Leap Forward programs were launched from 1958 to 1959. The militia became a nationwide mass movement: it was integrated into the structure of the communes in the countryside and grew enormously, to approximately 220 million members by 1959. Under the concept of "everyone a soldier," members of the communes simultaneously engaged in agriculture, industry, trade, and military work. The militia became the vehicle for mass mobilization for collective action as military organizational techniques and discipline were incorporated into the communes.[12] During this period the PLA had at first to share, and then gradually to relinquish, its authority and control over the militia to the communes and the party leadership within the communes. Simultaneously, the militia's status was elevated to a position coequal with that of the PLA in defending the countryside against possible enemy attack. These power shifts signaled the party's dissatisfaction with the army's desire to seek modernization in the midst of radicalized crash programs, and generated resentment and hostility within the PLA. But at this stage of development, the notion of the militia as a countervailing force to the regular army had not yet surfaced.

In early 1960, following the failure of the Great Leap, substantial changes were made in the militia's role.[13] The militia's priorities were reordered to place productive tasks before military training. To ensure responsible behavior of the militia and its cadres and to curb its wide-ranging activities, overall control of the militia's structure and training was returned to the PLA provincial and district commands. From 1960 to 1961, the militia was under tight political control and both its size and its activities were curtailed.[14]

On the eve of the Cultural Revolution, efforts were made to strengthen the political education of the militia so that it could become an instrument for political struggle. In 1967, in the midst of the Cultural Revolution, the army journal—then under the control of the radicals—defined the militia as not only "a partner and assistant to the PLA," but as "an important instrument for the dictatorship of the proletariat and a revolutionary weapon of the masses." The militia was asked to work with the regular army and the public security forces to suppress and smash the reactionaries and revisionists who wanted to restore capitalism.[15] The nature of the militia's participation in the Cultural Revolution, however, was largely dependent upon the stand taken by the local party authority and the PLA units in a given locality. In most rural areas, the local militia functioned as an integral part of the established party apparatus. When the authority of the party became disrupted as a result of the upheaval, the militia organization also became disrupted, or simply vanished. In other instances the local militia organization and personnel, which had established close ties with the county or municipal party committees, gave support to the established authorities in a showdown. We have well-documented case studies of the role played by the military and the militia in the provinces and cities, illustrating local armed resistance against the central authority during the Cultural Revolution.[16]

The Sino–Soviet border clashes in 1969 served as the primary reason to reactivate and strengthen the militia.[17] The campaign for war preparedness also revived charges against Liu Shaoqi and Peng Duhuai for their alleged inattention to the building up of the militia and for their overemphasis on development of a professional and modernized army. Many work conferences were held from 1969 to 1970. A constant theme at these conferences, as laid down by Chairman Mao, was that organizational control of the militia must be placed under the local party committees because they had a better grasp of the role of the militia in a "people's war."[18] To ensure the party's control over the militia, party committee members at the local level were designated to serve as leading cadres of the militia. Only party members could serve as commanders of the militia. Since the role of the militia was to assist the regular armed forces in defending against foreign incursion, the PLA chief of staff's office was responsible for developing a system that would utilize and manage militia weapons.[19]

The urban militia, as mentioned briefly in Chapter 2, was formed in 1973 by the radicals for the ostensible purpose of providing auxiliary service in case of foreign aggression. It soon became apparent that its real purpose was to provide the radicals with an "armed force"—a politically reliable instrument among the industrial workers in urban centers—for use in the political struggle for power.[20] Since the radical leaders, such as Zhang Chunqiao and Wang Hongwen, did not trust the political reliability of the regular PLA armed forces, an independent command structure was set up to direct the activities of the urban militia. In Shanghai, Beijing, Guangzhou, and Tianjin, the command headquarters of the workers' militia were controlled by leaders identified with the trade union federations in those cities. Both the urban militia and the trade union federations were under the control of the municipal party

committees, which were bastions of the radicals. The Shanghai urban militia was singled out by the radical-controlled mass media as a model for others to emulate.
Although the alleged coup plan of the Shanghai radicals who opposed Hua
Guofeng's appointment as successor to Mao never materialized in the crucial weeks
in late September 1976, there can be no doubt about the radicals' intention to use the
urban militia as a political instrument in any contest for power.[21]

The command structure and work of the militia as a whole were reorganized
following the arrest of the Gang of Four. Its overall role as an auxiliary to the regular armed forces in the event of a war has once again been revived.[22] The current
command of the militia is exercised by the PLA General Staff Office through the
People's Armed Forces units at the provincial military district level. The party shares
the responsibility of providing direction for the militia within PLA units.[23] As a result
of the use of urban militia units by the radicals during the contest for political power
in 1976, the militia today operates essentially in rural areas.[24] References in the 1978
state constitution to militia-building were deleted from the 1982 state constitution.
The role of the rural militia was curtailed and limited to auxiliary functions in the
event of a people's war.[25] Public security functions, once entrusted to the urban militia by the radicals, are no longer assigned to the militia. Militia units in rural areas
are still expected to engage in production, and military training is conducted under
the supervision of the regular PLA. China has not abandoned completely the concept
of a people's war. Marshal Nie Rongzhen reemphasized that China must not only
have a powerful regular army but also must organize the militia to fit the Maoist
doctrine of "everyone a soldier."[26] Deng Xiaoping also spoke of the militia's role in
civil air defense.[27]

Under the drive for military reform, to be discussed shortly, the people's militia
also underwent some significant changes.[28] There is no clear evidence that Mao's doctrine of people's war was abandoned entirely by Deng and his reformers. Militia training remained, with some modification, a function of the military regional commands.
Former party chief Hu Yaobang reportedly issued specific instructions on militia
training. His instructions reflected problems that needed corrective measures: too
many people involved in the militia; too much time spent on militia work; and too
heavy a burden carried by the populace for militia work. (One may argue whether Hu
had the power to give these instructions since he was not a member of the MAC.)[29]
MAC members monitored the party's instructions in the various military regions. In
fact, both PLA chief of staff Yang Dezhi and MAC vice-chairman Yang Shangkun
conducted militia inspections in various parts of China.[30] Reforming the people's militia took a two-pronged approach. One was to reduce the personnel involved in militia
work in the rural areas by cutting down the amount of time spent in military work,
and by curtailing support provided by the rural peasants. The other approach was to
elevate the professional-technical quality of militia training. Militia reform also centralized weapons management under the various regional commands.[31]

THE MILITARY IN CHINESE POLITICS

Militarism, as one of the major problems facing the Chinese, at least in the first half
of this century, continues to play an important—if not decisive—role in Chinese politics. The presence of militarism, its relation to social and political organizations, and

its effect upon the process of social and political transformation in Chinese communist society can be a useful framework for analyzing the military's role in politics.
Martin Wilbur defined militarism in Chinese political development as a "system of
organizing political power in which force is the normal arbiter in the distribution of
power and in the establishment of policy."[32] Modern Chinese political development
is, to a large extent, influenced by the power of armies, on one hand, and by the
techniques involved in the use of armies and in military organization, on the other.

For decades prior to the unification effort undertaken by the Chinese Nationalists in 1926, a system of regional military separatism dominated the political scene
in China. Under the system, independent military-political groupings, each occupying
one or more provinces, functioned as separate political entities and engaged in
internecine warfare in order to preserve their own separate regions and to prevent
their rivals from establishing a unified and centralized political system. To say that
contemporary China has been plagued by the problem of control by armies is really
an understatement. It is largely by military means and through military organization
and technique that the Chinese Nationalists tried, and the Chinese communists succeeded, in reestablishing a "unified hierarchical and centralized political system."[33]
The military thus constitutes a dominant group in society, and the military institution
has played a dominant role in political development.[34] The military has always occupied a special position in Chinese communist society. As mentioned in Chapter 4,
the Chinese Communist Party, for a long time, was the army. Party membership
grew from the 40,000 Long March survivors in 1935 to over 1.2 million members in
1945. Over 1 million of the total membership in 1945 constituted the military supply
system.[35] These people were regular members of either the army or the party, working without salary and under a military type of discipline. Robert Tucker has labeled
this unique system of militarizing the party as military communism, to distinguish it
from all other forms of communism.[36] It became evident in recent years that party
leadership has depended upon party members in the army to carry on political work,
to restore order, and to use the army as a coercive instrument in the contest for political power and succession.

The PLA's Political Role from 1949 to 1966

As we have noted, during the years immediately after the new regime came to
power, the PLA continued to govern the provinces under the military control commission.[37] Before the dissolution of military government in the provinces during 1953
and 1954, China became involved in the Korean War. The war made the military
leaders painfully aware of the need to modernize the armed forces with the most up-
to-date weaponry and combat skills. Figuring prominently in the issue of modernizing the military was the pressing policy question of whether to develop a nuclear
strategy to confront the United States in the Pacific.[38] These concerns of the military
were the basis for Marshal Peng Dehuai's criticism of Mao and the Great Leap programs. Peng's strategy for modernization was defeated at the Lushan party conference in the summer of 1959, and he was purged for daring to disagree with Mao's
policies on mass mobilization and the communes.

Lin Biao, who succeeded Peng as defense minister, launched a twofold ideological campaign under the Socialist Education Campaign.[39] The first part of the
campaign was aimed at tendencies toward professionalism, reliance on technical
skills and weaponry, and elitism within the PLA. Party cells, or committees, were

formed at the company level to supervise the work of the professionally trained military officers. Simultaneously, an intensive study of Mao's thought on politics and revolutionary military strategy was required of all PLA officers and soldiers. A massive printing of millions of copies of the "little red book," *Quotations from Chairman Mao Zedong*, was distributed first to the PLA ranks and later to the general public under the second part of the campaign: emulation of the PLA by the whole nation. The PLA was to be a model, a paradigm, of the new communist life. Under the direction of the military, political and ideological verbal symbols, or abbreviated slogans, were disseminated throughout the nation to reshape societal values and attitudes. PLA heroes and their diaries became key material in the campaign. The slogans, such as "self-sacrifice," "determination will prevail," and "primacy of politics," were closely related to Mao's policies for developing China.[40]

In 1965, politicization of the military reached its peak with the abolition of ranks and insignia for the PLA. This symbolized the PLA's return to its guerrilla image of a "proletarian army" of the masses waging class struggle under the firm control of the Mao-Lin faction of the party. The political and ideological work in the military was emphasized as the only way for the party to control governmental bureaucracies. Military officers increasingly were assigned positions of importance in the administrative agencies of the party and government.[41] These developments made it clear to the rest of Chinese society that it was the military, not the regular party under Liu Shaoqi and others opposed to Mao's concepts of reliance on politics, that was in control. It was also clear that Mao and Lin's strategy of "people's war," with its emphasis on reliance on the human factor and guerrilla tactics, was to be used in any possible confrontation with the United States in Indochina. The strategy had been elaborated to include a plan for China's survival in the event of nuclear war.[42] The acceptance of the strategy for people's war served as the basis for purging those senior PLA officers who advocated military professionalism and modernization. The stage was set for Mao, then a minority voice within the party, to mount a concerted attack against the bureaucratic party establishment, in the form of the Cultural Revolution.

The PLA in the Cultural Revolution, 1966–1976

During the initial stage of the Cultural Revolution—from April to December 1966—it was not the leaders' intention to directly involve the military. The major actors at the center invoked the military's power, prestige, and authority only to provide powerful backing for the radicalized students against the established party apparatus. The initial role of the military was essentially to present guidelines and to identify targets for the attack. In this initial phase, the military's own newspaper, *The Liberation Army Daily*, became the authoritative source of reports concerning the course of the upheaval. The military also provided the logistical support for the students who were moving en masse all over China to gain revolutionary experience by rebelling against the party apparatus. The logistical support included the use of military vehicles for transportation and army barracks for lodging.

The occasion for the PLA to intervene in the Cultural Revolution came in the early part of 1967, when the widespread breakdown of party and state authority resulted in bloodshed and disorder. Thus, in January, the Cultural Revolution was transformed into a gigantic onslaught on the party's machinery. The call for the PLA to intervene in the Cultural Revolution resulted primarily from rising resistance to the seizure of established party and government apparatuses by revolutionary rebel groups. In many instances the struggle for power involved rival groups and contending factions within the ranks of the revolutionary masses. The intervention of the PLA thus served two interrelated purposes: to restore law and order, and to throw the army's weight behind the Maoist radicals. In essence, the latter meant the PLA's entry into a factional struggle within the party. Once the local PLA commander decided to intervene, in the form of armed suppression, the action of the PLA was swift and decisive. Incidents of brutal suppression of the Red Guard groups became common, and February to May 1967 was a time of bloody armed struggle in all parts of China.

China Under Military Control

By September 1967 the central authorities finally realized that chaos and violence in the country could be halted only by placing the nation under military control. Besides providing the needed coercive force, military control would enable provincial party apparatuses to be reorganized and transformed into the new revolutionary committees.

The MAC was responsible for supervising the PLA main force once it had taken control of a city or a province. Initially this included (1) maintaining revolutionary discipline and protecting proletarian revolutionary groups; (2) supporting revolutionary factions within the public security bureau; and (3) purging the established public security bureau of antirevolutionary elements. Party newspapers and all broadcasting facilities were placed under PLA supervision, and the PLA was given the responsibility of supervising economic, financial, and relief activities. Nationally, military control was imposed on the country's communication and transportation systems. There was evidence that PLA officers were assigned to a number of ministries in the State Council at the government level. Senior PLA officers with managerial expertise were appointed directors or deputy directors in the State Planning Commission and in the ministries of finance, commerce, food supply, and foreign trade.[43]

By May 1968, with the active support of the PLA, twenty-four out of twenty-eight provinces and autonomous regions had established revolutionary committees based on the principle of the Three-Way Alliance (the mass organizations such as the Red Guard, the repentant party veterans, and the military) in place of the old party apparatus. Special PLA units—elements of the main force, under the exclusive direction of the MAC at the Central Committee level—were formed with specific instructions to help the localities complete the formation of the new revolutionary committees.

Authority for these special units was contained in a directive stating that the central forces were to act as the "representative in full authority" of the MAC and, as such, they were given power to supervise the local PLA units in implementing the directives of Beijing. Any resistance on the part of local PLA units to the orders, or refusal to cooperate with the special PLA units, could mean the arrest of their commanders and the disarming of their units as fighting forces. The directive was also explicit as to the authority given to the special PLA units in dealing with the revolutionary mass organizations to curb further armed struggle. It allowed arrest and punishment of those leaders of the contending factions who resisted the return of illegally seized weapons and ammunition; severe punishment of those who continued to incite armed bloodshed; returning fire on those who continued to incite the masses to attack the PLA; bringing conflicting leaders together for negotiation in order to achieve "Great Unity"; and finally, performance of educational and propaganda work among these Red Guard groups.[44]

The primary purpose of the special PLA units of the main force was to consolidate and accelerate the formation of the revolutionary committees in the provinces and the autonomous regions. Their major objective was to serve notice to the local military commanders to cut their local ties and regional predilections by lending their support to the revolutionary groups. Beijing had by now realized that infighting among the contending factions often was triggered by the alliance between the local PLA commands and the conservative party apparatus. The speedy establishment of unity among all revolutionary groups was retarded by the incessant fighting. Dispatching special PLA units into the regional and provincial military districts would also provide protection to the already hard-pressed groups loyal to Beijing. The immediate consequence of dispatching the special PLA units was the speedy establishment of the revolutionary committees in the remaining provinces of Yunnan, Fujian, and the autonomous regions of Xizang and Guangxi.

MILITARY POLITICS SINCE THE CULTURAL REVOLUTION

By the spring of 1969, when the Ninth Party Congress met, the military had been thrust by the Cultural Revolution into a dominant position in the provincial and municipal revolutionary committees. As we pointed out in Chapter 2, the revolutionary committees were temporary power structures established to reflect the alliance of the military, rehabilitated veteran party cadres, and the mass organizations, such as the Red Guard groups. The dominant position of the military from 1968 to 1975 was as follows: of the twenty-nine chairpersons for the provincial, autonomous regions and three centrally administered municipal revolutionary committees, twenty (68 percent) were affiliated with the PLA as either commanders or political commissars for provincial or regional military districts. Only nine (32 percent) of these chairpersons were party cadres, representing the old guard party bureaucratic power. Despite repeated pleas from Beijing that the Red Guard groups not be discriminated against, not a single Red Guard leader was ever appointed as chairperson of a provincial-level revolutionary committee. Leaders of the Red Guard groups made a better showing in the vice-chairperson distribution. Of the 181 known vice-chairpersons for these twenty-nine revolutionary committees, sixty-six (36 percent) were leaders of Red Guard groups. Sixty-three (34 percent) were PLA commanders and political commissars, and fifty-two (29 percent) were veteran party cadres. Again, the combined strength of the PLA and the veteran party cadres occupying the position of vice-chairperson in the revolutionary committees for the provinces overwhelmed those who represented the Red Guard groups. One other fact showed vividly the influence of the PLA in the provincial revolutionary committees: eight of thirteen PLA regional commanders (military regions of Guangzhou, Fuzhou, Shengyang, Nanjing, Wuhan, Xinjiang, Xizang, and Inner Mongolia) were concurrently serving

as chairpersons of the provincial revolutionary committees under their military jurisdictions. This alone demonstrated the ascendancy of the regional military's influence
in China's political development.

The dominant position of the military in the provinces continued in the period
of party rebuilding from 1970 to 1971. Of some 158 party secretaries of various
ranks in provincial party committees in 1971, about 60 percent were military officers
from regional and provincial commands, 34 percent were veteran party cadres, and
only 6 percent were leaders from the ranks of mass organizations.

The rapid expansion of military power in the provinces, and the continued
dominance of the PLA in Chinese politics in general (following the conclusion of the
Ninth Party Congress) became a major factor in the Lin Biao affair, which came to
a head in September 1971.[45] The key question raised in the Lin Biao affair was who
should have control of the political system in China: a civilian party under Mao, or
the military under Lin Biao. The purge of Lin was a direct consequence of the tensions that developed between the civilian party and the military as it expanded its
power, and the tensions that had developed between the central military command
and the regional military power base in the provinces. In the end, the powerful
regional commanders who opposed Lin had contributed significantly to his purge.[46]
The Lin Biao affair was an important benchmark in party–army relations. It also
meant that the rapid expansion of the military's role under Lin had constituted a
threat to the power and authority of Mao and Zhou Enlai. Events of the post-Lin
Biao period from 1971 to 1974 largely centered on restoring the party's control over
the military under Mao's 1929 dictum that "the party must command the gun."
These events can be summarized as follows:

First, a massive purge was undertaken at the central command structure level,
which had been the main base of Lin's support. In addition to the disappearance of
some nine senior military leaders—including the chief of staff and the commanders
of general logistics, the air force, and the navy—more than forty other ranking officers associated with the Lin group were purged.

Second, a movement was launched to reduce the involvement and role of the
military in politics. A January 4, 1973 announcement issued by the State Council,
headed by Zhou Enlai, and by the party's Military Affairs Committee, headed by
Zhou's close ally Marshal Ye Jianying, directed PLA units in all regions and
provinces to observe strictly the policies of the party. They stressed that the PLA's
role was primarily military, rather than political. Public media stressed the need to
observe military discipline and to concentrate on military affairs. Visitors to China
now found fewer military representatives on school and university campuses and in
factories. Coincident with the campaign to play down the role of the military in Chinese society was the reappearance of many party veterans who had been vilified during the Cultural Revolution.

Third, some analysts of Chinese politics suggest that there was also a deliberate attempt by Mao and Zhou Enlai to reduce the influence of the military in the
decision-making process at both the national level and the regional and provincial
levels.[47] Members of the military serving as party secretaries in the provinces
declined in numbers from ninety-five (60 percent) in the period from 1970 to 1971
to seventy-four (47 percent) in the period from 1974 to 1975. The most dramatic
decline in military participation in the political process came at the powerful Politburo level. In 1969 the twenty-five-member Politburo included thirteen PLA senior

officers, or 52 percent of the membership. In 1973 the twenty-one-member Politburo included only seven PLA senior officers, or 33 percent of the membership. Military representation on the Central Committee declined less drastically, from 43 percent of the full members on the Ninth Central Committee in 1969 to approximately 32 percent on the Tenth and Eleventh Central Committees. Interestingly, while PLA regional or provincial commanders holding concurrently the post of provincial party secretary decreased from fourteen to eight during the post-Lin period, their representation on the Central Committee remained fairly stable. The continued high participation rate in the Central Committee by the military commanders and political commissars for the regional and provincial commands apparently reflects their continuing importance in the Chinese political power structure.

The Tenth Party Congress of August 1973 not only officially disposed of the Lin Biao affair but approved the formation of a new power structure. The latter was based on the coalition of the forces under Premier Zhou and those following the party idealogues Jiang Qing, Zhang Chunqiao, Yao Wen-yuan, and the new rising star, Wang Hongwen, who was elected vice-chairperson of the CCP. The new power structure clearly revealed the ascendancy of Zhou and his veteran party cadres, who in the aftermath of the dominance exercised by Lin had received support from the majority of regional and provincial military commanders and political commissars. For the first time in decades, the new coalition was in a position in 1974 to make shifts in the personnel at the regional and provincial military commands: seven of the eleven commanders of the military regions were transferred or swapped posts. Ellis Joffe has pointed out several significant inferences that can be drawn from the reshuffling of the regional military commanders, many of whom held concurrently the position of first party secretary for a province. First, the removal of these military commanders from their bases of operations, some held since the early 1950s, strengthened immeasurably the center's control over the provinces. Second, the successful removal of the officers revealed their military discipline and their commitment to the center.[48]

The coalition formed in 1973 proved to be temporary and in many ways illusory. The heart of the new power structure was the veteran party administrators, reinforced by the key military figures brought to the center by Zhou. The weakest element of the coalition was the party's radical ideologues, the Gang of Four, who had tried unsuccessfully to organize the urban militia as a countervailing force to the PLA.

This brief study of the Chinese military's role in politics clearly shows that the PLA has been a major force in the party and government between 1969 and 1977. Approximately 31 percent of the regular members on the Eleventh Central Committee of the party, elected in 1977, were representatives of the PLA. Of the sixty-two PLA representatives on the Eleventh Central Committee, fifty-five, or 27 percent, were active PLA commanders and political commissars from the regional military commands. When this 27-percent representation of PLA members stationed in the provinces was added to the 40 percent representing provincial party secretaries of various ranks, it became evident that the provinces retained a formidable voice in the nation's highest decision-making council. Although the military's representation on the full membership of the Twelfth Central Committee (1982) declined in comparison to that on the Eleventh Central Committee (1977), it still represented 22 percent of the total. This, together with the representation of party and government adminis-

TABLE 8.2   PLA Representation on the 13th Central Committee (November 1987)

	FULL MEMBERSHIP (175)	ALTERNATE MEMBERSHIP (110)	TOTAL
PLA General Departments	5	3	8
Military Regions	19	15	34
Navy	2	3	5
Air Force	2	2	4
Total PLA Representation	28	23	51
Perentage of Committee	16%	20.9%	19.8%

Sources: Figures are obtained from *China News Analysis*, no. 1347 (November 15, 1987), p. 3, and *Zhengming*, 123 (January 1988), 42–43.

trators/technocrats, accounted for more than 74 percent of the total full membership of 210 on the Twelfth Central Committee.

For the Thirteenth Central Committee (see Table 8.2), military representation included 28, or 16 percent, of the full membership and 23, or 21 percent, of the alternate membership. Together the military was represented by 51 members, or about 20 percent of the total of 285 members.

For the Fourteenth Central Committee, elected in the fall of 1992, there has been an increase in PLA representation on the committee, from 20 percent of the total full and alternate membership to about 25 percent. However, significant changes have also taken place: the elder of the Yang brothers, Yang Shangkun, has retired, and the younger brother, Yang Baibing, has been purged from the powerful Military Affairs Committee. PLA General Liu Huaqing, 76, has been elevated to the Politburo's Standing Committee. The elder General Liu may have been placed on the Politburo's Standing Committee as a swing vote in case a deadlock should emerge among the evenly divided hard-line-inclined and reform-minded members of that highest decision-making body. General Liu has been considered Deng's close supporter within the high military echelon. In a move to gain support from the PLA, party and MAC chair, Jiang Zemin, not only has promoted several officers to the rank of general, but also has permitted MAC vice-chairman General Zhang Zhen and members of the military's high command to attend Politburo meetings without the right to vote.

MILITARY REFORM UNDER DENG XIAOPING

Nothing has really changed with regard to Mao's old dictum: political power grows out of the gun barrel, and the party must command the gun. Since Mao's death, the man in the party in command of the gun has been Deng Xiaoping. In 1974, when Deng was reinstated after being purged during the Cultural Revolution, one of the pivotal positions he held was that of chief of staff for the PLA. Because of Deng's many years of close association with the military—both as political commissar and as the party's general secretary—he was the only person in the top hierarchy after Mao's death who could command respect and support from most PLA officers.

Later, when Deng returned for the second time in 1977, he was not only the PLA's chief of staff but also the vice-chairperson of the MAC—the de facto political supervisor of the armed forces.

One of Deng's first goals was to consolidate his control over the central command structure of the armed forces. He accomplished the task in two carefully planned moves. One was to reshuffle the commanders and commissars for the military regions so as to ensure the retention of only those who supported his policies. By the spring of 1980, Deng was able to appoint ten of the eleven commanders for the eleven military regions. The only regional military commander who retained his appointment (uninterrupted since 1969) was Li Disheng of the Shengyang Military Region for the northeast provinces facing the Soviet border. Li was finally removed from that position in 1985, and subsequently was retired from the Politburo in the 1985 reshuffle, which installed a number of new Politburo members.[49] Li was reported to have been forced to retire because of his political views, which were considered contrary to Deng's.[50] (But that interpretation may not be correct because in 1985 Li was appointed vice-president of a newly established PLA University for Defense, a prestigious institution comparable to West Point. Li was said to have refused the PLA University presidency because of his advanced age.)[51] An extensive reshuffling and purge also were carried out in the provincial military districts. As a part of the ongoing PLA reorganization, the eleven military regional commands, as mentioned earlier, were reduced to seven through merger.

Deng's second move was to staff key military positions at the central command headquarters with his trusted associates. On the eve of the Twelfth Party Congress in September 1982, it was clear that Deng had established firm control over the central command structure. Deng was elected chairman of the MAC, a position comparable to supreme commander-in-chief for the armed forces. Yang Shangkun, his associate and a Politburo member, was made the permanent vice-chairman and general secretary for the MAC. Deng packed the standing committee of the MAC with his supporters. He promoted Yang Dezhi, the commander of the Chinese forces in the 1979 border war with Vietnam, to the position of chief of staff for the PLA. By 1981 all senior officers for the general logistics, rear services, and all commanders of the Chinese air force and navy were considered Deng's supporters.

Deng's next objective was to implement reforms in the command structure and in personnel. He recommended the following three reforms: (1) streamline the military command structure below the MAC level; (2) modernize officer training; (3) upgrade the competence of military officers. The PLA organizational structure was fragmented in such a way that there were separate commands for the air force, navy, artillery, armored units (tank corps), antichemical units, railway corps, engineering corps, and regional and provincial military districts. The thirty-eight army corps stationed in the military regions generally received their operational orders from the PLA general headquarters at the center.[52] Similarly, the air force, the navy, and the artillery in the military regions received their orders directly from their own headquarters in Beijing. Deng felt that it would be more efficient to have the forces and services all placed under the direct command of the military regions. For instance, the artillery corps would not be placed under the "dual command" of the military regions and the artillery's own headquarters.[53]

Deng also thought that reform was needed in PLA military officer corps training. Deng and his senior military associates believed that modern warfare requires knowledge and understanding about science and technology, and that special skills in modern warfare must be developed among the military officer corps through curriculum improvement in the military academies. The course content at the military academies seemed outdated in terms of tactics and strategies, and a large portion of the curriculum remained devoted to Mao's guerrilla strategy of a people's war.[54]

Since 1983 some actions have been taken to improve armed forces officers' training. A joint MAC and State Council decision was made to recruit university graduates below the age of 24 for PLA officers' training.[55] A military science degree was also established by the State Council as a forward step to encourage development in military science and modernization.[56] Special PLA cadre schools were set up in many provincial military districts to offer a year-long course in leadership training. After the year's training, graduates would be sent to the various military academies for further studies.[57] In the effort to upgrade the educational level of the officer corps, the air force seems to have taken the lead.[58] In December 1985 the new PLA University of Defense was established by merging the three separate military academies.[59] As of 1986 there were over one hundred technical military academies and specialized training schools, with "an enrollment of over 100,000 cadets, designed to produce a new generation of officers."[60]

Deng also felt the need to replace the large number of aging officers who clung to their posts but who had limited education and outdated concepts. These officers had little knowledge or understanding of modern military science and tactics. While they remained in their positions, artificial barriers had been erected between the armed forces and the service academies, preventing able young academy officers from receiving actual command posts.[61] Deng proposed a concerted campaign to elevate younger service academy officers with knowledge of modern science and with the needed stamina to command posts.[62]

By the summer of 1983, some measures had been introduced to support Deng's proposed reforms. One guaranteed aged officers a retirement pension equivalent to their full salary. In addition, a special bonus would be granted to every retired officer for each year of service. This meant that a military officer who served fifty years would receive an additional fifty yuan per month.[63] Housing allowance and a car would be added as special inducements for early retirement of high-ranking officers. For example, a political commissar could receive as much as 120,000 yuan in housing allowance and retirement.[64] Simultaneously, age limits were imposed on the commanders at various levels. The following age limits have been reported: corps commanders, 55; divisional commanders, 45; regimental commanders, 35; battalion commanders, 30; and company commanders, 25.[65] Finally, a system of rapid promotion for younger officers in the military was instituted to provide youthfulness and competence.

By 1986, PLA commanders and political commissars for the newly merged seven military regions were younger in age and better educated. One report stated that 91 percent of all newly appointed officers in the military regions had studied in the military academies and about 60 percent had completed their junior middle school education (or the equivalent of U.S. junior high education).[66] About 25 percent of the officers on the active list had a college education in 1986. The PLA as a whole has become a relatively young military force, with a vast majority of the recruits within the age range of 18 to 39; only 2.5 percent were 50 and over.[67] Han Huaizhi, deputy chief for the PLA general staff, stated that more than half the aged officers in the seven military regions had been retired.[68]

But some of the policies for military reform have aroused strong dissent within the military. Since the military has traditionally stood for Mao's ideological purity, the reassessment of Mao's role in party history generated some resentment within PLA ranks. The assessment of Mao as a man who made mistakes in his later years might be regarded as a political compromise to placate old guard military leaders who still view Mao as infallible. Deng's lengthy lecture at the 1978 All-Army Political Conference praising Mao and his three rules of discipline and eight points of attention, formulated in the guerrilla days during the 1930s, might also be viewed as a concession to the PLA old guard.

The campaign for "socialist spiritual civilization," articulated by Deng and Hu Yaobang, also caused controversy among the military.[69] This campaign reemphasized moral standards, education, culture, science, literature and arts, and a general knowledge of humankind.[70] Deng was reported to have summarized the "socialist spiritual civilization" campaign by coining the phrase: "To possess ideals, moral standards, civilization, and discipline."[71] When Deng instructed the military to emphasize culture and general knowledge as well as politics, some of the old guard military leaders protested. It was said that Wei Guoqing, then the director of the PLA general political department in charge of education and propaganda, did not share Deng's view on the importance of cultural emphasis in military training.[72] Yang Shangkun, then the MAC's general secretary, rebuked Wei by pointing out that both science and culture were equally important in military training.[73] Subsequently, Wei was replaced by Yu Quili, also a Politburo member. The removal of Wei indicated the continued presence of dissent in the military.

Deng Xiaoping was caught in another controversy with the military. A veteran army writer, Bai Hua, wrote a screenplay, *Bitter Love*, which was an angry film about the death of an artist persecuted during the Cultural Revolution. The screenplay cast the party in an unfavorable light and denigrated Mao by symbolism. The PLA condemned the author. On the other hand, the screenplay coincided with Deng's attempts to reassess Mao and the mistakes he made during the Cultural Revolution. In this case Deng sought a compromise solution that would placate the dissenters in the military. Evidently, in order to forestall a direct attack on the author and indirectly on Deng, Hu Yaobang pressured Bai Hua to make self-criticism, confessing his "ideological errors."

Another area of friction between Deng and the military was the low priority Deng gave to defense spending. China's defense outlay in 1979 was 22.2 billion yuan ($14.3 billion). It was reduced to 19.2 billion yuan ($13.0 billion) in 1980 and was further reduced in 1981 to 16.8 billion yuan ($9.9 billion).[74] Thus, the 1981 defense expenditure was down 5.4 billion yuan, or almost 25 percent, from the 1979 level. This reduction in military spending aroused the PLA's concern and criticism. The level of defense expenditure was held at about 17.8 billion yuan ($9.5 billion) for 1983 and 1984.[75] There was a further reduction in China's military expenditures for 1985 to about 10.5 percent from 14 percent in 1983, but the 1991–1992 budget called for military spending at about U.S. $16.25 billion, an increase of 12 percent from the 1990 U.S. $14.5 billion.[76] In terms of China's total national expenditures, defense spending represented only about 15 percent in 1982 and 14 percent in 1983. However, it must be pointed out that these defense figures, as reported by the Chinese, represented only a portion of the actual defense spending. If we use the methodology employed by the U.S. Defense Department, which includes all portions of defense expenditure, such as research and development and rocket space industries,[77] the 1983 figure of 17.8 billion yuan would have been increased to about 40 billion yuan or 30 percent of China's total state budget.[78]

However, China's defense budget, as approved by the Eighth NPC in April 1993, has been set at U.S. $17.5 billion, an almost 13 percent increase over the previous year. The increase was justified on the grounds that there will continue to be regional conflicts and wars, and China must be combat-ready to meet changing international situations.

One of the first consequences of the defense cuts in 1980 was the demobilization of some 400,000 soldiers.[79] The ultimate goal was eventually to reduce the total PLA strength of about four million soldiers by as much as a third. Even more dramatic was Deng Xiaoping's announcement in early June 1985 that one million soldiers, about 25 percent of the total 4.3 million armed forces, would have to be demobilized during 1985 and 1986 (see Table 8.3).[80] The reduction was made for two compelling reasons: to help reduce the national budget deficit and to modernize the armed forces by weeding out the aged, the less-educated, and the less-competent. Hu Yaobang, during his visit to New Zealand before his ouster, indicated the party's plan to reduce the armed forces by two million soldiers by the end of 1986.[81] The

TABLE 8.3   PLA Force Structure—1975, 1985, and Projected

	1975		1985	
	MANPOWER	*% OF TOTAL*	*MANPOWER*	*% OF TOTAL*
Ground Forces	2,800,000	86.2	3,500,000	80.5
Air Force	220,000	6.8	500,000	11.5
Navy	230,000	7.1	350,000	8.0
TOTAL	3,250,000		4,350,000	
Missiles (IRBM/MRBM)	80		110	
Missiles (ICBM)	0		0	

		PROJECTED	
		MANPOWER	*% OF TOTAL*
	Ground Forces	2,500,000	74.6
	Air Force	500,000	14.9
	Navy	350,000	10.5
	TOTAL	3,350,000	
	Missiles (IRBM/MRBM)	?	
	Missiles (ICBM)	?	

Sources: For past and current figures, see volumes of *The Military Balance*, London, International Institute for Strategic Studies.
John Frankenstein, "Military Cuts in China," *Problems of Communism*, xxxiv, 4 (July–August, 1985), 29. By permission of the publisher.

decision to demobilize one million soldiers in 1985–86 was reached in 1985 only after a lengthy debate that included some dissenting voices at the MAC meeting.[82] Tentative reassessment of the PLA demobilization program indicated that it had not accomplished its goal of reducing one million soldiers by the end of 1986. As of December 1986, only about 410,000 soldiers and officers had been retired from active duty.[83] Further accelerated demobilization had to be continued throughout 1987. In mid-December 1986 the MAC held a lengthy meeting, amid widespread student demonstrations, to address some of the problems in force reduction. One problem was resettlement. The central government was faced with the burden of finding suitable employment for the large number of demobilized soldiers. A number of them were placed in various public security positions.[84] Some participated in protest demonstrations as a way of expressing their resentment.[85] Reductions in military spending also meant the curtailment of benefits and privileges for the officers and soldiers.

An indirect cause of friction between the pragmatic leaders and the military was generated by the new agricultural policies for the communes. Peasant families have always provided the major source of recruitment for the PLA. The new liberal agricultural policies of fixing output quota at the household level and of permitting sideline production have brought general prosperity to rural peasants—so much so that those who stay on the farm are earning more than military recruits.[86] This has led to low morale in the military. Many soldiers are thinking of getting out of military service and returning to the rural communes. Aware of the morale problem within the military, Deng sought ways to boost spirits. One measure he suggested was to restore the rank and insignia that had been abolished in 1965 by Mao in his desire to make the army more egalitarian. The reinstitution of military rank for the officers and soldiers would mean more prestige, if not more pay.

For the officers, demobilization was more difficult to accomplish. Only 40 percent of the officers had opted for retirement at the end of 1986.[87] As a general rule, few soldiers and officers wanted to re-enter civilian life even if prior arrangements had been made in terms of jobs available for them and their spouses. In many cases retraining had to be provided for the demobilized soldiers to help them find suitable employment in industries.[88]

MILITARY MODERNIZATION: REVAMPING AN OUTDATED ARSENAL[89]

There has always been a demand for military professionalism and modernization. China's decision to develop a nuclear bomb in the early 1960s, the purge of Peng Dehuai, and the debate over Mao's military strategy all revolved around the question of military modernization and professionalism. This demand most likely became more urgent after 1969, as Sino–Soviet relations deteriorated and border incidents increased. After almost twenty years of debate and neglect, the new Chinese leadership has come out squarely on the side of military modernization. In an all-army political works conference, Hua Guofeng stated that "our army must speed the improvement of its weapons and equipment and raise its tactical and technical level."[90] By this, Hua meant the acquisition of modern arms and equipment, including missiles and nuclear weapons. Marshal Ye Jianying pointed out at the same conference that "a modern war will be more ruthless and more intense than past wars," and that the Chinese military establishment must devote its efforts to "more proficient techniques and tactics, military skills, and commandership."[91]

The theme of military modernization has been stressed continuously by Deng and Hu Yaobang former Politburo member Yang Shangkun, who was Deng's most valued supporter in the party's MAC, said that it was essential for the military to acquire modern "scientific, cultural, and technical knowledge." He made it abundantly clear that strength in war was more than a matter of the army's size—it must be seen "in the degree of modernization of equipment and the people's ability to use such equipment."[92] Yang Dezhi, the PLA chief of staff, also spoke of the urgent need to upgrade the technical level of military personnel through advanced training and education.[93] One Western military expert indicated that the Chinese military probably was fifteen years behind the U.S. military in technological training.[94]

The Chinese realize that the basic requirement for military modernization is the rapid development of heavy industries, as well as research in science and technology, which takes time. To fill the large deficiencies that exist in their technology, the Chinese at first thought they could embark on a program of weapons purchase from abroad. Chinese military missions, headed by senior military officers, most of whom were vilified for advocating military professionalism during the Cultural Revolution, shopped around in England, France, and West Germany with an eye toward the possible purchase of the latest weapons: tanks, antitank missiles, fighter planes, and helicopters. While the United States remained opposed to sales of sophisticated modern weapons to the Chinese, it had tacitly given approval to its allies in Western Europe to sell such weapons to China.[95] In 1978 an agreement was signed between China and West Germany, under which China was reportedly to have purchased 600 antitank missiles.[96] Then China and Italy reached an agreement for a missile guidance system and helicopters.[97] China's interest in the purchase of modern arms was also encouraged by a change in United States policy under the Carter administration. In January 1980 former Secretary of Defense Harold Brown paid a visit to China. He indicated to the Chinese that the United States was willing to sell, on a case-by-case basis, certain kinds of equipment, including trucks, communication gear, and possibly early warning radar systems. In 1980 the Pentagon also approved sales of battlefield radar and computers, helicopters, and transport planes.[98] In July 1980 the Chinese signed an agreement with France to purchase fifty helicopters costing about $57 million.[99] There were reports that the Chinese were interested in purchasing French Mirage F-1 fighter planes and heavy-duty helicopters.[100] In 1981 Canada offered to sell the Chinese certain defensive weapons, mostly aircraft and radar equipment.[101] Chinese agents also concluded an agreement with Great Britain for the purchase of Rolls-Royce supersonic jet engines.[102] The Chinese strategy may involve studying the mechanisms of the sophisticated modern weaponry purchased in limited quantities from the West, as a means of acquiring the needed weapon-making technology. This would be more beneficial for military modernization from a long-term point of view, and it would be less costly than massive purchases of the available modern weapons.

After many years of window shopping, the Chinese finally signed a letter of intent in November 1986 for the purchase from the U.S. of $550 million worth of radar, computer, and avionics equipment for jet fighters. It was a six-year agreement under which bids could be submitted by American firms to supply the sophisticated equipment by early 1987.[103] There was some expectation that these initial purchases would pave the way for subsequent U.S. sales of modern weaponry in areas where the Chinese defense needs were the greatest: artillery, antisubmarine warfare, and battlefield equipment.[104] The sale of sophisticated arms to China may raise a number of policy questions for the United States.[105] For instance, will China be more cooperative with the United States? Will a militarily strong China make Asia more secure? In addition, it must be kept in mind that while China attempted to upgrade her defense capability by purchasing sophisticated weapons from the United States, she also embarked on an accelerated program of arms sales abroad. China was said to have sold Iran more than $1 billion worth of jet fighters, tanks, and small arms.[106] In 1986, China held an international arms exhibition to display its military hardware, mostly a decade old in design, to buyers in the Third World nations.[107] China's active engagement in arms sales abroad may be motivated more by the need to earn foreign exchange than by the desire to export revolution to other parts of the world.

When we discuss the complex issue of Chinese military modernization, we need to keep in mind that there is a running debate among Chinese leaders on the priority of this issue—a conflict between the need to develop and modernize basic industries and the need to develop the military. The conflict has usually been resolved by placing military modernization second to the need for economic development.[108] In fact, the Chinese have always stressed the importance of economic development as basic to all progress. One of the reasons for the late Marshal Peng Dehuai's criticism of Mao's 1958 Great Leap policy was Peng's concern over the delay in modernizing China's military—a criticism that brought on Mao's wrath and led to Peng's eventual purge. Peng's concern stemmed from his experience in commanding Chinese forces in Korea during the early 1950s. Peng argued that a strong industrial base was the foundation for military modernization. Mao's view prevailed, and the concept of a revolutionary army with stress on the human element, not on sophisticated weapons, remained a basic military doctrine. After that the "people's war" concept dominated Chinese military thinking. Not until 1975, when the late premier Zhou Enlai proposed a ten-year modernization plan, was the issue of military modernization placed on a par with modernization of agriculture, industry, and science and technology. In fact, modernization of defense was not openly discussed by the Chinese leaders until 1977, when Mao had passed away and the Gang of Four had been arrested. Even in 1977 Marshal Ye insisted that modernization of China's basic industries was essential and necessary for its national defense.[109] (This view was not shared by one special interest group, the National Defense Industry Office within the Chinese defense establishment, which argued that modernization of defense industries would stimulate the growth of other industries and thus motivate the progress of the economy as a whole.)[110] In a frank speech to the Royal Institute of International Affairs in London in June 1986, six months before he was ousted, former party chief Hu Yaobang revealed that Chinese leaders had debated the question of priority between national economic development and defense modernization. He said the conclusion of the debate was "to concentrate on economic development vis-à-vis the national defense."[111]

The relegation of military modernization to a lower priority than the modernization of industry and agriculture is perhaps more understandable when one looks at the cost factor involved. The Rand Corporation estimated that China would have to spend between $41 billion and $63 billion in order to completely modernize her conventional fighting forces.[112] This estimate is for 3,000 to 8,000 new medium tanks, 8,000 to 10,000 armored personnel carriers, more than 20,000 heavy-duty trucks, 6,000 air-to-air missiles, and 200 to 300 fighter-bombers.[113] Closely linked to this enormous price tag of $41 billion to $63 billion was the lack of available foreign exchange needed to pay for the weapons. Western analysts speculated that one means of paying for the arms modernization would be to step up, as has already been done, exports from China of strategic metals, such as titanium, tantalum, and vanadium—all lightweight and heat-resistant metals used in aircraft.[114]

The inability and unwillingness of China to commit huge financial resources to large-scale purchases of modern, sophisticated weapons from abroad has forced China to develop several alternative military strategies for defense.[115] One is the development of nuclear weapons, on the ideological ground that the nuclear monopoly by the superpowers must be broken. China has detonated a hydrogen bomb from the air and has developed a creditable delivery system of tactical weapons with nuclear warheads. China also launched three new satellites in 1981 to ensure an early warning system against possible Soviet nuclear attack. In May 1980 China launched its first long-range ICBM, with a range of 6,000 miles, over the Pacific and missed the intended target by only twenty-seven miles. As mentioned earlier, China has not abandoned entirely the strategy of people's war. Many Chinese military officers still believe that a war could be fought under Chinese conditions. The editor of the *Beijing Review*, on the occasion of the 1982 Army Day celebration, said: "It is still fundamentally true that it is men, not materials, that decide the outcome of war. If a war breaks out, we will mobilize the masses of people to swamp the enemy in the ocean of people's war."[116] The PLA chief of staff, Yang Dezhi, while stressing the need for technical training of officers, also insisted that "in fighting a people's war today, the decisive factor is still a fighter's courage, consciousness and the mental preparation to sacrifice one's life."[117] The military action in the Falklands in 1982 certainly has forced many nations, including China, to reflect on the statement that "war remains first and foremost a human encounter."[118]

While the long-range goal is a modernized military, the Chinese military leaders recognize that the old military doctrine of people's war, or guerrilla warfare, must remain a basic ingredient in their war preparedness plans for some time to come.[119] But China's month-long military action in Vietnam in the spring of 1979 did alter that military approach, for the pace of China's invasion was rather slow, and casualties were high—20,000 killed and wounded. China's invasion of Vietnam showed that its military lacked mobility, which was the result of not having enough armored vehicles for combat purposes.[120]

Thus, China's military reform and modernization in the 1980s represented a basic modification to Mao's doctrine of people's war, which had dominated China's military strategy for decades.[121] Moreover, the Chinese seemed to be convinced, as they indicated to visiting American defense officials, that military modernization could be accomplished "within the framework of overall economic modernization."[122] The military, in conclusion, seemed to accept the fact that they will have to compete with other industries for priority in the national budget allocations.

CHINESE ARMS SALES ABROAD AND THE DEFENSE INDUSTRIES

In recent years there has been considerable concern over China's arms sales abroad. That concern has led to a probe of China's defense industries and China's military machine.[123] At a time when international superpower conflicts have been reduced after the collapse of the former Soviet Union, China's arms sales abroad have created apprehension, if not a feeling of instability and insecurity, in Asia. In this section we will discuss three aspects of the problem.

China's Arms Sales

For more than a decade China has been identified by international experts as one of the major suppliers not only of conventional weapons, but of ballistic missiles and nuclear technology as well, to the Islamic world and to North Korea. China's arms sales abroad began in the early 1970s, when it supplied Egypt with military weapons that included jet fighters and antisubmarine ships. During the eight-year war between Iran and Iraq in the 1980s, China exported arms to both belligerents in the Persian Gulf. In 1986 the world discovered that China had also provided Iran with the short-range antiship ballistic missile known as the "Silk Worm." The missiles have a 50-mile range and are packed with 1,000 pounds of warheads, three times as powerful as Exocet, the French-made missile that hit the United States naval vessel *Stark* in the Gulf in 1987.[124]

In the early 1980s China concluded a missile sales agreement with Saudi Arabia. It became known in 1985, through United States intelligence sources, that China had exported between 25 and 50 CSS-2 ballistic missiles with a range of 2,650 kilometers, capable of reaching most targets in the Middle East.[125] Soon China was ready to supply Syria with the M-9 short-range ballistic missile, but delivery was postponed after the United States protested. After the Soviet Union invaded Afghanistan, China delivered to Pakistan, its long-time ally and friendly neighbor, not only conventional weapons, but also M-11 short-range ballistic missiles, believed to have a range of 650 miles and capable of carrying nuclear warheads. With Chinese assistance, Pakistan has been developing nuclear bombs. Solid fuel surface-to-surface M-11 missiles have also been delivered by China to Syria, Iran, and Libya.

Wendy Frieman provides a picture which shows that China has made arms transfers to eight Islamic nations (Bangladesh, Egypt, Indonesia, Iran, Iraq, Pakistan, Saudi Arabia, and Syria) of a variety of ballistic missiles including short-range, intermediate-range, surface-to-air and antiship missiles.[126]

Under international pressure, particularly from the United States, China pledged to be bound by the 1987 Missile Technology Control Regime (MTCR), an international agreement signed by major Western powers but not by China, that sets guidelines intended to restrict the export and transfer of medium-range missiles and missile technology. China pledged to adhere to the MTCR guidelines and parameters in February 1992.

While it has been denied repeatedly by Chinese officials, U.S. intelligence sources have clear evidence that China continues to export M-11 missiles and technology to Pakistan. This was revealed in an intelligence briefing for members of the Senate Foreign Relations Committee in May 1993.[127] The United States is concerned about the M-11 missile transfers to Pakistan for possible nuclear bomb delivery systems, and it is applying leverage through a set of conditions attached to the 1993 extension of the "most-favored-nation" trade agreement with China. One such condition stipulated that China must show evidence of its adherence to the MTCR guidelines by 1994. (Earlier, the United States had imposed sanctions on the export of certain U.S. missile-related technology to China. In response, China had threatened in late August 1993 that it might not abide by the MTCR guidelines. In late 1993, the United States lifted the sanctions presumably in order to obtain concessions from China on human rights and trade issues.)

Motives behind China's Arms Sales

There may have been two major motives for China's continued sale of missiles and missile technology abroad. One is the profit motive. Arms export translates into foreign currency accumulation and a favorable balance of trade for China. In the 1980s when China was engaged in economic reform by stimulating the export trade, arms sales abroad earned an estimated U.S. $1.3 to $2 billion.[128] Eric Hyer estimated that during the Iran–Iraq war in the 1980s, arms sales to Iraq by China were worth about U.S. $5 billion and sales to Iran were worth about U.S. $3 billion.[129] Total arms sales by China to Saudi Arabia were valued at at least U.S. $2 billion in the 1980s.[130] The military dictatorship in Myanmar (Burma) purchased as much as U.S. $1.2 billion worth of jet fighters and other conventional weapons from China.[131] It has been reported that the Chinese also exported to the United States about two million guns between 1989 and 1991.[132]

The other motive behind Chinese arms sales abroad may be political or even ideological. Major arms transfers abroad to Third World nations who are China's friends or allies have the potential of altering the delicate regional balance in the Middle East and South Asia. A Chinese policy supporting the Third World allows China to develop a broad coalition all over the world. A united front of Third World nations implies a realignment in existing international relations.

China's Defense Industries[133]

China's defense industries are under the command of the PLA and those agencies controlled by the central government through several ministries in the State Council. The PLA command at the central level—that is, through the party's powerful Military Affairs Committee—controls the Commission of Science, Technology and Industry for National Defense (COSTIND), which in turn controls and operates some 50,000 factories for manufacturing weapons and civilian goods for consumption under economic reform. The State Council's two ministries for advanced technology development—the Ministry of Machine Building and Electronics Industry, and the Ministry of Aeronautics and Astronautics—maintain research and development facilities as well as factories for manufacturing consumer goods and weapons. In addition, Frieman identifies the China State Shipbuilding Corporation as responsible to both the military and the central government for operating hundreds of factories and research and development activities.[134] The PLA's general staff controls the Equipment Bureau, which provides weapons specifications to weapons factories, whereas the COSTIND is responsible for weapons research production and development. Both COSTIND and the State Council ministries mentioned here negotiate with certain export trading corporations for arms sales abroad. For instance, the New

Era Corporation and Poly Technologies serve as regulating firms under the command or control of COSTIND for a host of weapons export trading companies that have indirect relationships with the two State Council ministries (Machine Building and Aeronautics).

The Chinese policy on arms and missile sales abroad is generally a puzzle to the West.[135] That is, China's pledge to observe the Missile Technology Control Regime's guidelines and restrictions on the one hand, and the mounting intelligence evidence indicating otherwise on the other hand, illustrates the autonomous or separate relationship that has existed between the PLA high command and the State Council of the central government over the arms and missile sales issue.[136] Also, the PLA-controlled arms trading corporation negotiated the sale of 650-mile intermediate-range ballistic missiles to Saudi Arabia in spite of the foreign ministry's protest.[137] In addition, as pointed out by Peter Grier, one of the PLA-controlled arms export trading companies, Poly Technologies, has been headed by Deng Xiaoping's son-in-law since 1991.[138]

The Chinese defense industry bureaucracy maintains close ties with the powerful policymakers at the State Council level. There is a clear move by the defense industries to convert their factories into civilian uses.[139] It is therefore likely that Chinese defense industries may have acted independently, and that their bureaucracy is powerful enough to disregard the views of other central government agencies, including the Ministry of Foreign Affairs.

CIVIL–MILITARY RELATIONS TODAY: OPPOSITION AND DISSENT

The PLA has been viewed as "the repository of Mao's Thought" and as "the generator and legitimizer of the Chinese communist ideology."[140] For some time the military was the model of ideological purity and revolutionary character for the nation as a whole to emulate. Following Mao's death, Deng Xiaoping made efforts to develop military professionalism and combat capacity. By these efforts Deng hoped to minimize the PLA's political interventions. However, since 1978 the military has not been completely in agreement with Deng on central issues, including the de-Maoization and the economic reforms. Deng, as a pragmatic politician, has had to make concessions to the PLA from time to time in return for its support.

The military was said to have played an important role in the political struggle over Hu Yaobang's forced resignation as the party chief. It was reported that in December 1986, at the time of the student demonstrations, Deng presided over a large gathering of PLA leaders who pressured him to take action.[141] A week after that meeting, Deng met with other top party leaders and then ordered the crackdown on the students and intellectuals, who seemed to have lent their support to the student demonstrations.[142] While the PLA continued its support for Deng,[143] it steadfastly refused even to entertain the thought of naming Hu Yaobang concurrently as chairman of the party and of the MAC, a tradition long held by Mao. The military, in the view of Parris Chang, questioned Hu's ability to oversee the military apparatus and personnel even though Hu had been Deng's protégé for some time. The officer corps of the PLA was "antagonistic" toward Hu for his "excessive indictment of Mao's errors."[144] Rural economic prosperity brought on by the reforms deterred rural youth from joining the army; China's open door to "bourgeois tendencies"; and the forced retirement of many aged military officers—all these reform measures had brought on criticism within the PLA. One must also point out that these were the very measures initiated and supported by Deng himself, including the indictment of Mao's mistakes (see Chapter 3). It is possible that the leaders in the PLA ground forces, the so-called "military traditionalists," formed a temporary alliance with the orthodox hard-liners to block Hu's ascendancy.

There is really no general agreement among China scholars on the PLA's role in China's civil–military relations, a topic that has generated a cascade of literature in recent decades. (Many of these studies have been cited in the footnotes to this chapter.) Some analysts adhere to what Jencks has called "the factionalism school," which argues that many key military officers embraced Mao's ideological approach and would enter into a power struggle in due time to depose the reformers.[145] Then there is the "professional school," which believes that the Chinese military strives for professionalism and accepts civilian (party) supremacy.[146] Falling somewhere between these two opposing schools are an array of views, from the continued dominance of party-army personalities to the influence of the field army lineage on party politics.[147]

Deng Xiaoping, as an avid bridge player, has in his possession the trump card: his efforts toward military modernization were designed to lure the PLA's support for his reform policies.[148] By making his pledge to promote military professionalism and modernization, he obtained support from the military to weed out the "leftist thinkers" and the less-educated, aged soldiers. Today Deng still has the support and allegiance of the military as a whole. In an unprecedented press conference in 1987, Xu Xin, deputy chief of the PLA general staff, pledged the military's support to Deng and denied allegations that the military had played a key role in the ouster of Hu Yaobang in January 1987.[149]

THE PLA AFTER TIANANMEN

The massive deployment of units of the PLA, estimated at more than 150,000, was unprecedented and unnecessary for the purpose of suppressing student demonstrators at Tiananmen in 1989. The armed units dispatched to Tiananmen came from six military regions: the Beijing Military Region (including the 38th Army from the Beijing Garrison Command as well as the 24th, 27th, 28th, 63rd, 64th and 65th Armies); the Nanjing-Fuzhou Military Region (the 12th Army); the Lanzhou-Inner Mongolian Military Region (the 20th Army); the Shenyang Military Region (the 39th Army); the Jinan-Wuhan Military Region (the 54th Army); and the Guangzhou Military Region (the 12th Army and the 15th Air Force).

Initially the task of suppressing the students fell to the 38th Army of the Beijing Garrison Command. But two days after the imposition of martial law, the 38th Army had failed to implement orders from the central government to move on the students. There were at least two basic reasons why the 38th Army failed to move with deliberate speed on Tiananmen. One is thought to have been the professional younger officers' reluctance to be involved in using force to quell the student demonstration.[150] Another reason, as revealed by a former member of the 38th Army who was a doctoral candidate in political science at Stanford University in 1989, was that the 38th Army, stationed on the southern outskirts of Beijing, had enjoyed a close association with the people of the capital city, particularly the students who spent summers at the military camp and were recruited into the 38th Army as conscripts.[151]

Dissension within the PLA

The reluctance of the 38th Army to move against the students of Tiananmen was a symptom of a larger problem within the PLA concerning the use of force against civilians in a domestic disturbance. On May 22, 1989, seven senior military officers circulated a memorandum protesting the use of troops to put down the demonstration at Tiananmen. The letter urged that the PLA troops refrain from the use of force and that they not enter Beijing City.[152] The signers of the appeal included a former defense minister, a former deputy defense minister, a former army chief of staff when Deng came to power, a former commander of a military region, and one from the Chinese navy; the rest were senior officers of the military academy. Senior Army General Qin Jiwei, then the defense minister and a member of the Politburo, was also opposed to the use of troops to quell the disturbance. Two of China's most respected retired marshals, Ni Rongchen and Xu Xiangchen, tried to negotiate with the student leaders at Tiananmen. The two senior PLA marshals were said to have telephoned the martial law administrators, advising them against the use of force.[153]

Perhaps sensing the dissent and disagreement with the PLA over carrying out the martial law decree, or merely following past practice of using his personal prestige to win the support of the military regions, Deng Xiaoping convened an emergency meeting of the seven regional military commanders at Wuhan. The meeting was said to be stormy, and three regional military commanders expressed their opposition to the use of force.[154]

In the end, Deng's persuasion seemed to have prevailed, for by May 25 six of the seven regional military commanders pledged their support to the martial law decree—the one holdout was the pivotal Beijing Military Region. Soon after the agreement, troops began to be deployed from other parts of China, ostensibly for the purpose of enforcing martial law; but in reality they were intended to prevent a possible military rebellion by the 38th Army, or possibly by other military units.[155] The size of the military deployment, estimated at 150,000 troops, and the equipment employed (including tanks, heavy artillery, antiaircraft weapons, paratroopers, and missiles)[156] certainly indicated that they were not intended merely for suppression of the unarmed student demonstrators and the Beijing City residents who erected barriers to block the soldiers marching into Tiananmen. The troops that finally entered the square and opened fire on the students and residents near or on the square were the 27th Army from Hepei countryside, commanded by a relative of Yang Shangkun, then permanent general secretary for the MAC and a leader of the hard-liners. Recruits for the 27th Army were not urban youth, but mainly of peasant background.

The Purge and Continued Discontent within the PLA

The upshot of military dissent over the use of force at Tiananmen was a reorganization and a change of personnel—thus a purge—within the PLA command structure.

In the aftermath of Tiananmen, one of the most significant personnel changes for the PLA was Deng's resignation of his long-held chairmanship of the powerful MAC. His successor in that post, tantamount to commander-in-chief for the entire armed forces, was not Yang Shangkun, who reportedly coveted the position, but the

new party general secretary, Jiang Zemin, who up until
experience with the military. However, the real power of the
Shangkun, who became the first vice-chairman of the MAC.
brother, Yang Baibing, became permanent general secretary of the
been some complaints inside and outside the PLA that the Yangs have
itary their "family enterprise."[157]

By the spring of 1990 a major reshuffle of regional military comm
been completed by transfer of military commanders from one region to anoth
way of preventing their becoming entrenched within their local power bases.
there were no officially publicized dismissals of officers in the aftermath of Tiana
men, one Western source indicated that discharges or purges of 400 officers and
1,600 soldiers might have taken place within the PLA, either for refusal or inability
to carry out the martial law decree to crack down on the students.[158] On the whole,
there has been no purge at the highest military levels, mainly because the hard-liners
wanted to avoid the upheaval that might result from provoking the military officer
corps.[159] Contrary to the claim that the military had enhanced its political role,[160] the
PLA did not secure any new influential position in the reshuffle of the party's Politburo Standing Committee after having ousted Zhao Ziyang and Hu Qili, the two
reformers. However, there was a rise in the defense budget for 1990 to 28.97 billion
yuan, as compared with the 1989 budget of 24.5 billion yuan ($15 billion).

Promotion in the military in the aftermath of Tiananmen seems to have been
based on individuals' willingness to use force against the students under martial law,
and on personal loyalty to the Yang brothers, who were in control of the MAC and
its high command structure until 1992.[161]

In spite of purges within the military, younger officers who were promoted and
selected on the basis of professionalism and competence have been unhappy with the
present state of affairs in the PLA. Their chief complaints have been nepotism and
the reemphasis on political study or "redness" at the expense of military professional competence. While nepotism has been endemic within the party and the military,
the past decade's progress under Deng's military reform and modernization, which
stressed professionalism and competence, has been deemphasized. In its stead, the
traditional Maoist political and ideological study has become the order of the day—
six out of every ten hours must be spent on political sessions. The PLA's General
Political Department has ordered all officers to spend time attending political sessions studying Mao's thought and Marxism-Leninism. It was pointed out that bourgeois liberalization included ideas of "separation of army from politics." Party-controlled mass media and the PLA's own *Liberation Army Daily* have recently waged
a campaign to urge military officers to study a special circular that presented the
threefold tasks of "ensuring the absolute leadership of the party, ensuring a high
degree of stability and unity, and ensuring an everlasting political quality" for the
military.[162] The rationale for urging the need to engage in political study has been the
infiltration of "antagonistic forces" from outside to subvert the PLA's quality.[163]
Mao's old dictum that the guns must be in the party has been revived and stressed
as a priority for study by the younger officers, who seem to have been the opposition in recanting the ideological lines of yesteryear.

For the soldiers as well as the officers in the military, there is also the crisis of
the decline in the respect and prestige which the PLA had enjoyed before the Tiananmen crackdown. The traditional refrain that "the people love the PLA" is no longer
a cherished thought, after what happened to the students and the Beijing residents on

's, in addition to the loss of public image, onomic hardship brought on by inflation. eded provisions. They must, as always, factories to produce goods to be sold on budget[164]—about 80 percent of defense

motivated some officers from Shenyang, roduce a secret anti-Yang Shangkun cir- pport Jiang Zemin as party chief and of ral secretary for the MAC while concur- neral Political Department.[166] The resent- ntrol of the PLA by the Yang brothers r retired PLA generals confronted Jiang Zemin, the party chief, on the eve of the August 1, 1990 Army Day and registered their complaints and concerns.[167]

Presumably the removal of the Yang brothers from positions of power at the 1992 party congress assuaged the resentment against them within the PLA command. This was followed by a massive purge of nearly half the generals considered to be followers of the Yang brothers; this move is considered essential to ensure Deng's hand-picked successors' survival in case of a possible military coup in future power contests. As mentioned earlier, Jiang Zemin, the party head, is actively cultivating support from the PLA senior officers toward that end.

In short, in the aftermath of Tiananmen the Chinese military establishment is faced with internal dissension and discontent, not only for its role in the crackdown on the students, but over its ultimate place in society. Having lost its traditional pres- tige, the PLA is confronted with growing resentment and criticism, if not a risk of violence, from the populace. It will take more than political study or the emulation of Lei Feng to restore the PLA's relationship with the people. The Chinese military is now trying to resolve its political and professional identity. Ultimately, it must answer the basic questions of civil–military relations: Is it always the instrument of the party, and what must it do when there are contending factions within the party? How do the PLA officers and men reconcile the inevitable contradiction between "party reliability" and military professionalism?

In the final analysis, military professionalism will inevitably provoke a civil (party)–military crisis in the long run. In future power contests, the PLA officer corps, particularly the "frustrated modernizers," most likely will intervene as power brokers and kingmakers once the elders such as Deng Xiaoping have passed away and the inner party contest for succession begins in earnest.[168] Or, as a possible, if not probable, scenario, the military might intervene in a succession contest by placing the nation under military control as it did during the depth of the Cultural Revolu- tion, when widespread chaos and disorder prevailed nationwide.

NOTES

1. Hu Sheng, "On the Revision of the Constitution," *Beijing Review*, 18 (May 13, 1982), 16.
2. *Ta Kung Pao Weekly Supplement* (Hong Kong) (September 16, 1982), p. 5.
3. See Donald H. McMillen, "The Urumqi Military Region: Defense and Security in China's West,"

Asian Survey, vol. xxii, no. 8 (August 1982), 705–31; and Raphael Israeli, "The Muslim Minority in the People's Republic of China," *Asian Survey*, vol. xxi, no. 8 (August 1981), 901–19.

4. See William Whitson, "The Field Army in Chinese Communist Military Politics," *The China Quarterly*, 37 (January–March 1969), 1–30; and Jurgen Domes, *The Internal Politics of China, 1949–1972* (New York: Holt, Rinehart & Winston, 1973), pp. 21–26.

5. John Gittings, *The Role of the Chinese Army* (London: Oxford University Press, 1967).

6. Whitson, "The Field Army in Chinese Communist Military Politics," 7.

7. Ibid., 2–26. Also see Y.C. Chang, *Factionalism and Coalition Politics in China: The Cultural Revolution and Its Aftermath* (New York: Praeger Publishers, 1976), p. 77.

8. William L. Parish, Jr., "Factions in Chinese Military Politics," *The China Quarterly*, 56 (October–December 1973), 667–99; and Harvey W. Nelsen, "Military Forces in the Cultural Revolution," *The China Quarterly*, 51 (July–September 1972), 444–74.

9. See William Whitson, "The Field Army in Chinese Communist Military Politics," in William Whitson and Chu-Hsia Huang, *Chinese High Command: A History of Communist Military Politics, 1927–71* (New York: Praeger, 1973), pp. 498–517. Also see Shu-shin Wang, "Revamping China's Military," *Problems of Communism*, xxxiv, 2 (March–April, 1985), 114–117. For a review of other analytical theses on China's civil–military relations, see Harlan W. Jencks, "Watching China's Military: A Personal View," *Problems of Communism*, xxxv, 3 (May–June, 1986), 76–77; Parris Chang, "Chinese Politics: Deng's Turbulent Quest," *Problems of Communism*, xxxv, 1 (January–February, 1986), 1–21; and Jurgen Domes, *Peng Te-huai: The Man and the Image* (Stanford, Calif.: Stanford University Press, 1985).

10. See James C.F. Wang, "The Urban Militia as a Political Instrument in the Power Contest in China in 1976," *Asian Survey*, vol. xviii, no. 6 (June 1979), pp. 541–45.

11. Gittings, *The Role of the Chinese Army*, pp. 201–24.

12. Ibid.

13. Ibid.

14. Ibid.

15. *Renmin Ribao* (March 17, 1969), p. 1.

16. Philip Bridgham, "Mao's Cultural Revolution: The Struggle to Consolidate Power," *The China Quarterly*, 41 (January–March 1970), 1; Parris Chang, "Changing Patterns of Military Roles in Chinese Politics," in *The Military and Political Power in China in the 1970s*, ed. William Whitson (New York: Holt, Rinehart & Winston, 1972), pp. 47–70; Jurgen Domes, "The Cultural Revolution and the Army," *Asian Survey*, vol. viii, no. 5 (May 1968), 349–63; John Gittings, "Reversing the PLA Verdicts," *Far Eastern Economic Review*, 30 (July 25, 1968), 191–93; Ellis Joffe, "The Chinese Army in the Cultural Revolution: The Politics of Intervention," *Current Scene*, vol. viii, no. 18 (December 7, 1970), 1–25; Ellis Joffe, "The Chinese Army after the Cultural Revolution: The Effects of Intervention," *The China Quarterly*, 55 (July–September, 1973), 450–77; Thomas Jay Matthews, "The Cultural Revolution in Szechwan," in *The Cultural Revolution in the Provinces*, Harvard East Asian Monographs, no. 42 (Cambridge, Mass.: Harvard University Press, 1971), pp. 94–146; Margie Sargent, "The Cultural Revolution in Heilung-kiang," ibid., pp. 16–65; Vivienne B. Shue, "Shanghai After the January Storm," ibid., pp. 66–93; Harvey Nelsen, "Military Forces in the Cultural Revolution," *The China Quarterly*, 51 (July–September, 1972), 448–50; Ralph Powell, "The Party, the Government, and the Gun," *Asian Survey*, vol. x, no. 6 (June 1970), 441–71; William Whitson, *The Chinese Communist High Command: A History of Military Politics, 1927–69* (New York: Holt, Rinehart & Winston, 1971).

17. *Renmin Ribao* (March 29, 1969), p. 2.

18. Chiang Ye-shang, "Military Affairs for 1970," *The China Monthly*, 82 (January 1971), 11–12.

19. Based on monitored provincial broadcast. See *Chung-kung yen-chiu (Studies on Chinese Communism)*, vol. 6, no. 1 (January 1973), 40–41.

20. See "Failure of 'Gang of Four's' Scheme to Set Up a 'Second Armed Forces,' " *Peking Review* 13 (March 25, 1977), 10–12; " 'Gang of Four's' Abortive Counter-Revolutionary Coup," *Peking Review*, 25 (June 17, 1977), 22–25. Also see Wang, "The Urban Militia as a Political Instrument," 545–59.

21. "Failure of 'Gang of Four's' Scheme to Set Up a 'Second Armed Forces,' " pp. 10–12, " 'Gang of Four's' Abortive Counter-Revolutionary Coup," pp. 22–25; and Wang, "The Urban Militia as a Political Instrument," 545–59.

22. Nieh Jung-chen, "The Militia's Role in a Future War," *Peking Review*, 35 (September 1, 1978), 16–19.

23. See June T. Dreyer, "The Chinese People's Militia: Transformation and Strategic Role," paper presented at the 32nd annual meeting of the Association of Asian Studies, March 21, 1980.

24. See "Regulation on Militia Work," *Issues and Studies*, vol. xvi, no. 2 (February 1980), 76.

25. "The Concept of People's War," *Beijing Review*, 31 (August 2, 1982), 3.

26. See Nieh Jung-chen "The Militia's Role in a Future War," p. 19.

27. " 'August 1' Army Day," *Peking Review*, 31 (August 4, 1978), 3.

28. See Thomas C. Roberts, *The Chinese People's Militia and the Doctrine of People's War* (Washington, D.C.: National Defense University Press, 1983).

29. *Ming Pao Daily* (Hong Kong), (November 6, 1985), p. 3.

30. *Ming Pao Daily* (Hong Kong), (July 9, 1984), p. 8.

31. Ibid.

32. Martin Wilbur, "Military Separatism and the Process of Reunification under the Nationalist Regime, 1922–1937," in *China in Crisis*, vol. 1, no. 1, eds. Ho Pi-ting and Tang Tsou (Chicago: University of Chicago, 1968), p. 203.

33. Ibid.

34. Ibid.

35. Treadgold, *Soviet and Chinese Communism: Similarities and Differences*, (Seattle, Wash.: University of Washington Press, 1967), p. 25.

36. Robert C. Tucker, "On the Contemporary Study of Communism," *World Politics*, vol. xix, no. 2 (January 1967), 242–57.

37. Parris Chang, "Changing Patterns of Military Roles in Chinese Politics," in *The Military and Political Power in China in the 1970s*, ed. William Whitson (New York: Holt, Rinehart & Winston, 1972), p. 48.

38. See Alice Langley Hsieh, *Communist China's Strategy in the Nuclear Era* (Englewood Cliffs, N.J.: Prentice-Hall, 1962).

39. See Chalmers Johnson, "Lin Piao's Army and Its Role in Chinese Society," *Current Scene*, vol. iv, no. 13 (July 1, 1966), 1–10, and no. 14 (July 15, 1966), 1–11. Also see Ralph L. Powell, "The Increasing Power of Lin Piao and the Party-Soldiers, 1959–1966," *The China Quarterly*, 34 (April–June, 1968), 38–65; and Ellis Joffe, "The Chinese Army Under Lin Piao; Prelude to Political Intervention," in *China: Management of a Revolutionary Society*, ed. John M.H. Lindbeck (Seattle, Wash. and London: University of Washington Press, 1971), pp. 343–74.

40. See Mary Sheridan, "The Emulation of Heroes," *The China Quarterly*, 33 (January–March 1965), 47–72; and James C.F. Wang, "Values of the Cultural Revolution," *Journal of Communication*, vol. 27, no. 3 (Summer 1977), 41–46.

41. Powell, "The Increasing Power of Lin Piao and the Party-Soldiers, 1959–1966," 38–65.

42. See Lin Biao, "Long Live the Victory of People's War," *Peking Review*, 32 (August 4, 1967), 14–39.

43. *Renmin Ribao* (September 3, 1967), p. 1.

44. "Directive of the Central Committee, the State Council, Military Affairs Committee, and the Cultural Revolutionary Group Concerning the Dispatch of Central Support for the Left Units to Regional and Provincial Military Districts," *Studies on Chinese Communism*, vol. ii, no. 8 (August 31, 1968), 109–17; and *Renmin Ribao*, (September 7, 1968), pp. 1–4.

45. See Y.M. Kau, *The Lin Piao Affair: Power Politics and Military Coup* (White Plains, N.Y.: International Arts and Sciences Press, 1975), pp. xxi-xxviii; Ellis Joffe, "The Chinese Army after the Cultural Revolution," 468–77; and Parris Chang, "The Changing Patterns of Military Participation in Chinese Politics," *ORBIS*, vol. xvi, no. 3 (Fall 1972), 797–800.

46. Ellis Joffe, "The Chinese Army after the Cultural Revolution," 450–77. For the account of Biao's crash, see Cheng Huan, "The Killing of Comrade Lin Biao," *Far Eastern Economic Review* (July 22, 1972), 11–12; *The New York Times*, July 23, 1972, pp. 1, 16. For the official version, see Chou En-lai, "Report to the Tenth National Congress of the Communist Party of China," *Peking Review*, 35–36 (September 7, 1973), 18. Also see Philip Bridgham, "The Fall of Lin Biao," in *The China Quarterly*, 55 (July–September, 1973), 427–49; Ying-mao Kau and Pierre M. Perrolle, "The Politics of Lin Biao's Abortive Military Coup," *Asian Survey*, vol. xiv, no. 6 (June 1974), 558–77; and Y.M. Kau, *The Lin Biao Affair*, pp. xix-li.

47. See Parris Chang, "China Military," *Current History*, vol. 67, no. 397 (September 1974), 101–5; Ellis Joffe, "The PLA in Internal Politics," *Problems of Communism*, vol. xxiv, no. 6 (November–December 1975), 1–12.

48. Ellis Joffe, "The PLA in Internal Politics," 12.

49. *The New York Times* (September 17, 1985), p. 6. Also see *The Christian Science Monitor* (September 18, 1985), p. 9; and *Ming Pao Daily* (Hong Kong) (September 27, 1985), p. 8.

50. *The Wall Street Journal* (September 17, 1985), p. 3.

51. "A New Army for a New Society," *China News Analysis*, 1303 (February 1, 1986), 4.

52. Harvey W. Nelsen, *The Chinese Military System: An Organizational Study of the PLA* (Boulder, Colo.: Westview Press, 1977), 10.

53. See Lo Bing, "Inside Story About PLA Reform," *Zhengming* (Hong Kong), 66 (April 1983), 8.

54. William R. Heaton, Jr., "Professional Military Education in China: A Visit to the Military Academy of the PLA," *The China Quarterly*, 81 (March 1980), 122–28.

55. *Ming Pao Daily* (Hong Kong) (May 27, 1983), p. 1 and *Ta Kung Pao Weekly* (Hong Kong) (May 26, 1983), p. 1.

56. *Ming Pao Daily* (Hong Kong) (December 8, 1983), p. 1.

57. *Ming Pao Daily* (Hong Kong) (September 18, 1983), p. 1.

58. *Ming Pao Daily* (Hong Kong) (April 4, 1983), p. 1, and (May 25, 1983), p. 1.

59. *People's Daily* (October 28, 1985), p. 1.

60. See Paul H.B. Godwin, "Overview: China's Defense Modernization" in *China's Economy Looks Toward the Year 2000*, vol. 2. Joint Economic Committee, Congress of the United States (Washington, D.C.: U.S. Government Printing Office, (May 21, 1986), p. 143). Also see "For Peace and National Security," *Beijing Review*, 31 (August 3, 1987), 4.

61. *Ming Pao Daily* (Hong Kong) (March 6, 1983), p. 1.

62. See *Beijing Review*, 31 (August 4, 1978), 3–4. Also see *Ming Pao Daily* (Hong Kong) (March 6, 1983), p. 1.

63. *Ming Pao Daily* (Hong Kong) (March 24, 1982), p. 1.

64. Ibid.

65. *Zhengming* (Hong Kong), 66 (April 1983), 9.

66. "A New Army for a New Society," 3. Also see "For Peace and National Security," 4.

67. Ibid.

68. *Beijing Review*, 15 (April 14, 1986), 5.

69. On socialist spiritual civilization, see the following: *Beijing Review*, 45 (November 8, 1982), 13; *Beijing Review*, 37 (September 13, 1982), 21–26; *Beijing Review*, 47 (November 22, 1982), 3. Also see *Hongqi*, 15 (August 1, 1982), *Zhengming* (Hong Kong), 61 (November 1982), 8–9.

70. *Zhengming* (Hong Kong), 61 (November 1982), 8.

71. Ibid.

72. Ibid., and *Zhengming* (Hong Kong), 62 (December 1982), 9–10.

73. *Hongqi*, 15 (August 1, 1982), 8–9. Also see *Zhengming* (Hong Kong), 61 (November 1982), 9.

74. Wang Bingqian, "Report on Financial Work," *Beijing Review*, 39 (September 29, 1980), 17; "Report on the Final State Account for 1980 and Implementation of the Financial Estimates for 1981," *Beijing Review*, 2 (January 11, 1982), 16; and "Report on the Implementation of the State Budget for 1982 and the Draft Budget for 1983," *Beijing Review*, 3 (January 13, 1983), 16.

75. *Beijing Review* (October 27, 1986), 3.

76. Ibid., and Kathy Wilheim, "China Budget Hefty Increase for the Militia," Associated Press as reprinted from *Honolulu Star-Bulletin* (March 26, 1991), A-11.

77. See Edward Parris, "Chinese Defense Expenditures, 1967–83" in *China's Economy Looks Toward the Year 2000*, pp. 149–150.

78. Ibid. For a discussion on the relationship between economic development and defense needs, see Tai Ming Cheung, "Disarmament and Development in China: The Relationship between National Defense and Economic Development," *Asian Survey*, vol. xxviii, no. 7 (July 1988), 757–74.

79. *Far Eastern Economic Review* (September 25, 1981), 55.

80. *People's Daily* (June 11, 1985), p. 1.

81. *Asian Wall Street Journal* (April 15, 1985), p. 1; and *The New York Times* (April 21, 1985), p. 1.

82. Ibid.

83. *China Daily* (December 29, 1986), p. 1. Also see *Beijing Review*, 17 (April 28, 1986), 15–19.

84. *Far Eastern Economic Review* (September 25, 1981), 55.

85. *Ming Pao Daily* (Hong Kong) (July 6, 1981), p. 1.

86. *Far Eastern Economic Review* (September 25, 1981), 55. Also see Lo Bin, "Candid View of a PLA Divisional Cadre," *Zhengming* (Hong Kong), 65 (March 1983), 17.

87. *Zhengming*, 108 (October 1986), 8.

88. *People's Daily*, (November 1985), p. 4.

89. For recent articles on China's military modernization, see Christopher M. Clark, "Defense Modernization: How China Plans to Rebuild Its Crumbling Great Wall," *China Business Review* (July–August, 1984), 40–44; Jonathan Pollack, "The Men But Not the Guns," in *Far Eastern Economic Review* (December 18, 1981), 26–29; Robert S. Wong, "China's Evolving Strategic Doctrine," in *Asian Survey*, xxiv 10 (October 1984), 1040–55; Paul H.B. Godwin, "Overview: China's Defense Modernization," op. cit., 133–47; and Harlan Jencks, "Watching China's Military: A Personal View," op. cit., 74–76. Also see the following books: Charles D. Lovejoy, Jr. and Bruce W. Watson, eds., *China's Military Reforms: International and Domestic Implications* (Boulder, Colo.: Westview Press, 1986); Ellis Joffe, *The Chinese Army after Mao* (Cambridge, Mass.: Harvard University Press, 1987); Monte R. Bullard, *China's Political-Military Evolution: The Party and the Military in the PRC, 1960–1984* (Boulder, Colo.: Westview Press, 1985); and Jane Teufel Dreyer, "The Modernization of China's Military," *Problems of Communism*, vol. xxxix, no. 3 (May–June 1990), 104–121. Also see Ngok Lee, *China's Defence Modernization and Military Leadership* (Canberra: Australian National University Press, 1991).
90. "Chairman Hua's Speech at All-Army Political Work Conference," *Peking Review*, 24 (June 16, 1978), 10.
91. "Vice-Chairman Yeh Chien-ying's Speech," *Peking Review*, 25 (June 23, 1978), 12; also, *Peking Review*, 32 (August 5, 1977), 14.
92. " 'August 1' Army Day," *Beijing Review*, 32 (August 9, 1982), 6.
93. *Ta Kung Pao Weekly Supplement* (August 5, 1982), p. 3.
94. See Drew Middleton, "Supplying Weapons to China," New York Times Service, as reprinted in *Honolulu Star-Bulletin* (April 16, 1981), A-14.
95. *The New York Times* (May 18, 1978), A-6.
96. See Leo Y.Y. Liu, "The Modernization of the Chinese Military," *Current History* (September 1980), 11.
97. *Far Eastern Economic Review* (November 16, 1979), 21–22; and "Premier Hua Visits Italy: Building a Bridge of Friendship," *Beijing Review*, 45 (November 9, 1979), 13–14.
98. See *The New York Times* (May 30, 1980), p. 1; *Honolulu Advertiser* (May 30, 1980), A-1. Also see Christopher F. Chuba, "U.S. Military Support Equipment Sales to PRC," *Asian Survey*, vol. xxi, no. 4 (April 1981), 469–84. Also see Michael Gelter, "U.S. Willing to Sell Military Equipment to the Chinese," Washington Post Service, as reprinted in *Honolulu Advertiser* (January 25, 1981), A-20.
99. *Ming Pao Daily* (Hong Kong) (August 28, 1982), p. 1.
100. *Ming Pao Daily* (Hong Kong) (August 28, 1982), p. 1.
101. *Honolulu Advertiser* (August 21, 1981), B-1.
102. See Jonathan Pollack, *Defense Modernization in the PRC* (The Rand Corporation, N-1214-1-AP, 1979).
103. *Asian Wall Street Journal* (May 5, 1986), p. 1; *Business Week* (October 27, 1985), p. 63. Also see Roger W. Sullivan, "U.S. Military Sales to China: How Long Will the Window-Shopping Last?" *China Business Review* (March–April 1985), 6–9; and *Christian Science Monitor* (October 27, 1983), p. 4, and (June 11, 1984), p. 3.
104. *Ming Pao Daily* (Hong Kong) (May 9, 1986), p. 2.
105. *Asian Wall Street Journal* (May 5, 1986), p. 1 and 7. Also see *Business Week* (October 27, 1985), p. 63.
106. *Far Eastern Economic Review* (December 18, 1986), 23.
107. Ibid.
108. See Christopher F. Chuba, "U.S. Military Support Equipment Sales to the PRC," 483; Francis J. Romance, "Modernization of China's Armed Forces," *Asian Survey*, vol. xx, no. 3 (March 1980), 304–5; and Harlan W. Jencks, "Defending China in 1982," *Current History*, 476 (September 1982), 249.
109. *Peking Review* 21 (May 10, 1977), 18.
110. *Guangming Daily* (January 20, 1977), p. 5.
111. *Ta Kung Pao Weekly Supplement* (Hong Kong) (June 12, 1985), p. 1.
112. *The New York Times* (January 4, 1980), A-3.
113. Middleton, "Supplying Weapons to China"; and Pollack, *Defense Modernization in the PRC*. Also see Angus M. Fraser, "Military Modernization in China," *Problems of Communism* (September–December 1979), 34–49. For an earlier estimate see Edward N. Lutwak, "Problems of Military Modernization for Mainland China," *Issues and Studies*, vol. xiv, no. 7 (July 1978), 58.
114. Drew Middleton, "Sales of Rare Metals May Pay for China's Armed Buildup," New York Times

Service, as reprinted in *Honolulu Star-Bulletin* (December 31, 1981), A-34. Also see Chuba, "U.S. Military Support Equipment Sales to the PRC," 460–84; and Douglas T. Stuart and William T. Tow, "Chinese Military Modernization: The Western Arms Connection," *The China Quarterly*, 90 (June 1982), 262.

115. See Thomas W. Robinson, "Chinese Military Modernization in the 1980s," *The China Quarterly*, 90 (June 1982), 231–51.

116. "The Concept of People's War," p. 3.

117. *Ta Kung Pao Weekly Supplement* (July 29, 1982).

118. Jeffrey Record, "Men, Not Hardware, Still Decisive on Battlefield," Washington Post Service, as reprinted in *Honolulu Advertiser* (December 15, 1982), A-23.

119. Hsu Hsiang-chen, "Heighten Our Vigilance and Get Prepared to Fight a War," *Peking Review*, 32 (August 11, 1978), 8–11.

120. For an assessment of the Chinese military invasion of Vietnam, see Drew Middleton, "China's Lack of Mobility," New York Times News Service feature, reprinted in *Honolulu Star-Bulletin* (March 9, 1979), A-17.

121. See Paul H.B. Godwin, "Overview: China's Defense Modernization," op. cit., pp. 144–45; Robert S. Wong, "China's Evolving Strategic Doctrine," op. cit., pp. 1048–51; Harlan Jencks, "Watching China's Military," op. cit., p. 75; and Andrew Jencks, "People's War Under Modern Conditions: Wishful Thinking, National Suicide or Effective Deterrent," *China Quarterly*, 94 (June 1984), 305–19.

122. *Christian Science Monitor* (October 3, 1983), p. 13.

123. See Eric Hyer, "China's Arms Merchants: Profits in Command," *The China Quarterly*, 132 (December 1992), 1101–18; Dennis Van V. Kickey, "New Directions in China's Arms for Export Policy: An Analysis of China's Military Ties with Iran," *Asian Affairs: An American Review*, vol. 17, no. 1 (1990), 15–29; John Pomfret, "Reform Fuels China's Military Machines," *Asian Wall Street Journal* (30 June 1992), p. 8; and Wendy Frieman, "China's Defence Industries," *The Pacific Review*, vol. 6, no. 1 (1993), 51–62.

124. *The New York Times* (7 June 1987), p. 1.

125. Hyer, "China's Arms Merchants: Profits in Command," 1104.

126. Frieman, "China's Defence Industries," 52.

127. Ann Devroy, "New Evidence of Chinese Arms Sales," *The Washington Post*, reprinted in *The Honolulu Advertiser* (18 May 1993), A-6.

128. Hyer, "China's Arms Merchants: Profits in Command," 1101.

129. Ibid., 1103.

130. Ibid.

131. Ibid., 1105.

132. A *Washington Post* story from the Associated Press as reprinted in summary form in *The Honolulu Advertiser* (4 March 1993), A-12.

133. Frieman, "China's Defence Industries," 51–62. Also see Pomfret, "Reform Fuels China's Military Machine," p. 8 and *Far Eastern Economic Review*, October 14, 1993, pp. 64–66.

134. Frieman, "China's Defence Industries," 53.

135. Peter Grier, "China Arms Policy Puzzles West," *The Christian Science Monitor* (3 July 1992), p. 2.

136. See John L. Lewis, Hua Di and Xue-Letaè, "Beijing's Defense Establishment: Solving the Arms Export Enigma," *International Security*, vol. 15, no. 4 (Spring 1991).

137. Grier, "China Arms Policy Puzzles West."

138. Grier, "China Arms Policy Puzzles West." Also see *Far Eastern Economic Review*, October 14, 1993, p. 64.

139. See *Far Eastern Economic Review* (February 6, 1992), 40–43 and *Far Eastern Economic Review*, October 14, 1993, p. 68.

140. Alastair I. Johnston, "Changing Party–Army Relations in China, 1979–1984," *Asian Survey*, 24, 10 (October 1984), 1015.

141. See *Zhengming*, 111 (January 1987), p. 10.

142. Ibid.

143. See statement made by Xu Xin, PLA deputy chief-of-staff as printed in *Ming Pao Daily* (Hong Kong), (July 26, 1987), p. 1. Also see Jim Mann, "China's Army Backs Deng, Official Says," Los Angeles Times Service as reprinted in *Sunday Honolulu Star-Bulletin and Advertiser* (April 5, 1987), A-14.

144. See Alastair I. Johnston, "Changing Party–Army Relations in China," op. cit.

145. Harlan W. Jencks, *From Muskets to Missiles: Politics and Professionalism in the Chinese Army,*

1945–1984 (Boulder, Colo.: Westview Press, 1982), and his "Party and Military in China: Professionalism in Command?" *Problems of Communism*, 32 (September–October, 1983), 48–63. Also see Alastair Johnston, "Changing Party–Army Relations in China, 1979–1984," *Asian Survey*, xxiv, 10 (October 1984), 1012–39.

146. See Shu-shin Wang, "Revamping China's Military," *Problems of Communism* (March–April, 1985), 111–17.
147. See Parris Chang, "Chinese Politics: Deng's Turbulent Quest," *Problems of Communism*, (January–February, 1986). Also see William W. Whitson and Chen-hsia Huang, *Chinese High Command*, op. cit.
148. Monte R. Bullard and Edward C. O'Dowd, "Defending the Role of the PLA in the Post-Mao Era," *Asian Survey*, xxi, 6 (June 1986), 706–20. Also see Monte R. Bullard, *China's Political-Military Evolution: The Party and the Military in the PRC, 1960–1984* (Boulder, Colo. and London: Westview Press, 1985), p. 143.
149. See *Ming Pao Daily* (Hong Kong) (July 25, 1987), p. 1.
150. *The New York Times* (May 23, 1989), A-5.
151. Article by Yu Bin distributed by the Pacific News Service, as reprinted in the *Honolulu Star-Bulletin* (June 9, 1989), A-20.
152. *The New York Times* (May 23, 1989), A-1.
153. See June Teufel Dreyer, "The People's Liberation Army and the Power Struggle of 1989," *Problems of Communism*, vol. xxxviii, no. 5 (September–October 1989), 42; and *Zhengming* (Hong Kong), 143 (September 1989), p. 6.
154. Dreyer, "The People's Liberation Army," p. 42.
155. *Zhengming* (Hong Kong), 140 (June 1989), 10–11. Also see *The Christian Science Monitor* (May 14, 1990), p. 4.
156. *Zhengming* (Hong Kong), 140 (June 1989), 8 and 43.
157. See *Zhengming* (Hong Kong), 143 (September 1989), 6–7.
158. Ann S. Tyson's figure was based on PLA and Chinese sources in her article, which appeared in *The Christian Science Monitor* (May 14, 1990), p. 4.
159. See Dreyer, "The People's Liberation Army," p. 47.
160. See *Far Eastern Economic Review* (July 6, 1989), 12.
161. Ibid., p. 5.
162. See *People's Daily* (February 28, 1990), p. 1; and *Liberation Army Daily* (February 28, 1990), p. 1.
163. *People's Daily* (March 1, 1990), p. 1.
164. *The Christian Science Monitor* (May 14, 1990), p. 5.
165. *China Daily* (January 23, 1990), p. 1.
166. *Zhengming* (Hong Kong), 149 (March 1990), 6–8; and 147 (January 1990), 10.
167. *Zhengming* (Hong Kong), 155 (September 1990), 6–7.
168. See Harlan W. Jencks, "Civil–Military Relations in China: Tiananmen and After," *Problems of Communism*, XL 3 (May–June 1991), 27–28.

chapter nine

Maoist Mass Participation and Political Action before Deng's Reforms

One of the most dramatic and sometimes frightening aspects of the contemporary Chinese political scene has been the participation of millions of people in mass campaigns waged periodically by the regime for a variety of purposes—from the eradication of pests, to land reform, to socialist education, and finally to the Cultural Revolution. There were more than seventy-four mass campaigns waged on the national level from 1950 to 1978, and perhaps a third of that number waged locally over the same period. The average length of these mass campaigns has been between seventeen and eighteen months.[1] In addition to these campaigns, which generally involved the entire populace, peasants and urban residents were required to participate regularly in some sort of political activity—usually as participating members of "small groups,"[2] the organizational devices used to assure active participation by ordinary citizens in political action. The basic purpose of the extraordinary stress upon active mass participation and periodic Maoist mass campaigns waged prior to Deng's reforms in the early 1980s was to inculcate new values and to induce correct attitudinal and behavioral patterns essential for making political, social, and economic changes necessary in building a socialist society.

Before we take up such pertinent topics as the extent and manner of Maoist mass participation and the style, techniques, and significance of mass campaigns, a few words must be said about the Chinese masses. The Chinese population was estimated at 800 million in the mid-1960s, with a projected 2 percent annual growth rate.[3] This translated into an annual increase of approximately 16 million people in the already enormous population. Based on this projection, there was no question

' would have reached 1 billion. The State
a population of 975 million. In July 1982
ld's largest—assisted by more than five
the United States, and United Nations
eau announced that China's population
; of Taiwan, Hong Kong, and Macao.⁴
ipulation are party members or cadres,
t of the people. Roughly 80 percent of
and the remaining 20 percent reside
as large as that of the United States
ia's huge population is concentrated
..., the Huanghe and the Changjiang, and
....it of the land area is hilly or mountainous and is

ureat strides have been made since 1949 in raising the literacy rate in China.
At present, the literacy rate for adults is more than 65 percent, with a higher rate for
those who live in urban areas.⁵ Adult education, with political education as its main
content, has contributed to the gradual reduction of illiteracy among the adults in
China over the past three decades. While local dialects were a serious barrier to
effective political communication before 1949, adults below the age of 45 today can
converse effectively in the standard spoken language known as "Putonghua." It is a
common sight for visitors to China to see the simplified Chinese written characters
alongside the romanization, for standard uniform pronunciation in schools in various
regions of China. The Chinese masses, both rural and urban were constantly being
exposed before the 1980s to the networks of the political communication system:
controlled mass media in the form of newspapers, radio broadcasts, and wall posters;
the organizational units to which the masses in one way or another had become
attached; and the "small groups," or "xiaozu," into which the masses had been organized and through which mass mobilization efforts were achieved.

In Chapter 3 we discussed in detail the meaning and significance of mass line
in the thought of Mao. We may summarize the concept of Mao's mass line as a
process by which the leaders (cadres) and the people (masses) establish a close relationship: the cadres attempt to obtain willing compliance from the masses. In
essence, the mass line concept, as applied in practice, is a process of "mutual education of leaders and led," by which unity among the masses is achieved on a given
issue, and through which the masses can lend their overwhelming support by participating in the implementation of the decision.⁶ Thus, participation in Chinese politics
involved three sets of actors—the top leadership at the Politburo level, the cadres at
the middle level, and the masses at the bottom—and a host of actions, which included listening, learning, reacting, summing up, interpreting or reinterpreting changing
attitudes, and decision making.

It is plain that, unlike political participation in the United States, where there is
a wide variation in the degree of voluntary political involvement by people at various socioeconomic levels,⁷ a vast majority of Chinese citizens engaged in mandatory
activities. But discretionary participation, such as writing letters to the editors or contacting cadres, was low. It would be somewhat erroneous to assume that the vast
majority of Chinese who participated in formal and legal political activities were
automatically classified as activists. Chairman Mao once said that more than 60 per-

cent of the populace must be considered fence-sitting middle-of-the-roaders, and only about 20 percent as progressives or activists.[8] One study, based on information from refugees from mainland China, on frequency of political participation by mode, indicated that although a majority of Chinese did participate in various forms of political activity, their sincerity in participation varied with the mode: the more formal the mode of participation, the less sincerity there was on the part of the participants.[9] Still, the regime's institutionalization of mass participation in politics and in decision making had been highly successful in the past, especially when one considers the enormous size of China's population. Let us now turn to the fundamental question: in what ways have the Chinese masses participated in politics?

FORMS OF PARTICIPATION IN CHINA

There are a variety of ways in which the Chinese masses have participated in the "democratic management" of their political life. Mao's concept of mass line was enshrined in the 1982 state constitution, promulgated by the Fifth National People's Congress. That constitution states: "All state organs and functionaries must rely on the support of the people, keep close touch with them, heed their opinions and suggestions, accept their supervision and work hard to serve them."[10]

Elections and Voting

While voting in elections may be the single most important act of citizen participation in Western democracies, it is only one form of legally approved political action for the people of China. There are no direct nationwide elections in China. The election process in China also differs from that in Western democracies in several other crucial aspects.

First, the CCP manages the electoral process at all levels. Most important is CCP control of the election committees, which prepare approved slates of candidates for all elective offices, from the national to the basic level. Before 1980 these slates presented only one candidate for each office and thus determined the outcome of the election. Briefly from 1979 to 1980 some county elections for people's congresses allowed campaign rallies with speeches by candidates. The election law enacted in 1981–82 prohibited campaign rallies. The election process was used primarily as a vehicle to arouse interest and heighten political consciousness among the people. In late 1979, deputies to the county people's congresses were elected directly from a slate of candidates by secret ballot by the eligible voters. (The 1980 election of deputies from Hunan Teachers' College in Changsha attracted worldwide attention when students in Changsha demonstrated at the provincial party headquarters to protest school authorities' decision to add another candidate to the final list of nominees in an effort to head off the election of one of the candidates, Liang Heng, who had declared that he did not believe in Marxism.)[11] By 1981 it was reported that 95 percent of the 2,756 local governments at the county level had been elected by people's congresses.[12]

Second, all elections above the basic level are indirect. At the basic level, the people directly elect the people's congresses, according to Article 97. Basic-level congresses elect the county-level congresses, which in turn elect the provincial congresses. The provincial congresses then elect the National People's Congress. There is no breakdown of how many national deputies each provincial people's congress can elect, though 3,497 deputies met in March 1978 for the Fifth National People's Congress to adopt the new state constitution. In compiling the number of deputies to the provincial people's congresses, as reported in the government-controlled media, we arrive at a total of 28,709 deputies for the provinces and autonomous regions. Based on the reports of twenty-five provinces and autonomous regions, there was an average of 1,148 deputies for each province.[13]

Third, while the frequency of elections is prescribed by law, the legal schedule seldom has been followed in practice. There have been nine local elections since the founding of the People's Republic: 1953–54, 1956–57, 1958, 1961, 1963, 1966, 1979–81, 1986–87, and 1992–93. Both the 1953–54 and the 1956 elections had a respectable 86 percent voter turnout, somewhat below the usual turnout of over 90 percent for most communist countries.[14] Unfortunately, we have little information about the local elections after 1956.[15] But based on published accounts by the Chinese for the 1980 county-level elections, the typical local election process seemed to involve a number of procedures.[16] The first stage was the establishment of electoral districts for a county. Election districts were designated as follows: counties, if they had populations between 5,000 and 20,000; townships, if they had populations between 5,000 and 8,000; and industrial units, with requisite populations within the county. The local county and township governments decided their own ratios of population per deputy. For instance, in the local election for Tongxiang county in Zhejiang province in east China, it was decided that there would be one rural county deputy for every 1,600 people, and one township deputy for every 400 people.[17]

A second stage was to publicize the election laws, particularly reforms introduced in 1979, such as direct election at the county level and below, secret ballot, the requirement that a 50 percent majority is needed to win, and the mandate that there be more candidates than the number of elective offices on the ballot. Publicity about the election laws was carried out by "agitprop" teams dispatched to the villages and towns, by radio announcements, by wall posters, and by small study groups.

A third stage involved the registration of eligible voters. Article 34 of the 1982 constitution stipulates that anyone who is a citizen and who is at least 18 years old has the right to vote or to be a candidate for election, except for those deprived of political rights by law.

The fourth stage was the nomination of candidates. The CCP, other minor democratic parties, and the mass organizations were permitted to nominate candidates for election. A voter or a deputy could nominate candidates if seconded by three other persons. At this stage the list of candidates was announced and circulated publicly, and "consultations" were held among the voters' groups within the electoral districts. The purpose of the consultations was to allow the various groups, including the CCP, to screen out candidates and narrow the list to manageable proportions, so that only the preferred candidates could be presented for final balloting. In the case of Tongxiang county's 1980 election, there were more than 6,000 nominations for 500 deputy's seats in the preliminary round.[18] The list was finally narrowed down to a number between 750 and 1,000.[19] A voter could then raise objections to anyone on the list. Of course, most nominees on the list undoubtedly were CCP members. Even though some amendments were introduced in the fall of 1986 to make local direct elections more democratic, the situation remained largely unchanged. For instance, candidates were not to be designated by the higher level, but the practice continued nevertheless.[20] In fact, the December 1986 student demonstration in Anhui was triggered by the undemocratic procedures for local elections, to be discussed shortly. In a report to the March 1987 session of the Sixth NPC, the vice-chairman of its Standing Committee, Chen Pixian, admitted that at the local level voters were to vote for certain pre-designated candidates, and candidates "nominated in a legitimate manner" were to be excluded.[21] The revised election laws also state that no one is to be elected a deputy to the local levels of people's congresses merely as an "honorary title" without considering their qualifications. Evidently, at the grassroots level many elected deputies were not competent to serve or were not able to "handle social and political affairs."[22]

Next, the actual campaign for votes was initiated by the candidates and the voting groups who nominated them. Information about candidates was printed and distributed among the various voter groups and was also disseminated through posters on public bulletin boards and on the radio. Finally, balloting was held on election day, within the various electoral districts. Election day in China usually has been a festive day accompanied by fireworks and the beating of gongs. After the ballots were counted, the newly elected deputies made speeches at meetings called by the elections committee, which certified the final vote count. The institutionalization of direct election at the county level, expected to be extended to the provinces and the nation in the future, may in the long run provide a much healthier means through which popular energy can be channeled than the negative mass campaigns to which China has been accustomed for so long.

It should be noted that direct election of team leaders at the production team level, the lowest accounting and administrative unit in a rural commune, was more meaningful. At this level voting took place at regular intervals to elect cadres for the production team. Even though the slate of cadres to be elected by the team members must be approved by the brigade, the very process of election provided the team members with a significant opportunity to participate in selecting their leaders and, on some occasions, in contributing to the resolution of issues.[23]

Mass Organizations

In China thousands if not millions of people once participated daily in politics as members of a myriad of "mass organizations." These mass organizations have been described as the "organizational matrix" of the party's rule over the masses.[24] They served not only as institutions for political education but also as what Lenin termed the "transmission belt" for party policy. They were used as vehicles to gain support for policies and to mobilize the masses for implementing policies. The once enormous membership and widespread extension of the networks from these mass organizations assured participation in political action by millions of adults and youths. Although mass organizations still exist, they have declined in importance over the last several years. The mass organizations are formed on the basis of special interest or occupation and serve as "bridges and links" between the party and the masses.[25] The four largest and most active mass organizations—the Communist Youth League, the All-China Federation of Trade Unions, the All-China Women's Federation, and the peasants' associations—were reactivated following their disruption during the Cultural Revolution. All held national congresses in the fall of 1978.[26]

The Communist Youth League (CYL) of China reported a membership of over 48 million in 1978 under a new leadership approved by the party. About 26 million, or 54 percent, of the CYL membership were recruited between 1978 and 1982.[27] With the disbanding of the Red Guard organizations for secondary school students in November 1978, the CYL increased in size and importance. For instance, 2.7 million CYL members recruited between 1978 and 1982 were admitted into the CCP.[28] In the past the CYL has served as a vast reservoir for new party members and has provided political ideological education for China's youth. Many of the party's leaders have come up from the ranks of the CYL. Hu Yaobang, the party's former general secretary, was the head of the CYL for many years. Hu Qiaomu, a Politburo member elected in 1982 and director of the party's research department, was also at one time a key figure in the youth league. So was Hu Qili, now director of the Central Committee's General Office. Many secondary school students considered it necessary to join the CYL in order to ensure entrance to universities. Every other day the CYL publishes a journal, *China Youth*, which generally reflects the party's views on youth and their problems.[29] However, in spite of its renewed activities and the ascendance of former officers to positions of influence in the party, very little progress was made in the recruitment of new members for the CYL: 48 million during 1978 and 56 million during 1988, or about 25 percent of China's 250 million youth. Stanley Rosen offered at least two main reasons for the sluggishness in CYL recruitment: CYL's inability to provide channels "for upward mobility" and a decline in the willingness on the part of China's youth to become "activists."[30] In addition, the ideological approach of the CYL is no longer attractive to China's youth. A vice-minister for education reported that while 70–80 percent of Beida students signed up for a course on capitalism, only 7 percent elected Marxian economics for study.[31] As the doors of the universities were closed to a large number of youth and as fewer jobs were available in industries, the CYL was forced to center its work on preparing secondary school students "to lower their aspirations."[32] A survey conducted in the northeastern province of Heilongjiang found that by the mid-1980s students joined the CYL mainly for its educational or recreational activities.[33]

The All-China Federation of Trade Unions, an important mass organization in industrial centers, was most active prior to the Cultural Revolution. The upheaval disrupted the functioning of this workers' organization to such an extent that by January 1967 it was dissolved at both the national and the local levels. Many of the union leaders were purged by the Red Guards and were charged with being followers of the Liu Shaoqi line, with being opposed to the class struggle, and with emphasizing expertise in production.[34] From 1967 to 1973, workers were organized into revolutionary workers' congresses, dominated at the national level by radicals, such as Wang Hongwen and Ni Zhifu. The latter later lent his support to Hua Guofeng. During the period from 1973 to the arrest of the Gang of Four in October 1976, trade union committees in factories functioned as adjuncts of the factory revolutionary committees. These trade union committees were primarily responsible for political education of the workers and supervision of social insurance, welfare, and factory safety measures.[35] Whatever the current organizational structure, workers in factories frequently meet and actively participate in mass action, particularly with regard to production efficiency: "to lower costs, to raise productivity, to stimulate innovation and new design, to develop aspects of decision making, to improve proletarian work style."[36] In an address to the Ninth National Trade Union Congress in October 1978,

Politburo members Deng Xiaoping and Ni Zhifu urged the delegates to support the party's program for modernization and labor discipline and to observe the return to the system of decision making by the factory managers.[37] The role and functions of the All-China Federation of Trade Unions are being altered by changes brought about by economic reforms.[38] As a mass organization, the trade union congress traditionally had been the "transmission belt" for party directives and programs. Introduction of an individualized labor contract system in 1984 specified that industrial workers in a factory be hired based on competitive recruitment rather than assignment by the party. Reformers have advocated that full decision-making authority in factories be placed in the hands of the factory manager or director rather than the factory party secretary. Strong opposition to this reform from the orthodox hard-liners appears to have led to a compromise—a proposed law, drafted under the influence of Peng Zhen, that would place decision making in the workers' congress, which is indirectly controlled by the party branch secretary at the plant.

The All-China Women's Federation once had a membership of close to 100 million. However, it ceased to function as a mass organization in 1967, during the Cultural Revolution. The women's federation's basic function was to mobilize women in support of the various programs initiated by the party. Since women "shouldered half the sky," as the Chinese are fond of saying, this mass organization played an important role in the past in helping to obtain support for party programs and policies and in providing political education for its vast membership. The reactivated All-China Women's Federation selected the following items for its new program: promoting equal pay for equal work, with proper attention to conditions peculiar to women, such as pregnancies and maternity leaves; turning "petty housekeeping" into productive work and providing more time for rest and recreation; developing better educational care for children, and supporting family planning and planned population growth; and developing friendly contacts with women of other countries.[39]

The women's federation is supervised by a 250-member executive committee. The executive committee elects a chairwoman and numerous vice-chairpersons. Its vice-chairpersons generally include prominent women in the CCP and in other minor political parties that accept the leadership of the CCP. The executive committee of the women's federation includes model workers and women who have established reputations in various occupations, such as child care, family planning, health services, education, arts, culture, and sports.

The peasants' associations are another important mass organization. Inactive during the 1950s, the peasants' associations were reestablished in 1963 to serve as watchdog agencies to oversee the work performance and to monitor the behavior of the cadres, many of whom had engaged in antisocialist actions during the early 1960s, such as "eating too much or owning too much, extravagance and waste, nepotism, corruption, theft, and destruction of public property."[40] Under a June 1964 regulation, the peasants' associations were asked to participate in a host of governmental activities: public security surveillance over counterrevolutionary activities, propaganda and educational work among the people, and administrative consultation on commune policies prior to implementing any decisions by the cadres. Since the Cultural Revolution, the party branch at the basic level of rural communes has controlled and manipulated the mass organizations, such as the peasants' associations, the All-China Women's Federation, and the Communist Youth League.

Urban residents are organized into neighborhood communities, the lowest level of mass organization for urban areas. As pointed out in Chapter 7, the resident group is made up of fifteen to forty households. A small group of household representatives discusses and resolves neighborhood problems such as housing, social welfare, sanitation, marriage, and birth control.[41] A primary function of the resident group is political education of members living in the area. Thus, the resident groups in urban areas serve as instruments both for participatory democracy and for mass mobilization. They are comparable to production teams or brigades in rural communes.

Small Study Groups

No discussion of mass participation in China is complete without a close examination of the small group.[42] Across China, cadres in offices, workers in factories, peasants in communes, students in schools, soldiers in the armed forces, and residents in neighborhood committees are organized in small groups, known as the xiaozu. Everyone in China is also identified and referred to by the units (danwei) to which they belong.[43] Whereas a "xiaozu" is a small group formed for a political study purpose, a "danwei" is a larger organizational unit such as an office or a factory or a workplace. Usually the small groups are formed from the members of the lowest organizational unit in factories, offices, and communes.[44] Frequently, an entire class in a school, even at the primary level, becomes a small group.[45] It is a common practice to have representatives of the mass organizations—such as the peasants' associations, the trade union, or the Communist Youth League—work with the party committee at the lowest unit to organize these small groups.

The most important activity of the small groups is political study. In conversation with a small study group in a May Seventh cadre school near Beijing, where I visited in 1973, it was pointed out that political study for the group began with each member studying the works of Marx, Engels, and Mao on his or her own.[46] Sometimes they were asked to study an important editorial or special article in the *People's Daily*. A leader was generally assigned to the study group to answer questions about the reading content. Next, the group studied collectively, both engaging in group discussion and questioning each other's understanding of the reading material. Toward the end of the group's collective study, the group leader entered into the discussion by pointing out the important theoretical points and how they related to correct thinking and behavior, or simply the correct revolutionary line. After grasping the correct line, members of the group engaged in self-criticism for the purpose of making the necessary changes in their thinking and behavioral patterns. The author has been told that during the self-criticism stage, unity is reached by all members of the group on the meaning of the readings for their daily lives. In addition to political studies, small groups engage in problem solving for work units. Empirical studies, using refugees as informants, have indicated problems in the execution of small-group dynamics and have raised questions about the quality and sincerity of members' participation.[47] Boredom, disinterest, and deliberate reticence during group discussions are common in many office and factory units and in production brigades in the communes.

What can be said about the effects of small groups as an organizational technique in terms of implementing Mao's concept of mass line? First, there is no question, as James Townsend concluded, that the small group permitted personal participation in politics and thus made it real and meaningful.[48] Second, it is a very effective device for social control. Martin King Whyte employs a term, the "encapsulation" of the people, to describe how deviant behavior can be identified and corrected through mutual self-criticism and peer pressure.[49] The control that the regime exercises over its disciplined populace on the whole must be attributed to the workings of the small group. Third, it is a vehicle through which the party's directives and policies can be effectively communicated to the masses and can receive the necessary support for implementation. In the 1990s, small group political discussion has been mostly perfunctory if it is even held at work units.

Maoist Mass Campaigns

A Maoist mass campaign in China can be defined as a movement, conceived at the top, that encourages and promotes active participation by the masses in collective action, for the purpose of mobilizing support for or against a particular policy or program. Rarely has an important policy or program been launched without a mass campaign to support it. It is generally easy to detect the launching of such an effort. Since all mass campaigns require the active participation of the masses, the signal, or message, for the start of the campaign must be conveyed either in heavily couched ideological language or in "coded names" form, as Lucian Pye has pointed out.[50] The signal was sent through newspaper editorials or in statements made by key party leaders and displayed in newspaper headlines. First, an important speech—made by a key leader and accompanied by an editorial highlighting the major themes—was disseminated. Soon slogans embodying the key ideas of the campaign, as outlined in the published speech or editorial, appeared in the mastheads of newspapers, on walls, and on banners in communes and factories. These articles and editorials would become basic source material for small-group discussion and study. During the Cultural Revolution, activists in universities and high schools displayed their wall posters (dazibao) to pinpoint a particular theme or target to be struggled against in a campaign. Photographic displays or exhibits illustrating key leaders' ideas also appeared in prominent locations. It was a standard practice, for instance, for the government-owned and controlled printing corporation, the Xinhua Bookstore, to display photo exhibits outside the walls of its branch stores all over China.

Next, massive public rallies and demonstrations were staged and manipulated by the party. The rally in Tiananmen Square (October 24, 1976) for the campaign to criticize the Gang of Four drew a million people. In these campaign kickoffs, leading national, provincial, and local party and government cadres made repetitious speeches, outlining the purpose and targets for the campaign and exhorting the masses to participate and demonstrate their enthusiastic support.

Public rallies and demonstrations were followed by intensive study in numerous small groups, the intensity varying from one basic unit to another. For instance, it was not unusual for some factories to require daily political study by small groups for half an hour to one hour during the evening. Such was the case at the beginning of the anti-Lin Biao campaign in 1972.[51] As the campaign intensified, the small-group study in various basic units also became intense particularly when the stage of criticism and self-criticism was reached. In the early days, when the land reform program was launched, and at the time of the Cultural Revolution, struggle or accusation meetings took place when campaign procedure called for attacks, mostly verbal but sometimes physical, against the "enemy." Some campaigns called for the masses to make a sacrifice for the collective good. Sometimes the deeds of a model hero were used as examples, as in the early phases of the Cultural Revolution, when such PLA heroes as Lei Feng were used as models for emulation.[52]

From an organizational point of view, the key to the success of any mass campaign was in the cadres dispatched from the national and provincial party committees to the basic units in factories and production brigades in the communes. Work teams of these cadres were originally used during the Socialist Education Campaign from 1963 to 1965 to conduct on-the-spot investigations of corruption charges made against suspected cadres in the rural areas. Once the charges were substantiated through the teams' firsthand investigation among the peasants, the members of the teams were responsible for preparing and initiating mass criticism to end the corrupt practices within the cadre ranks. Finally, the teams were to recommend punishment for the wrongdoers and institute necessary changes. During the Cultural Revolution, Mao's thought propaganda teams were recruited among the PLA units and workers, primarily to mobilize the masses through discussion and study of Mao's teachings. Members of the work teams in a mass campaign were campaign supervisors, whose main task was to see that the masses participate in the movement through meetings and study sessions. Millions of cadres must have been recruited in urban areas to form these teams during the campaign against the Gang of Four.

Institutionalized mass campaigns had become an indispensable part of contemporary political life. The fact that there have been more than seventy campaigns waged at the national level since the founding of the republic in 1949 until the mid-1980s testifies to the frequency of their occurrence—an average of two per year. Charles Cell has classified mass campaigns into three basic groupings:[53] (1) campaigns waged on politics and economic development programs, frequently aimed at instituting basic changes; (2) ideological campaigns waged primarily to make social reforms or to induce new social values among the populace; and (3) campaigns waged to weaken or eliminate groups or individuals considered enemies of the people, such as landlords, counterrevolutionaries, and rightist elements. Some major mass campaigns, however, cannot readily be classified into any of these categories because of the multiplicity of themes. The Great Proletarian Cultural Revolution from 1966 to 1976 was such a campaign. However, the leaders now in power have indicated that large-scale mass campaigns cannot be undertaken in the future. They have argued that the large-scale class struggles after 1953 were wrong and were in fact harmful to China's socialist system. There has been no large-scale Maoist mass campaign waged since the 1984 campaign against spiritual pollution.

Wall Posters

Wall posters, a form of political communication closely associated with mass campaigns, have been common in major urban centers in China since the Cultural Revolution. Political messages written by hand on paper of various sizes and colors have been posted on walls and sidewalks in China as a form of protest since the days of the emperors, when this form of petition to redress wrongs was considered a right of the people, though the petitioner risked the consequences of arrest or physical abuse by authorities.

During the guerrilla days, the Chinese communist movement made wall posters a channel through which party members could voice their criticisms or complaints

about inner party affairs. Wall posters were institut
numerous mass campaigns were waged—for example,
campaign. Initially the 1957 campaign called for free cri
the slogan "let a hundred flowers bloom." But when the int
ed to the call by pointing out ills and defects in the Chinese
became the targets for attack, were called "rightists" and "cou
were subjected to vilification and purges. The behavior and thin
tuals were exposed in wall posters. It was then fashionable for a
character poster on a wall or bulletin board of a workplace for the p
ing a colleague or superior for his or her wrong political views, bad
ior, or even private life. Public exposure via wall posters reached its
the Cultural Revolution, when party leaders were attacked by wall poster
information deliberately provided by the radical leaders close to Mao. Li
malicious charges were made frequently, and the attackers were not re
reveal their identities. This practice of making malicious statements against
via wall posters gave the authors license to slander.

Too often these big-character posters publicized unsubstantiated rumor
sheer hearsay, but once posted, they caused irreparable damage to the persons und
attack. Since China is a closed society, wall-postering served a useful purpose, fre
quently giving insights into policy debates or pending inner party struggles among
the top leaders. A large portion of what we learned about the early phase of the Cultural Revolution came from wall posters tacked up by the feuding Red Guards.
Occasionally, wall posters—if they were spontaneous expressions—served as a
barometer of public opinion. The 1976 Tiananmen demonstration probably fell into
this category: poems posted and read orally on that spring Sunday morning conveyed
the public's respect for the departed premier and support for the purged Deng Xiaoping. This event is now viewed as something very positive, presaging the downfall of
the Gang of Four.[54]

In the final analysis, all wall poster campaigns, like all mass campaigns of the
past, can be abruptly terminated by the authorities. The flurry of free expression
exhibited on the Democracy Walls in Beijing was abruptly halted in March 1979 by
the authorities on the ground that it was excessive in criticizing the leaders and the
system. The 1984 spiritual pollution campaign was similarly terminated.

MASS CAMPAIGNS BEFORE DENG'S REFORMS

There have been a total of at least eight major and several minor mass campaigns
waged since the conclusion of the Cultural Revolution. Table 9.1 presents a summary of the general nature and duration of these recent mass movements. The first six
campaigns listed in Table 9.1—anti-Lin Biao, anti-Confucius, *Water Margin*, study
of the dictatorship of the proletariat, anti-capitalist roaders, and anti-Gang of Four—
were rectification campaigns aimed at the problem of leadership tension and crisis.
The modernization campaign launched in 1978 was for both economic and attitudinal purposes. The emulation campaign in railroads and the nationwide sanitation
campaign were directed at specific goals—railway reform and sanitation improvement. The following is a brief account of three important mass campaigns launched
since Mao's death.

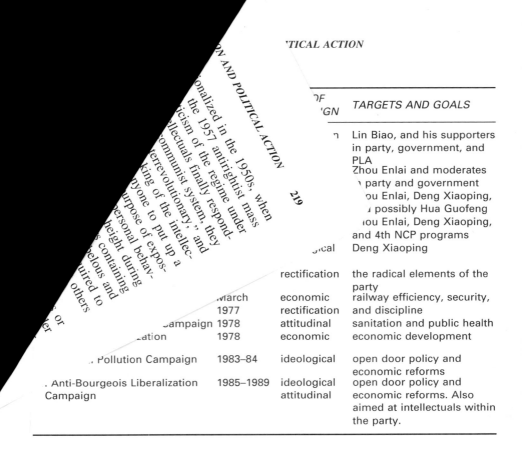

		OF	TARGETS AND GOALS
		'GN	
		า	Lin Biao, and his supporters in party, government, and PLA
			Zhou Enlai and moderates
			า party and government
			ฺou Enlai, Deng Xiaoping,
			ฺ possibly Hua Guofeng
			ฺou Enlai, Deng Xiaoping, and 4th NCP programs
		ฺ.cal	Deng Xiaoping
		rectification	the radical elements of the party
	March 1977	economic rectification	railway efficiency, security, and discipline
ฺampaign 1978		attitudinal	sanitation and public health
ฺation	1978	economic	economic development
. Pollution Campaign	1983–84	ideological	open door policy and economic reforms
. Anti-Bourgeois Liberalization Campaign	1985–1989	ideological attitudinal	open door policy and economic reforms. Also aimed at intellectuals within the party.

The Campaign to Criticize the Gang of Four, December 1976 to January 1978

This campaign was launched officially at the Second National Conference on Agriculture in December 1976. Hua Guofeng outlined the two-step development of the campaign: (1) to expose the radicals' plot to take over the party and state and (2) to reveal and criticize their past "criminal" and "counterrevolutionary" activities.[55] The conduct of this campaign closely followed the pattern of past campaigns that had the sanction of the leaders in control of the party. Party committees at all levels were used as focal centers for implementation. Work teams from urban areas in each province were dispatched to the countryside to help the communes prepare and organize meetings and study sessions. It has been reported that for the first several months of 1977, some 400,000 cadres assigned to these work teams were sent to the countryside in Anhui, Fujian, Henan, Shanxi, and Sichuan provinces alone.[56] The campaign was conducted both in public meetings and in small study groups. The mass media presented daily criticism of the "nation's scourge" (the misdeeds of the Gang of Four), and big-character posters proliferated. In official briefings in factories and communes, foreign visitors were told that production had increased since the downfall of the Gang of Four.

Exposés of various organizational units' struggles against the Gang of Four when they were in power gave a fairly good idea of how the radical leaders "interfered" in the work of every sector of society. They shed light on the conflicts over key issues between the radicals and the Zhou Enlai group. The theoretical group of the prestigious Chinese Academy of Sciences charged that the radicals considered scientific inquiry and pure research as "bourgeois in nature."[57] The mass criticism group of the State Planning Commission revealed that the Gang of Four was opposed to centralized planning, rational industrial management, training of skilled technicians, and importation of advanced technology from abroad.[58] The theoretical study group of the Ministry of Foreign Affairs criticized Jiang Qing for "issuing statements to foreigners without authorization" and for "divulging classified information of the party and the state," as well as for creating confusion in China's foreign trade.[59]

This mass outpouring of criticism against the radical leaders was also being used to mobilize public opinion in favor of the pragmatic policies and programs of Hua Guofeng and Deng Xiaoping, which were basically those endorsed by Zhou Enlai. The exposure of the wrongdoings of the radical leaders was intended to help explain the sweeping reversal of the Cultural Revolution policies of the past decade. The campaign was also intended to create a favorable climate for the new leaders to exercise control over their opposition. From September 1976 to the spring of 1977, there were reports of unrest and disorder in many parts of the country.[60] The intensive mass campaign allowed the new leaders to carry out the necessary purge within the party and governmental apparatus in order to consolidate their power. Hua's political report to the CCP Eleventh Party Congress in August 1977 made it very clear that the mass campaign would eradicate the Gang of Four's "pernicious influence in every field."[61] The purge was to extend to all individuals who were involved in the "conspiratory" activities of the Gang of Four.

The campaign against the Gang of Four was also accompanied by two minor mass movements: the emulation campaign in railway administration and the nationwide sanitation campaign. The first, primarily aimed at the railway workers, was intended to improve the efficiency of the railways. The second was a crash program to improve China's sanitation, and was reminiscent of the mass campaigns to eradicate pests in the early 1950s.

The Campaign against Spiritual Pollution, 1983–1984[62]

The spiritual pollution campaign had its origin in Deng Xiaoping's speech at the second session of the Twelfth CCP Central Committee, held in October 1983. Deng expressed his concern over the Western books, films, music, and audio/video recording tapes (some of which were regarded as vulgar even in Western countries) that accompanied the "open door," or "openness to the West" policy. (See Chapter 12 for more detail.) He issued a blunt warning that, unless some action was taken, the corrupt Western bourgeois culture would soon corrupt China's youth. Following Deng's speech on spiritual pollution, regulations were issued by the Beijing Municipal Government prohibiting, among many other things, long hair and mustaches on males and lipstick or jewelry on females. Within a short span of a few months, the campaign against spiritual pollution escalated into a mass campaign reminiscent of the 1957 antirightist campaign against the intellectuals. Party propaganda officials spoke about keeping the "bourgeois liberalization" trends out by putting in screens "to let in the fresh air but keep the insects out." By November, offices, schools, and factories held weekly study sessions that failed to generate much enthusiasm. There were outright confiscations of publications, videotapes, and films with "pornographic content" representing the "decadent capitalist" lifestyle. Liberal Marxist views were attacked in the mass media because these questioned the validity of socialism.

By the end of 1983 and the first month of 1984 a brake was applied to the spiritual pollution campaign to prevent it from escalating into a mass campaign nationwide. There were several reasons why it was halted. First, the campaign against things Western as bourgeois had affected the confidence of foreign investors—particularly those from the West—about China's ability to keep its door open. More important, perhaps, was the impact the campaign, if allowed to run its normal course, would have on Deng's economic reform that was so crucial to China's modernization. Hu Yaobang, then the party chief, told Western reporters that the Chinese propaganda apparatus had failed to limit the campaign as prescribed by the top leaders. The campaign was supposed to be confined to discussion and criticism within literary, artistic, and ideological circles. But, in this case, either the limit was not very clearly communicated to local party officials or its prescribed parameters were overrun. Thus it escalated into a repeat of the traditional type of mass campaign familiar to all before 1978.

The Anti-Bourgeois Liberalization Campaign, 1985 to 1989

According to a party directive, one of the charges leveled against the ousted party chief Hu Yaobang concerned his decision not to continue the 1983 campaign against "spiritual pollution"; that decision eventually led to the intensification of the anti-bourgeois liberalization campaign in 1985.[63] Hu's critics within the party hierarchy claimed that these two campaigns were "one and the same thing."[64]

To begin with, the sudden termination of the short-lived spiritual pollution campaign was followed by a period of liberalization. Literary and artistic figures, academicians, and intellectuals in general took advantage of another "let a hundred flowers bloom" campaign (the original call for free discussion issued by Mao that preceded the 1957 antirightist campaign) by demanding freedom in artistic expression and academic freedom in scientific research and experimentation. With the open door already an established state policy, Western concepts of democracy and the "freedom to create" surfaced among party reformers and intellectuals. Under the direction of Hu Yaobang and Hu Qili, numerous articles appeared in the media advocating respect for knowledge, talent, and academic research autonomy. Some scientists cried that "only by allowing free discussion can researchers distinguish between true and the false."[65] Fang Lizhi, China's "Sakharov" and professor of astrophysics, who was subsequently ousted as the vice-president of the Chinese University of Science and Technology, spoke of "intellectual ideology" and asserted that "the emergence and development of new theories necessitate creating the atmosphere of democracy and freedom in the universities."[66] However, the party, in clear language, issued the caveat that "freedom to create," or freedom to do research, was not the same thing as freedom of speech.[67]

Advocates for more freedom and less party interference in "artistic creation" and academic inquiry soon became targets for attack by the orthodox hard-liners. Chen Yun, the octogenarian in charge of the party's Discipline Inspection Commission, asked the party to pay serious attention to "decadent capitalist ideology" now surfacing in many areas of the socialist society.[68] Chen was concerned about party cadres and their children who "swarmed forward to do business" in connection with the open door policy.[69] Chen felt that there was some neglect in combating such corrosive ethics as "the capitalist philosophy, 'every man for himself. . .' which gives no regard to national human dignity" and does harm to socialism.[70] Economic crimes committed by cadres, obscene videotapes, and other vices representing "the decadent capitalist ideology which is characterized by the 'worship of money,' is asserting a serious corrosive influence on our party's work, habits, and social mores."[71] Peng Zhen, another critic from the orthodox hard-liners' camp, was concerned more about the publication of articles in the media expressing ideas on the obsolescence of Marxism and the superiority of capitalism. "Marxism-Leninism is revolutionary and not conservative," Peng lashed out at the reformers.[72] Hu Qiaomu, the Politburo member who supported the spiritual pollution campaign and allied with Chen Yu and Peng Zhen, labeled those intellectuals who questioned the validity of socialism and advocated some form of Western freedom as "representatives of bourgeois liberalization in China."[73]

Anti-bourgeois liberalization reached its height as a rectification campaign in early January 1987 when Hu Yaobang was forced to resign his position as the party chief. It was then decided that the campaign would be confined within the party. There was some fear that the campaign might get out of control and degenerate into another anti-intellectual campaign like that of 1957. However, Zhao Ziyang, the acting party chief, reassured everyone that party policy would not permit the campaign to spread outside the party organizations. But evidence seemed to indicate that Zhao's policy was not strictly followed. In a six-day boycott in June 1987, students at the Beijing Central Institute of Finance and Banking protested against the noise from a nearby cigarette factory. The students were ordered to write an essay on why bourgeois liberalization must be opposed, a familiar technique used in all previous mass campaigns that engaged the entire populace.[74] Students were sent down to factories and farms in the countryside as a way of correcting their bourgeois tendencies,[75] another familiar device for punishing dissenters. Zhao Ziyang told the delegates to the Thirteenth Party Congress that the campaign against bourgeois liberalization "has raised people's consciousness and has added to our experience of opposing wrong ideologies through education by positive examples" rather than through "political movements."[76]

The mass campaign, as we have seen in this section, has been a unique form of participation for the people of China. These movements have been employed for a variety of purposes: instilling ideological conformity, developing popular acceptance of economic programs, and resolving intraparty conflicts among leaders at the top. These mass movements also have been used to combat inertia of the masses and the cadres in implementing new economic programs, as well as to restrain cadre corruption by means of mass criticism. The mass campaigns launched in the post-Cultural Revolution era of the 1970s were mainly for rectification, to resolve conflicts among the top elites. In these mass campaigns, the shifting ideological pitch and targets for attack certainly created confusion and uncertainty for the populace as a whole. But, as Alan Liu has pointed out, the integrative effect of these mass campaigns for the Chinese nation has been valuable and lasting in terms of uniformity of language in political expression and the acquisition of the organization skills demanded by mass campaigns.[77] The Chinese, through these mass campaigns, have indeed become "organization people" in a society that traditionally has been full of centrifugal tendencies.

THE ANTI-BOURGEOIS LIBERALIZATION CAMPAIGN
SINCE TIANANMEN

For much of 1987–88, Zhao's attempt to limit the anti-bourgeois liberalization campaign to party organizations ran into opposition from the hard-liners, or gerontocrats, who harped on the lack of ideological leadership exhibited by Zhao, the party chief. At the summer top leadership meetings in Beidahe, the hard-liners pressured Deng to remove Zhao or to force him to make self-criticisms for errors in economic policies and ideological laxity.[78] At one time Zhao indicated his willingness to resign, but was persuaded by Deng to stay on.[79] While the hard-liners insisted on the full implementation of the anti-bourgeois liberalization campaign to prevent what they perceived as erosion of socialist values and rampant Westernization, the people and cadres alike were on the whole unenthusiastic or opposed to the campaign. For many, private enterprise was the new way of life, and they felt that opening up to the outside world was irreversible. In the ongoing battle between the hard-liners and the reformers, intellectuals and writers were expelled from the party. Progressive writers and reporters protested and ceased their writing entirely. Liu Binyan reported that intellectuals in the provinces boycotted the campaign altogether.[80] Chinese studying abroad signed petitions to protest the anti-bourgeois liberalization campaign.

In his June 9 speech to the PLA officers who took part in the crackdown on the students, Deng characterized the protest movement as an attempt to establish "a bourgeois republic entirely dependent on the West."[81] He described the state of affairs in China as "the confrontation between the *Four Cardinal Principles* and the bourgeois liberalization," and blamed the "poor work" done in the last ten years in political and ideological education of the students and masses as the main cause of the "turmoil" sparked by the Tiananmen demonstrations.[82] Jiang Zemin echoed Deng's theme in his speech on September 29, the fortieth anniversary of the founding of the People's Republic of China, saying, "Today, the *Four Cardinal Principles* and bourgeois liberalization stand in diametric opposition." And he called for the implementation of the "Four Basic Principles"—the socialist road, the dictatorship of the proletariat, the leadership of the party, and the study of Marxism-Leninism and Mao's thought—as the party's major task ahead.[83] Jiang emphasized the importance of constant communist ideological education among party members, the Communist Youth League, and advanced elements to resist "the influence of erroneous ideological and decadent ideas."[84] "The campaign is more than an ideological confrontation; it is a political struggle," cried Wang Renzhi, the new head of the party's Propaganda Department.[85]

If stripped of all ideological rhetoric, the campaign degenerated for some time into hostility toward the West. Schoolchildren were studying, as a part of ideological and political education, the Opium War and the injustices of Western imperialism of bygone years. Discussions of Western ideas of democracy and freedom and those officials who were sympathetic to such ideas were in danger of purge, or even arrest. Making contacts with foreigners became a risky business and foreigners were advised to avoid such contact with the Chinese people.[86] By the 1990s, the campaign

against bourgeois liberalization disappeared fr(
ers engaged in the promotion of market soc)
practices by party and government officials.

NOTES

1. Charles P. Cell, *Revolution at Work: Mobilizatio*. 1977).
2. Martin King Whyte, *Small Groups and Political Rituals in Cn*. ifornia Press, 1974).
3. John S. Aird, "Population Growth and Distribution in Mainland China, a. lation Figures," *The China Quarterly*, 73 (March 1978), 35–38, 44.
4. "The World's Biggest Census," *Beijing Review*, 32 (August 9, 1982), 16–25; and "Iı. Results," *Beijing Review*, 45 (November 8, 1982), 20–21. For the twenty-nine provinces, m. ties, and autonomous regions, the population was 1,008,175,288.
5. See Charles S. Taylor and Michael C. Hudson, *World Handbook of Political and Social Indicators* (New Haven, Conn.: Yale University Press, 1972), p. 232.
6. See Jack Gray and Patrick Cavendish, *Chinese Communism in Crisis: Maoism and the Cultural Revolution* (New York: Holt, Rinehart & Winston, 1968); and John W. Lewis, *Leadership in Communist China*, (New York: Holt, Rinehart and Winston) p. 70.
7. See Kenneth Prewitt and Sidney Verba, *Principles Of American Government*, 2nd ed. (New York: Harper & Row, 1977), pp. 65–67.
8. See "Speech at the Lushan Conference, 23 July 1959," in *Chairman Mao Talks to the People*, pp. 134–39.
9. V. C. Falkenheim, "Political Participation in the People's Republic of China" (unpublished paper presented at the 1978 annual meeting of the Association for Asian Studies, Chicago, March 31–April 2, 1978). Permission from author to make this reference.
10. See Article 27 of the 1982 Constitution, in Appendix A.
11. See Fox Butterfield, *China: Alive in the Bitter Sea*, (New York: Times Books, 1982) pp. 421–22. Laing Heng subsequently left China with his wife Judy Shapiro. Together they wrote a biography, *Son of the Revolution* (New York: Alfred A Knopf, 1983). Also see *The New York Times* (October 15, 1980); and Shan Zi, "Election in Changsha," *The Asia Record*, vol. 3, no. 3 (June 1982), 26.
12. "Election at the County Level," *Beijing Review*, 5 (February 1, 1982), 18. For a detailed study of the 1979 election law reform and county-level elections in 1980, see Brantly Womack, "The 1980 County-Level Elections in China: Experiment in Democratic Modernization," *Asian Survey*, vol. xxii, no. 3 (March 1982), 261–77.
13. *Renmin Ribao* (December 10, 1977), p. 1; (December 14, 1977), p. 1; (December 15, 1977), p. 1; (December 20, 1977), p. 1; (December 23, 1977), p. 1; (December 24, 1977), p. 1; (December 27, 1977), p. 1; (December 29, 1977), p. 1; (January 4, 1978), p. 1; (January 6, 1978), p. 1; (January 9, 1978), p. 1; (January 10, 1978), p. 1.
14. See James Townsend, *Political Participation in Communist China* (Berkeley, Calif.: University of California Press, 1969), p. 119. The figure of 86 percent turnout that Townsend used was based on Chinese reports compiled by the Union Research Service, Hong Kong. For a comparative voter turnout in different counties, see Gabriel A. Almond, *Comparative Politics Today: A World View* (Boston: Little, Brown, 1974), p. 60.
15. There are few statistics for local elections except for the 1953–54 election. See Townsend, *Political Participation in Communist China*, pp. 115–36.
16. For Chinese coverage of elections, see "Election of Deputies to a County People's Congress," *Beijing Review*, 8 (February 25, 1980), 11–19; *Beijing Review*, 18 (May 4, 1981), 5; and *Beijing Review*, 5 (February 1, 1982), 13–19. Also see Womack, "The 1980 County-Level Elections in China," pp. 266–70.
17. "Election of Deputies to a County People's Congress," p. 14.
18. Ibid., pp. 16–17.
19. Ibid.
20. See *Beijing Review*, 16 (April 20, 1987), 17, and commentary by a lawyer in a letter to the editor in *The New York Times* (January 16, 1987), p. 22.

(April 13, 1987), 5.

The Election of Production Team Cadres in Rural China: 1958–74," *The China Quar-*
1978), 273–96. For election of shop leaders in a factory, see Zhi Exiang, "The Elec-
Heads," *China Reconstructs*, vol. xxviii, no. 5 (May 1979), 6–8.
ett, *Communist China: The Early Years, 1949–55* (New York: Holt, Rinehart & Winston,
30.
RC's New Labor Organization and Management Policy," *Current Scene*, vol. xv, nos. 11 and
ovember–December 1977), 18–23; and Ni Chih-fu, "Basic Principle for Trade Union Work in
New Period," *Peking Review*, 44 (November 3, 1978), 7–13, 24.
lass Organizations Reactivated," *Peking Review*, 20 (May 19, 1978), 10–13; "Women's Movement
n China: Guiding Concepts and New Tasks," *Peking Review*, 39 (September 29, 1978), 5–11. See
also Ni Chih-fu, "Basic Principle for Trade Union Work in the New Period," p. 24.

27. "Communist Youth League Congress Opens," *Beijing Review*, 52 (December 27, 1982), 4.
28. Ibid.
29. See Butterfield, *China: Alive in the Bitter Sea*, pp. 142–43; Richard Bernstein, *From the Center of the Earth*, (Boston: Little, Brown, 1982), pp. 172–73; and Roger Garside, *Coming Alive: China After Mao*, (New York: McGraw-Hill, 1981), pp. 322–24, 210.
30. Stanley Rosen, "Prosperity, Privatization, and China's Youth," *Problems of Communism*, xxxiv, 2 (March–April, 1985), 26.
31. Ibid., p. 27.
32. Ibid., p. 28.
33. *China News Analysis*, 1328 (February 1, 1987), 2.
34. See *Peking Review*, 4 (January 26, 1968), 7. Also see "China's Trade Unions—An Interview with Chen Yu, Vice-Chairman of All China Federation of Trade Unions," *China Reconstructs*, vol. xxviii, no. 5 (May 1979), 9–12.
35. See Charles Hoffman, "Worker Participation in Chinese Factories," *Modern China: An International Quarterly*, vol. 3, no. 3 (July 1977), 296.
36. Ibid., p. 308.
37. "Greeting the Great Task," *Peking Review*, 42 (October 20, 1978), 5–8; and Ni Chih-fu, "Basic Principle for Trade Union Work," 10–13.
38. *China News Analysis*, 1320 (October 15, 1986), 8.
39. Kang Ke-ching, "Women's Movement in China: Guiding Concepts and New Tasks," *Peking Review*, 39 (September 29, 1978), 8–11. Also see "The Women's Movement in China—An Interview with Lou Qiong," *China Reconstructs*, vol. xxviii, no. 3 (March 1979), 33–36; Butterfield, *China: Alive in the Bitter Sea*, pp. 166–72; and David Bonavia, *The Chinese* (New York: Lippincott & Crowell, 1980), p. 165.
40. CCP Central Committee 23-Point Regulation on Cadres Policy, 1965. For details see Richard Baum, *Prelude to Revolution: Mao, the Party, and the Peasant Question, 1962–66* (New York: Columbia University Press, 1975), pp. 76–82.
41. "The Neighborhood Revolutionary Committee," in *China Reconstructs*, vol. xxii, no. 8 (August 1973), 2–3.
42. For an in-depth study of small groups, see Whyte, *Small Groups and Political Rituals in China*. Also see Townsend, *Political Participation in Communist China*, pp. 174–76.
43. For a more recent account of the small groups, see Butterfield, *China: Alive in the Bitter Sea*, pp. 40–42; and Bonavia, *The Chinese*, pp. 45–46.
44. Whyte, *Small Groups and Political Rituals in China*, p. 172; and Butterfield, *China: Alive in the Bitter Sea*, pp. 40–42, 323–26.
45. Whyte, *Small Groups and Political Rituals in China*, p. 105.
46. See James C. F. Wang, "May 7th Cadre School for Eastern Peking," *The China Quarterly*, 63 (September 1975), 524–25.
47. Whyte, *Small Groups and Political Rituals in China*, pp. 212–13; and Falkenheim, "Political Participation in the People's Republic of China." Permission to use the summary findings of the paper has been given by the author.
48. Townsend, *Political Participation in Communist China*, p. 176.
49. Whyte, *Small Groups and Political Rituals in China*, pp. 15–16, 233.
50. Lucian Pye, "Communications and Chinese Political Culture," *Asian Survey*, vol. xviii, no. 3 (March 1978), 228–30.

51. Conversation with Fred Engst, an American who worked

52. See Mary Sheridan, "The Emulation of Heros," *The Chin* 47–72; and James C. F. Wang, "Values of the Cultural Revolu 27, no. 3 (Summer 1977), 41–46.

53. See Charles P. Cell, "Making the Revolution Work: Mass Mobiliz Republic of China" (unpublished doctoral dissertation, University of M

54. "Tiananmen Incident: Completely Revolutionary Action," *Peking Review*, For examples of the poems posted at Tiananmen, see David S. Zweig, "The tion and the Fall of Teng Hsiao-p'ing," *The China Quarterly*, 74 (March 197 sion of the Tiananmen incident, see "The Truth about the Tiananmen Incident, (December 1, 1978), 6–17.

55. See "Speech at the Second National Conference on Learning from Tachai in Agric *Review*, 1 (January 1, 1977), 37.

56. "Marching to New Victories," *Peking Review*, 10 (March 4, 1977), 13.

57. "A Serious Struggle in Scientific and Technical Circles," *Peking Review*, 16 (April 15, 1976),

58. "Why did the 'Gang of Four' Attack 'The Twenty Points'?" *Peking Review*, 42 (October 14, 1 5–13.

59. "Premier Chou Creatively Carried Out Chairman Mao's Revolutionary Line in Foreign Affairs," *Peking Review*, 5 (January 28, 1977), 6–15.

60. See Jurgen Domes, "China in 1977: Reversal of Verdicts," *Asian Survey*, vol. xviii, no. 1 (January 1978), 3–9; and "The 'Gang of Four' and Hua Kuo-feng: Analysis of Political Events in 1975–76," *The China Quarterly*, 71 (September 1977), 492.

61. "Political Report to the Eleventh National Congress of the Communist Party of China, August 12, 1977," *Peking Review*, 35 (August 26, 1977), 44–45.

62. For a good discussion of the "spiritual pollution" campaign, see Thomas B. Gold, "Just in Time!: China Battles Spiritual Pollution on the Eve of 1984," *Asian Survey*, 24 (September 1984), 948–974, and David Bonavia, "Curbing the Zealots," *Far Eastern Economic Review* (December 15, 1983), 23.

63. See *The New York Times* (March 7, 1987), p. 12, and *Zhengming*, 113 (March 1987), 8.

64. *The New York Times* (March 7, 1987), p. 12.

65. *Beijing Review*, 21 (February 26, 1986), 16.

66. *Beijing Review*, 50 (December 15, 1986), 5, and *Renmin Ribao* (September 21, 1986), p. 3.

67. *Hongqi*, 21 (November 1, 1985), 9–13.

68. *Beijing Review*, 41 (October 14, 1985), 15.

69. Ibid.

70. Ibid.

71. Ibid., 16

72. *Beijing Review*, 20 (May 19, 1986), 15, and *Far Eastern Economic Review* (December 1, 1986), 51.

73. The following issues of *Zhengming*: 89 (March 1985), 7–10; 107 (September 1986), 8–9 and 12–13; and 110 (December 1986), 7–10.

74. See *Honolulu Advertiser* (June 17, 1987), C-1.

75. *Beijing Review*, 15 (April 13, 1987), 4.

76. "Advance Along the Road of Socialism with Chinese Characteristics," *Beijing Review*, 45 (November 9–15, 1987), 24.

77. *Communications and National Integration in Communist·China* (Berkeley, Calif.: University of California Press, 1971), pp. 115–16.

78. *Zhengming*, 131 (September 1988), 6–7, and 8–9. Also see the communique of the 4th Plenary Session of the 13th CCP Central Committee, *Beijing Review* (July 3–9, 1989), 13.

79. *Zhengming*, 132 (October 1988), 9.

80. Liu Binyan, *A Higher Kind of Loyalty* (New York: Pantheon Books, 1990), p. 270.

81. *Beijing Review* (July 10–16, 1989), 18.

82. Ibid., p. 20.

83. *Beijing Review* (October 9–15, 1989), 16.

84. Ibid., p. 20.

85. *Beijing Review* (April 23–29, 1990), 19.

86. See *The Wall Street Journal* (August 23, 1990), A-10.

acy,

ιt,

ιanmen

Mass Movement

CIPATION AND POLITICAL ACTION   227

in a factory in China from 1960–76.
Quarterly, 33 (January–March 1968),
tion," Journal of Communication, vol.

ation Campaigns in the People's
ichigan, 1973), pp. 26–28.
47 (November 24, 1978), 6.
Peita Debate on Educa-
8), 155–57. For a ver-
Peking Review, 45

lture," Peking

24–27.
977),

Before we discuss Chinese student dissent and the Tiananmen mass movement for democracy, we need to place these events in some conceptual framework. We may begin by describing a type of event that occurred frequently, in developing as well as developed nations, during the modern era, particularly during the turbulent times of the 1960s and 1970s—events that have been defined by Gabriel Almond and Bingham Powell as anomic activities. They often have erupted spontaneously in response to pent-up frustrations and the inability of governments to provide solutions to problems that beset societies.[1] Anomic behaviors, episodic and often violent, represent unconventional political action to address grievances and injustices and to demand action for change or reform. For American university students in the 1960s and 1970s, this meant street demonstrations for civil rights, anti-Vietnam war protests, and participatory democracy on campuses. From our American perspective and in view of the success of the civil rights movement and the antiwar demonstrations, Kenneth Prewitt and Sidney Verba, political scientists who have studied citizen participation in American politics, postulate that demonstrations, marches, and violence may be the "new political style."[2] However, direct political action has always been part of America's political process. The Boston Tea Party was a protest against British rule. In the First Amendment, the United States Constitution guarantees citizens the right to petition and to demonstrate peacefully. Some political scientists hold the view that exertion of public pressure on the decision makers through the use of demonstrations or protests may be essential to political change.[3] Protests, of course, are often employed "to resist change as well as to initiate it."[4] While protest politics is not new, it has become more frequent and more important in American politics since the 1960s. Whenever a large segment of the population takes part in a demonstration or protest, it can be considered an effective form of political participation. Finally, as pointed out by Almond and Powell, anomic political behavior can be the result of planning rather than spontaneity, or it may be the result of prolonged frustration and indignation.[5]

Now back to student protests in China. There has been a tradition in modern Chinese history to view protests and demonstrations by high school and college students as necessary anomic political behavior in the republican eras, beginning with the May Fourth Movement in 1919, to force change on the government, be it against warlords or the Nationalists. It will be recalled that the 1919 May Fourth Movement was a reaction by Chinese intellectuals to the encroachment of the West and Japan on Chinese political independence and territorial integrity. It also represented China's desperate search for ways to modernize the nation. Since then, student demonstrations have been the harbinger of change. Many leading members of the Chinese Communist Party made their debut in politics as participants in student demonstrations in the 1930s. The pages of modern Chinese history are colored with student demonstrations or similar anomic political behavior that too often ended in tragedy and bloodshed.

DEMOCRACY AND DISSENT IN CHINA: PROBLEMS IN EXERCISING POLITICAL RIGHTS

It is ironic to note that every constitution promulgated in China since 1954 has guaranteed certain basic political rights to citizens, but in practice these rights have on the whole been ignored by the party and government. The 1982 constitution is no exception. Article 35 of the 1982 constitution states that citizens of China "enjoy freedom of speech, of the press, of assembly, of association, of procession and of demonstration." On the surface, these words sound like the civil liberties guaranteed by the First Amendment in the American Constitution. In reality, the exercise of these "fundamental rights" by the citizens of China has always been restrained and restricted within the confines of the "Four Basic Principles," interpreted by Deng Xiaoping in 1978–79 to mean that the exercise of these political rights is guaranteed so long as they are not in conflict with "the socialist road, people's democratic dictatorship, leadership of the party, and essence of Marxism-Leninism-Mao's Thought." The following are case studies that illustrate the problem.

The Democracy Wall Movement Since 1978–1979[6]

For more than a year, between November 1978 and December 1979, worldwide attention was focused on the daily posting of handwritten messages on a brick wall, 12 feet in height and about 120 feet long, located at Changan Avenue near the Xidan crossing in the western district of downtown Beijing. Later, this wall came to be known as the Democracy Wall. Initially the appearance of the wall posters at the Xidan crossing may have had the blessing of the leadership faction, following the practice established during the early days of the Cultural Revolution. Some of the contents may have been leaked deliberately to the activists, who then aired them in the posters.

In March 1978 the first series of wall posters, in the form of poems, appeared on the Xidan Democracy Wall. Wu De, then the mayor of Beijing, and the Politburo members who had read the riot act to the 1976 demonstrators at Tiananmen, were attacked by name in the wall posters by some of the participants in the 1976 demonstration. This seemed to have signaled the events to come. The first officially approved act was the publication of a demand for a reversal of the verdict on the 1976 Tiananmen demonstration in the CYL periodical. By October 11, 1978, Wu was forced to resign as mayor of Beijing, and shortly thereafter hundreds of participants arrested in the 1976 Tiananmen riot were released and exonerated. During late October and early November, a sudden release of pent-up feelings increased the output of posters dramatically. This seemingly spontaneous outpouring of wall posters on the Democracy Wall might have coincided with the convening of the party's central work conference, which was planning the Third Plenum of the Eleventh Central Committee. During this period the leaders under Deng had locked horns with the "Whatever" faction on issues such as the new ideological line of "seeking truth from fact," the reversal of the 1976 Tiananmen demonstration verdict, the rehabilitation and exoneration of purged leaders of the Cultural Revolution, and, most important of all, the assessment of Mao and his role in the Cultural Revolution.

A study of the wall posters for that period revealed three main trends: the condemnation of political persecution authorized by Mao; petitions for the redress of personal grievances inflicted upon those who were persecuted during the Cultural Revolution; and the advocacy of democracy, justice, and human rights.[7] The proliferation of wall posters provided Deng Xiaoping with public support in his contest for power against the "Whatever" faction at the party's Third Plenum. As if by coincidence, decisions adopted by the party were identical to the concerns expressed by the posters on the Democracy Wall. For instance, the Third Plenum corrected the "erroneous conclusions" on veteran party leaders such as Peng Dehuai, Bo Yibo, and Yang Shangkun by exonerating and rehabilitating them.[8] The plenum also declared that the Tiananmen events of 1976 were "revolutionary actions."[9] It adopted the ideological line that "practice is the sole criterion for testing truth."[10] It was also decided to establish a discipline inspection commission within the party to enforce and investigate violation of party rules and regulations. While the plenum did not yet make an assessment of Mao's role in the Cultural Revolution, it hinted strongly that Mao, as a Marxist revolutionary leader, could not possibly be free of "shortcomings and errors."[11] It became evident that Deng Xiaoping had encouraged the wall posters when he told both a group of Japanese visitors and then Robert Novak, an American syndicated newspaper columnist, that the wall posters were officially tolerated.[12]

The Democracy Wall movement entered its second phase early in December 1978. In addition to candid expressions in support of sexual freedom and human rights, some criticisms of Deng Xiaoping now appeared. Deng then shifted his earlier stand and now expressed disapproval of the posters' criticism of the socialist system. There may have been other reasons for Deng's change of mind. It is possible that Deng had been subjected to criticism within the party for not having taken a stronger stand to curb the expressions of dissent at the Democracy Wall—members of the "Whatever" faction still sat on the Politburo even though they were criticized for their past role in the Cultural Revolution. Perhaps genuine concern about restoring stability and unity led to curbing the freewheeling activities at the wall. It was also very possible that Deng and his intimate colleagues were really apprehensive about the close contacts established by the participants with the foreign reporters who had been invited into the dissenters' homes to talk about democracy and human rights.[13]

During December 1978 activists associated with the Democracy Wall movement became dissatisfied with the success of their poster campaign and looked for ways to expand the campaign. They formed dissident organizations and study groups with names such as Enlightenment Society, China Human Rights Alliance, and the Thaw Society. Each published its own underground journals and offered them for sale at the Democracy Wall. Most publications were poorly produced with primitive mimeograph machines. Nevertheless, some of the underground publications soon attracted worldwide attention as American, British, Canadian, and French reporters were given copies for overseas consumption. Excerpts from underground journals, such as *Beijing Spring*, obviously inspired by the 1968 "Prague Spring" of the Soviet invasion of Czechoslovakia; *April Fifth Forum*, derived from the demonstration at Tiananmen on April 5, 1976; and *Tansuo (Exploration)*[14] were translated and published in foreign newspapers all over the world. The appearance of these underground journals, and the topics they discussed (freedom of speech, democracy, law and justice, human rights, and modernization of science and technology) were reminiscent of the May Fourth Movement sixty years earlier. The new movement spread to many provinces and cities in China. It also tried to forge an alliance with the many protest groups formed by demobilized soldiers and peasants who came to Beijing in increasing numbers. Then China launched its border war with Vietnam. Pressures now mounted on Deng Xiaoping to curb the dissident movement.

It was reported on March 16, 1979 that Deng informed the senior cadres of central government departments that a ban would be imposed on activities at the Democracy Wall.[15] When news of Deng's decision leaked out, Wei Jingsheng, an articulate editor, published an attack on Deng in a special issue of his underground journal, *Tansuo (Exploration)*. Deng did not at first place an immediate ban on dissident activities at the Democracy Wall. Instead, he outlined the "Four Basic Principles," which held that officials could accept wall poster dissent if it upheld the socialist road, the dictatorship of the proletariat, the leadership of the party, and Marxism-Leninism and Mao's thought.[16] Wei's editorials had slandered Marxism-Leninism and Mao's thought and had advocated the abandonment of the socialist system. Wei was arrested on March 29 along with thirty other dissidents. Simultaneously, the government-controlled mass media strongly criticized activities at the Democracy Wall. While the dissidents were under arrest, wall posters were allowed on the Democracy Wall, including ones that accused two leaders of the "Whatever" faction (Wang Dongxing and Chen Xilian) of alleged financial irregularities and misconduct. These wall posters were believed to have been sanctioned by the Deng group in its move to oust Politburo members who were key figures in the "Whatever" faction.[17]

Wei was not brought to trial until October 16; in a one-day trial he was sentenced to fifteen years' imprisonment for having supplied military intelligence to Western reporters (including names of commanders and troop numbers in China's war with Vietnam), for slandering Marxism-Leninism, and for encouraging the overthrow of the socialist system.[18] Wei subsequently appealed to the Beijing Municipal Higher Court, but his plea was rejected.[19] Meanwhile, on the recommendation of the Standing Committee of the National People's Congress, the Beijing Municipal Revolutionary Committee issued an order on December 6, 1979, which (1) prohibited wall posters on the Democracy Wall at Xidan but allowed such activities to take place at the Moon Altar Park, an area removed from downtown Beijing; (2) required registration of all those who wanted to display wall posters at the new site; (3) declared unlawful any disclosure of "state secrets" and false information; and (4) imposed punishments on those who created disturbances or riots at the new site.[20] On the night of December 7, a cleaning crew whitewashed the remaining posters still glued to the Democracy Wall at Xidan and thus ended the second phase of a movement that had attracted worldwide attention. (Wei was finally released from prison on September 13, 1993.)

The final phase of the Democracy Wall movement came in February 1980, when the Fifth Plenum of the Eleventh Central Committee decided to rehabilitate Liu Shaoqi, to remove the "Whatever" faction leaders from the Politburo, and to install Deng's close supporters Hu Yaobang and Zhao Ziyang to membership in the Politburo's Standing Committee.[21] With the removal of the "Whatever" faction from the Politburo, Deng proceeded to remove the last vestige of the Cultural Revolution: Article 45 of the 1978 state constitution, known as the "Sida" or the "four big rights"—*daming* ("speak out freely"), *dafang* ("air views fully"), *dabianlun* ("hold great debate"), and *dazibao* ("put up big-character posters"). In Deng's view the four big rights "had never played a positive role in safeguarding the people's democratic rights."[22] Instead, Deng argued that they had become weapons and tools employed by ultra-leftists like Lin Biao and the Gang of Four to advance their aims.[23] It was now the party's view that the very use of these rights had caused chaos during the Cultural Revolution decade. The wall posters, it was now charged, tended to incite "anarchism" and "factionalism."[24] Thus, Article 45 needed to be stricken from the 1978 constitution if political unity and stability were to be preserved.[25] The National People's Congress in its third session endorsed the party's stand, amending the 1978 constitution by deleting the "Sida" rights.[26] The removal of Article 45 ended China's youthful dissenters' brief flirtation with democracy and human rights. Having been encouraged initially by the forces under Deng to exercise the "Sida" rights, particularly the use of wall posters, to discredit Deng's opponents on the Politburo, the young dissenters were then "betrayed" by Deng as he gained power and control in the party and government. However, it might also be argued that to Deng and his colleagues, victims of the Cultural Revolution, any appearance of anarchy and chaos, reinforced by the pent-up energy and frustration of the young, constituted a serious threat to China's political stability. Deng and his supporters believed that the energy of the people must be directed toward modernization, not toward dissent. It could also be true, as many Western reporters and diplomats believe, that Deng had to crack down on the movement as a "tradeoff" for support from other leaders in his maneuvers to consolidate his power.[27]

STUDENT DEMONSTRATIONS FOR DEMOCRACY AND POLITICAL REFORM, 1986–1987

While 1985 was marked by the successful reshuffle of the Politburo, achieved by promoting a number of Deng's younger supporters, 1986 was marred by criticism and challenge mounted by the orthodox hard-liners that culminated by year's end with a massive student protest movement and the ouster of the party chief, Hu

Yaobang. The main cause of the student protests seemed to be the lack of democratic procedures in local direct elections and the slow pace of political reform. Once again Chinese university students dared to jeopardize their future careers by expressing dissent and criticism over the fundamental question in Chinese politics: the legitimacy of CCP rule.

On December 9, 1986, the anniversary of the 1935 nationwide protest against Japan's attack on China, students at the Anhui provincial capitol's China University of Science and Technology, known as "Keda," in Hefei and those in the city of Wuhan in Hubei province took to the streets, simultaneously chanting slogans for democracy and political reform. In the beginning the size of these protests was small. But, by December 12, the Hefei demonstration was estimated at 17,000. That same day the first of a series of big-character wall posters appeared on the campus of Beida in Beijing, the nation's capital, but without any street demonstration by the students. However, student demonstrations appeared on university campuses in six different provinces following the December 9 protests in Hefei and Wuhan.[28] On December 18, some 2,000 students marched on the streets of Kunming in the southwest. This demonstration was followed by a much larger student gathering in Shanghai. The number of protesters there was estimated from an official low count of 10,000 to more than 35,000 by Western observers.[29] On December 23, several thousand students from Quinghua University in Beijing took to the streets in freezing weather.[30] But much of the world's attention was drawn to the Shanghai protests, which involved students from fifty campuses in and around the largest city in China. The December 21 student demonstration in Shanghai was joined by industrial workers—a significant new development feared by the authorities.[31] At this point, student protests had spread to cities in eleven provinces.[32] On December 20, Beijing municipal authorities issued a set of regulations that made demonstrations and parades illegal unless permits were obtained five days before the event. Protest activities were also prohibited in areas that housed party and government offices.[33] Despite the ban, 3,000 students from Beida and some 5,000 more students from the People's University in Beijing staged their protests on Tiananmen Square on New Year's Day, 1987. The parade signaled a direct challenge to the authorities who had banned such activity in the capital. The next day, student protesters burned copies of the *Beijing Daily* for its inaccurate and distorted reporting on student demonstrations. At least twenty-four students were arrested on the square by the public security personnel, but released shortly thereafter.[34] Through a variety of means—including appeals from families of students, official warnings, propaganda in the media, rebukes from workers and peasants on television and radio, and deliberate isolation of students from the press—the wave of student protests was finally terminated.[35] Chinese officials attempted to minimize the magnitude of university student involvement in these protests by claiming that not more than a total of 40,000 had participated in the demonstrations, about 2 percent of the two million university students in China.[36]

By analyzing slogans, wall posters, and interviews with the protesters, it appears that student demands fell into four main categories: (1) democratization of local NPC election procedure; (2) the question of the party's legitimacy to rule; (3) exercise of basic freedoms; and (4) accelerating the tempo of political reform. In addition, the slogans and wall posters also revealed concerns about making decisions on their own careers, reform in higher education, and the rising consumer prices in urban areas.

The spark that initially ignited the student protests in Hefei and Wuhan was the undemocratic procedures superimposed on the nomination of candidates for local direct election to district NPC delegateship. What started out as a local issue soon spread like wildfire and expanded to the whole range of related issues of political rights and democracy. The issue of Hefei's Keda demonstration was the students' protest against the manner by which six candidates were nominated to represent the university district at the local NPC election. The issue was soon taken up by the protesters in Wuhan and Shanghai. The students wanted the right to nominate their own candidates and to campaign for nominated candidates before an election. Keda Vice-President Fang Lizhi later complained that students did not know anything about the six candidates proposed for the basic level, thus depriving the students of freedom of choice.[37] Another student protester offered the view that "people should be able to choose some of their representatives."[38]

On the issue of the party's legitimacy, student dissenters from 1986 to 1987 were quite blunt when they questioned the party's monopolizing power. In a dramatic encounter with the students in Shanghai, the city's party secretary was booed and was asked who, in fact, elected him in the first place.[39] A Beida student protester pointed out the need for more than one party and his preference for a multi-party system as in Japan.[40] Wall posters on display on the campus of Beida contained expressions such as: "Must we always obey the party?," "By party leadership, does it mean we cannot criticize the party?," "Party dictatorship that monopolizes everything will in the end bring despotism," "Party power must be checked and balanced," and "There must be separation of party and government."[41] In short, these expressions served as direct challenges to Deng's Four Basic Principles, which placed the party leadership at the center.

Students' demand for fundamental political freedoms, as seen from the wall posters, focused on the lack of free speech and a free press. They argued that it was necessary to put up the posters because it was "the only way to express opinions," and the wall posters became "the tool of speech and expression."[42] On many campuses it was a common practice to hold "bedroom conferences" in student dormitories to discuss issues of concern freely.[43] One issue that seemed to have been shared by all protesting university students was the lack of freedom and independence to choose their own careers. Wall posters demanded "self-determination" for their own lives.[44] With personal frustration came cynicism toward their own university educations, which did not even allow them to choose their own course work. The frustration and cynicism easily extended to doubts about socialism and the party's tight grip that monopolized power. Student dissenters in one Shanghai university issued a "manifesto" demanding the propagation of democratic ideals, opposition to bureaucratism, and greater freedom.[45] In defiance of Deng's Four Basic Principles, a Beida student told a Western reporter that he wanted "Western-style democracy and multi-party system."[46] An eight-page poster on the Beida campus stated bluntly that Western democracy was a better alternative for China.[47]

Student protesters' demand for democracy was also influenced by the extensive discussion on political reform in the summer of 1986, when mass media generated numerous articles and reports about the debate by party leaders on the issue. (See Chapter 4.) Student discussion of political reform at Hefei's Keda was singled out as a model in the early fall of 1986. The *People's Daily* ran a series of five articles in October and November, evidently with the backing of the reform leaders.[48] Fang Lizhi, the vice-president from Keda, was the most frequently quoted speaker on political reform by the mass media as he lectured at many universities in eastern China. Fang's ideas about the university as a marketplace of ideas freely exchanged, his criticism of the failure of socialism for thirty years in China, his advocacy of "complete Westernization," his criticism of Deng's Four Basic Principles as dogmatic, and, finally, his charge that democracy could only come from below and from individuals but not from above—all of these statements were well-publicized when the students took to the streets in early December in Hefei. Fang had told the university students that the power of the government came from the people, not from the party in control. He said that the NPC must not always be in unanimous agreement or be a perennial "rubber-stamp" to the party. Obviously referring to the short-lived spiritual pollution campaign from 1983 to 1984, Fang urged China to compete with the "assaults of Western culture, ideas, and goods" in order to yield better "ideological results."[49] He even jokingly wrote that "China not only should import new technology, but what is more important, China should import a prime minister."[50] Vividly displayed on Tiananmen Square was the slogan: "Support Reform."[51] To the student dissenters, protests and demonstrations "would serve as catalysts for further political reform."[52]

What were the consequences of the protests? One thing seems certain: there would be more time spent on ideological studies by the students. When Deng came to power in 1978, he vowed to reduce the time spent on political and ideological education in factories and schools. He wanted everyone to work hard and engage less in "empty talk." Now that approach might have to be modified in the light of the students' protests. A typical official response to the unrest was that more ideological work for students was necessary.[53] But if more ideological study were to be reimposed on university campuses, the party could be on the horns of a dilemma. To insist that more time be spent on ideological study could increase discontent and frustration among students. As pointed out in Chapter 3, few students today want to study Marxist ideology and economics on university campuses.[54] Past records show that the experience of students who spent time and effort on ideological studies was mostly negative.[55] To revive ideological studies in the universities might only build up more resentment and cynicism, sowing the seeds of future discontent and unrest among China's youth.

Another possible consequence to students, beyond additional ideological study, was the threat of being sent to do manual labor in factories and on farms in the countryside. He Dongchang, vice-minister for education, urged the revival of this Cultural Revolution practice as ideologically sound. An editorial comment was published later which stated that

> Correcting the mistakes of the Cultural Revolution does not mean negating the correct approaches such as integrating theory with practice, intellectuals with workers and farmers, and education with productive labor.[56]

The editorial comment added that manual labor for intellectuals was different from the "leftist mistakes" of the Cultural Revolution by rationalizing that "these activities will not affect normal teaching or lowering the colleges' theoretical requirement."[57] (He seemed to have forgotten the excessive application of Marxist theories during the Cultural Revolution.) A call was issued by CYL officials for students to offer themselves for work in "construction teams or battalions" or be sent down to poor areas to acquire practical experience.[58] The most immediate consequence to be felt personally by the student protesters was the fear that the party and government would institute punishment by assigning them to "undesirable jobs" upon graduation. The fear was intensified when the vice-minister for education indicated that "the employing organizations had the right to make their own choices," even if the party and government forgave them.[59]

Finally, there were signs of retrenchment in the push for more thorough political reform, even though Deng had indicated the speed-up on the eve of the Thirteenth Party Congress. Control would have to be reimposed on debates about political reform after a six-month freedom allowing lively discussion in the media and at the university campuses. The reformers' call for a revival of Mao's 1957 "let a hundred flowers bloom" concept had been muted since the January 1987 crackdown on the student protests, despite official insistence that it had not yet been abandoned. More importantly, Chinese intellectuals were once again silenced under the renewed campaign against "bourgeois liberalization." Officially, student protests were said to have been influenced by the intellectuals' call for "complete Westernization." Editorials from the *People's Daily* repeatedly called for party members to oppose "bourgeois liberalization," which now was defined as the "denial of the socialist system and the advocacy of the capitalist system."[60] The message was quite clear that the exploration of new ideas for political reform, which Fang Lizhi and others pushed for briefly in 1986, had to be stopped, and that there definitely were limits to criticizing and challenging the basic tenets of socialism. Thus, ironically, while the student protests and dissent in the winter of 1986–87 were motivated by the desire of the university students—the cream of China's future—to "quicken the pace" of political reform, these very disturbances in the end only made the CCP leadership on both ends of the opinion spectrum cautious about reform. In the final analysis, they dimmed the prospects for genuine political reform in China.

THE TIANANMEN MASS MOVEMENT: APRIL–JUNE 1989[61]

Reform in China entered a critical period from the summer of 1988 to the spring of 1989. The reformers' retail price reform, initiated by party chief Zhao Ziyang, had generated seemingly uncontrolled inflation of more than 30 percent. The government was experiencing a severe financial deficit and a host of other problems. The crime rate was rising rapidly and the nagging problem of widespread official corruption, brought on by economic reforms and the relaxation of control, became a source of major popular complaint. Leaders of the old generation expressed fear of the gradual erosion of socialist moral values such as selflessness and concern for the collective welfare.

Even more alarming to the old revolutionary veterans was the rising criticism by the intellectuals and concerned party members of the party's continued authoritarian rule and monopoly of power. Writers and scholars, many of them members of the party, demanded the release of political prisoners and observance of human rights. They not only expressed opposition to the mass campaigns of spiritual pollution and anti-bourgeois liberalization, but demanded political reform that would include proposals for a multi-party system and the speed-up of the privatization of enterprises. Zhao was already under attack by the hard-liners, made up mostly of old party conservative veterans, for not implementing fully the anti-bourgeois campaign, despite Zhao's attempt to appease the hard-liners by criticizing the intellectuals. The reform-minded intellectuals, protégés of the deposed Hu Yaobang and supporters of Zhao, needed a voice in the party's inner circle. Hu rose to the occasion, for he was still a member of the Politburo. Speaking at the April 8 enlarged meeting of the Politburo, he stated the case for the intellectuals and reformers in an emotional speech that was highly critical of the party for the poor state of education and the lack of improvement in the lives of the intellectuals. Additionally, Hu cited grain production problems.[62] Evidently under great emotional strain, Hu collapsed without completing his statement.[63] He was hospitalized and then went home to recuperate from a known heart problem.

However, the seeds of the 1989 Tiananmen protest were actually planted in the student demonstrations during 1986 and 1987. While those were terminated without bloodshed, the events that culminated in the removal of Hu Yaobang set the stage for an ongoing debate over the nature of Chinese socialism and the pace of economic and political reform. For much of 1988 and the early months of 1989, Chinese students abroad and intellectuals at home, many of them party members, petitioned the party in open letters for radical solutions to China's problems. There was a rising wave of intellectual discontent and criticism of the regime. It was against this background of dissent, coupled with the rising inflation and official corruption, that the spontaneous, student-led mass movement emerged in April 1989.

Genesis of the Protest[64]

University students at Beida, in cooperation with students from the People's University and the Central Institute for National Minorities, met secretly in the spring of 1988 to plan a national signature drive that would bring to the attention of CCP leaders—particularly Deng Xiaoping, Zhao Ziyang, Li Peng, and Wan Li—the problems of inflation, neglect of workers' living conditions, and lack of improvement in education.[65] Typically, the official response to the student unrest was to impose military training on the students or traditional downward transfer of students to factories and farms for the summer months.

For the university students there were the ringing messages of Fang Lizhi, who was invited to the Beida campus as an alumnus to give a lecture in early May commemorating the ninetieth anniversary of Beida's founding. Fang, already ousted from party membership and severely criticized by Deng, made three points: (1) there must be freedom of thought and speech; (2) modernization and science must be accompanied by democratic development; and (3) since the realization of democracy requires hard struggle, its attainment would be a complex process.[66]

The simmering student yearning for democracy and freedom of the press found expression a year later. A demonstration was planned for the seventieth anniversary of the 1919 May Fourth Movement. But the death on April 15 of Hu Yaobang, the deposed party chief, made it necessary for the student leaders to move up the date of the demonstration. For the second time in recent history, the death of a leader became the occasion for massive spontaneous demonstrations at Tiananmen. (The first time was April 1976 on the death of Zhou Enlai.) On the evening of Hu's death, poetry and commemorative mourning material appeared on the Beida campus. On April 16, the next day, students from five universities in Beijing—Beida, Qinghua,

Beijing Normal, Beijing Institute of Politics and Law, and the People's University—used the memorial for Hu as an occasion for criticism of the party. On April 17, Wang Dan, the student leader at Beida, made a speech in praise of the deceased Hu at a campus gathering. About one hundred students were in attendance. On the spot they decided to march on campus. Soon the modest gathering had swelled to about 5,000 students and it was decided to march for a distance of about 25 miles from the campus on the eastern side of the city to Tiananmen Square, at the heart of Beijing. Amidst shouting of slogans such as "Long Live Democracy" and "Down with Party Bureaucracy," there erupted, like a slow but steadily active volcano, the 1989 Tiananmen student demonstration that rocked China and captivated the world's attention for almost two months via live television coverage.

On April 18 there were approximately 100,000 student demonstrators at Tiananmen. They presented a list of demands:[67] the reevaluation of Hu Yaobang's career before his dismissal; the rehabilitation of three leading intellectuals—Fang Lizhi, Wang Ruowang, and Liu Binyan; public disclosure of party leaders' and their children's finances; freedom of the press; an increase in funding for education and the proper treatment of intellectuals; cancellation of the city's regulations against demonstrators; and reevaluation of the 1986 student protest movement. On April 19 these student demands on petitions were carried by 5,000 marchers to Zhongnanhai, the compound that houses the party and its leaders. The student marchers demanded a dialogue with the leaders, but they were met by police, who dispersed them.[68] At 10 o'clock that evening another demand for dialogue was made, with students shouting for Li Peng, the premier, to come out and receive them instead of sending three members of the National People's Congress. This was unavailing. On the morning of April 20, a contingent of 5,000 students marched again to Zhongnanhai to demand a dialogue with party leaders. This time, not only was there no dialogue, but they were attacked and beaten by the police. The marchers retreated to the square. The beating of the students prompted a group of 140 university professors to issue an open letter to the National People's Congress to force the leaders to have a dialogue with the students. The brutal treatment by the police also aroused concern and sympathy from many Beijing residents, who provided aid to the injured and now hungry students.

While the official memorial service for Hu Yaobang was being held inside the Great Hall of the People on April 22, attended by all the top leaders, including Deng Xiaoping and Li Peng, some 80,000 students were conducting their own memorial ceremonies on the square despite the city's last-minute curfew for the area. As the leaders were departing through the north gate of the Great Hall without confronting the demonstrating students, three student representatives went up the steps and knelt there for about forty minutes, appealing without avail for a dialogue with Premier Li. Meanwhile, the funeral cortege left the Great Hall on the square by a different route. The funeral procession was viewed in silence by over a million Beijing residents; some mourners wept.

By April 21–22 there were about 200,000 student marchers on the square, augmented by contingents from institutions of higher learning from Shanghai and nearby Tianjin, in addition to the students from some 30 universities in the Beijing area. They were coordinated by an interim student alliance or association formed under the leadership of Wuer Kaixi, Wang Dan, and a few others. Elsewhere in China there were riots: in Xian in the northwest, and in Chengsha and Wuhan in central China. The student marchers at Tiananmen called for a national strike on April 24 by sending their representatives to fifteen major cities to inform the people what had happened at Tiananmen and to solicit popular support for their cause. The students had no access to mass media; what had been reported in the press, in the students' view, were officially approved distortions.

On the evening of April 22, the Politburo decided not to be pressured by student protests to relax the campaign against bourgeois liberalization. The next day, April 23, Zhao Ziyang, the party chief left for North Korea as scheduled. On April 24 the students declared a class boycott of indefinite duration. However, in Zhao's absence, the Standing Committee of the Politburo met on April 24 and decided that the party must take action over the Tiananmen situation. But their decision had to be approved ultimately by Deng Xiaoping. So Premier Li and Yang Sungkun, then president of the PRC, went to see Deng, the paramount leader, now in semiretirement. Deng wanted to call in the military to crack down on the students, regardless of bloodshed and international repercussions.[69] But first, as a means of frightening the student marchers, a strongly worded statement was authorized to appear in the *People's Daily* on April 26. In the statement, entitled "Resolutely Oppose Rebellion," the Chinese authorities officially characterized the student protest as "dung luan" ("turmoil" or "rebellion") and as "counterrevolutionary insurrection" by a handful of people against the party and the socialist system.[70] To the students and the Chinese people the statement was an unmistakable warning of an impending military crackdown if the students did not disperse from Tiananmen. What followed on April 27 was a peaceful demonstration of 200,000, joined now by about one million Beijing residents, workers, and intellectuals who swarmed around the police. At major intersections people blocked the passage of armed vehicles headed for the square. What Deng feared most, a Poland-type opposition to communist control,[71] was now in the making.

The Escalation of the Demonstration

Undaunted by the provocative and strongly worded newspaper warning, the April 27 demonstration—peaceful, massive, but disciplined, involving 100,000 students and supported by the residents, sympathetic intellectuals, and workers—caused the authorities to hesitate, seeking some form of mediation. This time, at the invitation of the government-approved student associations, the State Council dispatched its spokesman, Yuan Mu, to meet with student representatives of the universities in the Beijing area. The government spokesman tried to tone down the official charge against the students, as contained in the April 26 statement, by implying that only a small minority would be considered instigators.

On May 2, student leaders from Beijing universities handed an appeal to the State Council and the National People's Congress for a dialogue. The appeal was refused by Yuan as the premier's representative. Meanwhile, Zhao, after his return from North Korea, had received a vague instruction from Deng to adopt a more conciliatory approach to the student demonstrators.[72] He was said to have sought "democratic and legal means with reason and discipline" to solve the problem.[73] Zhao even went so far as to suggest an official reaffirmation of the need for political reform and the retirement of party veterans above 75 years of age.[74] But even if this softening of the government position were true and understood by the demonstrating students, the protest at Tiananmen persisted without any slackening.

The May Fourth anniversary demonstration and parade at Tiananmen by some 100,000 students went on as scheduled, but it was more subdued. Some students were planning to return to classes. The government's reaction was restrained, as the meetings of the Asian Development Bank were being convened for the first time in China. However, the movement gathered new momentum and inspiration with the historic visit of former Soviet President Mikhail Gorbachev to China, an event that Deng Xiaoping considered to be a signal of normalization of Sino–Soviet relations and the crowning success in his stewardship since he assumed power in 1978. An escalation of the demonstration was underway as a final effort to induce the government to engage in a true dialogue to resolve the impasse.

The chief vehicle the students selected for the escalation was a hunger strike. On May 13 an initial group of 200 Beida students gathered on their campus to declare their pledge to fast until death if the government refused to meet their demands. The group marched to the Beijing Normal University campus; by then the number of students pledged to a hunger strike had reached 800. In the afternoon when they reached Tiananmen over 1,000 had joined their ranks seeking to force a dialogue with the government on the eve of the historic Sino–Soviet summit. Soon the total number of hunger strikers reached 3,000. The fasting students wore red and white headbands emblazoned with their college names and the Chinese characters for "hunger strike," a familiar device used by student demonstrators in Japan and South Korea.

Residents of Beijing poured into the square to show their support for the hunger-striking students, who endured hot sun during the day and chilling wind at night. Many fainted or suffered from stomach difficulties and had to be taken to hospitals in ambulances. By the third day of fasting, many felt dizzy and numb. Others, in a spirit of sacrifice, stopped taking water in addition to food. By May 17 a total of over 1,000 hunger-striking students had been hospitalized. And their demands had been reduced to two items: rescind the April 26 statement by recognizing the student demonstration as patriotic, and schedule a dialogue. They had expected the government to cave in and they were surprised when it did not budge.

On May 16, Gorbachev arrived and was officially received by Deng inside the Great Hall, out of sight and sound of the demonstrating students at Tiananmen, who now were joined by a throng of some 200 journalists and thousands of workers. A day before Gorbachev's arrival, Zhao proposed to the Politburo Standing Committee a four-point plan to resolve the conflict: (1) repudiation of the April 26 provocative editorial that officially labeled the student protest as rebellious; (2) investigation into corruption by high-level officials and their relatives; (3) public disclosure of finances of high-level party cadres; (4) elimination of special privileges for party officials.[75] But Zhao was outvoted 4 to 1 in the Politburo Standing Committee.

Popular pressure mounted the next day, May 17, in support of the students and for democratic reform as more than a million people took to the streets of Beijing and demanded the ouster of Deng and other leaders.[76] It seemed that the government had lost control and was paralyzed by the popular protests, not only at Tiananmen, but in many of the other cities as well. As more hunger-striking students became unconscious and were rushed to hospitals by ambulance, Zhao reportedly moved again on May 17 at top-level Politburo meetings to rescind the April 26 charges against the students; again his appeal was turned down by Li Peng and presumably by Deng. On May 19, Zhao, having offered his resignation, which was rejected by

Deng, made a last effort at mediation after a heated exchange with Deng. (Zhao was nevertheless voted out of office between May 19 and 20.)

Meantime, Premier Li issued a warning on Thursday, May 18, for restraint; this was ignored by another million protesters, who poured out of their homes, offices, and factories to show support for the students. However, Li, in a gesture of conciliation, did agree to hold a nationally televised meeting with the student leaders on May 18.[77] The televised meeting represented a faint effort by Li to get the students to call off the protest at the square for, as will be seen in the section to follow, by then a decision had been made at the top to use force on the protesters. The student leaders, such as Wuer Kaixi and Wang Dan, exhibited their impatience and frustration at the meeting by being discourteous to the premier.

At this point, the seventh day of the hunger strike, the month-old movement had reached a critical point: should they accede to the government ultimatum for a cessation of the strike, or persist on to the inevitable bloody crackdown? On the early morning of May 19, Zhao came to Tiananmen Square and begged the students to cease their hunger strike. That evening, after heated debate, the student leaders announced cessation of the hunger strike as 3,000 fasting students were on the verge of collapse and exhaustion. At 10:00 P.M. martial law was declared for the center of Beijing and the suburbs. The martial law order was broadcast six times each hour. The government sent troops into Beijing on Saturday, May 20 to restore order. Now an astounding event occurred and was viewed on worldwide television: as military vehicles and tanks moved to the outskirts of Beijing City, students and sympathetic residents climbed on army trucks to stop their advance. Residents along the major pathways also erected barricades to block the passage of the army vehicles. Millions of Beijing citizens held the PLA at bay in defiance of martial law. While the hunger strike had been called off, a student sit-in had begun at Tiananmen as barricades went up in Beijing City.

The Massacre on June 4, 1989

By June 2–3, it was estimated that there were at least 150,000 PLA soldiers, backed by armored vehicles and tanks, taking positions in various parts of the city and waiting to move into the square occupied by the students. The decision to order the PLA into the square was made on the afternoon of June 2 by Deng and Yang Shangkun, the three members of the Politburo's Standing Committee (Li Peng, Qiao Shi, and Yao Yilin), plus Wang Zhen and Bo Yibo, representing the retired hard-line party veterans. The die was cast. A last-minute telephone appeal by Zhao was futile.

On the morning of Saturday, June 3, in front of the Xinhua Gate leading to the compound of Zhongnanhai, the central government and CCP headquarters, 300 soldiers made a surprise move on the sit-in students from the Beijing Institute of Politics and Law. The students were beaten severely with hardened clubs. Meanwhile, thousands of soldiers and armed police came out of the west gate of Zhongnanhai and showered the civilians on Fuyou Street and Xidan with tear gas, blinding many. In the afternoon, thousands of police and soldiers were dispatched from the western end of the Great Hall on the edge of the square, but they were immobilized and mobbed by hundreds of residents, who overturned army vehicles and traffic control towers.

At 6:00 P.M., radio and television broadcast the government's emergency warnings to the residents to stay home. Instead, thousands of them defiantly rushed to the square. Three hours later great numbers of troops moved from the eastern suburbs, a heavily populated district of Beijing, where they encountered blockades erected by the residents. The students on the square were conducting classes beside the temporarily erected Goddess of Democracy statue, now a prominent site on the square. However, on the west of Tiananmen, facing Changan Avenue, peasant soldiers of the 27th Division from Hepei had opened fire with automatic weapons aimed indiscriminately at buildings and people.

As a long column of armored vehicles and tanks moved into the Xidan intersection, residents and workers tried desperately to erect barriers to stop the advancing vehicles. A dead silence followed; then the soldiers jumped out of their vehicles and opened fire on residents and students. On the east of the square two army tanks sped on Changan Avenue leading to Tiananmen and collided with each other. In the accident, one tank ran over four bystanders. The crowd went wild, forced the tank to stop, and set fire to it.

Around midnight, troops moved into the center of the square from the east and west. By 1:00 A.M. on June 4, an estimated 600 soldiers had taken control of the Great Hall. An hour later the students retreated to the Monument to the People's Heroes, ready to meet their death. They sang the Communist "Internationale" as they were surrounded by the advancing soldiers. In an attempt to avoid bloodshed, Hou Dejian, the famous Taiwan rock singer, and Liu Xiaobo, the young literary critic, who had been participating in the hunger strike, went to the PLA commanders to negotiate a peaceful retreat for the students on the square.

At 4:30 A.M., with the lights still turned off on the square, Hou Dejian, having won army consent to a peaceful retreat, appealed to the students to leave. But nine or ten minutes later, the lights came on and the soldiers rushed in, firing at the public address system, the banners, and the tents. At 4:55 A.M., students began to leave the square, moving westward to exit from Xidan. Tanks rolled in at 5:00 A.M. and overran the Goddess of Democracy statue and the tents. The soldiers were chasing and shooting randomly at the retreating students, who linked arms while singing the "Internationale." The shooting and carnage went on until sunrise; the casualties mounted.

There have been various estimates of the number of students killed on the early morning of June 4. The Chinese official figure, dubious at best, put the number at 23 students and 300 soldiers killed. The Beijing Red Cross put the figure at 2,600. Hong Kong newspapers gave much higher estimates, ranging from 3,500 to over 8,000. The best unofficial estimate of the number of students killed by the government troops puts the figure at between 1,000 and 1,500. Add to this the number of residents and bystanders killed on the street and the total fatalities could reach 3,000.[78] The brunt of the army's assault at Tiananmen was borne by the students from the provinces, because a majority of the marchers from Beijing campuses voted to withdraw from the square while those students who came from the provinces, constituting a minority of the total, remained.

Why the Tiananmen Movement

By reviewing post-Tiananmen analyses offered by China scholars, it is possible to discern a number of themes that serve to explain why the students demonstrated and why the movement ended in mass tragedy. First, there is the political culture thesis, which points out that the student demonstration escalated from "playfulness to moralizing, to shaming the government, to acting as a more righteous government." This caused not only great pain for the aged leaders, but anger to the extent that the "children" must be punished, in that they drove their father figure, Deng Xiaopeng, "into a fit of rage."[79]

Then there is the thesis of "leadership cleavages" along generational and ideological lines, starting with the emergence in 1988 of an influential group of older, conservative (leftist), and antireform party leaders; they were challenged by a corps of younger, pragmatic, but pro-reform intellectuals, many of them party members, who advocated more attention to human rights, privatization, and a multi-party political system for democratizing China.[80] Thus it was fundamentally an issue of "legitimacy" and "authoritarianism."[81] As a consequence of China's democracy movement, the 1989 Tiananmen protest sharpened the conflict between the intellectuals and the regime over "the nature of socialist democracy" and the appropriate speed with which to attain that goal.[82]

A third explanation for the Tiananmen massacre is that of "popular rebellion," which argues that the student demonstration at Tiananmen cannot be explained solely by student dissatisfaction with the regime in the reform decade. Rather, it was a "popular rebellion" that the regime was not able to control. The regime's ability to control demonstrations of this magnitude had been weakened by a divided top leadership.[83] The protest at Tiananmen became a "popular rebellion" only after the students had gained the support and sympathy of one of the contending factions, the reformers within the government and party under the leadership of Zhao Ziyang.[84]

Still another explanation is that the weakening of party control over the economic work units and the emergence, or reemergence, of a degree of "independent social identity" in associations and institutions in cities in the reformist 1980s "facilitated the development of a pro-democracy movement and open dissent." These institutions included universities, newspapers, and factories. In this view they provided both an impetus and a rationale for dissent and protest.[85] This thesis is explained in terms of two dimensions of political life that "underpin democratic theory and practice: the 'civil society' or the 'autonomy of individuals and groups' in their relation to the state, and 'public sphere' or the presence of a critical public which holds the government responsible for its actions."[86] Unlike the previous protests from 1978 to 1979 and from 1986 to 1987, the 1989 demonstration at Tiananmen "represented a dramatic enlargement of the scope of dissent" by support from the residents of the capital city. However, the reemergence of a "civil society" and a "public sphere" does not mean a movement of "society" against the "state" as in the case of the Solidarity struggle in Poland.[87] Rather, the 1989 Tiananmen protest resembled the 1956 Hungarian uprising in that it was a result of "growing restiveness among students and intellectuals exacerbated by existing divisions within the regime" that drew support and participation from the general population.[88] More importantly, the thesis of "civil society" points to the "potential for independent authority over politics"—that is, state-controlled institutions, such as the universities, newspapers, and factories, developed an independent social identity by forming "the social basis of protest against the regime itself," as had happened in Eastern Europe.[89]

David Strand's "civil society" thesis as an explanation for the eruption of the Tiananmen mass movement for democracy is expanded on by Barrett L. McCormick and his associates as "the expression of a fundamental conflict between a state with totalitarian intentions and an emerging civil society."[90] McCormick and his associates argue that an autonomous civil society has been growing in China for over a century, and that it has reemerged under Deng's reforms to come into conflict with "an increasingly uncertain and fragmented state." What happened in 1989 was the reemergence in China of "autonomous organizations" permitted by the party and the state—for example, private institutions such as the Beijing Social and Economic Science Research Institute, whose founders were arrested by the authorities after the Tiananmen massacre. Such research institutes and a host of entrepreneurial economic organizations provided inspiration and impetus for debate and discourse on government action or lack of action on societal problems. McCormick and associates present the thesis that the Tiananmen mass movement was a "civil disobedience movement" that had its roots in modern Chinese history (the 1919 May Fourth Movement), fostered and nurtured by the Hundred Flowers Bloom movement launched by Mao in the 1950s. The Tiananmen mass movement in 1989 was part of a continuing process for "democratic activism" and change.

Could the Tiananmen Massacre Have Been Averted?

The haunting questions raised by the 1989 student demonstrations are these: First, why was there no peaceful resolution to the student demands, so that bloodshed could have been avoided? Second, was there an opportunity for the reformers within the party to forge a coalition with the pro-democracy and pro-reform forces manifested in the student demonstration at Tiananmen for a united challenge to the hard-liners led by Deng?

In providing reasonable answers to these questions, one needs to consider the generational differences between the aging hard-liners led by Deng and Yang Shangkun and the young, mostly first- and second-year university students. As noted by Liu Binyan, the investigative reporter for the *People's Daily* who was expelled from party membership in 1987 for dissent, these university students valued highly their individuality and freedom, and were "contemptuous of all authority."[91] The movement produced a few leaders—Wang Dan, Wuer Kaixi (who was born a Uygur in Xinjiang but grew up in Beijing), and Chai Ling—who developed skills in organizing and coordinating massive student protest activities. Unlike the young students who took to the streets during the Cultural Revolution, the 1989 university protesters were fiercely independent and exercised great caution not to be used politically. They did not really care about ideology or loyalty to any political leader. They desired changes, political reform, the government's recognition of political rights as embodied in the 1982 constitution, and the end of the party's monopoly of power, even though initially they did not call for the removal of the party or its leaders. On the other hand, the hard-liners stood for loyalty and sacrifice for the socialist society for which they had fought hard as guerrillas in the 1930s and 1940s. The core of the hard-liner group, the so-called seven old party veterans, acting as an extralegal "inner cabinet"—Chen Yun, Deng Liqun, Hu Qiaomu, Peng Zhen, Wang Zhen, Yang Shangkun, and Bo Yibo—had been the victims of the Cultural Revolution. They were not so much opposed to reforms launched by Deng Xiaoping as they were obsessed by the need for stability and party control of the government. Because they had been victims of Red Guard abuse during the Cultural Revolution, they developed an aversion to student demonstrations for fear of chaos or "luan." Deng's main concern, as expressed in the April 26 editorial condemning the Tiananmen demonstration as "dung luan" or "turmoil," represented the typical mental outlook shared by the "gang of old men." For by 1987, when they forced Deng to dismiss his protégé, Hu Yaobang, from the party chief position, the hard-liners had gained in influence. Furthermore, these old party veterans were true believers in military solutions to political crises—a symptom of the guerrilla mentality that was the only experience they understood. Thus, from this perspective, the young and the old were on an irreversible collision course.

The students have been criticized for being too independent and uncompromising. The movement as a whole lacked "guidance in theory and in strategy."[92] It became a spontaneous movement with the naive expectation that the students could achieve "complete success at one stroke." For journalist Liu Binyan this attitude was reminiscent of "left tendencies" that prevented them from making concessions.[93] Wuer Kaixi, the exiled student leader, admitted later in Paris that at the time of the hunger strike he had urged the students to leave Tiananmen as a "tactical move" to provide the reformers within the party with a chance to get organized.[94] But Wuer was overruled by the students who wanted to stay and force the government to capitulate to their demands by lifting the martial law, removing the troops, guaranteeing no reprisals, and permitting a free press.

The independence exhibited by the students at Tiananmen in refusing to be used by any political bloc is illustrated by the failed negotiation with Yen Mingfu, who represented the State Council. Some of Zhao's supporters appealed to the students to end their hunger strike for the sake of long-term victory for the reform movement. Yen (a respected intellectual whose father was a close aide to the late Zhou Enlai), who speaks fluent Russian and has served as interpreter for former President Yang Shangkun, was dispatched to talk with the student leaders. The negotiation went well but in the end failed to produce an agreement because of the student leaders' insistence on television coverage of the entire negotiation proceedings. Yen appealed to the students to cool down the protest and to call off the hunger strike, so as not to provide the conservative hard-liners with the pretext to get tough and not to give them an excuse to blame or destroy the reform leaders for the disturbance. Yen was said to have argued in the inner council of the party for avoiding bloodshed by confrontation.[95] But there was no compromise or concession on the part of the students; instead they seemed to have relied on the public relations opportunities provided by worldwide television coverage to exact concessions from the government under Li Peng. (Singapore Prime Minister Lee Kuan Yew blamed television coverage for encouraging students to pursue the protest that led to the tragedy.)[96] This strategy on the part of the protesters may have played right into the hands of the conservative hard-liners. As worldwide TV coverage of the activities of the protesters intensified, the hard-liners' position toughened.

During the weeks preceding the June 4 crackdown, the student protesters' stance became increasingly intransigent. Wuer Kaixi, Wang Dang, and Shen Tong had gradually lost their leadership influence. Wuer lost his leadership position partly because he proposed withdrawal from Tiananmen to avert the impending slaughter by the army, and partly because of the power struggle among rival factions among the student protesters at Tiananmen. In retrospect, China's dissident intellectual, Fang Lizhi, remarked recently that "the movement was completely out of control" in the last weeks of the protest.[97]

To one observer, the only chance of defeating the hard-liners and their anti-reform influence was the alliance of the student democracy movement with the "pro-reform forces" in the party.[98] The failure of the 1989 democracy movement in China was laid squarely on the reform element in the Communist Party for its lack of ini-tiative and its indecisiveness in failing to forge a strong alliance with the students at Tiananmen.[99] Liu Binyan pointed out in retrospect that three "mistakes" were made by the reformers in the party and by Zhao Ziyang during these crucial weeks prior to the June 4 crackdown. First, the reformers within the party did not seize the initia-tive to make Li Peng conduct a genuine dialogue with the students. Zhao was blamed for his failure in early May to organize "a prestigious and influential group of leaders" to negotiate with the students.[100] Zhao had hesitated and had gone to the students on his own too late to alter the situation. Second, Zhao and his reformers within the party failed to maneuver, by available legal means, either a general con-ference of the party or the convening of the Standing Committee of the National People's Congress to rally support to oust Li Peng and avoid martial law. These moves were not attempted, even though for the period May 16 to 23 at least six senior military leaders had disagreed on the deployment of the PLA for internal political purposes,[101] and some party reformers had considered convening the NPC's Standing Committee as a method of opening debate over the martial law.[102] Thus, the chance was lost to legally outmaneuver the hard-liners; the seven members of the "gang of old men" and the four members on the Politburo's Standing Committee, with Deng's consent, were able to vote for the removal of Zhao as party chief.

The third mistake made by Zhao's reformers was their failure to use the news media, then sympathetic to the democracy movement, to generate public support by publicizing the urgent need for convening the Central Committee and the NPC to avert the impending disaster and to checkmate the hard-liners' next move. (In fact, many of the news media personnel had been actively participating in the protest at Tiananmen.) Liu Binyan later observed sorrowfully that because the reformers were not organized or united and because of Zhao's hesitancy and weak personality, the 1989 democracy movement was, in the end, crushed despite the military's own divided view about using force on the students.[103] The opportunity for forging an alliance between the party reformers and the forces for democracy was there, but it was lost for lack of initiative on the part of the reformers, so lamented by Liu Binyan.

However, Liu Binyan's criticism of Zhao's supporters within the party for fail-ing to seize the legal initiative to oust Li Peng may not be entirely accurate. For on May 19, on the eve of martial law, Zhao's supporters, party officials and intellectuals, issued a six-point statement that contained a demand for a special meeting of the NPC Standing Committee to review Li's actions and a special session of the party to restore Zhao to power.[104] Liu's criticism of the intellectuals' failure to join the protest-ing students may be too harsh. For during the demonstrations in May, large numbers of intellectuals—"professors, lecturers, research fellows, doctors, masters and staff members from research institutes and the Chinese Academy of Social Sciences, Bei-jing University, Qinghua University and 60 other units marched behind the banner of 'Chinese Intellectual Circles,' " and particularly notable were the journalists.[105]

The Aftermath: Repression of University Students

Following the killings and routing of the student demonstrators at Tiananmen, China entered a period of repression and economic retrenchment, brought on by international sanctions (to be discussed in Chapter 11). There were arbitrary arrests and detention of suspected agitators by the authorities throughout China. In Beijing alone, at least 400 persons were arrested, and nationwide the figure reached perhaps over 4,000 within a week of the massacre.[106] In some provinces the police conducted daily manhunts for student leaders and alleged counterrevolutionaries.

In the spring of 1990 the outside world learned from the Beijing officials that a total of 881 dissidents at Tiananmen had been released under pressure of world criticism of China's human rights violations and as a gesture to appease the United States, whose president was to decide whether to grant China most-favored-nation trade status. However, in early January 1991 legal action was taken, after several weeks of trial, against a dozen major activists in the 1989 Tiananmen demonstration. Among them were four student leaders, who received prison sentences of two to four years. These student leaders were all from universities in the Beijing area and were on the "most-wanted" list of the 21 students identified as ringleaders of the demonstration. Trials had been conducted in the early months of 1991 of a total of 787 protesters arrested in the 1989 Tiananmen crackdown.

University students in Beijing were placed under strict surveillance by the authorities for months after the massacre. The students on campuses were subjects of investigation for their activities at the time of the Tiananmen demonstration. Police went to the campuses with "wanted" lists of dissidents and their leaders. Students were instructed at campus rallies, sponsored by the investigating authorities, to cooperate, identify, or inform on the student leaders. In the annual July 1990 nationwide examination for the 2.8 million high school graduates, they were required to pass an ideological screening test by writing an essay on the reasons and lessons of the 1989 Tiananmen "rebellion and turmoil." All first-year university students were required to undergo military training to correct their ideological outlook. (In the fall of 1989 some 728 freshmen at Beijing University received ten months of ideological and physical training at an army camp.)

Yet, despite this regimentation and control, university students still exhibited occasional defiance. In one dialogue, Beijing students shouted criticisms and hissed a government official. Occasionally and mysteriously, anonymous posters have appeared on some of the university campuses. The dissident movement on Chinese university campuses is by no means completely crushed.

A significant development in the aftermath of the Tiananmen massacre has been the formation of a dissident movement outside of China by Chinese students studying abroad, exiled "Tiananmen warriors," and exiled intellectuals who keep alive the dream of democracy and reform in China.[107] Delegates from Chinese student groups around the world gathered initially in Paris on July 22, 1989 to form "The Front for Democracy in China." In September 1989 the Federation for a Democratic China (FDC) elected Yan Jiaqi (former president of the Institute of Political Science and a member of the brain trust for deposed party chief Zhao Ziyang) and Wuer Kaixi, the student leader at the Tiananmen demonstration, as the Federation's chairman and vice-chairman. (Yan Jiaqi has resigned recently from the movement.) The FDC issued a manifesto that pledged a worldwide united front by overseas Chinese to continue the struggle for democracy in China by peaceful and nonviolent means.[108] The dissident movement has received funding from overseas Chinese communities and the Hong Kong-based Democracy for China Alliance, which raised approximately HK $20 million (U.S. $2.5 million) from the colony's general population.[109] The mainstay of the overseas dissident movement for democracy in China has been the 40,000 Chinese students and scholars in the United States, plus their counterparts in other corners of the world. However, among these overseas student groups there is no consensus as to how to achieve the goal of a democratic China. Many members seem to advocate the overthrow of the CCP's monopoly of power and replacing it with a freely elected pluralist system of competing political parties. Some seem to believe that a democratic China could become a reality if there were genuine reform within the CCP.[110] A few exiled Tiananmen activists still believe that China can be changed if only the reformers within the party could depose hard-liners such as Li Peng.[111] Another problem for the dissident movement lies in the lack of a leader who could devote full time to organizing and fund-raising.[112] A few prominent exiled dissidents, such as Liu Binyan and Su Shaozhi (former head of the Institute of Economic Structural Reform, a think tank for Zhao Ziyang), have not become active in the movement. Only time will tell the eventual success or failure of the Chinese exiles abroad in their efforts to advance democracy in China.

THE STATE OF DISSENT IN THE 1990s

Four years after Tiananmen the mood concerning the historic event in China has been a mixed one. In the first place, for the general populace outside the capital city of Beijing, memories of the event are fading rapidly and generate very little anger and resentment toward the army crackdown on the student protestors. While four years ago student demonstrators demanded political reform and were against party-government corruption and nepotism, the major concerns today for the people in general are rising inflation and corruption, in that order.

In March 1993 the government, under pressure from the United States and European governments, and as a gesture to gain international support for China's application for GATT (General Agreement on Tariffs and Trade) membership and its bid to host the Olympics in the year 2000, released three leading student dissidents from jail. Among them was Wang Dan, 23, the most wanted of the student leaders at Tiananmen. Wang has reported that he has decided to seek readmission to Beijing University, but remains dedicated to continuing his work for a democratic China.[113] The Chinese government has taken some other conciliatory steps. For example, a noted intellectual and the grandfather of the dissident movement, Wang Raowang, was permitted to be a visiting scholar at Columbia University in New York after he was imprisoned for more than a year for leading a protest march in Shanghai in 1989. Other long-time dissidents, one who organized an independent trade union in China and one who was a democracy movement activist, were allowed to leave China to go abroad. (The trade union organizer, Han Dongfang, was denied reentry after authorities expelled him at the border of Hong Kong in late August 1993 by confiscating his Chinese passport; thus he became stateless.) Wei Jingsheng, the dissident imprisoned longest to his role at the Democracy Wall in 1978–79, was released, on Deng's orders almost fifteen years after his arrest. Wei's early release

may have been influenced by China's desire
year 2000.

On the other hand, there are still as n
who committed "crimes of counterrevolutic
(prison labor camps). Many of them must e
ing, whipping, shocking with electric batons
1992, dissidents, some of them ex-governm
or lent support to the protesting students, w
seven years.[115] A number of the dissident
courts were given five-year prison terms (
tionary activities related to the Tiananmen

Shen Tong, who escaped and was exiled in the United States.
1992 became the first student leader on the most-wanted list to return to China. Shen
Tong, who wrote his own personal account of the Tiananmen demonstration,[117] was
a Boston University graduate when he decided to return home. He was arrested by
public security officers at his family home. He was charged with violating the law by
opening a branch of the Democracy for China Fund in Newton, Massachusetts.[118]
However, he was subsequently released to permit his return to the United States.

Former Dissidents as Entrepreneurs

Perhaps the most interesting development in China's booming market economy
reform is the phenomenon of formerly imprisoned Tiananmen dissidents engaging in
entrepreneurial activities under the collective description of "going to the sea" or
"xia ha."[119] They represent the new breed of entrepreneurs known as the "turmoil
elite" who have pooled their skills and resources to go into business under Deng's
economic reforms. Most of the "turmoil elites," or "activists-turned-businessmen,"
have selected the economically booming southern Chinese provinces to conduct their
business. What they have in mind is the development of a middle class, like those in
Taiwan and South Korea that provided the impetus for the emergence of democratic
reform in those countries.[120] This new role for the Chinese democracy movement
activists resembles that of the 1960s American anti-Vietnam War activists who later
became Wall Street stockbrokers and business entrepreneurs.

As the Beijing government increasingly becomes overrun by "corrupt bureau-
crat-capitalist cliques," exiled dissidents like Liu Binyan, now at Princeton University, expect more Tiananmen incidents in the future with a different format in the continuing strife for "a future free society."[121]

A final comment may be in order: that is, despite some of the formidable
obstacles in the way of democratization for China—the lack of historical experience
with democracy and legal traditions, the monopoly of the CCP, the low level of education for the vast majority of the population, and poverty—there are, according to
Martin King Whyte, a number of forces that favor democracy in China.[122] Of those
discussed by Whyte, two major forces may eventually foster democracy in China: (1)
the decade-long economic reforms have weakened central party-government control
over society; and (2) the rapid changes in Asia, particularly in the former authoritarian regimes of Taiwan and South Korea, have produced economic growth and have
thereby encouraged the rise of an educated middle class. In turn this middle class has
demanded and obtained democratic reforms.[123]

ond and G. Bingham Powell, Jr., *Comparative Politics Today: A World View*, 2nd ed.
oronto: Little, Brown, 1980), p. 72.
ewitt and Sidney Verba, *Principles of American Government*, 3rd ed. (New York: Harp-
ow, 1977), pp. 71–72.
M. Burns, J.W. Peltason, and Thomas E. Cronin, eds., *Government by the People*, 14th ed.
glewood Cliffs, N.J.: Prentice Hall, 1990), pp. 227–28.
aymond Wolfinger, Martin Shapiro, and Fred Greenstein, eds., *Dynamics of American Politics*
(Englewood Cliffs, N.J.: Prentice Hall, Inc., 1976), p. 259.
5. Almond and Powell, *Comparative Politics Today*, p. 73.
6. For an excellent book on the subject see Andrew Nathan, *Chinese Democracy* (New York: Alfred A. Knopf, 1985). For the coverage of the Democracy Wall movement by Western reporters stationed in China, see Roger Garside, *Coming Alive: China After Mao*, (New York: McGraw-Hill, 1981), pp. 212–39; Fox Butterfield, *China Alive in the Bitter Sea*, (New York: Times Books, 1982) pp. 406–34; Richard Bernstein, *From the Center of the Earth*, (Boston: Little, Brown, 1982), pp. 215–42, 246–56; and John Fraser, *The Chinese: Portrait of a People* (New York: Summit Books, 1980), pp. 203–71. Also see Jay Matthews, "Dissident's Sentence Stirs Sharp Criticism," Washington Post Service, as reprinted in *Honolulu Advertiser* (October 26, 1979), and *Newsweek* (December 11, 1978), pp. 41–43. For an analysis of the movement as a whole, see Kjeld Erik Brodsguard, "The Democracy Movement in China, 1978–1979: Opposition Movements, Wall Posters Campaign, and Underground Journals," *Asian Survey*, vol. xx. no. 7 (July 1981), 747–74. For Chinese coverage in the *Beijing Review*, see the following issues: 8 (February 23, 1979), 6; 49 (December 7, 1979), 3–4; 50 (December 14, 1979), 6–7; 10 (March 10, 1980), 10; 17 (April 28, 1980), 3–5; 40 (October 6, 1980), 22–28; 45 (November 9, 1979), 17–20. For a collection of translations of writings by the Chinese on human rights, see James D. Seymour, ed. *The Fifth Modernization: China's Human Rights Movement, 1978–1979* (Stanfordville, N.Y.: Earl McColemen Enterprises, Inc. 1980). Also see Philip Short, *The Dragon and the Bear: China and Russia in the Eighties* (New York: William Morrow, 1982), pp. 252–64.
7. See Brodsguard, "The Democracy Movement in China, 1978–1979," pp. 759–61; and Garside, *Coming Alive: China After Mao*, pp. 213–22.
8. "Communiqué of the Third Plenary Session of the Eleventh Central Committee of the CCP," *Beijing Review*, 52 (December 29, 1978), 6.
9. Ibid., p. 13.
10. Ibid., p. 15.
11. Ibid.
12. Garside, *Coming Alive: China After Mao*, pp. 223–26. Also see Bonavia, *The Chinese*, p. 245.
13. Garside, *Coming Alive: China After Mao*, pp. 264–98.
14. See Brodsguard, "The Democracy Movement in China: 1978–1979," pp. 747–74. Also see "China's Dissidents," Washington Post Service, as reprinted in *Honolulu Advertiser* (September 15, 1979), A-17; and Melinda Liu, "Wei and the Fifth Modernization," *Far Eastern Economic Review* (November 27, 1979), 22–23.
15. Garside, *Coming Alive: China After Mao*, p. 256.
16. See *Hongqi*, 5 (May 4, 1979), 11–15. Also see David Bonavia, "The Flight form Freedom," *Far Eastern Economic Review* (October 26, 1979), 9–10.
17. *The New York Times* (July 1, 1979), p. 6.
18. "Wei Jingsheng Sentenced," *Beijing Review*, 43 (October 26, 1979), 6–7.
19. "The People's Verdict," *Beijing Review*, 46 (November 6, 1979), 15–16.
20. See *Beijing Review*, 50 (December 14, 1979), 6; *The New York Times* (December 9, 1979), p. 3; *The Christian Science Monitor* (December 11, 1979), p. 7; and *Ming Pao* (Hong Kong), December 9, 1979, p. 1.
21. "Communiqué of the Fifth Plenary Session of the Eleventh Central Committee of the CCP," *Beijing Review*, 10 (March 10, 1980), 8–9.
22. Ibid., p. 10.
23. "The 'Dazibao': Its Rise and Fall," *Beijing Review*, 40 (October 6, 1980), 23–24.
24. "Big Character Posters Not Equivalent to Democracy," *Beijing Review*, 17 (April 28, 1980), 4.
25. "Communiqué of the Fifth Plenary Session," p. 10.
26. "National People's Congress Ends Session," *Beijing Review*, 37 (September 15, 1980), 3.

27. See *Far Eastern Economic Review* (October 26, 1979), 9, and (October 19, 1979), 38–40.

28. *The Christian Science Monitor* (December 18, 1987), p. 1.

29. Washington Post Service as reprinted in *Honolulu Advertiser and Star-Bulletin*, Sunday Edition (December 21, 1986), A-34.

30. *The New York Times* (December 24, 1986), p. 3.

31. *Honolulu Advertiser* (December 22, 1986), D-4.

32. *Far Eastern Economic Review* (January 8, 1987), 9.

33. *The New York Times* (December 27, 1986), p. 1. And also see *Beijing Review*, 8 (February 8, 1987), 20.

34. *Asian Wall Street Journal* (January 1–2, 1987), p. 1.

35. Los Angeles Times Service as reprinted in *Honolulu Star-Bulletin*, A-21.

36. *Beijing Review*, 1 (January 5, 1987), 5. Also see *Time* (January 2, 1987), p. 38.

37. *Asian Wall Street Journal* (January 8, 1987), p. 7.

38. *Business Week* (January 19, 1987), p. 49.

39. *China News Analysis*, 1328 (February 1, 1987), 7.

40. *Asian Wall Street Journal* (January 8, 1987), p. 1.

41. *Far Eastern Economic Review* (January 15, 1987), 8–9.

42. Ibid., p. 9.

43. *China News Analysis*, 1328 (February 1, 1987), 3.

44. See *The Christian Science Monitor* (January 22, 1987), p. 14.

45. Ibid.

46. *Asian Wall Street Journal* (January 1–2, 1987), p. 1.

47. Ibid.

48. *Ming Pao Daily* (Hong Kong) (December 19, 1986), p. 2; and *China News Analysis*, 1328, 5.

49. See *Beijing Review*, 8 (February 23, 1987), 17–18. Also see *China News Analysis*, 1328, 4–5; and *Renmin Ribao* (September 21, 1986), pp. 3, 5–6.

50. See Jim Mann, "Dissident Shapes Up as China's Sakharov," Los Angeles Times Service as reprinted in *Honolulu Advertiser* (June 28, 1987), A-21. Also see Ge Sheng, "Fang Lizhi—A Model of Chinese Intellectuals," *China Spring Digest*, vol. 2, 1 (March–April 1987), 2–11.

51. Ibid.

52. *Far Eastern Economic Review* (January 15, 1987), 8; and *Business Week* (January 19, 1987), p. 49.

53. *Beijing Review*, 1 (January 5, 1987), 5.

54. Stanley Rosen, "Prosperity, Privatization, and China's Youth," *Problems of Communism*, vol. xxxiv, 2 (April–May 1985), p. 26.

55. *Beijing Review*, 15 (April 13, 1987), 1.

56. Ibid., p. 5.

57. *Los Angeles Times* (January 18, 1987), A-21.

58. *Beijing Review*, 8 (February 23, 1987), 15; and *Asian Wall Street Journal* (January 8, 1987), p. 1.

59. *People's Daily* (January 5 and 6, 1987), p. 1. Also see *Far Eastern Economic Review* (January 15, 1987), 9.

60. Ibid.

61. There is voluminous published material about the student protest and demonstration at Tiananmen. Reports and statements on the Tiananmen tragedy referenced in this chapter are culled from the following:

Harrison Salisbury, *Tiananmen Diary: Thirteen Days in June* (Boston: Little, Brown, 1989); *Massacre in Beijing: China's Struggle for Democracy* (New York: Warner, 1989); Melinda Liu, Orville Schell and Howard Chapnick, *Beijing Spring* (New York: Stewart, Tabori & Chang, 1989); Yi Mu, *Crisis at Tiananmen* (San Francisco: China Books Publishers, 1989); Scott Simmie and Bob Nixon, *Tiananmen Square* (Seattle: University of Washington Press, 1989); Michael Fathers and Andrew Higgins, *Tiananmen: The Rape of Peking* (Toronto and London: Doubleday, 1989); Liu Binyan, *"Tell the World": What Happened in China and Why* (New York: Pantheon, 1990); Andrew Nathan, *China's Crisis: Dilemmas of Reform and Prospects for Democracy* (New York: Columbia University Press, 1990); Han Minzhou (comp.), *A Book of Writings and Speeches from the Democracy Movement* (Princeton, N.J.: Princeton Press, 1990); John Roderice, ed., *China: From the Long March to Tiananmen Square* (New York: Henry Holt, 1990); Michael Oksenberg, ed., *Orthodoxy and Dissent in China, Spring 1989* (New York: M.E. Sharpe, 1990); Suzanne Ogden, ed., *China's Search for Democracy: The Student and Mass Movement of 1989* (New York: M.E. Sharpe, 1990); *Gate of Heavenly Peace: the Struggle for Democracy in China* (Toronto: Macmillan, 1990); *A Day in the Life of China* (San Francisco: Collins, and Hong Kong: Weldon Owen Publishing, 1990); Geremie Barmei and John Minford, *Seeds of Fire: Chinese Voices of Conscience* (New York: Hill & Wang, 1990); *Flames of Freedom: Chinese Voices of Protest* (New York: Hill & Wang, 1990); Yan Jiaqi, *History of the Chinese Cultural Revolution*, rev. (Honolulu: University of Hawaii Press, 1990); Steven M. Mosher, *China Misperceived* (New York: Basic Books, 1990); and Jonathan Spence, *Modern China* (New York: Norton, 1990).

Also, the following articles: James C. Hsuing, "From the Vantage of Beijing Hotel: Peering into the 1989 Student Unrest in China"; John C.H. Fei, "A Cultural Approach to the Beijing Crisis, 1989"; and William T. Liu, "A Social Study of the 1989 Beijing Crisis"—all the above appeared in *Asian Affairs: An American Review*, vol. 16, no. 2 (Summer 1989).

For more recent books on the Tiananmen mass movement and examination of the aftermath, see Geremie Barme and Linda Jaivin, *New Ghosts, Old Dreams: Chinese Rebel Voices* (New York: Times Books, 1992); Ann F. Thurston, *A Chinese Odyssey: The Life and Times of a Chinese Dissident* (New York: Scribner's, 1992); Shen Tong, *Almost a Revolution* (New York: Houghton-Mifflin, 1990); Chu Yuan Cheng, *Behind the Tiananmen Massacre: Social and Economic Ferment in China* (Boulder, Colo.: Westview Press, 1990); Lee Feigon, *China Rising: The Meaning of Tiananmen* (Chicago: Ivan R. Dee, 1990); and Mu Yi and Mark V. Thompson, *Crisis at Tiananmen: Reform and Reality in Modern China* (San Francisco: China Books and Periodicals, 1989).

62. See *Zhengming* (Hong Kong), 139, (May 1989), 8–9.
63. Ibid., p. 9.
64. In addition to the extensive daily news coverage of events at Tiananmen from April to June 1989 by major national newspapers such as *The New York Times, The Washington Post, The Los Angeles Times,* and *The Christian Science Monitor,* the following entries represent a collection of reporting and analyses of the Tiananmen protests: Lucian W. Pye, "Tiananmen and Chinese Political Culture," *Asian Survey,* vol. xxx, no. 4 (April 1990), 331–47; Alan P.L. Liu, "Aspects of Beijing's Crisis Management: The Tiananmen Square Demonstration," *Asian Survey,* vol. xxx, no. 5 (May 1990), 505–21; Corinna-Barbara Francis, "The Progress of Protest in China: The Spring of 1989," *Asian Survey,* vol. xxix, no. 9 (September 1989), 898–918; Lowell Dittmer, "The Tiananmen Massacre," *Problems of Communism,* vol. xxxviii, no. 5, (September–October 1989), 2–15; Andrew J. Nathan, "Chinese Democracy in 1989: Continuity and Change," *Problems of Communism,* vol. xxxviii, no. 5 (September–October 1989), 16–29; Andrew G. Walder, "The Political Sociology of the Beijing Upheaval of 1989," *Problems of Communism,* vol. xxxviii, no. 5 (September–October 1989), 30–40; and David Strand, "Protest in Beijing: Civil Society and Public Sphere in China," *Problems of Communism,* vol. xxxix, no. 3, (May–June 1990), 1–19.

Also see Li Lu, *Moving the Mountain: My Life in China* (London: Macmillan, 1990); and George Hicks, ed., *The Broken Mirror: China after Tiananmen* (London: Longman, 1990). For a good general introduction, accompanied by a collection of documents, see Michael Oksenberg and Marc Lambert, eds., *Beijing Spring, 1989—Confrontation and Conflict: The Basic Documents* (New York: M.E. Sharpe, 1990); and Corinna-Barbara Francis, "The Progress of Protest in China: The Spring of 1989," *Asian Survey,* vol. xxix, no. 9 (September 1989), 898–918. Also see Julia Kwong, "The 1986 Student Demonstrations in China: A Democratic Movement?" *Asian Survey,* vol. xxviii, no. 9 (September 1988), 970–1017.

65. See *Zhengming* (Hong Kong), 128, (June 1988), 8–9.
66. Ibid., p. 7.
67. See Liu Binyan, "*Tell the World*" p. 9; Julia Ching, *Probing China's Soul* (San Francisco: Harper & Row, 1990), pp. 17–18; and Dittmer, "The Tiananmen Massacre," p. 6.
68. *The New York Times* (April 19, 1989), A-1.
69. See Nicholas D. Kristof, "How the Hardliners Won," pp. 40–41; and Liu Binyan, "*Tell the World,*" p. 15.
70. *People's Daily,* overseas edition, (April 26, 1989), p. 1.
71. Dittmer, "The Tiananmen Massacre," p. 7.
72. *Ming Pao Daily* (Hong Kong) (May 16, 1989), p. 1; and Dittmer, "The Tiananmen Massacre," p. 7.
73. See *Zhengming* (Hong Kong), 140 (June 1989), 1.
74. *Ming Pao Daily* (Hong Kong) (June 1, 1989), p. 1.
75. Ibid. (May 21, 1989), p. 1.
76. *The New York Times* (May 18, 1989), A-1; and *The Asian Wall Street Journal* (May 18, 1989), p. 1.
77. *The New York Times* (May 19, 1989), A-1 and A-4. Also see *China Daily* (May 19, 1989), p. 1.
78. For some breakdown on the Tiananmen casualties see *The Massacre of June 1989 and Its Aftermath*

(New York: Amnesty International, USA, April 1990), p. 31; and *Preliminary Findings on Killings of Unarmed Civilians, Arbitrary Arrests and Summary Executions since June 3, 1989* (New York: Amnesty International, USA, August 1989), p. 23. Also see Julia Ching, *Probing China's Soul*, p. 32.

79. Lucian Pye, "Tiananmen and Chinese Political Culture," pp. 331–43. Also see Peter R. Moody, Jr., "The Political Culture of Chinese Students and Intellectuals: A Historical Examination," *Asian Survey*, vol. xxviii, no. 11 (November 1988), 1140–60.

80. Dittmer, "The Tiananmen Massacre," pp. 2–15.

81. Ibid., p. 2; and Pye, "Tiananmen and Chinese Political Culture," pp. 331–33.

82. See Andrew J. Nathan, "Chinese Democracy in 1989: Continuity and Change," pp. 16–27; and his *China's Crisis* (New York: Columbia University Press, 1990).

83. Andrew G. Walder, "The Political Sociology of the Beijing Upheaval of 1989," pp. 30–40.

84. Ibid. p. 38.

85. David Strand, "Protest in Beijing: Civil Society and Public Sphere," pp. 1–19.

86. Ibid., p. 2. Also see Barrett L. McCormick, Su Shaozhi, and Xiao Xiaoming, "The 1989 Democracy Movement: A Review of the Prospects for Civil Society in China," *Pacific Affairs*, vol. 65, no. 2 (Summer 1992), 182.

87. Strand, "Protest in Beijing," p. 11.

88. Ibid., p. 12.

89. Ibid., p. 18. Also see Michael D. Swaine, "China Faces the 1990s: A System in Crisis," *Problems of Communism*. vol. xxxix, no. 3 (May–June 1990), 20–35.

90. See "The 1989 Democracy Movement: A Review of the Prospects for Civil Society in China."

91. Liu Binyan, "*Tell the World*," p. 34.

92. Ibid., p. 27.

93. Ibid., p. 54.

94. For text of interview with Wuer Kaixi, see *Zhengming* (Hong Kong), 143 (September 1989), p. 28.

95. Nicholas D. Kristof, "How the Hardliners Won," *The New York Times Magazine* (November 12, 1989), pp. 66–67. Also see Dittmer, "The Tiananmen Massacre," p. 11. Transcript of Li Peng's speech about the failure of dialogues with the students can be found in *The New York Times* (May 20, 1989), A-4.

96. See Lee Kuan Yew's remarks in Hong Kong as reported in *The New York Times* (October 17, 1990), A-4.

97. See Li Lu, *Moving the Mountain: My Life in China*; and David Aikman, "Interview: The Science of Human Rights," *Time* (August 20, 1990), p. 12.

98. Liu Binyan, "*Tell the World*," p. 104.

99. Ibid.

100. Ibid., p. 105.

101. Ibid.; also see *The New York Times* (May 20, 1989), A-4.

102. Liu Binyan, "*Tell the World,*" p. 107; and Kristof, "How the Hardliners Won," p. 67.

103. *The New York Times* (May 23, 1989), A-1.

104. Nathan, "Chinese Democracy in 1989: Continuity and Change," 16 and 19.

105. "Protest in Beijing: Civil Society and Public Sphere," p. 16, as quoted from *People's Daily* (May 16, 1989). Also see Frank Tan, "The *People's Daily*: Politics and Popular Will—Journalist Defiance in China during the Spring of 1989," *Pacific Affairs*, vol. 63, no. 2 (Summer 1990), 151–169.

106. *The Massacre of June 1989 and Its Aftermath*, pp. 36–37.

107. For information on the overseas Chinese dissident movement for democracy in China, see *Far Eastern Economic Review* (August 24, 1989), 18–21; *Zhengming* (Hong Kong), 142 (August 1989), 22–23; *Zhengming* (Hong Kong), 146 (December 1989), 20–24; *Yazhou Zhoukan* (Hong Kong) (November 12, 1989), pp. 12–15; *Yazhou Zhoukan* (Hong Kong) (October 8, 1989), pp. 8–11; *Yazhou Zhoukan* (Hong Kong) (August 13, 1989), pp. 6–8. Notes taken by this author at a public lecture delivered by Yan Jiaqi, an exiled intellectual leader and a high official in the Chinese Academy of Social Sciences, on March 10, 1990 at the University of Hawaii at Manoa. Also see an interview with Yan Jiaqi in *Zhengming* (Hong Kong), 147 (January 1990), 66–72.

108. Text of the manifesto can be found in *Zhengming* (Hong Kong), 142 (August 1989), 23.

109. *Far Eastern Economic Review* (August 3, 1989), 29.

110. Ibid.

111. Ibid. Also see Liu Binyan, *China's Crisis, China's Hope* (Boston: Harvard University Press, 1990).

112. *Yazhou Zhoukan* (Hong Kong) (September 23, 1990), pp. 6–8.

113. See *Far Eastern Economic Review* (3 March 1993), 13.
114. *The New York Times* (September 1, 1992), A-4 and 5.
115. *The New York Times* (July 22, 1992), A-3.
116. *The New York Times* (February 19, 1992), p. 3; and (February 26, 1992), A-5.
117. Shen Tong, *Almost a Revolution* (New York: Houghton-Mifflin, 1990).
118. See Bob Hohler, "Arrest of Dissident on Return Is Cause Celebre," *Boston Globe* as reprinted in *The Honolulu Sunday Star-Bulletin and Advertiser* (September 6, 1992), A-36. Also see *Far Eastern Economic Review* (September 10, 1992), 13.
119. See *The Christian Science Monitor* (March 9, 1993), p. 6.
120. Ibid.
121. *China Focus* (A publication of the Princeton China Initiative), vol. 1, no. 4 (May 30, 1993), 3.
122. See Martin King Whyte, "Prospects for Democratization in China," *Problems of Communism*, vol. xli, no. 3 (May–June 1992), 59–62.
123. See James C.F. Wang, *Comparative Asian Politics: Power, Policy, and Change* (Englewood Cliffs, N.J.: Prentice-Hall, 1994), ch. 2, pp. 129–33 and 137–43.

chapter eleven

The Politics
of Modernization
Rural and Urban Economic Reforms

MODERNIZATION AS A CONCEPT

Modernization, in the social sciences, usually refers to a general approach that focuses on the dual process of improving and modifying traditional political institutions, typically of Third World nations, for the purpose of achieving industrialization or economic development. As discussed in Chapter 1, China began undergoing periods of political modernization in the 1860s and 1870s, advocating the need to acquire Western scientific and technological expertise, particularly in areas relating to military science. This was followed in 1895 by the "self-strengthening" movement for the study of Western ideas and methods, including railroad building and military reform. Certainly the 1919 May Fourth Movement was an important step in China's political modernization. As discussed in Chapter 1, this was basically an intellectual enlightenment movement that revolved around the themes of nationalism and a "New Society" that would advance "democracy and science." During the republican period of the Nationalists, earnest attempts were made to build modern political institutions in the areas of military organization, state bureaucracy, and education. Lastly, fundamental political modernization or changes have taken place in China since 1949, as discussed in previous chapters. Now, in this chapter, the focus will be on China's efforts at economic modernization in order to attain the goal of industrialization.

> . . . So the main task of socialism is to develop the productive forces, steadily improve the life of the people and keep increasing the material wealth of society. Therefore,

there can be no communism with pauperism, or socialism with pauperism. So to get rich is no sin . . .[1]

Deng Xiaoping
September 2, 1986

We are unanimous in the view that the economic structure is one of combining a planned economy with market regulation and we must never go back to the old road of a highly centralized economy.[2]

Jiang Zemin
July 6, 1990

The quotations above are from statements by China's two most powerful leaders at the height of the economic reform period from 1980 to June 1989, Deng Xiaoping (the paramount leader since 1978) and Jiang Zemin (the CCP general secretary). In a nutshell, the goal of China's modernization program is to improve the living standards of the people and the material wealth of the society. Deng made it clear that one cannot build socialism with pauperism or "blanket poverty," as Mao was fond of saying. Jiang defended the use of market forces and macroeconomic tools to invigorate the economy as the correct policy. Jiang vowed not to go back to a highly centralized, planned economy.

Let us begin our discussion of China's economic reform with an overview of China's economic development from 1953 to 1975.

ECONOMIC DEVELOPMENT

Overview of Economic Development Policies and Rate of Growth, 1953–1975

The development of the Chinese economy has not been a smooth process. On the contrary, it has been erratic and volatile. In the initial years, from 1949 to 1952, the regime's priority was to seek, as rapidly as possible, economic recovery and rehabilitation in the aftermath of a long period of war and the dislocation of the country's productive capacity. In 1953 the regime embarked on long-range planning of its economic development, employing the Stalinist model of centralized planning with emphasis on development of heavy industries. As was indicated in Chapter 2, the First Five-Year Plan was followed by a shift in development strategy in 1958, which placed emphasis on mass mobilization and intensive use of human labor under the Great Leap. While rapid economic recovery followed the failure of the Great Leap, this recovery was disrupted by the Cultural Revolution in the mid-1960s. The post-Cultural Revolution period, from 1969 to 1975, witnessed mixed emphases, both on local economic self-reliance and self-sufficiency and on continued selective centralized management of a number of heavy industries, transport, banking, and foreign trade. No major new economic policy was formulated until 1975, when Zhou Enlai consolidated his political power in the aftermath of the Lin Biao affair.

Between 1953 and 1975, covered by the economic development policies discussed above, the rate of economic growth in China was approximately 6 percent.

This was quite an impressive record when compared with other developing nations,[3] particularly in view of the size and density of China's population and the interruptions that occurred during the Great Leap and the Cultural Revolution.

Emergence of Pragmatic Development Policies

The reversal from a mass-mobilization-oriented strategy to a comprehensive and orderly planning strategy for modernization occurred at the beginning of 1975, when the Fourth National People's Congress convened to revise the 1954 constitution. Premier Zhou proposed a two-stage development for China's national economy: a comprehensive industrial system by 1980, and a comprehensive modernization program in agriculture, industry, national defense, and science and technology by the year 2000.[4] While preliminary discussions were held within the State Council's various functional ministries on the guidelines for implementing comprehensive plans to step up the economy, the radicals were set to attack any action that would reverse the gains made by the Cultural Revolution or restore "bourgeois rights." Yao Wenyuan, the radical's spokesperson, authored an article in the party's theoretical journal, *Hongqi (Red Flag)*, in which he raised at least four major points of disagreement with Zhou on the development of the economy.[5] First, Yao argued that a gap existed between the workers and peasants, between town and country, and between mental and manual labor, and that these differences must be removed or polarization and inequality would inevitably result. A comprehensive program of national economic development eventually would place the elite technocrats in a position of power and prestige and, thus, widen these gaps. Second, Yao argued that once the technocrats were in power, they would "restore capitalism in the superstructure" and would redistribute capital and power according to mental power and skills, rather than on the basis of "to each according to his work." Third, Yao attacked the plan for reintroducing material incentives to induce workers and peasants to produce more in the name of modernization. Wage incentives to "lure the workers" represented to Yao the corrupt practice of the bourgeois right. Fourth, Yao labeled the rationale for increasing agricultural and industrial production—the fact that the peasants "lacked food and clothing"—as nothing but a scheme to "undermine the socialist collective economy." Zhou and his supporters believed that raising the living conditions of the peasants would result in greater production, and that the only way to encourage the peasants to produce more was to provide them with incentives such as private plots and free markets. The radicals believed that using material incentives to spur production would alter the nature of the commune system, which was based on "the socialist collective economy."

The pragmatic planners under Premier Zhou ignored the radicals' attacks and continued to prepare comprehensive plans for modernization. Deng Xiaoping was brought back to the party in 1974 and the State Council after he was purged in 1966 to initiate a series of planning conferences within the central government, which would include members of China's scientific elite from the Chinese Academy of Sciences. These planning conferences produced three documents: a set of guidelines for the party and the nation for the modernization program, a twenty-point outline for the acceleration of industry, and a plan for the development of science and technology.[6] The radicals labeled these documents Deng's "three poisonous weeds." Deng was responsible for restoring centralized power in the administration of economic affairs to the State Council's functional ministries, with placing managers of enterprises in control in industrial plants, and with instituting rules and regulations in industrial plants for the purpose of restoring labor discipline.[7] Echoing the demand made by Zhang Chunqiao for the exercise of total dictatorship over the bourgeoisie, the mass criticism groups of China's two leading universities—Beijing and Qinghua—argued that scientific research institutions, which were dominated by the bourgeois intellectuals before the Cultural Revolution, must be in the hands of the masses. Scientific research must be carried on in an "open door" manner so that workers are integrated with the educated elite and so that theory is integrated with practice. The radicals at these universities argued that class struggle must continue and that "nonprofessionals can lead professionals."[8]

After the arrest of the Gang of Four, Hua Guofeng reintroduced Zhou Enlai's comprehensive plan for modernization and brought Deng back to revive his guidelines for accelerated industrial and scientific development. Hua pledged his support to these economic plans at the Eleventh Party Congress in August 1977, when he declared

> We must build an independent and fairly comprehensive industrial and economic system in our country by 1980. By then farming must be basically mechanized, considerable increases in production must be made in agriculture, forestry, animal husbandry, side-line production and fishery, and the collective economy of the people's communes must be further consolidated and developed.
>
> Scientific research ought to anticipate economic construction, but it now lags behind, owing to grave sabotage by the "Gang of Four." This question has a vital bearing on socialist construction as a whole and must be tackled in earnest.[9]

Hua presented a detailed set of development plans to the Fifth National People's Congress in March 1978. The plan consisted of two interrelated plans, comparable to Premier Zhou's 1975 two-stage development plan: a ten-year, short-term development plan, and a twenty-three-year, long-term comprehensive plan. The short-term plan called for 400 million metric tons of grain production, a 60 million-ton capacity for steel production, and an overall 10 percent per year increase in industrial production by 1985.[10] The ten-year plan also called for at least "85 percent mechanization in all major processes of farmwork" in the communes. The ten-year plan was to be followed by a series of five-year plans to push China "into the front ranks of the world economy."[11] Soon Hua launched a series of very ambitious but obviously exaggerated large-scale projects. These huge projects included a large opencast coal mines, oil field pipelines, modern iron and steel complexes, chemical fertilizer plants, farm machinery plants, and railway construction.

Readjustment, Restructuring, Consolidation, and Reform, 1978–1981

The modernization plan launched in 1978 was an ambitious one. It called for production of 60 million metric tons of steel by the year 2000, the mechanization of 85 percent of agriculture, and completion of 120 large-scale capital construction projects involving an investment of $360 billion. To the pragmatic leaders like Deng and Chen Yun, not only were the 1978 targets unrealistic, but the plan for implementing the program was unworkable and reminiscent of the 1958 "cash program." The 1978 plan laid undue emphasis on the development of heavy industry at the expense of consumer goods and light industries, they felt. The focal point of debate among the top leaders was again the question of priorities, as in 1958, and was inextricably intertwined with ideology. Hua Guofeng, as mentioned in Chapter 2, was blamed for the "Leftist tendency" in the 1978 program that resulted in imbalance and a national financial deficit. By the spring of 1979, it became obvious that the 1978 modernization plan needed revision. To understand China's economic readjustment from 1979 to 1981, we need to take a brief look at the economic problems that surfaced soon after the 1978 modernization plan was launched.[12]

First, there was the key conflict of industry versus agriculture. The orthodox Stalinist strategy of economic development, with emphasis on heavy industry, invariably placed a hardship on the agricultural sector. A leading Chinese economist pointed out that between 1949 and 1978, investment in heavy industry increased more than 90 percent, as compared to a mere 2.4 percent increase in agriculture.[13] The immediate consequence of a slow growth rate in agricultural output was China's dependence on grain purchases from abroad.

Second, there was the issue of heavy versus light industries. Because of the emphasis on investment in heavy industry, investment in light and consumer industries was insufficient to allow this sector to produce enough goods to meet the people's daily needs. In other words, "market supplies for the main light industrial goods have all along fallen short of needs."[14]

Third, experience had shown that in the development of heavy industry, excessive stress was placed on the development of metallurgical, machine-building, and processing industries. In the process, energy resources development (coal and electric power) and transport facilities were neglected. This resulted in a critical energy shortage, and transportation and communications services remained backward, as illustrated by the situation at the Baoshan steel complex near Shanghai.[15] When the giant Baoshan steel complex was almost completed in 1979, the Chinese discovered that there was not enough power available to turn the rolling steel mills, and that a new port was needed to handle the ores imported from Brazil and Australia.

Fourth, heavy industrial development required large-scale investment in capital construction projects. Too often these projects' requirements far exceeded the available personnel, machinery, finances, and material resources. For example, the Baoshan steel complex was constructed with Japanese, West German, and American know-how at a cost of about $27 billion—or an amount equal to about 40 percent of China's national budget for 1981. In addition, targets for most of the projects for 1978 and 1979 were unrealistic, reminiscent of the crash programs launched under the 1958 Great Leap. The shopping spree for modern equipment and contracts for capital construction projects resulted in a $6 billion deficit in China's national budget and consumed about $8 billion of China's foreign reserves. Finally, there was the need to upgrade the management efficiency in Chinese enterprises. Most Chinese factories were either overequipped with machines or overstaffed and were not operating at full capacity.

In April 1979 a central work conference was convened to discuss corrections and readjustments in the 1978 modernization program. Simultaneously, the Chinese central government was forced to revise, postpone, or cancel many contracts signed with foreign concerns, particularly Japanese firms. The NPC at its second session in June 1979 approved a series of urgent measures to readjust the modernization program by retrenchment.[16] First, it decided to readjust the priorities. Light and consumer industries were to be given equal, if not greater, emphasis with heavy industry. The overambitious plan for 60 million metric tons of steel by 1985 was revised to 45 million metric tons. Energy and power industries were scheduled to be developed and expanded more rapidly. Capital construction projects for heavy industries were to be curtailed, so that a large amount of investment funds would be freed. Second, it reached the conclusion that the economic management structure had to be overhauled. Enterprises were to be given real decision-making power and initiative. The concept of "egalitarian tendency" was discarded; those who had demonstrated success would now be given authority and reward. Provinces and localities were to be given increased power in planning, financing, and foreign trade. Third, it decided that factory managers must be given power in the operation of the plants to spur production. Managers were permitted to set prices for their own products; and they were allowed to apply to the banks to borrow operating funds and pay interest. Fourth, it mandated that all enterprises must produce quality products.

This austere readjustment program was to span the three-year period from 1979 to 1981. Reform measures in the economy would slow down China's planned growth rate from 12 percent in 1978 to about 7 percent in 1979 and to just over 5 percent in 1980.[17] These scaled-down goals represented an admission that the country had gone ahead too fast and was forced to apply the brakes.[18]

The 1979 economic reforms were intended to correct two basic problems: the overemphasis on the investment in and accumulation of heavy industries, discussed earlier, and the need for incentives to spur production. China's leading economists and planners such as Chen Yun (a Politburo member and former director of state planning) and Xue Muqiao (an adviser for state planning), argued that the "scale of economic construction must be commensurate with the nation's capabilities": the state should make a substantial investment in capital construction in heavy industries only when the people's livelihood had made marked improvement.[19] Chen Yun was quoted as saying that the distribution of the limited supply of raw materials should be given first to those industries "that ensure the production of people's daily necessities."[20] To proceed otherwise would be "Leftist thinking." It would be a "Leftist" error if the percentage of accumulation in national income—that is, the amount of money and material resources channeled into construction of large-scale heavy industrial projects as fixed assets and inventories—was disproportionately high. The accumulation ratio of fixed assets and inventories channeled into the building of heavy industrial projects was 36 percent of the national income.[21] When this imbalance occurred, Chen Yun was the most influential voice arguing for a reduction in capital construction investment and an increase in consumer goods industries.

The development strategy shift from heavy to light industries, in terms of state investment in the two sectors, was made not only because of the need to provide consumer goods for the rapidly increasing population, but also for more expedient reasons. Heavy industries consume an enormous quantity of energy resources. Light industries require less energy, and also provide more jobs. It has been pointed out that in China a 1 percent shift in the ratio from heavy to light industries saves 6 million tons of coal.[22] In addition, light industries produce China's export goods, which earn needed foreign exchange.

Planned Economy, Market Socialism, and the Sixth and Seventh Five-Year Plans

Since 1979 a familiar sight in many Chinese cities has been individual vendors, hawkers, and shopkeepers selling their goods and services—activities long prohibited by the government. When urban authorities began granting licenses to private entrepreneurs in 1979 for business, Westerners were delighted to be able to purchase fresh produce from the countryside and eat a good meal in a small family restaurant without waiting in line. Some 300,000 small private enterprises were reported to be operating in cities in 1979, with over 810,000 in existence at the end of 1980, and 2.6 million in 1983.[23]

The rationale for this new policy was that "individual economy," or private enterprise, should no longer be considered "capitalistic," and that it must be allowed to play a role in supporting the socialist economy.[24] Apparently, there was some resistance to the new policy. For example, the *People's Daily* accused the state commercial agencies of hanging on to the old practice of "monopoly economy."[25] Still, before 1966 there were at least two million small individual producers providing goods and services to meet the market demands that the state-owned economy failed to deliver.[26] These individual producers disappeared during the Cultural Revolution and were not revived until 1979, when economic readjustment and reform became necessary. The leadership hoped that the incentives provided by the "individual economy" would help spur production and fill gaps in the system once again. In addition, it was realized that the "individual economy" would open up jobs for the urban unemployed.

The existence of individual enterprises alongside the socialist collective enterprises raises serious questions, since the two are seemingly incompatible. It must be remembered that within the Soviet model of a centralized planned economy, China has had a pattern of alternating policy approaches over the extent to which market forces should play a role in the economy. These policies, as pointed out in Chapter 2, became the focus of debate and dissension among the top leaders. The fiasco of the 1958 Great Leap crash program paved the way for the economic readjustment and recovery in the 1960s, when there was a relaxation in strict control over market forces. The Cultural Revolution, with its excessive emphasis on the role of ideology, destroyed the gains made during the early 1960s, and with them went the permissible free markets for peasants and the profit-and-loss principle for industrial management. Now China once again returned to the pre-1966 policy of relaxing the state's control over market forces in the midst of a planned economy.

Under the 1979 adjustment, not only were market forces allowed in the "individual economy," but they were introduced into state enterprises as part of a series of reforms to generate growth. Many of the reforms had emerged from experiments conducted by Zhao Ziyang in enterprises selected as pilot projects in the province of Sichuan. During 1980–81 thousands of state enterprises were subjected to "market socialism" experiments through the introduction of the following reform measures:[27] (1) state-owned factories were allowed to produce for market demand as long as they fulfilled the assigned state quota; (2) state-owned enterprises were given the freedom to purchase needed raw material through the market, rather than remaining dependent on central allocation; (3) prices for the products were to be set by the supply and demand mechanism. In other words, for these enterprises microeconomic decisions on production would be governed by market forces, not by the state plan. All state-owned enterprises were to be responsible for their own profit and loss.

To some observers, it seems, the view is not widely accepted that what emerged in the early 1980s in China might be a variant of the Yugoslav and Hungarian market socialism that coexisted with the centralized planned economy.[28] The Chinese approach was best explained by Chen Yun, the architect of the current economic development strategy. Chen pointed out that "the planned economy is to play the major role and market regulation the supplementary role."[29] He decried the idea that planning should be abandoned once the incentive system has been introduced in enterprises and agriculture. Chen then illustrated the relative roles of planning and the market mechanism in this way: "We must have plans in running enterprises. In running socialist enterprises, we should take into consideration the following factors: whether there is a market for the products, where the raw materials come from and how enterprises are managed."[30] Chen's approach was to let the planned and the market economies coexist. Xue Muqiao, one of China's leading economists, argued that merchandise should be produced by enterprises in accordance with market demands. He condemned the old practice of state monopoly, which tended to choke market demands to death.[31] Xue advocated self-regulation of consumer goods by market demands, free markets for the peasants to sell their sideline products in the cities, and local autonomy for those provinces that were most adaptable to foreign trade.[32] Xue, however, insisted that basic items such as steel and petroleum be regulated under centralized planning. Premier Zhao told the NPC delegates that the proper relationship between the planned economy and market regulation was that "enterprises in the key branches of the economy or products vital to the economy must be organized mandatorily in accordance with the state plan; only those enterprises which were not considered vital to the economy were permitted, within the limits of the state plan, to produce items in accordance with changing market conditions."[33]

Thus it was under the strategy of a socialist planned commodity (market) economy that China launched its Sixth (1981–85) and Seventh (1986–90) Five-Year Plans.[34] As seen from Table 11.1, targets set for annual growth in industry and agriculture under the Sixth Five-Year Plan were "fulfilled" or "overfulfilled"—a point that Premier Zhao announced proudly to the NPC on March 25, 1986.[35] The combined actual gross value for industrial and agricultural output grew close to 12 percent annually under the Sixth Five-Year Plan, a remarkable accomplishment. The annual increase in the gross national product was 10 percent for the 1981–85 period, placing China in the ranks of the fastest-growing developing nations of the world for that period.

The Seventh Five-Year Plan, designed to "build a strong, wealthy country with a happy, prosperous people," contained certain key features. First, the plan set an annual growth rate at 7.5 percent, a restrained target after a 10 percent actual annual growth rate under the previous plan. Premier Zhao explained that a lower growth rate for the gross national product was set in order to keep the economy from overheating and to reduce the strain on the economy from inflation, overspending, energy deficiency, and transportation bottlenecks. Zhao warned that "the blind pursuit of an excessively high growth rate in disregard of actual conditions" was no longer to be tolerated.[36] The Seventh Five-Year Plan was designed for "health" and "stable" growth, he stated.

Second, the plan allocated the bulk of China's investment, about 500 billion renminbi (rmb), for energy development projects. The rational investment pattern

TABLE 11.1 China's Sixth (1981–85) and Seventh (1986–90) Five-Year Plans

	ACTUAL ANNUAL GROWTH 1981–85 (%)	TARGET ANNUAL GROWTH 1981–85 (%)	TARGET ANNUAL GROWTH 1986–90 (%)
Gross value of industrial and agricultural output	11%	4%	6.7% (Rmb 1,677 billiom)**
Gross value of industrial output	12	4	7.5 (Rmb 1,324 billion)
Gross value of agricultural output	8	4	4 (Rmb 353 billion)
Gross National Product	10	—	7.5 (Rmb 1,117 billion)
National income	—	4	6.7 (Rmb 935 billion)

*Value in 1990 at 1980 prices
**RMB: Renminbi (RMB 5.8 = $1.00 at 1993 exchange rate)
Source: *Far Eastern Economic Review* (April 10, 1986), p. 81. By permission of the publisher.

allowed increases in fixed investment only in energy, transport, telecommunications, and in science and education. Investment in processing industries, which put strains on energy and transportation, were cut back. In other words, China's weak infrastructure could no longer support a higher growth rate. Third, the plan stressed the importance of promoting science, education, and technological development. Total outlay for education amounted to 116 billion rmb, a 72 percent increase over the previous plan. Stress also was placed on improving instructional quality in education and teacher training. The educational system was projected to graduate 8 million teachers, 2.6 million university graduates, and 5 million advanced specialized personnel over the five-year period.[37] Fourth, the Seventh Five-Year Plan would double the growth in foreign trade from the previous plan. By 1990 China's trade volume was projected to U.S. $83 billion, or a 40 percent increase from 1985. Imports to China were projected to increase to about U.S. $45 billion by 1990, with emphasis on computer software, consumer durable goods, and advanced technology.[38] Premier Zhao pointed out that the plan would place a high priority on quality control of export products (textiles, light industrial goods, and processed foods) and the search for "larger international markets."[39] Fifth, the Seventh Five-Year Plan pledged to set "an appropriate rate for raising living standards" of the people. Specifically, the average annual growth rate for the rural peasants' net income was projected to rise by 7 percent, while urban industrial workers' wages would rise by only 4 percent.[40] However, by 1990 urban residents were projected to earn an average of 900 rmb, and rural residents 400 rmb.[41] Zhao warned that improvement in people's living standards must be based on the growth in production. He pointed out that limited funds would be available to raise the living standards for the population of over one billion: "If the people's level of consumption is raised too high, there will inevitably be a reduction in the accumulation of funds, an increase in production cost and a lack of strength for future economic development." He warned that "no development funds should be diverted for the purpose of raising living standards."[42]

A vital goal of the Seventh Five-Year Plan was to control demands for "nonproductive investment" by local governments under the reform for decentralized decision making. The previous plan had shown a rise in fixed asset investments in the form of the new buildings and factories that contributed to inflation and high prices for material. This had placed the planners in a dilemma: they must exercise restraint and control on local investments but, at the same time, must allow decentralized decision making at the local level. It has been proved that it is almost impossible to accomplish both tasks at the same time. In presenting the Seventh Five-Year Plan, Premier Zhao emphasized the need to raise productive efficiency as a whole. Increased efficiency may depend to a large extent on reform improvements in the management of enterprises, such as autonomy for the plant manager, control by the manager over loss and profit, and gradual price decontrol. In short, the success or failure of the plan may rest on solutions to the thorny problems that have hampered China's economic growth.

Under the Five-Year Plan for 1991–1995, China expects a slower growth rate of about 6 percent a year. The overall goal is to double its gross national product to U.S. \$538 billion by the year 2,000.

AGRICULTURAL (RURAL) REFORM: THE RESPONSIBILITY SYSTEM

The single most important change in recent years for the people's communes has been the introduction of the responsibility system for the peasants. It is, in essence, an incentive system. The system—introduced in 1978 but put into effect in 1980—is a modification of Liu Shaoqi's "Three Freedoms and One Guarantee," which was introduced in the early 1960s as a part of the economic recovery program after the failure of the Great Leap. Both Liu and his policy were attacked by the radicals during the Cultural Revolution as "revisionist" and "capitalist." Liu's policy included (1) free markets, (2) private plots, and (3) peasant responsibility for managing their own farms on the basis of contracts for fixed output quotas for each household. In 1978, at the Third Plenum of the Eleventh Central Committee, the party under the leadership of Deng Xiaoping revived the main features of the old Liu policy as a way to step up agricultural production.

The 1978 party resolution on agricultural reform urged that remuneration for work in the communes be based on the principle of "to each according to his work" by stressing quality of work. In addition, the party resolution directed that private plots and sideline production were now "necessary adjuncts of the socialist economy and must not be interfered with."[43] Central Committee Document No. 75, issued in November 1980, outlined a number of approved methods for use of the "responsibility system."[44] These methods were all based on contracts issued by the production teams to the peasants for specific quotas of output or work accomplished. Under all methods, pay was to be based on the level of production or work accomplished. The contracts, depending on local conditions and tradition, could be issued to individuals, to households, or to work teams. One type, "Baochan Daohu" ("to fix farm output quota for each household"), permitted a township to make land available to each household, usually a family, in accordance with its labor capacity. The production team and the household signed a contract fixing the quota the household was obligated to fulfill. This quota included a portion for the team's quota for the state and a portion to meet township expenses.

Another type of rural responsibility system was the concept of full responsibility to the household, "Baogan Daohu." Under this method the household signed a contract with the village to assume all responsibility for work on the land and to bear the entire responsibility for its own profit and loss.

Under this arrangement, land was contracted to the household on a per capita basis by the village. In addition, farm implements and draft animals were permanently assigned to the household under contract. The household not only had to meet the state procurement requirements, but it had to assume full responsibility for managing the land and fulfilling all its obligations to the collective—in this case, the village. After deduction of the various cost items for the state and the collective, the remainder of the earnings went to the household.

Unique advantages of the job responsibility system described above were: (1) encouraging peasants to work harder in order to receive more income; (2) allowing the peasants to manage their own production under the most favorable local conditions, rather than under the "commandism" of rural cadres—thus permitting the peasants to have more initiative and autonomy; and (3) avoiding the problem of constant complaints by peasants about unfair distribution of earnings. The advantages of the responsibility system, combined with the policy of private plots and free markets, gave a tremendous boost to peasant morale and resulted in increased output and work enthusiasm.

By 1981 the rural responsibility system had been adopted in all the provinces. By mid-1982, official figures reported that 90 percent of the villages in the townships had adopted some form of the responsibility system.[45] While there were differences in the methods or arrangements adopted, depending on type of produce and locale, on the whole the income of the peasants increased significantly under the incentive system.[46]

The introduction of the incentive system for agricultural production was not without criticism. Some felt that China was about to abolish the collective commune system. Others cried out that the new agricultural policy was a "bourgeois policy."[47] Defenders of the new policy countered that under it, peasants could expect increased income and general prosperity. Premier Zhao pointed out, when he introduced the agricultural reform experiment in Sichuan, that any innovation must be considered socialist as long as the means of production are publicly owned and as long as the Marxist principle of "to each according to his work" is observed.[48] One Western scholar noted: "In Guangdong, at least, it seems not to have weakened the commitment to a collective economy."[49] As a final note, the new reform in agricultural productivity eventually may remove some of the glaring shortcomings of the collective commune system in China; Premier Zhao pointedly told the NPC in December 1982:

> Many places report that, with the introduction of the responsibility system, production has gone up, the relationship between cadres and peasants has markedly improved and bureaucraticism, arbitrary orders, corruption, waste, and other obnoxious practices have declined sharply.[50]

Extension of Leased Land Under Contract

The success of the responsibility system in the countryside enabled the reformers to move a step further, to "legitimize" and "institutionalize" the widely accepted "Baogan Daohu," or simply "Da Baogan" system of leasing land owned collectively by the township under contract. This step had been termed the "second land reform" or the "decollectivization" of the communes in the countryside.[51] Party Document No. 1 of 1984 extended the duration of household contracts from a period of 3 to 5 years to 15 years. The 15-year extension of land contracted not only signified to peasants the legitimacy of the responsibility system, but also gave them a sense of permanence and stability in their contracts,[52] and alleviated the fear that the leased land contracts, the "Da Baogan," might be subject to shifting political winds. In addition, the longer period for leased land provided the peasants with "a greater incentive to invest in the land" and to make other improvements needed to enable the land to be continuously productive.[53] Inducing the peasants to invest capital and labor on the land also lightened the state's burden of providing subsidies to agricultural production.[54]

Another significant change endorsed by the party was the gradual abolition of the state monopoly to buy farm products. In its place, a new price system based on market demand was introduced. In other words, the state would gradually relinquish its position as the sole and exclusive purchasing agent for agricultural products at a fixed price. Instead of selling grain to the state grain bureau, the peasants now could enter into contracts with a variety of buyers and purchasing agents on the basis of 70 percent at above-quota price and 30 percent at the state quota price, depending on the quality of the product. Premier Zhao argued that the new rural reform not only would result in better quality but would entice the peasants to produce the needed marketable goods. In the past, the monopolistic price system tended to force the peasants to produce only grains and cotton, regardless of the market demands for other products, such as silk, jute, tea, and tobacco.[55]

Diversification and Specialization by Households

New rural policies contained in Document No. 1 (1984) also encouraged the rapid development of a new rural institution, the "special households" and "key-point households."[56] As of 1985–86, more than 25 million households in the countryside, or about 14 percent of the total rural population, were classified as "special" and "key point" households.[57] These households engaged not only in agricultural production, but in services, such as transport and commerce. Wan Li, a Politburo member and a vice-premier who was considered one of the key architects of rural reform, revealed that many peasants had become prosperous because of their expanded activities as "special households."[58] Based on the study of a county in Shanxi province, Wan Li distinguished several types of peasants involved in the specialized households: production and team leaders with managerial skills, demobilized soldiers, peasants with skills in specific grain or cash crop cultivation (such as silk, tobacco, livestock, poultry breeding, fishery cultivation, or forestry), and individuals providing services.[59]

Typically a specialized household signs a contract with the collective village for a piece of cultivatable land, forest, fruit orchard, fish pond, or grazing pasture. Under the contract, the specialized household is obligated to turn over a part of the income derived from the production to the collective, but is allowed to keep the rest. The specialized household must operate and manage its projects without any help from the township. It is the sole responsibility of the specialized household to make its own arrangements with other economic organizations based on market demand and supply. The state and the township come into the picture only when loans and credit are needed. While peasants engaged in specialized production must assume their own risks, they also keep profits.

The introduction of specialized households in rural China has provided a distinct shift in China's agriculture from basically subsistence farming—providing enough grain to feed the families—to commercial commodity production.[60] Peasants operating under the specialized household contracts enter into service trades, commodity production, manufacturing, and transportation of locally produced goods to distant locations. Thomas Bernstein sees the new development not only as a major shift to commodity production, but as a way of "unleashing the entrepreneurial talents of China's peasants."[61] The development of specialized households has enabled the peasants to diversify. Under this arrangement, peasants now grow any type of high-yield commercial commodity crop suitable to the land and able to be produced efficiently—so long as the grain quota imposed by the state is met. Diversification is not limited to farming, but extends to cottage industries as well.[62] The new system also allows more mobility for the peasants. During the off-season peasants may leave their villages for more lucrative jobs at construction sites in nearby towns or cities rather than remaining idle.[63] In interviewing Chinese immigrants in Hong Kong, Jonathan Ungar found that hired field hands have been allowed to move from poor farming areas to rich areas, thus opening for peasant families the alternative of mobility instead of being hopelessly bound to the poor villages as destitutes.

The need to encourage peasants to specialize and diversify led to another important change in rural China. Land contracted from the collective can now be transferred from one household to another, allowing for the more efficient households to replace the less efficient. Specialized households may also form partnerships and companies, either by themselves or in joint ventures with the state or the marketing cooperatives. They can even hire workers as "helpers" under "labor exchange."

Some of the specialized households have prospered and reportedly earned as much as 10,000 yuan (about U.S. $3,500) per year. On the other hand, the rate of failures and bankruptcy cases has been rising. In one county in Henan province, a survey showed that a total of 819 specialized households, about 3 percent of the total specialized households for the county, ended in bankruptcy. Reasons for failure included lack of technological know-how and managerial skills, inability to understand the need for financial skills, and the peasants' lack of the necessary skills and ties.[64]

Rural Surplus Labor and Rural Industries: "A Factory in Every Village"

As specialized households multiplied and agricultural production became more efficient, there arose a problem of rural surplus labor. In 1985 Xinhua news agency reported that as many as one-third of China's total rural labor force had been idled, or "freed" from farming.[65] In the eastern coastal province of Zhejiang, half of the rural labor force was reported to have gone into nonagricultural pursuits. From 1975 to 1985, some nine million peasants left their farms.[66] One expert on rural China has reported that 30 to 40 percent of China's rural labor force, about 370 million, most likely will be engaged in industries and sideline occupations in the future, thus creating "a class of landless landlords" in the future.[67] Instead of allowing the idled peasants to roam around or migrate to the already overpopulated cities, authorities permitted them to engage in nonagricultural activities in small towns created for them. Surplus rural workers and those unemployed seasonally could work in animal husbandry, fish farming, forestry, and other sideline production, or in the service trades.[68]

During the mid-1980s China began a program of rural industrialization using the slogan "A factory for every village."[69] The program was designed to utilize rural surplus labor in industries to process agricultural products. A number of small rural towns, particularly those with flourishing markets, developed rapidly. The rural cottage industries were owned by townships (formerly the entire commune), villages (formerly the production brigade), individual peasants, and rural cadres. From 1984 to 1985 the rural cottage industries employed 52 million, or 14 percent of the surplus rural labor force, and contributed about 40 percent of rural output.[70] In 1985, rural industries had absorbed 60 million surplus workers. The cottage industries operated outside of the centralized planning system and were independent of state-owned enterprises. Many were free-wheeling private business enterprises that contributed in some measure to the "overheating" of China's economy. The central authorities have tried to curb the rapid growth of rural industries by limiting lending and investment credits to village cottage industries.[71] Many observers doubt that these efforts will succeed, because rural industries can continue to expand by retaining profits and by issuing stock to workers in order to raise more investment capital.

Rural Reform: Cadres' Opposition and Accommodation

When the responsibility system was first introduced in 1978, rural cadres reacted with resentment and opposition to the change. Rural and "grassroot" party cadres were in many ways "earth emperors" over the peasants because of their power and authority to make decisions affecting life in the countryside. Under the collectivized commune system, rural party cadres could order what, when, and how to plant; they often mobilized the peasants for work on collective projects, such as water conservation and roads. Under the responsibility system, individual households could contract for collectively owned land and manage production by themselves. The responsibility system reduced the administrative cost at the brigade and team levels by the elimination of administrative staff in the collective.[72] Under the commune system the tasks such as record keeping, work assignment, and accounting were normal responsibilities of the cadres and the commune staff under their direction.[73] With the household contract system, these managerial tasks gradually decreased.[74] Moreover, rural party cadres soon discovered they no longer had the power to allocate funds for nonproductive party activities.[75] In the past, collective income had been appropriated by the rural party cadres to cover these overhead costs. As the rural cadres' managerial and supervisory tasks decreased, their income also declined. Provincial media reported many instances of rural cadres abandoning their posts as production team leaders and leaving these positions vacant.[76] However, many of the rural cadres who remained and accepted the responsibility system as a needed reform took the initiative by becoming "the middlemen brokering business deals and acting as entrepreneurs."[77]

With the declining functions of the commune, the 1982 state constitution, as discussed in Chapter 4, mandated the transfer of basic local governmental functions from the commune to the township people's government (see Article 95 in Appendix A).

In short, rural reform has created a new breed of local cadres: skilled, better educated, more technologically inclined, younger, and with the necessary "connections" to make things happen. Many former local cadres—brigade and team leaders—have abandoned their leadership positions to become prosperous holders of specialized household contracts.[78] To a large extent the local cadres have been the beneficiaries of the success of the rural reforms. It should be noted that a close relationship existed between the local cadres and the prosperous specialized households in the countryside, and the latter have often received "preferential treatment" in the contracting of land and distribution of sales contracts.[79]

Problems Resulting from Rural Reform

While the success of rural reform provided unprecedented prosperity for the peasants as a whole, it also created a number of problems for China's agrarian society.

One problem was the rise in rural violence from social tension generated by the reforms.[80] Household contracts created disputes over land and water rights.[81] A contributing factor to violence was the gradual erosion of local authority. Clashes among feuding peasants over ancestral temples and shrines became frequent.[82] Under the collective command structure, the local cadres had exercised a great deal of control over the lives of the peasantry. Now, under rural reform, that authority had been eroded to such an extent that local cadres could no longer restrain the feuding peasants from violence. Moreover, in many cases the restive local cadres served as instigators of violence. Large-scale looting led by local party cadres was reported frequently in China's local press.

Along with the rise of rural violence was the revival of feudalistic and superstitious practices. Feudal superstition, such as the use of Daoist priests to select tombs for the deceased and to conduct religious rituals, resurfaced in rural China.[83] There were even cases where work points were granted by party cadres for participating in these religious practices.[84] Gradually, kinship ties became more important than community interests.

Thomas Bernstein points out other side effects, or "unanticipated outcomes," of rural reform. Among these was a continuing reduction in arable land and forestry resources brought on by a steady housing construction boom in the countryside. Expansion in rural economic activities also siphoned off investment needed for irrigation projects.[85] Those familiar with China's farming have noted an increase in strip-farming—the division of land into tiny strips. William Hinton was alarmed by the neglect of rural education as the young were drawn into work for the households under household contracts.[86] Rural education was not only inferior in quality as compared with urban areas, but also in terms of the number of children attending schools. There seemed to be a general neglect of rural education as attention focused on those reform measures that would increase peasants' prosperity. Many of the collectives' tangible assets, including schools and machinery, were divided among contracting households. Other collective services also were neglected as the individual household contract system took root: social welfare for the aged, irrigation projects, and insecticide spraying. Finally, the differences between the poor and more prosperous peasants in the countryside became increasingly evident—a point that alarmed some China observers.[87]

URBAN REFORM: MEANING AND PROBLEMS

The average annual rate of growth for industrial production from 1953 to 1974 had been estimated at a very respectable rate of about 11 percent. The performance from 1975 to 1977 had been placed at a slightly lower rate, between 9 and 10 percent per year.[88] The official Chinese estimate put the annual growth rate from 1966 to 1977 at 12 percent.[89] In his presentation of the Sixth Five-Year Plan (from 1981 to 1985) to the NPC, Premier Zhao proposed a lower growth rate for industrial production than had existed during the previous twenty-eight years.[90] He pointed out candidly that although the growth rate for industrial output was not low in the past, the economic results—meaning quality, variety, and design of industrial products—had been "very poor." In the Sixth Five-Year Plan, he demanded better economic results. Before we discuss recent attempts to introduce reforms into the industrial system, it will be necessary to review very briefly some of the features of China's industrial system that made it possible for the nation to achieve a 10 to 11 percent average annual increase.

What were the key features of the Chinese industrial system? One obvious factor was the nationalization of basic industries. State ownership of all large enterprises since 1956 had enabled the state not only to establish a centralized budget process but also to reinvest a sizable share of earnings in new plants and equipment for increases in production. One specialist on the Chinese economy pointed out that by the end of the First Five-Year Plan, 75 percent of state revenues came from the earnings of state-owned enterprises, and that state revenues constituted one-third of China's national income.[91] Closely related to the capacity for reinvestment was the policy of keeping industrial wages at low levels; income not distributed to the workers could be reinvested.

Another key factor was the initial strategy of placing emphasis on the development of heavy industries, particularly machine tool factories and iron and steel plants. Iron and steel production remains the key to the future growth of China's industries.[92] Steel plants are located strategically in eight major centers, with the largest at Anshan in the northeast, producing about 25 percent of the total national output. During the 1980s a new steel plant, the Baoshan complex, was added to the Shanghai industrial region (with loans from Japan); there is also the Wuhan steel complex in central China. The nation now needs new mines for both coal and iron to feed the steel furnaces. In addition, efficient coal- and iron-mining equipment will have to be imported from abroad in order to boost production. Modern large-scale blast furnaces are needed. Most of the furnaces in use in 1978 were built by the Soviets in the 1950s.

Finally, emphasis on the development of a large number of medium-and small-scale, labor-intensive industries has been a major factor in the rapid gains in industrial production. These decentralized, relatively small enterprises take advantage of the abundance of labor in rural areas, using a minimum of capital goods, and thus freeing investment for heavy industry. The policy of "walking on two legs" therefore develops simultaneously heavy industry, which is capital-intensive and centralized, and medium to small industry, which is labor-intensive and decentralized. The small industries, with employment ranging from 15 to 600, are owned by either the state, the county, or the communes.[93] Many of the small- and medium-sized industries, such as cement, brick, fertilizer, and farm machinery plants, are linked to agricultural production. The importance of small-scale industries in rural communes can be illustrated by the following cycle of development: annual rainfall must be caught by dams and reservoirs, which are constructed with cement; with the availability of water for irrigation of the fields, more chemical fertilizer is needed to produce a higher yield of crops; with the prospect of a higher yield, agricultural machinery, such as tractors, harvesters, and water pumps, is needed. In one year, 54 percent of China's synthetic ammonia was produced by about 1,000 small fertilizer plants.[94] The United States' delegation on small-scale industry, which visited China in 1975, pointed out that these small-scale industries save time in construction, solve the problem of limited transport facilities for rural areas, and allow for the exploitation of available local resources.[95] These small-scale industries in rural areas also have the ideological justification of removing the urban–rural dichotomy.

Following on the heels of the emerging success in rural reform, the party authorized in the fall of 1984 a comprehensive set of directives for reform in the economic structure, known as urban reform.[96] The document on urban reform has been described as "socialism with Chinese characteristics."[97]

We may begin the discussion on urban reform by asking the following questions. Why urban reform? What were areas of concern for the party in October 1984? What problems were created as a result of urban reform? And finally, what are the political and economic implications of urban reform?

The party's 1984 document on urban reform called for a major overhaul of China's state-owned enterprises in urban areas. The reform was deemed necessary because of inherent defects in state-owned urban enterprises: the lack of distinction between governmental functions and enterprise management, and the rigid bureaucratic control exercised by the state over these enterprises. Further, market forces were seen as a means to stimulate worker initiative and enthusiasm. As a first step leading toward enterprise autonomy, the number of products regulated by centralized planning was reduced from 120 to 30. In other words, mandatory planning was retained for certain key products and resources. "Guided planning" still applied to other products and economic activities. Under "guided planning," market forces are permitted to operate for the production of minor industrial and consumer goods. Similarly, lesser industrial raw material and producer goods of local importance are permitted to be exchanged on the market.

Urban Reform–What Does It Mean?

A priority item for reform, according to the 1984 party document, was to invigorate the state-owned enterprises (numbering about 400,000 with a total labor force of more than 80 million) by separating the ownership from the operational functions. Instead of exercising "excessive and rigid control," the party document said, a state-owned enterprise "should be truly made a relatively independent economic entity." This meant that such enterprises must operate and manage their own affairs, assume responsibility for their own profits and losses, and develop themselves as "legal persons with certain rights and duties."[98] The party decision called for the factory managers to assume "full responsibility" and the party leaders in factories and service enterprises to "provide active support," without interference, to managers so as to establish unified direction in production and operation.[99] This meant that factory managers must have the right to determine matters such as job description and performance for workers as well as the right to set wages and bonuses. Full responsibility also implied that managers must be responsible for profit and loss. As a departure from previous reforms, the October 1984 urban reform advocated the practice of profit retention. In the past, profits from state-owned enterprises had to be returned to the state treasury. The state, then, reallocated these funds as supplies and resources needed for production according to the state plan.

Closely related to the reform in managerial autonomy was the introduction of the industrial contract responsibility system. Under the factory responsibility system, the workers and the factory director sign a contract with the state obligating them to turn over "a certain amount of taxes and profits to the state" and allowing them to keep for their own use "any or almost any amount above the set quota." However, they must make up any amount below the quota.[100] By 1986, 9,270 larger state-owned industrial enterprises, or about 75 percent of the total 12,380, had introduced the contract system. Under the system, the most qualified directors for the enterprises are selected competitively through public bidding. The ultimate objective of the industrial contract system is to enable each state-owned large enterprise to "either turn out cheap commodities of good quality or lag behind and be eliminated."[101] The 1984 party document recommended, based on selective experiments over the previous few years, the formation of "diverse economic forms" in the cities and "other diverse and flexible forms of cooperative management and economic associations among the state, collective and individual sectors of the economy." The party document then suggested that the state have collectives of individuals learn or run them on a contract basis, by relying on "voluntary participation and mutual benefit."[102] In a sense this was nothing new, because the mixture of public and private enterprises had been in operation since the early 1950s.[103] What was new was the scope of enterprise ownership reform. Between 1985 and 1987, all small-sized state-owned enterprises with fixed assets of less than 1.5 million yuan (about $400,000)—mostly retail service, repair, and catering businesses—were to be leased out under contract to individuals or cooperatives for a period of five years. These arrangements were to be managed independently without state supervision, provided rent and taxes were paid to the state treasury. These new arrangements, according to one estimate, accounted for more than half of the value of total gross industrial output in China in 1985.[104]

Existing large-scale state-owned enterprises not engaged in vital productive activities could voluntarily become joint stock companies with limited liability.[105] New companies thus formed became shareholding enterprises "with stocks purchased by workers and individuals outside the enterprises."[106] In the place of the heavy-handed government-party management style, a board of directors was to assume the overall management policies for the new shareholding enterprises. (It should be noted that the government retained 51 percent of the stock, or the controlling shares, for these large-scale enterprises.) The arrangement also applied to joint ventures with participation from foreign investors. Members of the boards of directors could be shareholding or non-shareholding, with the latter elected by and representing the interests of the workers and small individual shareholders.

Urban enterprise reform, in effect, created a "two-tier ownership" structure: large and key enterprises with their controlled subsidiaries as industrial combines engaged in high-tech development; and numerous small enterprises, cooperatives, and individual enterprises with mixed ownership devoted to the processing of farm and sideline production and improvement of services in both urban and rural areas. One immediate and tangible result of workers owning shares in the enterprises was increased initiative and productivity resulting from the pride of ownership and an incentive to be efficient.[107]

Urban Reform: Problems

One immediate result of urban reform was a rapid increase in output: a 23 percent growth rate for the first quarter of 1985 marked China as one of the world's overheated economies. Local authorities accumulated fixed assets by investing in plants, machinery, and other capital goods. This led to the reinstitution of administrative controls over credits and the money supply. By July 1986 the central government had to issue a new set of regulations to monitor fixed asset investment and placed all capital construction plans under state supervision.

Urban households immediately experienced the effect of price decontrol: food prices rose by as much as 37 percent in 1985. The official inflation rate was put at 6 percent in 1985, but the actual inflation rate was at least 20 percent for retail goods in urban areas. The authorities had not been able to devise a workable mechanism to prevent inflation for decontrolled prices, and soon it became necessary to reinstitute price controls for vegetables by placing a ceiling on their market prices. Then by January 1988 price ceilings were set for oil, gas, electricity, steel, timber, coal, and other raw materials.

Decentralization and decontrol under urban reform did not curb the growth of bureaucratic power and prerogatives. For more than thirty years, China had operated under a rigid system of centralized control. The party cadres, who held the decision-making power, had become a special privileged class. Reform in the urban areas yielded two conflicting trends. One was resistance, or foot-dragging, by the cadres against introduction of the market mechanism called for by the urban reform. Jan Prybyla has pointed out that "marketization," in fact, threatened the bureaucracy's role as planners and supervisors.[108] At the same time, bureaucrats in the cadre system were the ultimate survivors. They had access to both information and power. Therefore, they were in a position to exploit the new circumstances to enrich themselves. Soon they had transformed their position and seized the unique opportunities made available to form instant "briefcase companies" (these were bureaucratic entities organized overnight by the cadres who became the new owners of enterprises). Many of these bureaucrat-entrepreneurs now behaved "like capitalists" and committed economic crimes, such as black-marketeering, embezzling public funds or resources, and "lining their own pockets."[109]

While the 1984 party document mandated the party secretaries to gradually turn over managerial authority in the factories to plant managers (or directors), in reality party secretaries were unable to "break their habit" of making decisions in the plant. Often a factory director was not sure of his power vis-à-vis the party secretary's prerogatives.[110] Party committees in factories could still institute proceedings to overrule a factory manager's decisions by appealing to a higher party organization.[111] Then the turmoil caused by the 1986–87 student demonstrations provided the occasion for the orthodox hard-liners to launch an attack against the pragmatic reformers.

A set of new regulations on the factory responsibility system was announced.[112] The decision-making power in the factory was to be in the hands of the workers' congresses under the overall control of the All-China Federation of Trade Unions. Now it was the workers' congress, not the factory manager or party secretary, who had the right to adjust plans and wages, and to provide incentives and punishment leading up to dismissal, including the right to dismiss the factory manager. Factory managers could be appointed, elected by the workers, or recruited through open advertisement. In August 1987, it was reported that the manager responsibility system had been instituted in more than 30,000, or over 7.5 percent, of the 400,000 state-owned industrial enterprises.[113] Then, finally, in January 1988, after nine years of delay, the enterprise reform law was approved by the Standing Committee of the NPC for ratification. The new law would, in theory, grant power to the factory manager.

Large-scale state-owned enterprises in China are going through a difficult time. Some state-owned firms are in deep financial trouble because they no longer produce goods that people want or "they make too much of what people don't want."[114] Their goods are stockpiled in warehouses, and about 40 percent of these state-owned enterprises are in debt—estimated at U.S. $30–50 billion. Many are thinking of selling out to foreign investors.[115]

These enterprises were originally built with Soviet aid in the 1950s and their machinery had become obsolete over the years. For decades they operated under tight state controls and with government support. As the market economy grew under reforms, the state-owned enterprises failed to keep up, and many now face the inevitable prospect of closing down for good. In order to prevent bankruptcy of state-owned enterprises, the market device of security stock exchange—two established in the Shenzhen special economic zone bordering Hong Kong and one in Shanghai—has been employed without opting for privatization. A limited number of shares in stock ownership is given to individuals and to other government agencies.

THE CHINESE ECONOMY AFTER TIANANMEN: AUSTERITY, RETRENCHMENT, AND RECESSION

Long before the Tiananmen crackdown the Chinese economy was already in serious trouble. The reform decade, from 1978 to 1988, had brought on excessive growth that contributed to an overheated economy. Inflation for the urban areas was officially estimated at 18.5 percent in 1988, but the actual rate was over 30 percent. Industrial growth for the decade increased at an average rate of about 12 percent annually. In 1988 the total industrial growth rate was 20 to 21 percent against the official planned growth target of not more than 8 percent.[116] The "uncontrolled industrial investment hunger" was stimulated by the haphazard fixed investment initiated by provincial and local authorities without regard for conservation of resources and real market demand. As explained by Jan Prybyla:[117]

> This surge in economic activity placed enormous strain on scarce raw material and energy supplies and on the badly overburdened and bottlenecked transportation system. It also contributed to an already thriving black market and the concurrent corruption.

At the same time, after the peak 1984 production of 407 million tons, grain production had leveled off so that rationing for many key agricultural commodities had to be instituted.[118] In the first quarter of 1988 prices for fresh vegetables rose more than 48 percent and prices for nonstaple foods rose by 24 percent. Chinese consumers spent more than half of their income on food. This high inflation rate for the three-year period from 1986 to 1988 brought down real income for urban wage earners.[119]

After some heated and lengthy debate, Chinese leaders decided to inaugurate a price-reform policy—decontrol of prices in accordance with supply and demand and the introduction of a wage index to cost of living, insisted on by reform leader Zhao Ziyang. Decontrol in prices produced some panic in urban areas: "runs on the bank, a spending spree, stockpiling, and unauthorized price hikes."[120] The consumer panic was accompanied by deliberate increases in bonuses and subsidies to workers and staff in state enterprises, a hefty jump to 36 percent in the first seven months of 1988 as compared to the same period in 1987. At this juncture advocates of price reform, led by Zhao and his reformers, were in trouble and under criticism by the hard-liners. In fact, economic policy decision making was now taken away from the reformers and transferred to Li Peng and Yao Yilin, supporters of hard-liners on the Politburo at the CCP's Tenth Plenum in mid-August. By September and October, after more lengthy debate at party and State Council work conferences, Zhao admitted mistakes in economic policies and accepted the alternative of a new program of economic austerity and retrenchment. This policy included tightening credit for capital construction, reducing the purchasing power of various social groups, cracking down on corruption by cadres, recentralizing trade and foreign investment, reducing spending by party and government agencies, and reviving ideological indoctrination.[121]

The austerity and retrenchment policy adopted in the fall of 1988 meant a retreat in the partial market system experiment. What had been reinstituted was centralized "administrative command" and "compulsion."

Recession: The Tiananmen Aftermath

In the first six months after the military crackdown at Tiananmen, China was in an economic recession. Tightened and controlled credit and loan policies under the austerity program produced a slowdown in industrial output to a yearly gain of about 2.3 percent. Inflation was still estimated at 21.4 percent in 35 major cities for the first ten months of 1989.[122] As credit and loans became restricted and squeezed or not available at all, many factories ceased production. Enterprises or firms, established when credit and investment were readily obtainable and there was momentum for reform, now went bankrupt or fell deeply in debt. By the time the Tiananmen crackdown occurred, demand for durable consumer goods in urban areas had reached a saturation point and rural peasants were more interested in housing investment. The result was large inventories of durable goods and refrigerators and television sets in the warehouses.

The crackdown also brought fear and uncertainty to the flourishing rural enterprises, as now the political winds shifted to the right. By the end of 1989 many rural or village industries also stopped producing. About one million rural enterprises across China ceased production within one year of the austerity and retrenchment policy that began in the fall of 1988.[123] These small-scale but semiprivate rural industries depended on credit and loans from banks.

The industrial slowdown for both urban and rural sectors created serious unemployment problems after Tiananmen: in 1989 urban unemployment was 3.5 percent, or 5.4 million workers, out of a total labor force of more than 150 million.[124] The rural jobless rate for 1989 was estimated at 40 percent of the rural work force, or about 120 million in the countryside.[125] Urban workers bore the brunt of these stringent economic measures, for they had to endure wage cuts or unemployment. There were worker strikes in 1989 and small-scale protest marches in cities in western and central China.[126]

The overall goals for the austerity program and the tight money measures were to bring down the inflation rate to about 10 percent and the growth rate to 5 or 6 percent per year. The reinstitution of ideological studies in state-owned enterprises, a reaction to the student protests at Tiananmen, meant further loss in productivity, as workers spent time in political indoctrination instead of in production. As state-run enterprises slowed their productivity, the state was required to provide large amounts of money for resource purchasing and worker benefits, thus aggravating the state budget deficit. It has been estimated that the state must bail out the state-owned enterprises by as much as $12 billion, or about one-third of its revenue. To make up for the deficit, the government resorted to issuance of printed money, spurring more inflation. Furthermore, about 20 million workers, about one-fifth of the personnel in state enterprises, came to work each day and got paid even though there was no work to be done.[127]

Impact of Global Sanctions on the Chinese Economy in the Tiananmen Aftermath

Initial world reaction to the Tiananmen massacre included a tourism boycott and the withholding of foreign loans and investment from China. For the months from July to December 1989 China expected about one million tourists, whose spending would have enriched its treasury by about $2.2 billion in foreign currency. Instead, thanks to the global tourism boycott, only 500,000 tourists visited the country in the last six months of 1989, causing a loss of at least $1 billion in foreign exchange revenue. Most new hotels built by joint ventures in the 1980s suffered a low occupancy rate. Then many Western industrial nations withheld loans and extensions of credit to China for the remainder of 1989. For a while even Japan halted its aid projects to China. The World Bank stopped action on its seven loan projects for power, transport, and industrial development. (However, in May 1990 the World Bank decided to lend $300,000 for reforestation projects.)

The cumulative effects of withholding foreign loans and credit to China were delays in developing much-needed energy projects plus the drying up of funds for Chinese banks, which in turn contributed to recession. Direct foreign investment in China declined after Tiananmen. However, the gap seemed to have been filled by cumulative investment from Taiwan—$1 billion at the end of 1989, and then doubled in 1990.[128]

Easing Austerity to Revive the Sagging Economy

To relieve the deepening economic recession, Premier Li Peng announced in July 1990 a five-point plan to revive the sagging economy. A key point in the plan was to extend low-interest loans to state enterprises to reduce their debts. The beneficiaries of the new low-interest loans seemed to be those large-scale state enterprises engaged in export trade—grain procurement units and joint venture projects with foreign investment. The easing of credit and loan extension began in the spring of 1990 when the Industrial and Commercial Bank of China extended an initial amount of $510 million in new loans to industrial enterprises in major cities.[129] This was later increased to $1.06 billion.

Some of the large-scale state enterprises in the industrial northeast (including the giant Anshan Iron and Steel Works, Daqing Oil fields, Shenyang Electric Cable Plant, and other mining and chemical plants) have signed contracts with the state under which it has guaranteed energy, raw material, and transportation services in return for a commitment to meet fixed quotas for finished products and to pay taxes.[130] The new guaranteed loans would enable large-scale state enterprises to resolve their debt problems and develop new products. Since 1988, when the austerity program was initiated, many state enterprises have defaulted on bank loans. These loan arrangements were made at the provincial level without specific approval from the central government when decentralization reform was in vogue. Some of these loan arrangements involved joint venture or foreign investment. With tightening of credit under the austerity program, plant managers faced mounting problems of finding available working capital to purchase raw material and supplies, in addition to meeting their long-term debt obligations.[131] A plant manager's life was further complicated by the two-tiered pricing system for raw material and supplies: the low state-subsidized price and a market price.

The easing of credit and loan extension to state enterprises is aimed at revival of the sagging economy, but it also could create a new round of boom–bust cycles if it is not accompanied by price reform. Inflation, now at 10 percent—down from its high of 30 percent before the Tiananmen massacre—could easily increase again, in turn requiring the reinstitution of austerity measures.

In short, Chinese leaders embarked on two basic approaches to China's economic difficulties: continued austerity which ended in 1993, and the reinstitution of centralized administrative control immediately after Tiananmen, followed by easing of the austerity restrictions and emphasis on more growth. Under the Eighth Five-Year Plan (1991–95) some reform measures have been proposed in enterprise management, foreign trade, the financial system, and housing. However, the most important reform—doing away with the two-tiered price system (a fixed price on certain products and a floating or fluctuating price for the remaining goods produced) remains in controversy.

Crisis in the Rural Economy: An Overview

The Chinese grain harvest for 1990 reached a targeted record high of 422 million tons. But China's rural economy has been in crisis for several years due to a number of difficulties. Despite the grain increase, the total tonnage needed to feed the population, which is increasing by at least 15–20 million people annually, exceeds 422 million tons. China needs an additional 40–80 million tons of grain production per year before the year 2000 in order to adequately feed its people. One needs to bear in mind that in recent years a larger share of consumer spending, as much as 60 percent in 1988, has been for food.[132]

Then, there has been an increase in the consumption of meat and liquor, which require additional increases in grain production of about 20–40 million tons. Grain production can be increased in only three ways: an increase in land acreage for cultivation; improvement in existing land utilization; or the importation of grain from abroad. Arable acreage for agricultural production is shrinking rapidly in China. The reasons for this include the population increase, which places additional demands on land; peasants shifting production to more lucrative crops other than basic grain production; declining soil fertility; excessive use of chemical fertilizers; and soil erosion. Official estimates put the decline of arable land acreage for 1985 and 1986 at from 600,000 to one million hectares.[133]

Improvement of existing arable land means that, for an additional increase of 50 million tons of grain, there must be 15 million more tons of chemical fertilizers, 10 billion more kilowatt-hours of electricity, and 1.3 million more tons of diesel oil.[134] But agricultural investment credits have been on the decline, amounting to about 3 percent of total state spending for 1986–90, a 50 percent decrease as compared to 6 percent for 1981–85.[135] In 1979 total investment in agriculture was 5.8 billion yuan; but in 1986 it declined to about 3.5 billion yuan.[136] Realizing the difficulties in boosting grain production, the State Planning Commission revealed, in its draft 1990 plan to the NPC, a decision to invest an additional 1 billion yuan ($212 million) in agriculture, with most of the investment funds earmarked for irrigation facilities and grain and cotton production.[137] Agricultural investment loans and credit have been one of the hardest hit sectors since June 1989 due to the fact that overseas lending to Chinese agriculture had been suspended and delayed as a result of economic sanctions in reaction to the Tiananmen crackdown.

Importation of needed grain from abroad involves at least one major problem: China's foreign indebtedness and government deficit. In 1989, a good harvest year, grain imports reached almost 15 million tons. For 1990 the government tried to reduce grain imports—principally from Australia, Canada, the European Economic Community (EEC) group, and the United States.

Even if these difficulties in China's rural economy could be solved, either wholly or partially, grain production would still lag behind unless there is price reform in the government purchasing system. Grain purchasing by the government is operating on the old system of low administering price, currently at the 1989 level, rather than the market price for what is produced under state quotas. This policy provides little incentive for the peasants to grow grain, since other production costs such as fertilizer and pesticides have gone up many times. On top of the state-administered low price for grain are the unpaid debts local purchasing authorities owe to the peasants for "contracted purchases." The local authorities' inability to honor debts for purchases from the peasants is a direct result of the center-imposed austerity program over state funds that are made available to local authorities. The consequence is more discontent in the countryside.

After initial gains in the reform decade, since 1989 the gap in income between coastal urban areas and the hinterland has widened considerably. In 1984, as reported in one study, the rural–urban income ratio was 1 to 1.85, but in recent years the ratio has reached the pre-reform level of 1 to 2.[138] Average annual income for peasants was $137 in 1992 as compared with an average annual urban income of $313. The peasants have been burdened by local taxes and fees. Peasants have faced the constant problem of local governments' inability to pay cash—they have been paid by government IOUs that are honored slowly. Reports of peasant uprisings have become more frequent—a matter of concern for a party that came into power through the support of peasants. As many as sixty million peasants are migrating from their villages to cities for more lucrative jobs. As a way of ameliorating the peasant plight, in July 1993 the central government decreed that levying of arbitrary taxes on the peasants be banned. There is unhappiness and tension in the country-side, which the reformers cannot possibly ignore for long. Yet, as a test of a market-oriented economic strategy, much attention has been paid to the development of entrepreneurial rural communities in the coastal regions, such as the "Wenzhou Model," named after the eastern coastal town that emphasized "mass initiative" in household industries for export, long-distance trade with adjacent areas, and rapid growth in market towns.[139]

Curtailment in Rural Enterprise Expansion

China's economic retrenchment also hit hard at the growth of rural enterprises, which in 1989 stood at 18 million and employed more than 93 million people, or about 23 percent of the total rural labor force. After almost eleven years of promoting and encouraging rural enterprises by the state, the economic retrenchment policy for the rural enterprises launched in the fall of 1988 was aimed at the reduction of "large-scale infrastructure projects" and loans or credit extension. With curtailment of loans and credit control also came a drastic cut in fixed asset projects and payment for workers. The result has been merger or closing down of rural enterprises. Since the Tiananmen crackdown, party control has been exercised over rural enterprises that up to that time had been decentralized and autonomous. A deliberate policy also has been established to assist only those rural enterprises that are either labor-intensive or export-oriented.[140]

Rural enterprises have been the instruments of rural industrialization since the early 1980s. As of 1992 there were about 18.5 million rural enterprises employing 96 million people and contributing 25 percent of China's gross national product. A World Bank report predicted that by the year 2000 as many as 150 million would be employed by these rural enterprises.

DENGISM: CHINA AS AN ECONOMIC GIANT BY YEAR 2000

Deng Xiaoping's ideas and policies on economic reform over the past fifteen years (1978–93) have been collectively named the "Theory of Deng" or "Dengism." Basically, this is a collection of Deng's remarks concerning the building of socialism with Chinese characteristics that include market-style reforms and an open door to foreign investment. At the Fourteenth Party Congress, held in October 1992, Deng's ideas and policies on reform were elevated to the status of a theory: "Comrade Deng Xiaoping is the chief architect of our socialist reform, of the open door policy and of the modernization program."[141] Deng's theory is now regarded as "the product of the integration of the universal principle of Marxism-Leninism with the practice of the Chinese Second Revolution—economic construction, reform and opening to the outside world."[142] Reminiscent of the adulation for Mao, Deng was cited no fewer than thirteen times in Jiang Zemin's report to the party congress in 1992; an annotated dictionary, the *Thought of Deng Xiaoping*, has been published containing some 2,000 of Deng's speeches.

Finally, Deng's theory was enshrined by the Eighth National People's Congress, held March 15–31, 1993, which amended Article 15 of the 1982 state constitution by deleting the requirement for state enterprises to fulfill their obligations under the state plan. Words in the constitution that referred to a planned economy have been replaced by the words "socialist market economy." In short, Deng's market reform for China's economy has won the final battle over the hard-liners. Thus, as Deng Xiaoping approached his final years, he saw to it that market reform was firmly established as China's road to modernization.

China in 1992–93 was in the midst of a booming economy. In 1992 its domestic growth product (minus foreign investment) was over 12 percent. By 1993 it had become evident that China must once again apply the brakes to its fast-growing economy as banks began to face shortages of cash and inflation soared to more than 20–30 percent in most urban areas. Drastic measures had to be taken such as raising interest rates, reducing government operations by 20 percent, curbing bank lending for speculative investments, cutting down infrastructure spending, and calling a temporary halt to price decontrol. Some of these measures were recommended by The World Bank in its August 1993 report on China. The International Monetary Fund reported in the spring of 1993 that the Chinese economy had become the third largest in the world, next only to the United States and Japan, based on a new method of comparing a country's goods and services in terms of purchasing power instead of as compared with some other nation's currency.[143] By this new measure, China in 1992 produced $1.7 trillion in goods and services instead of $400 billion.[144]

CAN THE GOALS OF MODERNIZATION BE ACHIEVED?

In this chapter we have tried to present a picture of China's efforts to modernize after 1949, with emphasis on the post-Mao era. Modernization means industrialization and economic growth, supported and strengthened by a formula of universal education that emphasizes the learning of modern science and technology. The politics of modernization in China since 1949 has focused primarily, although not exclusively, on how China can be transformed into an industrialized nation, equal to other nations that are in the forefront of technological development. Because of the lack of unity among the leaders in answering this question, policies and programs for modernization have vacillated between the revolutionary mass mobilization model and the professional and orderly development model. The continuous conflict and ambivalence toward these strategies for modernization dominated the flow of Chinese politics during the past several decades. Beneath the struggle, however, is the pervasive feeling in Chinese society and among peoples of all developing nations that they want a better way of life in terms of both moral and material well-being; and that this can come about only through the continuous acquisition of knowledge in science and technology.

Will China be able to achieve its goal of modernization? The answer rests on a number of factors. One is the ability of the leaders to maintain unity and some degree of cohesiveness so as to provide the needed political stability and climate for orderly development. Another is China's ability to develop its energy resources and transportation facilities. Equally important is China's ability to curb its population growth in the next decade. China also needs to strengthen its educational system in order to pave the way for development in science and technology. Such development is also contingent upon China's willingness to keep her doors open to trade with other nations.

Let us examine briefly two important factors that could contribute to the successful implementation of China's modernization program before the year 2000: reform in the management system, and population control.

Reform in the Management System[145]

Managerial reform calls for the development of effective intermediate and lower-level leadership to implement the plans for modernization. This factor will be influenced or shaped to a large extent by the unity and cohesiveness at the top levels of leadership. Closely related to the development of effective leadership is the urgent need to *acquire* managerial skills in the industrial and agricultural sectors. While the American business community is beginning to unlock the secrets of Japanese management success,[146] the Chinese economy is characterized by inefficiency, waste, and poor management. We have mentioned earlier that corrective measures were introduced in order to make the Chinese economic system more efficient and productive. But a great deal still needs to be done to improve management techniques at the enterprise level.

Several years ago Sir Yue-Kong Pao, a Hong Kong-based shipping tycoon, complained that when he cabled Beijing on business matters, it usually took three to five days to get someone to reply. When he made a long-distance telephone call to Beijing, he found that no one seemed to be responsible for making any decisions. The problem here is that the Chinese management executive does not behave as a businessperson normally behaves elsewhere in the world. A Chinese management executive typically acts like a bureaucrat. Management decisions are made vertically. Clearance is required in the bureaucratic hierarchy before a decision can be made. There is also a tendency in Chinese bureaucratic management to place a high value on conformity.[147] The end result has been that no one wants to take a different approach or be innovative. Thus, the prevailing climate in Chinese organizations is one of "indifference or irrelevance."[148] Worse still, Chinese management executives make no decisions, nor do they take any risks at all.

A further problem is that workers in a Chinese factory are typically inexperienced and lack the skill required to do their jobs adequately.[149] This general lack of skill and experience extends to managers as well.[150] The concept of an unbroken "iron rice bowl" (job security) is so deeply implanted in the minds of Chinese workers that it is difficult to introduce any system of evaluation of job performance. The Chinese economist Xue Muqiao urged that the state institute "a system of examination, appraisal and promotion and transfer" for industrial workers as a basic management reform.[151] He also asked that incompetent workers be dismissed, a management right that most Chinese enterprises are very reluctant to exercise.

In 1980 the State Council issued a set of guidelines to allow enterprises to experiment with self-management. The guidelines, among other things, specified (1) that the type of merchandise produced must meet market demands; (2) that certain levels of profits must be retained for expansion and/or improvement of plant facilities; and (3) that enterprises must recruit their own workers.[152] Effective implementation of these reform measures, however, depends on the adoption of modern management techniques and some fundamental changes in the existing personnel system.

(Some provinces, such as Guangdong, have formed business management associations to study management skills, with a view toward improving provincial enterprise management.)[153] In short, managerial training for cadres in industry is urgently needed. In addition, China's pragmatic leaders must find ways to improve work efficiency by solving such problems as overstaffing, bureaucratic red tape, and endless meetings.

The need for managerial training is best demonstrated by the fact that about two-thirds of China's industrial managers have a very low level of educational attainment, not more than the equivalent of a secondary school education in America.[154] Only very recently have the Chinese begun to send cadres abroad for training in modern managerial skills. Management training under the State Economic Commission has involved only a small fraction of some nine million state cadres.[155] A German managerial consultant to China has suggested that a center for technical training and professional ethics education be established by every factory to upgrade quality control and reduce the waste of resources by factory workers.[156] The German consultant found it intolerable that a deputy factory director received only half of the wage paid to a factory storehouse keeper because the latter had longer service.[157]

Population Control[158]

As expected by many demographers, the July 1982 national census showed that China's total population was over one billion, with an annual growth rate of 1.5 percent. Of the total, 51.5 percent were male, and 48.5 percent were female. The far-ranging implication of this huge population for China's economic development is quite obvious. Premier Zhao told the 1982 NPC that "the execution of our national economic plan and the improvement of the people's living standards will be adversely affected" if population growth is not controlled.[159] This was certainly a most candid admission by a top Chinese leader that the Malthusian theory of population was valid—a theory that Mao Zedong never accepted as applicable to a socialist China. Premier Zhao directed that population growth be kept below 1.3 percent per annum, so that China's total population would not exceed 1.06 billion by 1985.[160]

How can China's population explosion be controlled? During the 1970s the much-publicized measure for population control was delayed marriage for the young. In addition, clinics were permitted to provide abortion services. Some birth control devices were disseminated in factories. Then, in 1977, the target became one child per family. As the 1982 census demonstrated, these measures were not able to check the enormous population growth. A major factor was the persistence of the traditional preference among the rural population for male offspring. While female infanticide was still an accepted practice in some rural areas, Premier Zhao condemned the practice.[161] The difficulty in controlling population growth was aggravated by the fact that 62 percent of the population in 1982 was under 35 years of age. As young people reach the age of marriage and childbearing, the total number of births can be expected to rise dramatically—unless strict control measures are imposed. So far, the one-child-per-couple policy has been observed widely only in the urban areas. Under this policy the state imposes punitive measures, such as a 2 percent reduction in salary, if a couple refuses abortion of their second child. Following the birth of the second child, a flat 15 percent salary reduction is imposed on the parents until the child has reached the age of seven. In urban areas couples have been encouraged to sign contracts pledging a one-child family in order to receive better and more spacious housing.[162] Obtaining general acceptance of the one-child-per-family policy among the peasants in rural China remains a Herculean task involving education, persuasion, and strong pressure from the state. Such efforts must be made, however, if China is to defuse its population bomb.

Unfortunately, resistance to the one-child family policy has been particularly prevalent in rural areas. There also have been "exceptions" granted in response either to "local conditions" or "hardships."[163] Exemptions from the policy were usually granted to sparsely populated areas or in cases where the first child was a girl. The most common complaint in rural areas against the harshness of the one-child family policy is the desire for a son. Under rural reform, a one-child family pledge has been incorporated into household contracts.[164] But the desire for a son is as strong as ever.

Some final comments about the single-child policy are in order. The one-child family policy is not national. Two obvious reasons serve to explain why no national law has been enacted to restrict family size to only one child: its controversial nature, and the possible effect on recruitment for the military, which traditionally exempted one-child families.[165] The single-child family policy is a temporary measure and is to remain in effect until the year 2000, when the Chinese population is expected to be 1.2 billion.[166] China was able to hold total population for the first half of the 1980s to a relatively stable level.[167] But by 1987 projections of demographic figures indicated a rising rate of growth. And if the birth rate is maintained at more than 1.5 or up to 2.0 percent, China will have a population of two billion by the year 2030.[168]

A national door-to-door census was taken in 1990; the result showed China's total population to be 1.13 billion. If the present trend of increasing population continues, there will be a growth of about 17 million more people each year, or close to two billion by the year 2035. Of more significance, a large component of China's population will be 65 and over, possibly 16 to 19 percent of the total by the year 2035.[169] This would mean further financial burden on families in providing support for their aging parents. The 12.45 percent increase in population since 1982 also raised doubt about the effectiveness of the one-child family policy.

A Chinese statistical report in 1993 indicated a drop in the birth rate from 21.1 per 1,000 population in 1987 to 18.2 in 1992.[170] Now Chinese women are estimated to have an average of 1.8 or 1.9 children in a lifetime, the same as in the United States.[171] A new population policy calls for compulsory sterilization in the villages for those childbearing women who have already borne children. Chinese public health officials have also prepared new legislation—the Draft Law on Eugenics and Health Protection—for the NPC to ratify in 1994. Though denied by officials, the proposed law advocates forced abortion and sterilization to prevent "inferior quality" births.[172]

NOTES

1. See *Beijing Review*, 38 (September 22, 1986), 5.
2. See *Beijing Review* (July 16–22, 1990), 7.
3. See Arthur G. Ashbrook, "China: Economic Overview, 1975," in *China: A Reassessment of the Economy*, Joint Economic Committee, U.S. Congress (Washington, D.C.: Government Printing Office, July 10, 1975), p. 24; and Jan S. Prybyla, "Some Economic Strengths and Weaknesses of the People's Republic of China," *Asian Survey*, vol. x, no. 12 (December 1977), 1122.

4. Chou En-lai, "Report on the Work of the Government," *Peking Review*, 4 (January 24, 1975), 23.
5. Yao Wen-yuan, "On the Social Basis of the Lin Biao Anti-Party Clique" *Hongqi*, 3 (1975), as translated in the *Peking Review*, 10 (March 7, 1975), 5–10.
6. For the full text of these three documents, see *Issues and Studies*, vol. xiii, no. 6 (June 1977), 107–15; no. 8 (August 1977), 77–99; no. 9 (September 1977), 63–70. For commentaries on the radicals' attack on Deng's three documents, see Chi Wei, "How the 'Gang of Four' Opposed Socialist Modernization," *Peking Review*, 11 (March 11, 1977), 6–9; Hsiang Chun, "An Attempt to Restore Capitalism Under the Signboard of Opposing Restoration," *Peking Review*, 34 (August 19, 1977), 29–32, 37; and Mass Criticism Group of State Planning Commission, "Why Did the 'Gang of Four' Attack 'The Twenty Points,' " *Peking Review*, 42 (October 14, 1977), 5–13.
7. Chang Ch'un-ch'iao, "On Exercising All-Round Dictatorship Over the Bourgeoisie," *Hongqi*, 4 (1975), as translated in *Peking Review*, 14 (April 4, 1975), 5–11. Also see Kao Lu and Chang Ko, "Comments on Teng Hsiao-p'ing's Economic Ideas of the Comprador Bourgeoisie," *Peking Review*, 35 (August 27, 1976), 6–9.
8. "Repulsing the Right Deviationist Wind in the Scientific and Technological Circles," *Peking Review*, 18 (April 30, 1976), 6–9.
9. Hua Kuo-feng, "Political Report to the Eleventh National Congress of the CCP," *Peking Review*, 35 (August 26, 1977), 50.
10. Hua Kuo-feng, "Report on the Work of the Government," *Peking Review*, 10 (March 10, 1978), 19.
11. Ibid.
12. "Readjusting the National Economy: Why and How?" *Beijing Review*, 26 (June 29, 1979). Also see a comprehensive survey of China's modernization efforts in Joseph Y.S. Cheng, ed., *China: Modernization in the 1980s* (New York: St. Martin's Press, 1989).
13. *China Trade Report* (April 1980), p. 9.
14. "Readjusting the National Economy: Why and How?" 14.
15. *Ming Pao* (Hong Kong) (June 14, 1979), p. 1. Also see Martin Weil, "The Baothan Steel Mill: A Symbol of Change in China's Industrial Development Strategy," *China Under the Four Modernizations*, Part 1, Joint Economic Committee, Congress of the United States (Washington, D.C.: Government Printing Office, August 13, 1982), pp. 365–91.
16. "Report on the Work of the Government," *Beijing Review*, 27 (July 6, 1979), 12–20; and *Far Eastern Economic Review* (October 5, 1979), 78–80.
17. See Lowell Dittmer, "China in 1981: Reform, Readjustment, Rectification," *Asian Survey*, vol. xxii, no. 2 (January 1982), 35.
18. These were the words used by Huang Hua, then minister for foreign affairs, in an interview in Ottawa, Canada. See Peter Stursberg, "Restructuring China Policy in the Wake of Chairman Mao," *The Canadian Journal of World Affairs* (May–June 1981), 5.
19. "Further Economic Readjustment: A Break with 'Leftist' Thinking," *Beijing Review*, 12 (March 23, 1981), 27. Also see Xue Muqiao, *Current Problems of the Chinese Economy* (Beijing: The People's Publishers, 1980).
20. "Further Economic Readjustment," p. 28.
21. See Nai-Ruenn Chen, "China's Capital Construction: Current Retrenchment and Prospects for Foreign Participation," *China Under the Four Modernizations*, Part 2, pp. 50–52; and Richard Y.C. Yin, "China's Socialist Economy in Action: An Insider's View," *Journal of Northeast Asian Studies*, vol. 1, no. 2 (June 1982), 97–98.
22. *Asiaweek* (February 20, 1981), p. 33.
23. Sidney Lens, "Private Enterprises in China," reprinted in *Honolulu Star-Bulletin* (October 1, 1981), A-19. Also see Takashi Oda, "Private Enterprise in China Fills the Gap," *The Christian Science Monitor* (February 2, 1983), p. 6; and Bradley K. Martin, "Capitalism with a Chinese Flavor," *Baltimore Sun*, as reprinted in *Honolulu Sunday Star-Bulletin and Advertiser* (December 21, 1980), C-19. For 1983 figure see Robert Delfs, "Private Enterprise Without Capitalism Is China's Goal: An Incentive Socialism," *Far Eastern Economic Review* (April 28, 1983), 40. Also see *The New Yorker* (January 23, 1984), pp. 43–85.
24. *People's Daily* (January 9, 1983), p. 1. Also see *Takung Pao* (Hong Kong) (June 2, 1983), p. 1.
25. *People's Daily* (January 9, 1983).
26. *Ming Pao Daily* (Hong Kong) (August 17, 1980), p. 1.
27. See David Bonavia, "Peking Watch," in *China Trade Report* (August 1982), p. 2, and (February 1, 1981), p. 10; Zhu Minzhi and Zou Siguo, "Chen Yun on Planned Economy," *Beijing Review*, 12 (March 12, 1982), 12.

28. *China Trade Report* (August 1982), p. 2, and (February 1981), p. 10.
29. Zhu Minzhi and Zou Siguo, "Chen Yun on Planned Economy," p. 12.
30. Ibid., p. 17.
31. *Hongqi*, 8 (April 6, 1982), 32.
32. Ibid., pp. 32–33.
33. "Report on the Sixth Five-Year Plan," *Beijing Review*, 25 (June 23, 1986), p. 26.
34. *Beijing Review*, 51 (December 20, 1982), 11–26; and *Beijing Review*, 16 (April 12, 1986), i–xx.
35. *Beijing Review*, 16 (April 12, 1986), i.
36. Ibid., p. vi. Also see *Far Eastern Economic Review* (April 10, 1986), 80.
37. *Beijing Review*, 16 (April 12, 1986), i.
38. See *China Trade Report* (May 1986), p. 41.
39. *Beijing Review*, 16 (April 12, 1986), x.
40. Ibid., p. xi.
41. *China Trade Report* (May 1986), p. 41.
42. *Beijing Review*, 16 (April 12, 1986), xi.
43. "Communiqué of the Third Plenary Session of the Eleventh Central Committee," *Beijing Review*, 10 (March 10, 1978), 12.
44. For the text of the document, see "Several Questions in Strengthening and Perfecting the Job-Responsibility System for Agricultural Production," *Issues and Studies*, vol. xvii, no. 5 (May 1981), 77–82. Also see "Rural Contract," *Beijing Review*, 45 (November 10, 1980) 5–6.
45. "A Programme for Current Agricultural Work," *Beijing Review*, 24 (June 14, 1982), 21.
46. See Graham E. Johnson, "The Production Responsibility System in Chinese Agriculture: Some Examples from Guangdong," *Pacific Affairs*, vol. 55, no. 3 (Fall 1982), 430–51.
47. "Let Some Localities and Peasants Prosper First," *Beijing Review*, 3 (January 19, 1981), 19–22; "System of Responsibility in Agricultural Production," *Beijing Review*, 11 (March 16, 1981), 3–4; and "Small Plots for Private Use," *Beijing Review*, 26 (June 29, 1981), 3–4.
48. "System of Responsibility in Agricultural Production," p. 4.
49. Johnson, "The Production Responsibility System," p. 451.
50. "Report on the Sixth Five-Year Plan," p. 33.
51. Y.Y. Kulh, "The Economies of the 'Second Land Reform' in China," *China Quarterly*, 101 (March 1985), 122–31. Also see Jonathan Unger, "The Decollectivization of the Chinese Countryside: A Survey of Twenty-Eight Villages," *Pacific Affairs*, vol. 58, no. 4 (Winter 1985–86), 585–606.
52. For the text of the document see "Circular of the Central Committee of the CCP on Rural Work During 1984" see *China Quarterly*, 101 (March 1985), 132–42. Also see N. Lardy, "Agricultural Reform in China," *Journal of International Affairs*, vol. 39 (Winter 1986), 97 and 99–100.
53. See Joseph Fewsmith, "Rural Reform in China: Stage Two," *Problems of Communism* (July–August 1985), 52–53 and *China Daily* (July 4, 1984), p. 1.
54. Fewsmith, "Rural Reform in China: Stage Two," p. 52. Also see Lardy, "Agricultural Reform in China," p. 99.
55. Ibid., p. 49.
56. See Kathleen Hartford, "Socialist Agriculture is Dead; Long Live Socialist Agriculture; Organizational Transformations in Rural China," *The Political Economy of Reform in Post-Mao China*, pp. 45–46; and *Beijing Review*, 9 (February 27, 1984), 4.
57. Fewsmith, "Rural Reform in China: Stage Two," pp. 52–53.
58. *Beijing Review*, 9 (February 27, 1984), 18.
59. Ibid.
60. See T. Bernstein, "Reforming Chinese Agriculture: The Consequences of Unanticipated Consequences," in *China Business Review* (May–April 1985), p. 46. Also see Fewsmith, "Rural Reform in China: Stage Two," p. 50.
61. Bernstein, "Reforming Chinese Agriculture" p. 52.
62. Unger, "The Decollectivization of the Chinese Countryside," p. 594.
63. Ibid., p. 599.
64. Ibid., p. 600–601.
65. Xinhua news release (January 8, 1985), p. 1.
66. See Patrice de Beer, "A Factory in Every Village," in *The Guardian* (July 14, 1985), p. 13.
67. *Beijing Review*, 18 (April 30, 1984), 18. Lardy also provided the percentage figure of 30% shift of surplus labor to nonagricultural activities. See "Agricultural Reform in China," *Journal of International Affairs*, 100.

68. *Beijing Review*, 47 (November 24, 1986), 16–18.
69. de Beer, "A Factory in Every Village," p. 13; and *Beijing Review*, 47 (November 24, 1986), 18–19.
70. *Beijing Review* (January 6, 1986), 4.
71. Ibid., and *Far Eastern Economic Review* (December 5, 1985), 65.
72. See *Far Eastern Economic Review* (July 11, 1985), 57, and *Ta Kung Pao Weekly Supplement* (May 1, 1986), p. 6. Also see *Beijing Review*, 26 (June 30, 1986), 14–17.
73. Richard J. Latham, "The Implications of Rural Reforms for Grass-Roots Cadres," *The Political Economy of Reform in Post-Mao China*, p. 165. Also see John P. Burns, "Local Cadre Accommodation to the 'Responsibility System' in Rural China," *Pacific Affairs*, vol. 58, no. 4 (Winter 1985–86), 607. Also see *China Daily* (January 16, 1986), p. 1.
74. Latham, "The Implications of Rural Reforms for Grass-Roots Cadres," p. 168; and Burns, "Local Cadre Accommodation," p. 613.
75. *People's Daily* (April 22, 1982), p. 2.
76. Burns, "Local Cadre Accommodation," p. 614 and p. 617.
77. Jean C. Oi, "Commercializing China's Rural Cadres," *Problems of Communism* (September–October, 1986), 2.
78. Ibid., 10.
79. Ibid., 13.
80. See Elizabeth J. Perry, "Rural Collective Violence: The Fruits of Recent Reform," *The Political Economy of Reform in Post-Mao China*, pp. 175–192.
81. Ibid., p. 180.
82. Ibid.
83. Ibid., p. 183.
84. Ibid.
85. "Reforming Chinese Agriculture," pp. 46–47.
86. "Transformation in the Countryside, Part I," *Beijing Review* 9 (February 27, 1984), p. 9.
87. Ibid., p. 11. Also see Lardy, "Agricultural Reform in China," p. 101. For an overview of rural changes, see Kathleen Hartford and Steven M. Goldstein, eds., *Single Sparks: China's Rural Revolutions* (Armonk, N.Y.: M.E. Sharpe, 1989).
88. See "PRC Economic Performance in 1975," *Current Scene*, vol. xiv, no. 6 (June 1976), 1–14; and "The PRC Economy in 1976," *Current Scene*, vol. xv, nos. 4 and 5 (April–May 1977), 1–10.
89. Hua Kuo-feng, "Report on the Work of Government," p. 20.
90. "Report on the Sixth Five-Year Plan," p. 12.
91. Robert F. Dernberger, "Past Performance and Present State of China's Economy," in *China's Future: Foreign Policy and Economic Development in the Post-Mao Era*, eds. Allen S. Whiting and Robert F. Dernberger (New York: McGraw-Hill, 1977), pp. 95, 140.
92. For information on China's steel production, see Alfred H. Usack, Jr., and James D. Egan, "China's Iron and Steel Industry," in *China: A Reassessment of the Economy*, pp. 264–88.
93. American Rural Small-Scale Industry Delegation, *Rural Small-Scale Industry in the People's Republic of China* (Berkeley, Calif.: University of California Press, 1977), p. 1. Also, for an article on the evolution of China's policy toward the development of small industries, see Carl Riskin, "Small Industry and the Chinese Model of Development," *The China Quarterly*, 46 (April–June 1971), 245–73; and Carl Riskin, "China's Rural Industries: Self-Reliant System or Independent Kingdom?" *The China Quarterly*, 73 (March 1978), 77–98.
94. Chaing Hung, "Small and Medium-sized Industries Play Big Role," *Peking Review*, 45 (November 7, 1975), 23–25.
95. See *Rural Small-Scale Industries in the People's Republic of China*; and "Small Enterprises," *Peking Review*, 46 (November 15, 1974), 22.
96. See *Beijing Review*, 44 (October 29, 1984), i–xvi.
97. *Far Eastern Economic Review* (November 1, 1984), 24.
98. *Beijing Review*, 44 (October 29, 1984), vi.
99. Jan S. Prybyla, "China's Economic Experiment," *Problems of Communism*, Vol. xxxiii, 1 (January–February, 1989), p. 34.
100. *Beijing Review*, 34 (August 24, 1987), 4. Also see *Beijing Review*, 29 (February 10, 1984), xi.
101. *Beijing Review*, 34 (August 24, 1987), 5.
102. *Beijing Review*, 44 (October 29, 1984), xiii.
103. Prybyla, "China's Economic Experiment," p. 34.
104. Ibid. For a discussion of China's industrial policy, see Yu-Shan Wa, "Reforming the Revolution: Industrial Policy in China," *The Pacific Review*, vol. 3, no. 3 (1990), 243–56.

105. *Beijing Review*, 52 (December 29, 1986), 18.
106. Ibid.
107. See *Asian Wall Street Journal* (January 20, 1987), p. 1, and *The Wall Street Journal* (February 2, 1987), p. 22.
108. Prybyla, "China's Economic Experiment," p. 38.
109. Ibid., p. 37.
110. See *Wall Street Journal* (February 6, 1985), p. 31.
111. See *Far Eastern Economic Review* (January 29, 1987), 14.
112. Ibid.
113. See *China Daily* (August 16, 1987), p. 1.
114. *The Christian Science Monitor* (December 5, 1991), p. 8.
115. Ibid.
116. *China News Analysis*, 1385 (May 15, 1989), 3; and Jan S. Prybyla, "China's Economic Experiment: Back from the Market," *Problems of Communism*, vol. xxxviii, no. 1 (January–February 1989), 3–4.
117. Prybyla, "China's Economic Experiment," 4. Also see his "Why China's Economic Reform," *Asian Survey*, vol. xxix, no. 11 (November 1989), 1017–32.
118. Prybyla, "China's Economic Experiment," p. 3. And also see Joseph Fewsmith, "Agricultural Crisis in the PRC," *Problems of Communism*, vol. xxxvii, no. 6 (November–December 1988), 78–93.
119. See Lowell Dittmer, "China in 1988: The Continued Dilemma of Socialist Reform," *Asian Survey*, vol. xxix, no. 1 (January 1989), 21.
120. Dittmer, "China in 1988," 22. Also see Li Peng's report on the work of the government in *Beijing Review* (April 16–22, 1990), ix.
121. Dittmer, "China in 1988," 24–25.
122. *The Christian Science Monitor* (November 29, 1989), p. 8.
123. Ibid., p. 3.
124. *Far Eastern Economic Review* (July 9, 1990), 49.
125. Ibid.
126. *The Wall Street Journal* (July 27, 1990); *Far Eastern Economic Review* (January 25, 1990), 46; and *The New York Times* (October 28, 1989), p. 2.
127. *The Wall Street Journal* (February 20, 1990), A-10.
128. *The Wall Street Journal* (August 17, 1990), A-7B.
129. *The Wall Street Journal* (March 15, 1990), A-11.
130. *Far Eastern Economic Review* (March 22, 1990), 51; and (April 5, 1990), 38.
131. *The Wall Street Journal* (April 13, 1990), A-1.
132. Chu-yuan Cheng, "China's Economy in Retrenchment," *Current History* (September 1990), 253.
133. *People's Daily* (May 18, 1987); and Vaclar Smil, "Feeding China's People," *Current History* (September 1990), 276–77.
134. *Far Eastern Economic Review* (August 30, 1990), 54.
135. Ibid., p. 55.
136. *China News Analysis*, 1401 (January 1, 1990), 5.
137. *Beijing Review* (April 2–8, 1990), 7.
138. See Zheng Yi, "The Perils Faced by Chinese Peasants," *China Focus*, vol. 1, no. 3 (30 April 1993), 1.
139. See Alan P.L. Liu, "The Wenzhou Model of Development and China's Modernization," *Asian Survey*, vol. xxxii, no. 8 (August 1992), 696–711. Also see *People's Daily* (19 October 1992), p. 5.
140. *China News Analysis*, 1405 (March 1, 1990), 4.
141. Jiang Zenin, "Accelerating Reform and Opening Up," *Beijing Review* (26 October–1 November 1992), 16.
142. Li Haibo, "The Man Who Makes History," *Beijing Review* (12–18 October 1992), 17.
143. The New York Times Service as reprinted in the *Honolulu Star-Bulletin* (20 May 1993), A-12.
144. Ibid.
145. See the following article for a discussion of China's management problems: Xue Muqiao, "On Reforming the Economic Management System, I, II, III," *Beijing Review*, 5 (February 4, 1980), 16–21; 12 (March 24, 1980), 21–25; and 14 (April 7, 1980), 20–26; Richard Y.C. Yin, "China's Socialist Economy in Action," *Journal of Northeast Asian Studies*, vol. 1, no. 2 (June 1982), 105–9; and James O'Toole, "The Good Managers of Sichuan," *Harvard Business Review*, vol. 59, no. 3 (May–June 1981), 28–40.
146. See at least two of the more popular books on Japanese management theories: William Ouchi, *Theory Z: How American Business Can Meet the Japanese Challenge* (New York: Addison Wesley,

1980); and Richard T. Pascale and Anthony G. Athos, *The Art of Japanese Management: Applications for American Executives* (New York: Warner Books, 1982).

147. David A. Hayden. "The Art of Managing Chinese Ventures," *Asian Wall Street Journal Weekly* (July 6, 1981), p. 12.

148. Ibid., p. 12.

149. Frank Ching, "Poor Management and Irresponsible Workers Frustrate Foreign Partners in Chinese Factory," *Asian Wall Street Journal Weekly* (December 15, 1980), p. 2.

150. O'Toole, "The Good Managers of Sichuan," p. 38. Also see *Ta Kung Pao Weekly Supplement* (December 2, 1982), p. 11.

151. Xue Muqiao, "On Reforming the Economic Management System (I)," *Beijing Review*, 12 (March 12, 1980), 24.

152. "On Reforming the Economic Management System (I)," p. 25.

153. *Ta Kung Pao Weekly Supplement* (December 22, 1980), p. 6.

154. Malcolm Warner, "The 'Long March' of Chinese Management Education, 1979–84," *China Quarterly*, 106 (June 1986), 326.

155. Ibid., pp. 340–341.

156. *Ta Kung Pao Weekly Supplement* (Hong Kong) (January 23, 1986), p. 10.

157. Ibid.

158. For China's 1982 population census, see "The World's Biggest Census," *Beijing Review*, 32 (August 9, 1982), 16; "The 1982 Census Results," *Beijing Review*, 45 (November 8, 1982), 20–21; and "Report on the Sixth Five-Year Plan," p. 18.

159. "The 1982 Census Results," 20; and "Report on the Sixth Five-Year Plan," p. 181.

160. "Report on The Sixth Five-Year Plan," p. 18.

161. Ibid.

162. See Michele Vink, "China's Draconian Birth Control Program Weighs Heavily on Its Women," *Asian Wall Street Journal Weekly* (November 23, 1981), pp. 1, 21.

163. See Jeffrey Wasserstrom, "Resistance to One Child Family," *Modern China*, vol. 10, no. 3 (July 1984), 345–72.

164. See Joyce K. Kallgren, "Politics, Welfare, and Change: The Single Child Family in China," in Elizabeth Perry and Christine Wong, ed., *The Political Economy of Reform in Post-Mao China*, p. 151.

165. Ibid.

166. Wang Wee's statement in an interview in *Honolulu Star-Bulletin* (August 17, 1984), A-4.

167. See *The Christian Science Monitor* (February 18, 1987), p. 8.

168. See *Honolulu Advertiser* (July 31, 1987), A-21.

169. For results of 1990 census, see *Beijing Review* (December 17–23, 1990), 27.

170. See Nicholas D. Kristoff, "China's Crackdown on Births: A Stunning and Harsh Success," *The New York Times* (25 April 1993), p. 6.

171. Ibid.

172. See *Honolulu Star Bulletin*, December 20, 1993, A-1. And a comment from an editorial in *The New York Times*, December 27, 1993, A-14.

chapter twelve

The Politics
of Modernization
Education, Science/Technology,
Open Door Policy,
and the Intellectuals

Two important factors have influenced, if not dominated, Chinese educational policies since 1949. First, education has been used as an instrument for the inculcation of new values and beliefs to build a new socialist revolutionary society. Second, changes in the content and form of education invariably have been intertwined with the shifting policies and strategies of economic development. Although the basic goal of the regime has been to construct a socialist state, the implementation of this basic goal has involved periodic shifts in emphasis between "red" (politics) and "expert" (technology). Let us begin our discussion by examining the educational policies that governed the administration of schools and universities prior to the advent of the Cultural Revolution in 1966.

EDUCATIONAL POLICIES BEFORE THE CULTURAL REVOLUTION

The very first governmental decree on education, "Decision of The Reformation of the Education System," promulgated in October 1951, was intended to provide for formal education stressing both technical training and the learning of the new socialist values.[1] Chinese educational reform in the early 1950s was modeled on the Soviet approach to education, which stressed technical training to develop specialized skills. This emphasis on technical training was in harmony with the need to develop adequate personnel to implement the First Five-Year Plan (1953–57). There was a great increase in the number of special technical schools at the secondary and university levels to help produce skilled workers to fill the estimated 1 million positions that would be required by the industrial plants transferred from the Soviet Union.[2] In many instances the length of schooling at the secondary and university levels was increased to ensure the quality of technical training. In addition, spare-time educational opportunities were made available for workers and peasants who were to be trained as semi-skilled workers.[3] Student enrollment in spare-time primary and middle schools increased from a combined total of less than 2 million in 1953 to about 9 million in 1957.[4] The Great Leap placed increased emphasis on the need to combine education and productive labor. With the introduction of communes in the countryside and the stress on self-sufficiency, local communities assumed the full responsibility for maintaining schools. A summary of the Chinese educational system on the eve of the Cultural Revolution follows.

Primary Schools

On the advice of Soviet advisers, the length of primary schooling was initially reduced by one year, to a term of five years, to extend the system and to produce more graduates. By 1953 the length of primary schooling had reverted to six years. In rural areas the length of primary schooling was usually limited, perhaps to three or four years, with many of the schools on a half-study, half-work basis. Initially, primary school was neither compulsory nor universal. During the first ten years of the regime's rule, enrollment in primary schools increased from a little over 24 million in 1949 to 51 million in 1953 and to over 86 million in 1958.[5] Between 1953 and 1958, approximately 27.5 million adult peasants and workers enrolled in spare-time primary schools.[6] The curriculum for primary schools contained a heavy emphasis on political and ideological value formation as well as the usual subjects: Chinese language, arithmetic, and introduction to general science.

Secondary Schools

There were several types of secondary, or middle, schools prior to the Cultural Revolution. The first kind were the general, academically oriented secondary schools, which included three years at the junior level and three years at the senior level. These schools were found exclusively in urban areas before 1958. Second were vocational schools, which emphasized practical training and teacher education. The length of attendance at these vocational schools was usually three to four years. Third were specialized polytechnic secondary schools that prepared students for work in industry, agriculture, public health, and commerce and trade. These specialized secondary schools emphasized little solid academic instruction and were almost exclusively found in urban areas before 1958. Most of the vocationally oriented and specialized schools were on a half-study, half-work basis. The Great Leap and the communization programs expanded the half-study, half-work vocational schools into the communes, where agricultural production became the main content of instruction. There were enormous increases in enrollment in all types of secondary schools.[7] In 1953 enrollment in middle schools, including spare-time schools, was at 3.3 million; enrollment in secondary technical schools, including spare-time schools, was about 1.7 million. By 1958 enrollment in middle schools, including spare-time schools, was over 9 million; enrollment in secondary technical schools, including spare-time schools, was 1.4 million. A large percentage of the middle school enrollment was in the countryside. By 1958 the educational thrust was to teach whatever was required by the communes to help agricultural production. In addition to a heavy emphasis on agricultural subjects, rural middle schools' curricula included political and ideological studies and arithmetic. Spare-time rural secondary specialized schools now began to teach machinery repair and tractor driving.

The mushrooming of secondary schools, and their tremendous increase in enrollment, soon presented problems as regarded the job situation in the urban areas. The First Five-Year Plan's economic acceleration had encouraged migration to the urban areas, but the number of jobs generated by the economy simply could not keep pace with the potential workers who flocked to the urban areas. Two basic changes in China's educational policy were made to meet this problem: first, the number of spare-time specialized secondary schools was reduced; and second, all graduates from primary and secondary schools who could neither find jobs in factories nor go on to technical colleges or universities were sent to the countryside to engage in agricultural production. This was the beginning of the youth rustication program, which dispatched over 20 million young people to rural areas from 1966 to 1977.

The problems of rapid migration to the urban centers and the resultant unemployment in urban areas were solved in 1958 by the Great Leap, which called for mass mobilization and labor-intensive production in the countryside. Students were told to participate as farmers or workers after school. Expansion of half-study, half-work schools resumed in both urban and rural areas. In addition, political education became an even more essential part of the curriculum, to inculcate the values of being both "red" and "expert."[8]

Higher Education

Leo Orleans identified five different types of higher educational institutions in China prior to the Cultural Revolution.[9] There were comprehensive universities, comparable to American universities, with the traditional academic departments. These were four-year institutions of higher learning with full-time students. Then there were the polytechnic institutions, such as the famous Qinghua University, located in Beijing—a sort of Chinese M.I.T. Below these two types of universities were the new institutions of higher learning that proliferated during and after the Great Leap: (1) vocationally organized, specialized colleges; (2) enterprise-controlled spare-time industrial colleges for workers already employed by the industries; and (3) the low-quality and highly questionable institutions known as workers' and peasants' colleges, which mushroomed during the Great Leap. While comprehensive and polytechnic universities numbered between twenty and forty before 1966, the new institutions grew by the hundreds. Enrollment in institutions of higher education in 1949 was about 117,000. In 1959 the total figure had reached 810,000.[10]

Entrance to comprehensive and polytechnic universities was based on passing the entrance examination. A large percentage of students who were admitted to university work in the period under discussion were those who wanted to be engineers and scientists. The areas of specialization were determined according to the state plan and personnel needs in the scientific and technological fields. During the author's visits in 1973 to Beijing University, Qiaodung University in Xian, and Fudan University in Shanghai, it was pointed out by the faculties that before 1960, science instruction at the university level was under the influence of the Soviet

Union, in terms of textbooks, laboratories, and equipment. Before the withdrawal of Soviet aid in June 1960, some 7,500 Chinese students had gone to the Soviet Union for either postgraduate work or specialized training. According to Leo Orleans, the total number of graduates from these institutions of higher learning from 1949 to 1966 was 1.7 million, with 34 percent in engineering, 27 percent in education, 11 percent in medicine, 8 percent in agriculture and forestry, 6 percent in natural sciences, and 5 percent in finance and economics.[11]

Before the Cultural Revolution, Chinese university education was modeled on the European system, with a great deal of formalism and rigidity. The role of the professor was to give formal lectures in class, with no opportunity for questions and answers or interaction between the instructor and the students. As the doors of higher education opened to students of worker and peasant backgrounds (in 1957 about 36 percent of the university student body in China came from that social background), a serious problem of academic deficiency occurred among the students. Instructors were unwilling to provide remedial work for those who needed it, and were often contemptuous of those who were academically ill-prepared for university work.[12] Therefore, tension existed in the relationship between the students and their professors, coupled with feelings of resentment on the part of students who could not contact their instructors.[13] We will see later how this "feudal relationship" was corrected after the Cultural Revolution.

THE CULTURAL REVOLUTION AND EDUCATIONAL REFORM

It must be kept in mind that for at least two years, from 1966 to 1968, all schools and universities were closed because of the disruption caused by the students' participation in the Cultural Revolution. When the central government ordered the schools to reopen and students to return to their classes in late 1967 and early 1968, the normal combined length of attendance for both primary and middle schools was shortened from twelve years to nine years.[14] Most rural areas shortened the combined length of attendance in both primary and middle schools to a bare seven years. It was reasoned that by the time the youngsters completed their middle school educations, they would be 15 or 16, "a suitable age to begin taking part in farm work." Those who finished the shortened secondary education in urban areas were expected to work in factories to gain practical experience. Upon reaching the age of 15 or 16, all youths who had completed secondary education were required to render at least three years of practical work or service before considering entrance to higher education. This requirement for three years of practical work experience relieved some of the pressure for entrance to colleges and universities. University education, particularly at technical colleges, was shortened to three years or less.

The Cultural Revolution severely condemned the system of evaluating student performance by examination. Entrance examinations and the practice of holding students back a year for failure to pass the examinations were labeled as the "revisionist line of education." Entrance examinations for universities were abolished when these institutions were reopened in 1970. In their place a system of nominations and recommendations was adopted for all institutions of higher learning. The new system called for the following methods of nomination: (1) self-nomination by individual students; (2) nomination by the masses; and (3) recommendation by the party leadership. High school graduates thus nominated then had to be approved by the institutions. The purpose of the new system was to enable youngsters from a "revolutionary social background"—workers, poor and lower-middle peasants, members of the army, and youths who had gone down to live with the peasants—to have the opportunity to enter universities. Clearly, the system was designed to meet complaints at the time that the universities, the road to one's future station in life, had become the preserve of the elite and tended to exclude those political activists who were endowed with revolutionary fervor. The new admissions policy was aimed not only at greatly increasing recruitment of youths from the proper "revolutionary social background," but it limited admissions to those who had acquired practical experience, either as workers in factories or in communes. In 1970 most universities required two or three years of practical experience prior to entrance. Thus, under the new system—with its lack of entrance examinations—150,000 workers, peasants, and PLA members were admitted to universities from 1970 to 1973. With the admission of large numbers of students who did not have adequate preparation, academic standards had to be lowered and remedial classes organized.

The administration and management of education during the Cultural Revolution was taken out of the hands of the professional educators. Local revolutionary committees began taking control of the schools in October 1968 through the dispatch of worker and peasant "Mao's Thought Propaganda Teams," with the active participation of PLA soldiers.[15] These teams ended strife among the students[16] and worked with the students and teachers to reorganize educational content, placing more emphasis on the study of Mao's thought and relating education to productive labor. In addition to the revolutionary committees that administered the schools and universities, there was a "Revolution in Education Committee" on campuses to provide daily guidance in carrying out the reform measures in these institutions, particularly in higher education.[17] Members of these educational committees were cadres and teachers. At Fudan University in Shanghai, where the author visited in 1973, cadres who were workers in the revolutionary committee dominated the university's administration; the leading cadre who directed Fudan University was a skilled worker in a textile factory in Shanghai.

In rural areas primary schools were run by the production brigades, and secondary schools by the communes. This meant that the revolutionary committees on the communes were in full charge of education. Two reasons were generally given for the reform. One was purely ideological: "Since the fundamental question of revolution is political power" and the "fundamental question of revolution in education is also the question of power," proletarian education must be in the hands of the people in order to prevent the growth of the revisionist educational line. The second was more practical: "We (lower-middle peasants) can decide the teaching contents and, in a way we see fit, plan when classes take place."[18] Another important fact was that in brigade-run schools, teachers were members of the same commune, "eating the same kind of food and living in the same kind of housing as the poor and lower-middle peasants."[19] In urban areas primary schools were generally run by neighborhood revolutionary committees or street committees; secondary schools were run by neighborhood revolutionary committees and factories located in the area. The new revolutionary management of schools by local units reflected the Cultural Revolution's emphasis on decentralization. It also relieved the state from spending enormous amounts of money for primary and secondary education.

THE NEW EDUCATIONAL POLICY AFTER MAO[20]

In a speech to the Chinese Scientific and Technical Congress in the spring of 1980, Hu Yaobang, then the CCP general secretary, said that China's young people must become the effective force and reserve in science and technology. He also indicated that the education of China's youth was the key to building this reserve. In a major speech to the 1978 National Educational Work Conference, Deng Xiaoping outlined China's new educational policy, which was formulated to meet the needs of modernization.[21] First, Deng urged that educational quality be improved at the primary and secondary school levels—"We must fill out the courses in primary and secondary schools with advanced scientific knowledge"—by upgrading the curriculum content and reinstituting the examination system.[22] Then he called for a tightening of school discipline, with emphasis on elevating students' moral, intellectual, and physical levels. Third, Deng reiterated the important role education must play in China's modernization. Last, he asked for respect for the teachers and care for their well-being in terms of better working conditions and compensation. Let us now review briefly the changes that have taken place since the pragmatists came to power.

In primary schools major changes were made in the length of schooling and instructional content. In 1977 the 9.8 million primary schools, with a total enrollment of 146 million students, did not provide all youngsters with a five-year primary education. In fact, the goal announced in 1977 of guaranteeing eight years of schooling in rural areas and ten years in urban areas was simply a wish that was not possible to fulfill.

In 1981 many urban primary schools provided six years of schooling for children between the ages of 7 and 12, and rural schools offered four to five years of primary education. As compared to what existed during the Cultural Revolution, the length of primary schooling had been extended somewhat. However, leading educators spoke out at the June 1983 session of the Chinese People's Political Consultative Conference in favor of a compulsory six-year primary education for rural areas in order to eradicate illiteracy, which was estimated to affect 25 percent of the total population.

The new primary school curriculum was designed to give children "a sounder education," developing their moral, intellectual, and physical well-being.[23] Instructional content at the primary level, at least in urban areas such as Beijing and Shanghai, consisted of the Chinese language (children were expected to master 2,000 characters), arithmetic, general science, and foreign language (English, Russian, Japanese, or German in the third year). Urban primary schools added subjects such as music, art, ethics, and geography to the curriculum, to replace political-ideological studies. Primary schools in China in this period became more conventional and academically oriented. Also, more emphasis was given to moral education—including instruction on being "polite, honest, brave, industrious, modest and economical," helpful to others, and good in personal hygiene—as well as to love the "socialist motherland."[24] Many of these conventional moral instructions were incorporated in the rules of conduct for pupils.[25] Good students were now expected to be all-around persons, not only excelling in examinations but also being sound "ideologically, intellectually, and physically."[26]

Work-study programs were again instituted in many schools. On-campus factories or workshops in urban areas, and farm plots in rural areas, were provided so that youngsters could engage in practical work projects. It was reported that 431,000 of

China's one million primary and secondary schools have in the early 1980s instituted work-study programs in the form of small-scale factories, farms, and tree nurseries.[27] A basic purpose of these programs was to train students so that they will
eventually become "workers with a socialist consciousness and culture."[28]

In 1979 there was a shift of emphasis in the role of secondary education in
China. The pre-1965 policy of stressing vocational training was revived.[29] Secondary
schools were now entrusted with the dual task of producing graduates for university
work and good workers for society.[30] Vocational classes in secondary and middle
schools were designed to equip students with marketable and productive skills. Many
urban secondary schools offered training in tourism, foreign trade, commerce, electrical appliance repair, sewing, food preparation and service, and printing.[31] Emphasis was put on vocational education for several reasons. One reason was to redress
the past overemphasis on general education. There was a shortage of skilled personnel at the entry and intermediate levels in factories and enterprises. In addition, millions of secondary school graduates simply could not find jobs because of their lack
of technical training. Finally, institutions of higher learning in China could absorb
only 3 to 4 percent of each year's secondary school graduates.[32]

Former Premier Zhao indicated that under the Sixth Five-Year Plan (1981–1985)
China would produce a trained and skilled labor force large enough to meet rising
demands in industries and enterprises.[33] The newly instituted policy for secondary
schools included the following reforms: (1) the addition of more vocational and technical courses in the secondary school curriculum; (2) conversion of some middle
schools into vocational or agricultural schools that would take in junior middle school
(junior high) graduates and provide them with three years of vocational training; and
(3) new technical schools.[34] However, graduates of vocational schools would not be
provided with jobs automatically. They must pass examinations before employment,
with placement depending on skill and performance.[35] In 1982 some 630,000 new students reportedly were enrolled in vocational and secondary schools.[36] While the post-
Mao policy for secondary education placed emphasis on vocational and technical
training, most urban areas also embarked on the development of academically oriented secondary schools, known as "key schools." In the 1950s, "key schools" devoted
their efforts to producing quality education. They received special government funds
and had the best-trained teachers and the best facilities. Students selected for the "key
schools" were generally the brightest and best-qualified intellectually. The unique features of "key schools," once attacked by the radicals as "revisionist" and elitist, were
revived in 1978 in many urban areas. A deputy director of education for the Shanghai
municipality told a visiting group of American educators that the city was moving
rapidly toward the establishment of a network of "key schools" with ample budgets
and superior teachers for the brightest students.[37]

A significant reform in higher education since 1976 has been the reintroduction
of competitive examinations for university entrance. From 1970 to 1976, the radicals
had imposed a "recommendation model"[38] for university entrance, where graduates of
secondary schools were able to apply for university entrance after two or three years
of practical work. Applicants would be screened by their own work units on the
basis of their work records as well as political factors. Final admission was based on
review by provincial authorities and university administrations. For a brief period,
between 1973 and 1974, Zhou Enlai experimented with combining recommendations
with a "cultural examination" system. The experiment was abandoned after radicals
mounted an attack on the examination system and on Zhou himself.[39]

In 1977 the government revived the examination system for university entrance. In the summer of that year, approximately 5.7 million young people took the entrance examinations, which were administered on a nationwide basis. The leading universities admitted over 1,100 successful candidates, with a large percentage coming from peasant and cadre family backgrounds.[40] The total number of candidates admitted to colleges in 1977 reached 278,000. For the three-year period between 1977 and 1979, some 738,000 new students were admitted to the universities via competitive examinations, as follows: 278,000 in 1977, 290,000 in 1978, and 270,000 in 1979.[41] The total number of secondary school graduates or equivalents who took the examinations was 5.7 million in 1977, 5 million in 1978, and 4.6 million in 1979.[42] But the level of annual admissions to universities averaged less than 300,000. This meant that only a very small percentage of the millions of applicants were successful in gaining admittance each year. Even under the Sixth Five-Year Plan, not more than 400,000 were accommodated in 1985.[43] The problem remains as to how to provide further education for the unsuccessful candidates who desire it.

To help fill the need for large numbers of skilled and technically competent personnel for modernization, the Chinese in the post-Mao period devised alternative educational programs. One program used television and radio for instruction in urban centers such as Beijing and Shanghai. For example, courses in mechanical engineering, electronics, chemistry, physics, and mathematics were offered as key components of a three-year program. Students who successfully completed the TV university program were given diplomas and recognized as bona fide college graduates by the state.[44] In 1979 the Central Broadcasting and Television University in Beijing granted graduation certificates to half a million students.[45] At that time 1.3 million enrolled college students were mainly factory workers, miners, teachers, and military personnel.[46]

Another innovation was the establishment of affiliated colleges by regular accredited institutions of higher learning on campuses of secondary schools. Students attending affiliated colleges were regular workers in factories, seeking advanced training in specialized skills.[47] Spare-time colleges were yet another way to provide technical training for the young. Trade union federations organized classes for workers who were selected by competitive examination to enroll in these colleges to study economic law and management.[48] Finally, admittance of additional students to universities on a self-paying basis provided opportunities to secondary school graduates. A number of universities in Beijing have opened their doors to those who failed the entrance examinations but who can pay a tuition of 20 yuan (about $10) per term. These students are not allowed to stay in dormitories. Upon graduation, the self-paid students receive certificates and apply for jobs themselves instead of being assigned by the state.[49]

REFORM IN THE EDUCATIONAL SYSTEM, 1985

The buzzword in China in 1984 and 1985 was reform. Not only were there major decisions on rural and urban reform, but on educational reform as well. The party's decision on educational reform was made public on May 28, 1985, following a national educational conference in Beijing.[50] The conference, the first since 1978, listened to appeals and pep talks by China's reform leaders, such as Deng Xiaoping and Wan Li, on the need to place educational reform on a par with economic reform.[51] The conference identified some of the urgent problems in China's educational system. The party's subsequent educational reform was aimed at providing remedies.

Top on the agenda for major educational reform was the party's decision to call for nine years of compulsory education for all school-age children. The decision was followed by a national law on compulsory education, enacted by the NPC in the spring of 1986.[52] The new law called for a step-by-step implementation of compulsory nine-year elementary education, beginning with urban areas by 1990, most rural areas by 1995, and for all backward areas by the end of this century. Under the law, school-age children in all rural areas would be guaranteed a nine-year compulsory education by the year 2000. The Seventh Five-Year Plan (1986–90) increased educational outlays by 72 percent to 116.6 billion yuan (about $40 billion). Under the national compulsory education law, local governments were permitted to collect "educational funds." The new law mandated that parents send their children to schools and, thus, made illegal the traditional practice of sending children into the field to work. The law prohibited recruitment of school-age children for employment. It also prohibited local government officials from engaging in the practice of diverting (or misappropriating) funds earmarked for education, and local government was prohibited from seizing educational buildings for noneducational use.

Another weakness in China's educational system was the low social status of teachers. Added to the persistent problem of low teachers' morale was the widespread practice of recruiting teachers into lucrative employment in noneducational areas. Vice-premier Wan Li told the national educational conference in May 1985 that luring teachers away from schools with higher pay was analogous to "killing the goose that lays the golden egg."[53] The average monthly wage for a teacher was about 50 to 60 yuan, the equivalent of U.S. $20, one of the lowest wages paid in China. It was no wonder that many teachers had left that profession. Wan emphasized at the 1985 national conference that teachers must receive an annual increase in salary in order to reduce the rate of attrition.[54] Primary and middle school teachers did receive raises as well as special seniority pay in 1985. The fact remains, however, that few secondary school graduates have opted for teacher training, and the shortage of qualified schoolteachers has deepened as a result.[55] In a recent report on rural education, the local government for the ancient city of Luoyang in north China showed that only 20 percent of its 50,000 primary school teachers had graduated from teacher-training school and were considered qualified.[56] To implement the nine-year compulsory education law by the end of this century, an additional 30,000 trained teachers will be required for primary and junior middle schools in Luoyang alone.[57] The problem of a teacher shortage is probably found in most parts of the nation. China faces an enormous task if the nine-year compulsory education program is to be successfully implemented.

Reform in Higher Education

In higher education, the main problem has been the limited number of students who can be admitted into the universities. In 1985 about 1.7 million secondary school graduates took the grueling, three-day nationwide entrance examination in the hot and humid month of July, but only 560,000, or about one out three, were admitted to the universities. China expects to increase total university enrollment to 7 million by the year 2000, as compared to 1.7 million in 1985–1986 and 1.9 million in 1987. Only a slight yearly increase is expected in the total number of institutions of higher learning, numbered at 1,016 in 1986 and 1,054 in 1987.[58] By the year 2000 only about 8 to 9 percent of those who take the national entrance examinations will be admitted to the universities. This leaves a large number of disappointed, if not psychologically damaged, youth to be absorbed into gainful employment. It also creates the prospect of discontent and unrest among a significant number of talented young people.

A possible solution lies in the expansion of vocational education and training—a neglected area that needs to be emphasized. It is estimated that by the turn of the century China will need as many as 17 million polytechnic school graduates.[59] One estimate made during the reform period of the mid-1980s put the number of junior and middle-level technicians and managers required for 1990 at eight million—an enormous increase that could only be fulfilled by expanded vocational education and training. The 1985 party decision on educational reform made it very clear that vocational and technical school graduates must be given preference in job assignments.[60] In 1984 there were only 3.7 million students enrolled in technical vocational schools, compared to over 45.5 million students enrolled in general middle schools.[61] The dire need for skilled technicians in all fields resulted in an upsurge in part-time education for workers and staff members in state-owned enterprises. Special courses were designed in areas such as computers, drafting, and accounting. Government departments, factories, and trade union congresses set up schools to promote vocational education. Special courses were offered over radio and television or through correspondence arrangements. Television and radio universities graduated 160,000 students in 1984.[62] These electronic universities, "Dianda" as they are known in Chinese, enrolled over one million students in the mid-1980s.[63] It seems obvious that only through expanded funding by the central and local governments for vocational education could the unemployed youth become skilled workers in a rapidly expanding but increasingly technically oriented economy.[64] In response to the urgent need for trained skilled workers, a number of short-term vocational courses were offered by many institutes of higher learning, leading up to degrees comparable to two-year vocational degrees in American community colleges.[65] Thus the emphasis was less on theoretical instruction in mathematics and hard sciences and more on the acquisition of practical knowledge and skills. Other structural reform measures for higher education included the extension of well-known universities from developed coastal areas to the hinterland and border regions, with increased funding and establishment of facilities for post-graduate study, as part of an ongoing effort to encourage scientific research at the universities.

The single most important reform in higher education in the mid-1980s was the recognition by the state and party of the need to grant more autonomy to the universities by dismantling centralized control.[66] There had been too much rigid control over schools and universities by the party. In June 1986 the State Council announced a set of regulations dealing with the management, or decision-making, power of the universities. As a part of the ongoing decentralization in the economic system, the university presidents were granted autonomous power to make decisions regarding university governance and management, finances (including the right to allocate funds and collect fees from students), construction of buildings, and personnel matters involving job and teaching assignments.[67] Under the regulations, a university president presumably could appoint and dismiss other university officials, teachers, and staff. Faculty also could determine their own academic curricula, as well as having the right to select their own teaching material. On paper at least, these reform measures seemed to provide university administrators and faculty with the instruments to fend off control and constant political interference from the party bureaucrats. These reform measures have not been entirely successful. The vice-president for Heftel's Science and Technology University was dismissed by Deng Xiaoping and expelled from party membership in January 1987 after student protests erupted in many cities. This occurred two and half years before the 1989 mass protest.

Another important reform decision made in the mid-1980s was that the state no longer be "responsible for all cash outlays for universities and colleges."[68] Students were to help pay for part of their education or participate in part-work, part-study programs. A new scholarship and loan program was established to reward students who (1) had excellent scholastic standing (350 yuan a year); (2) wanted to specialize in teacher training or other high-demand fields such as agriculture or forestry (400 yuan a year); and (3) opted to work in the poor and border areas (500 yuan a year).[69] A student loan program was established to enable needy students to borrow a maximum of 300 yuan a year without interest. In 1987, the scholarship and loans were made available at 85 selected institutions under experimental pilot programs.

EDUCATION IN CHINA AFTER TIANANMEN

China's educational system is beset with persistent problems that have been aggravated by the effects of the 1989 Tiananmen upheaval. These problems include the declining school attendance of school-age children caused by the rural reform or the responsibility incentive system; the intense competition and pressure between lower schools to promote their better students, thus placing undue stress on passing examinations rather than on learning; the continued problem of illiteracy affecting over 230 million among China's rural population; and the "brain drain," or loss, of some of China's best minds to advanced industrialized nations. Out of a total of more than 64,000 Chinese students who have been sent abroad to study since 1978, only about 22,000 had returned by 1990.[70] Complicating these educational problems are the shortage of qualified teachers and the low pay for the profession. In 1988 about 40 percent of primary school teachers and 47 percent of secondary school teachers were not qualified or trained.[71]

The austerity program, which was launched in the fall of 1988, and the policy changes since the Tiananmen upheaval in June 1989, have made the situation worse in rural areas, in particular in terms of availability of local financial resources for basic education. Since local taxes paid by rural enterprises and local individual entrepreneurs finance rural basic educational institutions, the austerity program (see Chapter 11) has caused a sharp reduction in local tax revenues. Many such tax-producing rural enterprises suffered losses or went bankrupt, a familiar occurrence in the latter part of 1989. As a result, the much-heralded goal of compulsory education has not been achieved. In short, the educational level of the Chinese has moved backward. The nation ranked sixtieth among 122 nations in the proportion of people over 25 years of age who have received higher or secondary education, and eightieth among 139 nations for the entrance rate of secondary school children.[72]

Certainly the most significant development that has taken place in the early 1990s has been in the area of vocational education. In October 1991 the State Council decided to expand and strengthen vocational education for the purpose of meeting growing national needs for manpower training, which have resulted from continued economic reform. Vocational education in the early 1990s focused on the development of polytechnic, skilled-worker, and secondary vocational schools. As mentioned earlier, China will need about 17 million polytechnic school graduates by the turn of the century. Government figures now show that in 1990 China had about 4,000 polytechnic schools, with 2.2 million students; this has been augmented by over 4,000 skilled-worker schools, with 1.3 million students, and over 9,000 secondary vocational schools, with almost 3 million students. Many state-owned enterprises, such as the Anshen Iron and Steel Company and some of the automobile factories, have participated in the vocational education program. Local governments at the county level are expected to operate at least one vocational school devoted to agricultural skills.

Another development in the 1990s addresses the need for university education to place some emphasis on its mission, not only in arts and sciences, but in manufacturing and trade as well. The prestigious Beijing University (Beida) has established on campus the Beida Fangzheng Company, which specializes in electronic typesetting with Chinese characters for domestic and foreign markets. The academic department of biology ran the Beida Weimin Bioengineering Company in cooperation with some eighteen high-tech-oriented enterprises formed and managed by the university. In addition, Beida has expanded its graduate programs by offering advanced degrees.

During my recent visit to Guangzhou in south China, it was common to see private school newspaper advertisements offering training in skills in order to meet industry's demands under economic reform and the economic boom. In Guangzhou alone there were hundreds of these private schools, with an annual student enrollment of 60,000.

DISCONTENT AMONG YOUTH

About 160 million young people who were between the ages of 8 and 18 at the time of the Cultural Revolution have been termed the "lost generation." These youths, who were in their mid-twenties to mid-thirties in 1980, had their educations interrupted by the great upheaval. Among this group, at least 20 million secondary school graduates were sent down to the countryside under the xiafang movement, or "the downward transfer."

The bulk of the "lost generation" suffered widespread discontent and disillusionment.[73] Many of these young people faced a "crisis of confidence" in attitudes toward the CCP and China's socialist system. Those dissenters who formed the core of the 1978–1979 Democracy Wall movement, discussed in Chapter 10, were drawn largely from this age group. Having wasted their time in the Cultural Revolution, many of them now possessed neither the education nor the necessary skills to be gainfully employed. Rural youth fared much better, in that they always knew there would be little opportunity for them if they migrated to the cities to find jobs in the factories. Today, with the new incentive system in the countryside, more rural youngsters prefer to remain on the farm.

As a group, Chinese youth and students want more or less the same things that their counterparts in other countries want—good jobs, material goods, and a secure future as they grow up and mature. Having learned what happened to the youth during the Cultural Revolution decade, Chinese youth and students of today are more skeptical about marching behind any ideological banner. In fact, a chief characteristic of China's youth and students of today is their disillusionment about communism as preached by Marx, Lenin, and Mao Zedong. In the later 1970s the discontent and unrest of youth was expressed via demonstrations, wall posters, and disruption of city traffic. Although these feelings of discontent have been suppressed by the authorities since the Democracy Wall movement, the underlying problems of this group remain. One problem facing youth is unemployment within their ranks. It is common to find thousands upon thousands of young people between the ages of 22 and 35 jobless in the cities. Some years ago, approximately 75 percent of the secondary school graduates in the city of Shanghai could not find jobs. While it is true that the relaxed policy of permitting individual enterprises to operate in the urban areas has relieved some of the pressure of joblessness for the young, unemployed urban youth are still a source of dissent in China today. The youth of China have entered the period of "awakening" after having gone through periods of "blind faith" and "skepticism." It is in the awakening state that the young are seeking answers to their practical problems for which China's socialism does not seem to have the answers.

In the mid-1980s, the total youth population in China, age 15–18, was about 250 million. Although they may be less cynical than their elders—the "Lost Generation" described earlier—nevertheless, these youngsters are more individualistic in their orientation and outlook. Their hero is not the party's national folk hero Lei Feng, the embodiment of selflessness and a "serve-the-people" attitude towards life. Instead their national hero, as portrayed in popular cinema, is that of a "smoking, drinking, snappy dresser" who has his or her own opinion about things and who despises "rigid bureaucratic thinking."[74] While their elders accepted state-assigned jobs, today's 15- to 18-year-old youths want some freedom of choice. In the past, their elders opted for membership in the Communist Youth League (CYL); the teenagers nowadays shy away from it. As we pointed out in Chapter 9, the total CYL membership was about 52 million in 1985—a bare 20 percent of China's 250 million youth in the mid-1980s.[75] Teenagers are extremely interested in the outside world, particularly the West. They tend to flock to foreign visitors and are eager to practice their foreign languages, knowing that for most of them travel abroad is only a dream. With the latest campaign against "bourgeois liberalization," youth in China have become more cautious in contacting foreigners. Of course, most of them have impressions of an affluent West that may be superficial or even naïve, gleaned from an occasional movie, TV, or imported magazines. But these superficial impressions of a superior material Western civilization compel them to reflect upon their own society under socialism. They ask disturbing questions about the socialist state and the validity of Marxism. Forums sponsored by the CYL revealed that a majority of the youth were "unclear" about the "superiority of socialism" and expressed a lack of confidence in the modernization goals, Marxism, and Mao's thought.[76] Thus, the future outlook for China's youth seems rather bleak. If their pent-up energy is not

channeled toward useful ends, if their disillusionment about the system is not alleviated, and if they are not made a useful part of the march toward modernization, then
they will remain a potential source of unrest in the future. (See Chapter 10 for a discussion of student demonstrations and dissent.)

THE ROLE OF SCIENCE AND TECHNOLOGY
IN MODERNIZATION

A historic milestone was reached in the spring of 1978 when some 6,000 scientists
and technicians gathered in Beijing to discuss and endorse the plans for China's
development of modern science and technology. In his keynote address to the conference, Deng Xiaoping, then vice-premier of the State Council, criticized the party
for not providing adequate services, supplies, and working conditions for scientists.[77]
This was certainly a far cry from the days when the intellectuals, scientists, and technicians were labeled, by Yao Wenyuan, "an exploiting class" with strong bourgeois
prejudices,[78] and when Deng himself was charged by the radicals with advocating the
"poisonous weed" of advanced scientific development.

Since 1949 science policy has vacillated between professional orientation and
mass mobilization, depending on China's development policies.[79] William Whitson
has noted that during each alternation the leadership embraced a different set of
approaches toward the identifiable issues of planning, the role of self-sufficiency,
and the place of technology transfers from abroad.[80] During the First Five-Year Plan,
professionals and technical bureaucrats held a position of dominance. Consequently,
they emphasized centralized planning and control over the allocation of resources,
importation of some 300 complete industrial plants from the Soviet Union, and scientific and technical training of Chinese in the Soviet Union. Following the withdrawal of Soviet aid in 1960, the Great Leap altered the basic approach from professionalism—with heavy reliance on technological transfers from abroad—to Mao's
approach of self-reliance and "disdain" for foreign technology. The alternating pattern reappeared with some variations during the periods of economic recovery following the Great Leap and the Cultural Revolution.

The Cultural Revolution disrupted the scientific community in a number of
ways. Scientists and technicians were criticized for their professional sins: their
aloofness from and disinterest in politics; their privileged status and high salaries;
and their theoretical research, unrelated to practical problems. Established in 1958
under the supervision of the State Council, the State Scientific and Technological
Commission was supposed to provide direction for scientific research, administer scientific and technological programs, and approve funds for research. The organization's leading members, however, were subjected to Red Guard criticism and harassment for their "elitist" orientation. Many of the scientific cadres associated with the
commission were sent to the countryside for rehabilitation through physical labor,
and the commission disappeared as an organization.

The Chinese Academy of Sciences, which conducts research in the various
physical and social sciences, both directly and through affiliate members, was subjected to criticism and purges. At the height of the upheaval, it was reported that
thousands of its members had been sent to the factories and communes for physical

labor.[81] The president of the academy, the late Guo Moruo, a noted historian, managed to survive by making self-criticism in which he repudiated all his previous writings. Typically, the academy's affairs were taken over by a revolutionary committee, with the PLA and the masses participating in decision making. Members were forced to spend long hours in political reeducation and ideological remolding.

Some members of the academy were sent to factories and communes to engage in applied research. Many of the research institutes of the academy decentralized their operations during the Cultural Revolution by establishing provincial and local branches, which proliferated and duplicated activities. Although the Cultural Revolution strategy did not contribute to basic scientific research, some observers in the West viewed some of the reforms in science and technology as innovative from a developmental perspective. Genevieve Dean has argued that China's urgent need was for the application of innovative native technology to solve immediate problems of development, and that high-level research was too sophisticated to be of any use to the ordinary peasants and workers.[82] C. H. G. Oldham and Rennselaer Lee saw the prospect of mass participation in developing native technology, based on local initiative and resources, as enriching the economic life of the Chinese.[83] Oldham noted that mass training of ordinary workers as "amateur technicians" might be viewed as a beginning step toward the eventual formation of a "highly specialized corps of technicians."[84]

In contrast to Mao and the radicals, who questioned both the practicality and the ideological impact of modern science, Deng Xiaoping and his pragmatic colleagues see the "mastery of modern science and technology" as the key to modernization. They have admitted frankly that China lags behind some of the advanced countries, such as the United States, by as much as fifteen to twenty years in food production.[85] To catch up with the ever-expanding body of world knowledge, China plans to learn from the advanced nations and to develop her own scientific capabilities. Modernization, or "the mastery of modern science and technology," as Deng would phrase it, has involved at least a three-pronged approach since 1978: the recruitment of a "mammoth force" of scientific and technical personnel, the strengthening of China's scientific and technological institutions, and the acquisition of advanced technology from abroad.

Recruitment of Scientific and Technological Personnel

In 1978 Politburo member Fang Yi, then a vice-premier in the State Council, presented an outline of the national plan for science and technological development, in which he called for the recruitment of a force of 800,000 "professional scientific researchers" between 1978 and 1985.[86] It was obvious that there was a serious shortage of trained technical personnel. The government pointed out that in 1979 only 300,000 scientific and technological (S & T) personnel were working in the 2,400 national research organizations and 600 universities.[87] Richard Suttmeier estimated that almost 41 percent of the 1.3 million university graduates from 1978 to 1985 (or 553,500 to be exact) would need to be in science and engineering, and all would need to be engaged in research in order to meet the targeted personnel needs set by the national plan.[88] What was even more urgent was the need to provide a professional corps of what Suttmeier called "research S & T personnel capable of exercising scientific leadership and of conducting independent research."[89] S & T personnel would be much more highly trained than the present vast number of "scientific and technology workers" in state enterprises and organizations. It was estimated that a total of more than 5.7 million "scientific and technological workers" were employed by state enterprises in 1981.[90]

As urged by Politburo member Chen Yun, China must still recruit scientific and technological specialists as advisors in policymaking.[91] According to Suttmeier, there were ways that China could possibly overcome the huge gap in scientific leadership needs. One was to reinstitute postgraduate work for mid-career training.[92] In August 1981 the Chinese Academy of Sciences, the Academy of Social Sciences, and the Ministry of Education authorized 11,000 postgraduate students to sit for master's degree examinations, and 420 to sit for the doctoral degree.[93] Another way was to send postgraduate students abroad for advanced training in science and technology. There were about 40,000 Chinese students and scholars in the United States, a majority of them doing advanced studies in the sciences. Scientific training could also be obtained through exchanges with foreign countries. For instance, since the normalization of relations in January 1979, China's scientific contacts with the United States have expanded considerably. Under the Science and Technology Agreement, signed on January 31, 1979, during Deng's visit to the United States, numerous accords were concluded for cooperative exchanges. These included such subject areas as agriculture, space science, higher-energy physics, information science, meteorology, atmospheric science, marine and fishery science, medicine, hydroelectric power, earthquake science, and environmental protection.[94] In May 1982 more agreements were reached on cooperative programs on transportation, nuclear research, and aeronautics. These were set up under the auspices of a U.S.–China Joint Commission on Cooperation in Science and Technology.[95] A typical pattern under these agreements was to bring Chinese scientists to the United States and send American scientists to China as advisors.

A related problem in expanding recruitment of scientific personnel was how to use their talent to the fullest, a point stressed clearly by Deng at a meeting with the leaders of the State Planning Commission.[96] Generally, since the scientists were also intellectuals, they were often despised by many. Deng hit hard on this point in 1978 when he talked to the first national science conference. He publicly rejected the radicals' assertion that scientists were not part of the productive forces, and instead contended that "brain workers who serve socialism" were part of the working people. At the conference Deng clearly repudiated the treatment of intellectuals and technicians over the past decade and went on to ask that the party stop interfering in the work of scientific and research institutions and restore the decision-making authority on technical matters to the directors and deputy directors of these agencies. The party committee's work in a scientific institution should be judged by the scientific results and the training of competent scientific personnel, Deng demanded.[97]

Strengthening Chinese Scientific and Technological Institutions

To supervise the development program in science, the Fifth National People's Congress reinstated the State Scientific and Technological Commission and elevated it to ministerial status under the State Council. This commission is, in essence, an overall policymaking body. The commission and its counterparts in the provinces act as scientific advisors to the party committees and government on economic development projects. The commission also has sponsored a series of national conferences on science and technology. Together with the State Planning Commission and the State Economic Commission, they plan, coordinate, and implement scientific research. A key role in scientific research was given to the prestigious Chinese Academy of Sciences. The academy provided funds and direction for 117 research institutes with a combined staff totaling 75,000.[98] Until 1981 the leadership of the academy was in the hands of party committees within each of the research institutes; since then party committees in these institutes were told that they must confine their work to political and ideological matters.[99]

Under the Sixth Five-Year Plan, allocations for education, science, culture, and public health accounted for almost 16 percent of all state expenditures. Funds allocated for science and technology were earmarked for expanding both basic and applied research to meet economic development needs.[100] To what extent Marxist ideology would continue to play a role in research on social and natural sciences remained to be seen.[101] However, in a subsequent policy outline, the State Scientific and Technological Commission stated that it was important to establish "an atmosphere of seriousness and truth seeking," and that research conclusions should be based on facts and "objective law." The commission declared that the time had come "to put a stop to the evil trends of opportunism and falsification."[102] A problem that remains in Chinese politics is the bureaucratic maze that sooner or later may disrupt scientific and technological policies. Despite the institutional reforms, the formulation of major scientific policies was done jointly by no less than six state agencies under the State Council: the state Planning Commission, the Economic Commission, the Capital Construction Commission, the Agriculture Commission, the Energy Commission, and the Machine Building Industry Commission.[103] This bureaucratic decision making will inevitably hamper China's progress in scientific and technological programs.

Reform in Science and Technology in the 1980s

From 1978 to 1981 the goal for the development of science and technology was to catch up with the world's advanced industrial powers, such as Japan and the United States, by the year 2000. But that goal was unrealistic and unattainable because the strategy was predicated on the construction of large-scale projects under a "crash program," as we discussed in Chapter 11. Research in science and technology emphasized basic research that had little to do with the improvement of China's economy. By 1981, as China was pursuing economic adjustment and reform, the emphasis on science and technology began to shift. Deng Xiaoping urged establishment of a linkage between science and technology as tools for economic development.[104] It was felt that economic growth was dependent upon steady progress in developing new technologies. In other words, "technological transformation" became a basic strategy in economic development. This meant an overall revamping in the structural, organizational, and managerial aspects for science and technology.

One of the first major decisions made was to shift emphasis from basic to applied research. Scientific and technological research must be "integrated" with economic production. Some Chinese leaders hoped that China could reach the 1960–1970 technical level of the West and Japan by the year 2000.[105] In order to achieve the revised goal, a number of reforms were introduced in 1985. "Horizontal links" were established between scientific research institutes and industries and between enterprises and local governments. Failure to link science research institutes to industries meant that many industries' problems remained unsolved or that research findings were not utilized by industries.[106] Formerly there was no coordination between various sectors doing research: "The military and civilian sectors, the various governmental departments and administrative regions of the country were also severely cut off from each other."[107] Under the reform, scientific research institutes were now responsible for disseminating applied research findings on technological development to industries and enterprises.

Another reform was the commercialization of technological development. Hundreds of large-scale "technological transaction fairs" were held to enable research institutes to exhibit and sell their technological innovations to industries. These fairs were held in key industrial cities, such as Shanghai, Wuhan, and Tianjin. By 1986 some 1,400 technological centers had been formed to handle these exhibits and fairs. Even more significant was the introduction of a contract system by some 600 research institutes. An institute engaged in applied research projects could contract for its projects with local governments and enterprises for a fee for services, a percentage of profits earned, or simply a bonus award.[108] The income derived from these contracts was to be retained by the institutes as an alternate or additional source of funding. These project contracts were awarded on the basis of bidding for costs by competing research institutes.[109] The contract system for technological research reportedly was borrowed from the Romanian system.[110] However, research institutes still could receive funding from two other sources: "by undertaking major state scientific research projects through which state funds are made available and by applying for funds from science foundations controlled by the academy and the state."[111] The contract system presumably would provide more autonomy for the research institutes in managing their activities and would perhaps lessen to some extent the rigid control exercised by the government.

A third area of reform in science and technology concerned efficient use of the talents of scientific and technological personnel. One commentator complained that "researchers in China were not fully appreciated" and were poorly understood by the bureaucrats in government and the party.[112] A majority of China's researchers associated with the Academy of Sciences were aged senior and middle-level cadres. They might be eager to conduct independent research, but they received only about $300 per person for research, a level of investment inconsequential by Western standards. Too often researchers were assigned to other jobs for lack of research funds. The system stifled initiative and made inefficient use of talent. Only recently has any effort been made to retrain factory managers and research and development personnel with the aim of eventually placing them in positions of authority or where they could use their expertise productively. A final comment: it is obvious that reform in science and technology depends on freedom from political interference and the right amount of independent inquiry and academic discussion in scientific research. Ideological labels such as "rightists" have been used in the past against scientists and researchers whose task was to discover knowledge and truth. The stirrings of political winds in January 1987 and the renewed campaign against "bourgeois liberalization" after the 1989 Tiananmen crackdown revived bitter memories of a political climate that had stifled research in science and technology and had restricted development for more than two decades.

THE OPEN DOOR POLICY: ACQUISITION
AND TRANSFER OF SCIENCE AND TECHNOLOGY

China's main strategy for technological transfer in the 1970s was purchase from abroad—frequently acquiring complete industrial plants. This strategy was called "turnkey," because the complete facility required only the keys to open it for operation. Between 1972 and 1975, China imported some 170 complete industrial plants, valued at $2.6 billion, from eight European nations, Japan, the United States, and the Soviet Union.[113] Most of these plants were for basic industries, such as steel, electricity, petroleum, and chemical fertilizer. The Chinese could expand capital formation by copying a complete imported plant, which was a "carrier of new technology."[114] Former vice-premier Fang Yi made it very clear in 1978 that "an important way to develop science and technology at high speed is to utilize fully the latest achievements in the world of science and technology and absorb their quintessence." He said, "We should introduce selected techniques that play a key and pace-setting role."[115] During a brief spell of euphoria from 1977 to 1978, proposed contracts for purchasing technology from abroad proliferated; however, financial realities forced a readjustment of priorities in 1979. The government then made efforts to address the questions of how to digest and absorb foreign technology and how to deal with the problem of financing. The purchase of complete sets of equipment was not always satisfactory. At times imported equipment was found to be unsuitable for the intended localities. In other cases there was too much equipment imported, or the technology imported was inappropriate. There was a failure generally "to study the equipment, and master and spread knowledge of its use."[116]

The policy for scientific and technological purchases from abroad consists of the following guidelines:[117] (1) purchases must be selective—"We should start by considering our national economic requirements, our technical base, etc., not just go after the newest and most advanced"; (2) foreign technology "must be integrated with China's own research projects, otherwise there can be no true digestion and absorption"; and (3) scientists must study foreign scientific techniques through published journals, conferences, and exchanges. The policy in science and technology calls for "buying techniques, software and samples of machinery." The Chinese are trying to restrict purchases of equipment to what will be the most useful for their technological development, or as the Chinese say, "To buy hens for them to lay eggs." Hu Yaobang told the 1982 party congress: "We must refrain from indiscriminate import of equipment, and particularly of consumer goods that can be manufactured and supplied at home."[118] It is interesting to note that the Reagan administration granted China a "friendly but non-allied" status to permit it to purchase higher-level electronics and computers under some restrictive guidelines. The Chinese have also discovered three effective ways to acquire advanced foreign technology rapidly: joint ventures with foreign business concerns, countertrade factors, and special economic zones for trade and foreign investment. These strategies are key components of the new open door policy.

The Open Door Policy

Of the reforms instituted by China's pragmatic leaders under Deng Xiaoping, the policy of opening China's doors to foreign investment has been one of the most significant departures from decades of largely self-imposed ideological rigidity under Mao. The purpose of the "open door" "kaifang zhenze" was stated in the communiqué of the third session of the Eleventh Central Committee in December 1978:

> We are now. . . adopting a number of major new economic measures, on conscientiously transforming the system and methods on terms of equality and mutual benefit with other countries on the basis of self-reliance, striving to adopt the world's advanced technologies and equipment and greatly strengthening scientific and educational work to meet the needs of modernization.[119]

The party's 1978 decision to open up China to the outside world was included in the 1982 state constitution adopted by the Sixth National People's Congress.[120] The open door policy involved, in addition to the acquisition of advanced equipment, the acquisition of what is known as "codified technology," such as blueprints and drawings, and "undocumented technology," or technical information and skills.[121]

Let us review briefly the various methods China has employed to acquire advanced technology.

Joint Venture.[122]   The idea of cooperative business ventures between a communist nation and a capitalist one was pioneered by the Yugoslavs in 1967. In July 1979 the Fifth NPC at its second session adopted a joint venture law governing both Chinese and foreign investments.[123] The law contains three basic provisions:[124] (1) protection by the Chinese government of investment by a foreign concern in a joint venture; (2) a pledge by the foreign concern that the technology or equipment contributed from abroad "shall be truly advanced and appropriate to Chinese needs"; and (3) a guarantee of the retention by the foreign concern in the joint venture of the net profits after appropriate Chinese income taxes are paid.[125] The joint venture law also serves as a framework allowing foreign investors to negotiate and enter into contracts with the Chinese government. While the law defines the role of foreign investment on Chinese soil, its emphasis is on the advanced technology a foreign investor or firm can share with the Chinese. A usual format in such arrangements is the 51/49 percent joint ownership agreement between the Chinese government and foreign firms. The Chinese provide land, labor, and the necessary infrastructure, and the foreign investor provides the investment capital and equipment.

Since 1979 there have been more than 2,000 joint venture agreements concluded, totaling about $16 billion. Many of these agreements, however, were merely pledges, and actual operations remained unfulfilled. The actual amount contracted and spent for joint ventures amounted to only about $4.8 to $5.0 billion by 1986.[126] Most investments came from Japan, the United States, France, West Germany, Australia, and Switzerland. A model of this type of investment was the China–Schindler joint venture, involving a Swiss manufacturer in partnership with Jardine Matheson of Hong Kong.[127] They formed a partnership to set up factories in China to produce lifts, or elevators. In its first year of operation (from 1980 to 1981), this joint venture yielded about $3.5 million in profits. Another such arrangement was the joint $51 million deal between China and American Motors Corporation (AMC) to produce Jeeps and Jeep engines at Beijing Auto Works. According to the contract, AMC was to invest $8 million initially, with another $8 million in advanced technology, to assist in the modernization of Beijing Auto Works. For AMC the advantage lay in cheap labor costs, enabling AMC's Chinese-made Jeeps to compete favorably in the Southeast Asian market.[128]

The original expectation was that the newly modernized Beijing auto plant would be able to produce 20,000 Cherokee Jeeps a year by 1990, using mostly locally made components and material.[129] However, the AMC–China joint venture ran into a number of problems from 1985 to 1986, and its Jeep production was interrupted for about seven weeks in 1986. One problem in the venture was the Chinese regulation that prohibited the company from obtaining foreign exchange needed to pay for imported components. The original joint venture agreement called for Beijing Auto Works to follow the new design for the Cherokee Jeep by using Chinese components, but the vehicles assembled with Chinese components were defective. AMC wanted to import about 90 percent of the Cherokee Jeep components as an alternative. As a partner in the joint venture, AMC had expected to pay for the imports with the United States dollar earnings from the sale of the Jeeps. But the second problem was that the Chinese foreign exchange regulation reduced the amount of foreign exchange allotted to the joint venture and added a 60 percent duty on imported parts.[130] After seven weeks of negotiation (during which the case received worldwide publicity threatening China's reputation as a country that welcomed foreign investment), Chinese authorities made changes in the foreign exchange regulation to permit buyers of Cherokee Jeeps to pay in United States dollars to enable the joint venture to import the needed spare parts.

The AMC joint venture episode illustrates some of the frustrations experienced by foreign investors in joint ventures with China. A major problem was converting Chinese currency earnings into United States dollars. The new 1986 currency exchange regulations seem to have eased the problem. In February 1986 the new regulations permitted joint ventures that were short of hard currency to sell their products in China for needed hard currency or to reinvest their earnings in Chinese currency (renminbi) in Chinese enterprises that earn hard currencies.[131] But the new regulations on joint ventures also discriminate against small foreign investors by allowing no debt on paid-up capital—a rule designed to prevent financially unsound foreign investors from entering the Chinese market.[132] The new regulations may discourage formation of more joint ventures. In any event, by the late 1980s the Chinese were beginning to take a tougher stance in approving joint ventures.[133]

Countertrade Factors. Countertrade factors is another technique for obtaining foreign investment and technology.[134] The following scenario illustrates the technique. Assume that China wishes to import advanced mining equipment, to develop its coal resources. Under countertrade factors, payment for the equipment would be deferred until the coal mined with the equipment is sold to the exporter. This device enables China to acquire technology in exchange for the product the technology will produce. It preserves China's limited foreign exchange reserves. As of 1982 China's foreign exchange and gold reserves were estimated at 12.6 million troy ounces.[135] But official foreign reserves declined from $16.7 billion in 1984 to about $10.9 billion at mid-year 1985.[136] This technique also provides a good way to reduce foreign trade deficits.

Special Economic Zones.[137]   Special economic zones (SEZ) are really free trade or tax-free zones that provide customs exemptions and preferential treatment to balance foreign trade. Since 1979 the Chinese government has established four such zones in southern China, all ports opening into the South China Sea: Zhuhai, facing the Portuguese colony of Macao; Shenzhen, near Xianggang (Hong Kong); and Shantou and Xiamen, in Fujian province. One of the main objectives was to have these specially designated zones serve as "bridges for introducing foreign capital, advanced technology and equipment and as classrooms for training personnel capable of mastering advanced technology."[138] Some of these zones, such as Shenzhen and Zhuhai, were multipurpose zones where a host of economic activities could take place: industry, commerce, housing, agriculture, and tourism. The other two zones would primarily process exports. Imports into all zones are tax-free, except for cigarettes and alcohol, which have a reduced tariff. Workers in the zones are hired by contract under a basic wage scale, with a flexible floating wage system. Chinese currency at present is the only currency permitted in these zones. But eventually, foreign currencies will be permitted under special regulations. Most of the funds for investment in these special economic zones come from foreign investors.[139]

By the end of 1992, special economic zones in coastal southern China had helped to boost the regional growth rate to China's highest: 19.5 percent for Guangdong and 21.7 percent for Fujian. The per capita income for Guangdong in 1992 was over $3,000, and for Fujian it was over $2,000.[140] The economic boom in Guangdong has been helped by foreign investment—particularly by Hong Kong capital in the Shenzhen special economic zone. That SEZ is known for its property speculation and its stock market.

The open door policy has brought many benefits to China, particularly in invigorating the domestic economy, as stressed by Deng Xiaoping, the architect of that policy.[141] It has also created unrealistic expectations among China's youth, and raised questions about the gradual erosion of socialist ideology, as discussed in Chapter 10. There has been some criticism from foreign business executives also. In contrast to the original enthusiasm, some of them no longer see the Chinese investment climate as conducive to profitable business.[142] The soaring costs of doing business in China have led to complaints.[143] Bureaucratic delays in negotiating contracts for joint ventures have become more than just matters of annoyance. Added to these complaints is the problem of arbitrary taxes and charges that make doing business in China rather unattractive.[144] Former United States Ambassador Winston Lord was quoted as saying that many businesspeople were utterly frustrated by "high costs, price-gouging, tight foreign exchange controls, limited access to the Chinese market, bureaucratic foot-dragging, lack of qualified local personnel and unpredictability."[145] For 1992, China signed a total of over 40,000 foreign investment agreements totaling $58 billion, but only about $16 billion of these funds was actually used.[146] A large percentage of total actual investments by foreign businesses traditionally has come from overseas Chinese in Hong Kong.[147]

Doubts have been raised about the open door policy in the light of the 1986–1987 campaign against "bourgeois liberalization." Chinese leaders now in power maintain that there will be no retrogression on reform measures such as the open door policy.[148] There were even indications that China might double its efforts in opening its doors to the world.[149]

THE TREATMENT OF CHINESE INTELLECTUALS[150]

As of 1982 there were about 20 million intellectuals in China—defined as anyone who has had more than secondary education. Thus, a teacher, a university professor, a technician, a writer, or an engineer is defined as an intellectual. It is believed that the vast majority of them are not CCP members. In most societies this category of educated person is treated with respect and valued as a precious human resource. In China this was not the case between 1957 and 1978. In 1957 Chinese intellectuals were labeled "rightists"; they were suspected, put down, and despised. From 1957 through the decade of the Cultural Revolution (from 1966 to 1976), Chinese intellectuals were not only labeled as "rightist" but as "the stinking ninth category" by the radicals. They were despised and persecuted merely because they possessed education, knowledge, and skills. The Cultural Revolution radicals did not consider them productive members of the socialist society. To the radical ideologues, it was better to be a peasant or a worker than a "stinking" intellectual.

When the pragmatic reformers came back to power in 1977, they set out to correct this negative attitude toward the intellectuals. The new leaders realized that China's modernization could not possibly proceed without the people who possessed the "brain power." In 1978 Deng quoted Marx and Lenin to prove that scientists and technological personnel were integral parts of the productive force. "Intellectuals," Deng cited Lenin as saying, "engage in scientific and technical work who themselves are not capitalists but scholars."[151] Deng went on to say that "brain workers who serve socialism are a part of the working people."[152] He argued further that so long as intellectuals were not opposed to the party or socialism, "we should, in line with the party's policy of uniting with, educating and remolding the intellectuals, bring out their specialized abilities, respect their labor and take interest in their progress, giving them a warm helping hand."[153]

However, "Leftist" attitudes toward intellectuals lingered on into the era of the Sixth Five-Year Plan. The truth of the matter is that many intellectuals were still not given full opportunities to apply their specialized knowledge and skill. In an article in *Hongqi* (*Red Flag*), Politburo member Nie Rongzhen made it clear that the middle-aged intellectuals—about five million men and women in their forties and fifties, serving as the backbone of China's modernization program—continued to receive low wages and to face many difficulties.[154] Marshal Nie, in the winter of 1982, urged that provisions be made to take good care of the middle-aged intellectuals, who could provide enormous contributions to China's modernization. Nie indicated that in many government units, the intellectuals were still not being treated well and were not trusted.[155] There were frequent stories in the mass media about how some intellectuals were mistreated, demoted, and castigated by jealous local people. While most workers had received two wage increases since 1977, middle-aged intellectuals with twenty years of service received only one raise, a mere 7 yuan, or the equivalent of $3.50. They were also given cramped housing arrangements. During the author's visit to China, some middle-aged intellectuals spoke about "three heavies and two neglects"; namely, heavy family burden, heavy responsibility, and heavy pressure at work; and inadequate remuneration and meager living conditions.[156] Discrimination against the intellectuals continued mainly because of the lingering fear among the people of the "bourgeois academic authority." For many intellectuals the memory of their persecution after 1957 was too vivid for them to be optimistic about the future. Unless the pragmatic leaders successfully reverse the anti-intellectual climate, China's success in modernization will be in jeopardy.

Some developments concerning China's intellectuals need to be discussed here. One is the decision by the national conference in January 1986 to have a system of professional titles for those engaged in intellectual endeavors.[157] The new system was designed to provide better monetary rewards and promotional advancement for individuals working in science, technology, and higher education. Under this system, salary is based on professional title rather than on educational background or seniority in length of service. Under the old system a young scientist could not attain a position commensurate with his or her ability and competence. Now workers in professional fields may be given a professional title, such as engineer, researcher, economist, or editor. Hiring, salary, and promotion are in accordance with their professional title, which, in turn, is based on ability and competence. The system was instituted as an experiment in July 1985 in the Academies of Sciences and Social Sciences, the State Education Commission, and the ministries of agriculture, health, and mineral resources.

While Chinese intellectuals welcomed the "new deal" accorded to them in status, compensation, and career advancement, they also realized that their fate is still subject to the constantly shifting political winds. It has always been hard for intellectuals to know for sure how far they can go in expressing their thoughts. Their confidence in the party's willingness to provide an environment of relaxation and liberalization was jolted when the crusade against "spiritual pollution" was launched by the ideologues in 1983. Although the spiritual pollution campaign was abruptly terminated, it deeply shocked the intellectuals. Then, at the end of 1984, authors, artists, and writers were given an enormous boost on the issue of artistic free expression. In a speech to the Fourth Congress of the Writers' Association, Politburo member Hu Qili said: "Writers must have the freedom to choose material, themes and artistic methods and to express their own feeling and thoughts so that they could produce touching and inspiring works."[158] Hu's speech was interrupted thirty-three times by applause from the 12,500 members present. This speech, along with demands from intellectuals for freedom to think, ushered in a period of "freedom of creation." Professor Fang Lizhi made speeches stating that the "emergence and development of new theories necessitates creating an atmosphere of democracy and freedom in the universities, an atmosphere of intellectual ideology."[159] The "freedom of creation" and thought was cut short by the 1987 crackdown on student protest and demonstration as the campaign against "bourgeois liberalization" intensified. Fang Lizhi and other outspoken intellectuals were dismissed from their posts and expelled from party membership. This was followed by more expulsions and dismissals of authors, writers, and journalists. Once again Chinese intellectuals had to exercise caution, despite the official position that intellectuals were not the target in the fight against "bourgeois liberalization."[160] Premier Li Peng reemphasized that the party "will not change its policy on intellectuals, whose skills and knowledge are indispensable to China's drive for modernization." But for many Chinese intellectuals there is a crisis of confidence in the party. That pledge by Li has not been fulfilled, and a widespread feeling of fear and oppression has developed among Chinese intellectuals since the June 4 killings at Tiananmen.

CHINESE INTELLECTUALS AFTER TIANANMEN

In his report to the Seventh NPC Standing Committee on June 30, 1989, Chen Xiton, mayor of Beijing, charged that a handful of China's intellectuals, inside and outside the CCP, had engineered the Tiananmen "conspiracy" to "overthrow" the party's leadership.[161] He then presented a list of allegedly incriminating political assemblies, seminars, big-character posters, and joint petitions organized by Chinese intellectuals, who had used their positions in various institutions to criticize the party for its failure to act on inflation, corruption, and the slowdown in reform. One of these petitions was Fang Lizhi's open letter to Deng Xiaoping, co-signed by forty-two scientists and thirty-two other intellectuals, urging the release of political prisoners.[162]

Mayor Chen's report on this situation was, however, only a culmination of a long-standing antagonism between the government and China's intellectual vanguard—an antagonism that was destined to reach a breaking point in June 1989 at Tiananmen Square. By January 1989 the government's relationship with the intellectuals had reached the point of confrontation. In fact, the party leaders' relationship with Chinese intellectuals had already gone sour during the December 1986–87 student demonstration, when the party's response was to expel from party membership those intellectuals—Fang Lizhi, Wang Ruowang, and Liu Binyan—who were openly critical of the campaign against "bourgeois liberalization." This was the beginning of the "desertion of the intellectuals," as scientists, writers, and some journalists—many of them party veterans—protested and withdrew from party membership.[163]

Provocative new ideas being advanced by young social science researchers in 1988 and 1989 also generated official wrath. One such idea was the concept of "New Authoritarianism" that surfaced just prior to Hu Yaobang's death on April 15, 1989. Researcher Wu Jianliang, working in the party's general office, advocated that the government be entrusted to a leader who is committed to modern economic views; protection of individual freedom; and opening the country to foreign capital, culture, and technology.[164] Another idea advocated by the now-exiled political scientist Yan Jiaqi and many other intellectuals was direct popular election of delegates to the NPC.

The Tiananmen crackdown not only silenced the intellectuals, but forced a number of them into exile. Moreover, scholars, researchers, and thinkers in the prestigious Chinese Academy of Social Sciences—the bastion of new ideas for solving China's social and economic problems—were subjected to indoctrination and intimidation by the regime. They were forced to attend periodic political study sessions. When not forced into political indoctrination, Chinese intellectuals have merely kept silent, waiting quietly for a leadership change.[165] Immediately after Tiananmen their research institutions were placed under military control, and directors for these institutions have been interrogated. Dissidents have been dismissed and expelled from the party after investigation.

A year after the Tiananmen crackdown, the new party chief, Jiang Zemin, made overtures to appease the alienated Chinese intellectuals, who as of 1989 numbered more than 22 million. He praised them as "an excellent contingent" supporting Deng's "Four Basic Principles": the leadership of the party, and the socialist road, the dictatorship of the proletariat, Marxism-Leninism and Mao's thought. However, Jiang warned that China's young intellectuals, almost half of the total 22 million, have some "shortcomings and deficiencies" due to their lack of experience in life. He reiterated the traditional national attitudes toward intellectuals, such as "inadequate attention" to and lack of appreciation for their work. He pointed out that their living and working conditions still need improvement.[166] He paid lip service to academic freedom and literary creativeness. He assured them that "academic disputes on scientific and cultural issues must not be subject to official sanction." What this presages for the future in terms of an improvement in official status is hard to predict. Meanwhile, the bulk of China's intellectuals are anything but pessimistic; they wait silently, but hopefully, for a change.

Some encouraging signs have emerged as China has decided to continue full speed ahead with economic reform. One such sign is monetary reward for scientific intellectuals in order to encourage applied or practical research to enhance production.[167] One engineer in the Zhuhai SEZ received a cash reward of $200,000, a car, and an apartment for designing a method of extracting a clotting agent from animal blood and helping to open a factory to produce it. A biologist in Beijing was granted a cash reward of about $4,000 for breeding better pigs. Finally, in its decision to move forward in establishing a socialist market economy, the CCP's Central Committee laid stress on the need for trained skilled workers and professionals in all fields.[168]

NOTES

1. Hung-ti Chu, "Education in Mainland China," *Current History*, vol. 59, no. 349 (September 1970), 168–70; and Leo A. Orleans, "Communist China's Education: Policies, Problems, and Prospects," in *India and China: Studies in Comparative Development*, ed. Kuan-I Chen and Jogindar Uppal (New York: Free Press, 1971), pp. 276–77.
2. Joel Glassman, "Educational Reform and Manpower Policy in China: 1955–1958," *Modern China*, vol. iii., no. 3 (July 1977), 265–66.
3. Ibid., pp. 268–69.
4. Ibid., p. 272.
5. The figure for 1949 was taken from "Primary Schools in China," *Peking Review*, 36 (September 8, 1978), 15. Figures for 1953 and 1958 were taken from State Statistical Bureau of 1960, as reprinted in Glassman, "Educational Reform and Manpower Policy in China," pp. 212, 281.
6. Glassman, "Educational Reform and Manpower Policy in China," pp. 212, 281.
7. Ibid. p. 268.
8. Ibid., p. 280; Hung-Ti Chu, "Education in Mainland China," p. 181; and Orleans, "Communist China's Education," p. 282.
9. Orleans, "Communist China's Education," p. 282–83.
10. Hung-Ti Chu, "Education in Mainland China," p. 169; and Orleans, "Communist China's Education," p. 282.
11. Orleans, "Communist China's Education," p. 288.
12. Philip E. Ginsburg, "Development and Educational Process in China," *Current Scene*, vol. xiv, no. 3 (March 1976), 3–4. Also see *Survey of China Mainland Press* (SCMP), no. 784, pp. 22–23.
13. Ginsburg, "Development and Educational Process in China," p. 4.
14. "It is Essential to Rely on the Poor and Lower-Middle Peasants in the Educational Revolution in the Countryside," *Peking Review*, 39 (September 27, 1968), 21.
15. See Ellen K. Ong, "Education in China since the Cultural Revolution," *Studies in Comparative Communism*, vol. iii, nos. 3 and 4 (July–August 1970), 158–75.
16. See William Hinton, *Hundred Day War: The Cultural Revolution at Tsinghua University* (New York and London: Monthly Review Press, 1972).
17. Robert McCormick, "Revolution in Education Committees," *The China Quarterly*, 57 (January–March 1974), 134–39.

18. "Power Is the Fundamental Question of Revolution in Education," *Peking Review*, 51 (December 21, 1968), 8.
19. Ibid., p. 8.
20. For facts and figures about Chinese education since 1978 from the *Beijing Review*, see the following issues: 37 (September 14, 1981), 7–8; 6 (February 6, 1982), 28; 42 (October 18, 1982), 23; and 47 (November 22, 1982), 27. Also see Michael W. Kirst, "Reflections on Education in China," *Phi Delta Kappan*, vol. 60, no. 2 (October 1978), 124–25; Ralph W. Tyler, "Chinese Education," *Phi Delta Kappan*, vol. 60, no. 1 (September 1978), 26–29; "A Glimpse at Chinese Education," *Today's Education* (September/October 1979), 48–50; H. William Koch, "People and Publishing in China," *Physics Today*, vol. 32, no. 8 (August 1979), 32–37; Frank F. Wong, "Education and Work in China: What Can We Learn from China's Experience?" *Change: The Magazine of Higher Learning* (November–December 1980), 24–58; A. Tom Grunfeld, "Innovations in Post-Secondary Education in China," *The China Quarterly*, 90 (June 1980), 281–85; John J. Cogan, "China's Fifth Modernization: Education," *Phi Delta Kappan*, vol. 62, no. 4 (December 1980), 268–72; Jonathan Unger, "The Chinese Controversy Over Higher Education," *Pacific Affairs*, vol. 53, no. 1 (September 1980), 29–47; Ann Kent, "Red and Expert: The Revolution in Education at Shanghai Teachers' University, 1975–76," *The China Quarterly*, 86 (June 1981), 304–21; Zhang Suchu, "Rice Paddy Educations for China's Elite," Los Angeles Times Service, as reprinted in *Honolulu Advertiser* (July 19, 1982), A-7; Takashi Oka, "China Schools: Less Rote, More Ideology," *The Christian Science Monitor* (August 3, 1981), p. 3; Suzanne Pepper, "China's Schools Turning an Old Leaf," *Asian Wall Street Journal Weekly* (September 21, 1981), p. 11; "China's Nagging Educational Dilemma," *Asian Wall Street Journal Weekly* (December 28, 1981), p. 11; Edward J. Kormondy, "The PRC: Revitalizing an Educational System," *Change: The Magazine of Higher Learning*, vol. 14, no. 5 (July–August 1982), 33–35.
21. Deng Xiaoping, "Speech at the National Education Work Conference," pp. 6–12.
22. Ibid., p. 7.
23. "Six-Year Curriculum Restored in Primary Schools," *Beijing Review*, 49 (December 8, 1980), 6.
24. "Moral Education in the Schools," *Beijing Review* (December 7, 1981), 21.
25. "Good Marks Are Not Everything," *Beijing Review*, 16 (April 19, 1982), 8–9.
26. Ibid., p. 9.
27. "Work-Study Programmes in Primary and Middle Schools," *Beijing Review*, 45 (November 8, 1982), 21.
28. Ibid., p. 21.
29. For discussion on vocational training at secondary schools, see the following issues of *Beijing Review*; 28 (July 13, 1979) 7–8; 35 (September 1, 1980), 5–6; 46 (November 17, 1980), 7–8; and 25 (June 21, 1982), 8–9.
30. "Reforming Middle School Education," *Beijing Review*, 35 (September 1, 1980), 5.
31. "Vocational and Technical Education," *Beijing Review*, 25 (June 21, 1982), 8.
32. Statistical data came from the following issues of *Beijing Review*: 28 (July 13, 1979), 7; and 46 (November 17, 1980), 7.
33. See Premier Zhao's report in *Beijing Review*, 51 (December 20, 1982), 16.
34. "Reforming Middle School Education," p. 6.
35. "Vocational and Technical Education," *Beijing Review*, 25 (June 21, 1982), 8.
36. Ibid., p. 8.
37. "Education: Apex and Base of a Pyramid," *Beijing Review*, 20 (May 18, 1979), 6. Information about Shanghai "key schools" program was based on notes taken by the author at the group interview, August 6, 1979.
38. See Unger, "The Chinese Controversy Over Higher Education," pp. 29–47; also see Dale Bratton, "University Admission Politics in China, 1970–1978," *Asian Survey*, vol. xix, no. 10 (October 1979), 1008–22.
39. See Unger, "The Chinese Controversy Over Higher Education," pp. 36–38; and *Ming Pao Daily* (Hong Kong) (April 30, 1977).
40. "New College Student," *Peking Review*, 16 (April 21, 1978), 11.
41. "Affiliated Colleges Set Up," *Beijing Review*, 3 (January 19, 1979), 31; and 41 (October 12, 1979), 6.
42. "New College Student," *Beijing Review*, 41 (October 12, 1979), 6.
43. "Report on the Sixth Five-Year Plan," *Beijing Review*, 51 (December 20, 1982), 15.
44. "TV University," *Beijing Review*, 7 (February 16, 1979), 7; and 1 (January 5, 1981), 8.

45. "China's TV Universities," *Beijing Review*, 1 (January 5, 1981), 8.
46. "TV University," 7. Also see Edward J. Kormondy, "The PRC: Revitalizing an Educational System," *Change: The Magazine of Higher Education*, vol. 14. no. 5 (July–August, 1982), 34–35.
47. "Affiliated Colleges Set Up," 31.
48. "Spare Time College for Beijing's Staff and Workers," *Beijing Review*, 11 (March 16, 1981), 31.
49. "Open More Avenues for Education," *Beijing Review*, 30 (July 28, 1980), 19; and 39 (September 29, 1980), 6.
50. *Beijing Review*, 2 (May 27, 1985), 3; and 3 (June 6, 1985), 16.
51. *Ta Kung Pao Weekly Supplement* (Hong Kong), (May 23, 1985), p. 1. Also see *Beijing Review*, 21 (May 27, 1985), 6; 23 (June 10, 1985), 15; and 24 (June 17, 1985), 19.
52. *Beijing Review* (May 12, 1986), 4–5.
53. *Beijing Review*, 21 (May 27, 1985), 6.
54. *Ta Kung Pao Weekly Supplement* (Hong Kong) (May 23, 1985), p. 1.
55. *Beijing Review*, 19 (May 13, 1985), 4.
56. *Beijing Review*, 33 (August 18, 1986), 22.
57. Ibid.
58. *Beijing Review*, 47 (November 24, 1986), 14; and 34 (August 24, 1987), 6.
59. *Beijing Review*, 29 (July 21, 1986), 4.
60. *Beijing Review*, 23 (June 10, 1985), 16.
61. Ibid. Also see Austin Swanson and Zhang Zhian, "Education Reform in China," *Phi Delta Kappan* (January 1987), pp. 373–378.
62. *Beijing Review*, 7–8 (February 18, 1985), 30.
63. Ibid. And also see Robert McCormick, "The Radio and Television Universities and the Development of High Education in China," *China Quarterly*, 105 (March 1986), 74–94.
64. McCormick, "The Radio and Television Universities," 93–94.
65. *Beijing Review*, 47 (November 24, 1986), 15.
66. *Beijing Review*, 24 (June 16, 1986), 5. Also see Swanson and Zhang Zhian, "Education Reform in China," pp. 373–78.
67. Ibid. Also see Swanson and Zhang Zhian, "Education Reform in China," p. 371.
68. *Beijing Review*, 34 (August 24, 1987), 6.
69. Ibid.
70. *China News Analysis*, 1377 (January 15, 1989), 1–9, and 1414 (July 15, 1990), 1–3.
71. *China News Analysis*, 1414 (July 15, 1990), 5.
72. *Beijing Review* (July 17–23, 1989), 25.
73. Thomas B. Gold, "Alienated Youth Cloud China's Future," *Asian Wall Street Journal Weekly* (May 18, 1981), p. 13; John Roderick, "China's Youth Problem," Associated Press, as reprinted in *Honolulu Star-Bulletin* (September 15, 1980), A-21; and Richard Critchfield, "Youth Turn out Dogma, Turn on Radios," *The Christian Science Monitor* (August 1, 1980), p. 13. Also see Mary-Louise O'Callaghan, "A Streak of Individualism in China's Youth," *The Christian Science Monitor* (July 22, 1983), p. 3.
74. *The Christian Science Monitor* (July 22, 1983), p. 3.
75. Stanley Rosen, "Prosperity, Privatization, and China's Youth," *Problems of Communism*, xxxiv, 2 (March–April, 1985), 3.
76. Ibid., p. 13.
77. Teng Hsiao-p'ing, "Speech at Opening Ceremony of National Science Conference (March 18, 1978)," *Peking Review*, 12 (March 24, 1978), 17.
78. Theoretical Group of the Chinese Academy of Sciences, "A Serious Struggle in Scientific and Technical Circles," *Peking Review*, 16 (April 15, 1977), 24–27.
79. Richard Suttmeier, "Science Policy Shifts, Organizational Change and China's Development," *The China Quarterly*, 62 (June 1975), 207–41. Also see William W. Whitson, "China's Quest for Technology," *Problems of Communism*, xii (July–August 1973), 16–30.
80. Whitson, "China's Quest for Technology," 17–18.
81. Bruce J. Esposito, "The Cultural Revolution and China's Scientific Establishment," *Current Scene*, vol. xii, no. 4 (April 1974), 2–3.
82. Genevieve Dean, "China's Technological Development," *New Scientist* (May 18, 1972), 371–73.
83. C. H. G. Oldham, "Technology in China: Science for the Masses?" *Far Eastern Economic Review* (May 16, 1968), 353–55; and Rennselaer W. Lee, III, "The Politics of Technology in Communist China," in *Ideology and Politics in Contemporary China*, ed. Chalmers Johnson (Seattle, Wash. and London: University of Washington Press, 1973), pp. 301–25; Jonathan Unger, "Mao's Million Ama-

teur Technicians," *Far Eastern Economic Review* (April 3, 1971), 115–18.

84. Oldham, "Science and Technological Policies," in *China's Developmental Experience*, ed. Michael Oksenberg (New York, Washington, and London: Praeger Publications, 1973), pp. 80–94.

85. Teng Hsiao-p'ing, "Speech at Opening Ceremony of National Science Conference," p. 10; and Hua Kuo-feng, "Raise the Scientific and Cultural Level of the Entire Chinese Nations," *Peking Review*, 31 (March 13, 1978), 6–14.

86. "Outline National Plan for Development of Science and Technology, Relevant Policies and Measures," *Beijing Review*, 14 (April 7, 1978), 7.

87. "30th Anniversary of Chinese Academy of Sciences," *Beijing Review*, 46 (November 16, 1979), 3.

88. Richard Suttmeier, "Politics, Modernization, and Science," *Problems of Communism*, vol. xxx, no. 1 (January–February 1981), 30.

89. Ibid., p. 30.

90. "Updating Science and Technology," *Beijing Review*, 7 (February 14, 1983), 16.

91. See "Outline Report on Policy Governing the Development of Our National Science and Technology the State Science and Technology Commission (February 23, 1981)," in *Issues and Studies*, vol. xviii, no. 5 (May 1982), 88–101.

92. Suttmeier, "Politics, Modernization, and Science," p. 31.

93. See *Ming Pai Daily* (Hong Kong) (February 20, 1982), p. 1; and *Ta Kung Pao Weekly Supplement* (August 6, 1981), p. 4.

94. See *GIST*, Bureau of Public Affairs, Department of State, March, 1981.

95. *Honolulu Advertiser* (May 11, 1983), H-1.

96. *Ta Kung Pao Weekly Supplement* (December 2, 1982), p. 1.

97. Teng Hsiao-p'ing, "Speech at Opening Ceremony of National Science Conference," p. 15 and p. 17.

98. *Ta Kung Pao Weekly Supplement* (Hong Kong) (May 14, 1981), p. 1.

99. Ibid., p.1; and issue of May 21, 1981, p.3.

100. "Report on the Sixth Five-Year Plan," p. 16.

101. See James Reardon-Anderson, "Science and Technology in Post-Mao China," *Contemporary China*, vol. 2, no. 4 (Winter 1978), 42–43.

102. "Outline Report on Policy Governing the Development of Our National Science and Technology," p. 99.

103. Ibid., p. 94.

104. *Beijing Review*, 11 (March 18, 1985), 6.

105. See Richard Conrou, "Technological Change and Industrial Development" in Graham Young, ed., *China's Dilemma of Modernization* (London: Croom Helm, 1985), pp. 118–23.

106. *Beijing Review*, 24 (June 16, 1984), p. 22. Also see Dennis Fred Simon, "S & T Reforms," *China Business Review* (March–April 1985), 31.

107. *Beijing Review*, 24 (June 16, 1984), 22.

108. "S & T Reforms," p. 32.

109. Ibid.

110. *Beijing Review*, 24 (June 16, 1984), 22.

111. Ibid. For an overview of science and reform, see Richard P. Suttmeier, "Reform, Modernization, and the Changing Constitution of Science in China," *Asian Survey*, vol. xxix, no. 10 (October 1989), pp. 999–1015.

112. Ibid., p. 27.

113. See Dave L. Denny, "International Finance in the People's Republic of China," in *China: A Reassessment of the Economy*, pp. 701–2. Also see Kent Morrison, "Domestic Politics and Industrialization in China: The Foreign Trade Factor," *Asian Survey*, vol. xviii, no.7 (July 1978) 690–98.

114. Shannon Brown, "Foreign Technology and Economic Growth," *Problems of Communism*, xxvi (July–August 1977), 30–32.

115. "Outline Report on Policy Governing the Development of Our National Science and Technology," p. 93.

116. "On China's Economic Relations with Foreign Countries," *Beijing Review*, 22 (May 31, 1982), 15.

117. "Outline Report on Policy Governing the Development of Our National Science and Technology," p. 93.

118. "Creating a New Situation in All Fields of Socialist Modernization," *Beijing Review*, 51 (December 20, 1985), p. 20.

119. "Communique of the Third Plenary Session of the Eleventh Central Committee of the Communist Party of China," *Peking Review*, 52 (December 29, 1978), 11.

120. See Appendix A, p. 320.

121. *China's Open Door Policy: The Quest for Foreign Technology and Capital* (Vancouver, Canada: University of British Columbia Press, 1984), p. 23.
122. For joint venture projects and laws, see Peter Nehemkis and Alexis Nehemkis, "China's Law on Joint Ventures," *California Management Review*, vol. xxii, no. 4 (Summer 1980), 37–46; *Law of the PRC on Joint Ventures Using Chinese & Foreign Investment*, Wen Wei Po (Hong Kong), July 1979; James Roselle, "Local Lenders May Aid China Venture," *Asian Wall Street Journal Weekly* (September 7, 1981), p. 12; Frank Ching, "China Is Adopting Cautious Approach to Joint Ventures," *Asian Wall Street Journal Weekly* (July 27, 1981), p. 4; Phijit Chong, "More Clues to a Taxing Puzzle," *Far Eastern Economic Review* (March 21, 1980), 99; *Joint Venture Agreements in the People's Republic of China*, U.S. Department of Commerce, 1982; and David C. Brown, "Sino-Foreign Joint Ventures: Contemporary Developments and Historical Perspective," *Journal of Northeast Asian Studies*, vol. 1, no. 4 (December 1982), 25–55. Also for a recent study on doing business in China, see Graeme Browning, *If Everybody Bought One Shoe: American Capitalism in Communist China* (New York: Hill and Wang, 1989).
123. Nehemkis and Nehemkis, "China's Law on Joint Ventures," pp. 37–46. Also see Lev P. Deliusin, "Reforms in China: Problems and Prospects," *Asian Survey*, vol. xxvii, no. 11 (November 1988), 1101–16. For a thorough treatment of the origin, direction, content and the future of reform, see Harry Harding's *China's Second Revolution: Reform after Mao* (Washington, D.C.: The Brookings Institution, 1987).
124. "The Law of PRC on Joint Ventures Using Chinese and Foreign Investment," *Beijing Review*, 29 (July 20, 1979), 24–26.
125. Ibid., 24.
126. *Asian Wall Street Journal* (July 19, 1986), p. 4.
127. *China Trade Report* (October 1981), p. 8.
128. *Newsweek* (May 16, 1983), pp. 75–76. For a discussion on the history and the partnership of AMC in China, see Jim Mann, *Beijing Jeep: The Short, Unhappy Romance of American Business in China* (New York: Simon and Schuster, 1989).
129. *China Daily* (September 17, 1986), p. 4.
130. *China Business Review* (July–August, 1986), 34.
131. *China Trade Report* (March 1986), p. 1.
132. *Ta Kung Pao Weekly Supplement* (Hong Kong), January 30, 1986, p. 4.
133. See *China Trade Report* (March 1986), p. 1; and *Asian Wall Street Journal* (January 15, 1986), p. 3.
134. See Robert D. Dennis, "The Countertrade Factor in China's Modernization Plan," *The Columbia Journal of World Business*, vol. xvii, no. 1 (Spring 1982), 67–75. Also see Stephen Markschild, "Compensation Trade: The Chinese Perspective," *China Business Review* (January–February 1982), 50–52.
135. *Ta Kung Pao Weekly Supplement* (March 11, 1982), p. 6.
136. See John Stuermen, "The Foreign Exchange Situation," *China Business Review* (January–February, 1986), 14–17.
137. See, "New SEZ Regulations Made Public," *Ta Kung Pao Weekly Supplement* (December 24, 1981), pp. 1, 3; *China Trade Report* (April 1982), p. 10, and (April 1983), p. 6. Also see a special article in *Beijing Review*, 50 (December 14, 1981), 14–21; John J. Putnam, "Special Economic Zones: China's Opening Door," *National Geographic*, vol. 164, no. 1 (July 1982), 64–83.
138. Xu Dixin, "China's Special Economic Zones," *Beijing Review*, 50 (December 14, 1981), 14–17.
139. See *China Trade Report* (April 1982), p. 10, and (April 1983), p. 6; and *Ta Kung Pao Weekly Supplement* (August 20, 1981), p. i, and (December 24, 1981), p. 1.
140. See *The Christian Science Monitor* (April 2, 1993), p. 1.
141. See *China Daily* (August 23, 1986), p. 1.
142. *Asian Wall Street Journal* (July 19, 1986), p. 1.
143. See *Asian Business* (May 1986), pp. 60–61.
144. *Asian Wall Street Journal* (July 19, 1986), p. 1.
145. Ibid.
146. See *Beijing Review*, January 11–17, 1993, p. 5.
147. Ibid. Also see Stanley B. Lubman, "Equity Joint Ventures in China: New Legal Framework, Continuing Questions," in *China's Economy Looks Toward the Year 2000*, Joint Economic Committee, U.S. Congress, vol. 2 (May 21, 1986), pp. 432–43.
148. See *Beijing Review*, 9 (March 2, 1987), p. 4 and p. 14.

149. See *Ming Pao Daily* (Hong Kong), February 10, 1987, p. 1.
150. For more discussion about the Chinese intellectuals, see Jerome B. Grieder, *State in Modern China: A Narrative History* (New York: Free Press, 1981); Merl *Intellectuals: Advise and Dissent* (Cambridge, Mass.: Harvard University Press, I Kraus, "Intellectuals and the State in China," *Problems of Communism*, vol. xxxi, I ber–December 1982), 81–84; Takashi Oka, "China Tries to Use Once-Scorned Intellectu ernizing," *The Christian Science Monitor* (February 4, 1983), pp. 1, 6; Fox Butterfield, "Cl secution of Intellectuals," New York Times Service, reprinted in *Honolulu Star-Bulletin* (De 10, 1981), A-2, and *China: Alive in the Bitter Sea*, pp. 416–19; *Hongqi*, 24 (December 16, 1 4–12; and Gerald Chen, "The Middle-aged Intellectuals," *Ta Kung Pao Weekly Supplement* (Se tember 23, 1982), p. 14.
151. Teng Hsiao-p'ing, "Speech at Opening Ceremony of National Science Conference," *Peking Review*, 11.
152. Ibid., 12.
153. Ibid., 15.
154. *Hongqi*, 24 (December 16, 1982), 10.
155. Ibid.
156. Notes taken on author's visits in 1978 and 1979. Also see *Ming Pao Daily* (Hong Kong) (March 6, 1983), p. 1; and *Beijing Review*, 49 (December 6, 1982), 3–4.
157. *Ta Kung Pao Weekly Supplement* (Hong Kong) (January 16, 1986), p. 7.
158. *The New York Times* (January 1, 1985), p. 4.
159. *Beijing Review*, 50 (December 15, 1986), 17.
160. *Beijing Review*, 4 (January 26, 1987), 9. For recent cases of expulsion from the party membership, see *Ming Pao Daily* (Hong Kong) (August 25, 1987), p. 1.
161. *Beijing Review* (July 17–23, 1989), i–iv.
162. See "Chinese Democracy in 1989: Continuity and Change," *Problems of Communism*, May 30, 1972, p. 24.
163. See "Chinese Democracy in 1989," p. 24; and Liu Binyan, *A Higher Kind of Loyalty*, (New York: Pantheon Books, 1990), pp. 265–268.
164. *China News Analysis*, 1387 (June 15, 1989), 6.
165. Washington Post Service as reprinted in *The Honolulu Advertiser* (July 23, 1990), A-5.
166. *Beijing Review* (May 14–20, 1990), 9.
167. See *Hawaii Tribune Herald* (Hilo) (October 18, 1992), p. 7.
168. See *Beijing Review*, November 22–28, 1993, pp. 27–28.

Intellectuals and the
Goldman, China's
981); Richard C.
o. 6 (Novem-
ls for Mod-
ina's Per-
ember
982),

endix A

on of the People's Republic of China (1982)

TABLE OF CONTENTS*

PREAMBLE

China is one of the countries with the longest histories in the world. The people of all nationalities in China have jointly created a splendid culture and have a glorious revolutionary tradition.

Feudal China was gradually reduced after 1840 to a semi-colonial and semi-feudal country. The Chinese people waged wave upon wave of heroic struggles for national independence and liberation and for democracy and freedom.

Great and earth-shaking historical changes have taken place in China in the 20th century.

The Revolution of 1911, led by Dr. Sun Yat-sen, abolished the feudal monarchy and gave birth to the Republic of China. But the Chinese people had yet to fulfill their historical task of overthrowing imperialism and feudalism.

After waging hard, protracted and tortuous struggles, armed and otherwise, the Chinese people of all nationalities led by the Communist Party of China with Chairman Mao Zedong as its leader ultimately, in 1949, overthrew the rule of imperialism, feudalism and bureaucrat-capitalism, won the great victory of the new-democratic revolution and founded the People's Republic of China. Thereupon the Chinese people took state power into their own hands and became masters of the country.

After the founding of the People's Republic, the transition of Chinese society from a new-democratic to a socialist society was effected step by step. The socialist transformation of the private ownership of the means of production was completed, the system of exploitation of man by man eliminated and the socialist system established. The people's democratic dicta-

---

Beijing Review, 52 (December 27, 1982), 10–52. (Adopted on December 4, 1982, by the Fifth National People's Congress of the People's Republic of China at its fifth session.)

torship led by the working class and based on the alliance of workers and peasants, which is in essence the dictatorship of the proletariat, has been consolidated and developed. The Chinese people and the Chinese People's Liberation Army have thwarted aggression, sabotage and armed provocations by imperialists and hegemonists, safeguarded China's national independence and security and strengthened its national defence. Major successes have been achieved in economic development. An independent and fairly comprehensive socialist system of industry has in the main been established. There has been a marked increase in agricultural production. Significant progress has been made in educational, scientific, cultural and other undertakings, and socialist ideological education has yielded noteworthy results. The living standards of the people have improved considerably.

Both the victory of China's new-democratic revolution and the successes of its socialist cause have been achieved by the Chinese people of all nationalities under the leadership of the Communist Party of China and the guidance of Marxism-Leninism and Mao Zedong Thought, and by upholding truth, correcting errors and overcoming numerous difficulties and hardships. The basic task of the nation in the years to come is to concentrate its effort on socialist modernization. Under the leadership of the Communist Party of China and the guidance of Marxism-Leninism and Mao Zedong Thought, the Chinese people of all nationalities will continue to adhere to the people's democratic dictatorship and follow the socialist road, steadily improve socialist institutions, develop socialist democracy, improve the socialist legal system and work hard and self-reliantly to modernize industry, agriculture, national defence and science and technology step by step to turn China into a socialist country with a high level of culture and democracy.

The exploiting classes as such have been eliminated in our country. However, class struggle will continue to exist within certain limits for a long time to come. The Chinese people must fight against those forces and elements, both at home and abroad, that are hostile to China's socialist system and try to undermine it.

Taiwan is part of the sacred territory of the People's Republic of China. It is the lofty duty of the entire Chinese people, including our compatriots in Taiwan, to accomplish the great task of reunifying the motherland.

In building socialism it is imperative to rely on the workers, peasants and intellectuals and unite with all the forces that can be united. In the long years of revolution and construction, there has been formed under the leadership of the Communist Party of China a broad patriotic united front that is composed of democratic parties and people's organizations and embraces all socialist working people, all patriots who support socialism and all patriots who stand for reunification of the motherland. This united front will continue to be consolidated and developed. The Chinese People's Political Consultative Conference is a broadly representative organization of the united front, which has played a significant historical role and will continue to do so in the political and social life of the country, in promoting friendship with the people of other countries and in the struggle for socialist modernization and for the reunification and unity of the country.

The People's Republic of China is a unitary multinational state built up jointly by the people of all its nationalities. Socialist relations of equality, unity and mutual assistance have been established among them and will continue to be strengthened. In the struggle to safeguard the unity of the nationalities, it is necessary to combat big-nation chauvinism, mainly Han chauvinism, and also necessary to combat local-national chauvinism. The state does its utmost to promote the common prosperity of all nationalities in the country.

China's achievements in revolution and construction are inseparable from support by the people of the world. The future of China is closely linked with that of the whole world. China adheres to an independent foreign policy as well as to the five principles of mutual respect for sovereignty and territorial integrity, mutual non-aggression, non-interference in each other's internal affairs, equality and mutual benefit, and peaceful coexistence in developing diplomatic relations and economic and cultural exchanges with other countries; China consistently opposes imperialism, hegemonism and colonialism, works to strengthen unity with the people of other countries, supports the oppressed nations and the developing countries in their just struggle to win and preserve national independence and develop their national economies, and strives to safeguard world peace and promote the cause of human progress.

This Constitution affirms the achievements of the struggles of the Chinese people of all nationalities and defines the basic system and basic tasks of the state in legal form; it is the fundamental law of the state and has supreme legal authority. The people of all nationalities, all state organs, the armed forces, all political parties and public organizations and all enterprises and undertakings in the country must take the Constitution as the basic norm of conduct, and they have the duty to uphold the dignity of the Constitution and ensure its implementation.

CHAPTER ONE
GENERAL PRINCIPLES

Article 1   The People's Republic of China is a socialist state under the people's democratic dictatorship led by the working class and based on the alliance of workers and peasants.

The socialist system is the basic system of the People's Republic of China. Sabotage of the socialist system by any organization or individual is prohibited.

Article 2   All power in the People's Republic of China belongs to the people.

The organs through which the people exercise state power are the National People's Congress and the local people's congresses at different levels.

The people administer state affairs and manage economic, cultural and social affairs through various channels and in various ways in accordance with the law.

Article 3   The state organs of the People's Republic of China apply the principle of democratic centralism.

The National People's Congress and the local people's congresses at different levels are instituted through democratic election. They are responsible to the people and subject to their supervision.

All administrative, judicial and procuratorial organs of the state are created by the people's congresses to which they are responsible and under whose supervision they operate.

The division of functions and powers between the central and local state organs is guided by the principle of giving full play to the initiative and enthusiasm of the local authorities under the unified leadership of the central authorities.

Article 4   All nationalities in the People's Republic of China are equal. The state protects the lawful rights and interests of the minority nationalities and upholds and develops the relationship of equality, unity and mutual assistance among all of China's nationalities. Discrimination against and oppression of any nationality are prohibited; any acts that undermine the unity of the nationalities or instigate their secession are prohibited.

The state helps the areas inhabited by minority nationalities speed up their economic and cultural development in accordance with the peculiarities and needs of the different minority nationalities.

Regional autonomy is practised in areas where people of minority nationalities live in compact communities; in these areas organs of self-government are established for the exercise of the right of autonomy. All the national autonomous areas are inalienable parts of the People's Republic of China.

The people of all nationalities have the freedom to use and develop their own spoken and written languages, and to preserve or reform their own ways and customs.

Article 5   The state upholds the uniformity and dignity of the socialist legal system. No law or administrative or local rules and regulations shall contravene the Constitution.

All state organs, the armed forces, all political parties and public organizations and all enterprises and undertakings must abide by the Constitution and the law. All acts in violation of the Constitution and the law must be looked into.

No organization or individual may enjoy the privilege of being above the Constitution and the law.

Article 6   The basis of the socialist economic system of the People's Republic of China is socialist public ownership of the means of production, namely, ownership by the whole people and collective ownership by the working people.

The system of socialist public ownership supersedes the system of exploitation of man by man; it applies the principle of "from each according to his ability, to each according to his work."

Article 7   The state economy is the sector of socialist economy under ownership by the whole people; it is the leading force in the national economy. The state ensures the consolidation and growth of the state economy.

Article 8   Rural people's communes, agricultural producers' co-operatives, and other forms of co-operative economy such as producers', supply and marketing, credit and consumers' co-operatives, belong to the sector of socialist economy under collective ownership by the working people. Working people who are members of rural economic collectives have the right, within the limits prescribed by law, to farm private plots of cropland and hilly land, engage in household sideline production and raise privately owned livestock.

The various forms of co-operative economy in the cities and towns, such as those in the handicraft, industrial, building, transport, commercial and service trades, all belong to the sector of socialist economy under collective ownership by the working people.

The state protects the lawful rights and interests of the urban and rural economic collectives and encourages, guides and helps the growth of the collective economy.

Article 9   Mineral resources, waters, forests, mountains, grassland, unreclaimed land, beaches and other natural resources are owned by the state, that is, by the whole people, with the exception of the forests, mountains, grassland, unreclaimed land and beaches that are owned by collectives in accordance with the law.

The state ensures the rational use of natural resources and protects rare animals and plants. The appropriation or damage of natural resources by any organization or individual by whatever means is prohibited.

Article 10   Land in the cities is owned by the state.

Land in the rural and suburban areas is owned by collectives except for those portions which belong to the state in accordance with the law; house sites and private plots of cropland and hilly land are also owned by collectives.

The state may in the public interest take over land for its use in accordance with the law.

No organization or individual may appropriate, buy, sell or lease land, or unlawfully transfer land in other ways.

All organizations and individuals who use land must make rational use of the land.

Article 11   The individual economy of urban and rural working people, operated within the limits prescribed by law, is a complement to the socialist public economy. The state protects the lawful rights and interests of the individual economy.

The state guides, helps and supervises the individual economy by exercising administrative control.

Article 12   Socialist public property is sacred and inviolable.

The state protects socialist public property
tive property by any organization or individual b

Article 13 The state protects the right
savings, houses and other lawful property.
The state protects by law the right of citiz

Article 14 The state continuously rais
results and develops the productive forces by enh
raising the level of their technical skill, disser
improving the systems of economic administratic
instituting the socialist system of responsibility
of work.

The state practises strict economy and con
interests of the collective and the individual as w
ed production, gradually improves the material a

Article 15 The state practises econom
ownership. It ensures the proportionate and co
through overall balancing by economic planning
the market.

Disturbance of the orderly functioning of
economic plan by any organization or individual

Article 16 State enterprises have decisi
ment within the limits prescribed by law, on cor
by the state and fulfil all their obligations under
State enterprises practise democratic man,nt;
staff and in other ways in accordance with the la

Article 17 Collective economic organiz
ducting independent economic activities, on cor
state plan and abide by the relevant laws.
Collective economic organizations practise
the law, with the entire body of their workers ele
and deciding on major issues concerning operatic

Article 18 The People's Republic of Ch
economic organizations and individual foreigners
forms of economic co-operation with Chinese ent
accordance with the law of the People's Republic

All foreign enterprises and other foreign (
joint ventures with Chinese and foreign investmei
the People's Republic of China. Their lawful rig
the People's Republic of China.

Article 19 The state develops socialist
the scientific and cultural level of the whole natic
The state runs schools of various types, m
versal, develops secondary, vocational and high
tion.

The state develops educational facilities of

on the support of the people, keep in close
ons, accept their supervision and work hard

order and suppresses treasonable and other
ions that endanger public security and disrupt
ities, and punishes and reforms criminals.

People's Republic of China belong to the people.
ce, resist aggression, defend the motherland, safe-
ipate in national reconstruction, and work hard to

ionization, modernization and regularization of the
tional defence capability.

division of the People's Republic of China is as follows:
nto provinces, autonomous regions and municipalities
nt;
us regions are divided into autonomous prefectures, coun-
s;
ous counties are divided into townships, nationality town-

der the Central Government and other large cities are divided
tonomous prefectures are divided into counties, autonomous

s, autonomous prefectures and autonomous counties are nation

ate may establish special administrative regions when necess
d in special administrative regions shall be prescribed by law e
s Congress in the light of the specific conditions.

People's Republic of China protects the lawful rights and inte
ese territory, and while on Chinese territory foreigners must
s Republic of China.

Republic of China may grant asylum to foreigners who req

/O
MENTAL RIGHTS AND DUTIES
S

33 All persons holding the nationality of the People's Rep
citize... ne People's Republic of China.
All citizens of the People's Republic of China are equal before the
Every citizen enjoys the rights and at the same time must perform
by the Constitution and the law.

Article 34 All citizens of the People's Republic of China w
of 18 have the right to vote and stand for election, regardless of na

. Appropriation or damage of state or collec-
y whatever means is prohibited.

‎ ‎ens to own lawfully earned income,

‎ ‎perty.

‎ ‎mic

pation, family background, religious belief, education, property status, or length of residence, except persons deprived of political rights according to law.

Article 35 Citizens of the People's Republic of China enjoy freedom of speech, of the press, of assembly, of association, of procession and of demonstration.

Article 36 Citizens of the People's Republic of China enjoy freedom of religious belief.

No state organ, public organization or individual may compel citizens to believe in, or not to believe in, any religion; nor may they discriminate against citizens who believe in, or do not believe in, any religion.

The state protects normal religious activities. No one may make use of religion to engage in activities that disrupt public order, impair the health of citizens or interfere with the educational system of the state.

Religious bodies and religious affairs are not subject to any foreign domination.

Article 37 The freedom of person of citizens of the People's Republic of China is inviolable.

No citizen may be arrested except with the approval or by decision of a people's procuratorate or by decision of a people's court, and arrests must be made by a public security organ.

Unlawful deprivation or restriction of citizens' freedom of person by detention or other is prohibited; and unlawful search of the person of citizens is prohibited.

Article 38 The personal dignity of citizens of the People's Republic of China is inviolable. Insult, libel, false charge or frame-up directed against citizens by any means is prohibited.

The home of citizens of the People's Republic of China is inviolable. Unlawful search of, or intrusion into, a citizen's home is prohibited.

‎ ‎freedom and privacy of correspondence of citizens of the People's ‎ ‎tected by law. No organization or individual may, on any ground, ‎ ‎d privacy of citizens' correspondence except in cases where, ‎ ‎w or of investigation into criminal offences, public security or ‎ ‎d to censor correspondence in accordance with procedures

‎ ‎ple's Republic of China have the right to criticize and ‎ ‎nctionary. Citizens have the right to make to relevant ‎ ‎s or exposures of, violation of the law or derelic- ‎ ‎v; but fabrication or distortion of facts with the ‎ ‎ma‎ ‎by citizens, the state organ concerned ‎ ‎certaining the facts. No one may suppress ‎ ‎ainst the citizens making them. ‎ ‎ment of their civic rights by any state ‎ ‎ordance with the law.

‎ ‎nina have the right as well as the ‎ ‎ions for employment, strengthens labour

l

ary.

nact-

rests of
bide by

uest it for

ublic of China are

law.
the duties prescribed

o have reached the age
ionality, race, sex, occu-

n-
the

with
sonnel

r foreign
o various
izations in

, as well as
by the law of
by the law of

d works to raise

mpulsory and uni-
s preschool educa-

to wipe out illiteracy

protection, improves working conditions and, on the basis of expanded production, increases remuneration for work and social benefits.

Work is the glorious duty of every able-bodied citizen. All working people in state enterprises and in urban and rural economic collectives should perform their tasks with an attitude consonant with their status as masters of the country. The state promotes socialist labour emulation, and commends and rewards model and advanced workers. The state encourages citizens to take part in voluntary labour.

The state provides necessary vocational training to citizens before they are employed.

Article 43   Working people in the People's Republic of China have the right to rest.

The state expands facilities for rest and recuperation of working people, and prescribes working hours and vacations for workers and staff.

Article 44   The state prescribes by law the system of retirement for workers and staff in enterprises and undertakings and for functionaries of organs of state. The livelihood of retired personnel is ensured by the state and society.

Article 45   Citizens of the People's Republic of China have the right to material assistance from the state and society when they are old, ill or disabled. The state develops the social insurance, social relief and medical and health services that are required to enable citizens to enjoy this right.

The state and society ensure the livelihood of disabled members of the armed forces, provide pensions to the families of martyrs and give preferential treatment to the families of military personnel.

The state and society help make arrangements for the work, livelihood and education of the blind, deaf-mute and other handicapped citizens.

Article 46   Citizens of the People's Republic of China have the duty as well as the right to receive education.

The state promotes the all-round moral, intellectual and physical development of children and young people.

Article 47   Citizens of the People's Republic of China have the freedom to engage in scientific research, literary and artistic creation and other cultural pursuits. The state encourages and assists creative endeavours conducive to the interests of the people that are made by citizens engaged in education, science, technology, literature, art and other cultural work.

Article 48   Women in the People's Republic of China enjoy equal rights with men in all spheres of life, political, economic, cultural and social, including family life.

The state protects the rights and interests of women, applies the principle of equal pay for equal work for men and women alike and trains and selects cadres from among women.

Article 49   Marriage, the family and mother and child are protected by the state.

Both husband and wife have the duty to practise family planning.

Parents have the duty to rear and educate their minor children, and children who have come of age have the duty to support and assist their parents.

Violation of the freedom of marriage is prohibited. Maltreatment of old people, women and children is prohibited.

Article 50   The People's Republic of China protects the legitimate rights and interests of Chinese nationals residing abroad and protects the lawful rights and interests of returned overseas Chinese and of the family members of Chinese nationals residing abroad.

Article 51   The exercise by citizens of the People's Republic of China of their freedoms and rights may not infringe upon the interests of the state, of society and of the collective, or upon the lawful freedoms and rights of other citizens.

Article 52   It is the duty of citizens of the People's Republic of China to safeguard the unity of the country and the unity of all its nationalities.

Article 53   Citizens of the People's Republic of China must abide by the Constitution and the law, keep state secrets, protect public property and observe labour discipline and public order and respect social ethics.

Article 54   It is the duty of citizens of the People's Republic of China to safeguard the security, honour and interests of the motherland; they must not commit acts detrimental to the security, honour and interests of the motherland.

Article 55   It is the sacred obligation of every citizen of the People's Republic of China to defend the motherland and resist aggression.
It is the honourable duty of citizens of the People's Republic of China to perform military service and join the militia in accordance with the law.

Article 56   It is the duty of citizens of the People's Republic of China to pay taxes in accordance with the law.

CHAPTER THREE
THE STRUCTURE OF THE STATE

Section I
The National People's Congress

Article 57   The National People's Congress of the People's Republic of China is the highest organ of state power. Its permanent body is the Standing Committee of the National People's Congress.

Article 58   The National People's Congress and its Standing Committee exercise the legislative power of the state.

Article 59   The National People's Congress is composed of deputies elected by the provinces, autonomous regions and municipalities directly under the Central Government, and by the armed forces. All the minority nationalities are entitled to appropriate representation.
Election of deputies to the National People's Congress is conducted by the Standing Committee of the National People's Congress.
The number of deputies to the National People's Congress and the manner of their election are prescribed by law.

Article 60   The National People's Congress is elected for a term of five years.
Two months before the expiration of the term of office of a National People's Congress, its Standing Committee must ensure that the election of deputies to the succeeding National People's Congress is completed. Should exceptional circumstances prevent such an election, it may be postponed by decision of a majority vote of more than two-thirds of all those on the Standing Committee of the incumbent National People's Congress, and the term of office of the incumbent National People's Congress may be extended. The election of deputies to the

succeeding National People's Congress must be completed within one year after the termination of such exceptional circumstances.

Article 61   The National People's Congress meets in session once a year and is convened by its Standing Committee. A session of the National People's Congress may be convened at any time the Standing Committee deems this necessary, or when more than one-fifth of the deputies to the National People's Congress so propose.

When the National People's Congress meets, it elects a presidium to conduct its session.

Article 62   The National People's Congress exercises the following functions and powers:

(1)   to amend the Constitution;

(2)   to supervise the enforcement of the Constitution;

(3)   to enact and amend basic statutes concerning criminal offences, civil affairs, the state organs and other matters;

(4)   to elect the President and the Vice-President of the People's Republic of China;*

(5)   to decide on the choice of the Premier of the State Council upon nomination by the President of the People's Republic of China, and to decide on the choice of the Vice-Premiers, State Councillors, Ministers in charge of ministries or commissions and the Auditor-General and the Secretary-General of the State Council upon nomination by the Premier;

(6)   to elect the Chairman of the Central Military Commission and, upon his nomination, to decide on the choice of all the others on the Central Military Commission;

(7)   to elect the President of the Supreme People's Court;

(8)   to elect the Procurator-General of the Supreme People's Procuratorate;

(9)   to examine and approve the plan for national economic and social development and the reports on its implementation;

(10)   to examine and approve the state budget and the report on its implementation;

(11)   to alter or annul inappropriate decisions of the Standing Committee of the National People's Congress;

(12)   to approve the establishment of provinces, autonomous regions, and municipalities directly under the Central Government;

(13)   to decide on the establishment of special administrative regions and the systems to be instituted there;

(14)   to decide on questions of war and peace; and

(15)   to exercise such other functions and powers as the highest organ of state power should exercise.

Article 63   The National People's Congress has the power to recall or remove from office the following persons:

(1)   the President and the Vice-President of the People's Republic of China;

(2)   the Premier, Vice-Premiers, State Councillors, Ministers in charge of ministries or commissions and the Auditor-General and the Secretary-General of the State Council;

(3)   the Chairman of the Central Military Commission; and others on the Commission;

(4)   the President of the Supreme People's Court; and

(5)   the Procurator-General of the Supreme People's Procuratorate.

Article 64   Amendments to the Constitution are to be proposed by the Standing Committee of the National People's Congress or by more than one-fifth of the deputies to the National People's Congress and adopted by a majority vote of more than two-thirds of all the deputies to the Congress.

---

*Previously translated as Chairman and Vice-Chairman of the People's Republic of China.—*Tr.*

Statutes and resolutions are adopted by a majority vote of more than one half of all the deputies to the National People's Congress.

Article 65   The Standing Committee of the National People's Congress is composed of the following:

the Chairman;
the Vice-Chairmen;
the Secretary-General; and
members.

Minority nationalities are entitled to appropriate representation on the Standing Committee of the National People's Congress.

The National People's Congress elects, and has the power to recall, all those on its Standing Committee.

No one on the Standing Committee of the National People's Congress shall hold any post in any of the administrative, judicial or procuratorial organs of the state.

Article 66   The Standing Committee of the National People's Congress is elected for the same term as the National People's Congress; it exercises its functions and powers until a new Standing Committee is elected by the succeeding National People's Congress.

The Chairman and Vice-Chairmen of the Standing Committee shall serve no more than two consecutive terms.

Article 67   The Standing Committee of the National People's Congress exercises the following functions and powers:

(1)   to interpret the Constitution and supervise its enforcement;

(2)   to enact and amend statutes with the exception of those which should be enacted by the National People's Congress;

(3)   to enact, when the National People's Congress is not in session, partial supplements and amendments to statutes enacted by the National People's Congress provided that they do not contravene the basic principles of these statutes;

(4)   to interpret statutes;

(5)   to examine and approve, when the National People's Congress is not in session, partial adjustments to the plan for national economic and social development and to the state budget that prove necessary in the course of their implementation;

(6)   to supervise the work of the State Council, the Central Military Commission, the Supreme People's Court and the Supreme People's Procuratorate;

(7)   to annul those administrative rules and regulations, decisions or orders of the State Council that contravene the Constitution or the statutes;

(8)   to annul those local regulations or decisions of the organs of state power of provinces, autonomous regions and municipalities directly under the Central Government that contravene the Constitution, the statutes or the administrative rules and regulations;

(9)   to decide, when the National People's Congress is not in session, on the choice of Ministers in charge of ministries or commissions or the Auditor-General and the Secretary-General of the State Council upon nomination by the Premier of the State Council;

(10)   to decide, upon nomination by the Chairman of the Central Military Commission, on the choice of others on the Commission, when the National People's Congress is not in session.

(11)   to appoint and remove the Vice-Presidents and judges of the Supreme People's Court, members of its Judicial Committee and the President of the Military Court at the suggestion of the President of the Supreme People's Court;

(12)   to appoint and remove the Deputy Procurators-General and procurators of the Supreme People's Procuratorate, members of its Procuratorial Committee and the Chief Procu-

rator of the Military Procuratorate at the request of the Procurator-General of the Supreme People's Procuratorate, and to approve the appointment and removal of the chief procurators of the people's procuratorates of provinces, autonomous regions and municipalities directly under the Central Government;

(13)   to decide on the appointment and recall of plenipotentiary representatives abroad;

(14)   to decide on the ratification and abrogation of treaties and important agreements concluded with foreign states;

(15)   to institute systems of titles and ranks for military and diplomatic personnel and of other specific titles and ranks;

(16)   to institute state medals and titles of honour and decide on their conferment;

(17)   to decide on the granting of special pardons;

(18)   to decide, when the National People's Congress is not in session, on the proclamation of a state of war in the event of an armed attack on the country or in fulfillment of international treaty obligations concerning common defence against aggression;

(19)   to decide on general mobilization or partial mobilization;

(20)   to decide on the enforcement of martial law throughout the country or in particular provinces, autonomous regions or municipalities directly under the Central Government; and

(21)   to exercise such other functions and powers as the National People's Congress may assign to it.

Article 68   The Chairman of the Standing Committee of the National People's Congress presides over the work of the Standing Committee and convenes its meetings. The Vice-Chairmen and the Secretary-General assist the Chairman in his work.

Chairmanship meetings with the participation of the Chairman, Vice-Chairmen and Secretary-General handle the important day-to-day work of the Standing Committee of the National People's Congress.

Article 69   The Standing Committee of the National People's Congress is responsible to the National People's Congress and reports on its work to the Congress.

Article 70   The National People's Congress establishes a Nationalities Committee, a Law Committee, a Finance and Economic Committee, an Education, Science, Culture and Public Health Committee, a Foreign Affairs Committee, an Overseas Chinese Committee and such other special committees as are necessary. These special committees work under the direction of the Standing Committee of the National People's Congress when the Congress is not in session.

The special committees examine, discuss and draw up relevant bills and draft resolutions under the direction of the National People's Congress and its Standing Committee.

Article 71   The National People's Congress and its Standing Committee may, when they deem it necessary, appoint committees of inquiry into specific questions and adopt relevant resolutions in the light of their reports.

All organs of state, public organizations and citizens concerned are obliged to supply the necessary information to those committees of inquiry when they conduct investigations.

Article 72   Deputies to the National People's Congress and all those on its Standing Committee have the right, in accordance with procedures prescribed by law, to submit bills and proposals within the scope of the respective functions and powers of the National People's Congress and its Standing Committee.

Article 73   Deputies to the National People's Congress during its sessions, and all those on its Standing Committee during its meetings, have the right to address questions, in accordance with procedures prescribed by law, to the State Council or the ministries and commissions under the State Council, which must answer the questions in a responsible manner.

Article 74   No deputy to the National People's Congress may be arrested or placed on criminal trial without the consent of the Presidium of the current session of the National People's Congress or, when the National People's Congress is not in session, without the consent of its Standing Committee.

Article 75   Deputies to the National People's Congress may not be called to legal account for their speeches or votes at its meetings.

Article 76   Deputies to the National People's Congress must play an exemplary role in abiding by the Constitution and the law and keeping state secrets and, in production and other work and their public activities, assist in the enforcement of the Constitution and the law.

Deputies to the National People's Congress should maintain close contact with the units which elected them and with the people, listen to and convey the opinions and demands of the people and work hard to serve them.

Article 77   Deputies to the National People's Congress are subject to the supervision of the units which elected them. The electoral units have the power, through procedures prescribed by law, to recall the deputies whom they elected.

Article 78   The organization and working procedures of the National People's Congress and its Standing Committee are prescribed by law.

Section II
The President of the People's Republic of China

Article 79   The President and Vice-President of the People's Republic of China are elected by the National People's Congress.

Citizens of the People's Republic of China who have the right to vote and to stand for election and who have reached the age of 45 are eligible for election as President or Vice-President of the People's Republic of China. The term of office of the President and Vice-President of the People's Republic of China is the same as that of the National People's Congress, and they shall serve no more than two consecutive terms.

Article 80   The President of the People's Republic of China, in pursuance of decisions of the National People's Congress and its Standing Committee, promulgates statutes; appoints and removes the Premier, Vice-Premiers, State Councillors, Ministers in charge of ministries or commissions, and the Auditor-General and the Secretary-General of the State Council; confers state medals and titles of honour; issues orders of special pardons; proclaims martial law; proclaims a state of war; and issues mobilization orders.

Article 81   The President of the People's Republic of China receives foreign diplomatic representatives on behalf of the People's Republic of China and, in pursuance of decisions of the Standing Committee of the National People's Congress, appoints and recalls plenipotentiary representatives abroad, and ratifies and abrogates treaties and important agreements concluded with foreign states.

Article 82   The Vice-President of the People's Republic of China assists the President in his work.

The Vice-President of the People's Republic of China may exercise such parts of the functions and powers of the President as the President may entrust to him.

Article 83   The President and Vice-President of the People's Republic of China exercise their functions and powers until the new President and Vice-President elected by the succeeding National People's Congress assume office.

Article 84   In case the office of the President of the People's Republic of China falls vacant, the Vice-President succeeds to the office of President.

In case the office of the Vice-President of the People's Republic of China falls vacant, the National People's Congress shall elect a new Vice-President to fill the vacancy.

In the event that the offices of both the President and the Vice-President of the People's Republic of China fall vacant, the National People's Congress shall elect a new President and a new Vice-President. Prior to such election, the Chairman of the Standing Committee of the National People's Congress shall temporarily act as the President of the People's Republic of China.

Section III
The State Council

Article 85   The State Council, that is, the Central People's Government, of the People's Republic of China is the executive body of the highest organ of state power; it is the highest organ of state administration.

Article 86   The State Council is composed of the following:

the Premier;
the Vice-Premiers;
the State Councillors;
the Ministers in charge of ministries;
the Ministers in charge of commissions;
the Auditor-General; and
the Secretary-General.

The Premier has overall responsibility for the State Council. The ministers have overall responsibility for the respective ministries or commissions under their charge.

The organization of the State Council is prescribed by law.

Article 87   The term of office of the State Council is the same as that of the National People's Congress.

The Premier, Vice-Premiers and State Councillors shall serve no more than two consecutive terms.

Article 88   The Premier directs the work of the State Council. The Vice-Premiers and State Councillors assist the Premier in his work.

Executive meetings of the State Council are composed of the Premier, the Vice-Premiers, the State Councillors and the Secretary-General of the State Council.

The Premier convenes and presides over the executive meetings and plenary meetings of the State Council.

Article 89   The State Council exercises the following functions and powers:

(1)   to adopt administrative measures, enact administrative rules and regulations and issue decisions and orders in accordance with the Constitution and the statutes;

(2)   to submit proposals to the National People's Congress or its Standing Committee;

(3)   to lay down the tasks and responsibilities of the ministries and commissions of the State Council, to exercise unified leadership over the work of the ministries and commissions

and to direct all other administrative work of a national character that does not fall within the jurisdiction of the ministries and commissions;

(4)   to exercise unified leadership over the work of local organs of state administration at different levels throughout the country, and to lay down the detailed division of functions and powers between the Central Government and the organs of state administration of provinces, autonomous regions and municipalities directly under the Central Government;

(5)   to draw up and implement the plan for national economic and social development and the state budget;

(6)   to direct and administer economic work and urban and rural development;

(7)   to direct and administer the work concerning education, science, culture, public health, physical culture and family planning;

(8)   to direct and administer the work concerning civil affairs, public security, judicial administration, supervision and other related matters;

(9)   to conduct foreign affairs and conclude treaties and agreements with foreign states;

(10)   to direct and administer the building of national defence;

(11)   to direct and administer affairs concerning the nationalities, and to safeguard the equal rights of minority nationalities and the right of autonomy of the national autonomous areas;

(12)   to protect the legitimate rights and interests of Chinese nationals residing abroad and protect the lawful rights and interests of returned overseas Chinese and of the family members of Chinese nationals residing abroad;

(13)   to alter or annul inappropriate orders, directives and regulations issued by the ministries or commissions;

(14)   to alter or annul inappropriate decisions and orders issued by local organs of state administration at different levels;

(15)   to approve the geographic division of provinces, autonomous regions and municipalities directly under the Central Government, and to approve the establishment and geographic division of autonomous prefectures, counties, autonomous counties and cities;

(16)   to decide on the enforcement of martial law in parts of provinces, autonomous regions and municipalities directly under the Central Government;

(17)   to examine and decide on the size of administrative organs and, in accordance with the law, to appoint, remove and train administrative officers, appraise their work and reward or punish them; and

(18)   to exercise such other functions and powers as the National People's Congress or its Standing Committee may assign it.

Article 90   The Ministers in charge of ministries or commissions of the State Council are responsible for the work of their respective departments and convene and preside over their ministerial meetings or commission meetings that discuss and decide on major issues in the work of their respective departments.

The ministries and commissions issue orders, directives and regulations within the jurisdiction of their respective departments and in accordance with the statutes and the administrative rules and regulations, decisions and orders issued by the State Council.

Article 91   The State Council establishes an auditing body to supervise through auditing the revenue and expenditure of all departments under the State Council and of the local governments at different levels, and those of the state financial and monetary organizations and of enterprises and undertakings.

Under the direction of the Premier of the State Council, the auditing body independently exercises its power to supervise through auditing in accordance with the law, subject to no interference by any other administrative organ or any public organization or individual.

Article 92   The State Council is responsible, and reports on its work, to the National

People's Congress or, when the National People's Congress is not in session, to its Standing Committee.

Section IV
The Central Military Commission

Article 93 The Central Military Commission of the People's Republic of China directs the armed forces of the country.

The Central Military Commission, is composed of the following:

the Chairman;
the Vice-Chairmen; and
members.

The Chairman of the Central Military Commission has overall responsibility for the Commission.

The term of office of the Central Military Commission is the same as that of the National People's Congress.

Article 94 The Chairman of the Central Military Commission is responsible to the National People's Congress and its Standing Committee.

Section V
The Local People's Congresses and the Local People's Governments at Different Levels

Article 95 People's congresses and people's governments are established in provinces, municipalities directly under the Central Government, counties, cities, municipal districts, townships, nationality townships and towns.

The organization of local people's congresses and local people's governments at different levels is prescribed by law.

Organs of self-government are established in autonomous regions, autonomous prefectures and autonomous counties. The organization and working procedures of organs of self-government are prescribed by law in accordance with the basic principles laid down in Sections V and VI of Chapter Three of the Constitution.

Article 96 Local people's congresses at different levels are local organs of state power.

Local people's congresses at and above the county level establish standing committees.

Article 97 Deputies to the people's congresses of provinces, municipalities directly under the Central Government, and cities divided into districts are elected by the people's congresses at the next lower level; deputies to the people's congresses of counties, cities not divided into districts, municipal districts, townships, nationality townships and towns are elected directly by their constituencies.

The number of deputies to local people's congresses at different levels and the manner of their election are prescribed by law.

Article 98 The term of office of the people's congresses of provinces, municipalities directly under the Central Government and cities divided into districts is five years. The term of office of the people's congresses of counties, cities not divided into districts, municipal districts, townships, nationality townships and towns is three years.

Article 99 Local people's congresses at different levels ensure the observance and implementation of the Constitution, the statutes and the administrative rules and regulations in their respective administrative areas. Within the limits of their authority as prescribed by law, they adopt and issue resolutions and examine and decide on plans for local economic and cultural development and for the development of public services.

Local people's congresses at and above the county level examine and approve the plans for economic and social development and the budgets of their respective administrative areas, and examine and approve reports on their implementation. They have the power to alter or annul inappropriate decisions of their own standing committees.

The people's congresses of nationality townships may, within the limits of their authority as prescribed by law, take specific measures suited to the peculiarities of the nationalities concerned.

Article 100   The people's congresses of provinces and municipalities directly under the Central Government, and their standing committees, may adopt local regulations, which must not contravene the Constitution, the statutes and the administrative rules and regulations, and they shall report such local regulations to the Standing Committee of the National People's Congress for the record.

Article 101   At their respective levels, local people's congresses elect, and have the power to recall, governors and deputy governors, or mayors and deputy mayors, or heads and deputy heads of counties, districts, townships and towns.

Local people's congresses at and above the county level elect, and have the power to recall, presidents of people's courts and chief procurators of people's procuratorates at the corresponding level. The election or recall of chief procurators of people's procuratorates shall be reported to the chief procurators of the people's procuratorates at the next higher level for submission to the standing committees of the people's congresses at the corresponding level for approval.

Article 102   Deputies to the people's congresses of provinces, municipalities directly under the Central Government and cities divided into districts are subject to supervision by the units which elected them; deputies to the people's congresses of counties, cities not divided into districts, municipal districts, townships, nationality townships and towns are subject to supervision by their constituencies.

The electoral units and constituencies which elect deputies to local people's congresses at different levels have the power, according to procedures prescribed by law, to recall deputies whom they elected.

Article 103   The standing committee of a local people's congress at and above the county level is composed of a chairman, vice-chairmen and members, and is responsible, and reports on its work, to the people's congress at the corresponding level.

The local people's congress at and above the county level elects, and has the power to recall, anyone on the standing committee of the people's congress at the corresponding level.

No one on the standing committee of a local people's congress at and above the county level shall hold any post in state administrative, judicial and procuratorial organs.

Article 104   The standing committee of a local people's congress at and above the county level discusses and decides on major issues in all fields of work in its administrative area; supervises the work of the people's government, people's court and people's procuratorate at the corresponding level; annuls inappropriate decisions and orders of the people's government at the corresponding level; annuls inappropriate resolutions of the people's congress at the next lower level; decides on the appointment and removal of functionaries of state organs within its jurisdiction as prescribed by law; and, when the people's congress at the corresponding level is not in session, recalls individual deputies to the people's congress at the next higher level and elects individual deputies to fill vacancies in that people's congress.

Article 105   Local people's governments at different levels are the executive bodies of local organs of state power as well as the local organs of state administration at the corresponding level.

Local people's governments at different levels practise the system of overall responsibility by governors, mayors, county heads, district heads, township heads and town heads.

Article 106   The term of office of local people's governments at different levels is the same as that of the people's congresses at the corresponding level.

Article 107   Local people's governments at and above the county level, within the limits of their authority as prescribed by law, conduct the administrative work concerning the economy, education, science, culture, public health, physical culture, urban and rural development, finance, civil affairs, public security, nationalities affairs, judicial administration, supervision and family planning in their respective administrative areas; issue decisions and orders; appoint, remove and train administrative functionaries, appraise their work and reward or punish them.

People's governments of townships, nationality townships and towns carry out the resolutions of the people's congress at the corresponding level as well as the decisions and orders of the state administrative organs at the next higher level and conduct administrative work in their respective administrative areas.

People's governments of provinces and municipalities directly under the Central Government decide on the establishment and geographic division of townships, nationality townships and towns.

Article 108   Local people's governments at and above the county level direct the work of their subordinate departments and of people's governments at lower levels, and have the power to alter or annul inappropriate decisions of their subordinate departments and people's governments at lower levels.

Article 109   Auditing bodies are established by local people's governments at and above the county level. Local auditing bodies at different levels independently exercise their power to supervise through auditing in accordance with the law and are responsible to the people's government at the corresponding level and to the auditing body at the next higher level.

Article 110   Local people's governments at different levels are responsible, and report on their work, to people's congresses at the corresponding level. Local people's governments at and above the county level are responsible, and report on their work, to the standing committee of the people's congress at the corresponding level when the congress is not in session.

Local people's governments at different levels are responsible, and report on their work, to the state administrative organs at the next higher level. Local people's governments at different levels throughout the country are state administrative organs under the unified leadership of the State Council and are subordinate to it.

Article 111   The residents' committees and villagers' committees established among urban and rural residents on the basis of their place of residence are mass organizations of self-management at the grass-roots level. The chairman, vice-chairmen and members of each residents' or villagers' committee are elected by the residents. The relationship between the residents' and villagers' committees and the grass-roots organs of state power is prescribed by law.

The residents' and villagers' committees establish committees for people's mediation, public security, public health and other matters in order to manage public affairs and social services in their areas, mediate civil disputes, help maintain public order and convey residents' opinions and demands and make suggestions to the people's government:

Section VI
The Organs of Self-Government of National Autonomous Areas

Article 112   The organs of self-government of national autonomous areas are the people's congresses and people's governments of autonomous regions, autonomous prefectures and autonomous counties.

Article 113   In the people's congress of an autonomous region, prefecture or county, in addition to the deputies of the nationality or nationalities exercising regional autonomy in the administrative area, the other nationalities inhabiting the area are also entitled to appropriate representation.

The chairmanship and vice-chairmanships of the standing committee of the people's congress of an autonomous region, prefecture or county shall include a citizen or citizens of the nationality or nationalities exercising regional autonomy in the area concerned.

Article 114   The administrative head of an autonomous region, prefecture or county shall be a citizen of the nationality, or of one of the nationalities, exercising regional autonomy in the area concerned.

Article 115   The organs of self-government of autonomous regions, prefectures and counties exercise the functions and powers of local organs of state as specified in Section V of Chapter Three of the Constitution. At the same time, they exercise the right of autonomy within the limits of their authority as prescribed by the Constitution, the law of regional national autonomy and other laws, and implement the laws and policies of the state in the light of the existing local situation.

Article 116   People's congresses of national autonomous areas have the power to enact autonomy regulations and specific regulations in the light of the political, economic and cultural characteristics of the nationality or nationalities in the areas concerned. The autonomy regulations and specific regulations of autonomous regions shall be submitted to the Standing Committee of the National People's Congress for approval before they go into effect. Those of autonomous prefectures and counties shall be submitted to the standing committees of the people's congresses of provinces or autonomous regions for approval before they go into effect, and they shall be reported to the Standing Committee of the National People's Congress for the record.

Article 117   The organs of self-government of the national autonomous areas have the power of autonomy in administering the finances of their areas. All revenues accruing to the national autonomous areas under the financial system of the state shall be managed and used by the organs of self-government of those areas on their own.

Article 118   The organs of self-government of the national autonomous areas independently arrange for and administer local economic development under the guidance of state plans.

In exploiting natural resources and building enterprises in the national autonomous areas, the state shall give due consideration to the interests of those areas.

Article 119   The organs of self-government of the national autonomous areas independently administer educational, scientific, cultural, public health and physical culture affairs in their respective areas, protect and cull through the cultural heritage of the nationalities and work for the development and prosperity of their cultures.

Article 120   The organs of self-government of the national autonomous areas may, in accordance with the military system of the state and concrete local needs and with the approval of the State Council, organize local public security forces for the maintenance of public order.

Article 121   In performing their functions, the organs of self-government of the national autonomous areas, in accordance with the autonomy regulations of the respective areas, employ the spoken and written language or languages in common use in the locality.

Article 122   The state gives financial, material and technical assistance to the minority nationalities to accelerate their economic and cultural development.

The state helps the national autonomous areas train large numbers of cadres at different levels and specialized personnel and skilled workers of different professions and trades from among the nationality or nationalities in those areas.

Section VII
The People's Courts and the People's Procuratorates

Article 123   The people's courts in the People's Republic of China are the judicial organs of the state.

Article 124   The People's Republic of China establishes the Supreme People's Court and the local people's courts at different levels, military courts and other special people's courts.

The term of office of the President of the Supreme People's Court is the same as that of the National People's Congress; he shall serve no more than two consecutive terms.

The organization of people's courts is prescribed by law.

Article 125   All cases handled by the people's courts, except for those involving special circumstances as specified by law, shall be heard in public. The accused has the right of defence.

Article 126   The people's courts shall, in accordance with the law, exercise judicial power independently and are not subject to interference by administrative organs, public organizations or individuals.

Article 127   The Supreme People's Court is the highest judicial organ.

The Supreme People's Court supervises the administration of justice by the local people's courts at different levels and by the special people's courts; people's courts at higher levels supervise the administration of justice by those at lower levels.

Article 128   The Supreme People's Court is responsible to the National People's Congress and its Standing Committee. Local people's courts at different levels are responsible to the organs of state power which created them.

Article 129   The people's procuratorates of the People's Republic of China are state organs for legal supervision.

Article 130   The People's Republic of China establishes the Supreme People's Procuratorate and the local people's procuratorates at different levels, military procuratorates and other special people's procuratorates.

The term of office of the Procurator-General of the Supreme People's Procuratorate is the same as that of the National People's Congress; he shall serve no more than two consecutive terms.

The organization of people's procuratorates is prescribed by law.

Article 131   People's procuratorates shall, in accordance with the law, exercise procuratorial power independently and are not subject to interference by administrative organs, public organizations or individuals.

Article 132   The Supreme People's Procuratorate is the highest procuratorial organ.

The Supreme People's Procuratorate directs the work of the local people's procuratorates at different levels and of the special people's procuratorates; people's procuratorates at higher levels direct the work of those at lower levels.

Article 133   The Supreme People's Procuratorate is responsible to the National People's Congress and its Standing Committee. Local people's procuratorates at different levels are responsible to the organs of state power at the corresponding levels which created them and to the people's procuratorates at the higher level.

Article 134   Citizens of all nationalities have the right to use the spoken and written languages of their own nationalities in court proceedings. The people's courts and people's procuratorates should provide translation for any party to the court proceedings who is not familiar with the spoken or written languages in common use in the locality.

In an area where people of a minority nationality live in a compact community or where a number of nationalities live together, hearings should be conducted in the language or languages in common use in the locality; indictments, judgments, notices and other documents should be written, according to actual needs, in the language or languages in common use in the locality.

Article 135   The people's courts, people's procuratorates and public security organs shall, in handling criminal cases, divide their functions, each taking responsibility for its own work, and they shall co-ordinate their efforts and check each other to ensure correct and effective enforcement of law.

CHAPTER FOUR
THE NATIONAL FLAG, THE NATIONAL EMBLEM
AND THE CAPITAL

Article 136   The national flag of the People's Republic of China is a red flag with five stars.

Article 137   The national emblem of the People's Republic of China is Tian An Men in the centre illuminated by five stars and encircled by ears of grain and a cogwheel.

Article 138   The capital of the People's Republic of China is Beijing.

Appendix B

The Constitution
of the Communist Party
of China (1982)

General Programme

The Communist Party of China is the vanguard of the Chinese working class, the faithful representative of the interests of the people of all nationalities in China, and the force at the core leading China's cause of socialism. The Party's ultimate goal is the creation of a communist social system.

The Communist Party of China takes Marxism-Leninism and Mao Zedong Thought as its guide to action.

Applying dialectical materialism and historical materialism, Marx and Engels analysed the laws of development of capitalist society and founded the theory of scientific socialism. According to this theory, with the victory of the proletariat in its revolutionary struggle, the dictatorship of the bourgeoisie is inevitably replaced by the dictatorship of the proletariat, and capitalist society is inevitably transformed into socialist society in which the means of production are publicly owned, exploitation is abolished and the principle "from each according to his ability and to each according to his work" is applied; with tremendous growth of the productive forces and tremendous progress in the ideological, political and cultural fields, socialist society ultimately and inevitably advances into communist society in which the principle "from each according to his ability and to each according to his needs" is applied. Early in the 20th century, Lenin pointed out that capitalism had developed to the stage of imperialism, that the liberation struggle of the proletariat was bound to unite with that of the oppressed nations of the world, and that it was possible for socialist revolution to win victory first in countries that were the weak links of imperialist rule. The course of world history during the past half century and more, and especially the establishment and development of the socialist system in a number of countries, has borne out the correctness of the theory of scientific socialism.

The development and improvement of the socialist system is a long historical process. Fundamentally speaking, the socialist system is incomparably superior to the capitalist system, having eliminated the contradictions inherent in the capitalist system, which the latter itself is incapable of overcoming. Socialism enables the people truly to become masters of the country, gradually to shed the old ideas and ways formed under the system of exploitation and private ownership of the means of production, and steadily to raise their communist consciousness and foster common ideals, common ethics and a common discipline in their own ranks. Socialism can give full scope to the initiative and creativeness of the people, develop the productive forces rapidly, proportionately and in a planned way, and meet the growing material and cultural needs of the members of society. The cause of socialism is advancing and is bound gradually to triumph throughout the world along paths that are suited to the specific conditions of each country and are chosen by its people of their own free will.

The Chinese Communists, with Comrade Mao Zedong as their chief representative, created Mao Zedong Thought by integrating the universal principles of Marxism-Leninism with the concrete practice of the Chinese revolution. Mao Zedong Thought is Marxism-Leninism applied and developed in China; it consists of a body of theoretical principles concerning the revolution and construction in China and a summary of experience therein, both of which have been proved correct by practice; it represents the crystallized, collective wisdom of the Communist Party of China.

The Communist Party of China led the people of all nationalities in waging their prolonged revolutionary struggle against imperialism, feudalism and bureaucrat-capitalism, winning victory in the new-democratic revolution and establishing the People's Republic of China—a people's democratic dictatorship. After the founding of the People's Republic, it led them in smoothly carrying out socialist transformation, completing the transition from New

---

Beijing Review, 38 (September 20, 1982), 8–21. (Adopted by the Twelfth National Congress of the Communist Party of China on September 6, 1982.)

Democracy to socialism, establishing the socialist system, and developing socialism in its economic, political and cultural aspects.

After the elimination of the exploiting classes as such, most of the contradictions in Chinese society do not have the nature of class struggle, and class struggle is no longer the principal contradiction. However, owing to domestic circumstances and foreign influences, class struggle will continue to exist within certain limits for a long time, and may even sharpen under certain conditions. The principal contradiction in Chinese society is that between the people's growing material and cultural needs and the backward level of our social production. The other contradictions should be resolved in the course of resolving this principal one. It is essential to strictly distinguish and correctly handle the two different types of contradictions— the contradictions between the enemy and ourselves and those among the people.

The general task of the Communist Party of China at the present stage is to unite the people of all nationalities in working hard and self-reliantly to achieve, step by step, the modernization of our industry, agriculture, national defence and science and technology and make China a culturally advanced and highly democratic socialist country.

The focus of the work of the Communist Party of China is to lead the people of all nationalities in accomplishing the socialist modernization of our economy. It is necessary vigorously to expand the productive forces and gradually perfect socialist relations of production, in keeping with the actual level of the productive forces and as required for their expansion. It is necessary to strive for the gradual improvement of the standards of material and cultural life of the urban and rural population, based on the growth of production and social wealth.

The Communist Party of China leads the people, as they work for a high level of material civilization, in building a high level of socialist spiritual civilization. Major efforts should be made to promote education, science and culture, imbue the Party members and the masses of the people with communist ideology, combat and overcome decadent bourgeois ideas, remnant feudal ideas and other non-proletarian ideas, and encourage the Chinese people to have lofty ideals, moral integrity, education and a sense of discipline.

The Communist Party of China leads the people in promoting socialist democracy, perfecting the socialist legal system, and consolidating the people's democratic dictatorship. Effective measures should be taken to protect the people's right to run the affairs of the state and of society, and to manage economic and cultural undertakings; and to strike firmly at hostile elements who deliberately sabotage the socialist system, and those who seriously breach or jeopardize public security. Great efforts should be made to strengthen the People's Liberation Army and national defence so that the country is prepared at all times to resist and wipe out any invaders.

The Communist Party of China upholds and promotes relations of equality, unity and mutual assistance among all nationalities in the country, persists in the policy of regional autonomy of minority nationalities, aids the areas inhabited by minority nationalities in their economic and cultural development, and actively trains and promotes cadres from among the minority nationalities.

The Communist Party of China unites with all workers, peasants and intellectuals, and with all the democratic parties, non-party democrats and the patriotic forces of all the nationalities in China in further expanding and fortifying the broadest possible patriotic united front embracing all socialist working people and all patriots who support socialism or who support the reunification of the motherland. We should work together with the people throughout the country, including our compatriots in Taiwan, Xianggang (Hongkong) and Aomen (Macao) and Chinese nationals residing abroad, to accomplish the great task of reunifying the motherland.

In international affairs, the Communist Party of China takes the following basic stand: It adheres to proletarian internationalism and firmly unites with the workers of all lands, with the oppressed nations and oppressed peoples and with all peace-loving and justice-upholding organizations and personages in the common struggle against imperialism, hegemonism and colonialism and for the defence of world peace and promotion of human progress. It stands for the development of state relations between China and other countries on the basis of the five principles of mutual respect for sovereignty and territorial integrity, mutual non-aggression, non-interference in each other's internal affairs, equality and mutual benefit, and peaceful co-existence. It develops relations with Communist Parties and working-class parties in other countries on the basis of Marxism and the principles of independence, complete equality, mutual respect and non-interference in each other's internal affairs.

In order to lead China's people of all nationalities in attaining the great goal of socialist modernization, the Communist Party of China must strengthen itself, carry forward its fine traditions, enhance its fighting capacity and resolutely achieve the following three essential requirements:

First, a high degree of ideological and political unity. The Communist Party of China makes the realization of communism its maximum programme, to which all its members must devote their entire lives. At the present stage, the political basis for the solidarity and unity of the whole Party consists in adherence to the socialist road, to the people's democratic dictatorship, to the leadership of the Party, and to Marxism-Leninism and Mao Zedong Thought and in the concentration of our efforts on socialist modernization. The Party's ideological line is to proceed from reality in all things, to integrate theory with practice, to seek truth from facts, and to verify and develop the truth through practice. In accordance with this ideological line, the whole Party must scientifically sum up historical experience, investigate and study actual conditions, solve new problems in domestic and international affairs, and oppose all erroneous deviations, whether "Left" or Right.

Second, wholehearted service to the people. The Party has no special interests of its own apart from the interests of the working class and the broadest masses of the people. The programme and policies of the Party are precisely the scientific expressions of the fundamental interests of the working class and the broadest masses of the people. Throughout the process of leading the masses in struggle to realize the ideal of communism, the Party always shares weal and woe with the people, keeps in closest contact with them, and does not allow any member to become divorced from the masses or place himself above them. The Party persists in educating the masses in communist ideas and follows the mass line in its work, doing everything for the masses, relying on them in every task, and turning its correct views into conscious action by the masses.

Third, adherence to democratic centralism. Within the Party, democracy is given full play, a high degree of centralism is practised on the basis of democracy and a sense of organization and discipline is strengthened, so as to ensure unity of action throughout its ranks and the prompt and effective implementation of its decisions. In its internal political life, the Party conducts criticism and self-criticism in the correct way, waging ideological struggles over matters of principle, upholding truth and rectifying mistakes. Applying the principle that all members are equally subject to Party discipline, the Party duly criticizes or punishes those members who violate it and expels those who persist in opposing and harming the Party.

Party leadership consists mainly in political, ideological and organizational leadership. The Party must formulate and implement correct lines, principles and policies, do its organizational, propaganda and educational work well and make sure that all Party members play their exemplary vanguard role in every sphere of work and every aspect of social life. The Party must conduct its activities within the limits permitted by the Constitution and the laws of the state. It must see to it that the legislative, judicial and administrative organs of the state and the economic, cultural and people's organizations work actively and with initiative, independently, responsibly and in harmony. The Party must strengthen its leadership over the trade unions, the Communist Youth League, the Women's Federation and other mass organizations, and give full scope to their roles. The Party members are a minority in the whole population, and they must work in close co-operation with the masses of non-Party people in the common effort to make our socialist motherland ever stronger and more prosperous, until the ultimate realization of communism.

CHAPTER 1
MEMBERSHIP

Article 1   Any Chinese worker, peasant, member of the armed forces, intellectual or any other revolutionary who has reached the age of 18 and who accepts the Party's programme and Constitution and is willing to join and work actively in one of the Party organizations, carry out the Party's decisions and pay membership dues regularly may apply for membership of the Communist Party of China.

Article 2   Members of the Communist Party of China are vanguard fighters of the Chinese working class imbued with communist consciousness.

Members of the Communist Party of China must serve the people wholeheartedly, dedicate their whole lives to the realization of communism, and be ready to make any personal sacrifices.

Members of the Communist Party of China are at all times ordinary members of the working people. Communist Party members must not seek personal gain or privileges, although they are allowed personal benefits and job functions and powers as provided for by the relevant regulations and policies.

Article 3   Party members must fulfill the following duties:

(1)   To conscientiously study Marxism-Leninism and Mao Zedong Thought, essential knowledge concerning the Party, and the Party's line, principles, policies and decisions; and acquire general, scientific and professional knowledge.

(2)   To adhere to the principle that the interests of the Party and the people stand above everything, subordinate their personal interests to the interests of the Party and the people, be the first to bear hardships and the last to enjoy comforts, work selflessly for the public interest, and absolutely never use public office for personal gain or benefit themselves at the expense of the public.

(3)   To execute the Party's decisions perseveringly, accept any job and fulfill actively any task assigned them by the Party, conscientiously observe Party discipline and the laws of the state, rigorously guard Party and state secrets and staunchly defend the interests of the Party and the state.

(4)   To uphold the Party's solidarity and unity, to firmly oppose factionalism and all factional organizations and small-group activities, and to oppose double-dealing and scheming of any kind.

(5)   To be loyal to and honest with the Party, to match words with deeds and not to conceal their political views or distort facts; to earnestly practise criticism and self-criticism, to be bold in exposing and correcting shortcomings and mistakes in work, backing good people and good deeds and fighting against bad people and bad deeds.

(6)   To maintain close ties with the masses, propagate the Party's views among them, consult with them when problems arise, listen to their views and demands with an open mind and keep the Party informed of these in good time, help them raise their political consciousness, and defend their legitimate rights and interests.

(7)   To play an exemplary vanguard role in production and other work, study and social activities, take the lead in maintaining public order, promote new socialist ways and customs and advocate communist ethics.

(8)   As required by the defence of the motherland and the interests of the people, to step forward and fight bravely in times of difficulty and danger, fearing neither hardship nor death.

Article 4   Party members enjoy the following rights:

(1)   To attend pertinent Party meetings and read pertinent Party documents, and to benefit from the Party's education and training.

(2)   To participate in the discussion, at Party meetings and in Party newspapers and journals, of questions concerning the Party's policies.

(3)   To make suggestions and proposals regarding the work of the Party.

(4)   To make well-grounded criticism of any Party organization or member at Party meetings; to present information or charges against any Party organization or member concerning violations of discipline and of the law to the Party in a responsible way, and to demand disciplinary measures against such a member, or to demand the dismissal or replacement of any cadre who is incompetent.

(5)   To vote, elect and stand for election.

(6)   To attend, with the right of self-defence, discussions held by Party organizations to decide on disciplinary measures to be taken against themselves or to appraise their work and behaviour, while other Party members may also bear witness or argue on their behalf.

(7)   In case of disagreement with a Party decision or policy, to make reservations and present their views to Party organizations at higher levels up to and including the Central Committee, provided that they resolutely carry out the decision or policy while it is in force.

(8)   To put forward any request, appeal or complaint to higher Party organizations up to and including the Central Committee and ask the organizations concerned for a responsible reply.

No Party organization, up to and including the Central Committee, has the right to deprive any Party member of the above-mentioned rights.

Article 5   New Party members must be admitted through a Party branch, and the principle of individual admission must be adhered to. It is impermissible to drag into the Party by any means those who are not qualified for membership, or to exclude those who are qualified.

An applicant for Party membership must fill in an application form and must be recommended by two full Party members. The application must be accepted by a general membership meeting of the Party branch concerned and approved by the next higher Party organization, and the applicant should undergo observation for a probationary period before being transferred to full membership.

Party members who recommend an applicant must make genuine efforts to acquaint themselves with the latter's ideology, character and personal history, to explain to each applicant the Party's programme and Constitution, qualifications for membership and the duties and rights of members, and must make a responsible report to the Party organization on the matter.

The Party branch committee must canvass the opinions of persons concerned, inside and outside the Party, about an applicant for Party membership and, after establishing the latter's qualifications following a rigorous examination, submit the application to a general membership meeting for discussion.

Before approving the admission of applicants for Party membership, the next higher Party organization concerned must appoint people to talk with them, so as to get to know them better and help deepen their understanding of the Party.

In special circumstances, the Central Committee of the Party or the Party committee of a province, an autonomous region or a municipality directly under the Central Government has the power to admit new Party members directly.

Article 6   A probationary Party member must take an admission oath in front of the Party flag. The oath reads: "It is my will to join the Communist Party of China, uphold the Party's programme, observe the provisions of the Party Constitution, fulfill a Party member's duties, carry out the Party's decisions, strictly observe Party discipline, guard Party secrets, be loyal to the Party, work hard, fight for communism throughout my life, be ready at all times to sacrifice my all for the Party and the people, and never betray the Party."

Article 7   The probationary period of a probationary member is one year. The Party organization should make serious efforts to educate and observe the probationary members.

Probationary members have the same duties as full members. They enjoy the rights of full members except those of voting, electing or standing for election.

When the probationary period of a probationary member has expired, the Party branch concerned should promptly discuss whether he is qualified to be transferred to full membership. A probationary member who conscientiously performs his duties and is qualified for membership should be transferred to full membership as scheduled; if continued observation and education are needed, the probationary period may be prolonged, but by no more than one year; if a probationary member fails to perform his duties and is found to be really unqualified for membership, his probationary membership shall be annulled. Any decision to transfer a probationary member to full membership, prolong a probationary period, or annul a probationary membership must be made through discussion by the general membership meeting of the Party branch concerned and approved by the next higher Party organization.

The probationary period of a probationary member begins from the day the general membership meeting of the Party branch admits him as a probationary member. The Party standing of a member begins from the day he is transferred to full membership on the expiration of the probationary period.

Article 8 Every Party member, irrespective of position, must be organized into a branch, cell or other specific unit of the Party to participate in the regular activities of the Party organization and accept supervision by the masses inside and outside the Party. There shall be no privileged Party members who do not participate in the regular activities of the Party organization and do not accept supervision by the masses inside and outside the Party.

Article 9 Party members are free to withdraw from the Party. When a Party member asks to withdraw, the Party branch concerned shall, after discussion by its general membership meeting, remove his name from the Party rolls, make the removal publicly known and report it to the next higher Party organization for the record.

A Party member who lacks revolutionary will, fails to fulfill the duties of a Party member, is not qualified for membership and remains incorrigible after repeated education should be persuaded to withdraw from the Party. The case shall be discussed and decided by the general membership meeting of the Party branch concerned and submitted to the next higher Party organization for approval. If the Party member being persuaded to withdraw refuses to do so, the case shall be submitted to the general membership meeting of the Party branch concerned for discussion and decision on a time limit by which the member must correct his mistakes or on the removal of his name from the Party rolls, and the decision shall be submitted to the next higher Party organization for approval.

A Party member who fails to take part in regular Party activities, pay membership dues or do work assigned by the Party for six successive months without proper reason is regarded as having given up membership. The general membership meeting of the Party branch concerned shall decide on the removal of such a person's name from the Party rolls and report the removal to the next higher Party organization for approval.

CHAPTER II
ORGANIZATIONAL SYSTEM OF THE PARTY

Article 10 The Party is an integral body organized under its programme and Constitution, on the principle of democratic centralism. It practices a high degree of centralism on the basis of a high degree of democracy. The basic principles of democratic centralism as practised by the Party are as follows:

(1) Individual Party members are subordinate to the Party organization, the minority is subordinate to the majority, the lower Party organizations are subordinate to the higher Party organizations, and all the constituent organizations and members of the Party are subordinate to the National Congress and the Central Committee of the Party.

(2)   The Party's leading bodies of all levels are elected except for the representative organs dispatched by them and the leading Party members' groups in non-Party organizations.

(3)   The highest leading body of the Party is the National Congress and the Central Committee elected by it. The leading bodies of local Party organizations are the Party congresses at their respective levels and the Party committees elected by them. Party committees are responsible, and report their work, to the Party congresses at their respective levels.

(4)   Higher Party organizations shall pay constant attention to the views of the lower organizations and the rank-and-file Party members, and solve in good time the problems they raise. Lower Party organizations shall report on their work to, and request instructions from, higher Party organizations; at the same time, they shall handle, independently and in a responsible manner, matters within their jurisdiction. Higher and lower Party organizations should exchange information and support and supervise each other.

(5)   Party committees at all levels function on the principle of combining collective leadership with individual responsibility based on division of labour. All major issues shall be decided upon by the Party committees after democratic discussion.

(6)   The Party forbids all forms of personality cult. It is necessary to ensure that the activities of the Party leaders be subject to supervision by the Party and the people, while at the same time to uphold the prestige of all leaders who represent the interests of the Party and the people.

Article 11   The election of delegates to Party congresses and of members of Party committees at all levels should reflect the will of the voters. Elections shall be held by secret ballot. The lists of candidates shall be submitted to the Party organizations and voters for full deliberation and discussion. There may be a preliminary election in order to draw up a list of candidates for the formal election. Or there may be no preliminary election, in which case the number of candidates shall be greater than that of the persons to be elected. The voters have the right to inquire into the candidates, demand a change or reject one in favour of another. No organization or individual shall in any way compel voters to elect or not to elect any candidate.

If any violation of the Party Constitution occurs in the election of delegates to a local Party congress, the Party committee at the next higher level shall, after investigation and verification, decide to invalidate the election and take appropriate measures. The decision shall be reported to the Party committee at the next higher level for checking and approval before it is formally announced and implemented.

Article 12   When necessary, Party committees of and above the county level may convene conferences of delegates to discuss and decide on major problems that require timely solution. The number of delegates to such conferences and the procedure governing their election shall be determined by the Party committees convening them.

Article 13   The formation of a new Party organization or the dissolution of an existing one shall be decided upon by the higher Party organizations.

Party committees of and above the county level may send out their representative organs.

When the congress of a local Party organization at any level is not in session, the next higher Party organization may, when it deems it necessary, transfer or appoint responsible members of that organization.

Article 14   When making decisions on important questions affecting the lower organizations, the leading bodies of the Party at all levels should, in ordinary circumstances, solicit the opinions of the lower organizations. Measures should be taken to ensure that the lower organizations can exercise their functions and powers normally. Except in special circumstances, higher leading bodies should not interfere with matters that ought to be handled by lower organizations.

Article 15   Only the Central Committee of the Party has the power to make decisions on major policies of a nationwide character. Party organizations of various departments and localities may make suggestions with regard to such policies to the Central Committee, but shall not make any decisions or publicize their views outside the Party without authorization.

Lower Party organizations must firmly implement the decisions of higher Party organizations. If lower organizations consider that any decisions of higher organizations do not suit actual conditions in their localities or departments, they may request modification. If the higher organizations insist on their original decisions, the lower organizations must carry out such decisions and refrain from publicly voicing their differences, but have the right to report to the next higher Party organization.

Newspapers and journals and other means of publicity run by Party organizations at all levels must propagate the line, principles, policies and decisions of the Party.

Article 16   Party organizations must keep to the principle of subordination of the minority to the majority in discussing and making decisions on any matter. Serious consideration should be given to the differing views of a minority. In case of controversy over major issues in which supporters of the two opposing views are nearly equal in number, except in emergencies where action must be taken in accordance with the majority view, the decision should be put off to allow for further investigation, study and exchange of opinions followed by another discussion. If still no decision can be made, the controversy should be reported to the next higher Party organization for ruling.

When on behalf of the Party organization, an individual Party member is to express views on major issues beyond the scope of existing Party decisions, the content must be referred to the Party organization for prior discussion and decision, or referred to the next higher Party organization for instructions. No Party member, whatever his position, is allowed to make decisions on major issues on his own. In an emergency, when a decision by an individual is unavoidable, the matter must be reported to the Party organization immediately afterwards. No leader is allowed to decide matters arbitrarily on his own or to place himself above the Party organization.

Article 17   The central, local and primary organizations of the Party must all pay great attention to Party building. They shall regularly discuss and check up on the Party's work in propaganda education, organization and discipline inspection, its mass work and united front work. They must carefully study ideological and political developments inside and outside the Party.

CHAPTER III
CENTRAL ORGANIZATIONS OF THE PARTY

Article 18   The National Congress of the Party is held once every five years and convened by the Central Committee. It may be convened before the due date if the Central Committee deems it necessary or if more than one-third of the organizations at the provincial level so request. Except under extraordinary circumstances, the congress may not be postponed.

The number of delegates to the National Congress of the Party and the procedure governing their election shall be determined by the Central Committee.

Article 19   The functions and powers of the National Congress of the Party are as follows:

(1)   To hear and examine the reports of the Central Committee;

(2)   To hear and examine the reports of the Central Advisory Commission and the Central Commission for Discipline Inspection;

(3)   To discuss and decide on major questions concerning the Party;

(4)   To revise the Constitution of the Party;

(5)   To elect the Central Committee; and

(6)   To elect the Central Advisory Commission and the Central Commission for the Discipline Inspection.

Article 20   The Central Commission of the Party is elected for a term of five years. However, when the next National Congress is convened before or after its due date, the term shall be correspondingly shortened or extended. Members and alternate members of the Central Committee must have a Party standing of five years or more. The number of members and alternate members of the Central Committee shall be determined by the National Congress. Vacancies on the Central Committee shall be filled by its alternate members in the order of the number of votes by which they were elected.

The Central Committee of the Party meets in plenary session at least once a year, and such sessions are convened by its Political Bureau.

When the National Congress is not in session, the Central Committee carries out its decisions, directs the entire work of the Party and represents the Communist Party of China in its external relations.

Article 21   The Political Bureau, the Standing Committee of the Political Bureau, the Secretariat and the General Secretary of the Central Committee of the Party are elected by the Central Committee in plenary session. The General Secretary of the Central Committee must be a member of the Standing Committee of the Political Bureau.

When the Central Committee is not in session, the Political Bureau and its Standing Committee exercise the functions and powers of the Central Committee.

The Secretariat attends to the day-to-day work of the Central Committee under the direction of the Political Bureau and its Standing Committee.

The General Secretary of the Central Committee is responsible for convening the meetings of the Political Bureau and its Standing Committee and presides over the work of the Secretariat.

The members of the Military Commission of the Central Committee are decided on by the Central Committee. The Chairman of the Military Commission must be a member of the Standing Committee of the Political Bureau.

The central leading bodies and leaders elected by each Central Committee shall, when the next National Congress is in session, continue to preside over the Party's day-to-day work until the new central leading bodies and leaders are elected by the next Central Committee.

Article 22   The Party's Central Advisory Commission acts as political assistant and consultant to the Central Committee. Members of the Central Advisory Commission must have a Party standing of 40 years or more, have rendered considerable service to the Party, have fairly rich experience in leadership and enjoy fairly high prestige inside and outside the Party.

The Central Advisory Commission is elected for a term of the same duration as that of the Central Committee. It elects, at its plenary meeting, its Standing Committee and its Chairman and Vice-Chairmen, and reports the results to the Central Committee for approval. The Chairman of the Central Advisory Commission must be a member of the Standing Committee of the Political Bureau. Members of the Central Advisory Commission may attend plenary sessions of the Central Committee as non-voting participants. The Vice-Chairmen of the Central Advisory Commission may attend plenary meetings of the Political Bureau as non-voting participants and, when the Political Bureau deems it necessary, other members of the Standing Committee of the Central Advisory Commission may do the same.

Working under the leadership of the Central Committee of the Party, the Central Advisory Commission puts forward recommendations on the formulation and implementation of the Party's principles and policies and gives advice upon request, assists the Central Committee in investigating and handling certain important questions, propagates the Party's major principles and policies inside and outside the Party, and undertakes such other tasks as may be entrusted to it by the Central Committee.

Article 23 Party organizations in the Chinese People's Liberation Army carry on their work in accordance with the instructions of the Central Committee. The General Political Department of the Chinese People's Liberation Army is the political-work organ of the Military Commission; it directs Party and political work in the army. The organizational system and organs of the Party in the armed forces will be prescribed by the Military Commission.

CHAPTER IV
LOCAL ORGANIZATIONS OF THE PARTY

Article 24 A Party congress of a province, autonomous region, municipality directly under the Central Government, city divided into districts, or autonomous prefecture is held once every five years.

A Party congress of a county (banner), autonomous county, city not divided into districts, or municipal district is held once every three years.

Local Party congresses are convened by the Party committees at the corresponding levels. Under extraordinary circumstances, they may be held before or after their due dates upon approval by the next higher Party committees.

The number of delegates to the local Party congresses, at any level and the procedure governing their election are determined by the Party committees at the corresponding levels and should be reported to the next higher Party committees for approval.

Article 25 The functions and powers of the local Party congresses at all levels are as follows:

(1) To hear and examine the reports of the Party committees at the corresponding levels;

(2) To hear and examine the reports of the commissions for discipline inspection at the corresponding levels;

(3) To discuss and decide on major issues in the given areas; and

(4) To elect the Party committees and commissions for discipline inspection at the corresponding levels and delegates to the Party congresses at their respective next higher levels.

The Party congress of a province, autonomous region, or municipality directly under the Central Government elects the Party advisory committee at the corresponding level and hears and examines its reports.

Article 26 The Party committee of a province, autonomous region, municipality directly under the Central Government, city divided into districts, or autonomous prefecture is elected for a term of five years. The members and alternate members of such a committee must have a Party standing of five years or more.

The Party committee of a county (banner), autonomous county, city not divided into districts, or municipal district is elected for a term of three years. The members and alternate members of such a committee must have a Party standing of three years or more.

When local Party congresses at various levels are convened before or after their due dates, the terms of the committees elected by the previous congresses shall be correspondingly shortened or extended.

The number of members and alternate members of the local Party committees at various levels shall be determined by the next higher committees. Vacancies on the local Party committees at various levels shall be filled by their alternate members in the order of the number of votes by which they were elected.

The local Party committees at various levels meet in plenary session at least once a year.

Local Party committees at various levels shall, when the Party congresses of the given areas are not in session, carry out the directives of the next higher Party organizations and the decisions of the Party congresses at the corresponding levels, direct work in their own areas and report on it to the next higher Party committees at regular intervals.

Article 27   Local Party committees at various levels elect, at their plenary sessions, their standing committees, secretaries and deputy secretaries and report the results to the higher Party committees for approval. The standing committees at various levels exercise the powers and functions of local Party committees when the latter are not in session. They continue to handle the day-to-day work when the next Party congresses at their levels are in session, until the new standing committees are elected.

Article 28   The Party advisory committee of a province, autonomous region or municipality directly under the Central Government acts as political assistant and consultant to the Party committee at the corresponding level. It works under the leadership of the Party committee at the corresponding level and in the light of the relevant provisions of Article 22 of the present Constitution. The qualifications of its members shall be specified by the Party committee at the corresponding level in the light of the relevant provisions of Article 22 of the present Constitution and the actual conditions in the locality concerned. It serves a term of the same duration as the Party committee at the corresponding level.

The advisory committee of a province, autonomous region or municipality directly under the Central Government elects, at its plenary meeting, its standing committee and its chairman and vice-chairmen, and the results are subject to endorsement by the Party committee at the corresponding level and should be reported to the Central Committee for approval. Its members may attend plenary sessions of the Party committee at the corresponding level as non-voting participants, and its chairman and vice-chairmen may attend meetings of the standing committee of the Party committee at the corresponding level as non-voting participants.

Article 29   A prefectural Party committee, or an organization analogous to it, is the representative organ dispatched by a provincial or an autonomous regional Party committee to a prefecture embracing several counties, autonomous counties or cities. It exercises leadership over the work in the given region as authorized by the provincial or autonomous regional Party committee.

CHAPTER V
PRIMARY ORGANIZATIONS OF THE PARTY

Article 30   Primary Party organizations are formed in factories, shops, schools, offices, city neighbourhoods, people's communes, co-operatives, farms, townships, towns, companies of the People's Liberation Army and other basic units, where there are three or more full Party members.

In primary Party organizations, the primary Party committees, and committees of general Party branches or Party branches, are set up respectively as the work requires and according to the number of Party members, subject to approval by the higher Party organizations. A primary Party committee is elected by a general membership meeting or a delegate meeting. The committee of a general Party branch or a Party branch is elected by a general membership meeting.

Article 31   In ordinary circumstances, a primary Party organization which has set up its own committee convenes a general membership meeting or delegate meeting once a year; a general Party branch holds a general membership meeting twice a year; a Party branch holds a general membership meeting once in every three months.

A primary Party committee is elected for a term of three years, while a general Party branch committee or a Party branch committee is elected for a term of two years. Results of the election of a secretary and deputy secretaries by a primary Party committee, general branch committee or branch committee shall be reported to the higher Party organizations for approval.

Article 32   The primary Party organizations are militant bastions of the Party in the basic units of society. Their main tasks are:

(1)   To propagate and carry out the Party's line, principles and policies, the decisions of the Central Committee of the Party and other higher Party organizations, and their own decisions; to give full play to the exemplary vanguard role of Party members, and to unite and organize the cadres and the rank and file inside and outside the Party in fulfilling the tasks of their own units.

(2)   To organize Party members to conscientiously study Marxism-Leninism and Mao Zedong Thought, study essential knowledge concerning the Party, and the Party's line, principles and policies, and acquire general, scientific and professional knowledge.

(3)   To educate and supervise Party members, ensure their regular participation in the activities of the Party organization, see that Party members truly fulfill their duties and observe discipline, and protect their rights from encroachment.

(4)   To maintain close ties with the masses, constantly seek their criticisms and opinions regarding Party members and the Party's work, value the knowledge and rationalization proposals of the masses and experts, safeguard the legitimate rights and interests of the masses, show concern for their material and cultural life and help them improve it, do effective ideological and political work among them, and enhance their political consciousness. They must correct, by proper methods, the erroneous ideas and unhealthy ways and customs that may exist among the masses, and properly handle the contradictions in their midst.

(5)   To give full scope to the initiative and creativeness of Party members and the masses, discover advanced elements and talented people needed for the socialist cause, encourage them to improve their work and come up with innovations and inventions, and support them in these efforts.

(6)   To admit new Party members, collect membership dues, examine and appraise the work and behaviour of Party members, commend exemplary deeds performed by them, and maintain and enforce Party discipline.

(7)   To promote criticism and self-criticism, and expose and overcome shortcomings and mistakes in work. To educate Party and non-Party cadres; see to it that they strictly observe the law and administrative discipline and the financial and economic discipline and personnel regulations of the state; see to it that none of them infringe the interests of the state, the collective and the masses; and see to it that the financial workers including accountants and other professionals who are charged with enforcing laws and regulations in their own units do not themselves violate the laws and regulations, while at the same time ensuring and protecting their right to exercise their functions and powers independently in accordance with the law and guarding them against any reprisals for so doing.

(8)   To educate Party members and the masses to raise their revolutionary vigilance and wage resolute struggles against the criminal activities of counter-revolutionaries and other saboteurs.

Article 33   In an enterprise or institution, the primary Party committee or the general branch committee or branch committee, where there is no primary Party committee, gives leadership in the work of its own unit. Such a primary Party organization discusses and decides on major questions of principle and at the same time ensures that the administrative leaders fully exercise their functions and powers, but refrains from substituting itself for, or trying to take over from; the administrative leaders. Except in special circumstances, the general branch committees and branch committees under the leadership of a primary Party committee only play a guarantory and supervisory role to see that the production targets or operational tasks assigned to their own units are properly fulfilled.

In Party or government offices at all levels, the primary Party organizations shall not lead the work of these offices. Their task here is to exercise supervision over all Party members, including the heads of these offices who are Party members, with regard to their implementation of the Party's line, principles and policies, their observance of discipline and the law, their contact with the masses, and their ideology, work style and moral character; and to assist the office heads to improve work, raise efficiency and overcome bureaucratic ways, keep them informed of the shortcomings and problems discovered in the work of these offices, or report such shortcomings and problems to the higher Party organizations.

CHAPTER VI
PARTY CADRES

Article 34   Party cadres are the backbone of the Party's cause and public servants of the people. The Party selects its cadres according to the principle that they should possess both political integrity and professional competence, persists in the practice of appointing people on their merits and opposes favouritism; it calls for genuine efforts to make the ranks of the cadres more revolutionary, younger in average age, better educated and more professionally competent.

Party cadres are obliged to accept training by the Party as well as examination and assessment of their work by the Party.

The Party should attach importance to the training and promotion of women cadres and cadres from among the minority nationalities.

Article 35   Leading Party cadres at all levels must perform in an exemplary way their duties as Party members prescribed in Article 3 of this Constitution and must meet the following basic requirements:

(1)   Have a fair grasp of the theories of Marxism-Leninism and Mao Zedong Thought and the policies based on them, and be able to adhere to the socialist road, fight against the hostile forces disrupting socialism and combat all erroneous tendencies inside and outside the Party.

(2)   In their work as leaders, conduct earnest investigations and study, persistently proceed from reality and properly carry out the line, principles and policies of the Party.

(3)   Be fervently dedicated to the revolutionary cause and imbued with a strong sense of political responsibility, and be qualified for their leading posts in organizational ability, general education and vocational knowledge.

(4)   Have a democratic work style, maintain close ties with the masses, correctly implement the Party's mass line, conscientiously accept criticism and supervision by the Party and the masses, and combat bureaucratism.

(5)   Exercise their functions and powers in the proper way, observe and uphold the rules and regulations of the Party and the state, and combat all acts of abusing power and seeking personal gain.

(6)   Be good at uniting and working with a large number of comrades, including those who hold differing opinions, while upholding the Party's principles.

Article 36 Party cadres should be able to co-operate with non-Party cadres, respect them and learn open-mindedly from their strong points.

Party organizations at all levels must be good at discovering and recommending talented and knowledgeable non-Party cadres for leading posts, and ensure that the latter enjoy authority commensurate with their posts and can play their roles to the full.

Article 37 Leading Party cadres at all levels, whether elected through democratic procedure or appointed by a leading body, are not entitled to lifelong tenure, and they can be transferred from or relieved of their posts.

Cadres no longer fit to continue working due to old age or poor health should retire according to the regulations of the state.

CHAPTER VII
PARTY DISCIPLINE

Article 38 A Communist Party member must consciously act within the bounds of Party discipline.

Party organizations shall criticize, educate or take disciplinary measures against members who violate Party discipline, depending on the nature and seriousness of their mistakes and in the spirit of "learning from past mistakes to avoid future ones, and curing the sickness to save the patient."

Party members who violate the law and administrative discipline shall be subject to administrative disciplinary action or legal action instituted by administrative or judicial organs. Those who have seriously violated criminal law shall be expelled from the Party.

Article 39 There are five measures of Party discipline: warning, serious warning, removal from Party posts and proposals for their removal from non-Party posts to the organizations concerned, placing on probation within the Party, and expulsion from the Party.

The period for which a Party member is placed on probation shall not exceed two years. During this period, the Party member concerned has no right to vote, elect or stand for election. A Party member who during this time proves to have corrected his mistake shall have his rights as a Party member restored. Party members who refuse to mend their ways shall be expelled from the Party.

Expulsion is the ultimate Party disciplinary measure. In deciding on or approving an expulsion, Party organizations at all levels should study all the relevant facts and opinions and exercise extreme caution.

It is strictly forbidden, within the Party, to take any measures against a member that contravene the Party Constitution or the laws of the state, or to retaliate against or frame up comrades. Any offending organization or individual must be dealt with according to Party discipline or the laws of the state.

Article 40 Any disciplinary measure against a Party member must be discussed and decided on at a general membership meeting of the Party branch concerned, and reported to the primary Party committee concerned for approval. If the case is relatively important or complicated, or involves the expulsion of a member, it shall be reported, on the merit of that case, to a Party commission for discipline inspection at or above the county level for examination and approval. Under special circumstances, a Party committee or a commission for discipline inspection at or above the county level has the authority to decide directly on disciplinary measures against a Party member.

Any decision to remove a member or alternate member of the Central Committee or a local committee at any level from posts within the Party, to place such a person on probation within the Party or to expel him from the Party must be taken by a two-thirds majority vote at a plenary meeting of the Party committee to which he belongs. Such a disciplinary measure against a member or alternate member of a local Party committee is subject to approval by the higher Party committees.

Members and alternate members of the Central Committee who have seriously violated criminal law shall be expelled from the Party on decision by the Political Bureau of the Central Committee; members and alternate members of local Party committees who have seriously violated criminal law shall be expelled from the Party on decision by the standing committees of the Party committees at the corresponding levels.

Article 41   When a Party organization decides on a disciplinary measure against a Party member, it should investigate and verify the facts in an objective way. The Party member in question must be informed of the decision to be made and of the facts on which it is based. He must be given a chance to account for himself and speak in his own defence. If the member does not accept the decision, he can appeal, and the Party organization concerned must promptly deal with or forward his appeal, and must not withhold or suppress it. Those who cling to erroneous views and unjustifiable demands shall be educated by criticism.

Article 42   It is an important duty of every Party organization to firmly uphold Party discipline. Failure of a Party organization to uphold Party discipline must be investigated.

In case a Party organization seriously violates Party discipline and is unable to rectify the mistake on its own, the next higher Party committee should, after verifying the facts and considering the seriousness of the case, decide on the reorganization or dissolution of the organization, report the decision to the Party committee further above for examination and approval, and then formally announce and carry out the decision.

CHAPTER VIII
PARTY ORGANS FOR DISCIPLINE INSPECTION

Article 43   The Party's Central Commission for Discipline Inspection functions under the leadership of the Central Committee of the Party. Local commissions for discipline inspection at all levels function under the dual leadership of the Party committees at the corresponding levels and the next higher commissions for discipline inspection.

The Party's central and local commissions for discipline inspection serve a term of the same duration as the Party committees at the corresponding levels.

The Central Commission for Discipline Inspection elects, in plenary session, its standing committee and secretary and deputy secretaries and reports the results to the Central Committee for approval. Local commissions for discipline inspection at all levels elect, at their plenary sessions, their respective standing committees and secretaries and deputy secretaries. The results of the elections are subject to endorsement by the Party committees at the corresponding levels and should be reported to the higher Party committees for approval. The First Secretary of the Central Commission for Discipline Inspection must be a member of the Standing Committee of the Political Bureau. The question of whether a primary Party committee should set up a commission for discipline inspection or simply appoint a discipline inspection commissioner shall be determined by the next higher Party organization in the light of the specific circumstances. The committees of general Party branches and Party branches shall have discipline inspection commissioners.

The Party's Central Commission for Discipline Inspection shall, when its work so requires, accredit discipline inspection groups or commissioners to Party or state organs at the central level. Leaders of the discipline inspection groups or discipline inspection commissioners may attend relevant meetings of the leading Party organizations in the said organs as non-voting participants. The leading Party organizations in the organs concerned must give support to their work.

Article 44   The main tasks of the central and local commissions for discipline inspection are as follows: to uphold the Constitution and the other important rules and regulations of the Party, to assist the respective Party committees in rectifying Party style, and to check up on the implementation of the line, principles, policies and decisions of the Party.

The central and local commissions for discipline inspection shall carry out constant education among Party members on their duty to observe Party discipline; they shall adopt decisions for the upholding of Party discipline, examine and deal with relatively important or complicated cases of violation of the Constitution and discipline of the party or the laws and decrees of the state by Party organizations or Party members; decide on or cancel disciplinary measures against Party members involved in such cases; and deal with complaints and appeals made by Party members.

The central and local commissions for discipline inspection should report to the Party committees at the corresponding levels on the results of their handling of cases of special importance or complexity, as well as on the problems encountered. Local commissions for discipline inspection should also present such reports to the higher commissions.

If the Central Commission for Discipline Inspection discovers any violation of Party discipline by any member of the Central Committee, it may report such an offence to the Central Committee, and the Central Committee must deal with the case promptly.

Article 45   Higher commissions for discipline inspection have the power to check up on the work of the lower commissions and to approve or modify their decisions on any case. If decisions so modified have already been ratified by the Party committee at the corresponding level, the modification must be approved by the next higher Party committee.

If a local commission for discipline inspection does not agree with a decision made by the Party committee at the corresponding level in dealing with a case, it may request the commission at the next higher level to re-examine the case; if a local commission discovers cases of violation of Party discipline or the laws and decrees of the state by the Party committee at the corresponding level or by its members, and if that Party committee fails to deal with them properly or at all, it has the right to appeal to the higher commissions for assistance in dealing with such cases.

CHAPTER IX
LEADING PARTY MEMBERS' GROUPS

Article 46   A leading Party members' group shall be formed in the leading body of a central or local state organ, people's organization, economic or cultural institution or other non-Party unit. The main tasks of such a group are: to see to it that the Party's principles and policies are implemented, to unite with the non-Party cadres and masses in fulfilling the tasks assigned by the Party and the state, and to guide the work of the Party organization of the unit.

Article 47   The members of a leading Party members' group are appointed by the Party committee that approves its establishment. The group shall have a secretary and deputy secretaries.

A leading Party members' group must accept the leadership of the Party committee that approves its establishment.

Article 48   The Central Committee of the Party shall determine specifically the functions, powers and tasks of the leading Party members' groups in those government departments which need to exercise highly centralized and unified leadership over subordinate units; it shall also determine whether such groups should be replaced by Party committees.

CHAPTER X
RELATIONSHIP BETWEEN THE PARTY
AND THE COMMUNIST YOUTH LEAGUE

Article 49   The Communist Youth League of China is a mass organization of advanced young people under the leadership of the Communist Party of China; it is a school where large numbers of young people will learn about communism through practice; it is the Party's assistant and reserve force. The Central Committee of the Communist Youth League functions under the leadership of the Central Committee of the Party. The local organizations of the Communist Youth League are under the leadership of the Party committees at the corresponding levels and of the higher organizations of the League itself.

Article 50   Party committees at all levels must strengthen their leadership over the Communist Youth League organizations and pay attention to the selection and training of League cadres. The Party must firmly support the Communist Youth League in the lively and creative performance of its work to suit the characteristics and needs of young people, and give full play to the League's role as a shock force and as a bridge linking the Party with the broad masses of young people.

Those secretaries of League committees, at or below the county level or in enterprises and institutions, who are Party members may attend meetings of Party committees at the corresponding levels and of their standing committees as non-voting participants.

Appendix B-1

Revision of Some Articles of the Constitution of the Communist Party of China (1987)

The 13th National Congress of the Chinese Communist Party has decided to make the following revisions* of some articles of the constitution of the Communist Party of China:

1. In the first paragraph of Article 11, the sentences, "There may be a preliminary election in order to draw up a list of candidates for the formal election. Or there may be no preliminary election, in which case the number of candidates shall be greater than that of the persons to be elected," are replaced by "the election procedure of nominating a larger number of candidates than the number of persons to be elected may be used directly in a formal election. Or this procedure may be used first in a preliminary election in order to draw up a list of candidates for the formal election."

2. In the first paragraph of Article 16, the sentences, "Party organizations must keep the principles of subordination of the minority to the majority in discussing and making decisions on any matter. Serious consideration should be given to the differing views of a minority. In case of controversy over major issues in which supporters of the two opposing views are nearly equal in number, except in emergencies where action must be taken in accordance with the majority view, the decision should be put off to allow for further investigation, study and exchange of opinions followed by another discussion. If still no decision can be made, the controversy should be reported to the next higher Party organization for ruling," are *replaced by* "When discussing and making decisions on any matter, Party organizations must keep to the principle of subordination of the minority to the majority. A vote must be taken when major issues are decided on. Serious consideration should be given to the differing views of a minority. In case of controversy over major issues in which supporters of the two opposing views are nearly equal in number, except in emergencies where action must be taken in accordance with the majority view, the decision should be put off to allow for further investigation, study, and exchange of opinions followed by another vote. Under special circumstances, the controversy may be reported to the next higher Party organization for ruling."

3. The following paragraph is added to the end of Article 19: "The powers and functions of the National Conference of the Party are as follows: to discuss and make decisions on major questions; to replace members and elect additional members of the Central Committee, the Central Advisory Commission, and the Central Commission for Discipline Inspection. The number of members and alternate members of the Central Committee to be replaced or newly elected shall not exceed one-fifth of the respective totals of members and alternate members of the Central Committee elected by the National Congress of the Party."

4. In the first paragraph of Article 21, the sentence, "The Political Bureau, the Standing Committee of the Political Bureau, the Secretariat and the General Secretary of the Central Committee of the Party are elected by the Central Committee in plenary session," is *replaced by* "The Political Bureau, the Standing Committee of the Political Bureau and the General Secretary of the Central Committee of the Party are elected by the Central Committee in plenary session."

The third paragraph of Article 21, "The Secretariat attends to the day-to-day work of the Central Committee under the direction of the Political Bureau and its Standing Committee," is *replaced by* "The Secretariat is the working body of the Political Bureau of the Central Committee and its Standing Committee. The members of the Secretariat are nominated by the Standing Committee of the Political Bureau of the Central Committee and are subject to endorsement by the Central Committee in plenary session."

---

*Adopted at the 13th CPC National Congress on November 1, 1987.
Source: *Beijing Review* (November 16–22, 1987), 33–34.

The fifth paragraph of Article 21, "The members of the Military Commission of the Central Committee are decided on by the Central Committee. The Chairman of the Military Commission must be a member of the Standing Committee of the Political Bureau," is *replaced by* "The members of the Military Commission of the Central Committee are decided on by the Central Committee."

5. In the second paragraph of Article 22, the sentences, "The Central Advisory Commission is elected for a term of the same duration as that of the Central Committee. It elects, at its plenary meeting, its Standing Committee and its Chairman and Vice-Chairmen, and reports the results to the Central Committee for approval. The Chairman of the Central Advisory Commission must be a member of the Standing Committee of the Political Bureau," are *replaced by* "The Central Advisory Commission is elected for a term of the same duration as that of the Central Committee. It elects, at its plenary meeting, its Standing Committee and its Chairman and Vice-Chairmen, and reports the results to the Central Committee for approval."

6. The first paragraph of Article 30, "Primary Party organizations are formed in factories, shops, schools, offices, city neighbourhoods, people's communes, co-operatives, farms, townships, towns, companies of the People's Liberation Army and other basic units, where there are three or more full Party members," is *replaced by* "Primary Party organizations are formed in factories, shops, schools, offices, city neighbourhoods, co-operatives, farms, townships, towns, villages, companies of the People's Liberation Army and other basic units, where there are three or more full Party members."

7. The following paragraph is added before the first paragraph of Article 33: "In an enterprise or an institution where the system of administrative leader assuming full responsibility is practiced, the primary Party organization guarantees and supervises the implementation of the principles and policies of the party and the state in its own unit. Such a primary Party organization should concentrate on strengthening Party building, doing effective ideological and political work and mass work, support the administrative leaders in fully exercising their powers and functions according to regulations, and offer views and suggestions on major issues."

In the first paragraph of Article 33, the sentence, "In an enterprise or institution, the primary Party committee or the general branch committee or branch committee, where there is no primary Party committee, gives leadership in the work of its own unit," is *replaced by* "In an institution where the system of administrative leader assuming full responsibility has not yet been practiced, the primary Party committee or, where there is no primary Party committee, the general branch committee or branch committee provides leadership in the work of its own unit."

8. In the third paragraph of Article 43, the sentences, "The Central Commission for Discipline Inspection elects, in plenary session, its standing committee and secretary and deputy secretaries and reports the results to the Central Committee for approval. Local commissions for discipline inspection at all levels elect, at their plenary sessions, their respective standing committees and secretaries and deputy secretaries. The results of the elections are subject to endorsement by the party committees at the corresponding levels and should be reported to the higher Party committees for approval. The First Secretary of the Central Commission for Discipline Inspection must be a member of the Standing Committee of the Political Bureau," are *replaced by* "The Central Commission for Discipline Inspection elects, in plenary session, its standing committee and secretary and deputy secretaries and reports the results to the Central Committee for approval. Local commissions for discipline inspection at all levels elect, at their plenary sessions, their respective standing committees and secretaries and deputy secretaries. The results of the elections are subject to endorsement by the Party committees at the corresponding levels and should be reported to the next higher Party committees for approval."

9. In Article 46, the sentence, "A leading Party members' group shall be formed in the leading body of a central or local state organ, people's organization, economic or cultural institution or other non-Party unit," is *replaced by* "A leading Party members' group may be formed within the leading body elected by the national or a local people's congress, the national or a local committee of the Chinese People's Political Consultative Conference, people's organization or other non-Party unit."

10. Article 48, "The Central Committee of the Party shall determine specifically the functions, powers and tasks of the leading Party members' groups in those government departments which need to exercise highly centralized and unified leadership over subordinate units; it shall also determine whether such groups should be replaced by Party committees," is *replaced by* "The Central Committee of the party shall determine specifically whether Party committees should be formed in those government departments which need to exercise highly centralized and unified leadership over subordinate units; it shall also determine specifically the powers, functions and tasks of such committees."

Index